CURLFRIENDS
NEW IN TOWN

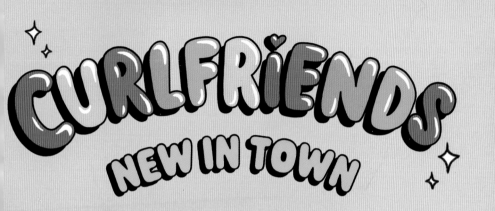

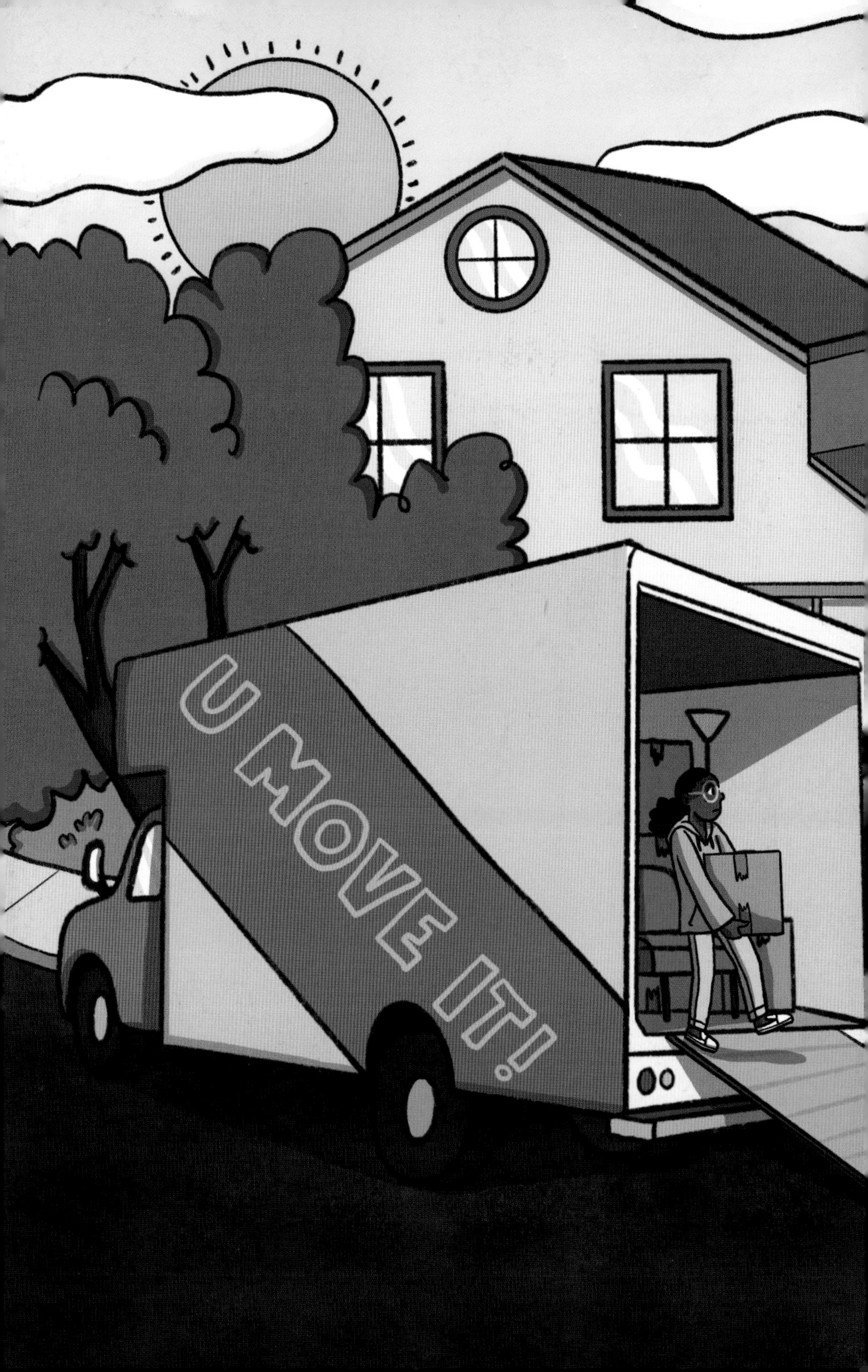
U MOVE IT!

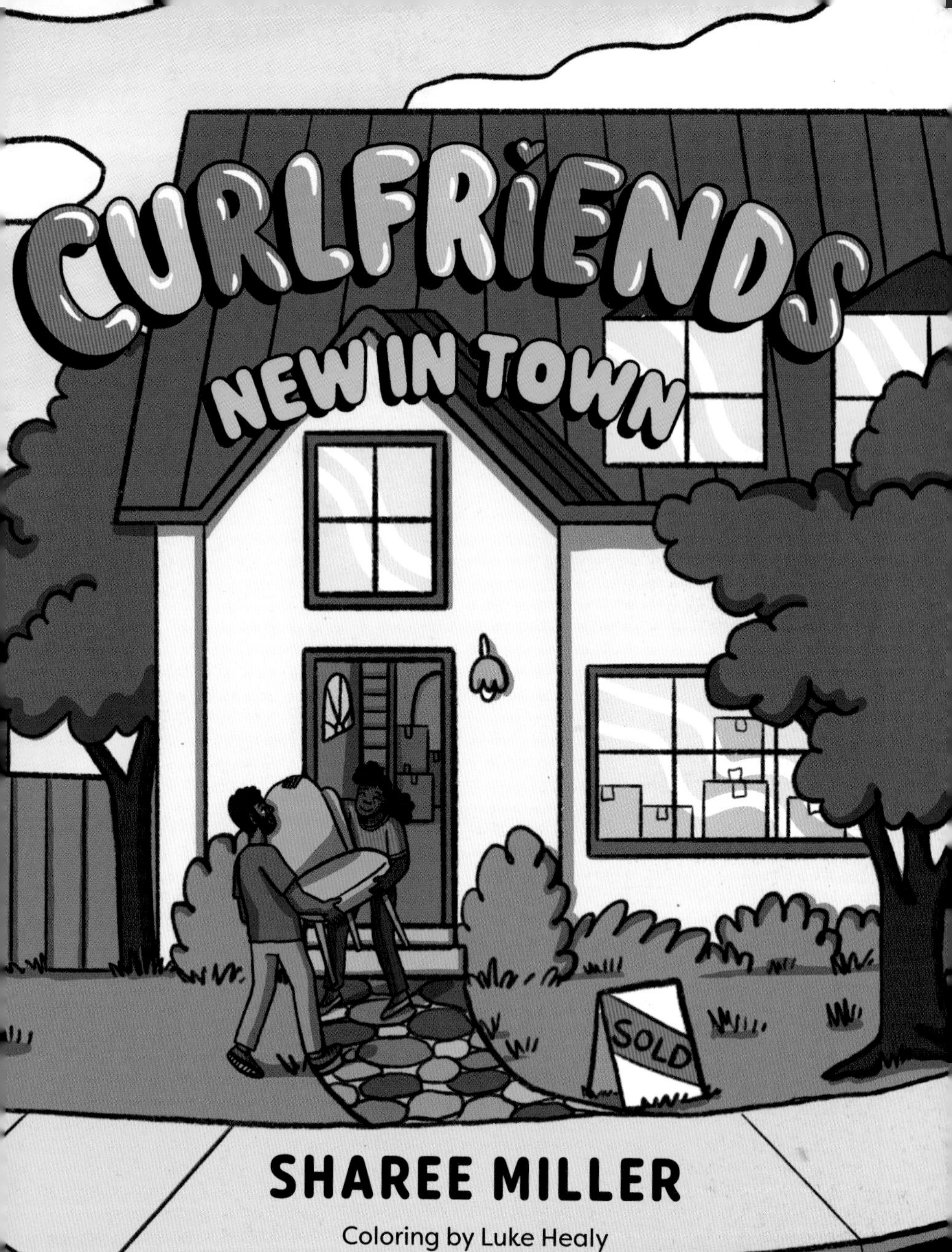
CURLFRIENDS
NEW IN TOWN
SOLD
SHAREE MILLER
Coloring by Luke Healy

To my dad and my sister Adrienne

About This Book

The illustrations for this book were created by sketching in pencil, inking in Procreate, and coloring in Photoshop. This book was edited by Andrea Colvin and Nikki Garcia and designed by Jenny Kimura. The production was supervised by Bernadette Flinn, and the production editor was Marisa Finkelstein. The text was set in Sunbird Medium, and the display type was hand lettered by the artist.

This book is a work of fiction. Names, characters, places, and incidents are the product of the author's imagination or are used fictitiously. Any resemblance to actual events, locales, or persons, living or dead, is coincidental.

Copyright © 2023 by Sharee Miller
Letterer: AndWorld Design

Cover illustration copyright © 2023 by Sharee Miller. Cover design by Jenny Kimura.
Cover copyright © 2023 by Hachette Book Group, Inc.

Hachette Book Group supports the right to free expression and the value of copyright. The purpose of copyright is to encourage writers and artists to produce the creative works that enrich our culture.

The scanning, uploading, and distribution of this book without permission is a theft of the author's intellectual property. If you would like permission to use material from the book (other than for review purposes), please contact permissions@hbgusa.com. Thank you for your support of the author's rights.

Little, Brown Ink
Hachette Book Group
1290 Avenue of the Americas, New York, NY 10104
Visit us at LBYR.com

First Edition: October 2023

Little, Brown Ink is an imprint of Little, Brown and Company. The Little, Brown Ink name and logo are trademarks of Hachette Book Group, Inc.

The publisher is not responsible for websites (or their content) that are not owned by the publisher.

Little, Brown and Company books may be purchased in bulk for business, educational, or promotional use. For information, please contact your local bookseller or the Hachette Book Group Special Markets Department at special.markets@hbgusa.com.

Library of Congress Cataloging-in-Publication Data
Names: Miller, Sharee (Illustrator) | Title: Curlfriends : new in town / Sharee Miller. | Description: First edition. | New York : Little, Brown and Company, 2023. | Series: Curlfriends ; 1 | Audience: Ages 8–12. | Summary: Eager to make a good first impression at her new middle school, thirteen-year-old Charlie does her best to fit in until she meets a group of diverse Black girls who show her the importance of authenticity. | Identifiers: LCCN 2022060940 | ISBN 9780316591454 (trade paperback) | ISBN 9780316591478 (hardcover) | ISBN 9780316591447 (ebook) | Subjects: CYAC: Graphic novels. | Individuality—Fiction. | Middle schools—Fiction. | Schools—Fiction. | Friendship—Fiction. | African Americans—Fiction. | LCGFT: Graphic novels. | Classification: LCC PZ7.7.M553 Cu 2023 | DDC 741.5/973—dc23/eng/20221221 | LC record available at https://lccn.loc.gov/2022060940

ISBNs: 978-0-316-59147-8 (hardcover), 978-0-316-59145-4 (paperback), 978-0-316-59144-7 (ebook), 978-0-316-59326-7 (ebook), 978-0-316-59328-1 (ebook)

PRINTED IN CHINA

1010

Hardcover: 10 9 8 7 6 5 4 3 2 1
Paperback: 10 9 8 7 6 5 4 3 2 1

CHAPTER 1

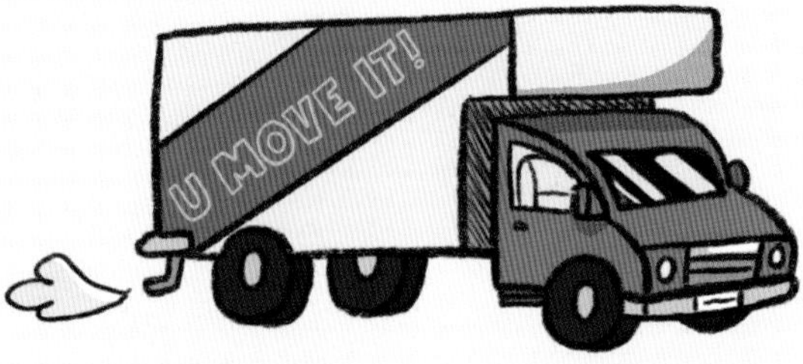
U MOVE IT!

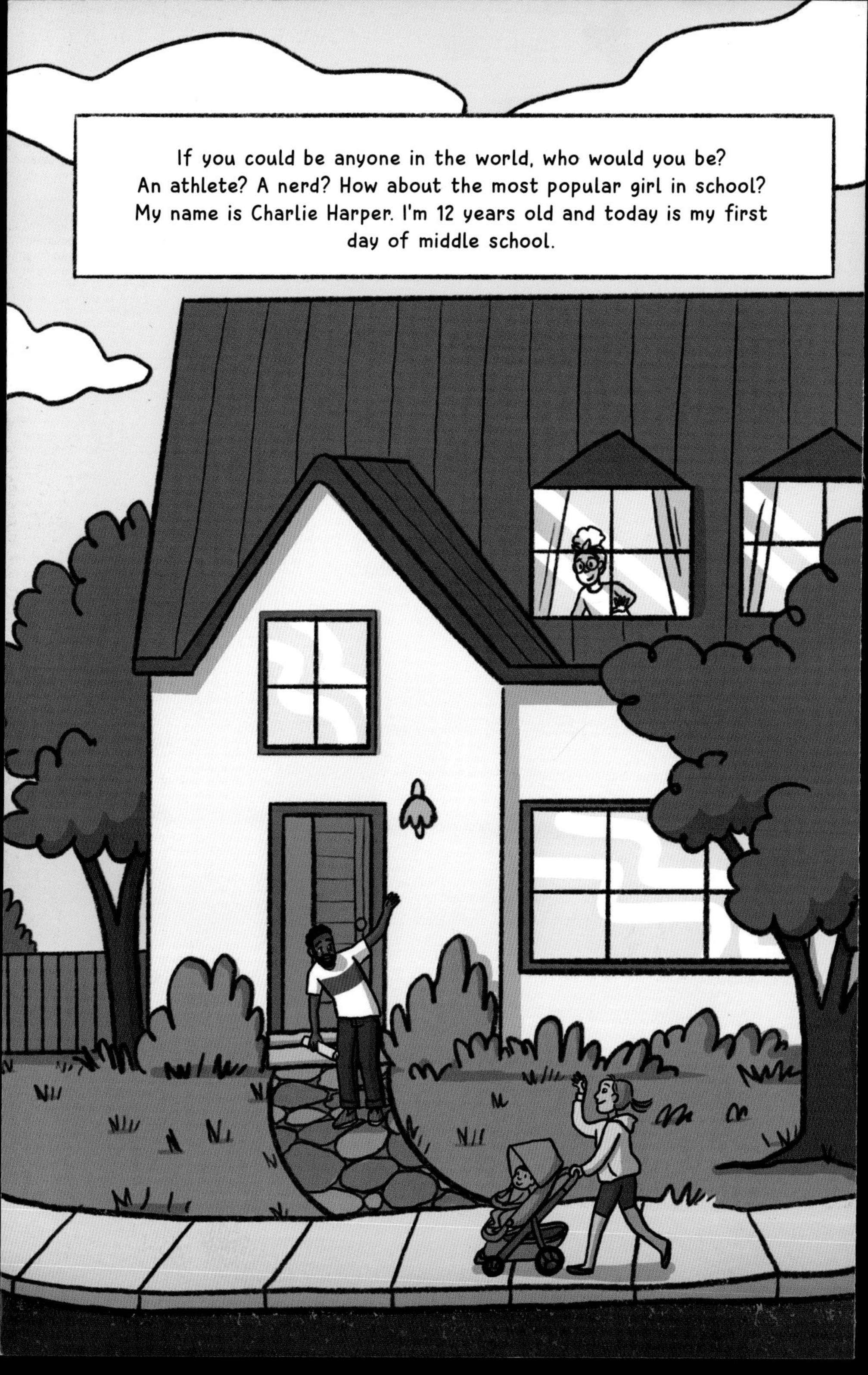
If you could be anyone in the world, who would you be? An athlete? A nerd? How about the most popular girl in school? My name is Charlie Harper. I'm 12 years old and today is my first day of middle school.

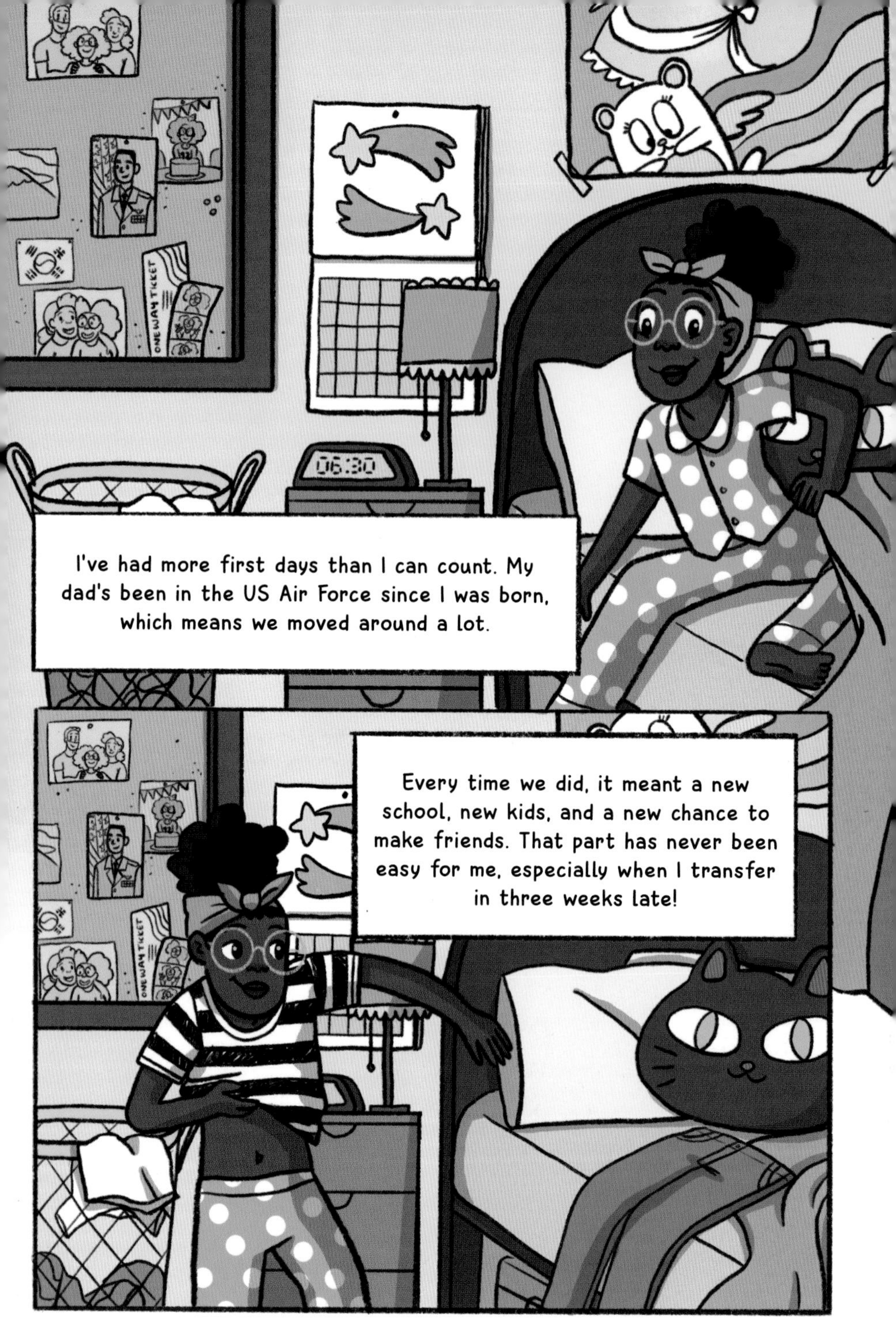
ONE WAY TICKET
06:30
I've had more first days than I can count. My dad's been in the US Air Force since I was born, which means we moved around a lot.
ONE WAY TICKET
Every time we did, it meant a new school, new kids, and a new chance to make friends. That part has never been easy for me, especially when I transfer in three weeks late!

Sometimes it feels impossible to fit in. I've always been labeled before I could make friends.

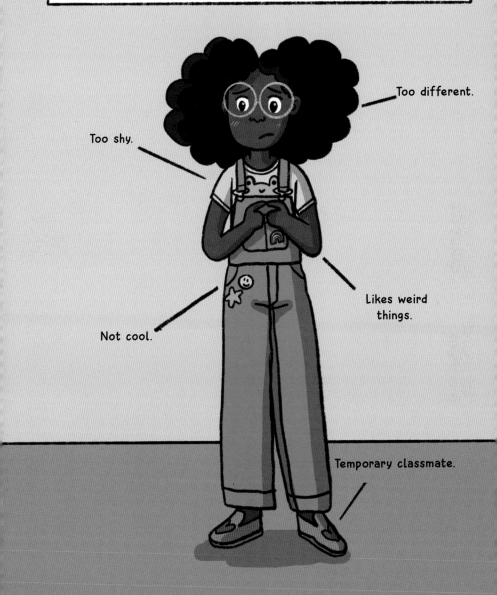

Too different.

Too shy.

Likes weird things.

Not cool.

Temporary classmate.

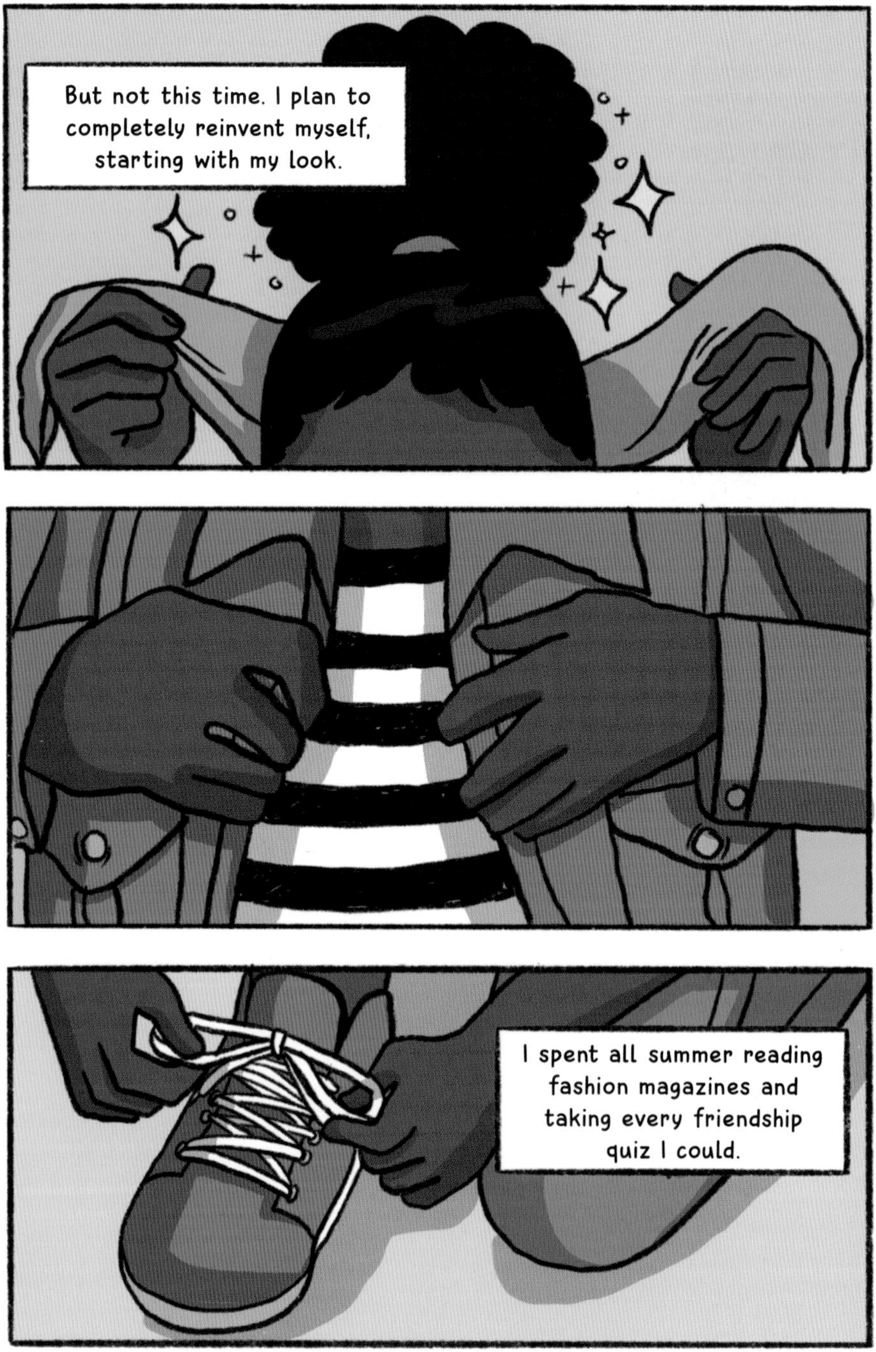
But not this time. I plan to completely reinvent myself, starting with my look.
I spent all summer reading fashion magazines and taking every friendship quiz I could.

I've never studied this much in my life, but all my preparation is about to pay off. My mom always says you only get one chance at a first impression, so today must go perfect.

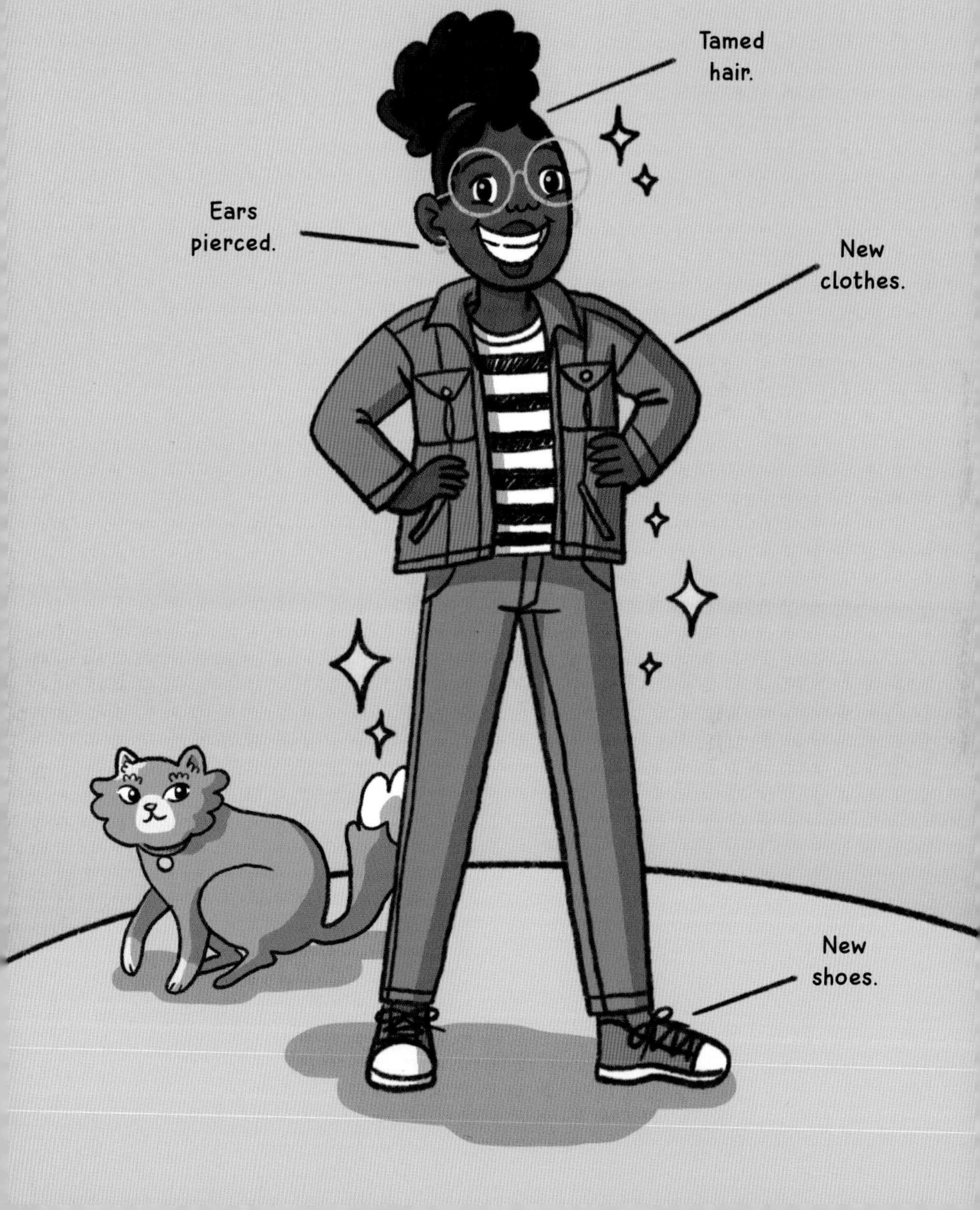
Tamed hair.
Ears pierced.
New clothes.
New shoes.

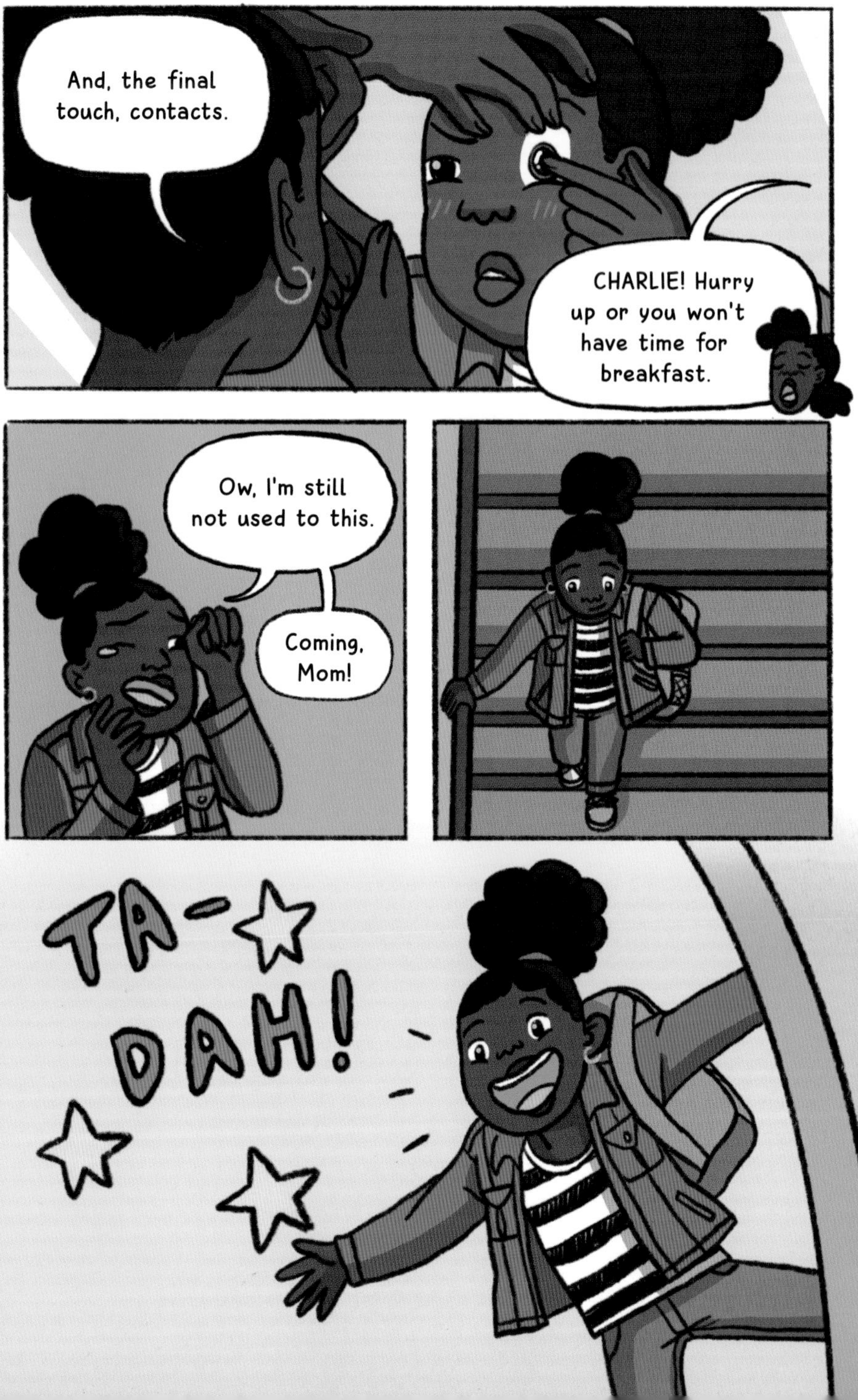
And, the final touch, contacts.
CHARLIE! Hurry up or you won't have time for breakfast.
Ow, I'm still not used to this.
Coming, Mom!
TA-DAH!

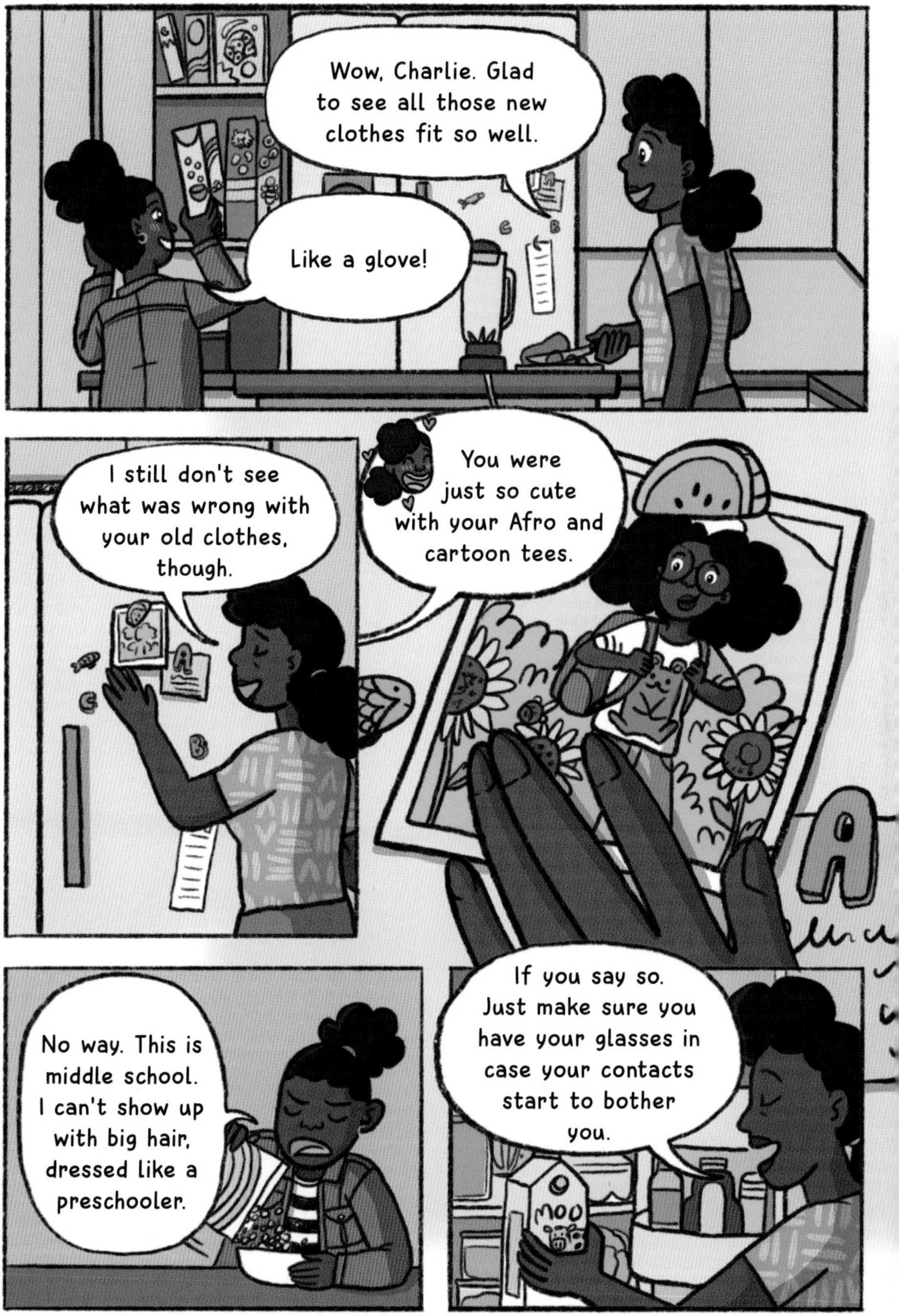
Wow, Charlie. Glad to see all those new clothes fit so well.
Like a glove!
I still don't see what was wrong with your old clothes, though.
You were just so cute with your Afro and cartoon tees.
No way. This is middle school. I can't show up with big hair, dressed like a preschooler.
If you say so. Just make sure you have your glasses in case your contacts start to bother you.
MOO

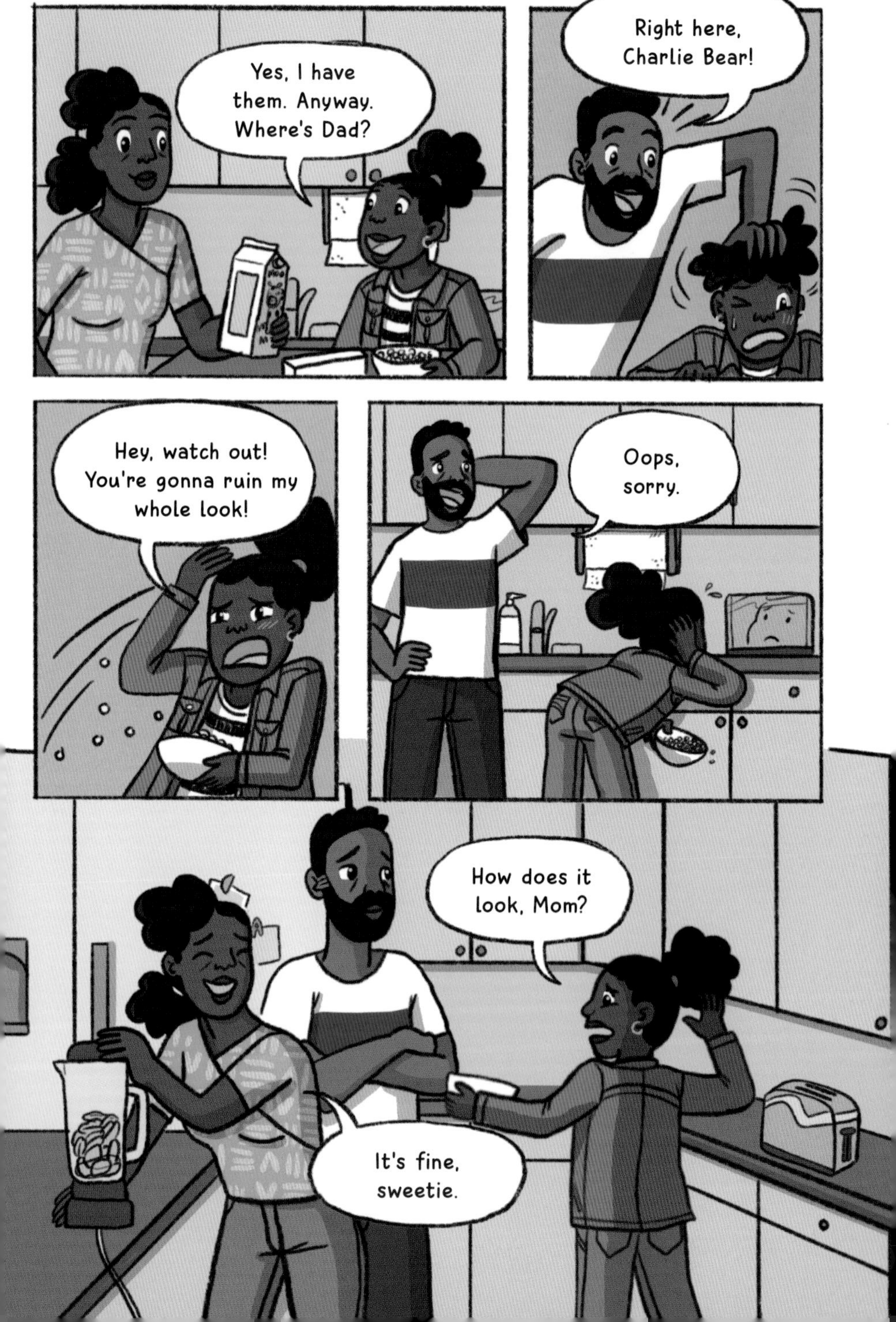
Yes, I have them. Anyway. Where's Dad?
Right here, Charlie Bear!
Hey, watch out! You're gonna ruin my whole look!
Oops, sorry.
How does it look, Mom?
It's fine, sweetie.

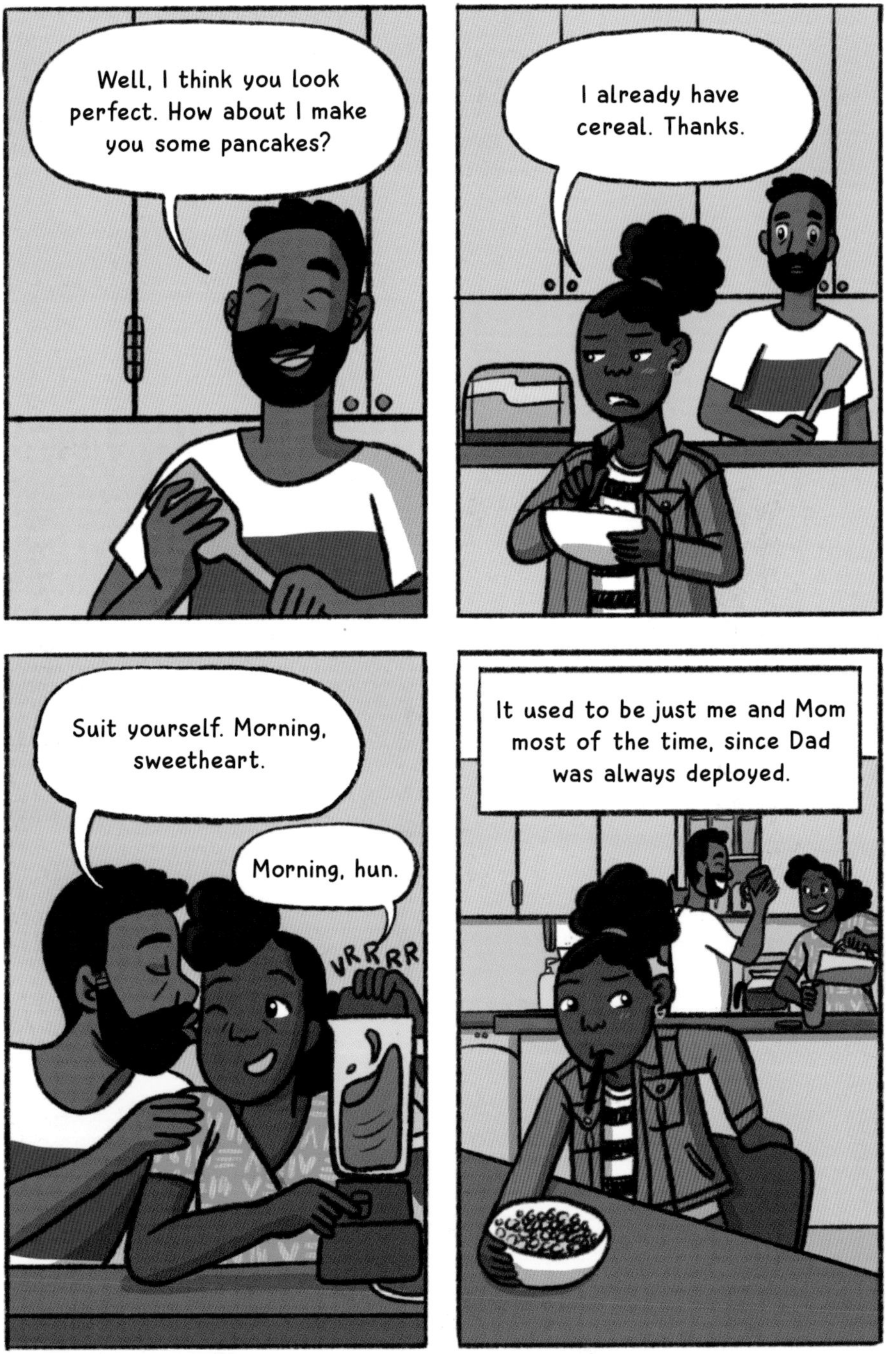
Well, I think you look perfect. How about I make you some pancakes?
I already have cereal. Thanks.
Suit yourself. Morning, sweetheart.
Morning, hun.
VRRRR
It used to be just me and Mom most of the time, since Dad was always deployed.

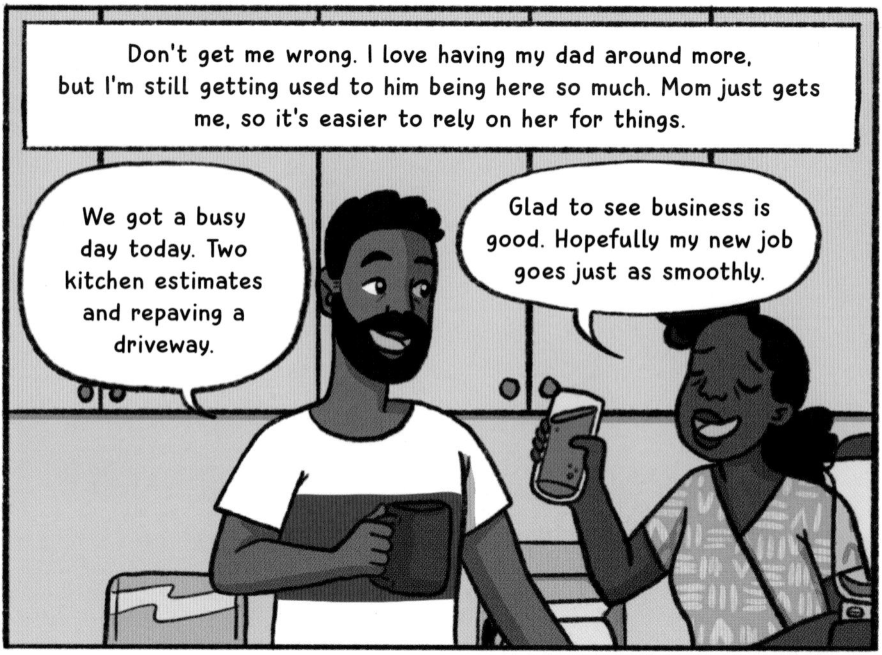
Don't get me wrong. I love having my dad around more, but I'm still getting used to him being here so much. Mom just gets me, so it's easier to rely on her for things.
We got a busy day today. Two kitchen estimates and repaving a driveway.
Glad to see business is good. Hopefully my new job goes just as smoothly.

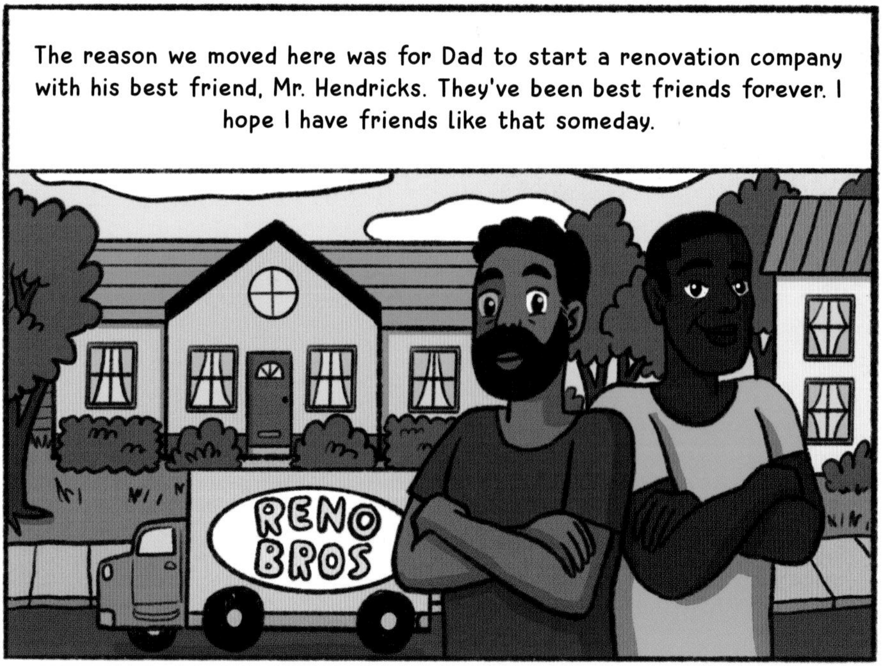
The reason we moved here was for Dad to start a renovation company with his best friend, Mr. Hendricks. They've been best friends forever. I hope I have friends like that someday.
RENO BROS

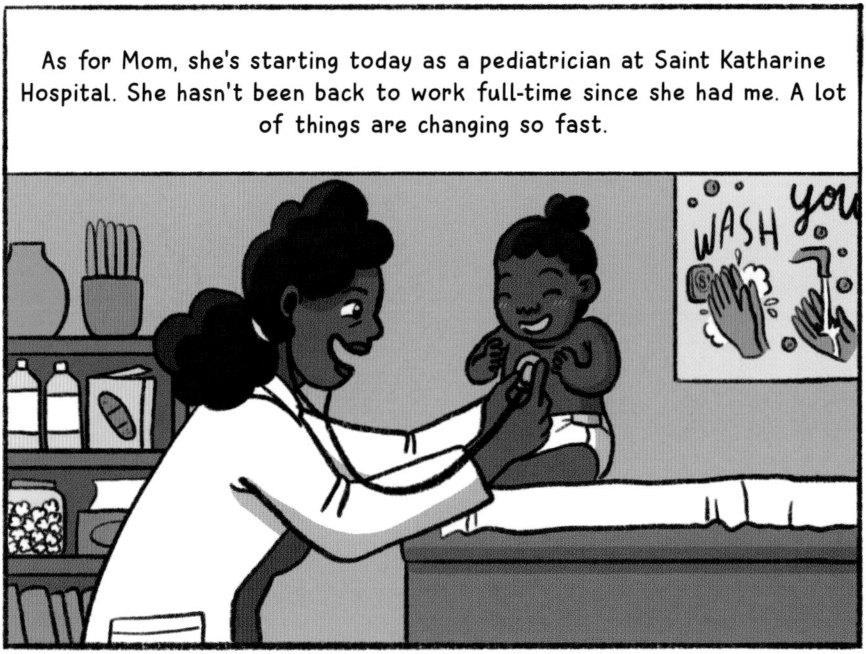
As for Mom, she's starting today as a pediatrician at Saint Katharine Hospital. She hasn't been back to work full-time since she had me. A lot of things are changing so fast.
WASH you

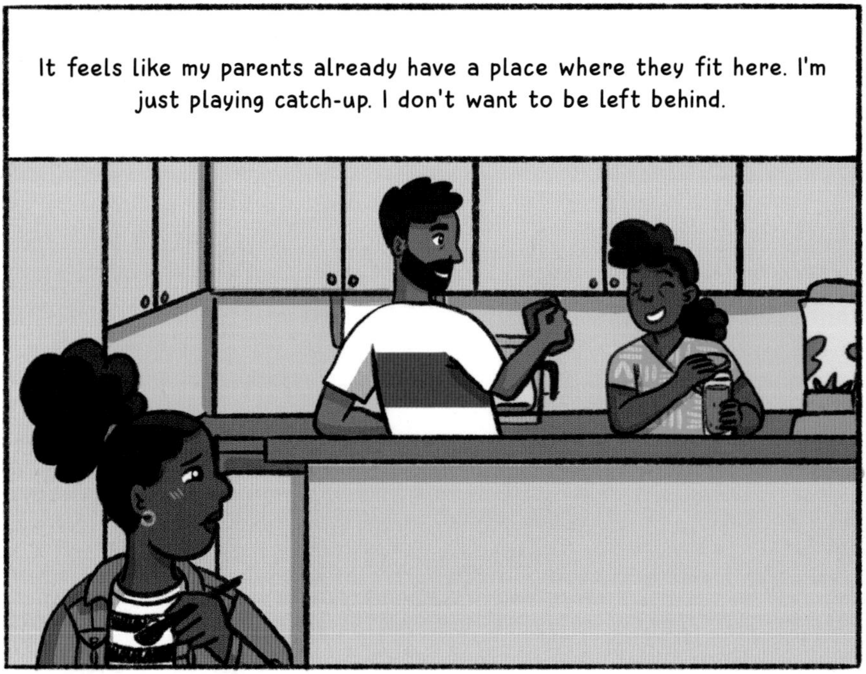
It feels like my parents already have a place where they fit here. I'm just playing catch-up. I don't want to be left behind.

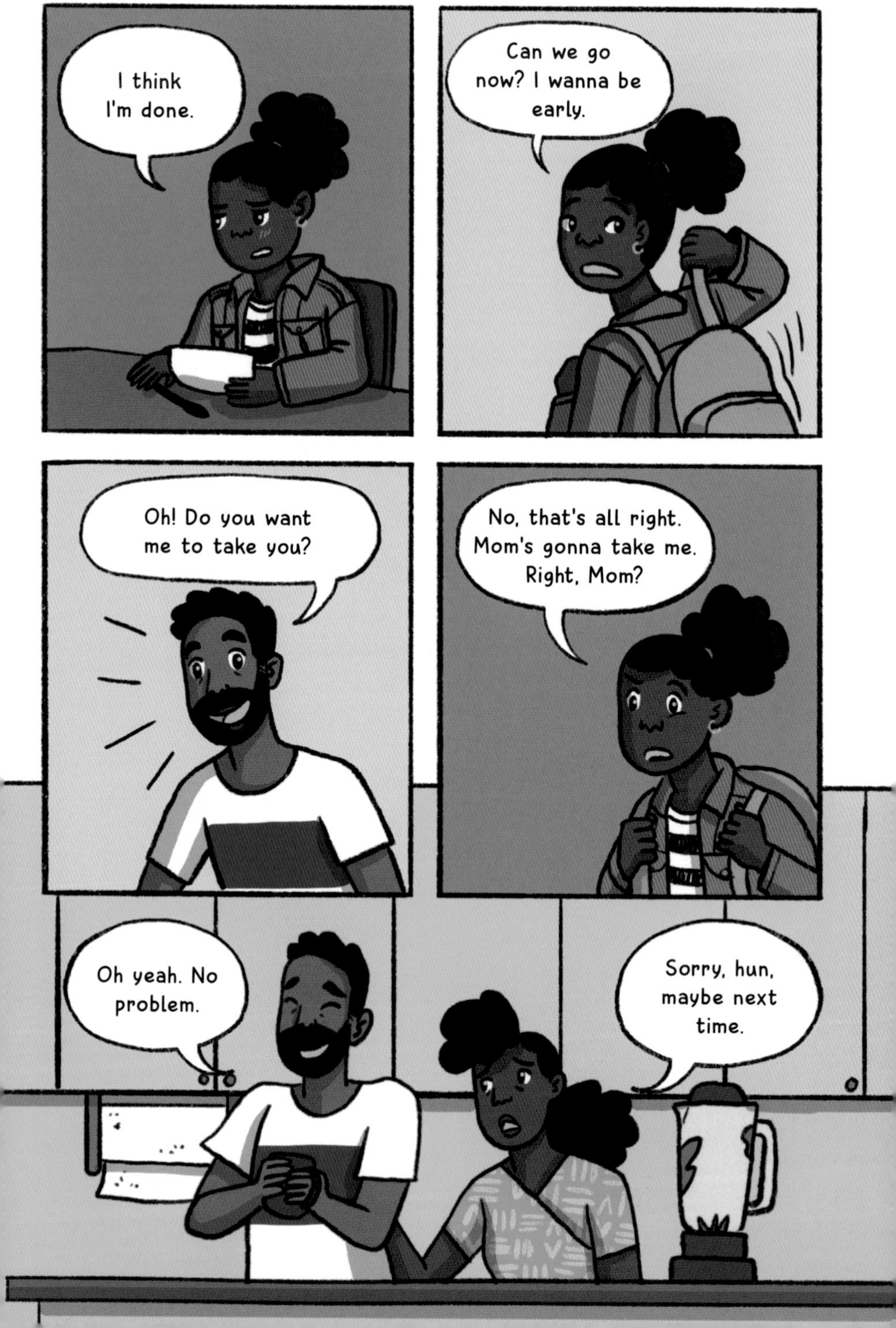
I think I'm done.
Can we go now? I wanna be early.
Oh! Do you want me to take you?
No, that's all right. Mom's gonna take me. Right, Mom?
Oh yeah. No problem.
Sorry, hun, maybe next time.

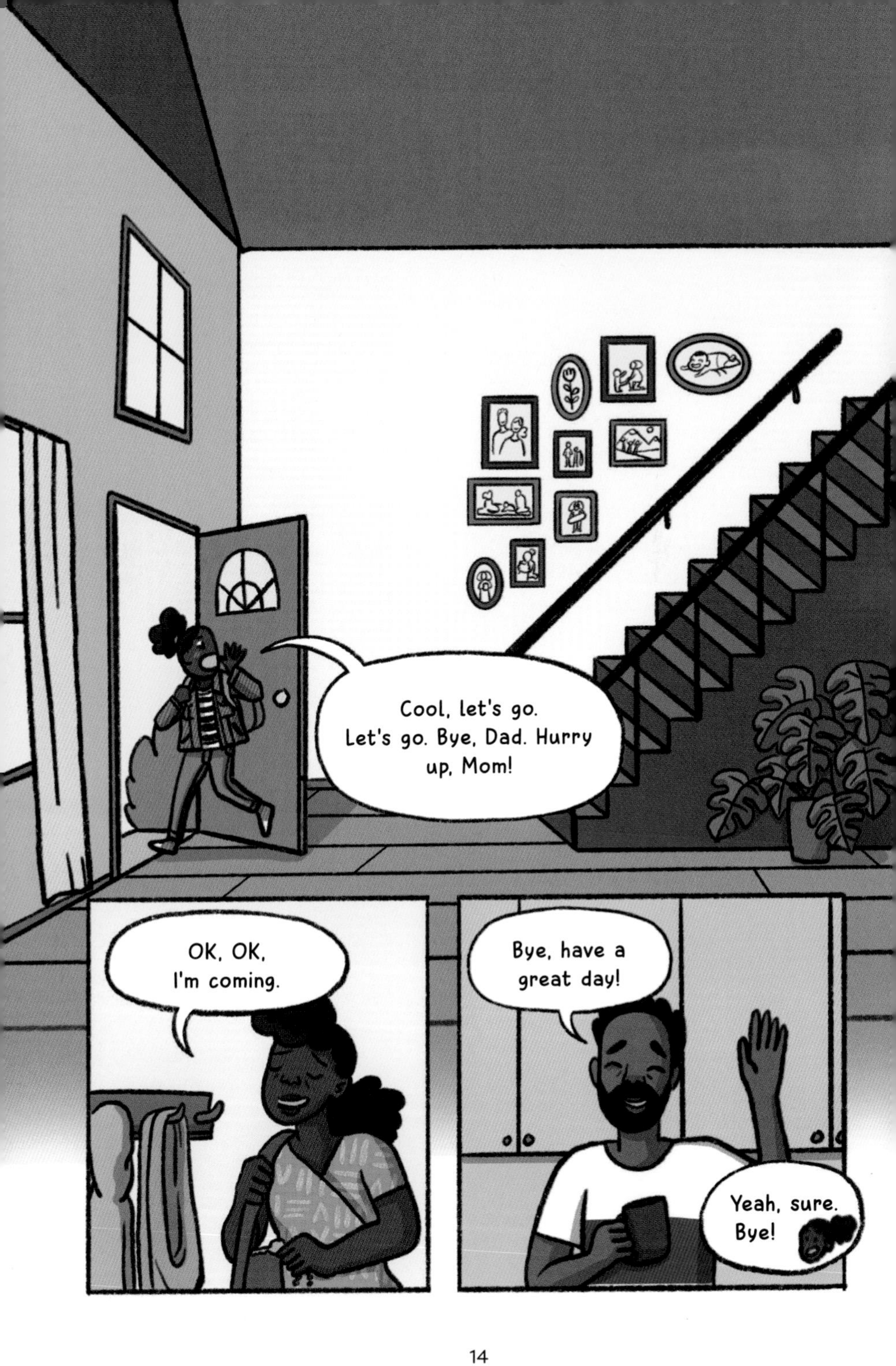
Cool, let's go. Let's go. Bye, Dad. Hurry up, Mom!
OK, OK, I'm coming.
Bye, have a great day!
Yeah, sure. Bye!

CHAPTER 2

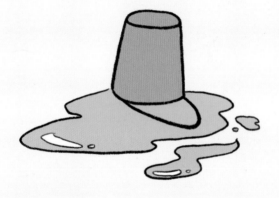

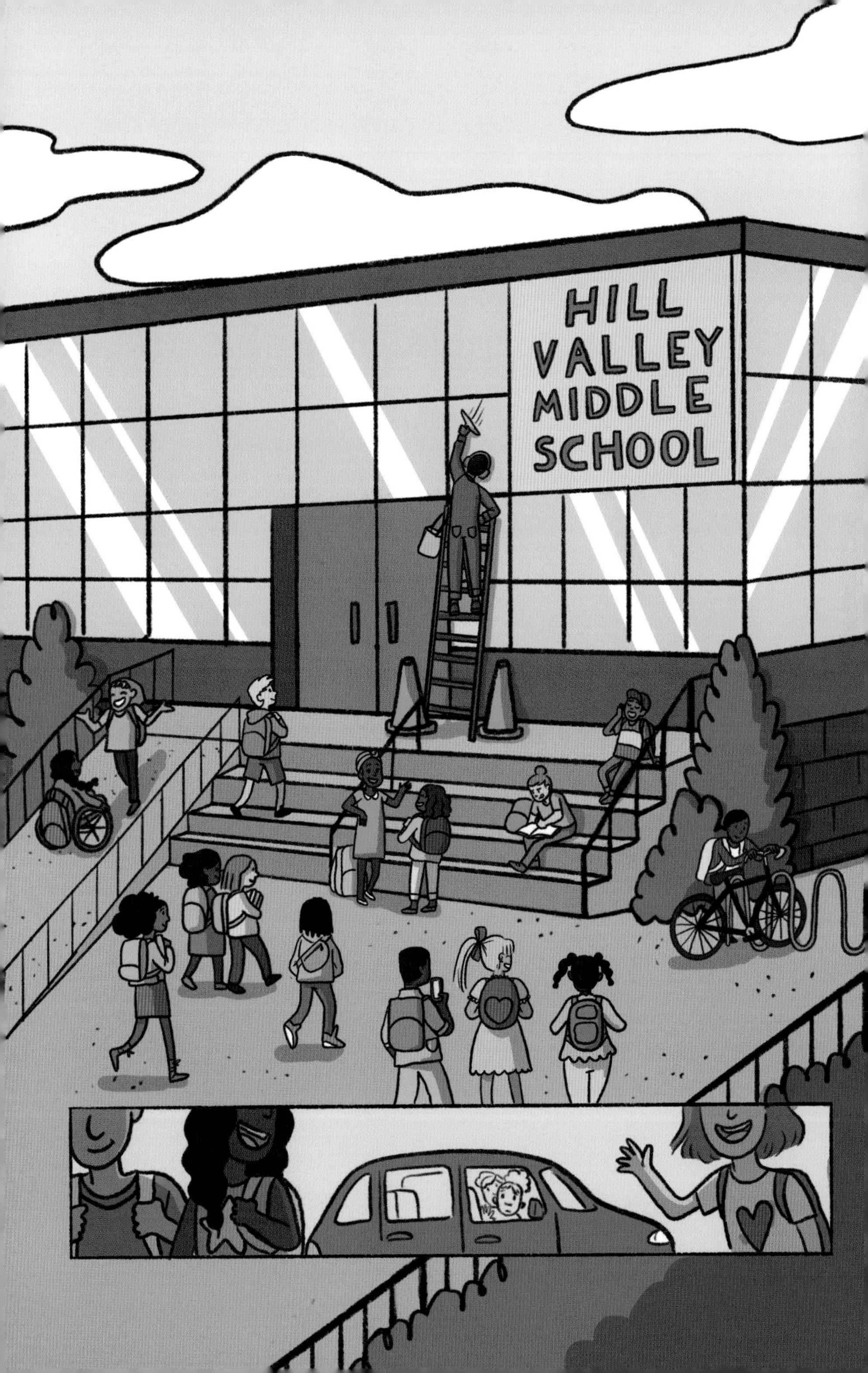
HILL VALLEY MIDDLE SCHOOL

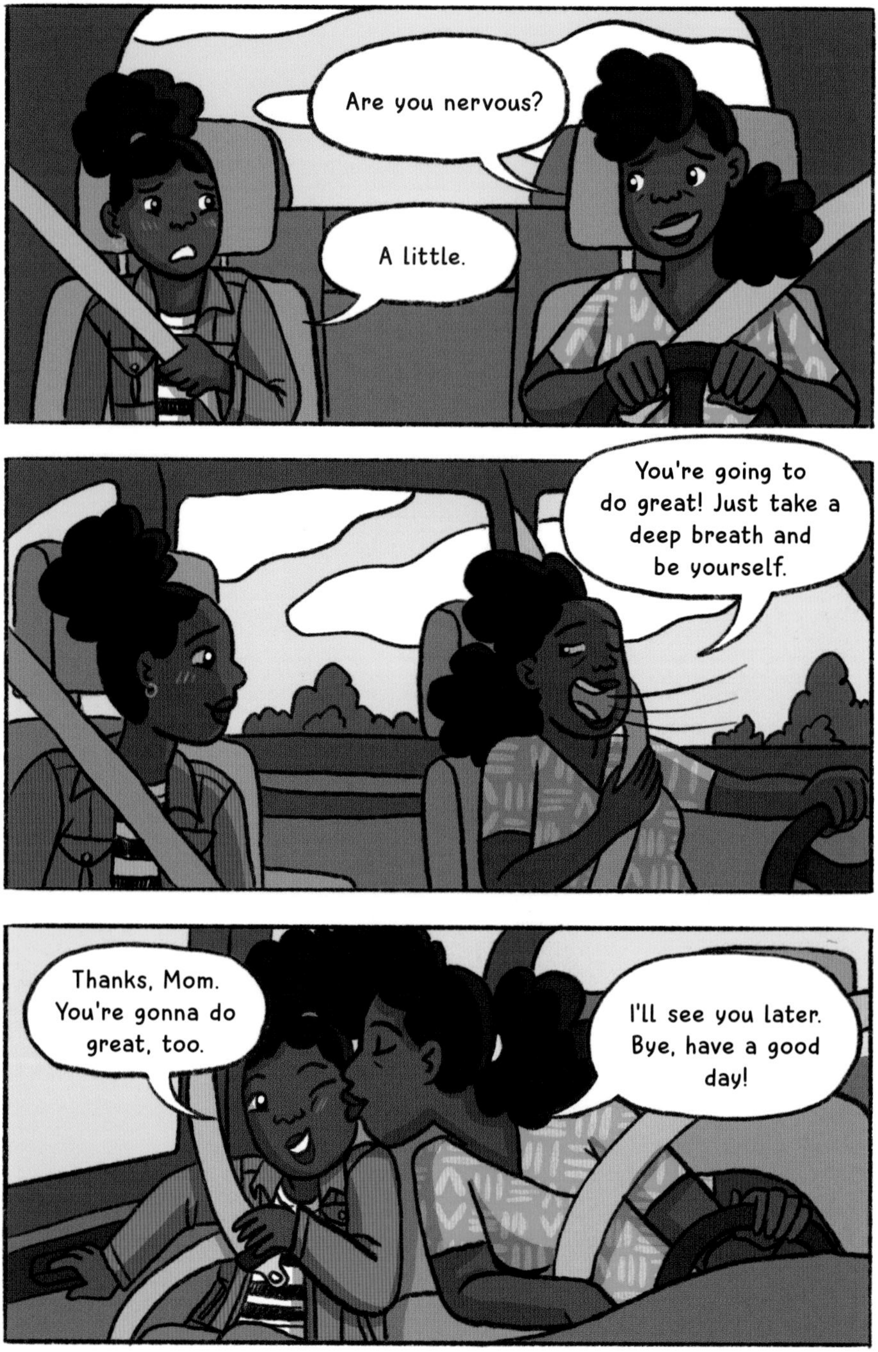
Are you nervous?
A little.
You're going to do great! Just take a deep breath and be yourself.
Thanks, Mom. You're gonna do great, too.
I'll see you later. Bye, have a good day!

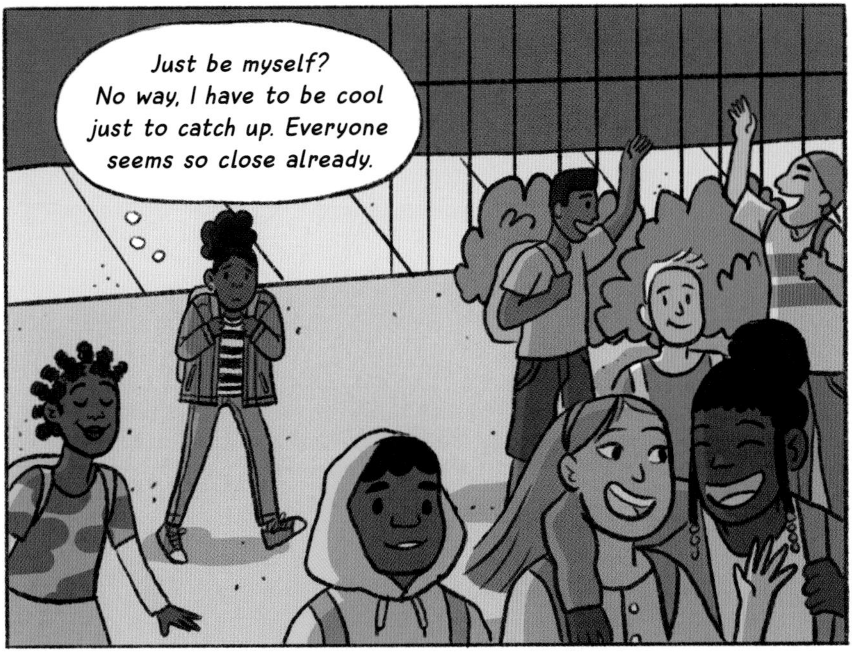
Just be myself? No way, I have to be cool just to catch up. Everyone seems so close already.

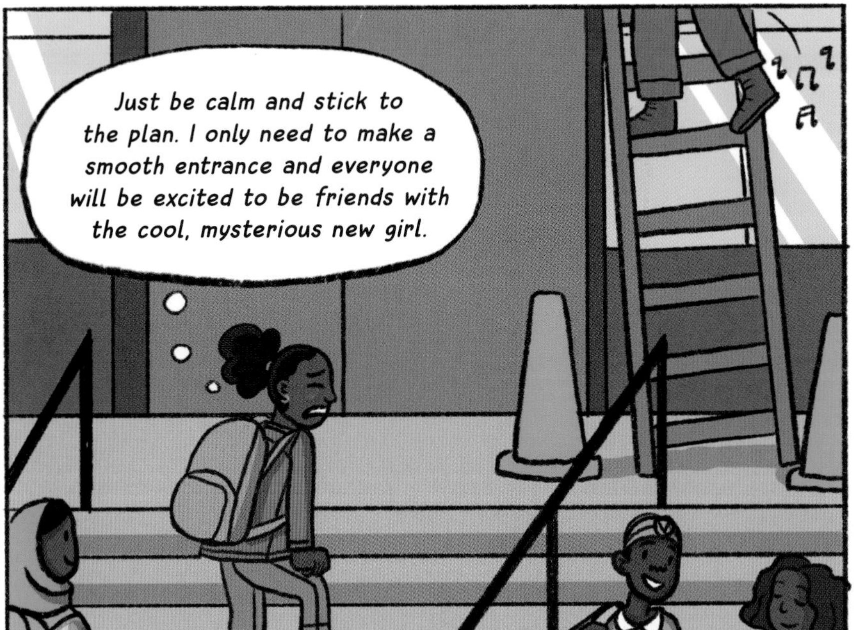
Just be calm and stick to the plan. I only need to make a smooth entrance and everyone will be excited to be friends with the cool, mysterious new girl.

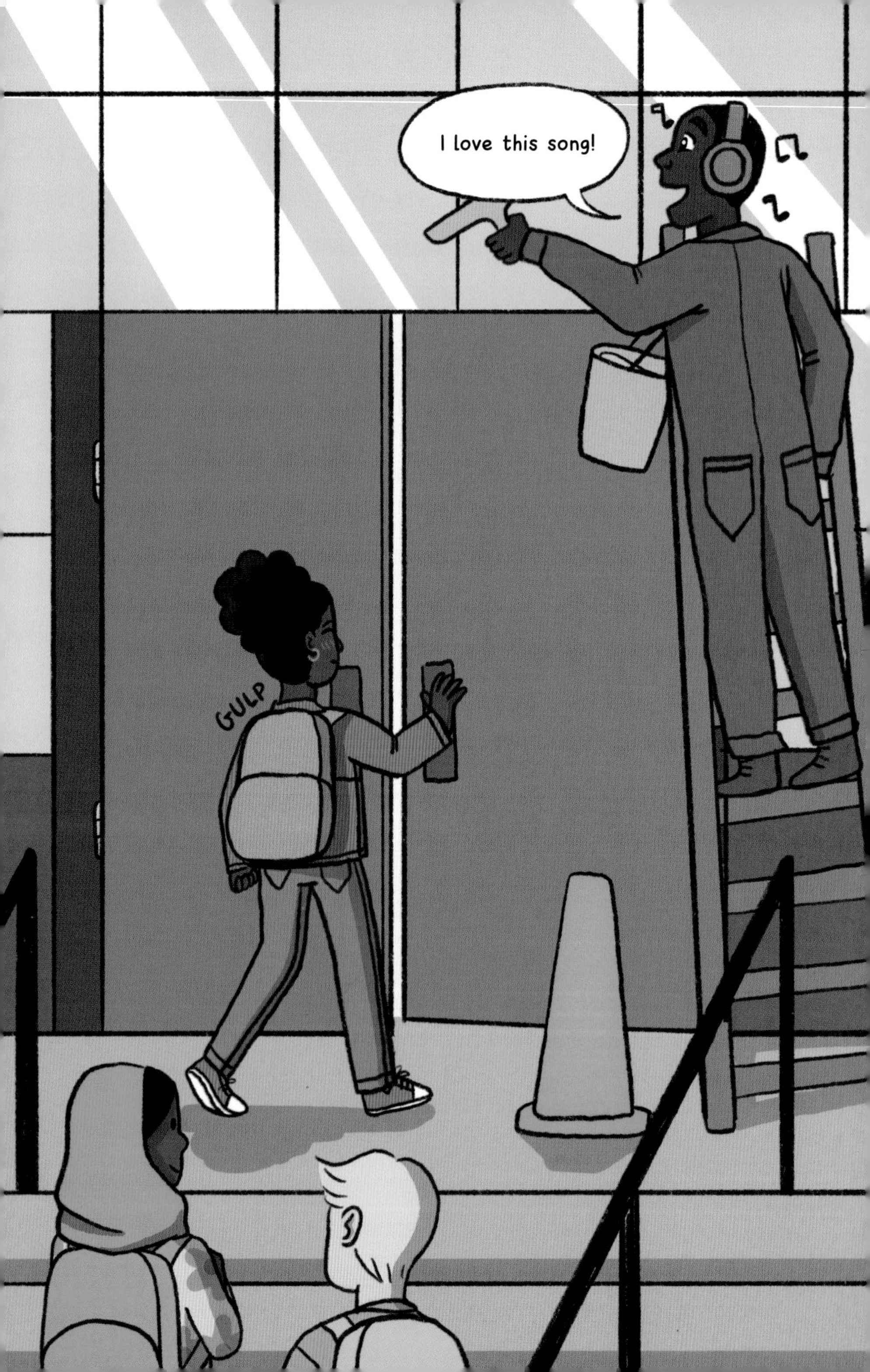
I love this song!
GULP

Oh yeah!
SPLASH
EEEEEEK!!

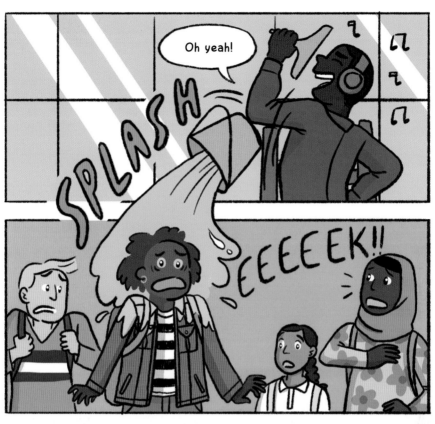

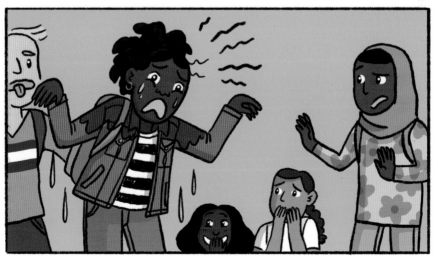

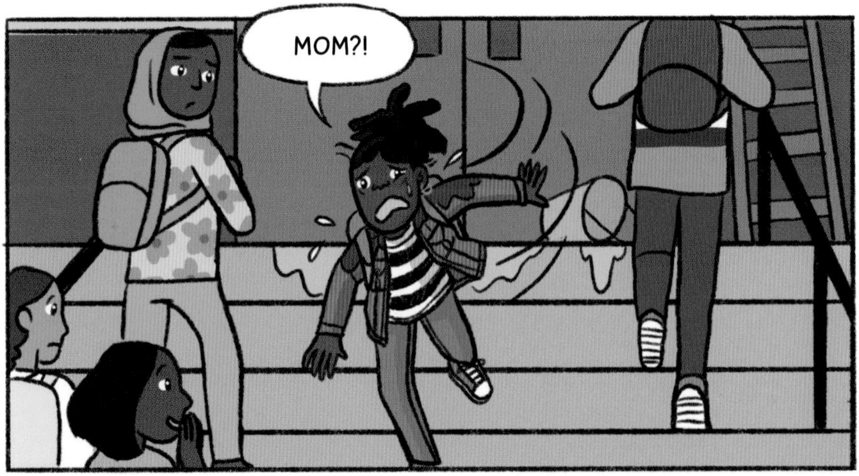
MOM?!
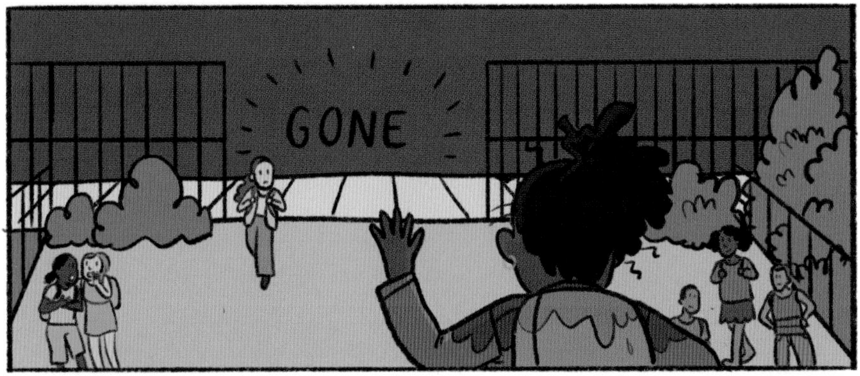
GONE
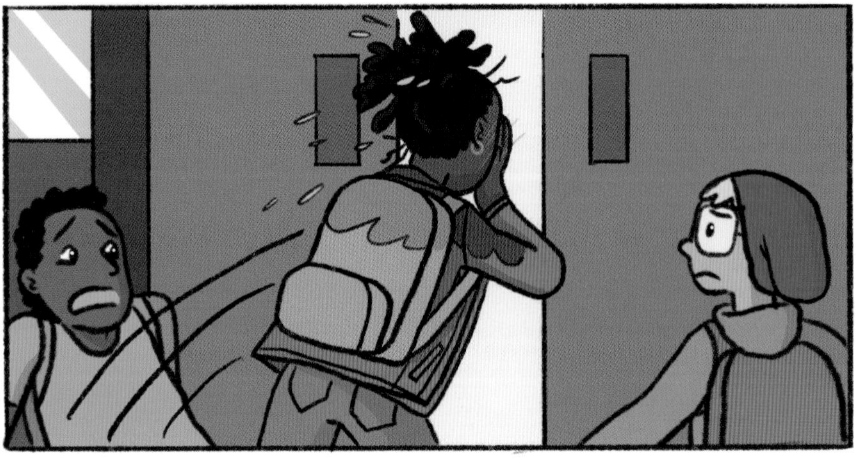

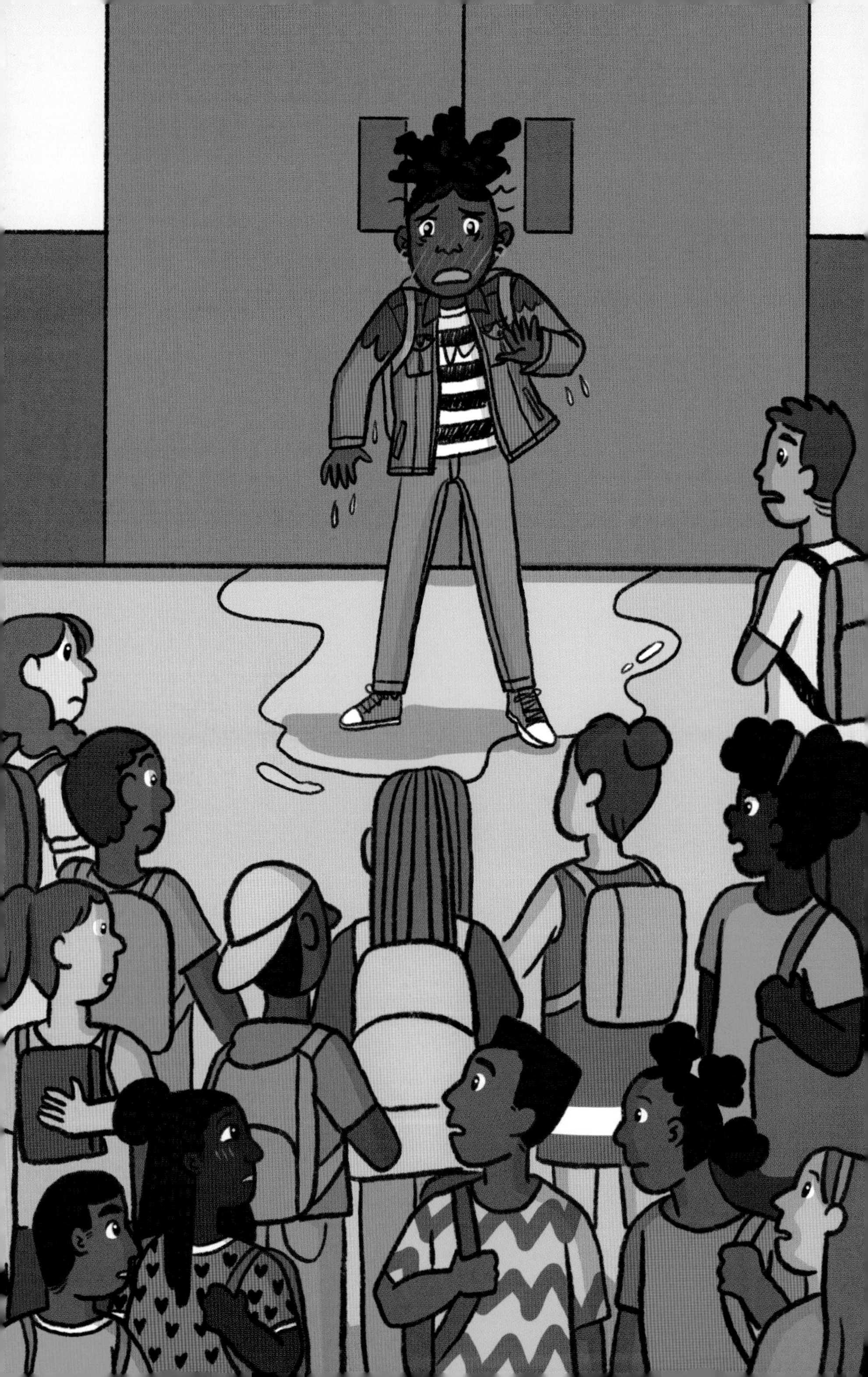

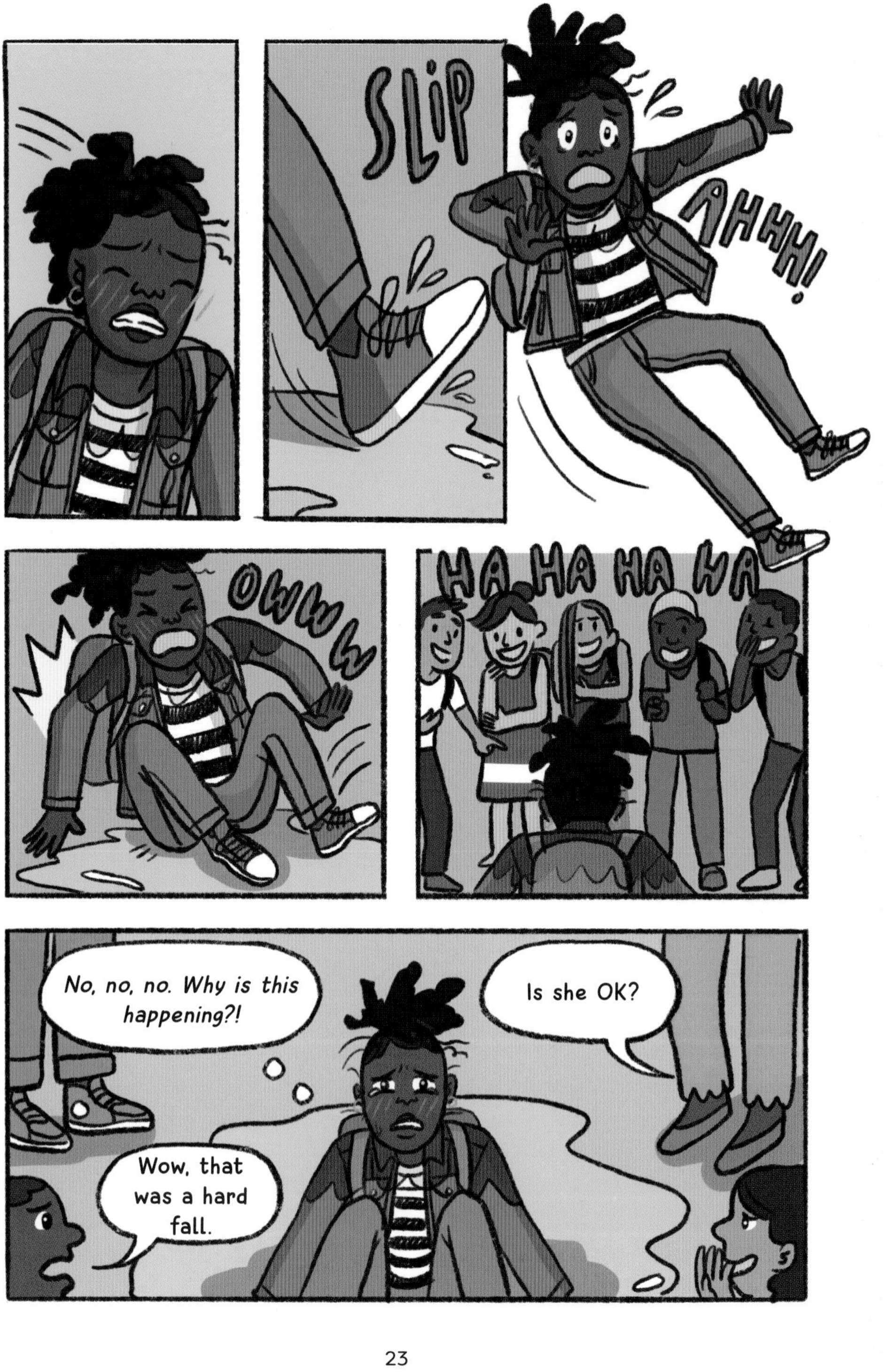
SLIP
AHHH!
OWWW
HA HA HA HA
No, no, no. Why is this happening?!
Is she OK?
Wow, that was a hard fall.

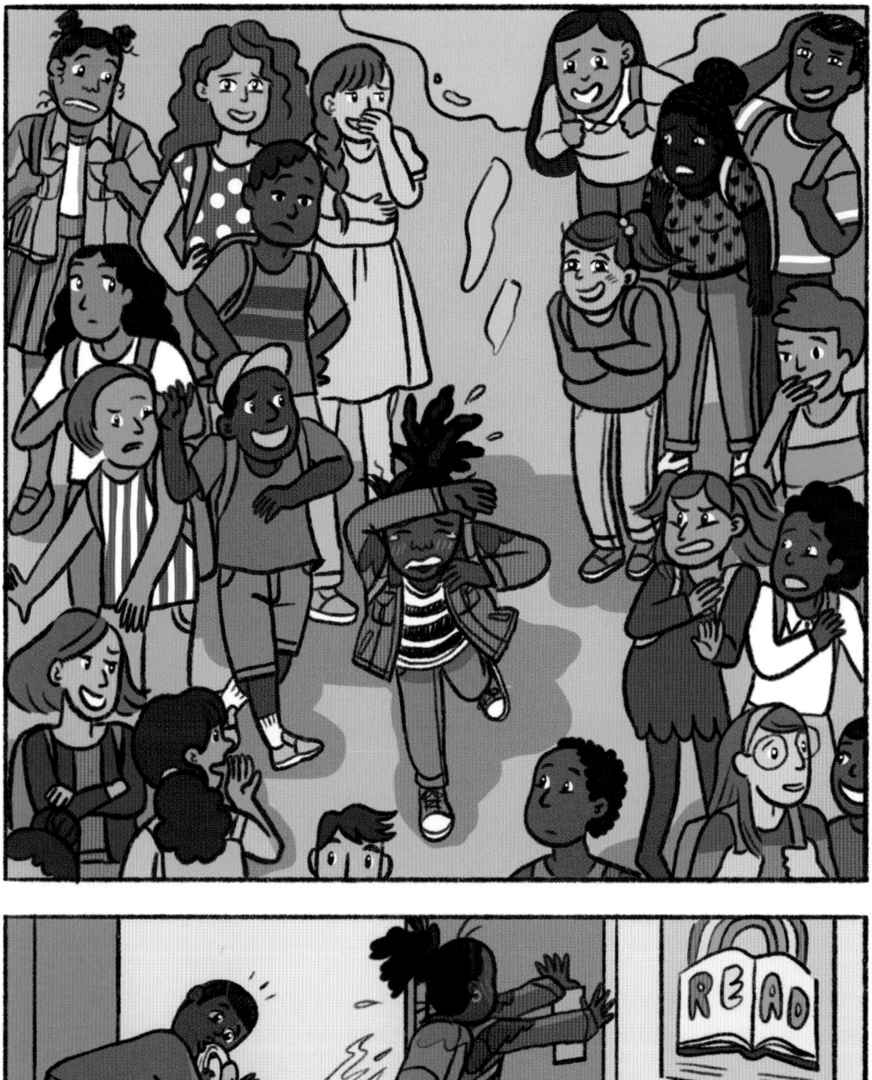

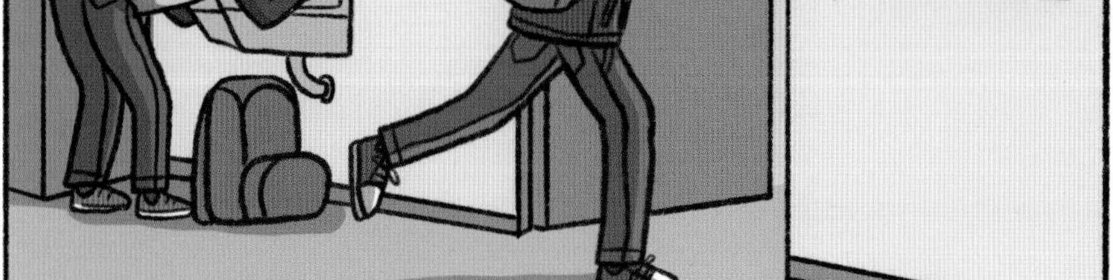
READ

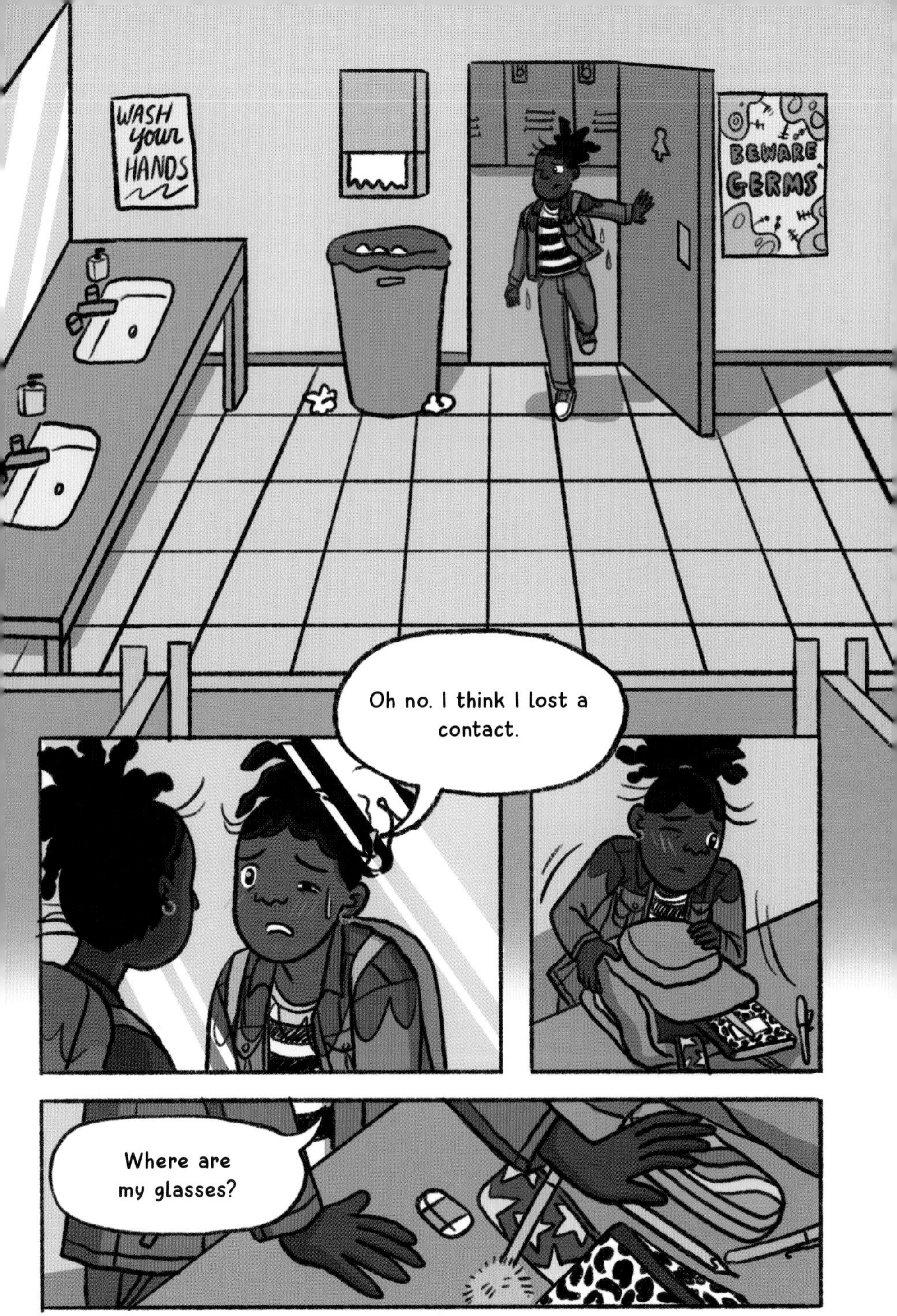
WASH your HANDS
BEWARE GERMS
Oh no. I think I lost a contact.
Where are my glasses?

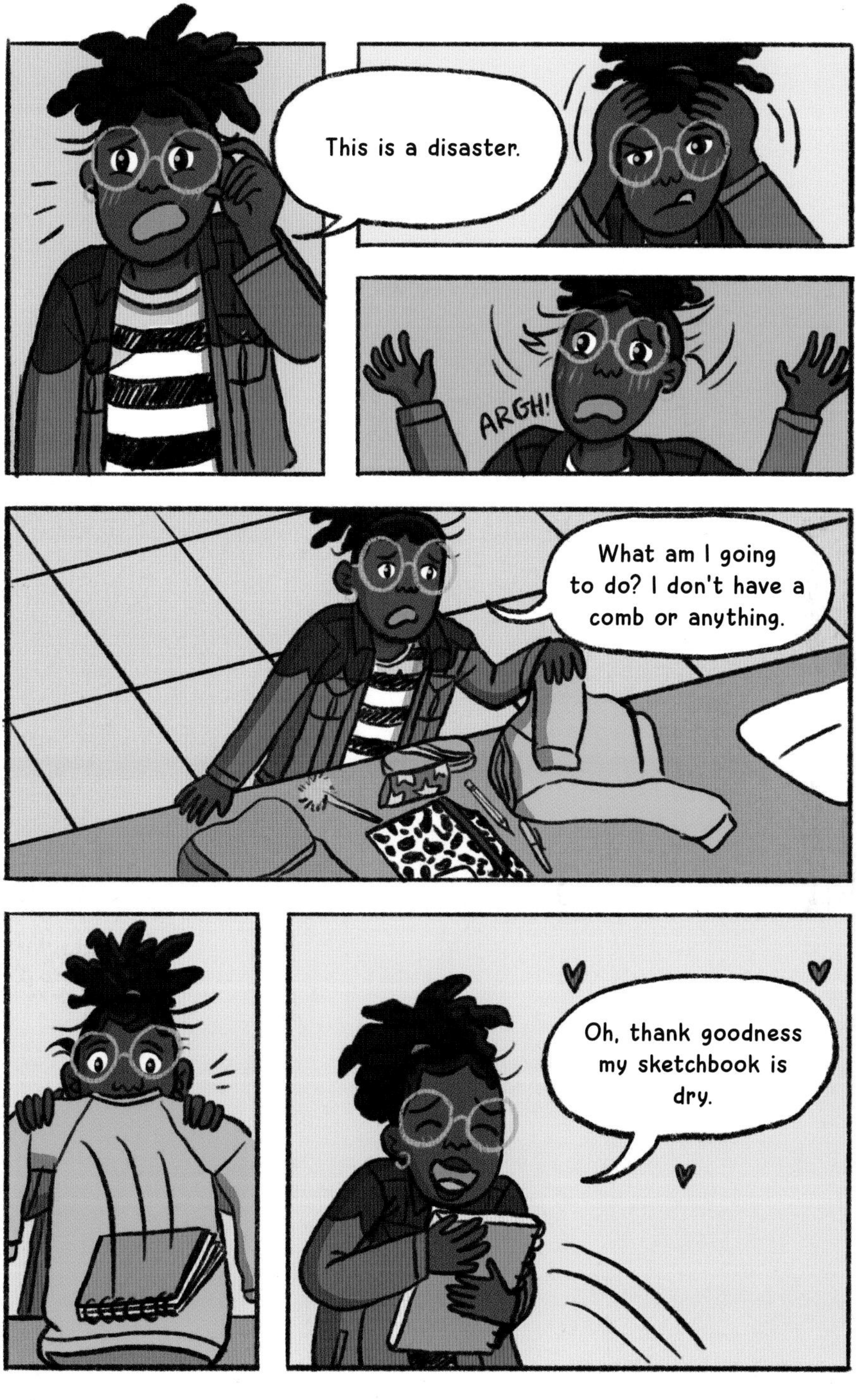
This is a disaster.
ARGH!
What am I going to do? I don't have a comb or anything.
Oh, thank goodness my sketchbook is dry.

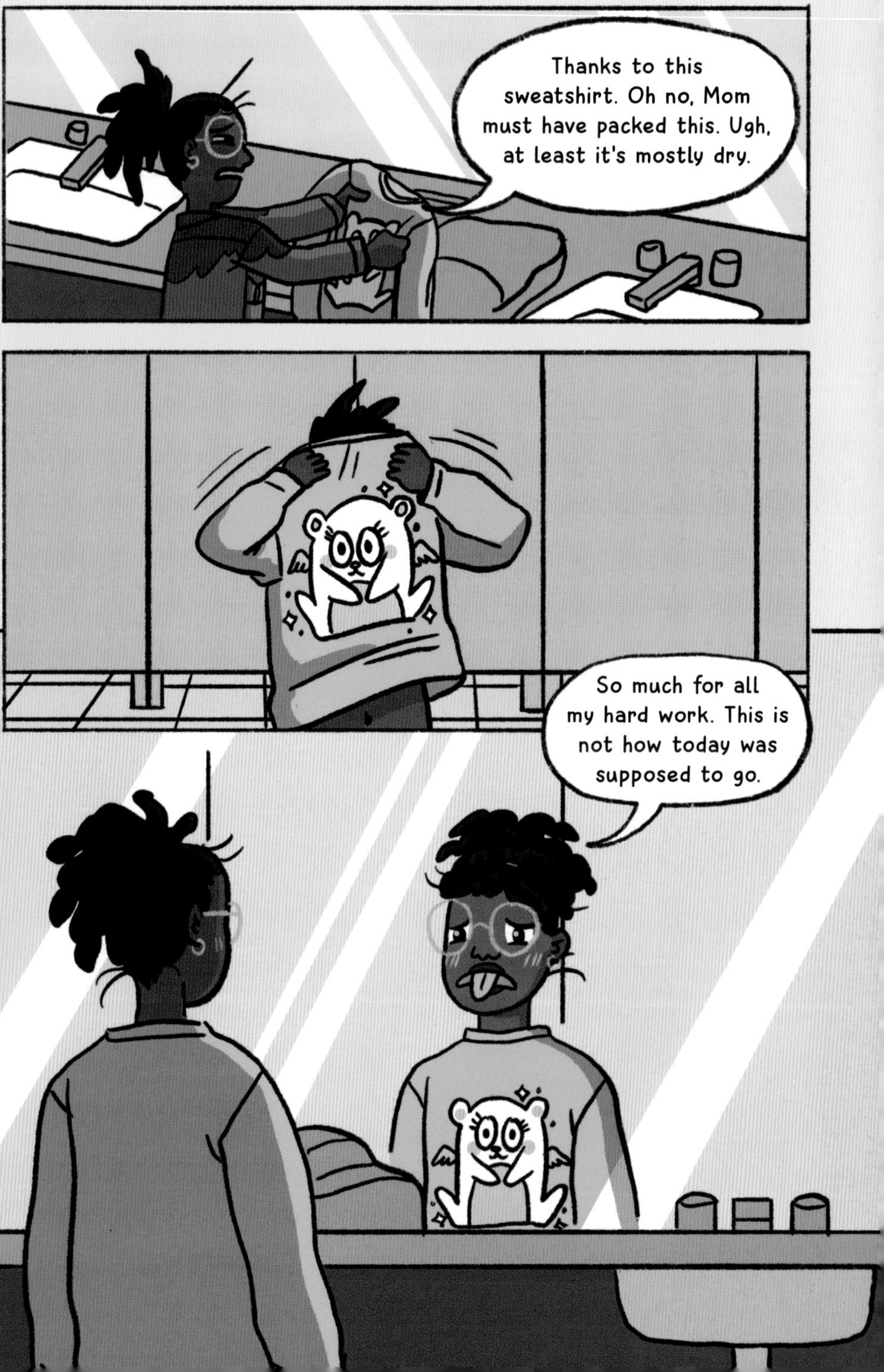
Thanks to this sweatshirt. Oh no, Mom must have packed this. Ugh, at least it's mostly dry.
So much for all my hard work. This is not how today was supposed to go.

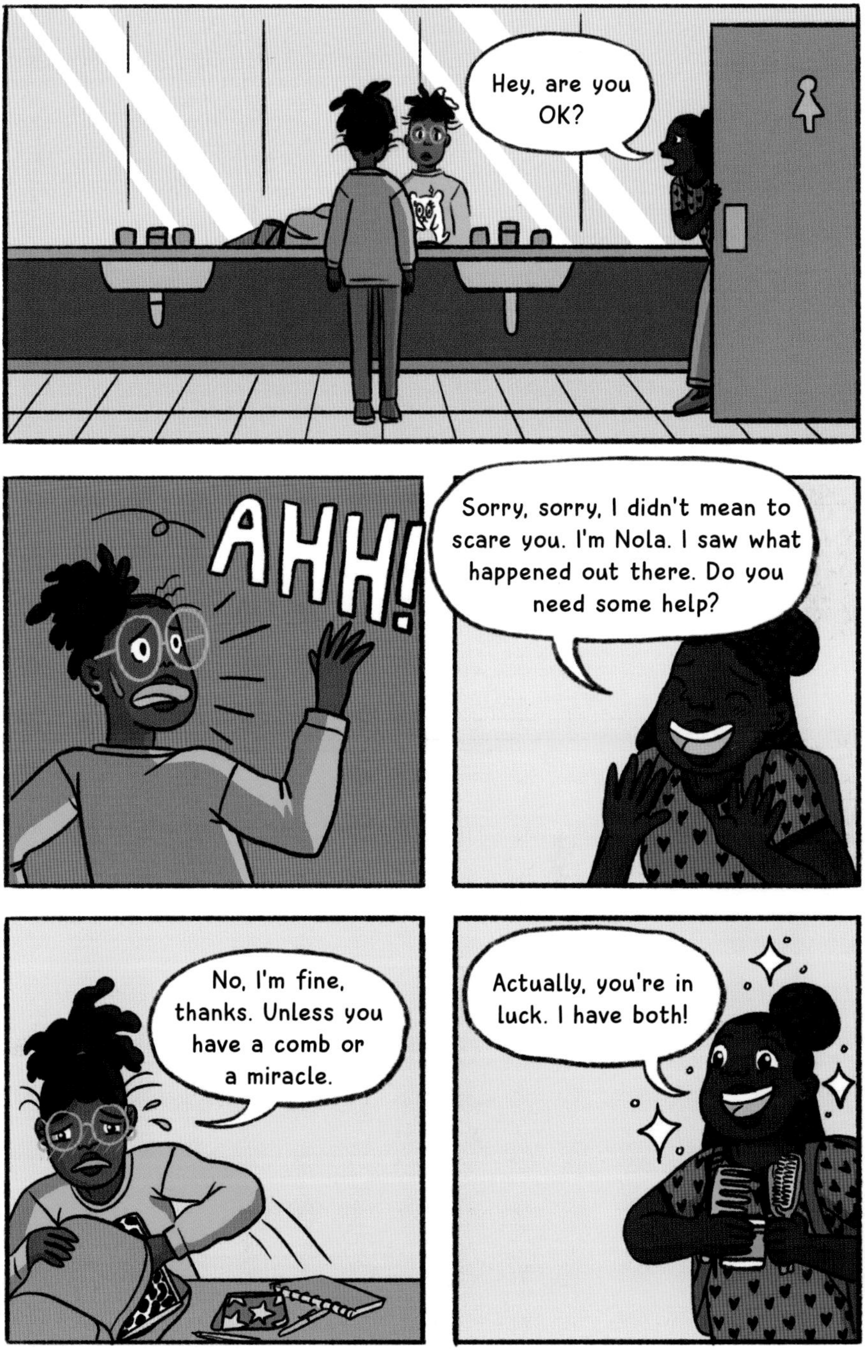
Hey, are you OK?
AHH!
Sorry, sorry, I didn't mean to scare you. I'm Nola. I saw what happened out there. Do you need some help?
No, I'm fine, thanks. Unless you have a comb or a miracle.
Actually, you're in luck. I have both!

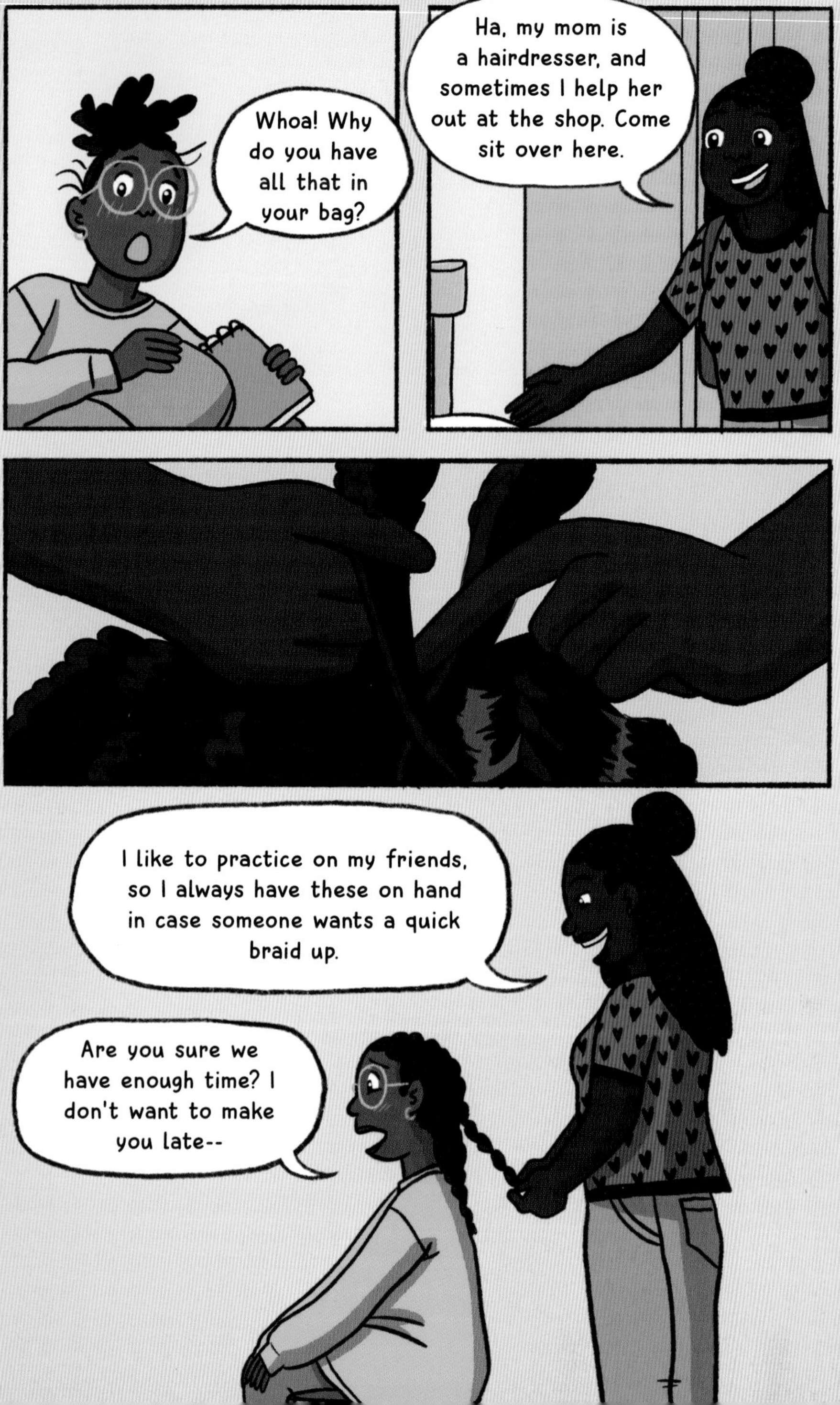
Whoa! Why do you have all that in your bag?
Ha, my mom is a hairdresser, and sometimes I help her out at the shop. Come sit over here.
I like to practice on my friends, so I always have these on hand in case someone wants a quick braid up.
Are you sure we have enough time? I don't want to make you late--

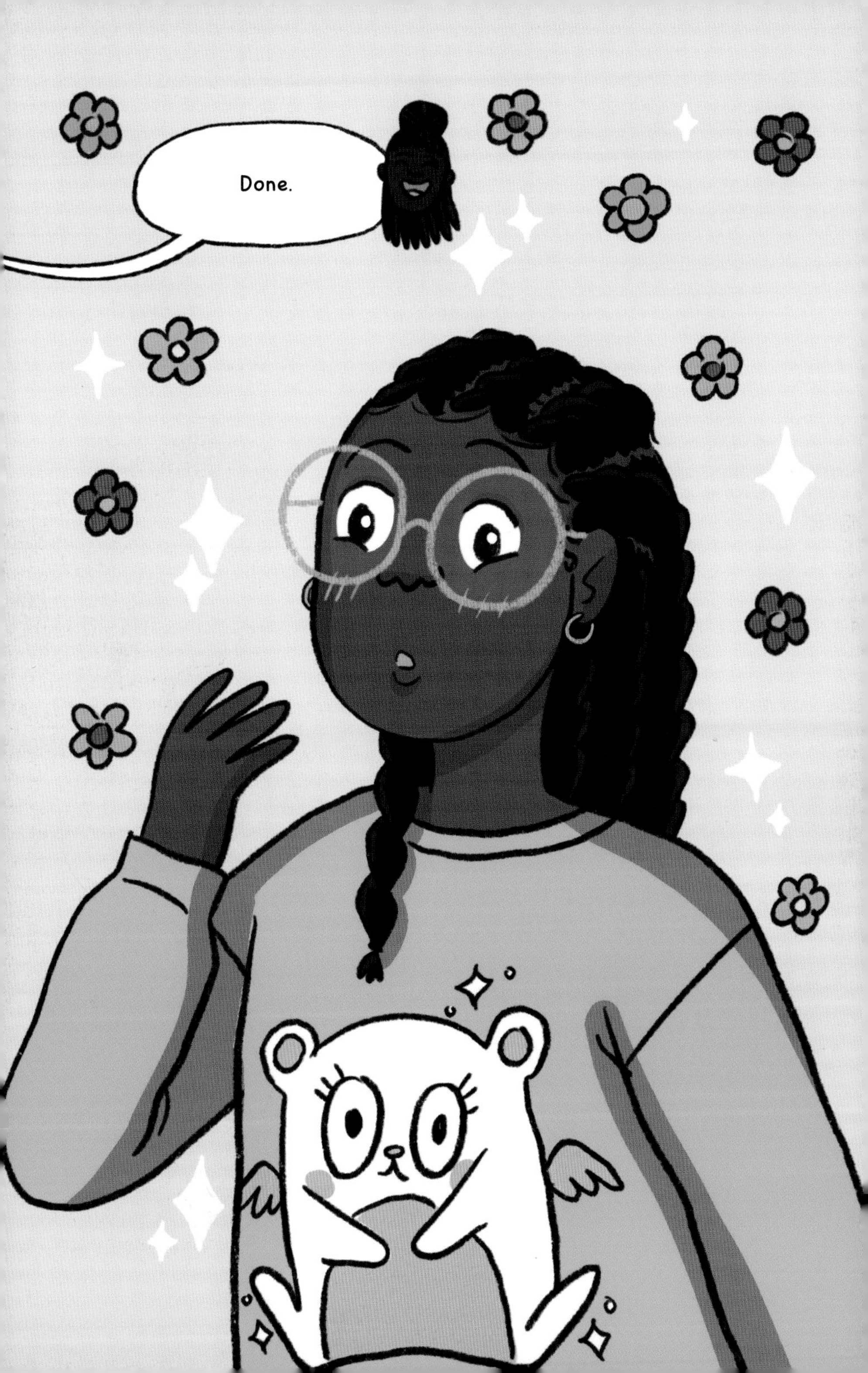
Done.

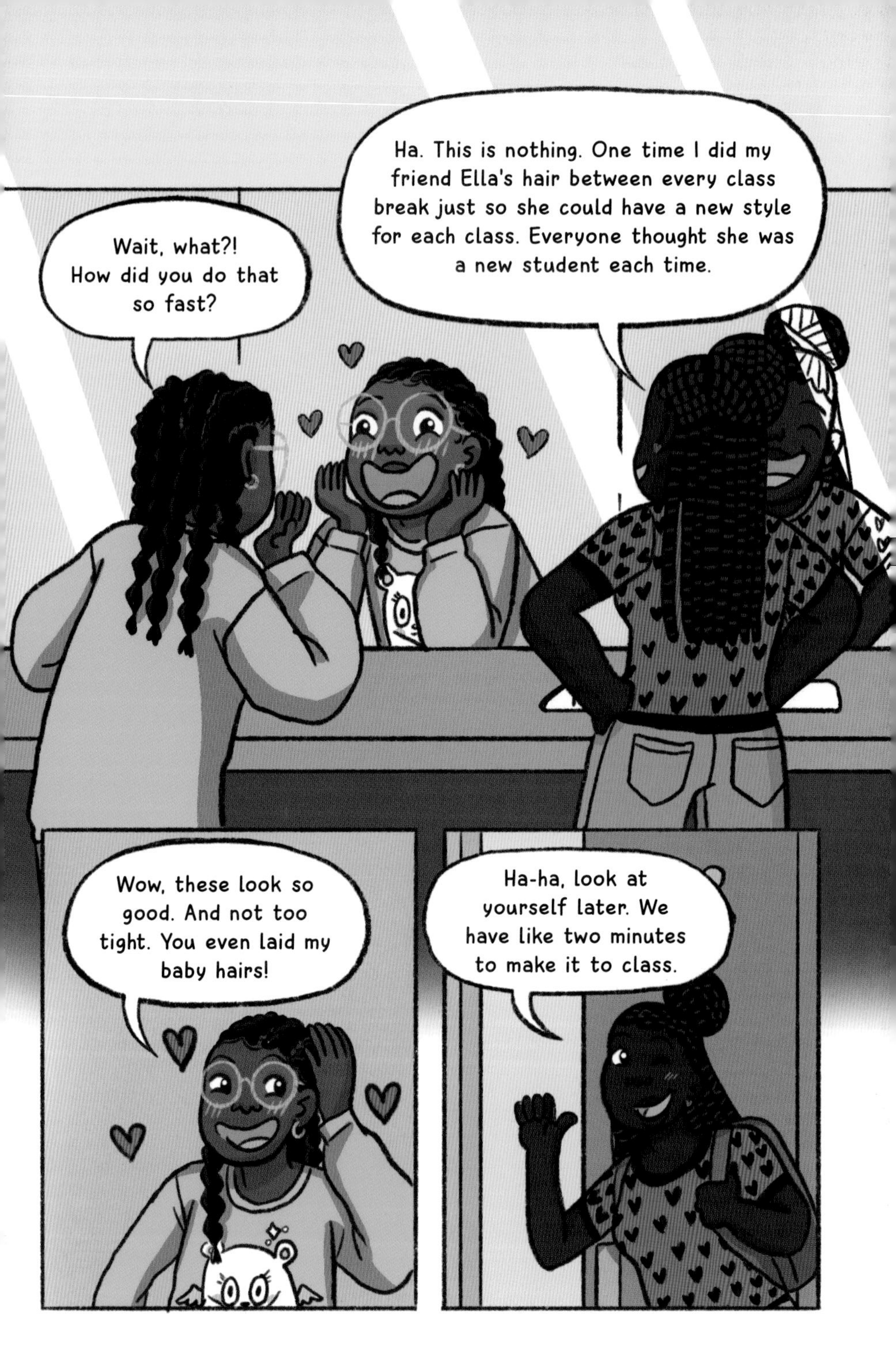
Wait, what?! How did you do that so fast?
Ha. This is nothing. One time I did my friend Ella's hair between every class break just so she could have a new style for each class. Everyone thought she was a new student each time.
Wow, these look so good. And not too tight. You even laid my baby hairs!
Ha-ha, look at yourself later. We have like two minutes to make it to class.

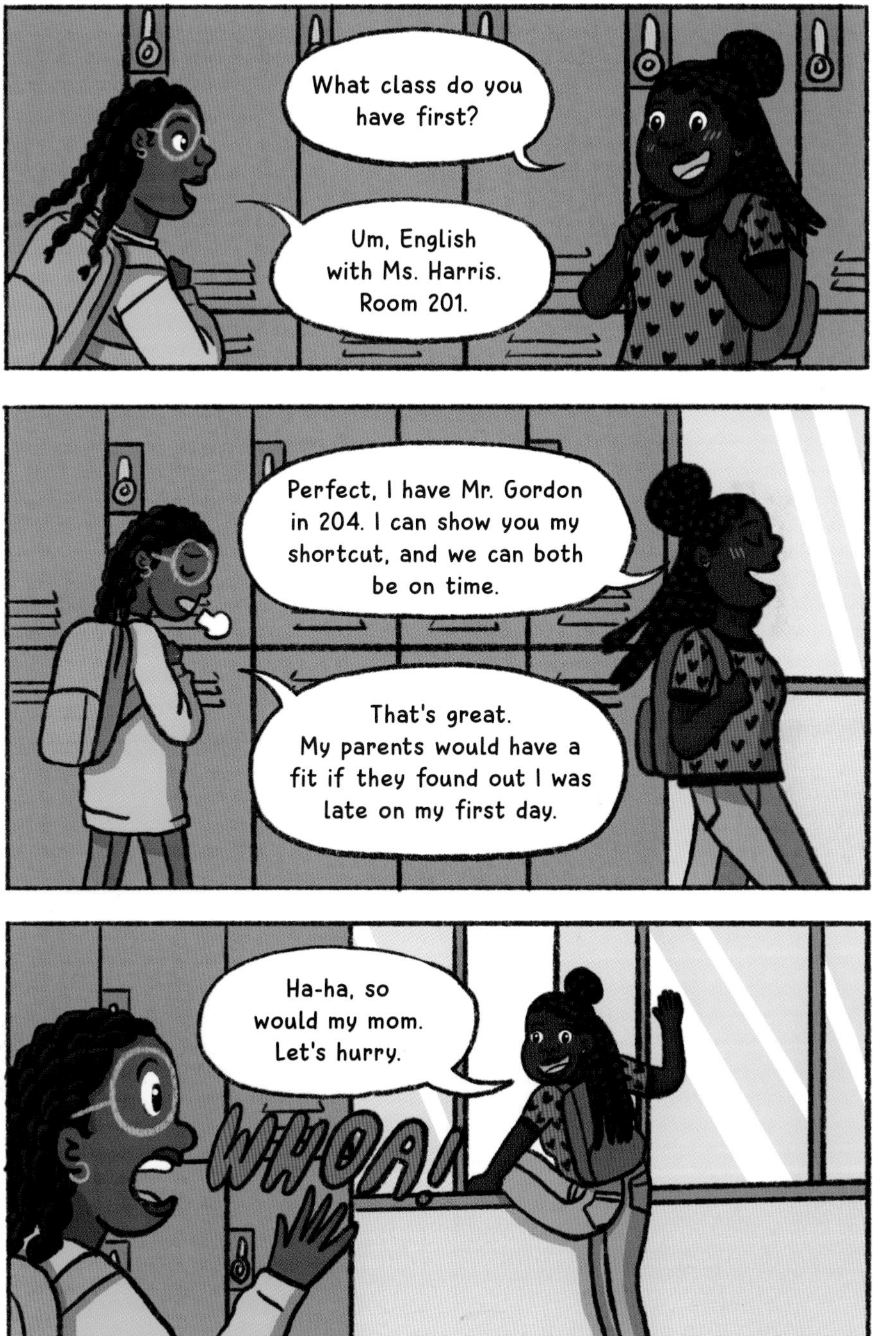
What class do you have first?
Um, English with Ms. Harris. Room 201.
Perfect, I have Mr. Gordon in 204. I can show you my shortcut, and we can both be on time.
That's great. My parents would have a fit if they found out I was late on my first day.
Ha-ha, so would my mom. Let's hurry.
WHOA!

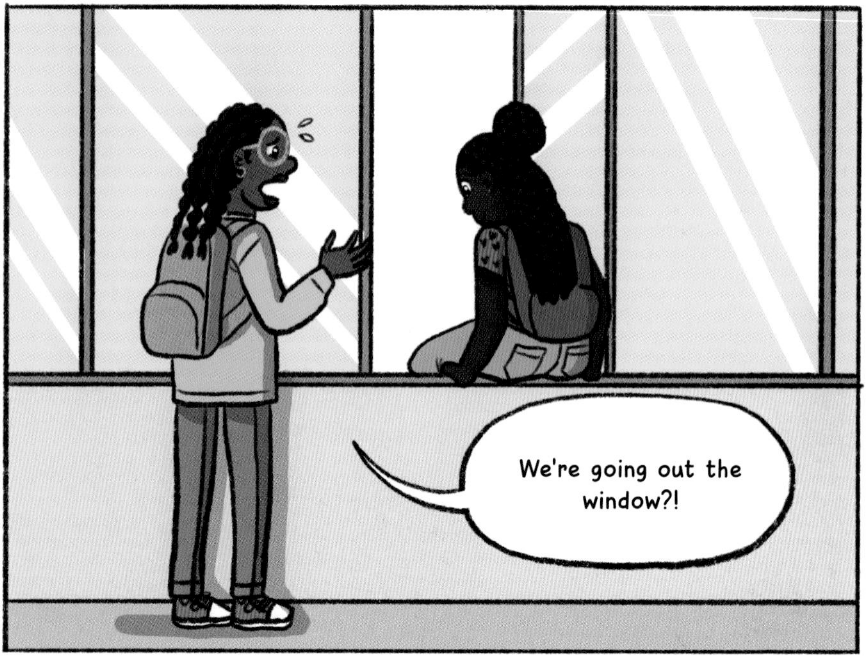
We're going out the window?!

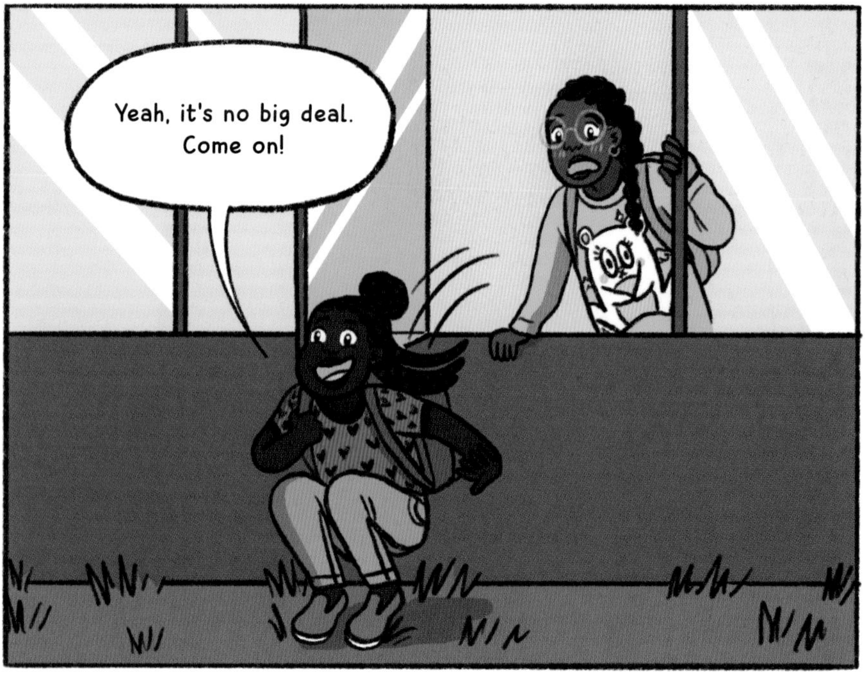
Yeah, it's no big deal. Come on!

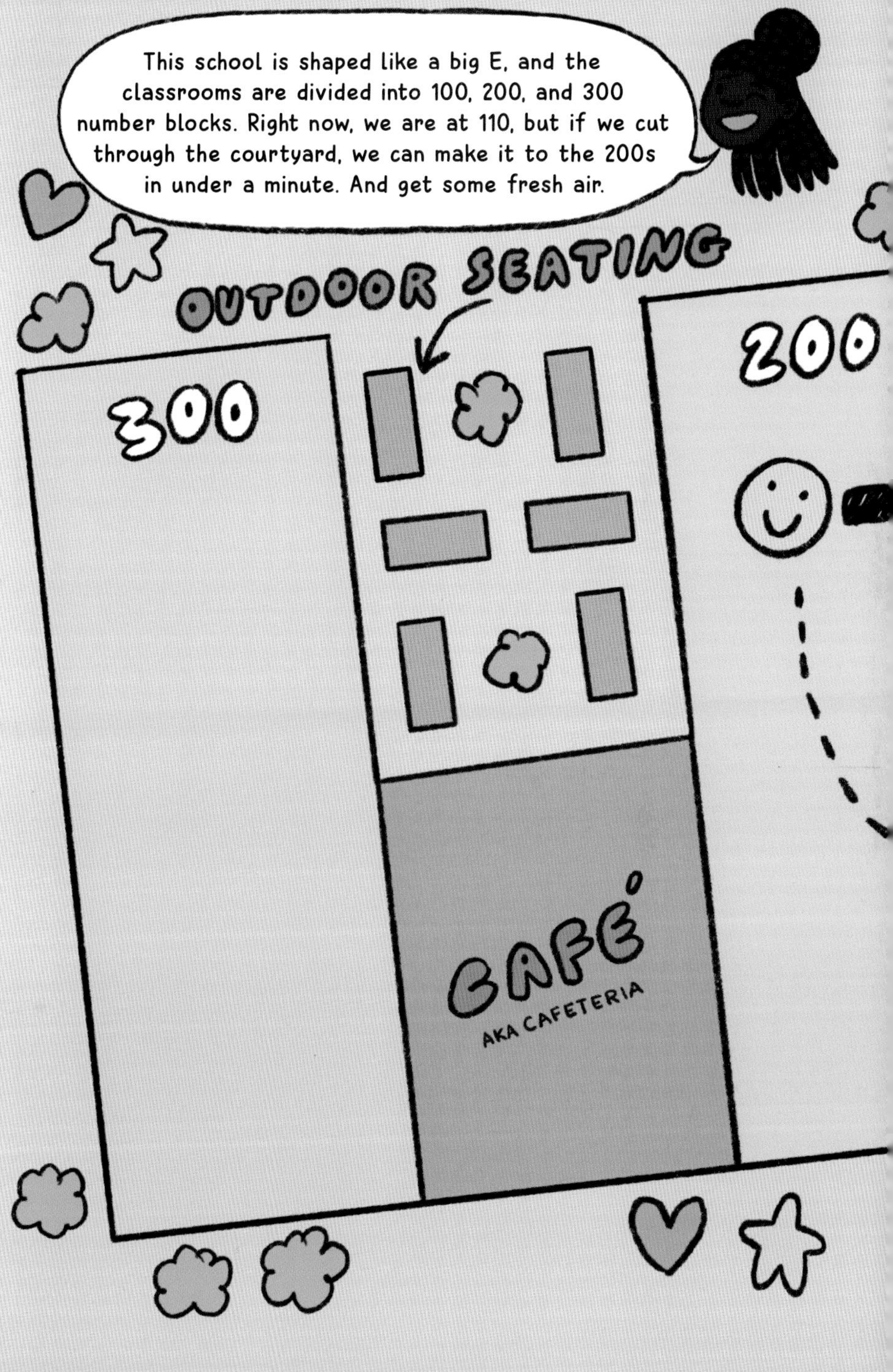
This school is shaped like a big E, and the classrooms are divided into 100, 200, and 300 number blocks. Right now, we are at 110, but if we cut through the courtyard, we can make it to the 200s in under a minute. And get some fresh air.
OUTDOOR SEATING
300
200
CAFÉ
AKA CAFETERIA

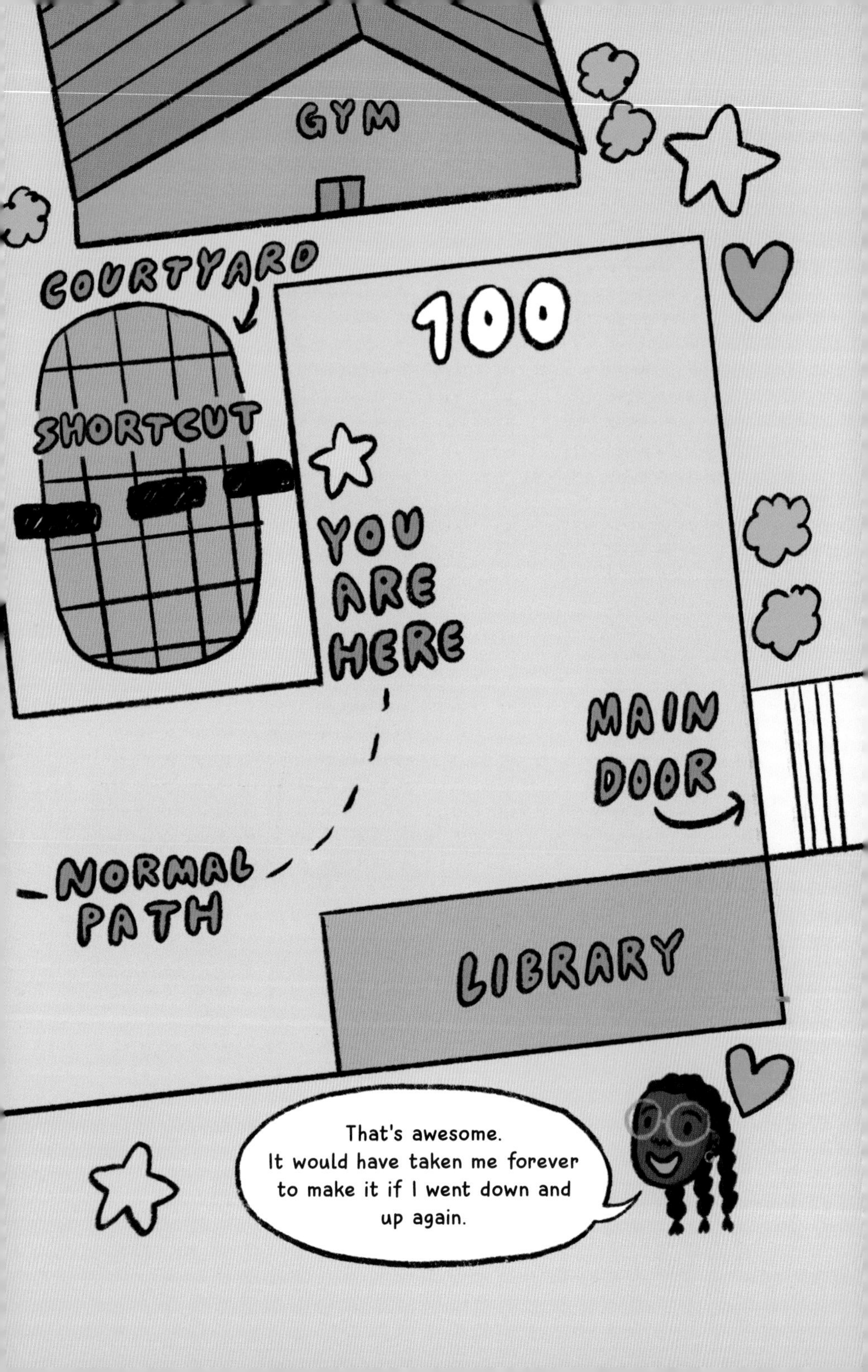
GYM
COURTYARD
100
SHORTCUT
YOU ARE HERE
MAIN DOOR
NORMAL PATH
LIBRARY
That's awesome. It would have taken me forever to make it if I went down and up again.

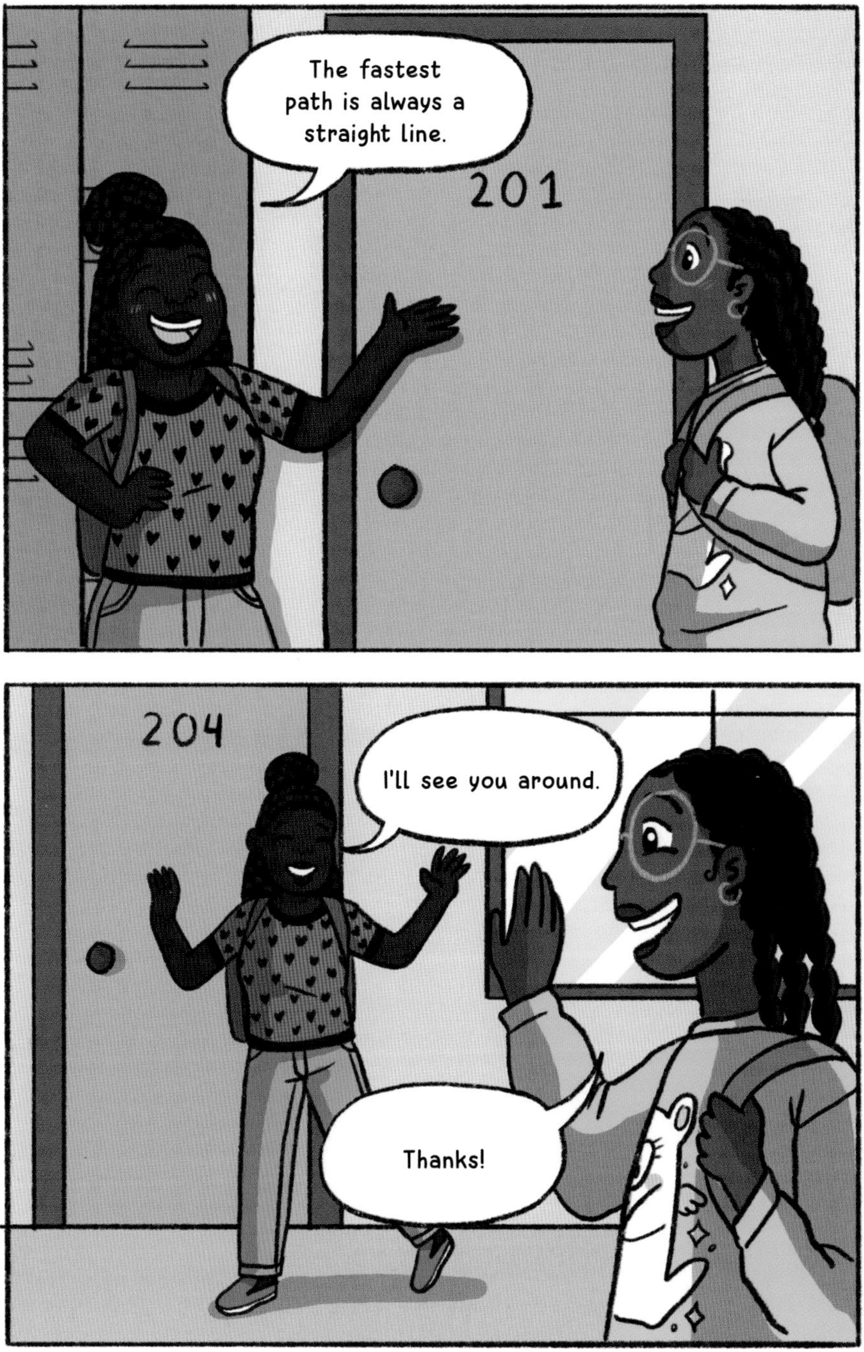
The fastest path is always a straight line.
201
204
I'll see you around.
Thanks!

CHAPTER 3

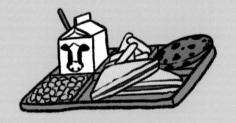

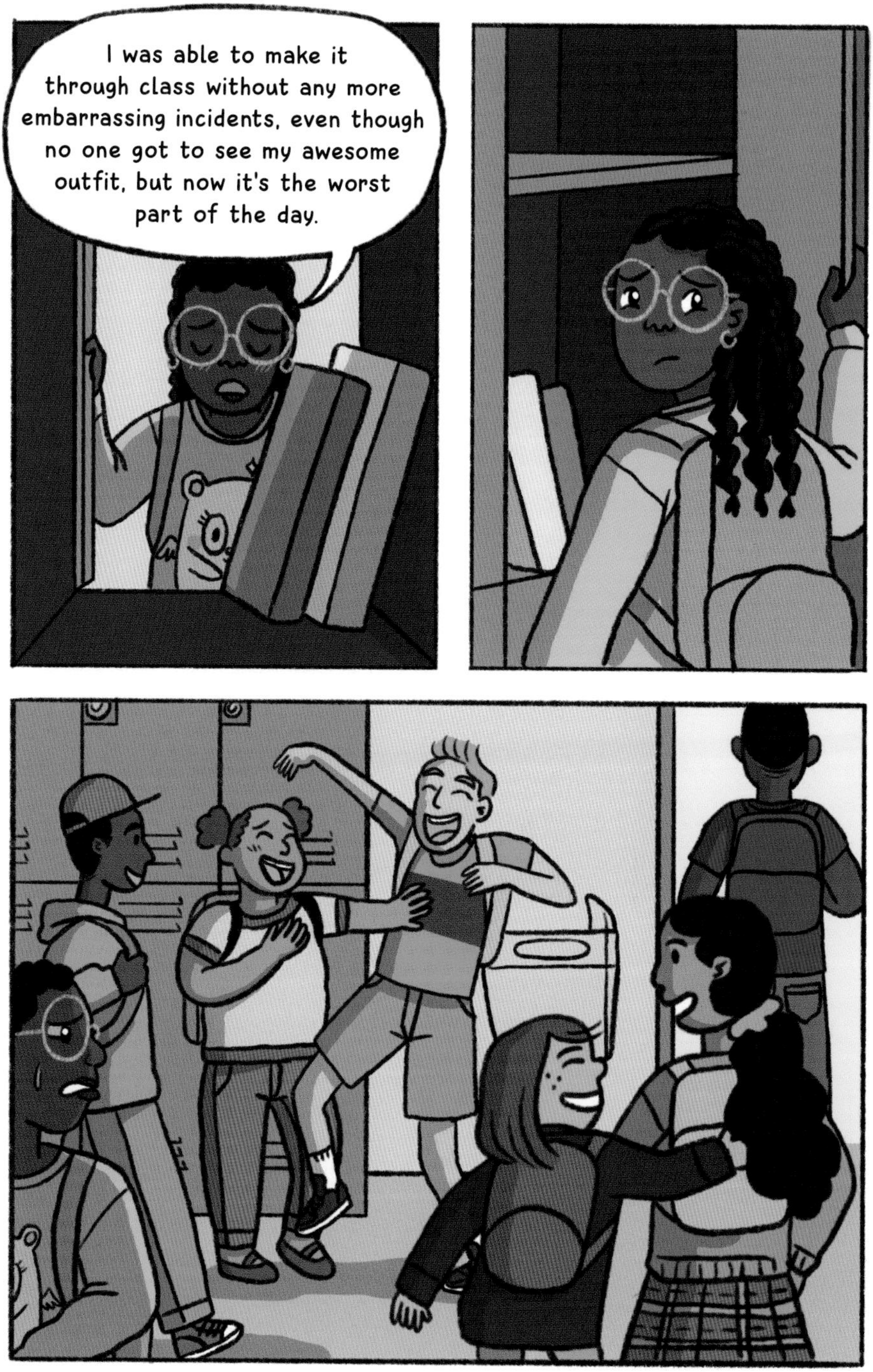
I was able to make it through class without any more embarrassing incidents, even though no one got to see my awesome outfit, but now it's the worst part of the day.

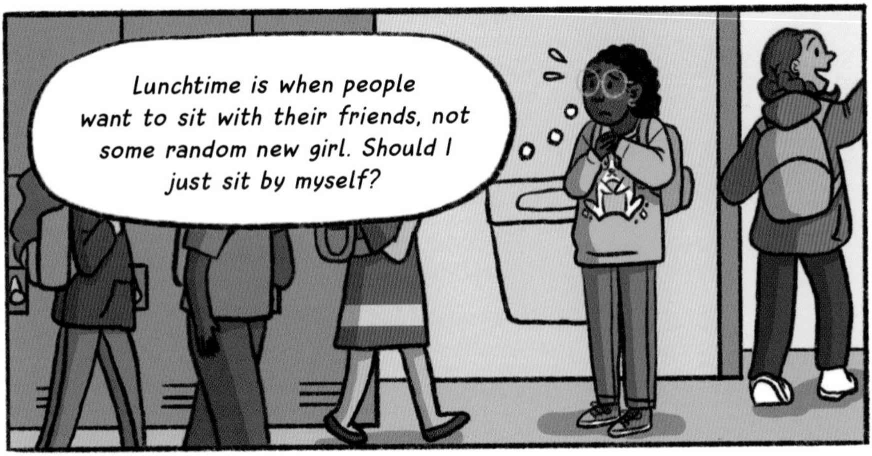
Lunchtime is when people want to sit with their friends, not some random new girl. Should I just sit by myself?

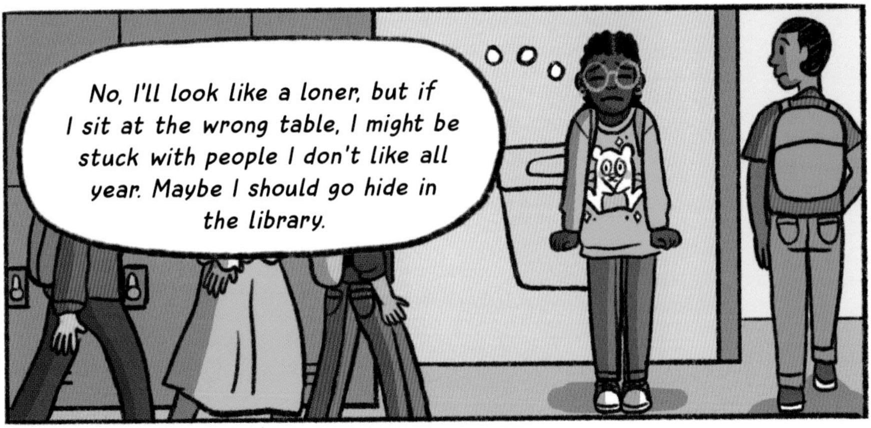
No, I'll look like a loner, but if I sit at the wrong table, I might be stuck with people I don't like all year. Maybe I should go hide in the library.

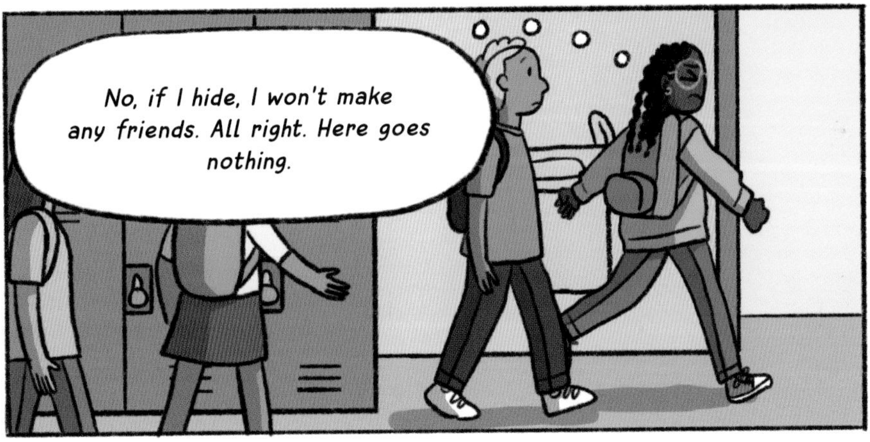
No, if I hide, I won't make any friends. All right. Here goes nothing.

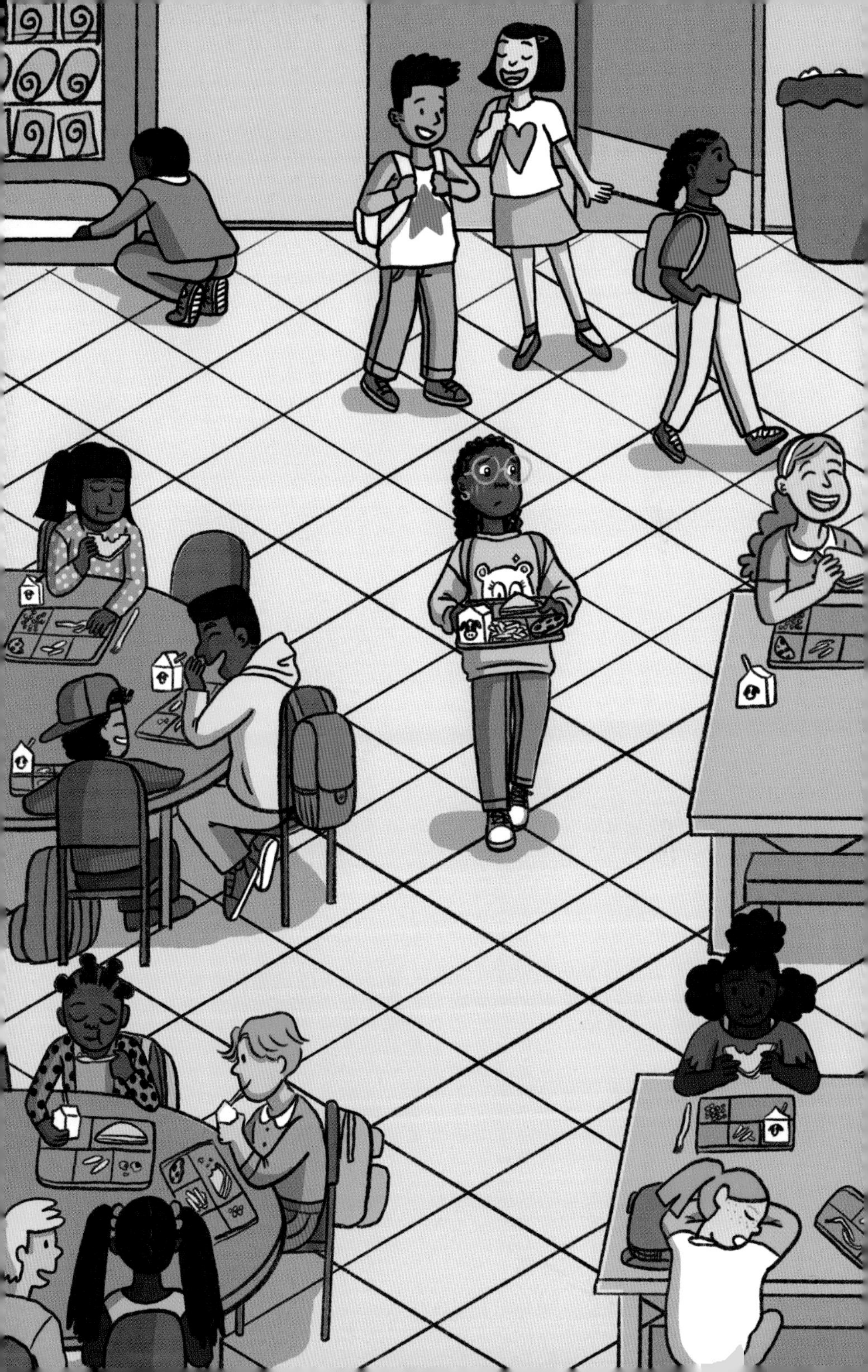

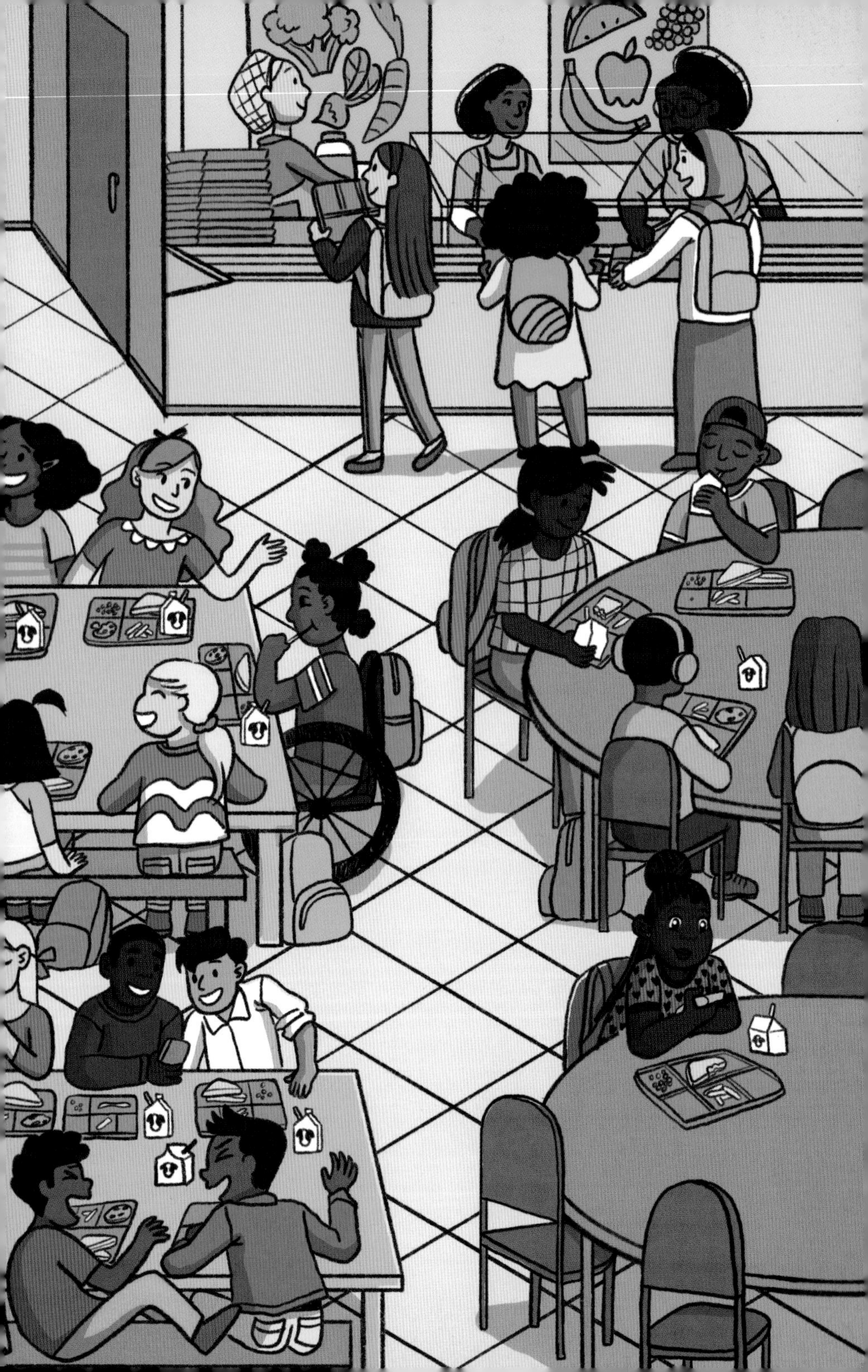

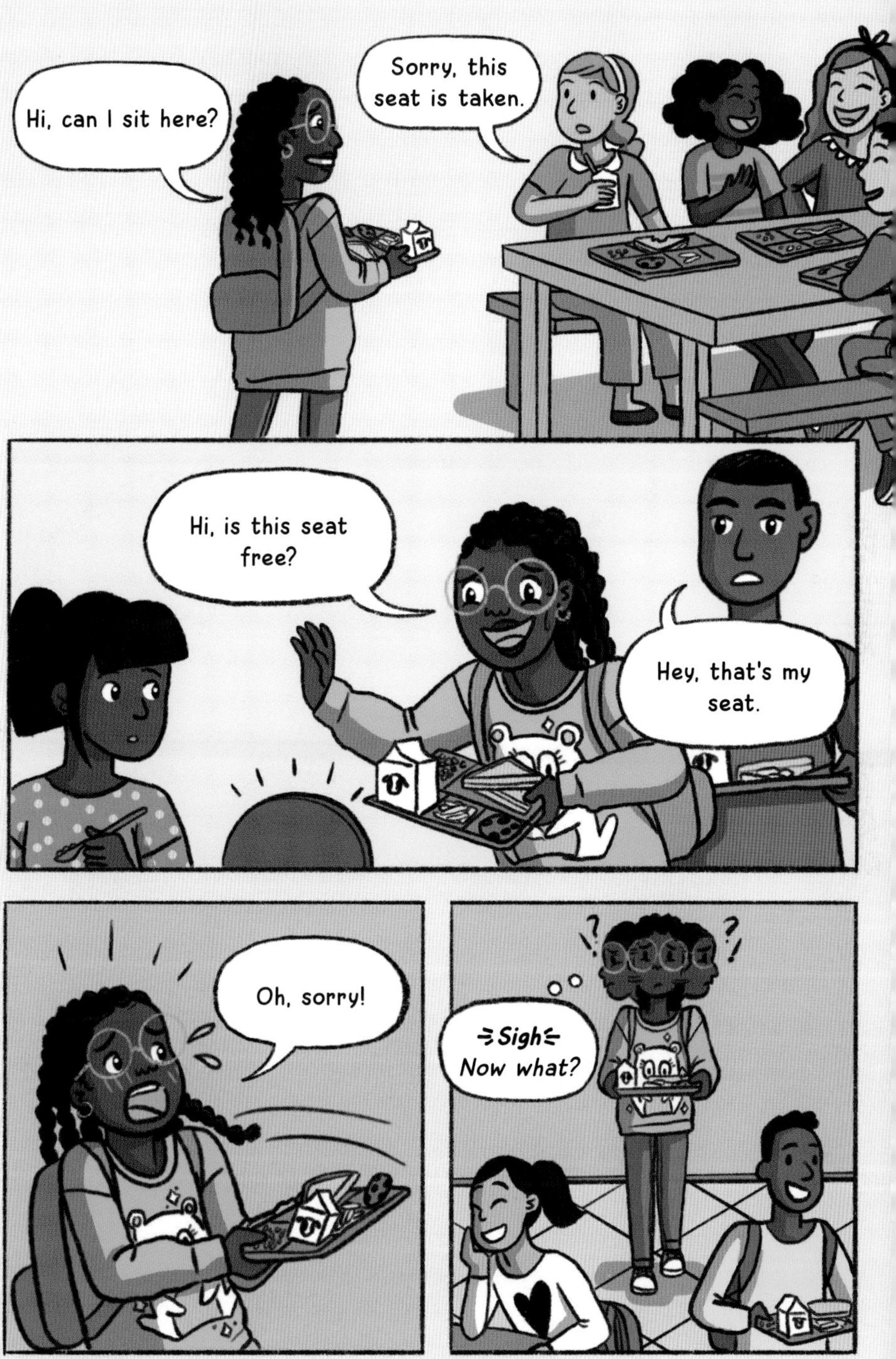
Hi, can I sit here?
Sorry, this seat is taken.
Hi, is this seat free?
Hey, that's my seat.
Oh, sorry!
Sigh
Now what?

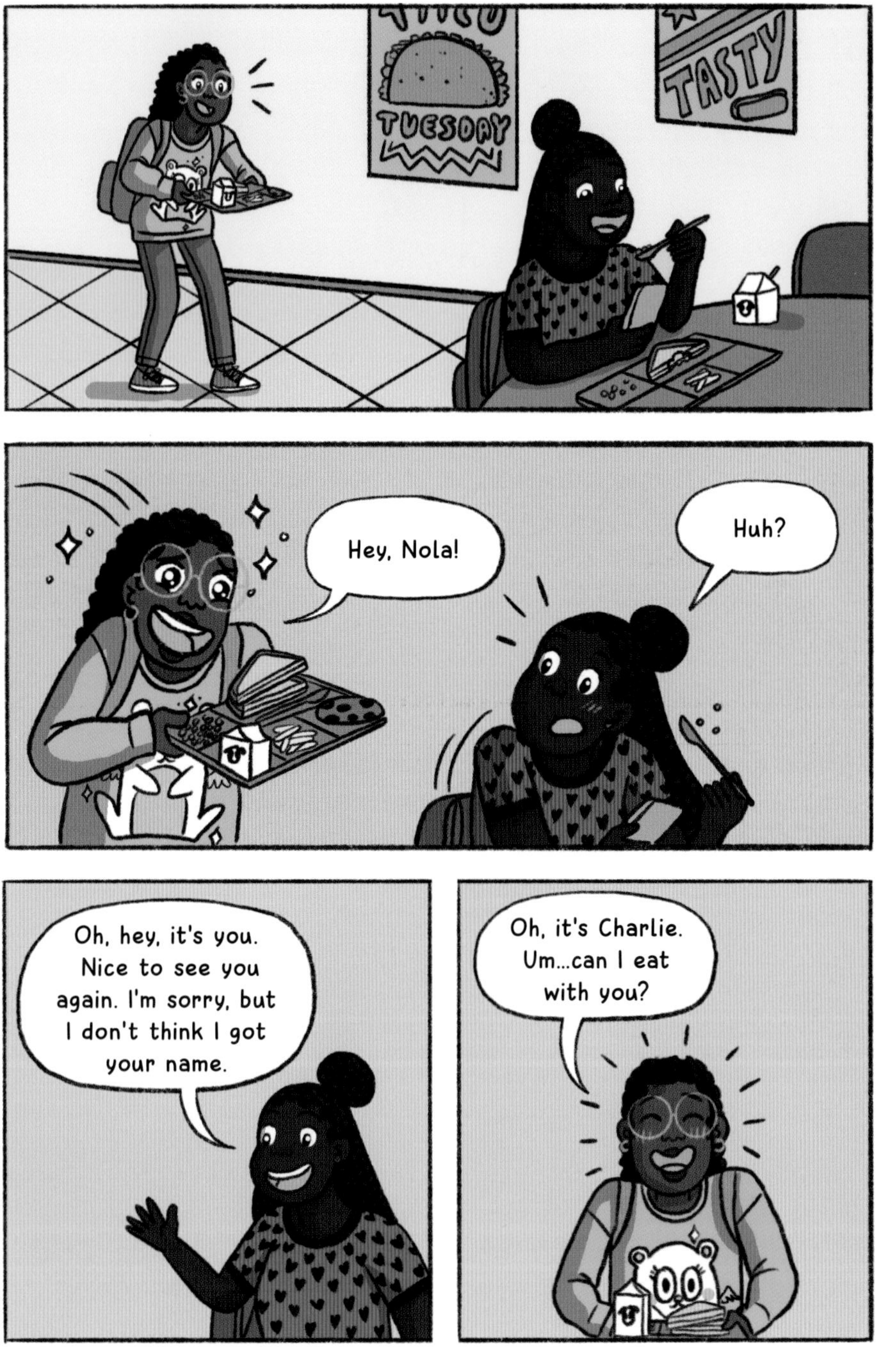
TUESDAY
TASTY
Hey, Nola!
Huh?
Oh, hey, it's you. Nice to see you again. I'm sorry, but I don't think I got your name.
Oh, it's Charlie. Um...can I eat with you?

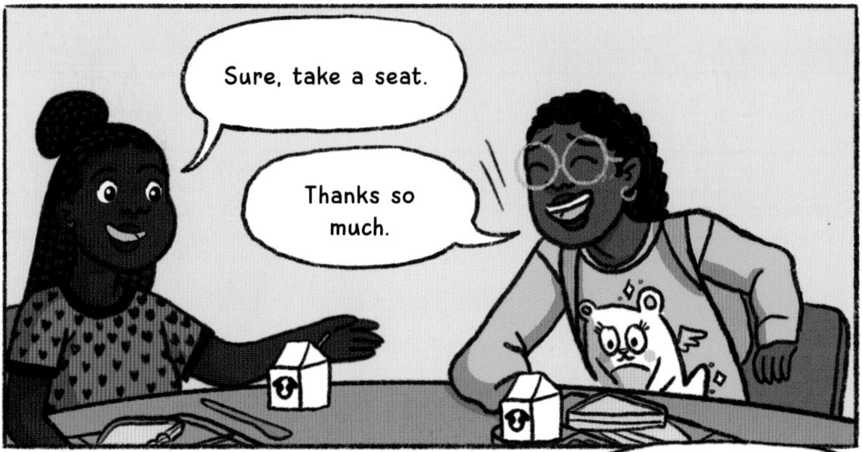
Sure, take a seat.
Thanks so much.

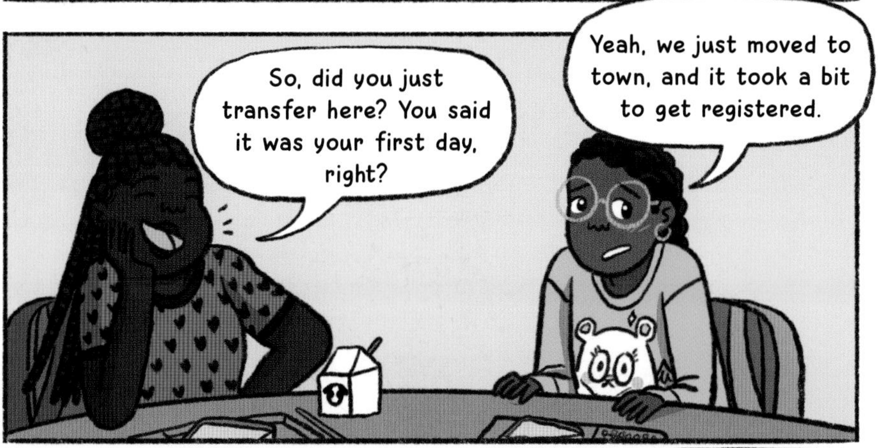
So, did you just transfer here? You said it was your first day, right?
Yeah, we just moved to town, and it took a bit to get registered.

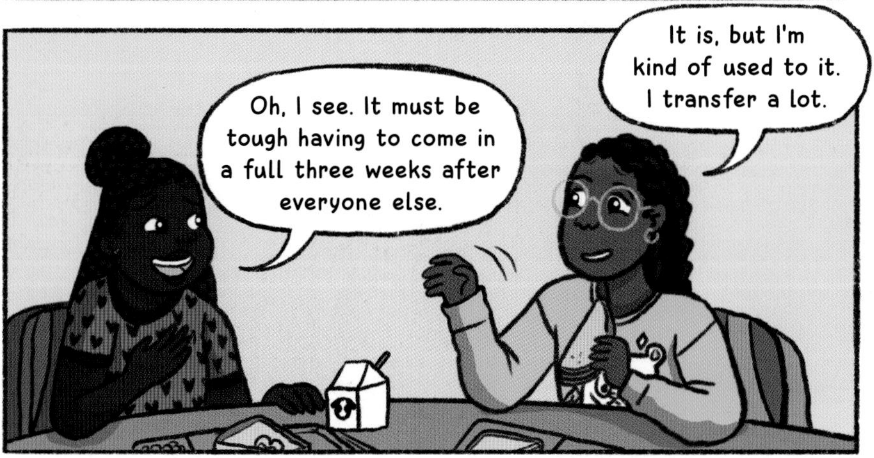
Oh, I see. It must be tough having to come in a full three weeks after everyone else.
It is, but I'm kind of used to it. I transfer a lot.

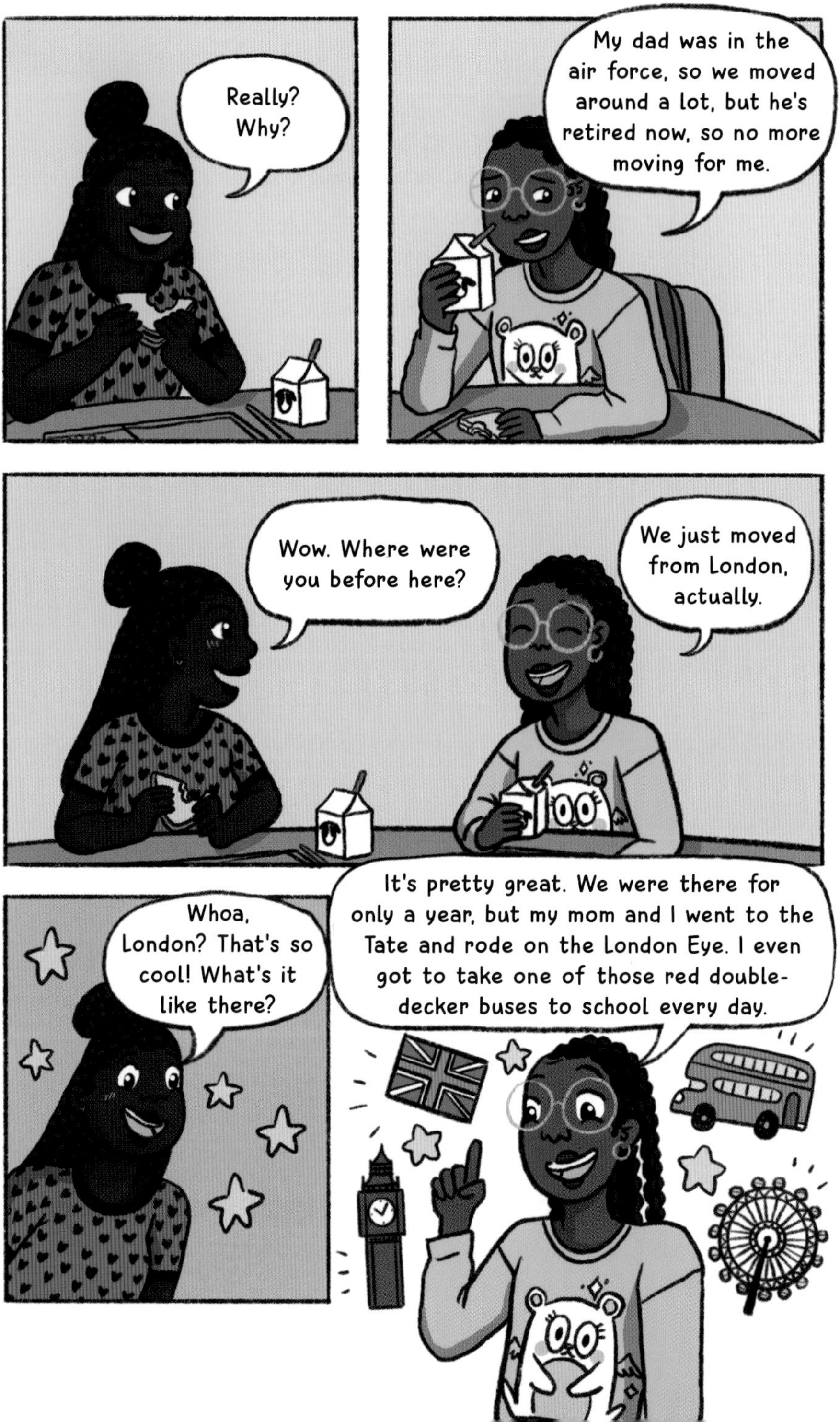
Really? Why?
My dad was in the air force, so we moved around a lot, but he's retired now, so no more moving for me.
Wow. Where were you before here?
We just moved from London, actually.
Whoa, London? That's so cool! What's it like there?
It's pretty great. We were there for only a year, but my mom and I went to the Tate and rode on the London Eye. I even got to take one of those red double-decker buses to school every day.

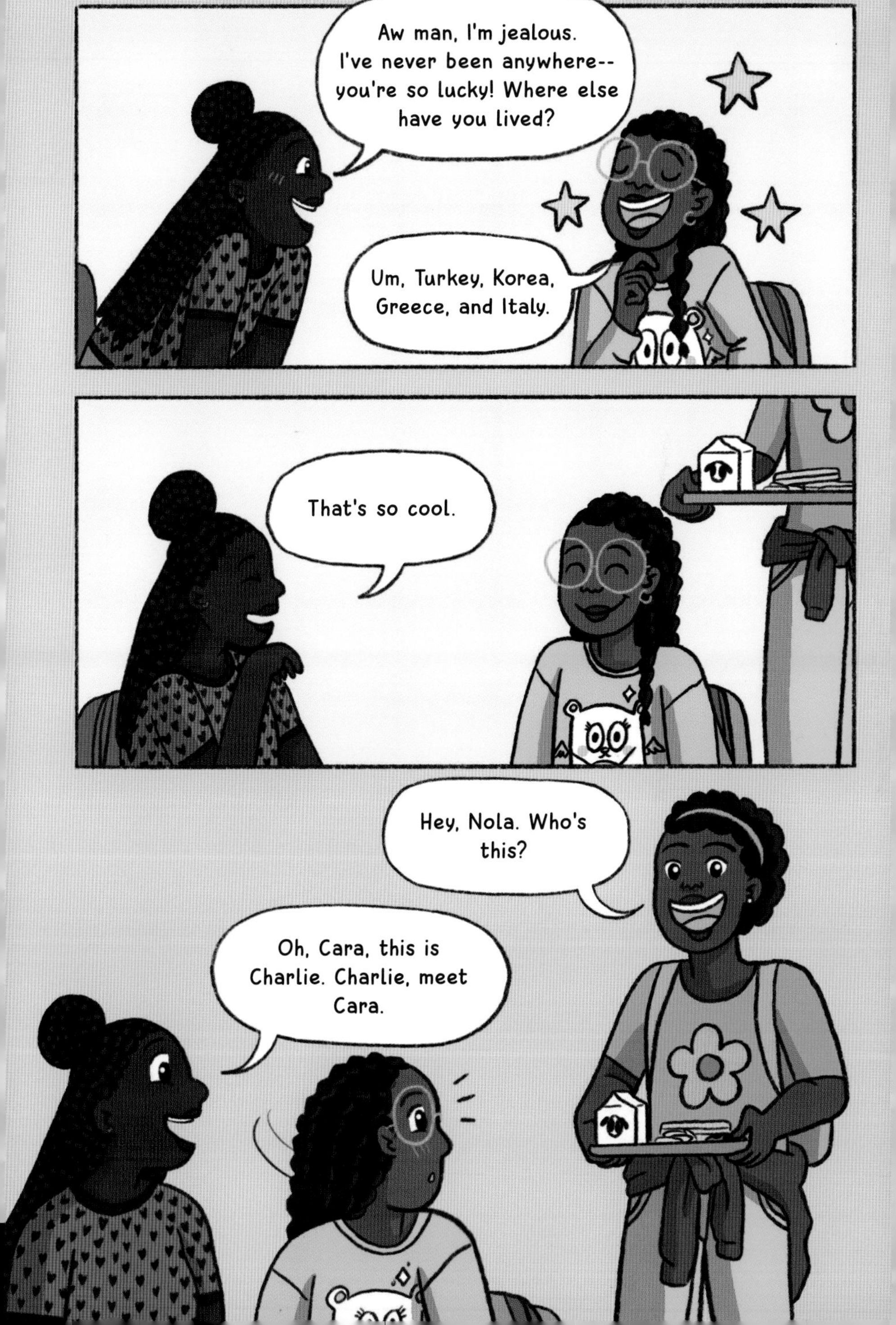
Aw man, I'm jealous. I've never been anywhere-- you're so lucky! Where else have you lived?
Um, Turkey, Korea, Greece, and Italy.
That's so cool.
Hey, Nola. Who's this?
Oh, Cara, this is Charlie. Charlie, meet Cara.

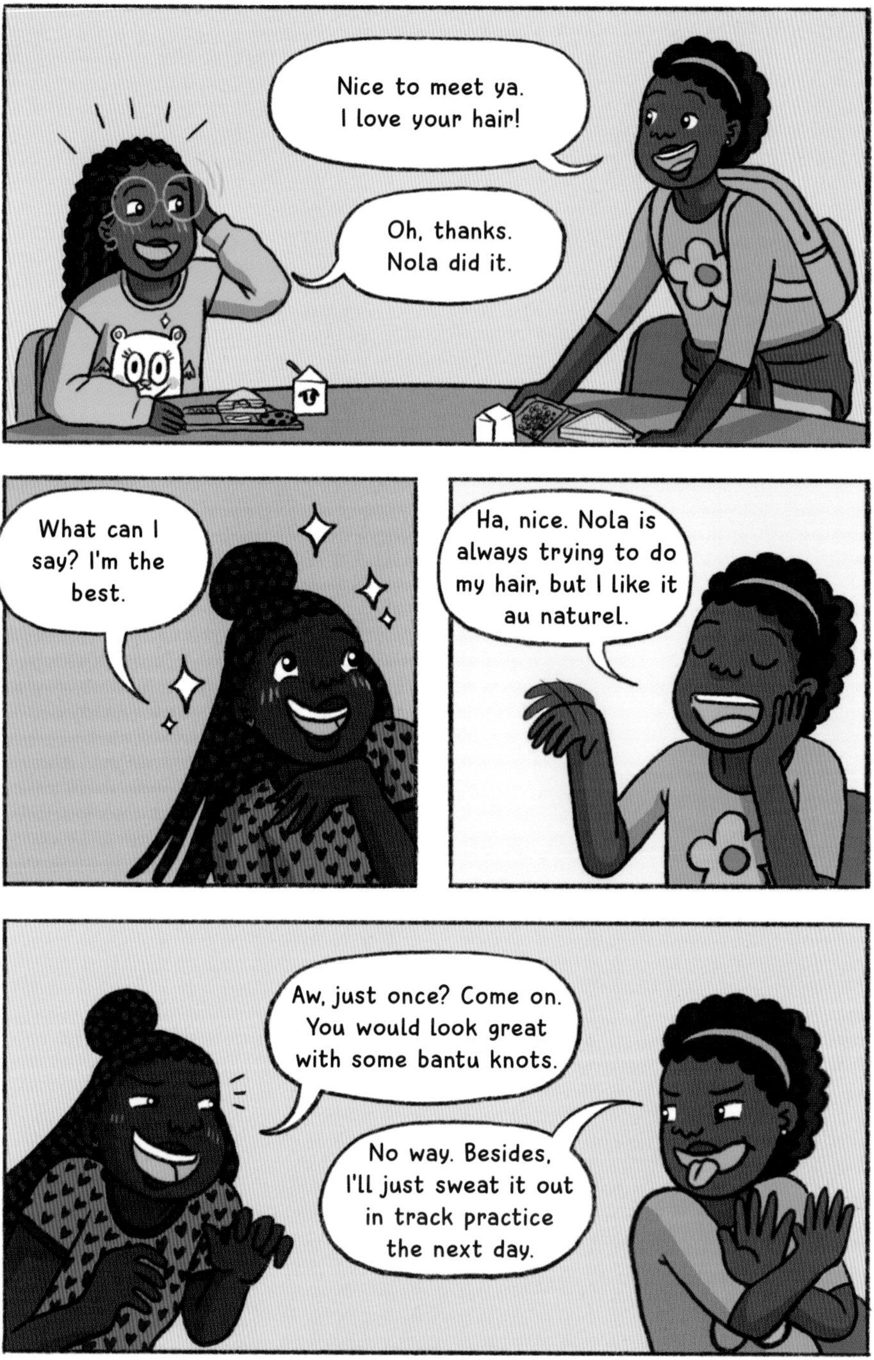
Nice to meet ya. I love your hair!
Oh, thanks. Nola did it.
What can I say? I'm the best.
Ha, nice. Nola is always trying to do my hair, but I like it au naturel.
Aw, just once? Come on. You would look great with some bantu knots.
No way. Besides, I'll just sweat it out in track practice the next day.

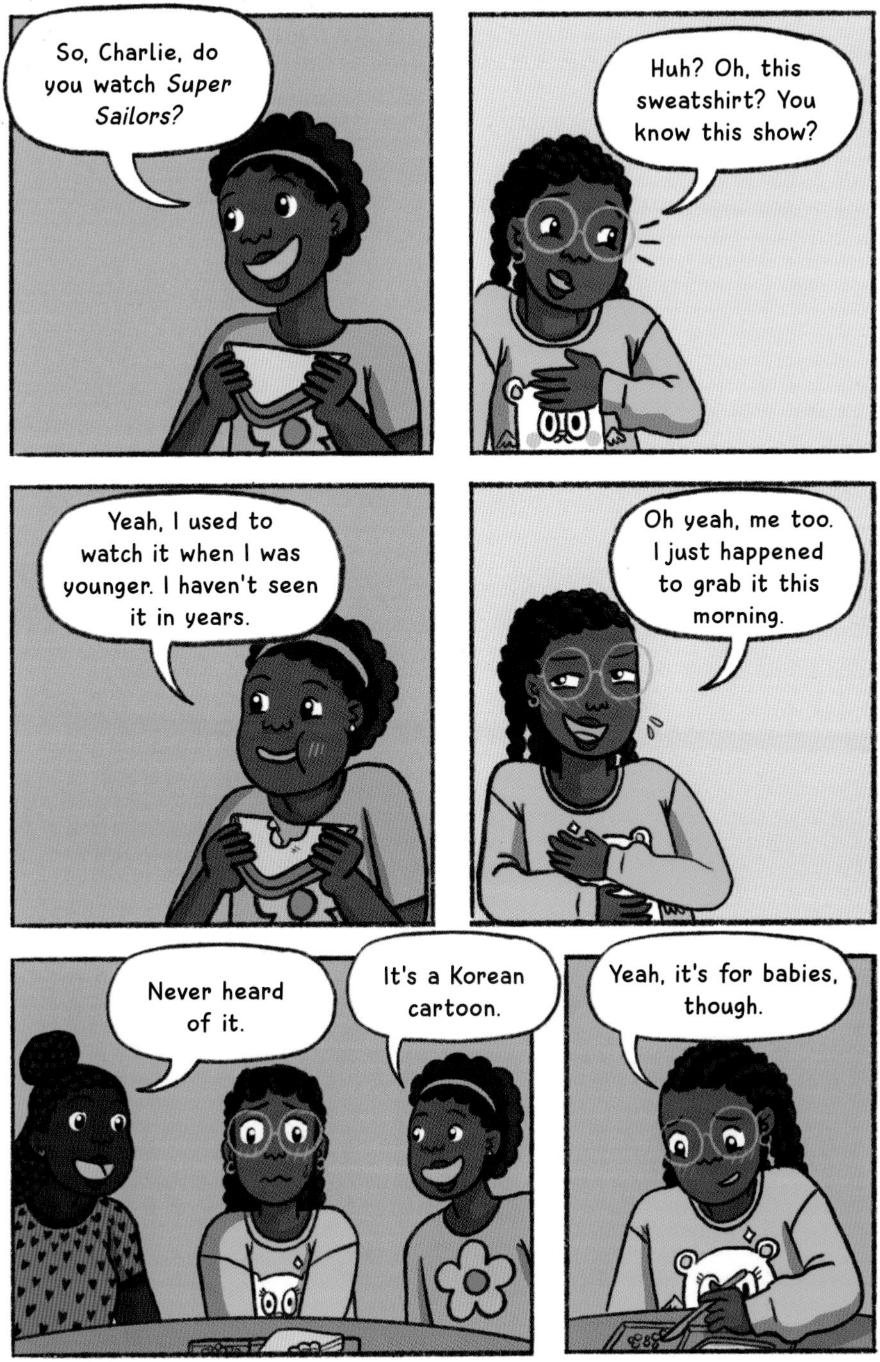
So, Charlie, do you watch *Super Sailors?*
Huh? Oh, this sweatshirt? You know this show?
Yeah, I used to watch it when I was younger. I haven't seen it in years.
Oh yeah, me too. I just happened to grab it this morning.
Never heard of it.
It's a Korean cartoon.
Yeah, it's for babies, though.

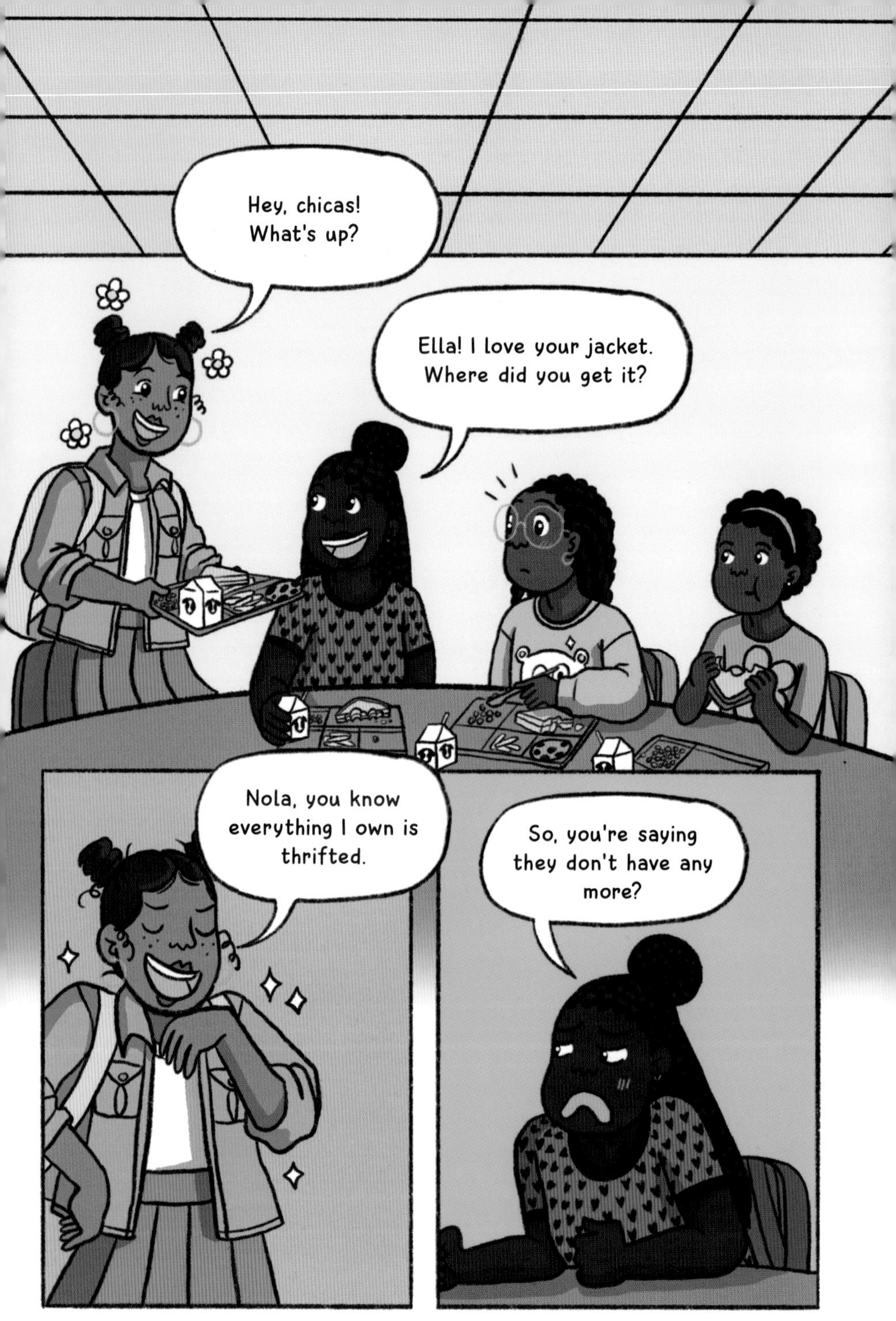
Hey, chicas! What's up?
Ella! I love your jacket. Where did you get it?
Nola, you know everything I own is thrifted.
So, you're saying they don't have any more?

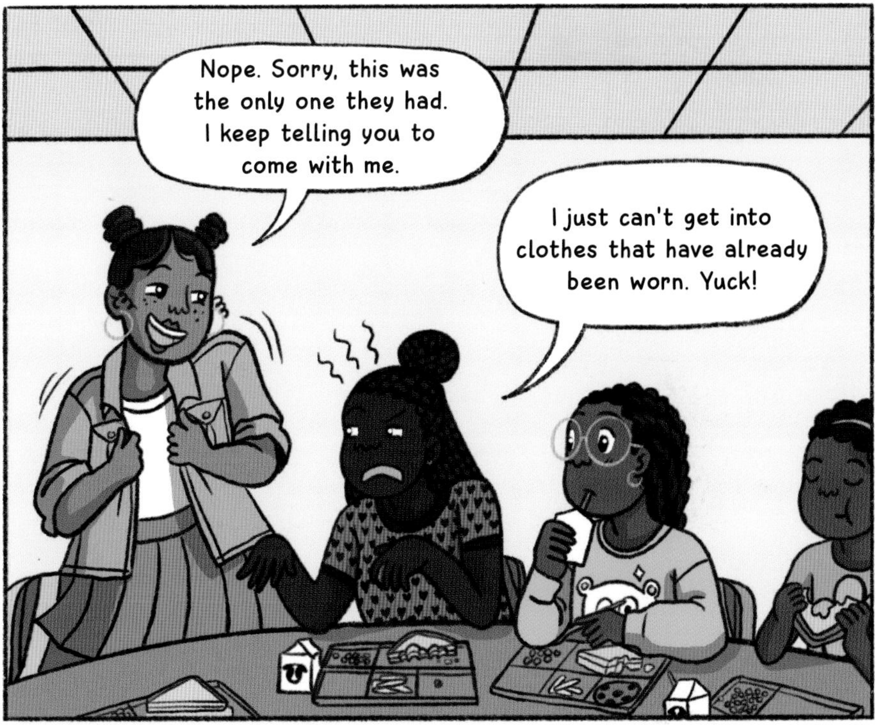
Nope. Sorry, this was the only one they had. I keep telling you to come with me.
I just can't get into clothes that have already been worn. Yuck!
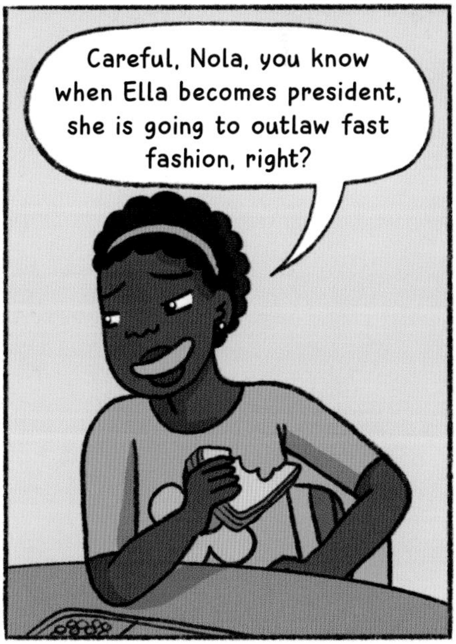
Careful, Nola, you know when Ella becomes president, she is going to outlaw fast fashion, right?
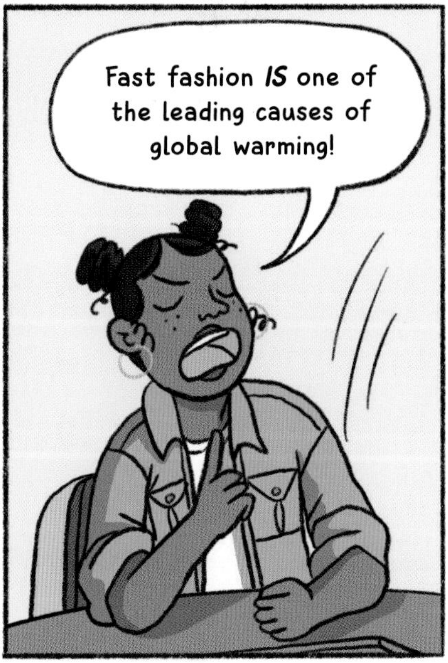
Fast fashion *IS* one of the leading causes of global warming!

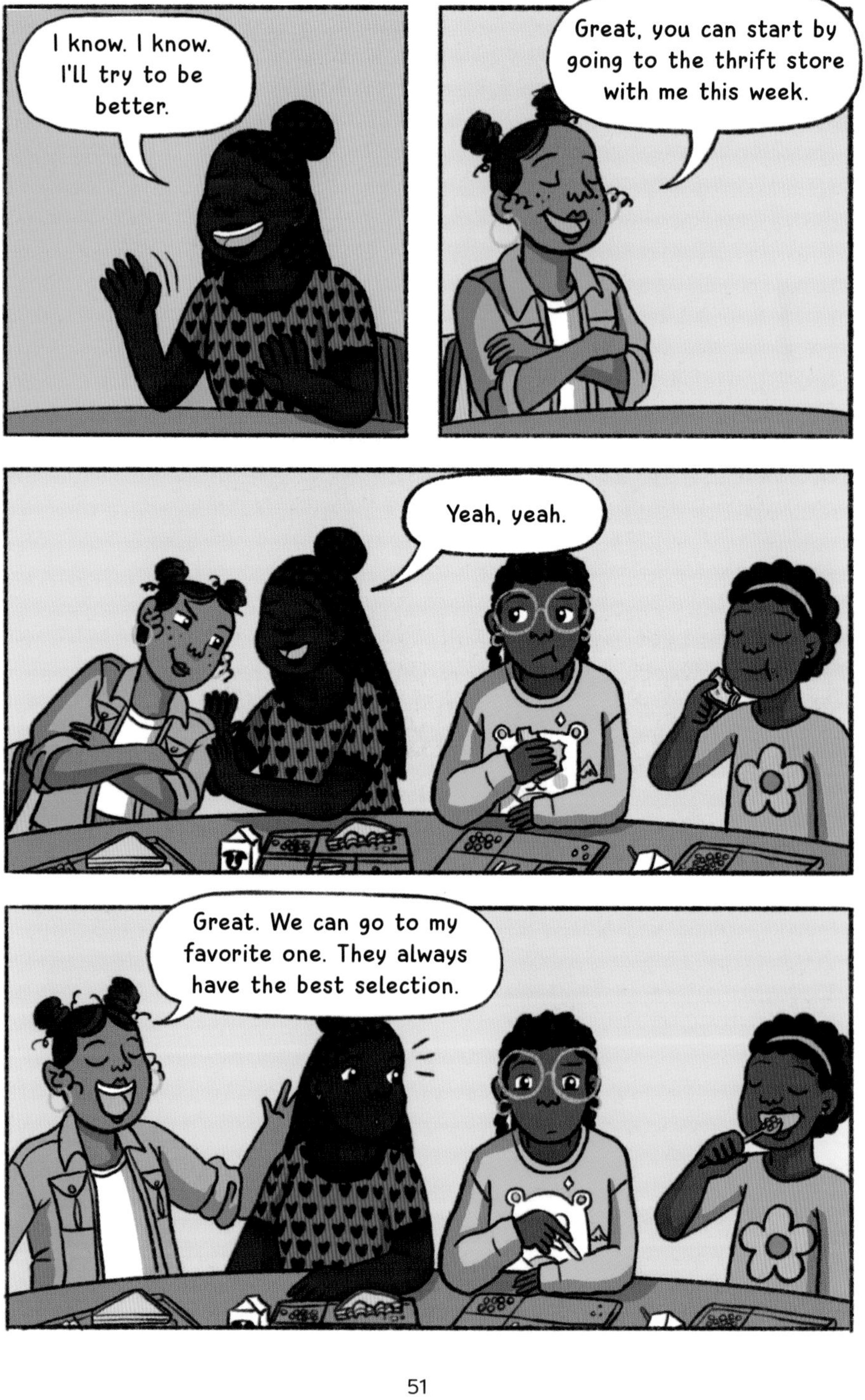
I know. I know. I'll try to be better.
Great, you can start by going to the thrift store with me this week.
Yeah, yeah.
Great. We can go to my favorite one. They always have the best selection.

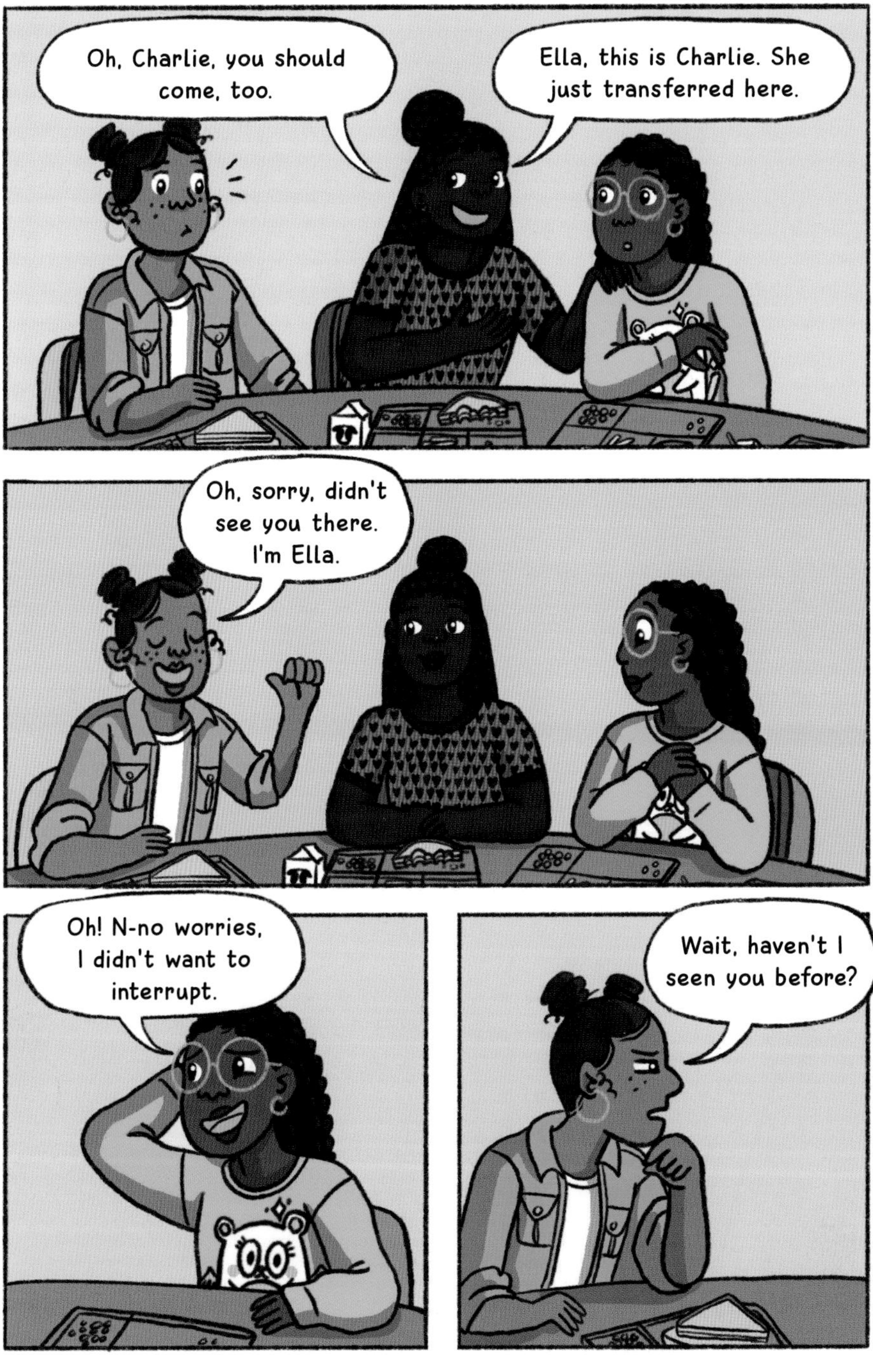

Oh, Charlie, you should come, too.
Ella, this is Charlie. She just transferred here.
Oh, sorry, didn't see you there. I'm Ella.
Oh! N-no worries, I didn't want to interrupt.
Wait, haven't I seen you before?

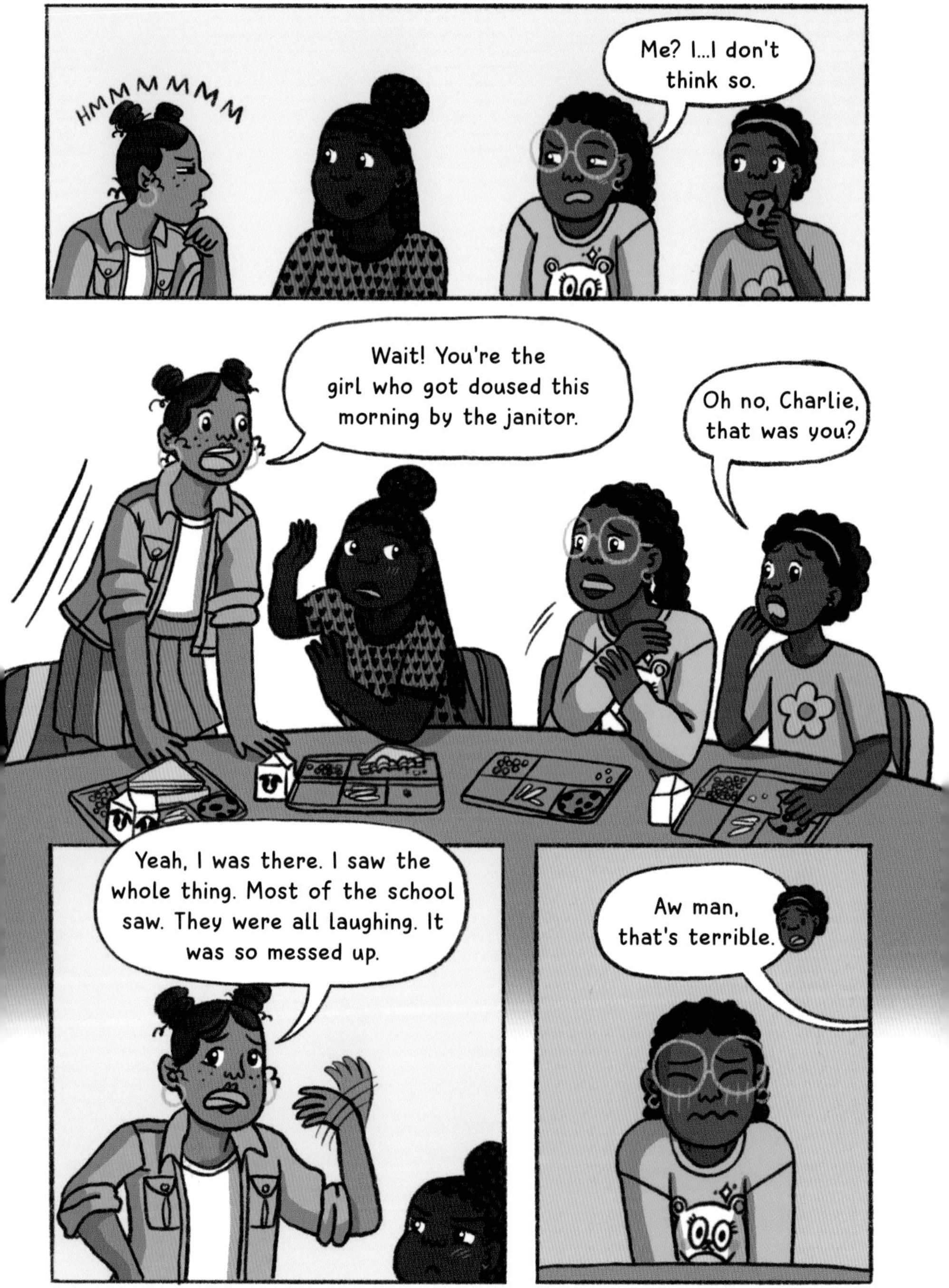
HMMMMMMM
Me? I...I don't think so.
Wait! You're the girl who got doused this morning by the janitor.
Oh no, Charlie, that was you?
Yeah, I was there. I saw the whole thing. Most of the school saw. They were all laughing. It was so messed up.
Aw man, that's terrible.

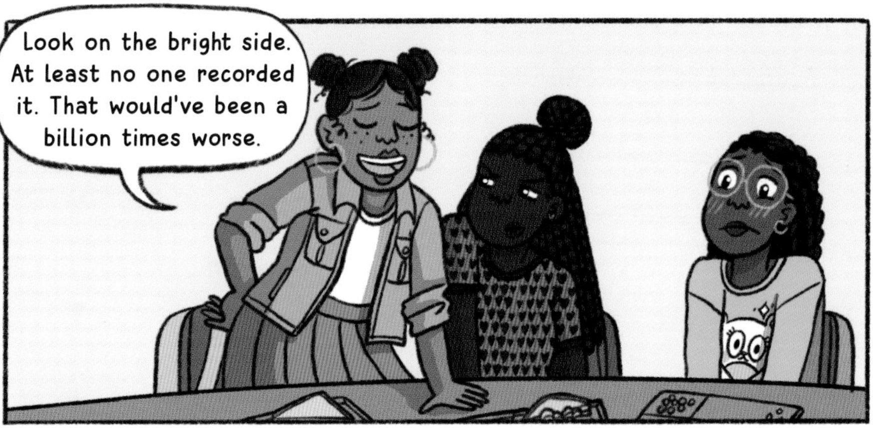
Look on the bright side. At least no one recorded it. That would've been a billion times worse.

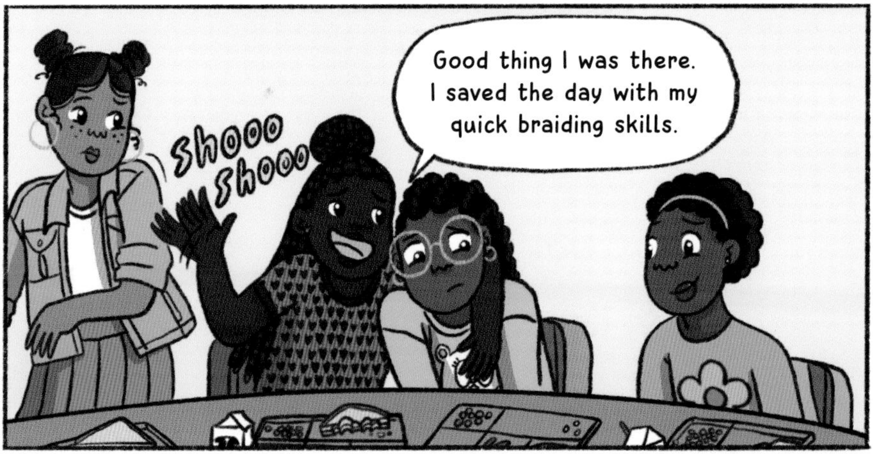
shooo shooo
Good thing I was there. I saved the day with my quick braiding skills.

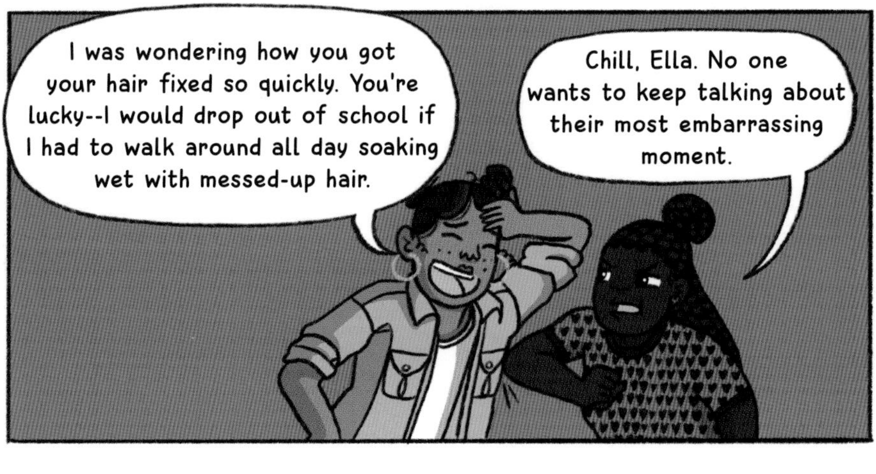
I was wondering how you got your hair fixed so quickly. You're lucky--I would drop out of school if I had to walk around all day soaking wet with messed-up hair.
Chill, Ella. No one wants to keep talking about their most embarrassing moment.

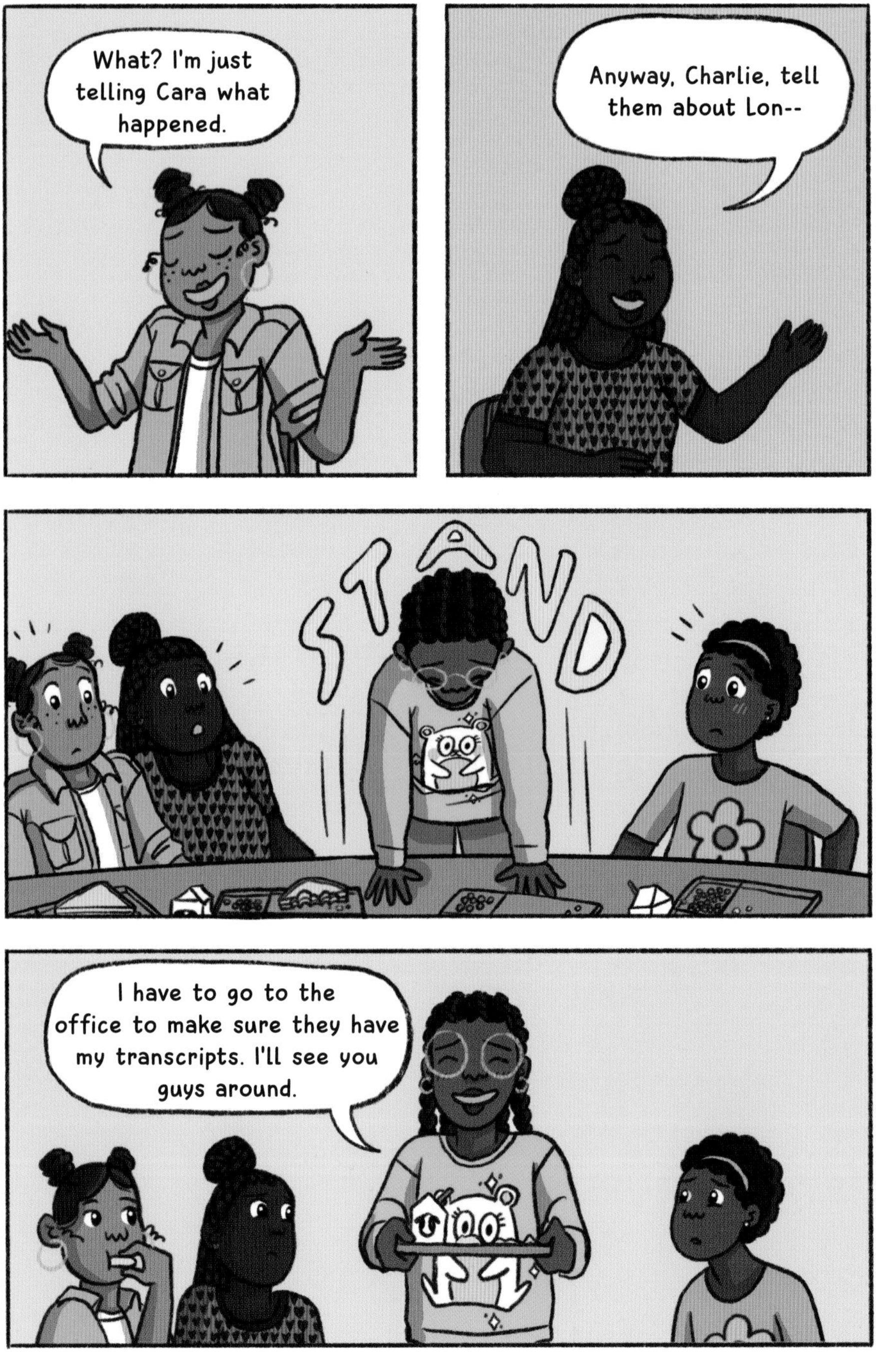
What? I'm just telling Cara what happened.
Anyway, Charlie, tell them about Lon--
STAND
I have to go to the office to make sure they have my transcripts. I'll see you guys around.

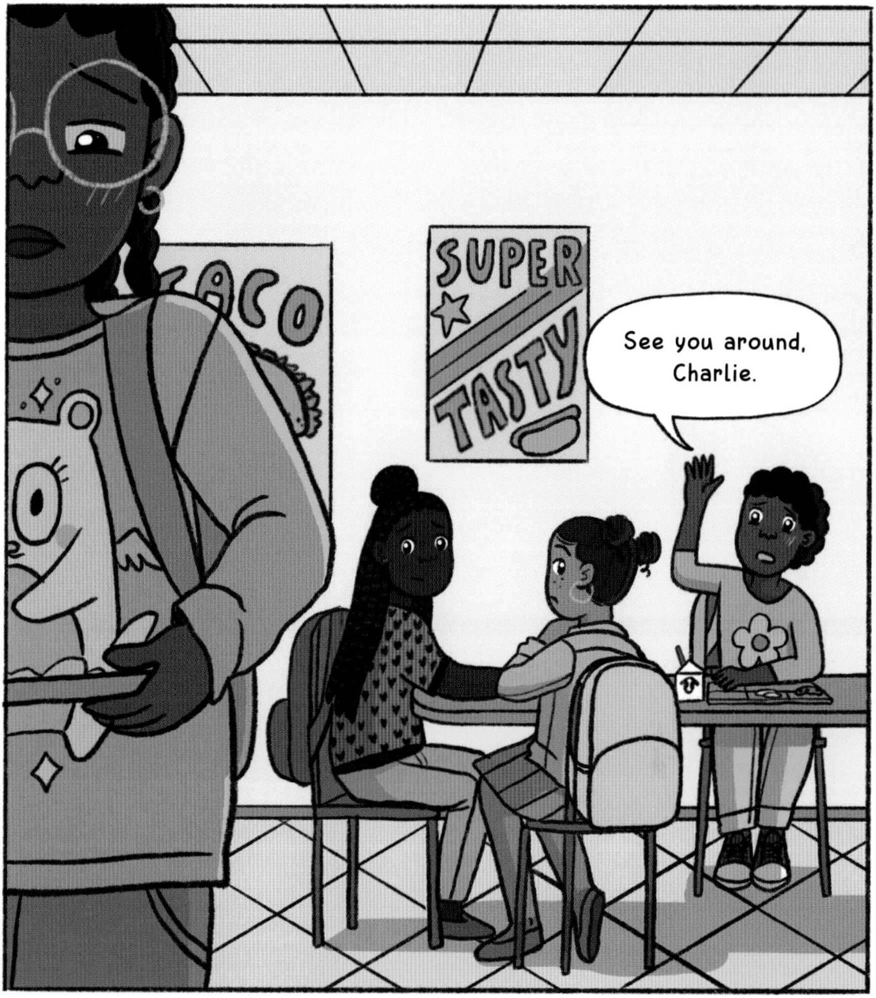
SUPER TASTY
ACO
See you around, Charlie.

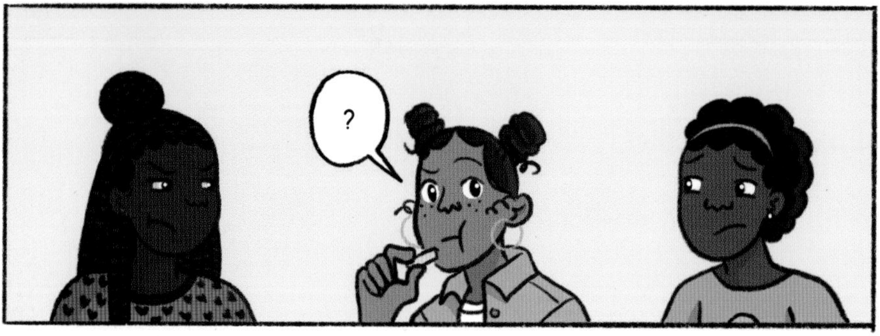
?

CHAPTER
4

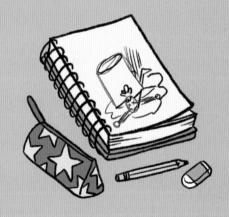

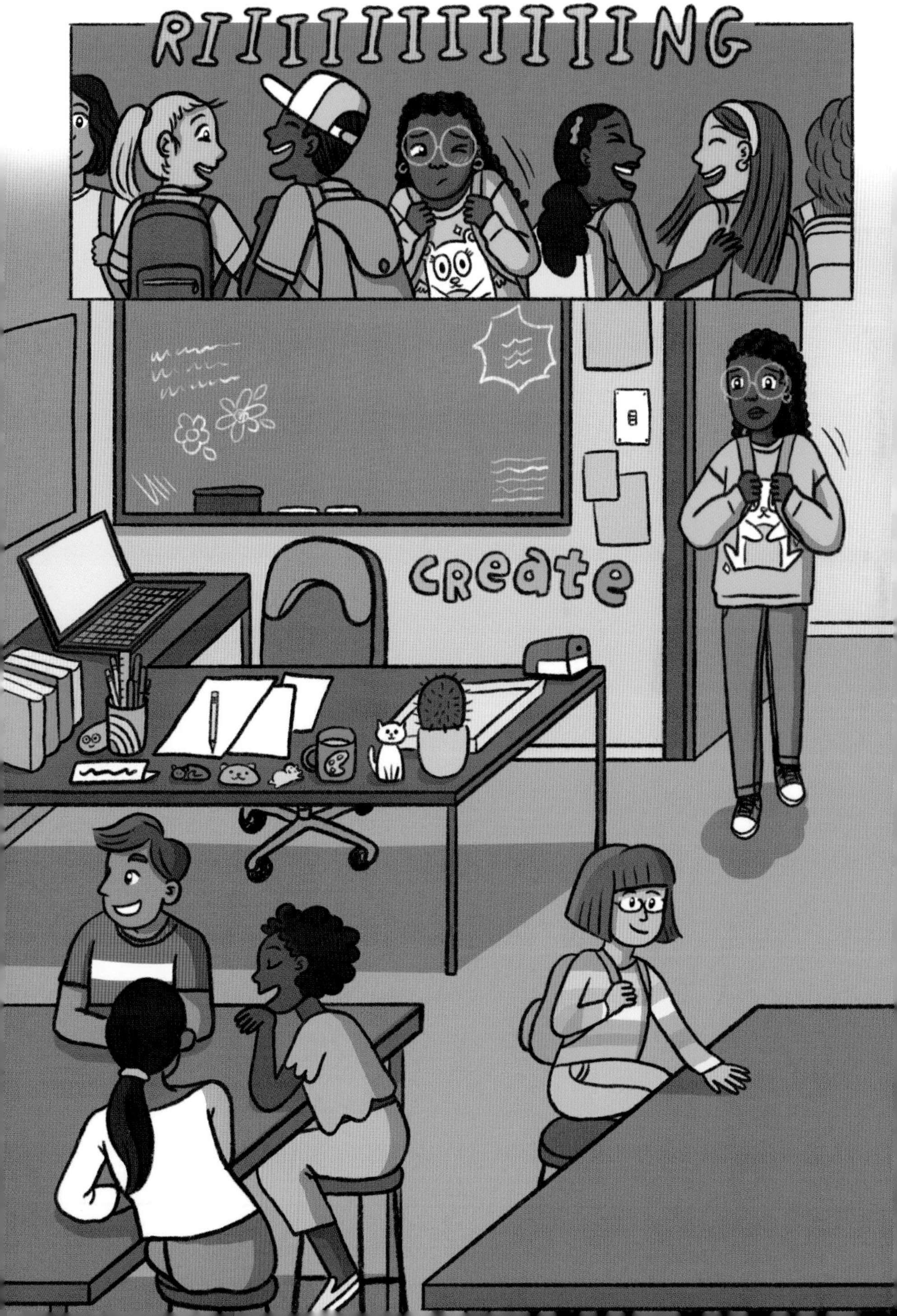
RIIIIIIIIIIING
create

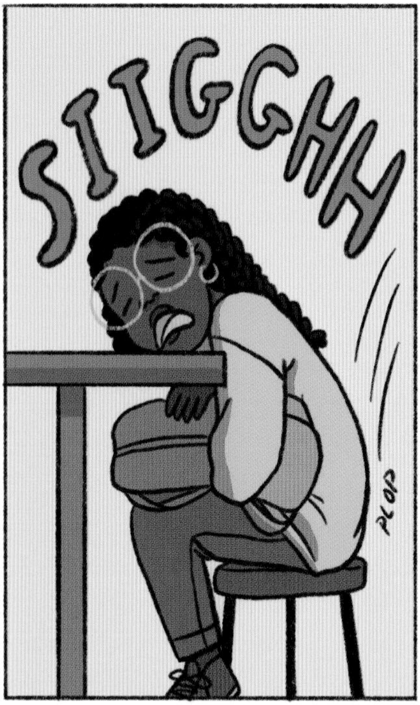
SIIGGHH
PLOP

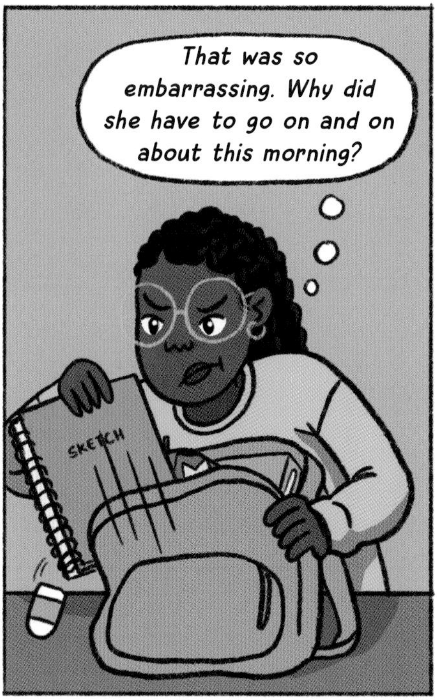
That was so embarrassing. Why did she have to go on and on about this morning?
SKETCH

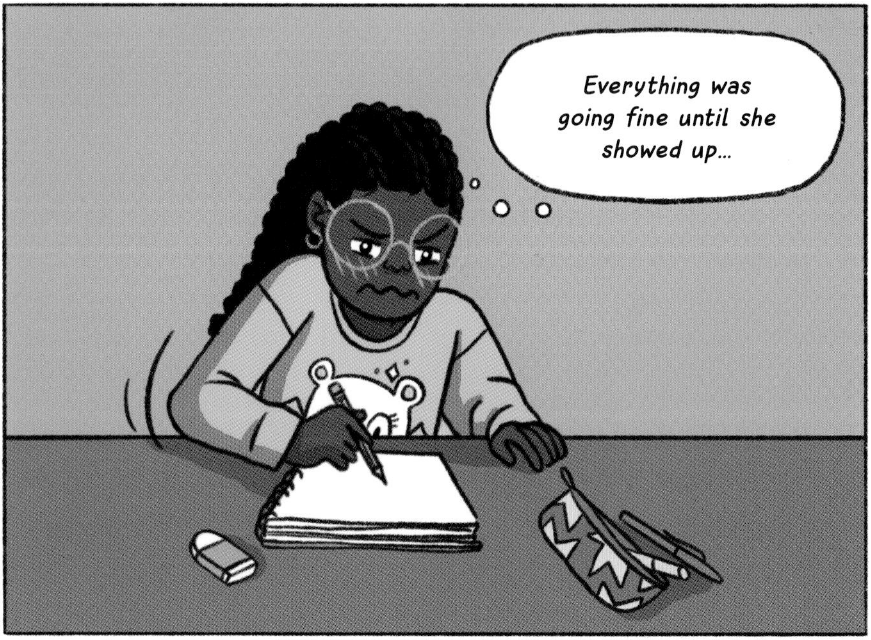
Everything was going fine until she showed up...

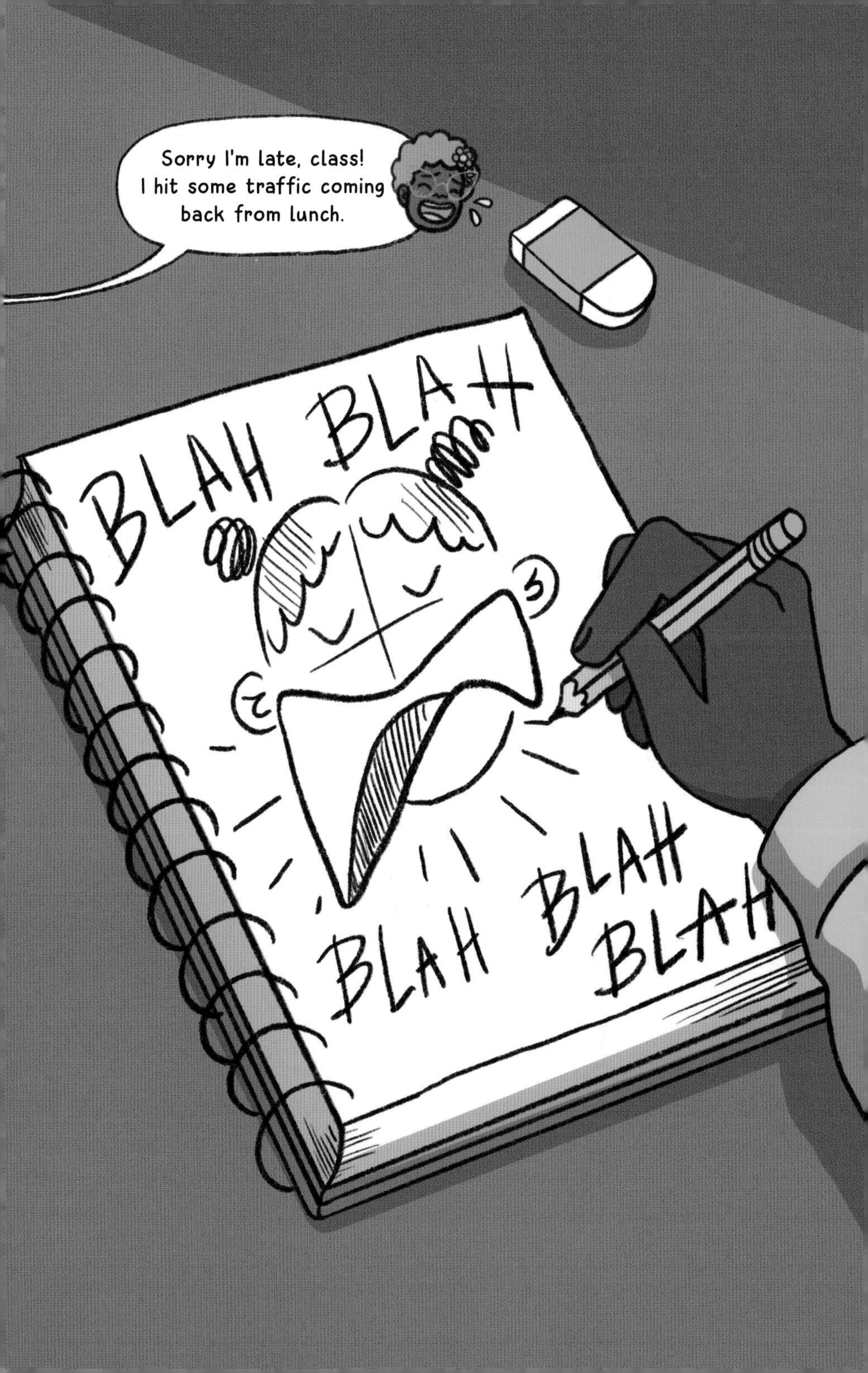
Sorry I'm late, class! I hit some traffic coming back from lunch.
BLAH BLAH
BLAH BLAH BLAH

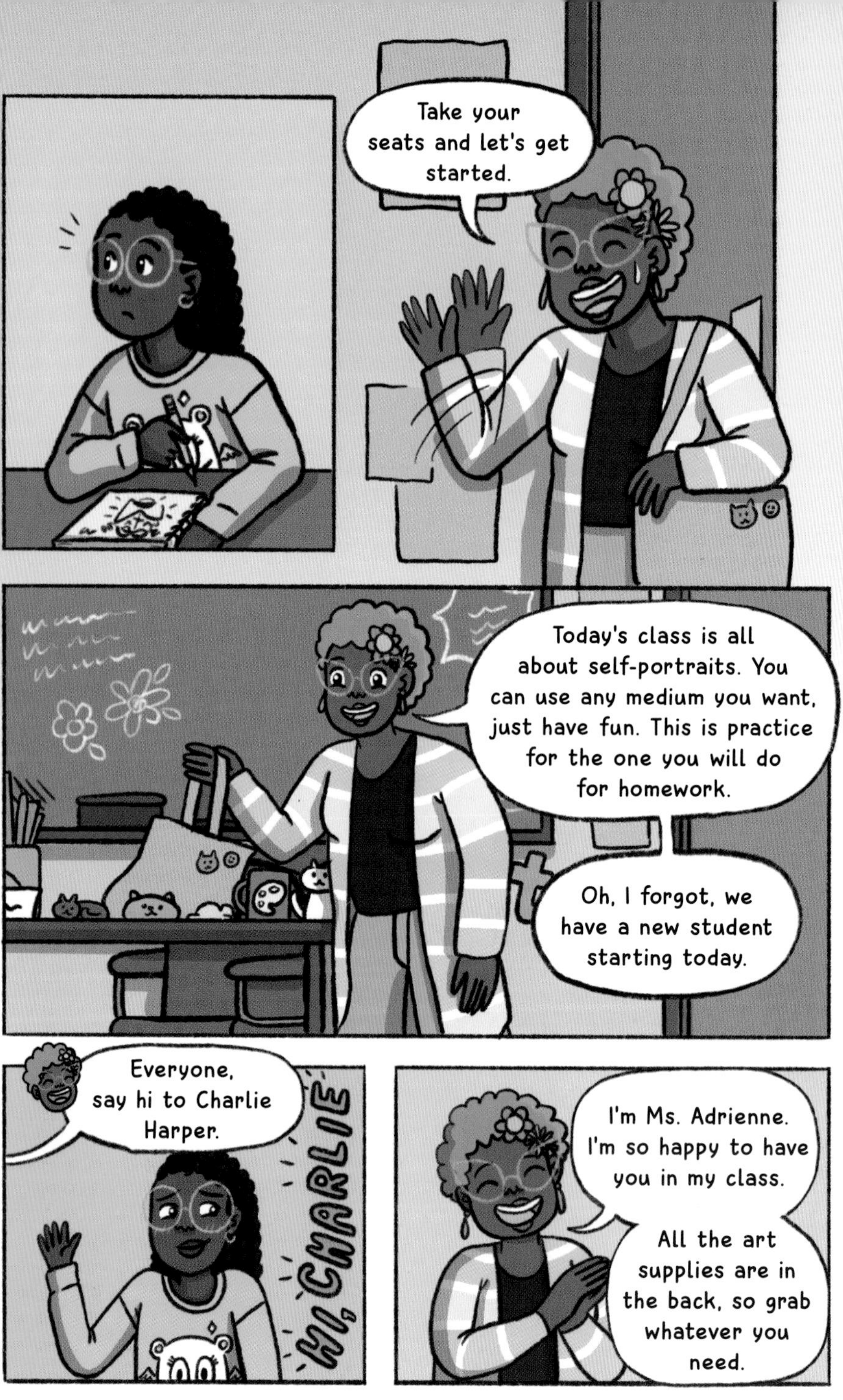
Take your seats and let's get started.
Today's class is all about self-portraits. You can use any medium you want, just have fun. This is practice for the one you will do for homework.
Oh, I forgot, we have a new student starting today.
Everyone, say hi to Charlie Harper.
HI, CHARLIE
I'm Ms. Adrienne. I'm so happy to have you in my class.
All the art supplies are in the back, so grab whatever you need.

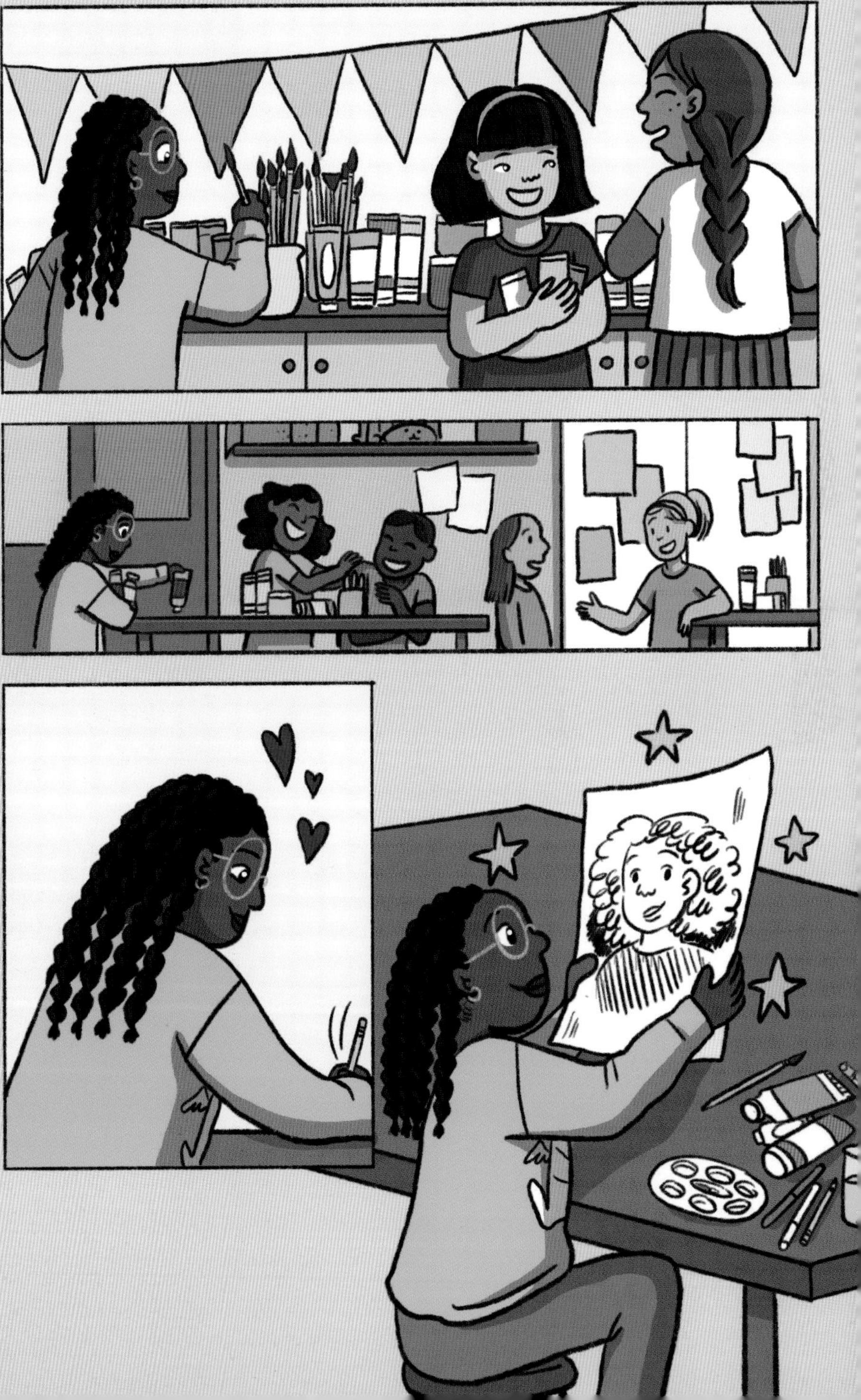

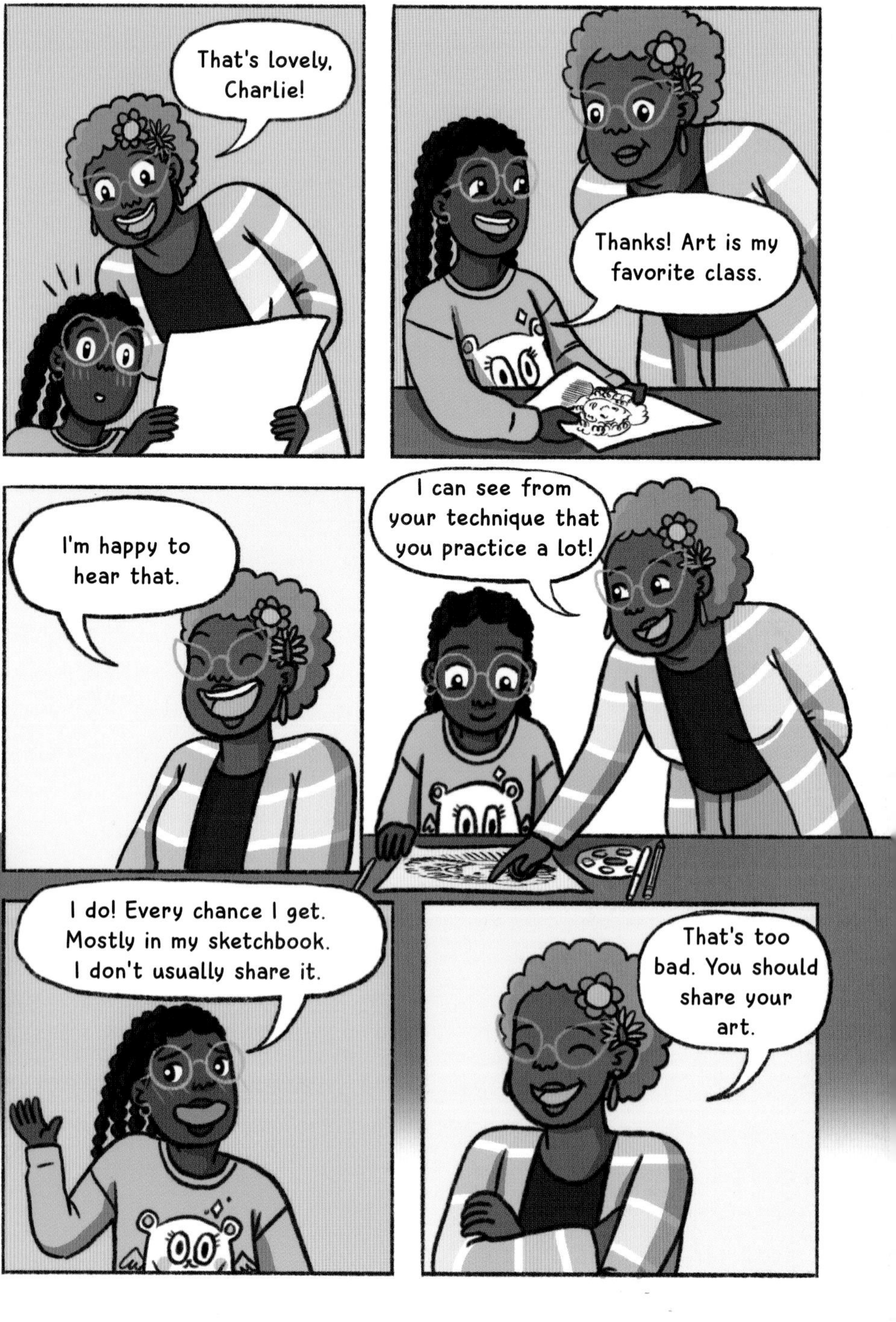
That's lovely, Charlie!
Thanks! Art is my favorite class.
I'm happy to hear that.
I can see from your technique that you practice a lot!
I do! Every chance I get. Mostly in my sketchbook. I don't usually share it.
That's too bad. You should share your art.

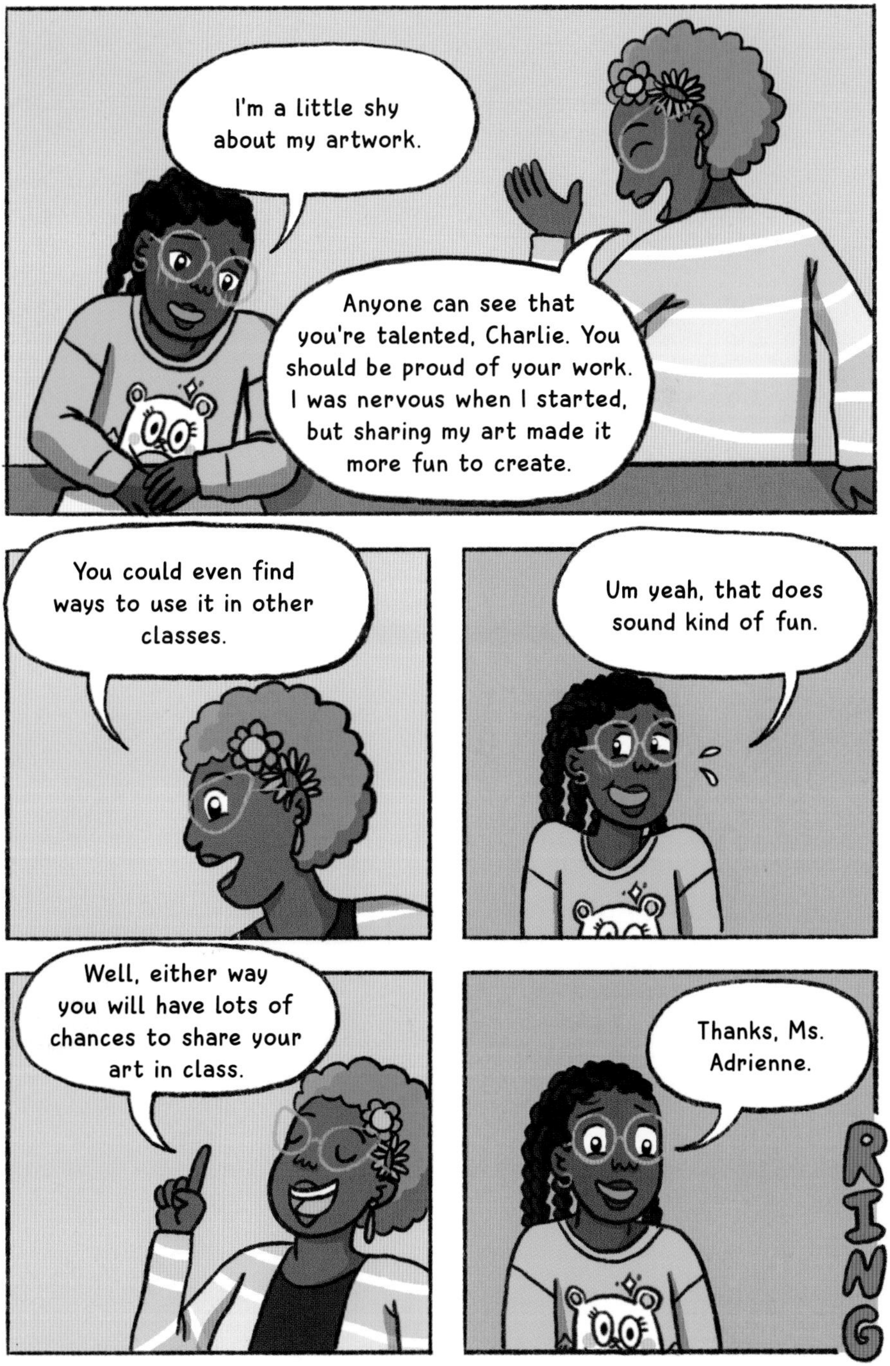
I'm a little shy about my artwork.
Anyone can see that you're talented, Charlie. You should be proud of your work. I was nervous when I started, but sharing my art made it more fun to create.
You could even find ways to use it in other classes.
Um yeah, that does sound kind of fun.
Well, either way you will have lots of chances to share your art in class.
Thanks, Ms. Adrienne.
RING

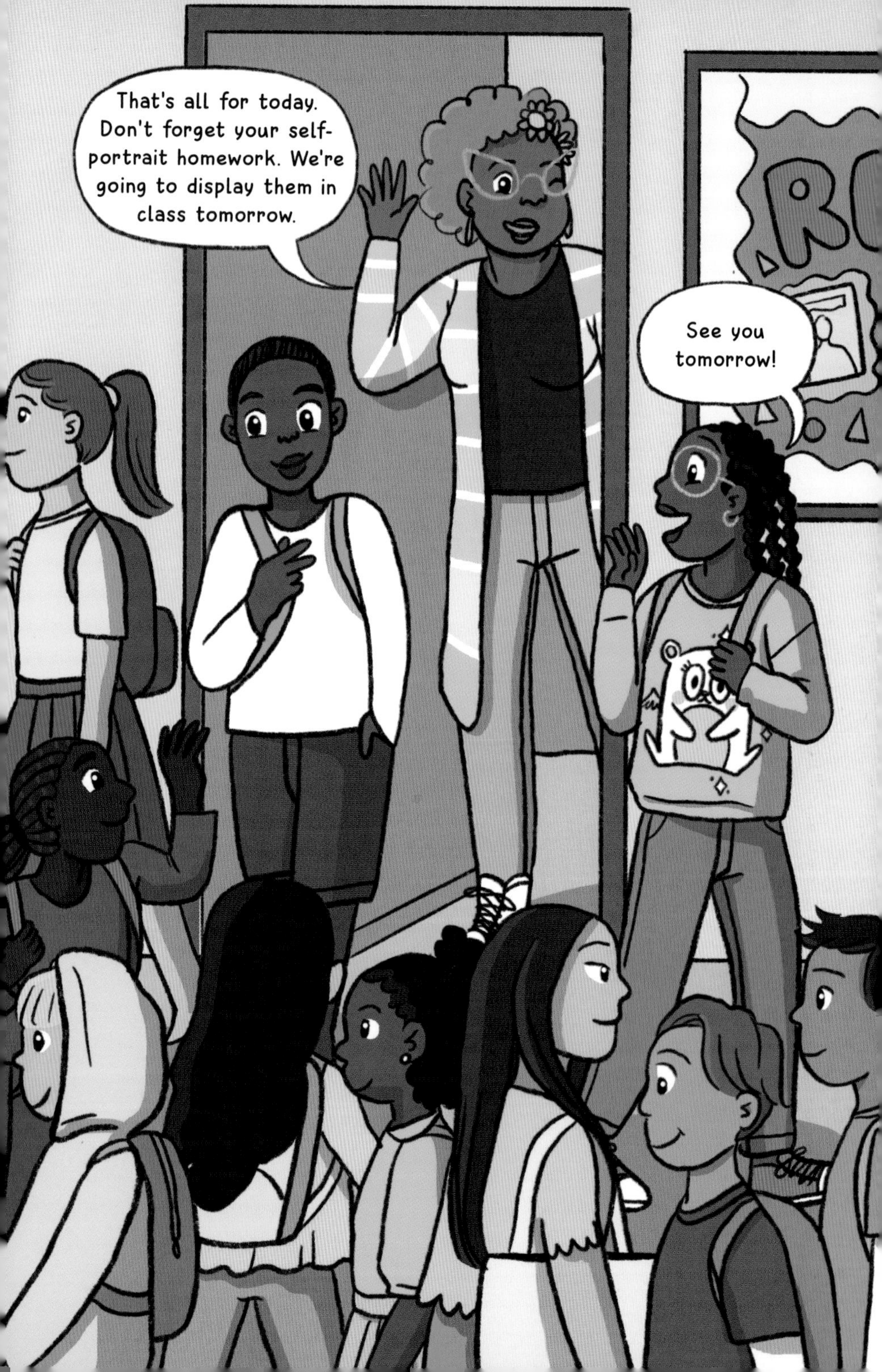
That's all for today. Don't forget your self-portrait homework. We're going to display them in class tomorrow.
See you tomorrow!

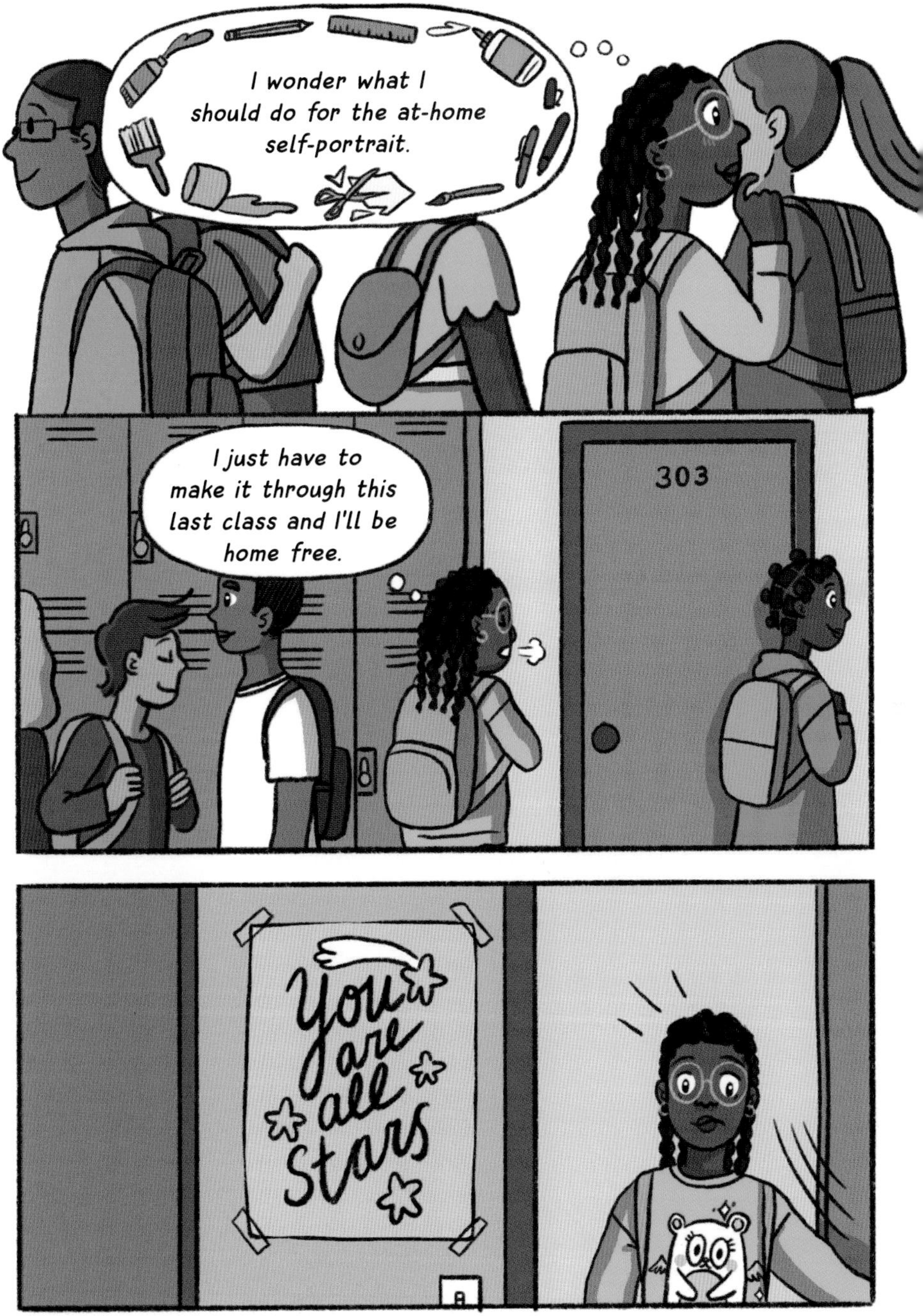

I wonder what I should do for the at-home self-portrait.
303
I just have to make it through this last class and I'll be home free.
You are all Stars

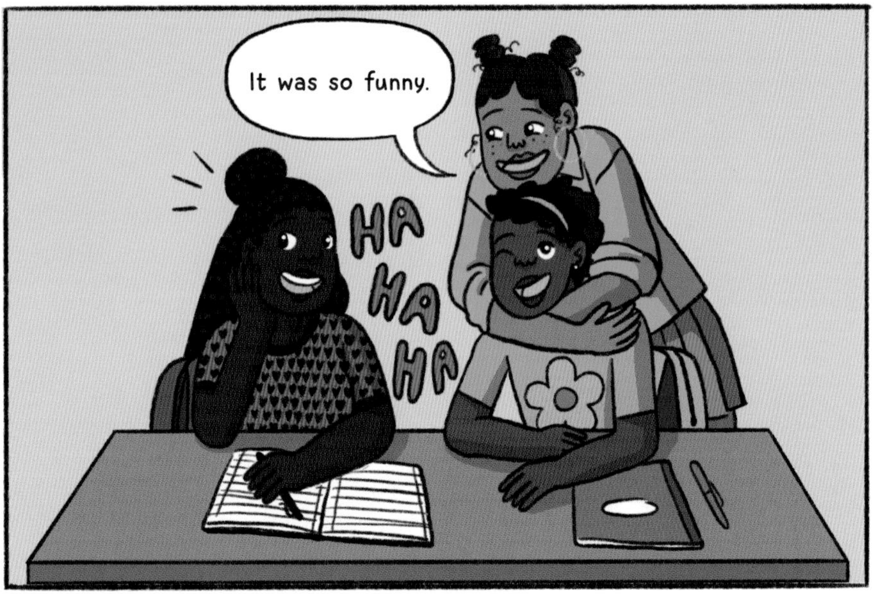
It was so funny.
HA HA HA

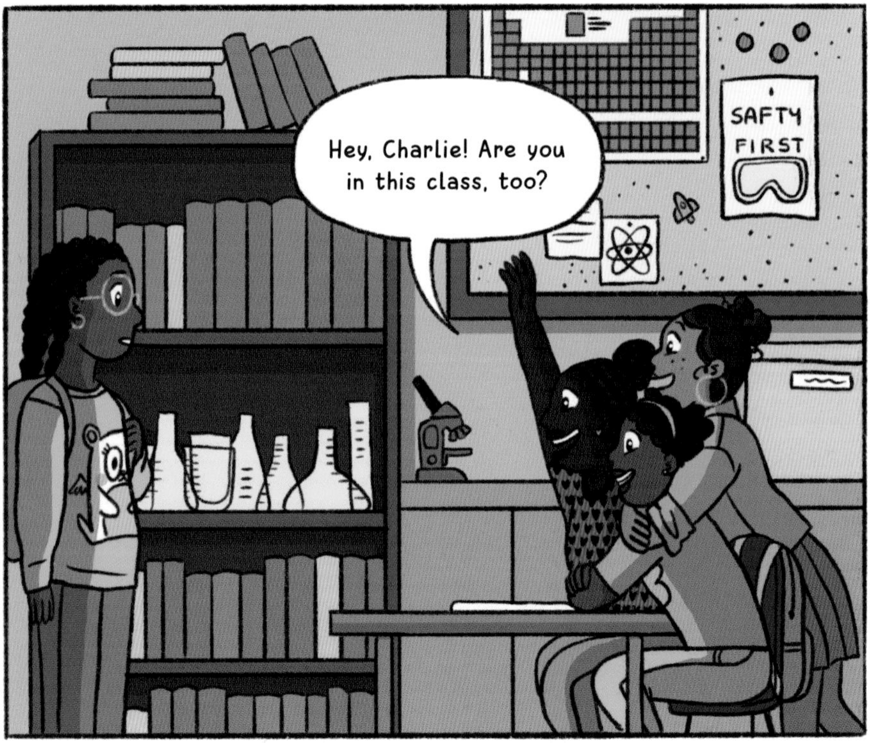
Hey, Charlie! Are you in this class, too?
SAFTY FIRST

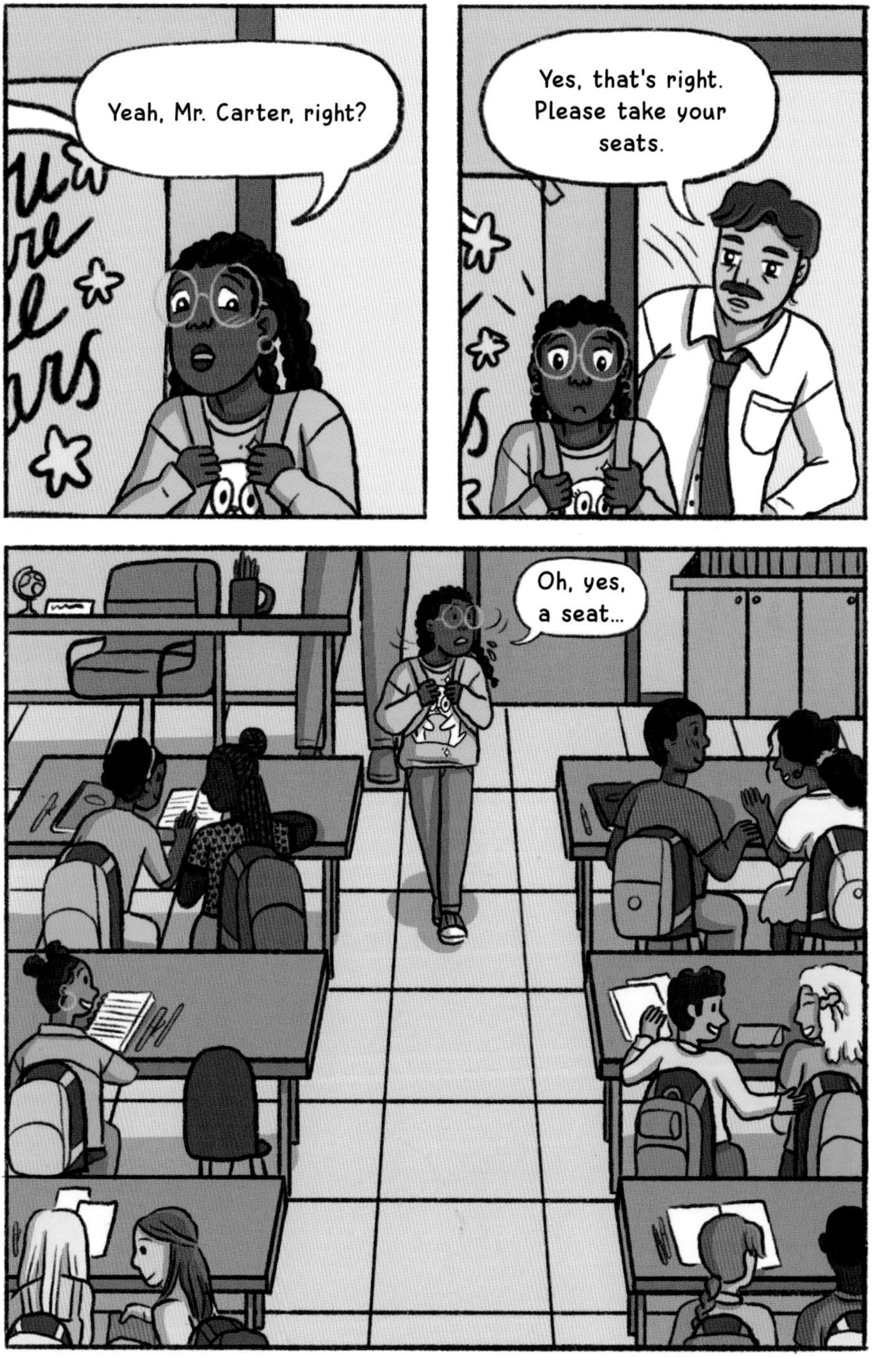
Yeah, Mr. Carter, right?
Yes, that's right. Please take your seats.
Oh, yes, a seat...

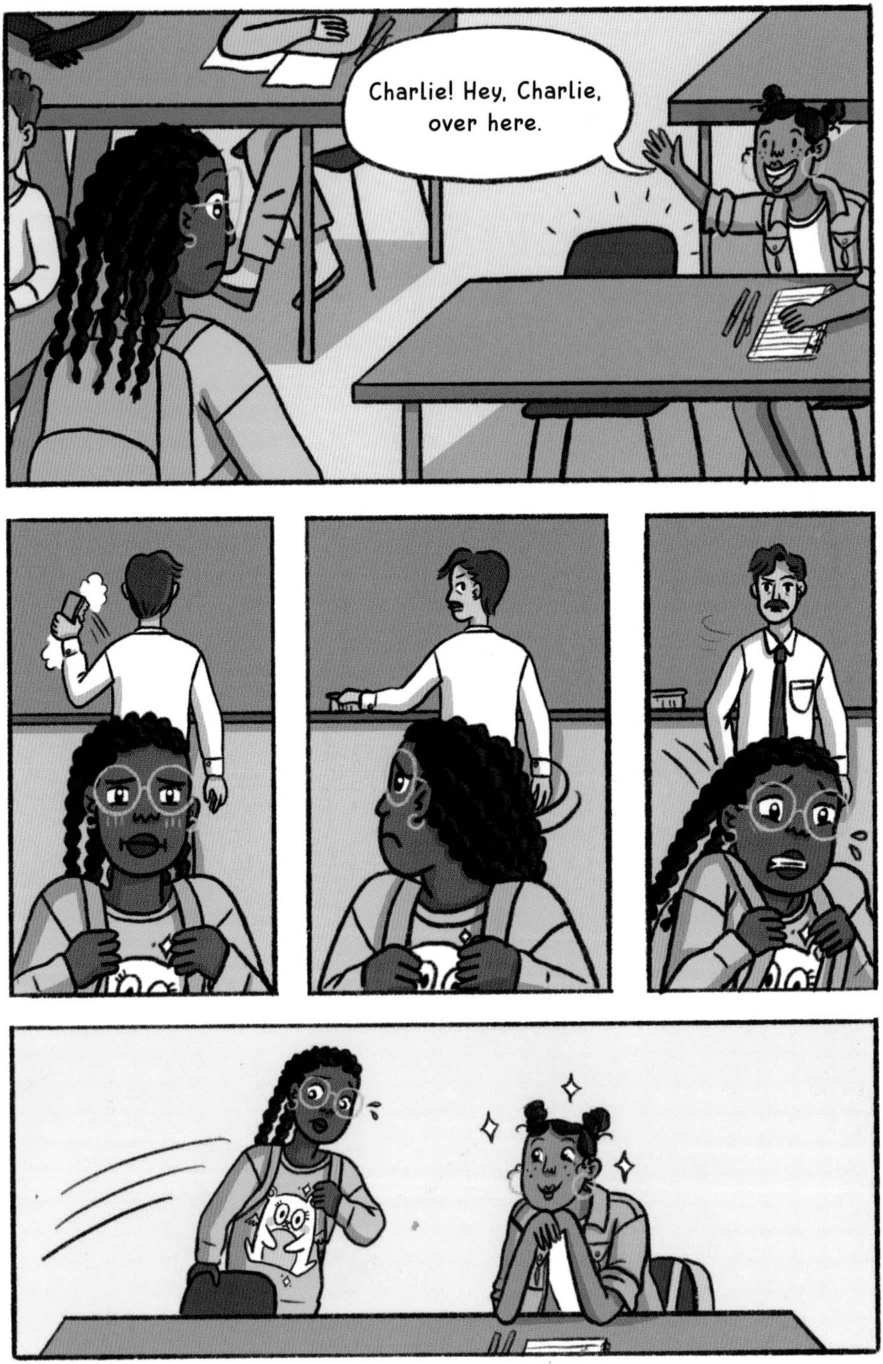
Charlie! Hey, Charlie, over here.

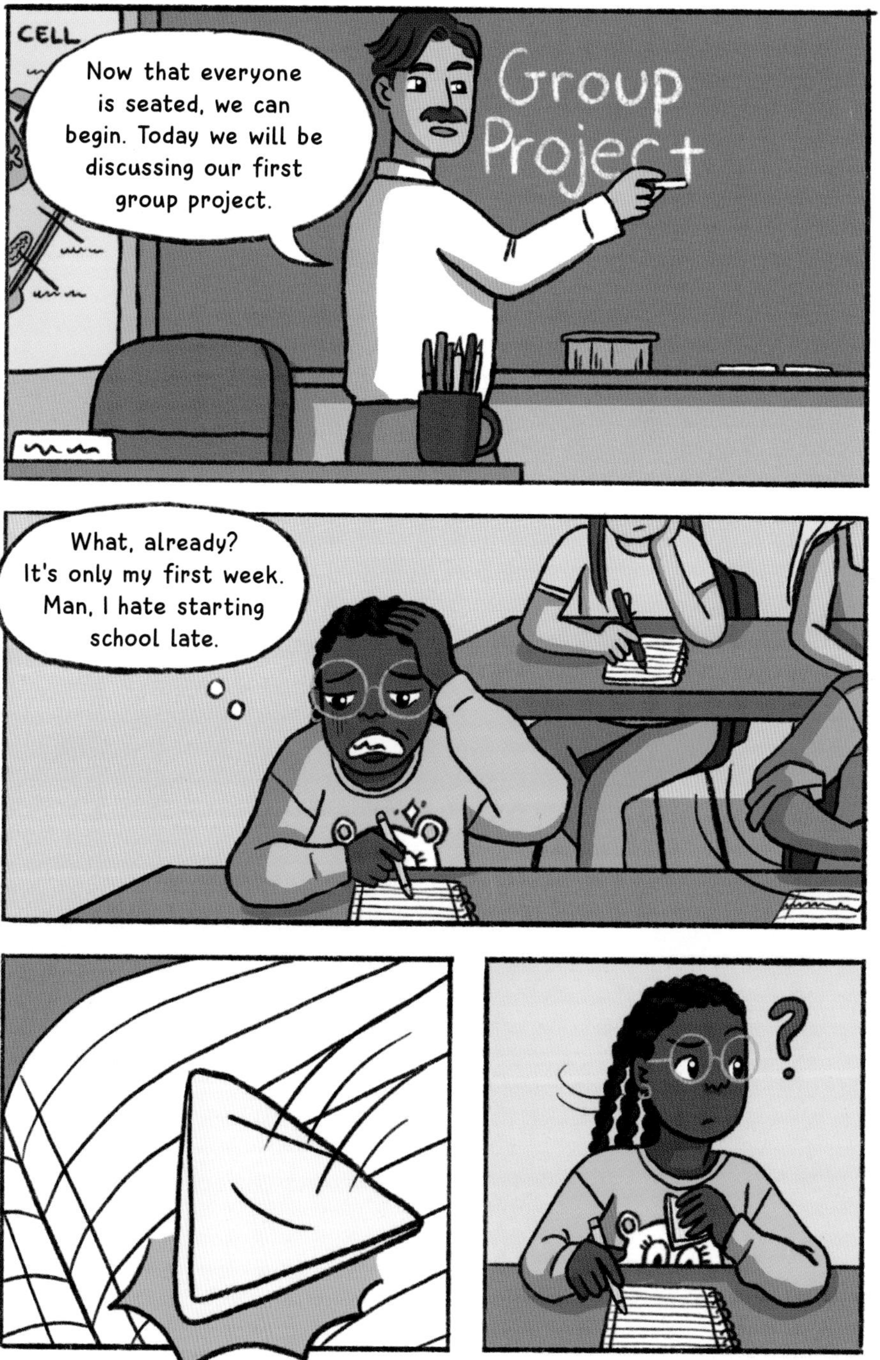
CELL
Now that everyone is seated, we can begin. Today we will be discussing our first group project.
Group Project
What, already? It's only my first week. Man, I hate starting school late.
?

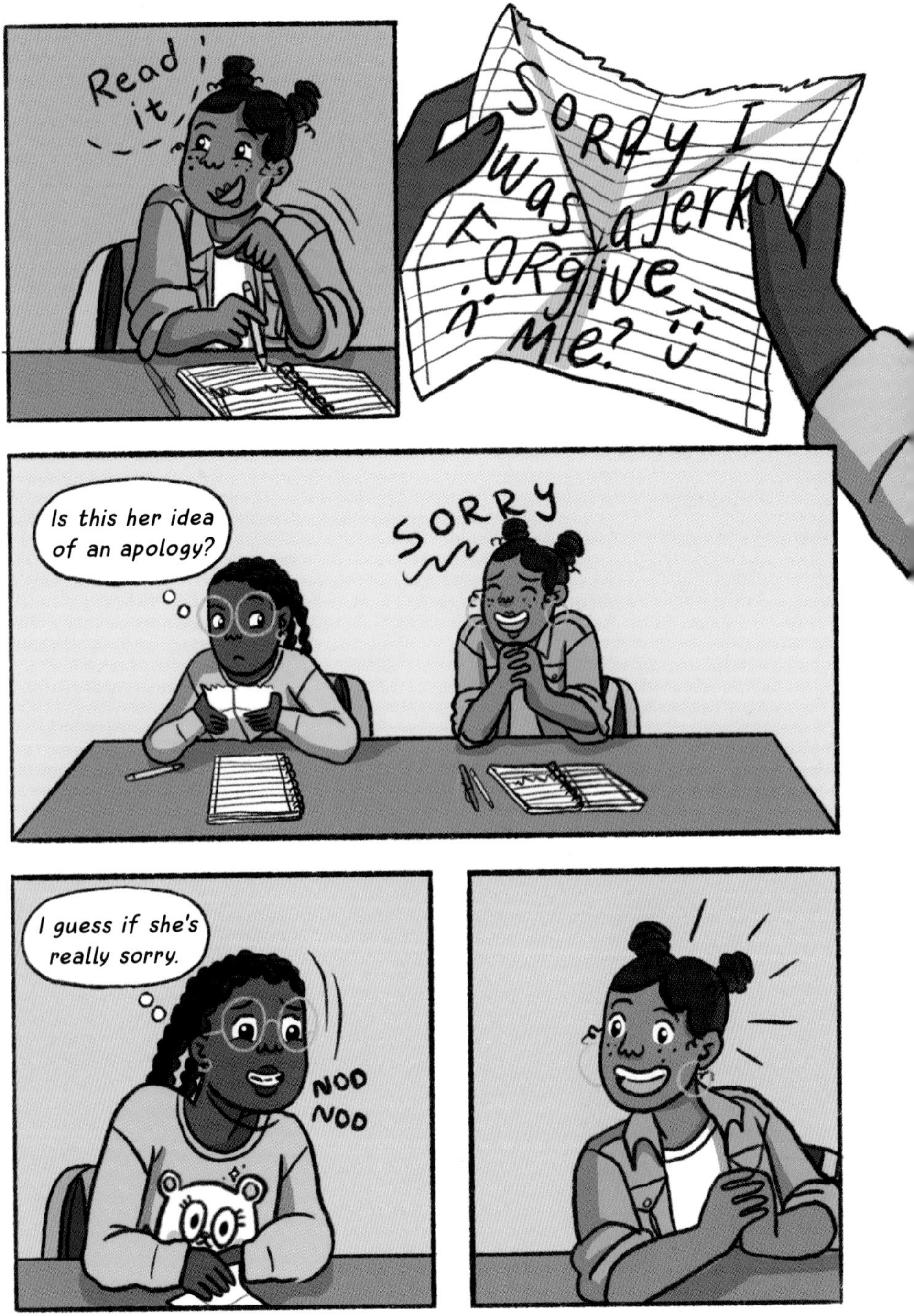
Read it
SORRY I was a jerk FORgive me? :)
Is this her idea of an apology?
SORRY
I guess if she's really sorry.
NOD NOD

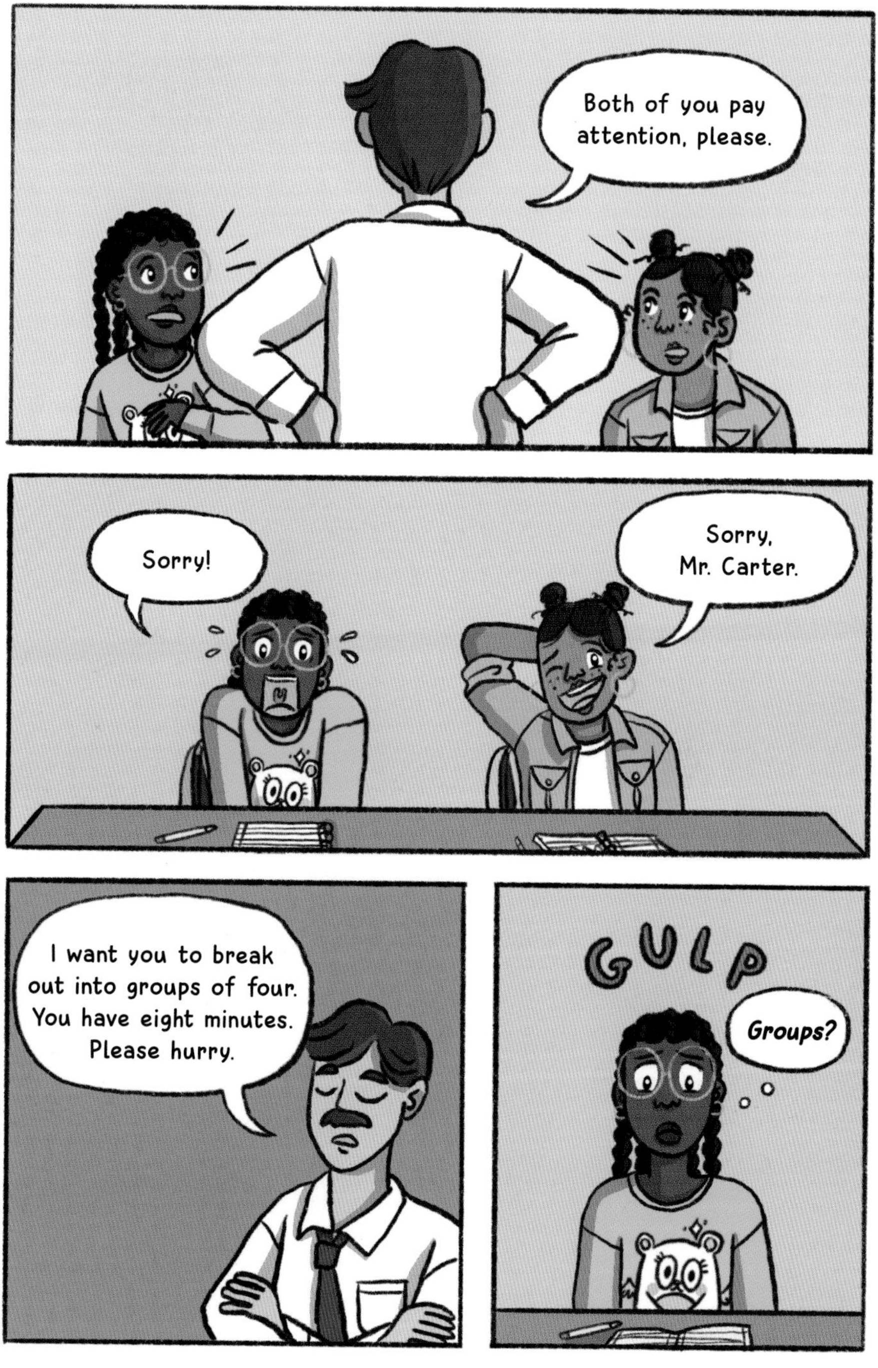
Both of you pay attention, please.
Sorry!
Sorry, Mr. Carter.
I want you to break out into groups of four. You have eight minutes. Please hurry.
GULP
Groups?

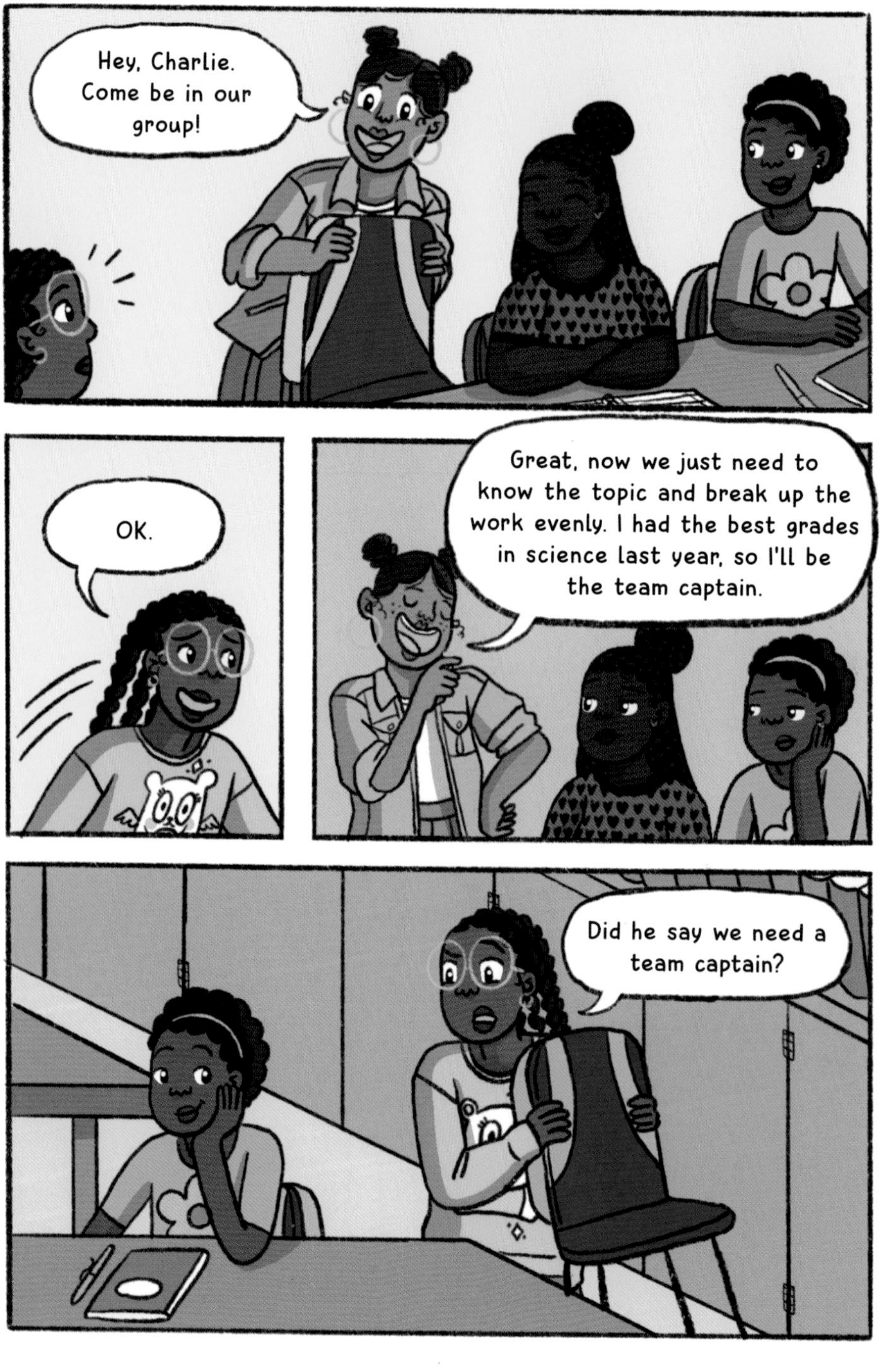
Hey, Charlie. Come be in our group!
OK.
Great, now we just need to know the topic and break up the work evenly. I had the best grades in science last year, so I'll be the team captain.
Did he say we need a team captain?

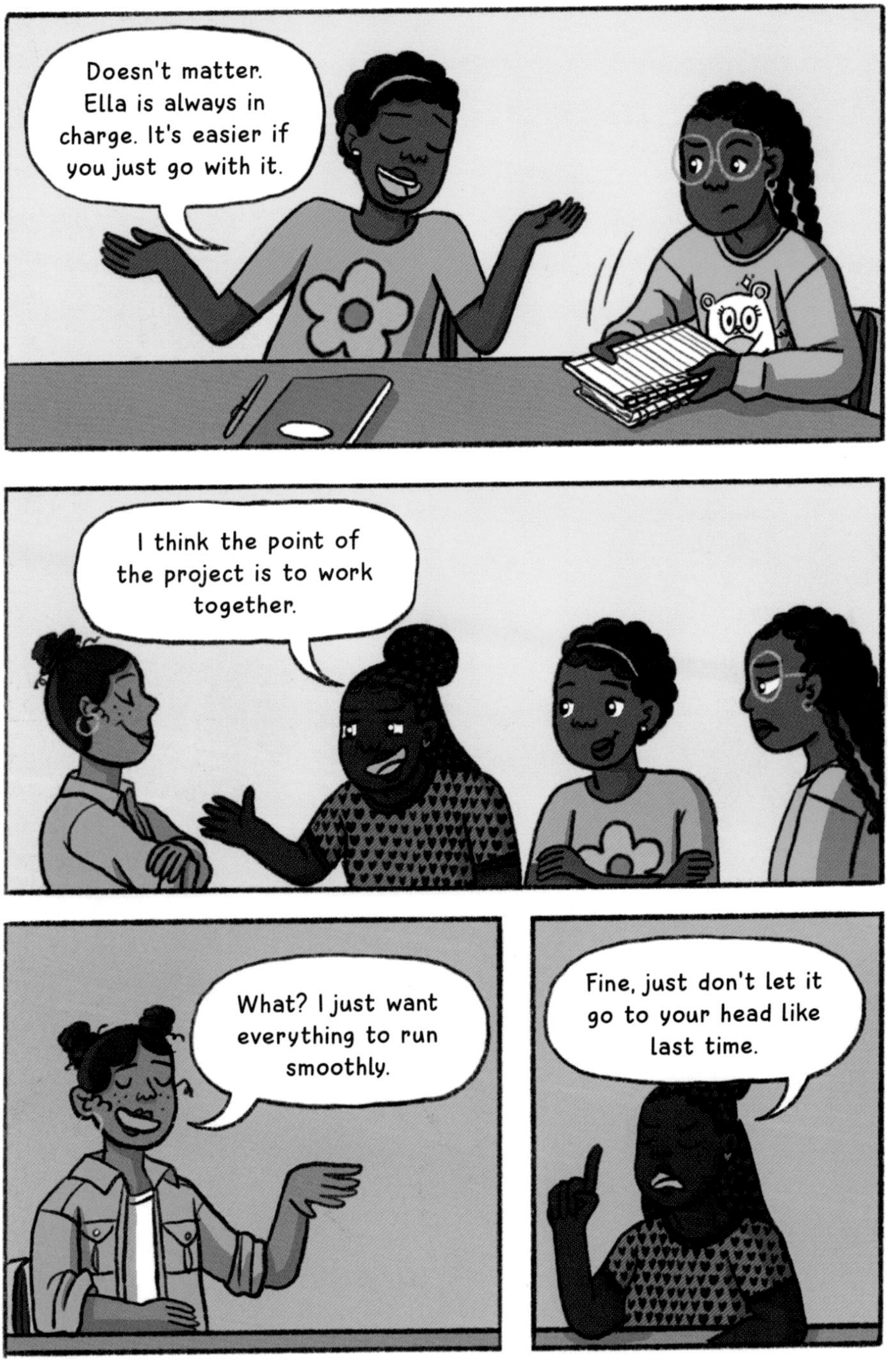
Doesn't matter. Ella is always in charge. It's easier if you just go with it.
I think the point of the project is to work together.
What? I just want everything to run smoothly.
Fine, just don't let it go to your head like last time.

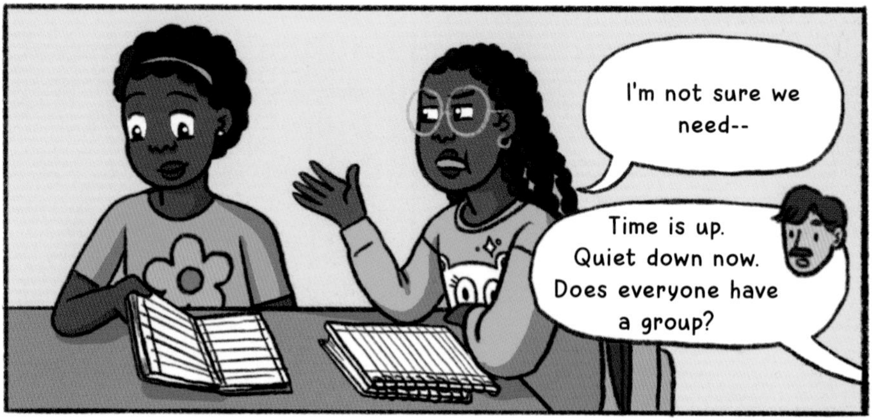
I'm not sure we need--
Time is up. Quiet down now. Does everyone have a group?

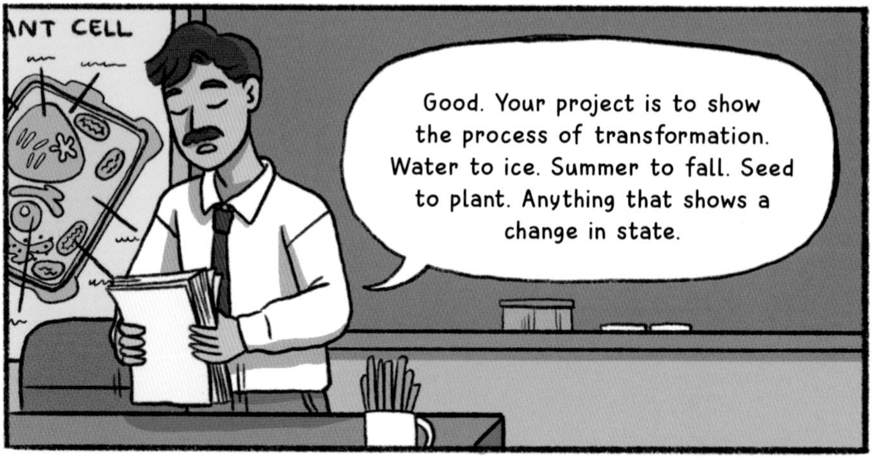
ANT CELL
Good. Your project is to show the process of transformation. Water to ice. Summer to fall. Seed to plant. Anything that shows a change in state.

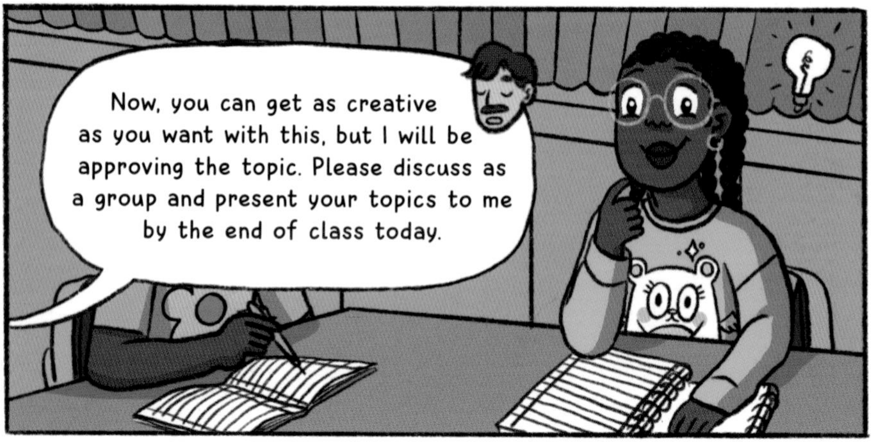
Now, you can get as creative as you want with this, but I will be approving the topic. Please discuss as a group and present your topics to me by the end of class today.

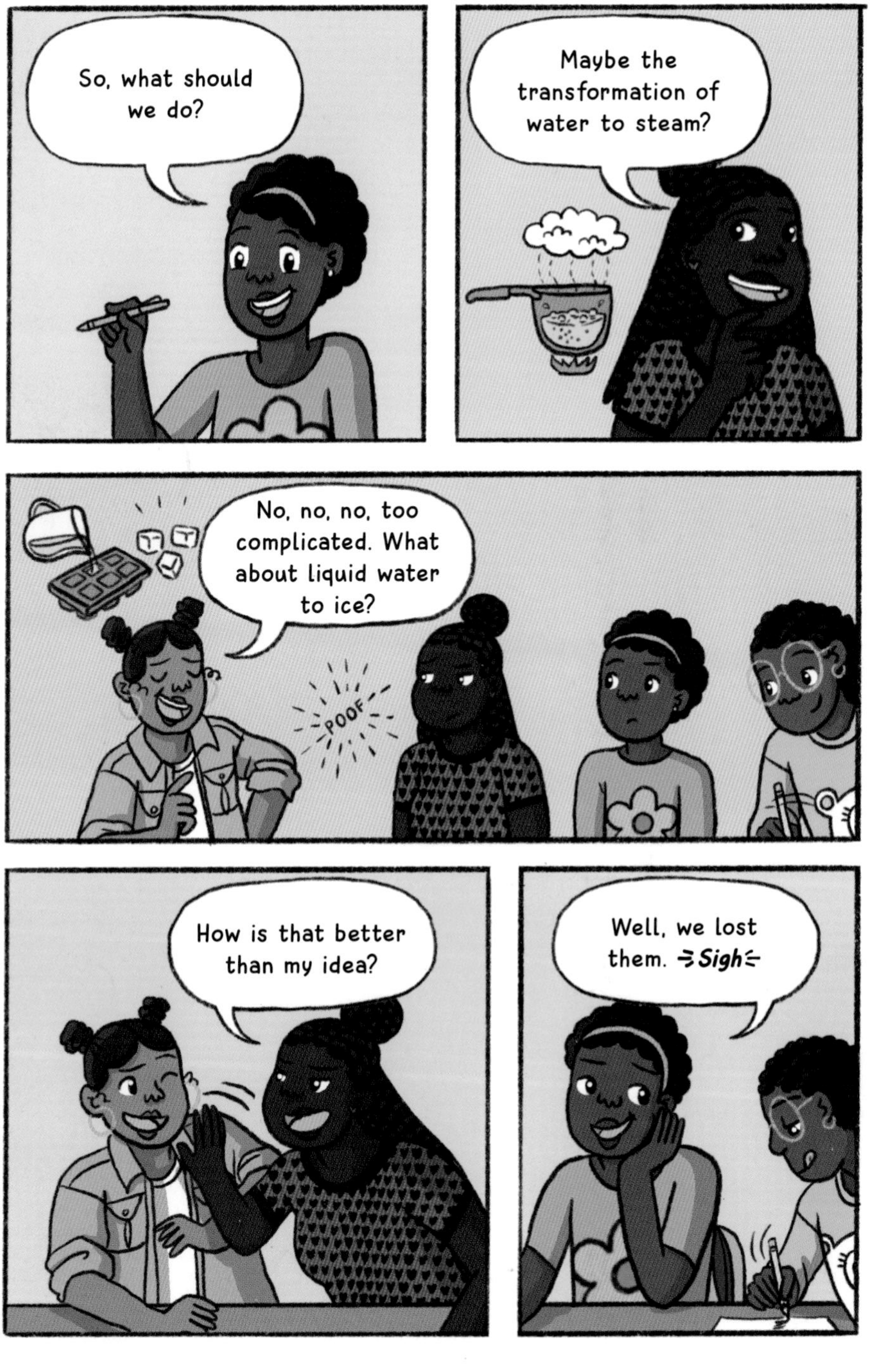
So, what should we do?
Maybe the transformation of water to steam?
No, no, no, too complicated. What about liquid water to ice?
POOF
How is that better than my idea?
Well, we lost them. Sigh

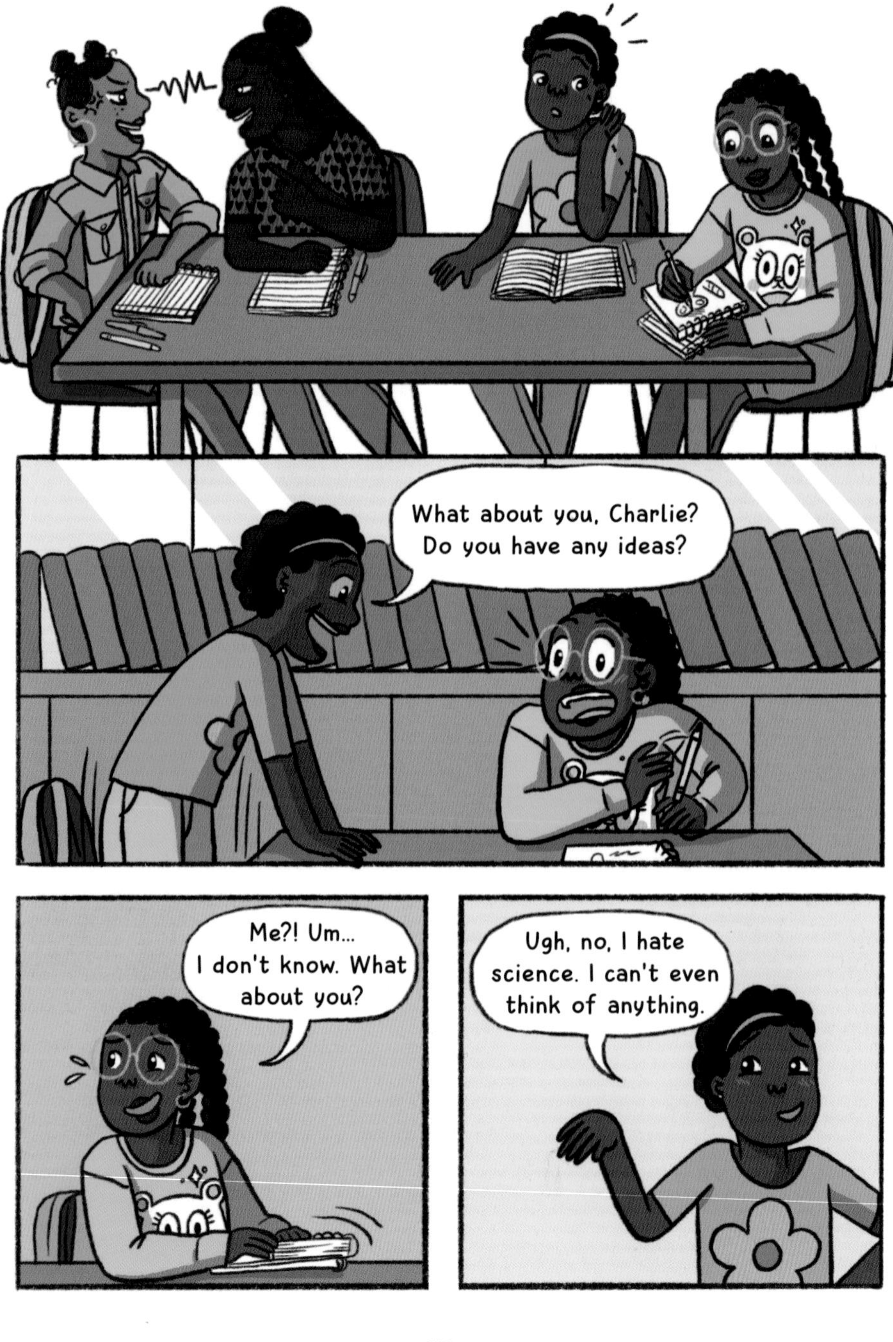
What about you, Charlie? Do you have any ideas?
Me?! Um... I don't know. What about you?
Ugh, no, I hate science. I can't even think of anything.

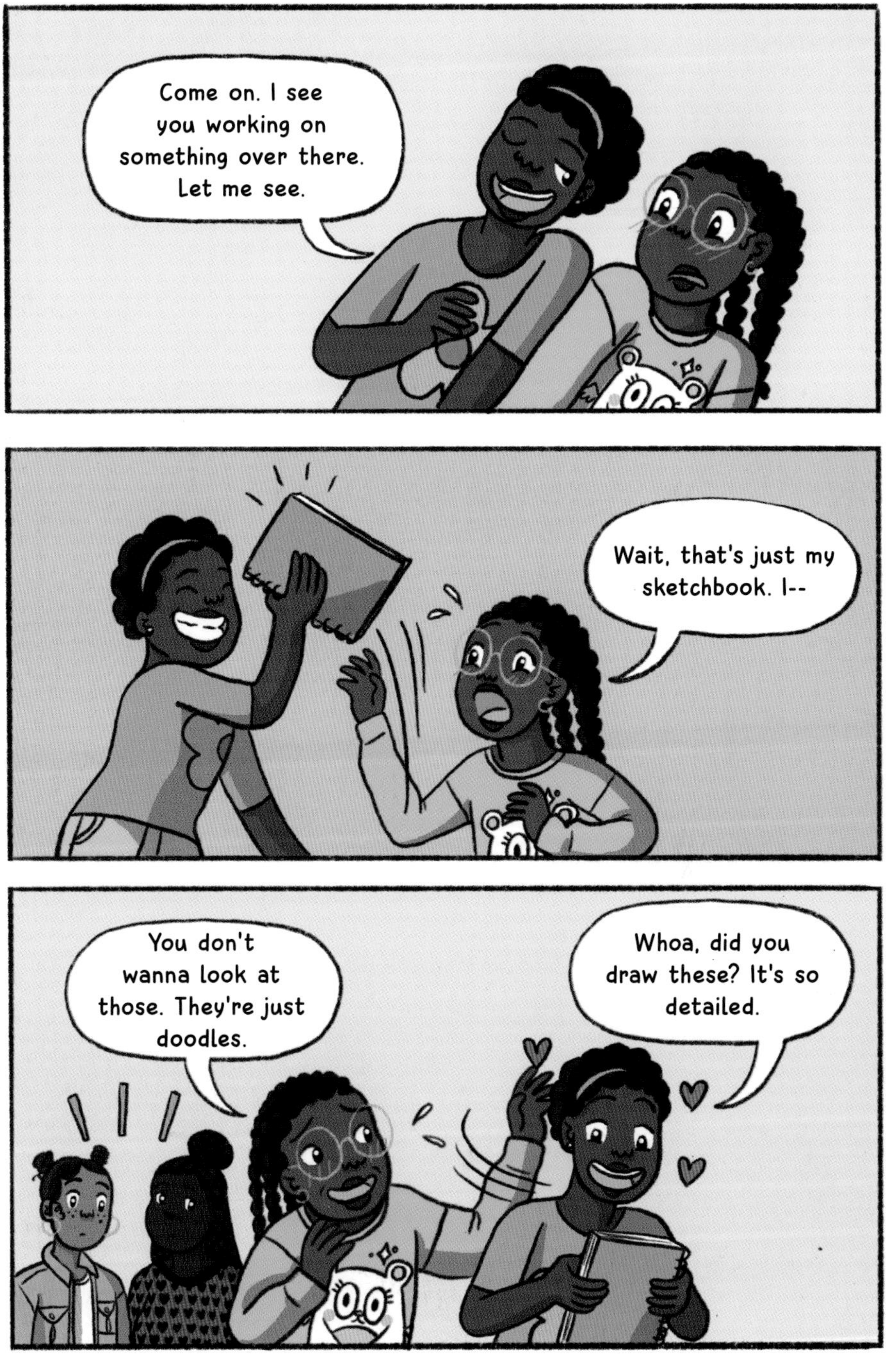
Come on. I see you working on something over there. Let me see.
Wait, that's just my sketchbook. I--
You don't wanna look at those. They're just doodles.
Whoa, did you draw these? It's so detailed.

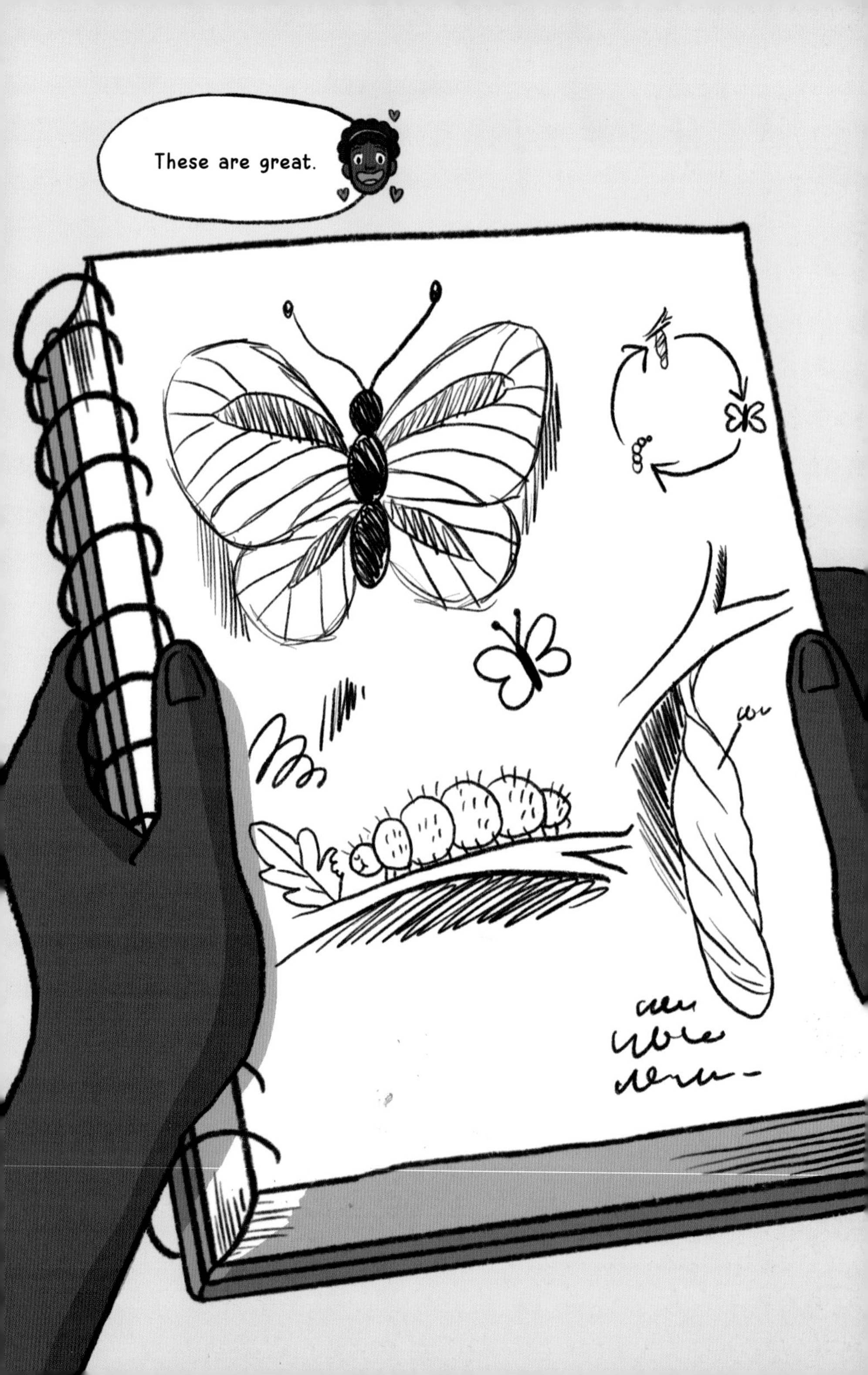
These are great.

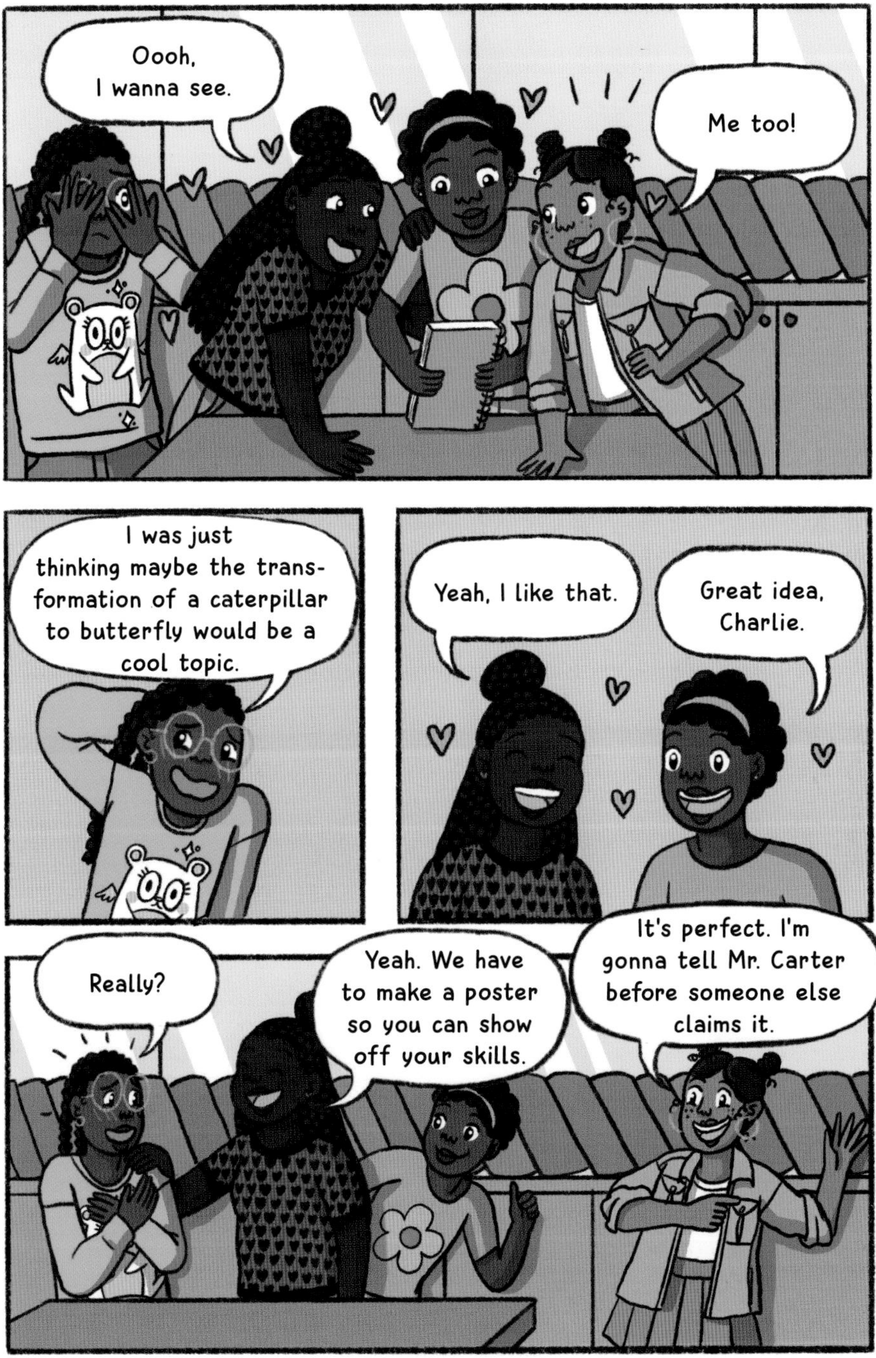
Oooh, I wanna see.
Me too!
I was just thinking maybe the trans-formation of a caterpillar to butterfly would be a cool topic.
Yeah, I like that.
Great idea, Charlie.
Really?
Yeah. We have to make a poster so you can show off your skills.
It's perfect. I'm gonna tell Mr. Carter before someone else claims it.

CHAPTER
5

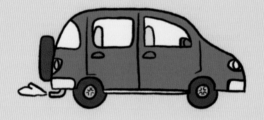

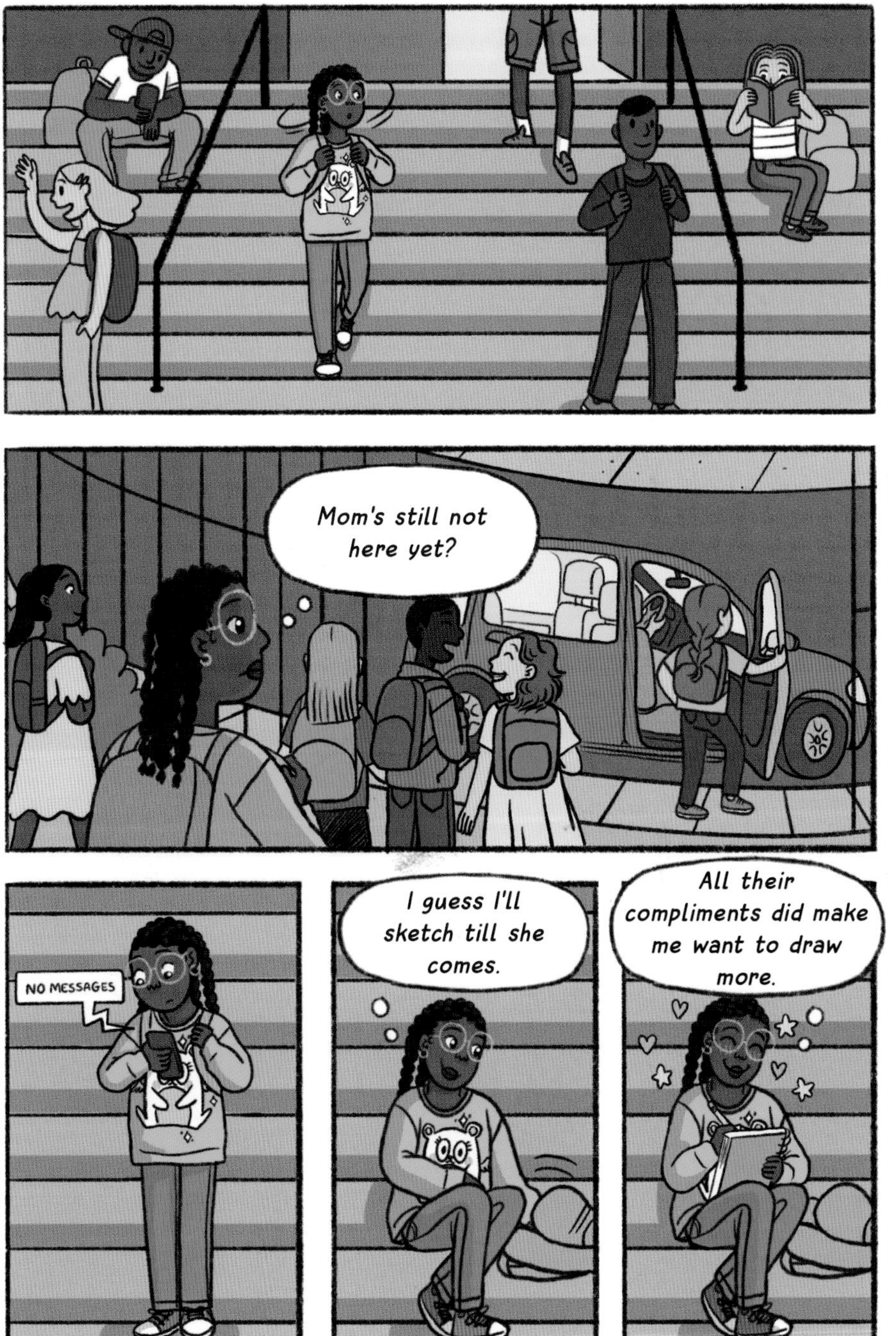
Mom's still not here yet?
NO MESSAGES
I guess I'll sketch till she comes.
All their compliments did make me want to draw more.

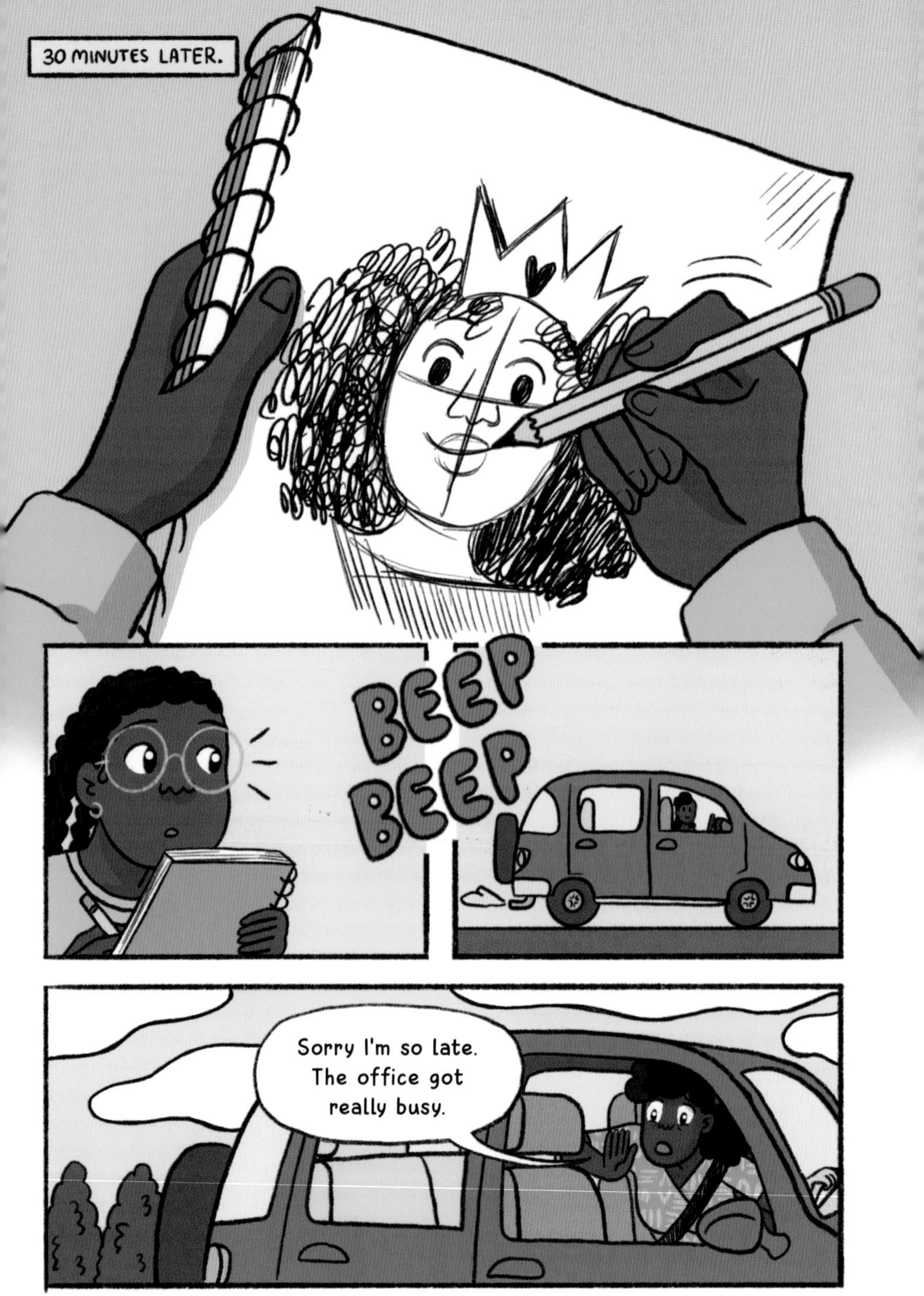
30 MINUTES LATER.
BEEP BEEP
Sorry I'm so late. The office got really busy.

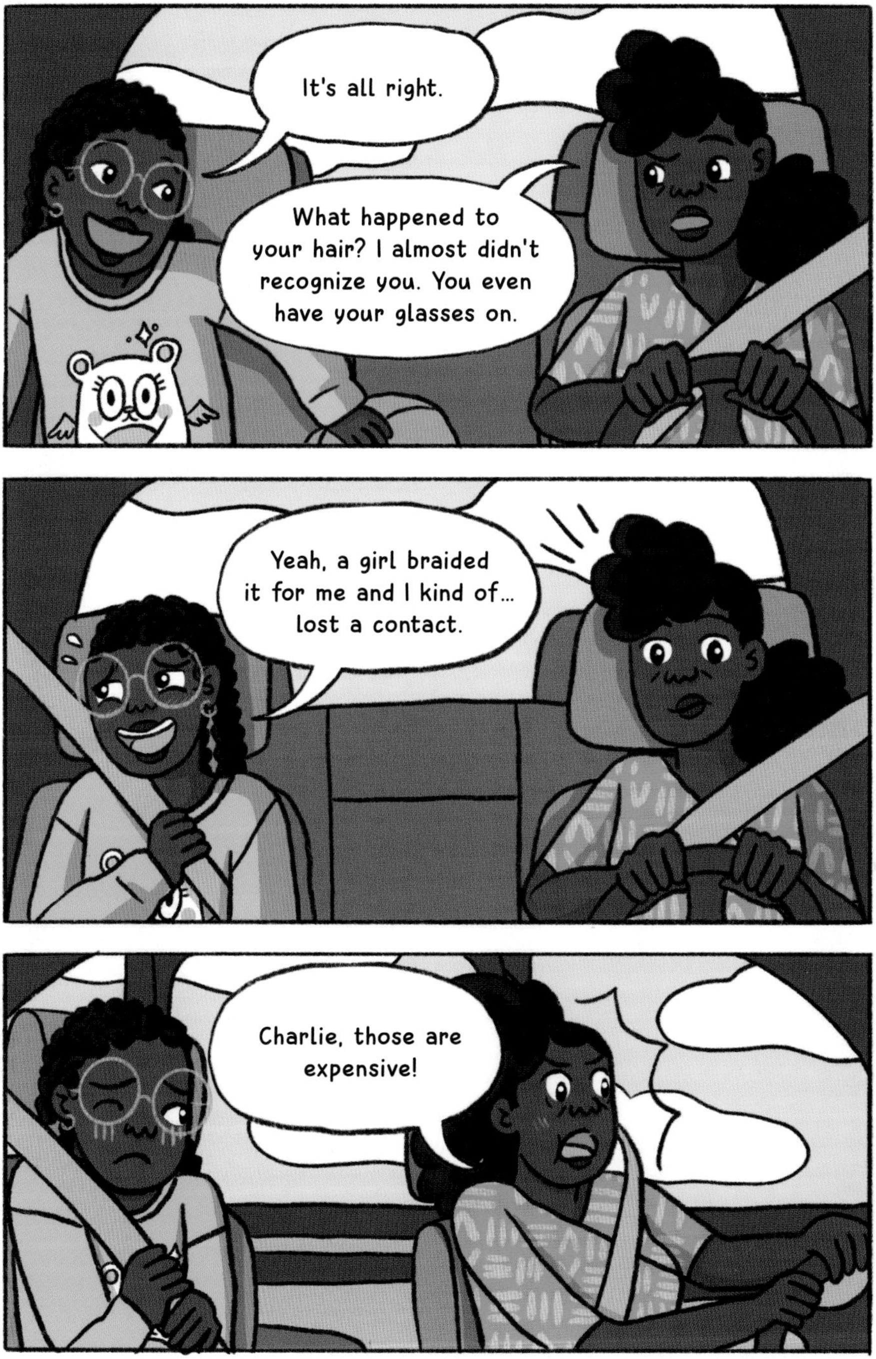
It's all right.
What happened to your hair? I almost didn't recognize you. You even have your glasses on.
Yeah, a girl braided it for me and I kind of... lost a contact.
Charlie, those are expensive!

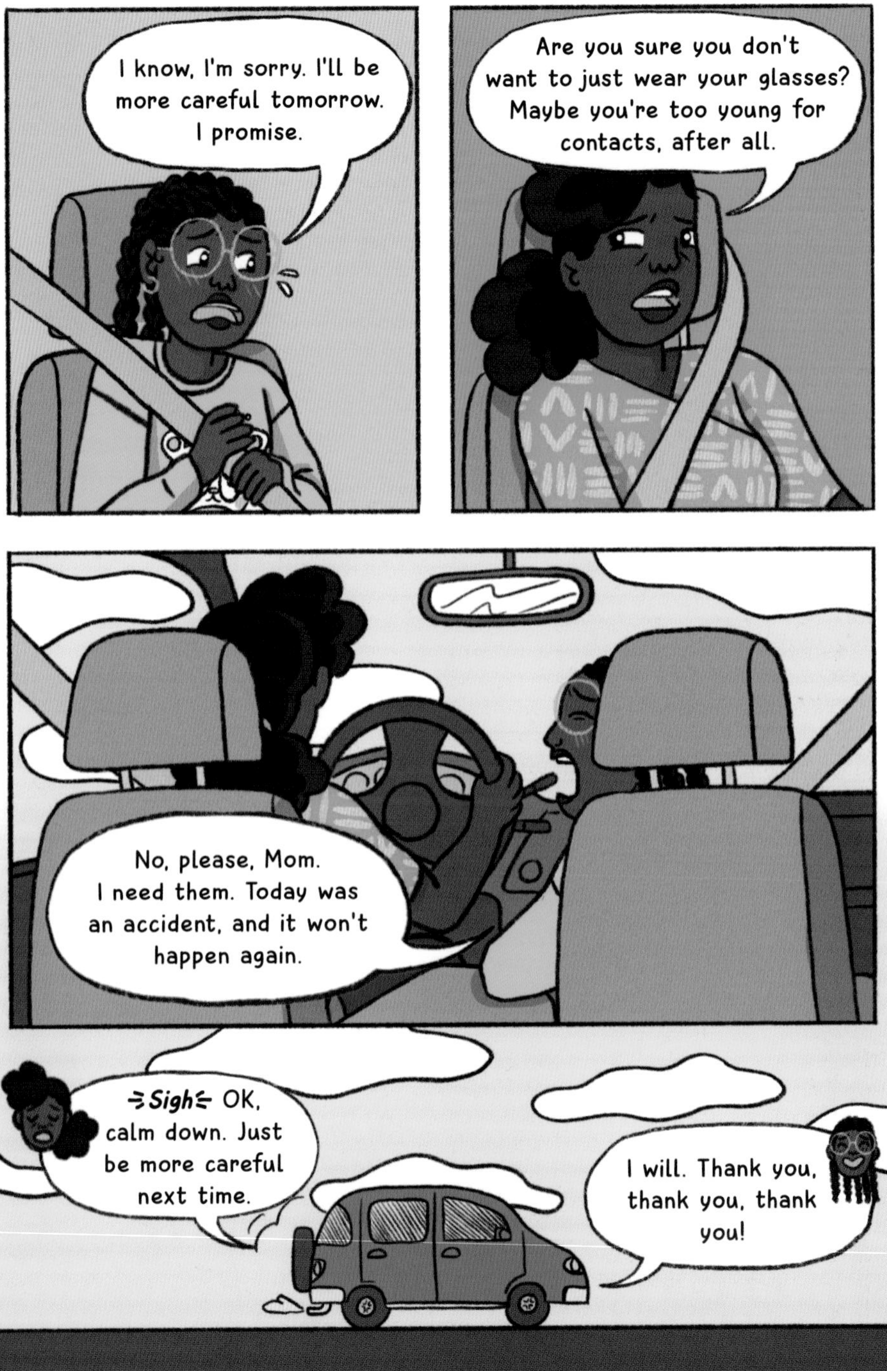
I know, I'm sorry. I'll be more careful tomorrow. I promise.
Are you sure you don't want to just wear your glasses? Maybe you're too young for contacts, after all.
No, please, Mom. I need them. Today was an accident, and it won't happen again.
Sigh OK, calm down. Just be more careful next time.
I will. Thank you, thank you, thank you!

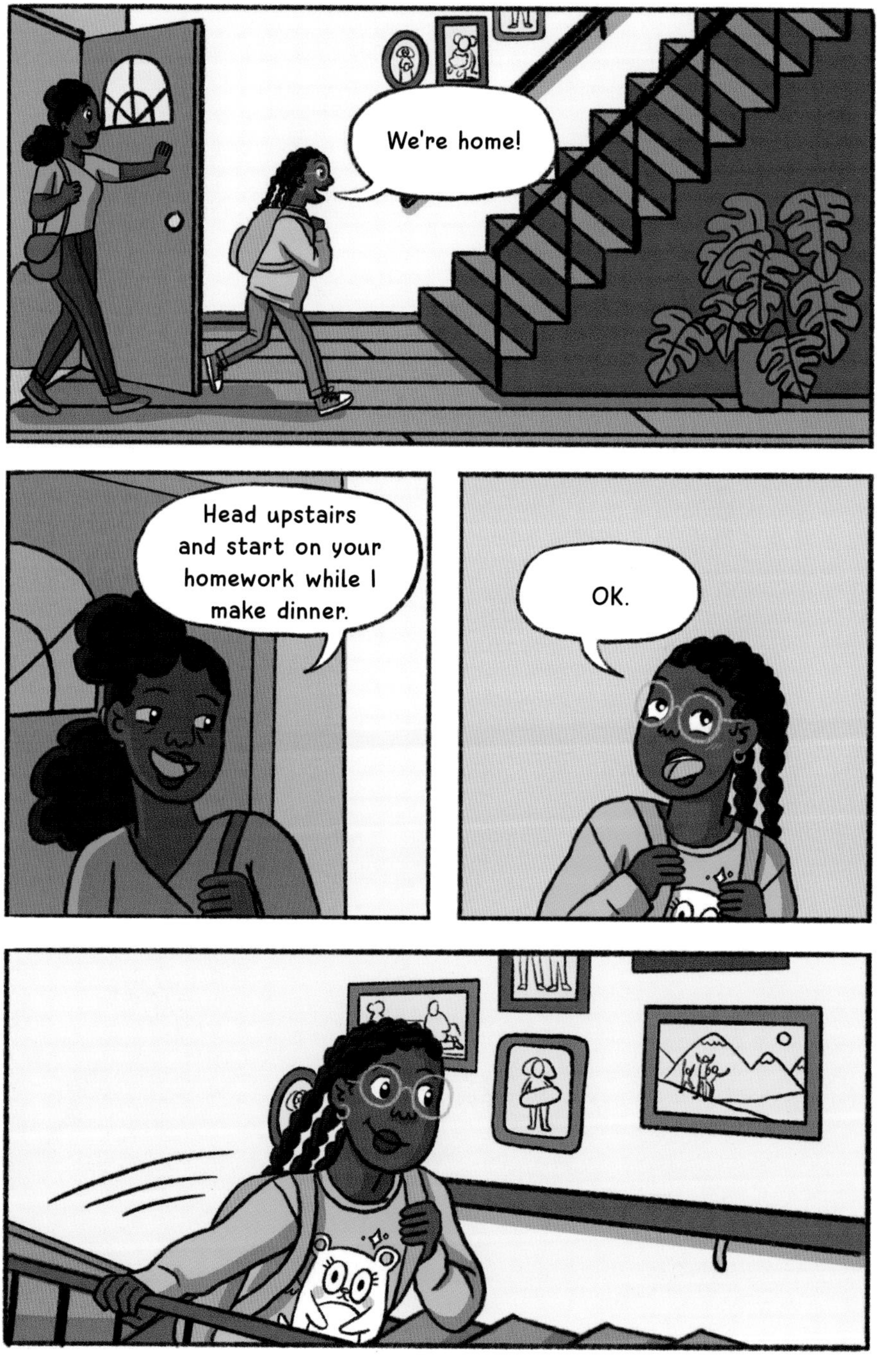
We're home!
Head upstairs and start on your homework while I make dinner.
OK.

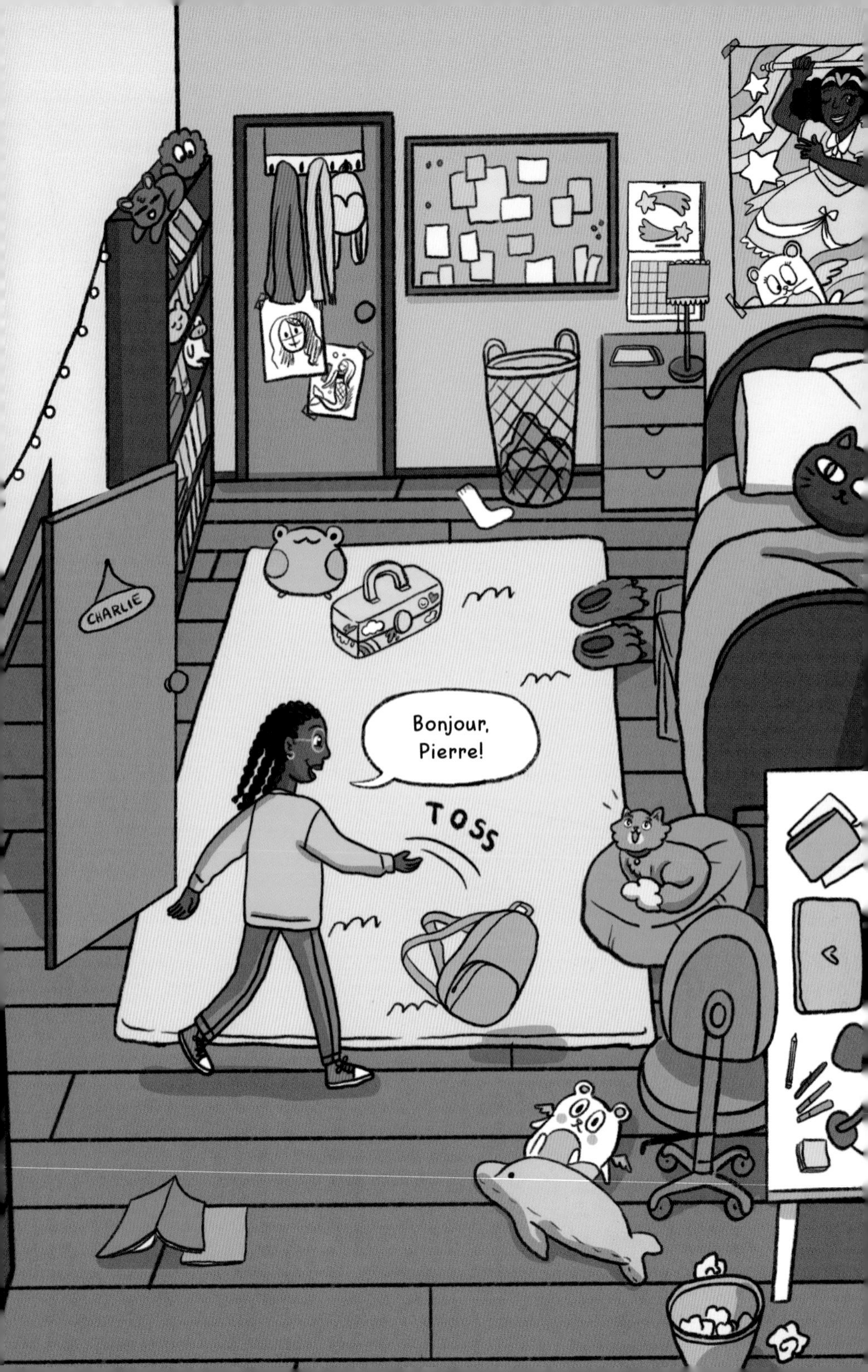

CHARLIE
Bonjour, Pierre!
TOSS

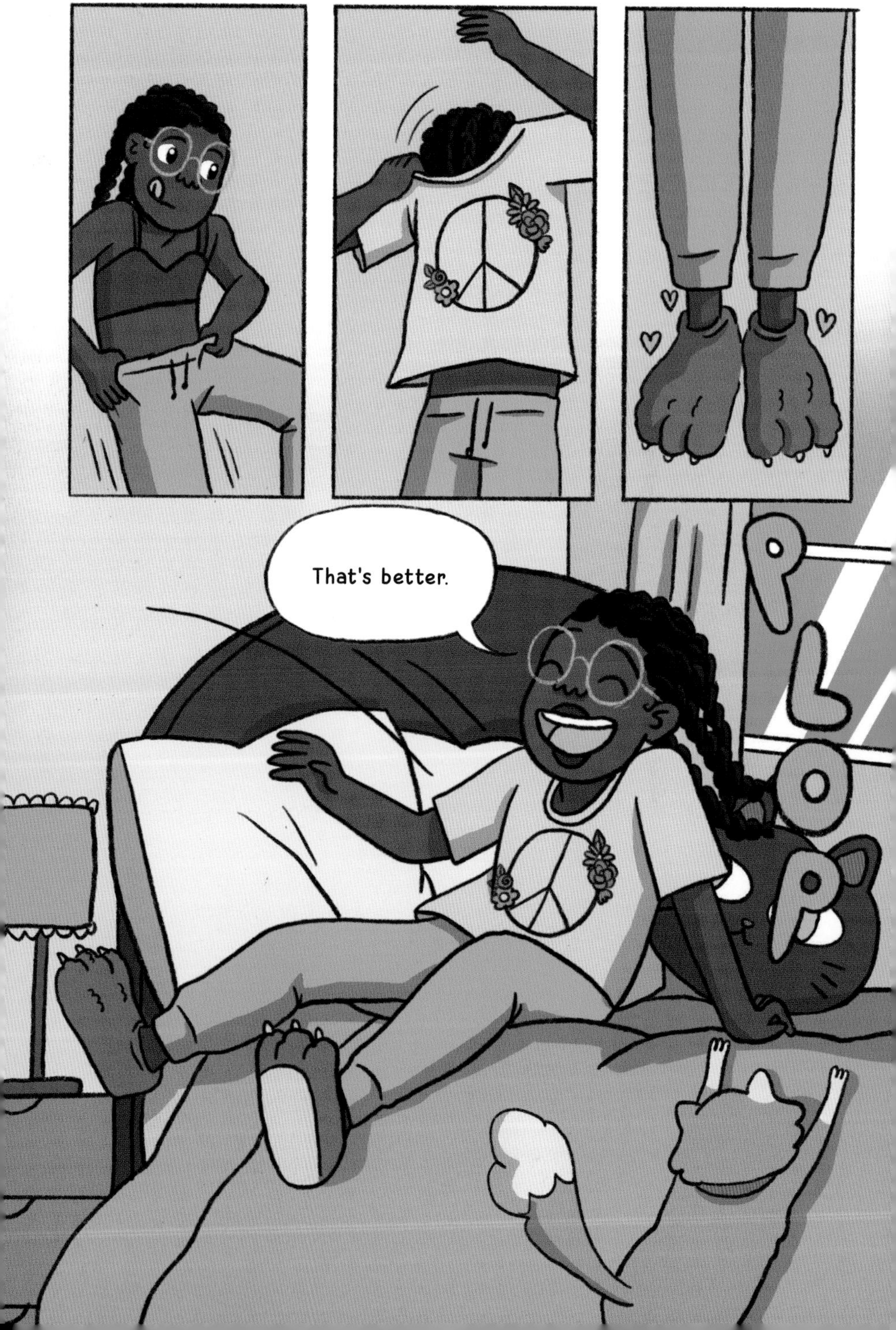
That's better.
PLOP

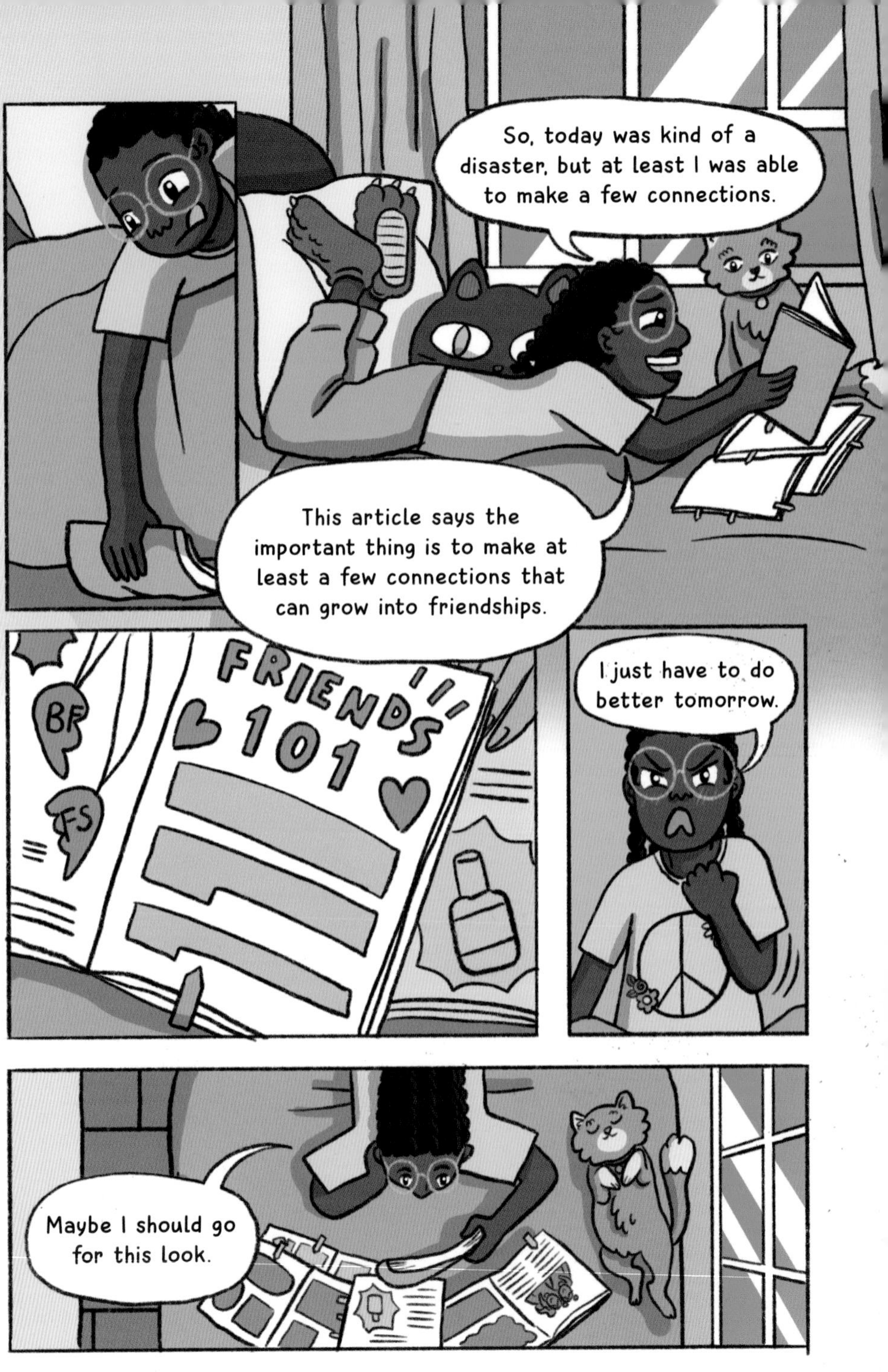
So, today was kind of a disaster, but at least I was able to make a few connections.
This article says the important thing is to make at least a few connections that can grow into friendships.
FRIENDS 101
BF
FS
I just have to do better tomorrow.
Maybe I should go for this look.

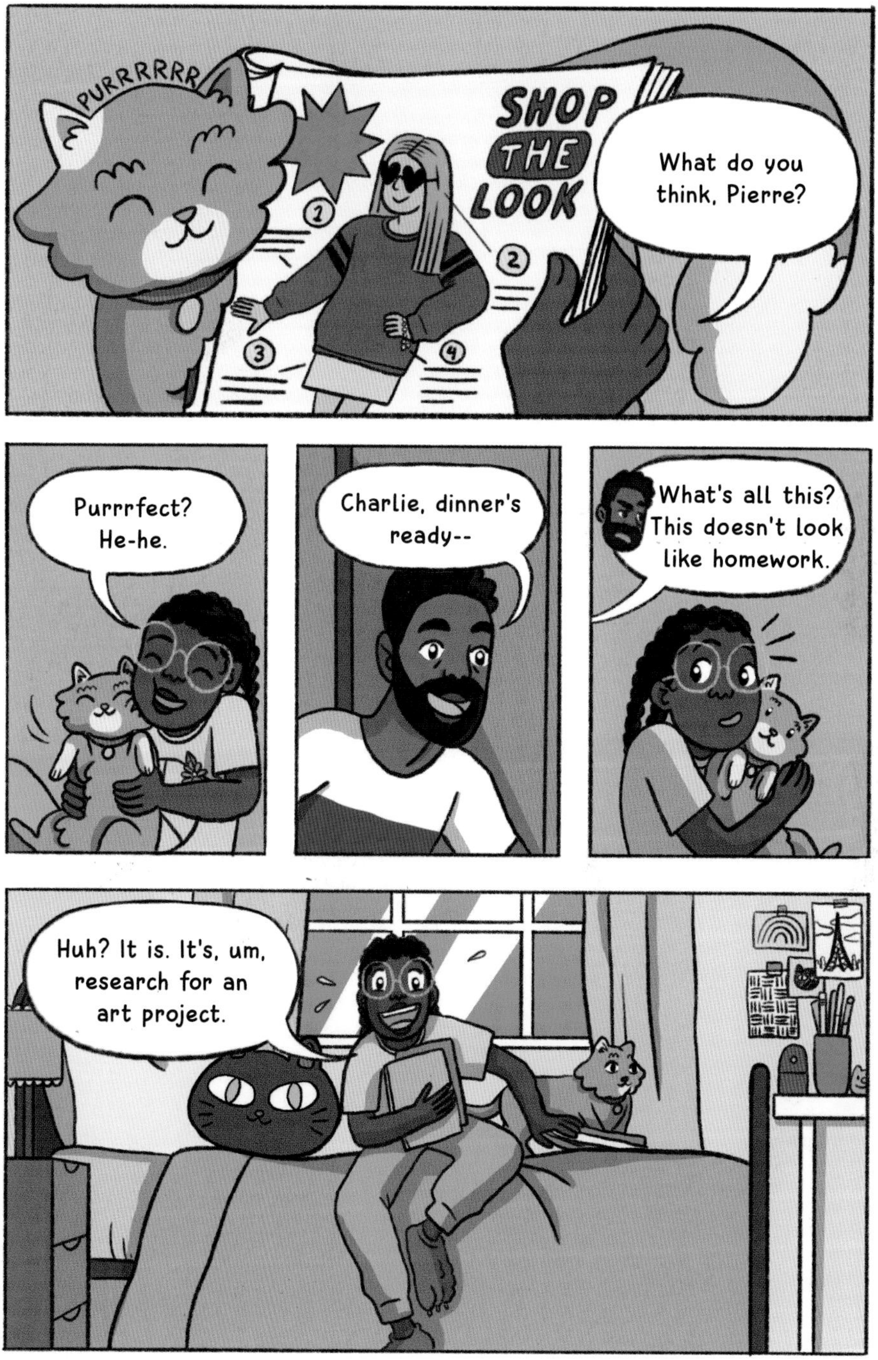
PURRRRRR
SHOP THE LOOK
1
2
3
4
What do you think, Pierre?
Purrrfect? He-he.
Charlie, dinner's ready--
What's all this? This doesn't look like homework.
Huh? It is. It's, um, research for an art project.

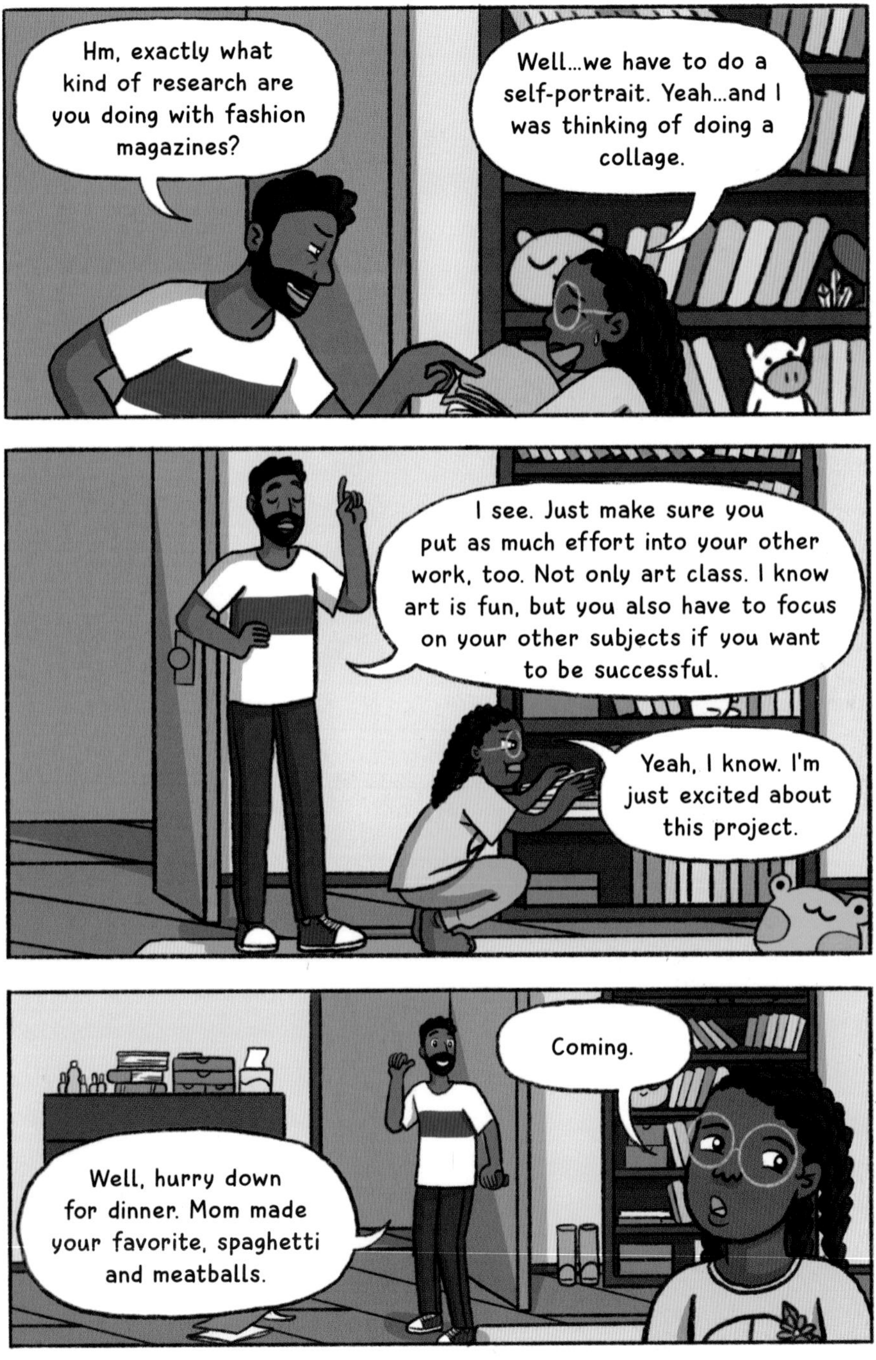

Hm, exactly what kind of research are you doing with fashion magazines?
Well...we have to do a self-portrait. Yeah...and I was thinking of doing a collage.
I see. Just make sure you put as much effort into your other work, too. Not only art class. I know art is fun, but you also have to focus on your other subjects if you want to be successful.
Yeah, I know. I'm just excited about this project.
Well, hurry down for dinner. Mom made your favorite, spaghetti and meatballs.
Coming.

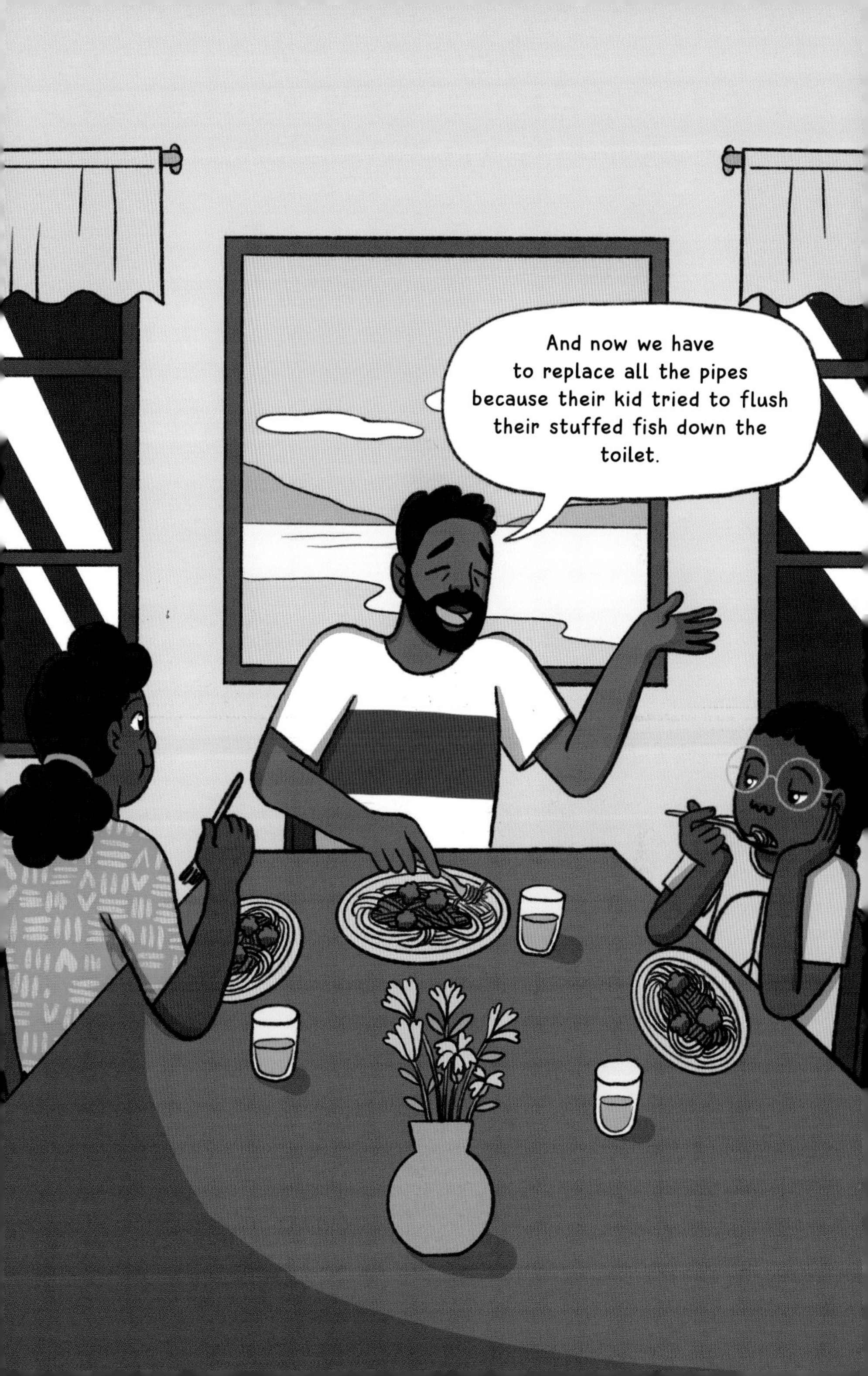
And now we have to replace all the pipes because their kid tried to flush their stuffed fish down the toilet.

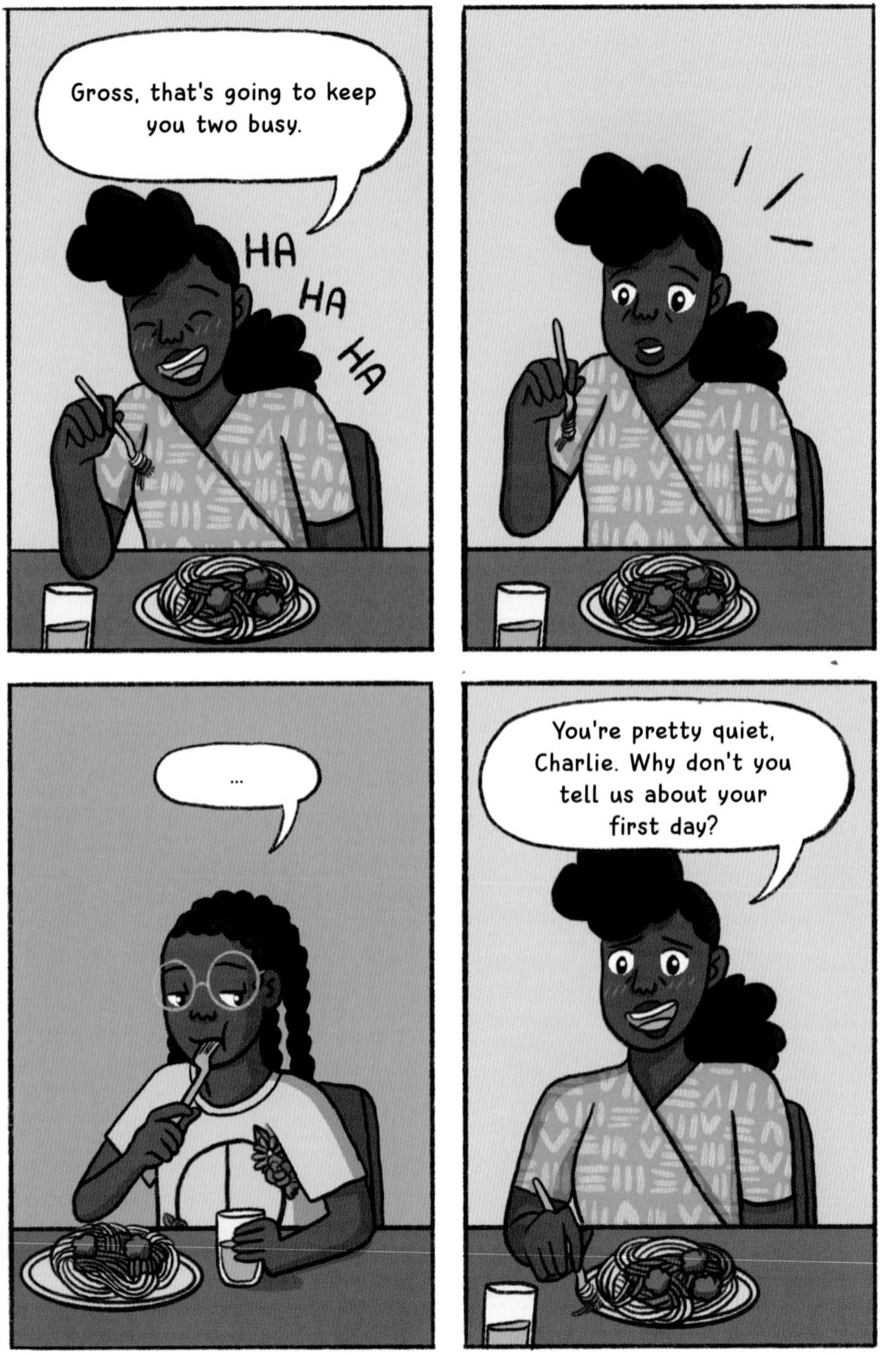
Gross, that's going to keep you two busy.
HA HA HA
...
You're pretty quiet, Charlie. Why don't you tell us about your first day?

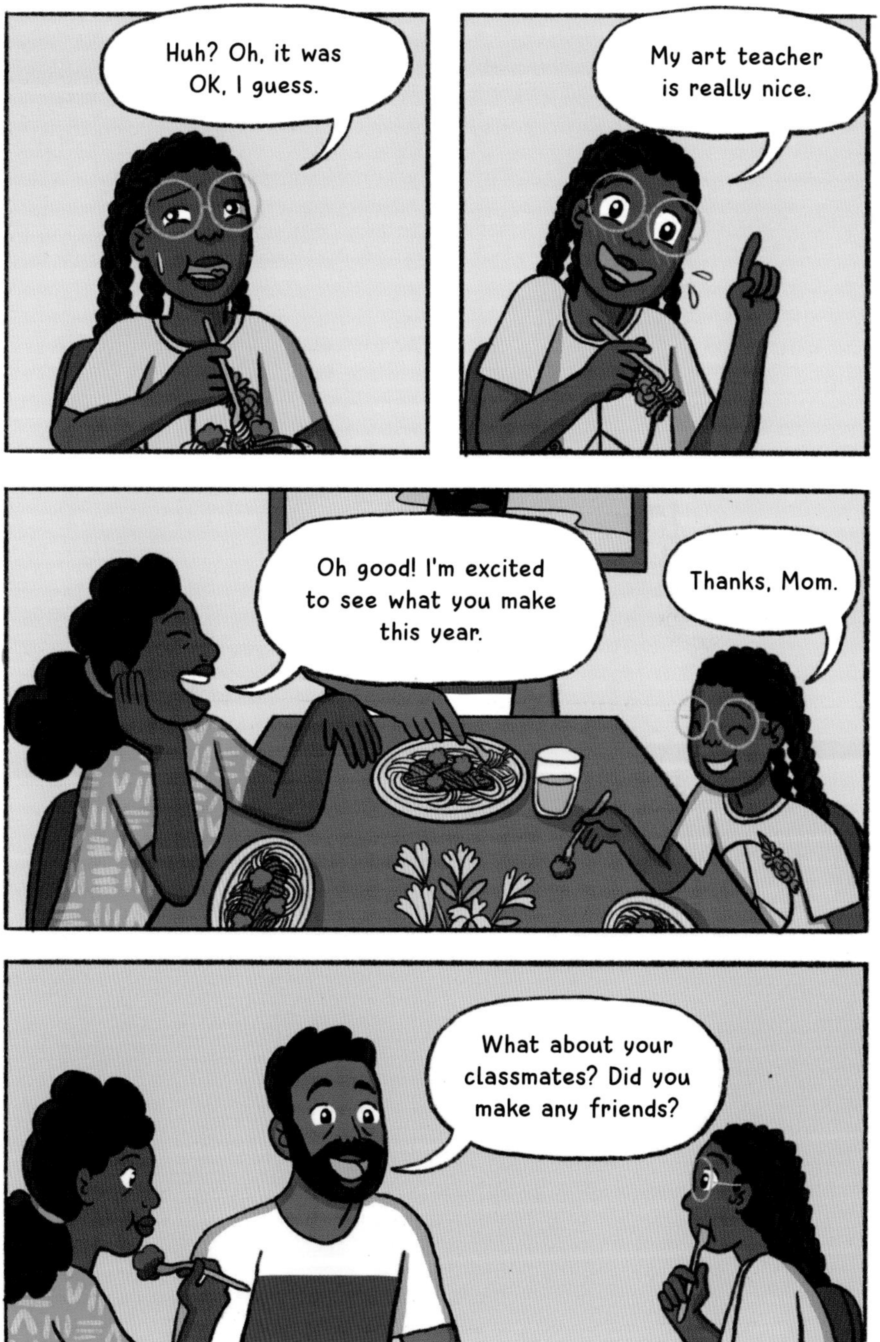
Huh? Oh, it was OK, I guess.
My art teacher is really nice.
Oh good! I'm excited to see what you make this year.
Thanks, Mom.
What about your classmates? Did you make any friends?

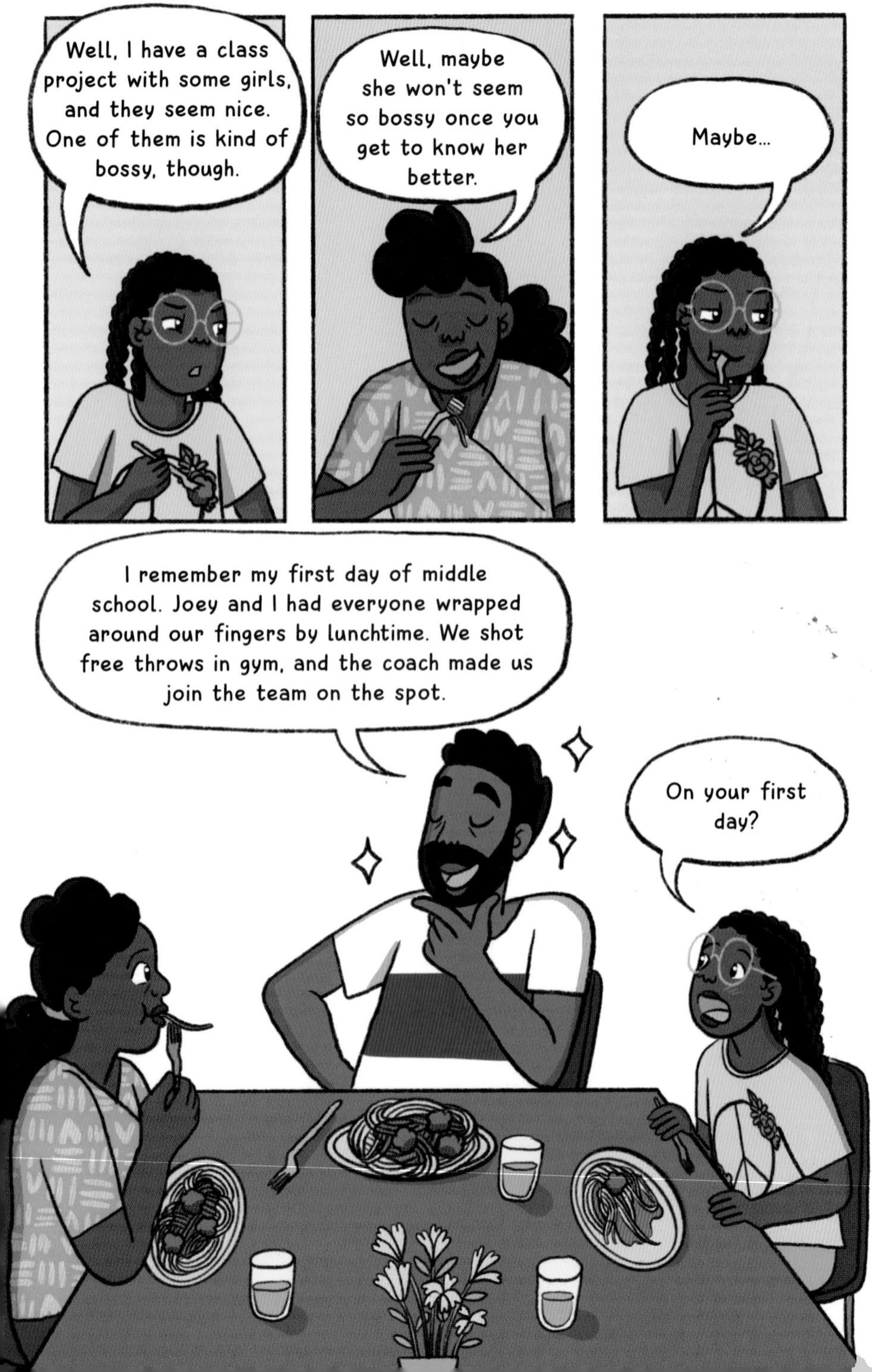
Well, I have a class project with some girls, and they seem nice. One of them is kind of bossy, though.
Well, maybe she won't seem so bossy once you get to know her better.
Maybe...
I remember my first day of middle school. Joey and I had everyone wrapped around our fingers by lunchtime. We shot free throws in gym, and the coach made us join the team on the spot.
On your first day?

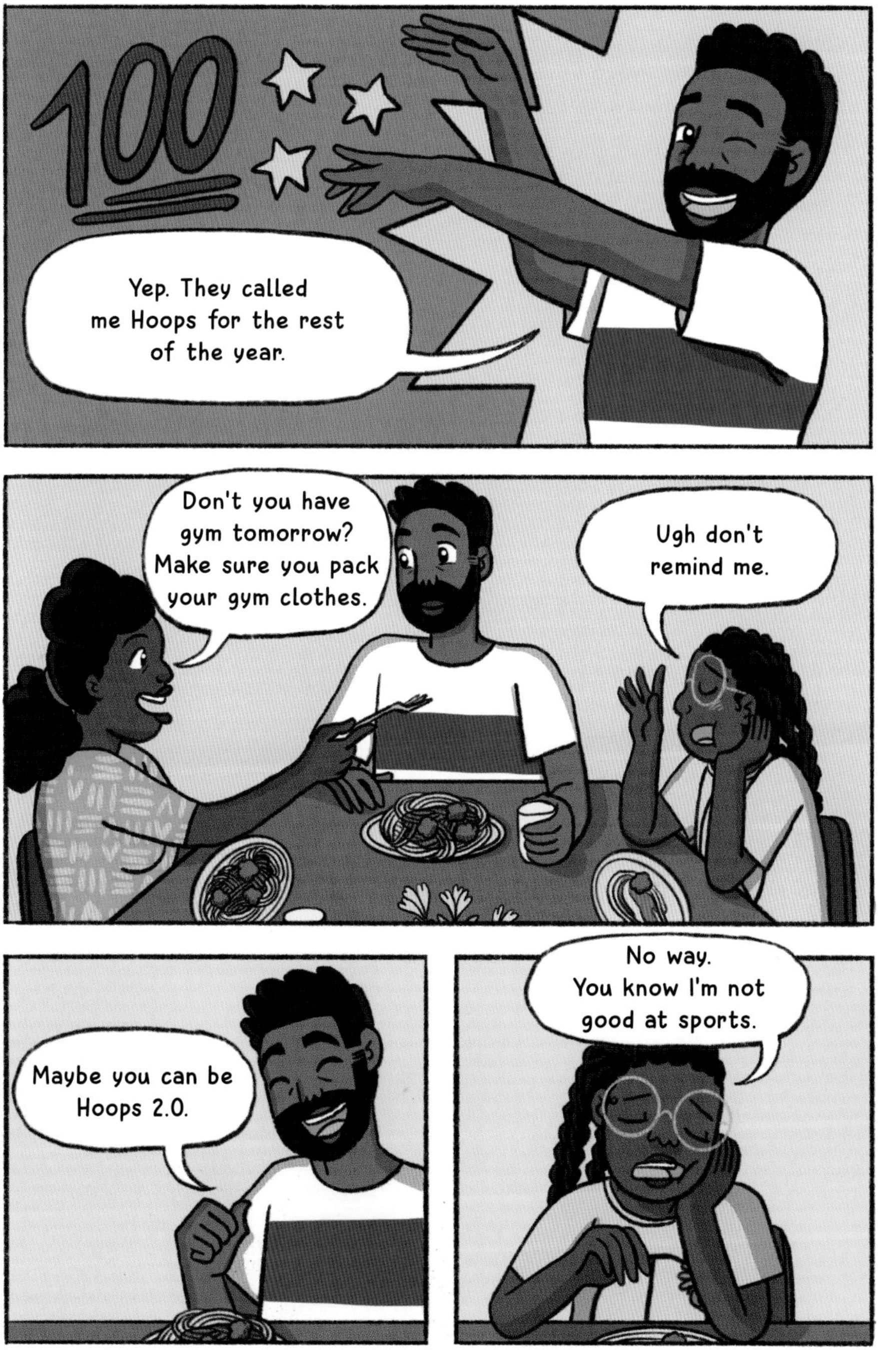
100
Yep. They called me Hoops for the rest of the year.
Don't you have gym tomorrow? Make sure you pack your gym clothes.
Ugh don't remind me.
Maybe you can be Hoops 2.0.
No way. You know I'm not good at sports.

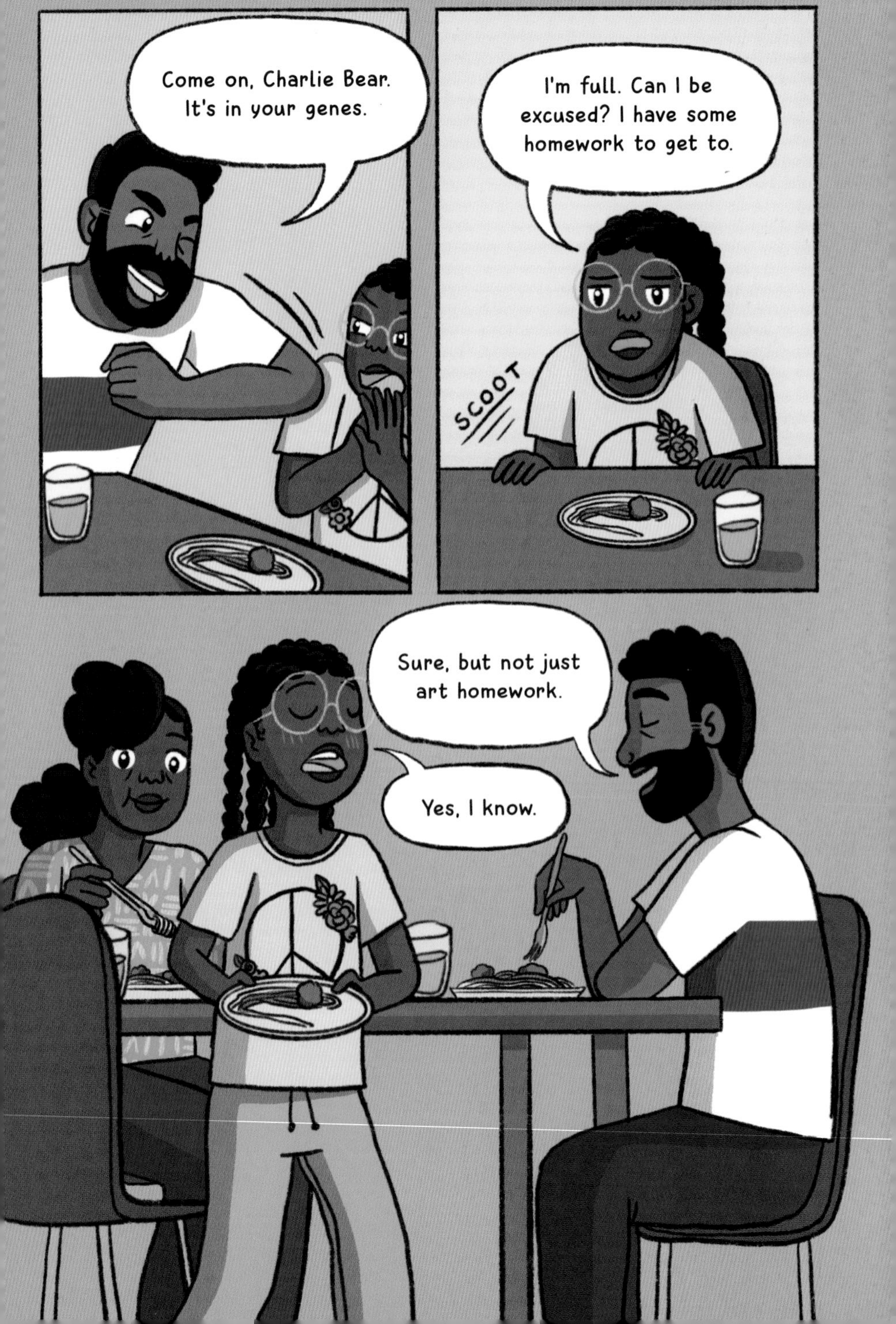
Come on, Charlie Bear. It's in your genes.
I'm full. Can I be excused? I have some homework to get to.
SCOOT
Sure, but not just art homework.
Yes, I know.

CHAPTER
6

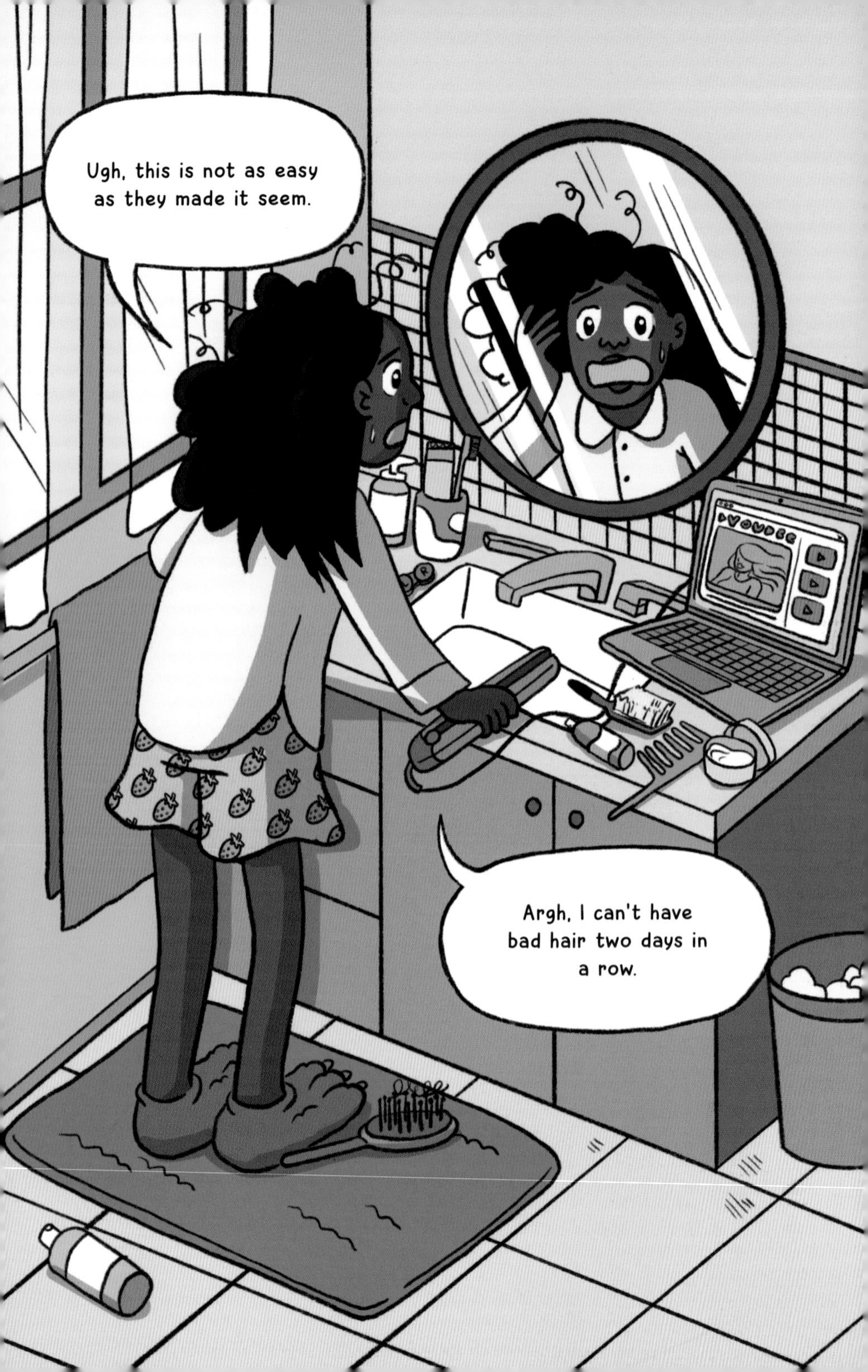
Ugh, this is not as easy as they made it seem.
Argh, I can't have bad hair two days in a row.

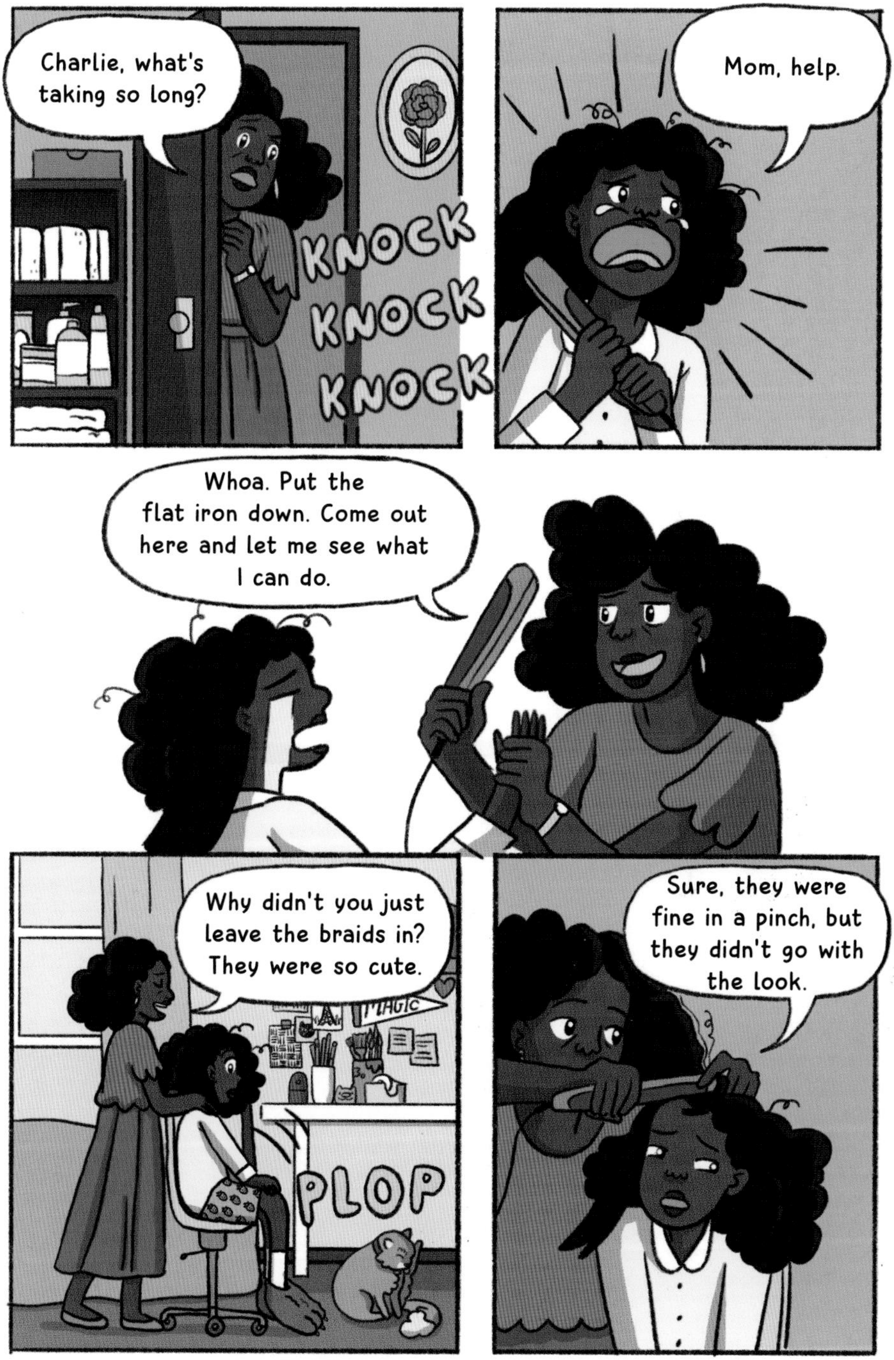
Charlie, what's taking so long?
KNOCK KNOCK KNOCK
Mom, help.
Whoa. Put the flat iron down. Come out here and let me see what I can do.
Why didn't you just leave the braids in? They were so cute.
PLOP
MAGIC
Sure, they were fine in a pinch, but they didn't go with the look.

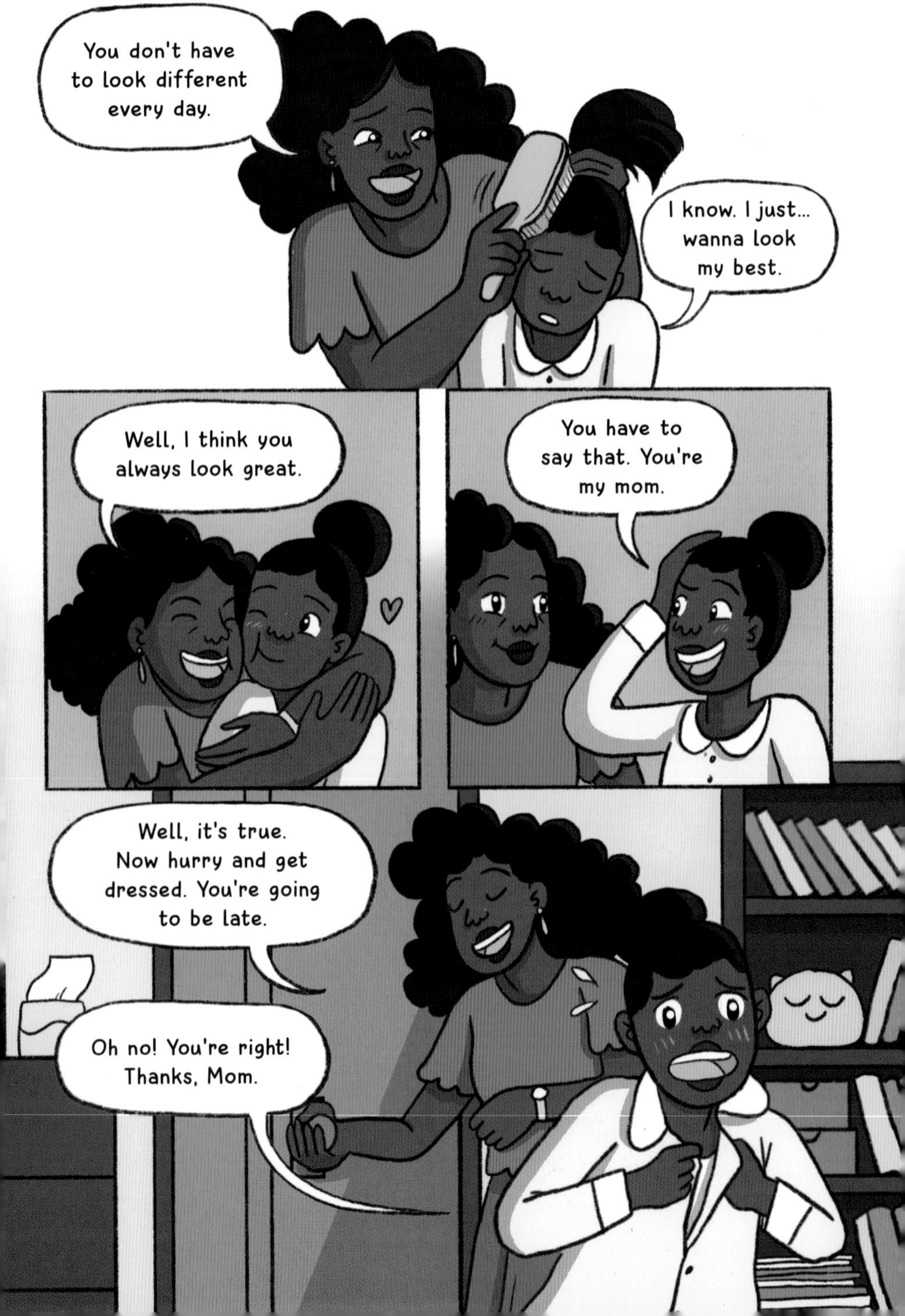
You don't have to look different every day.
I know. I just... wanna look my best.
Well, I think you always look great.
You have to say that. You're my mom.
Well, it's true. Now hurry and get dressed. You're going to be late.
Oh no! You're right! Thanks, Mom.

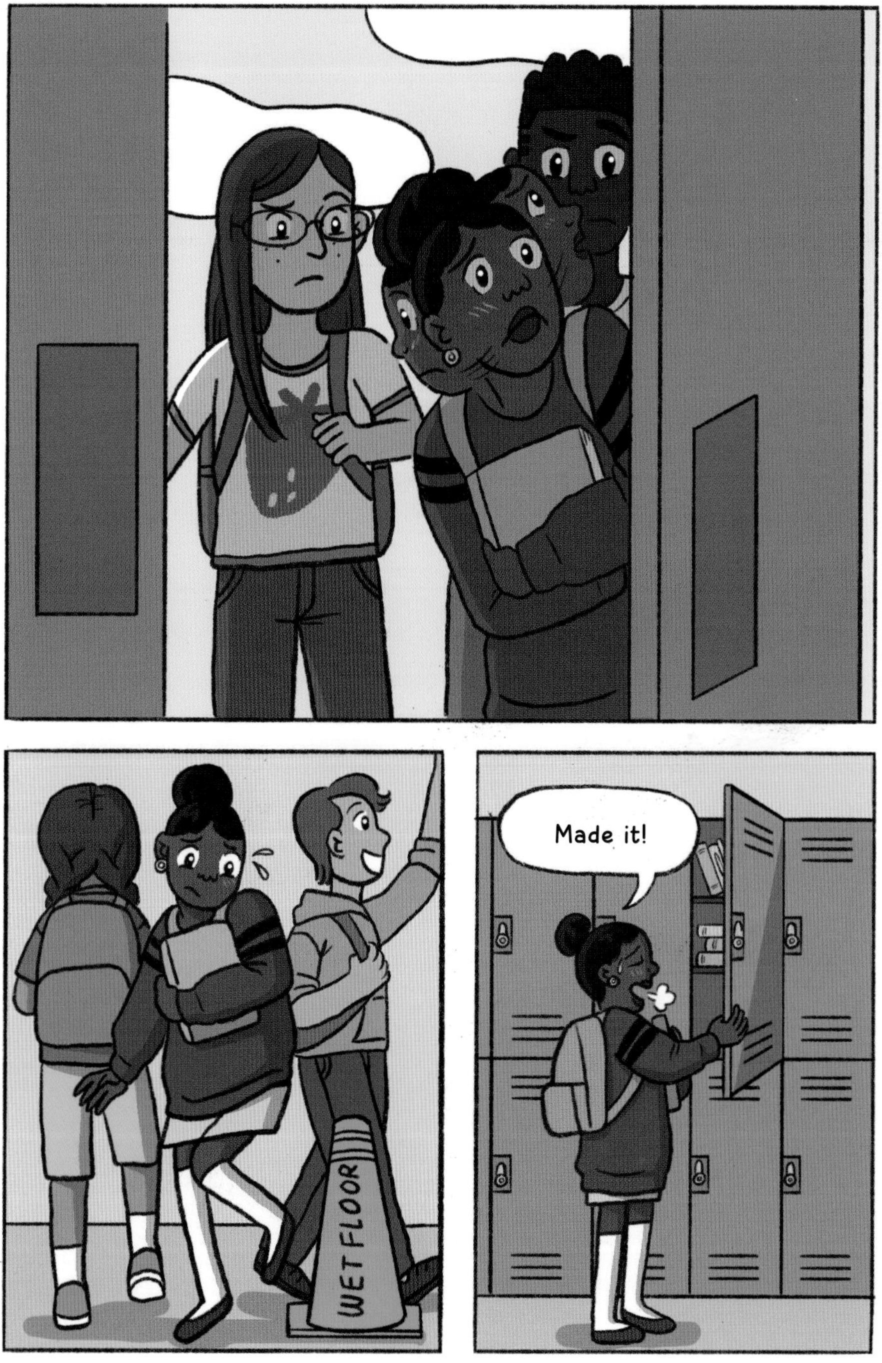
WET FLOOR
Made it!

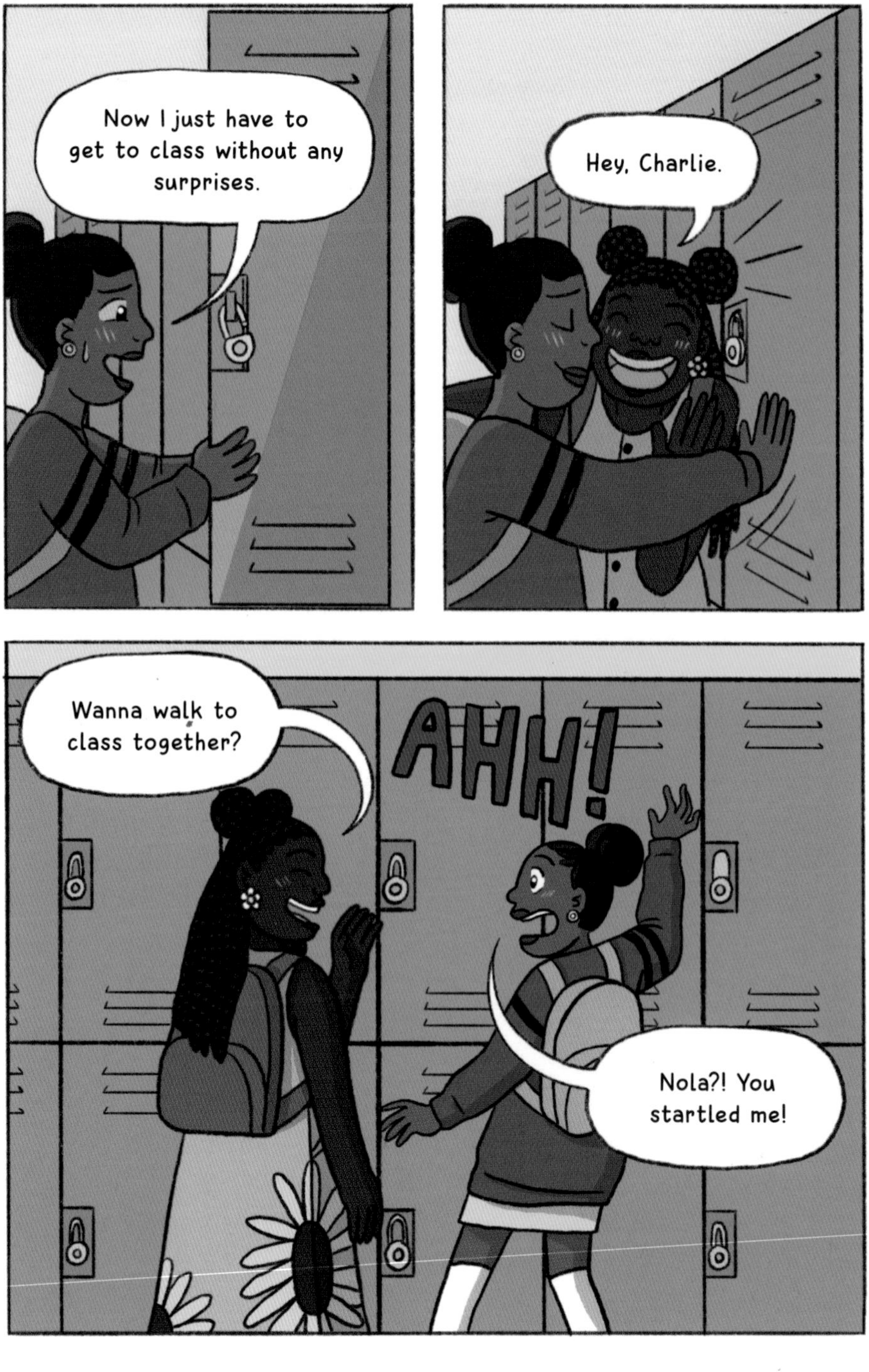
Now I just have to get to class without any surprises.
Hey, Charlie.
Wanna walk to class together?
AHH!
Nola?! You startled me!

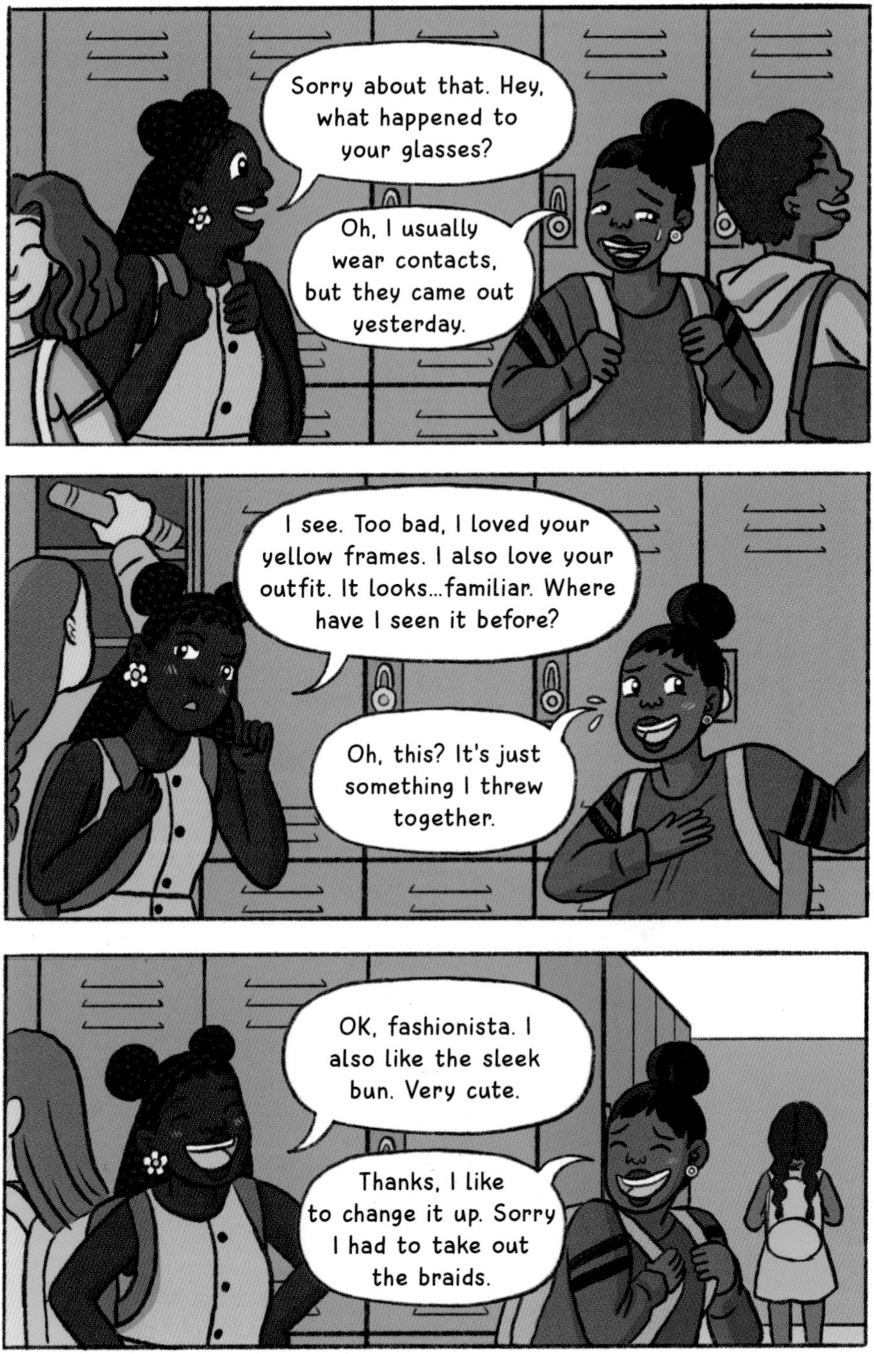
Sorry about that. Hey, what happened to your glasses?
Oh, I usually wear contacts, but they came out yesterday.
I see. Too bad, I loved your yellow frames. I also love your outfit. It looks...familiar. Where have I seen it before?
Oh, this? It's just something I threw together.
OK, fashionista. I also like the sleek bun. Very cute.
Thanks, I like to change it up. Sorry I had to take out the braids.

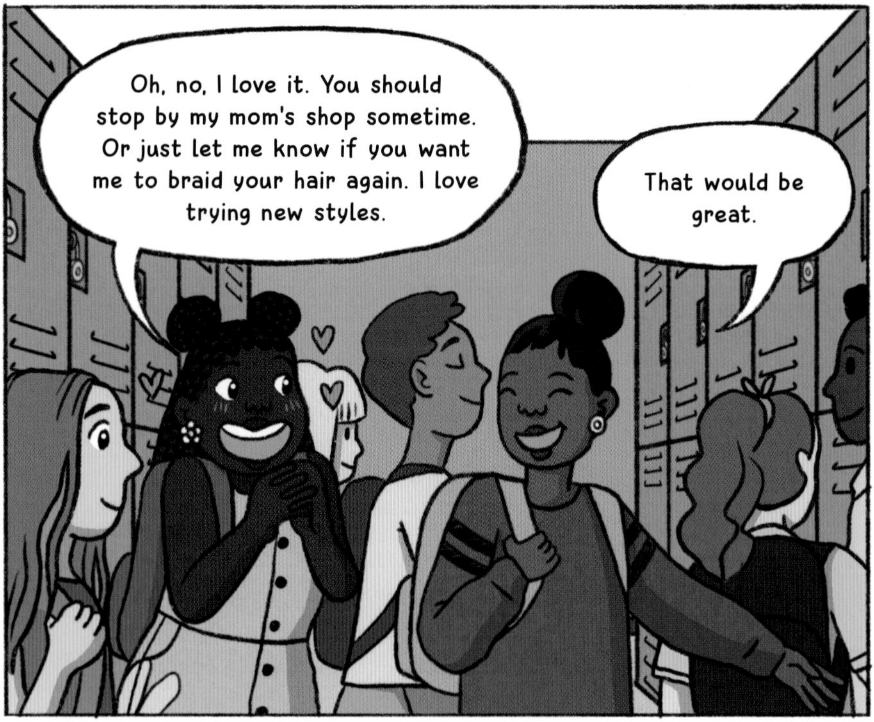
Oh, no, I love it. You should stop by my mom's shop sometime. Or just let me know if you want me to braid your hair again. I love trying new styles.
That would be great.

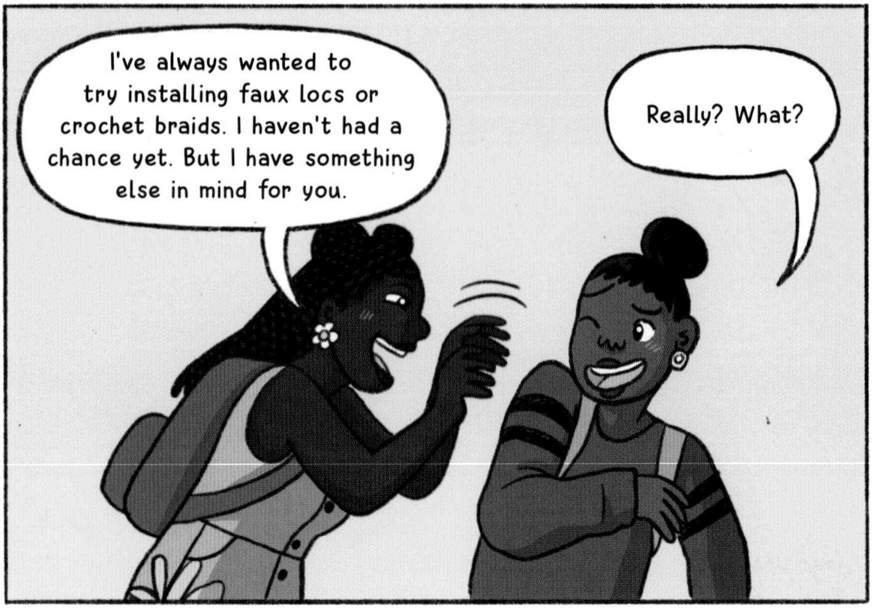
I've always wanted to try installing faux locs or crochet braids. I haven't had a chance yet. But I have something else in mind for you.
Really? What?

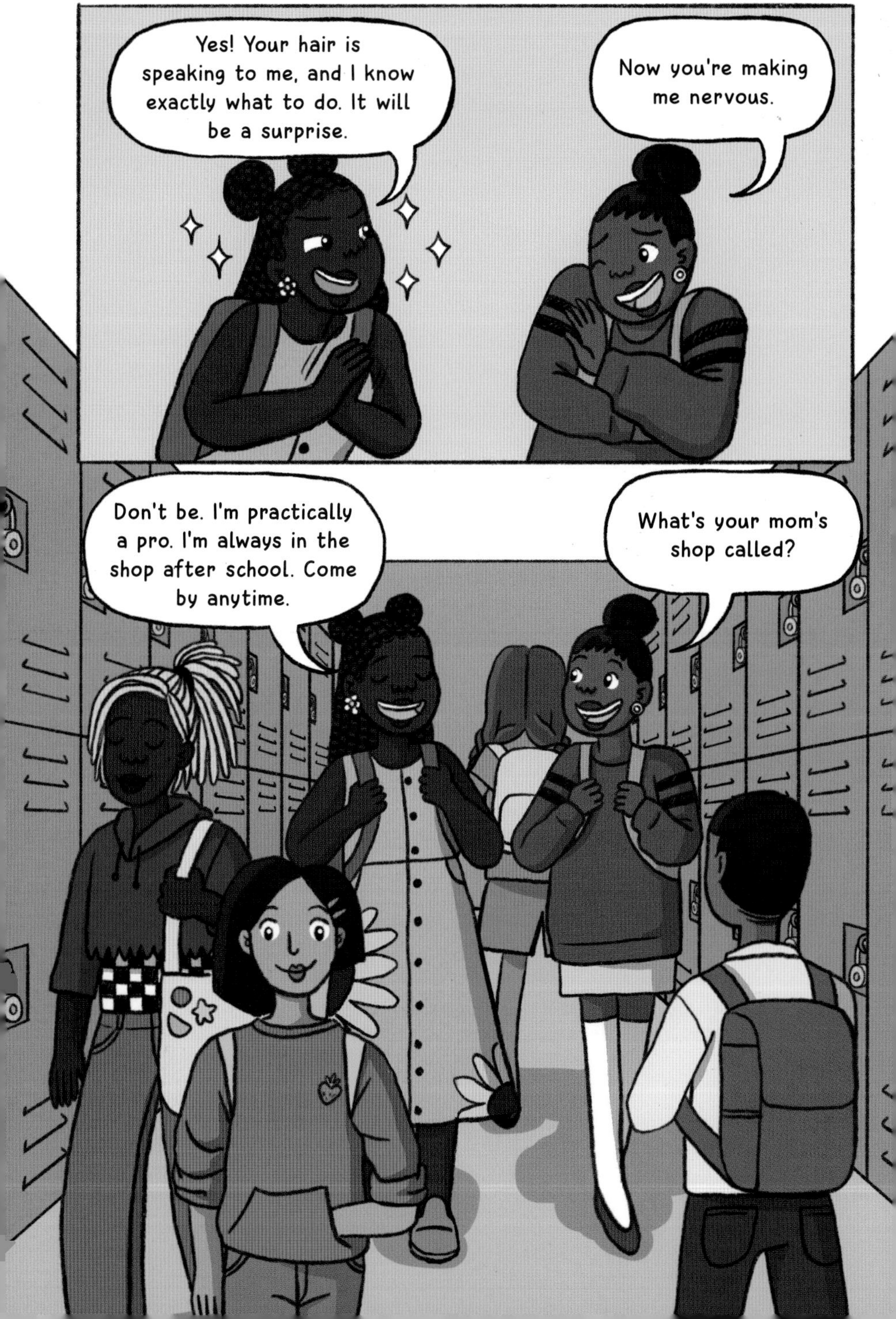
Yes! Your hair is speaking to me, and I know exactly what to do. It will be a surprise.
Now you're making me nervous.
Don't be. I'm practically a pro. I'm always in the shop after school. Come by anytime.
What's your mom's shop called?

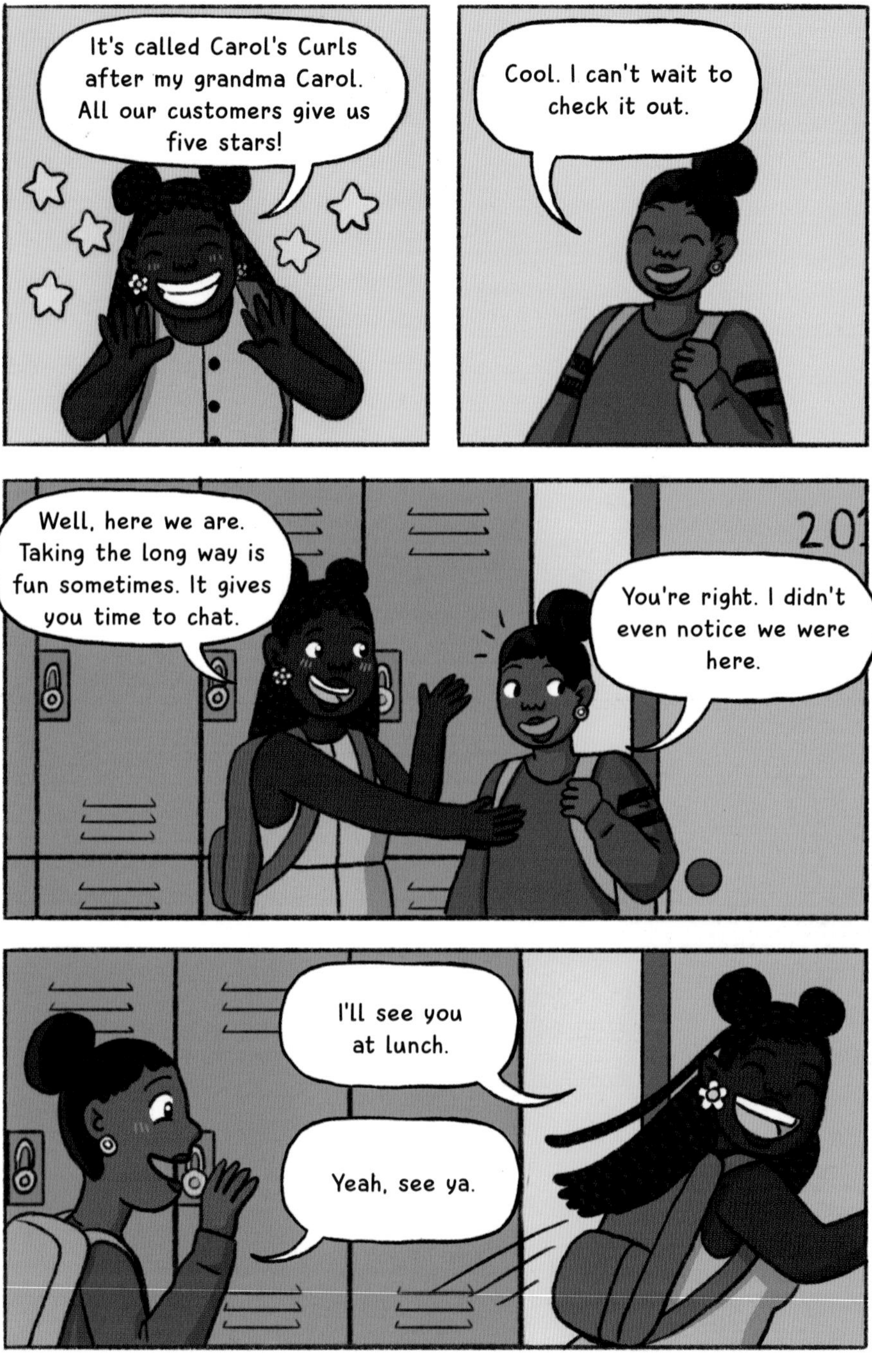
It's called Carol's Curls after my grandma Carol. All our customers give us five stars!
Cool. I can't wait to check it out.
Well, here we are. Taking the long way is fun sometimes. It gives you time to chat.
You're right. I didn't even notice we were here.
I'll see you at lunch.
Yeah, see ya.

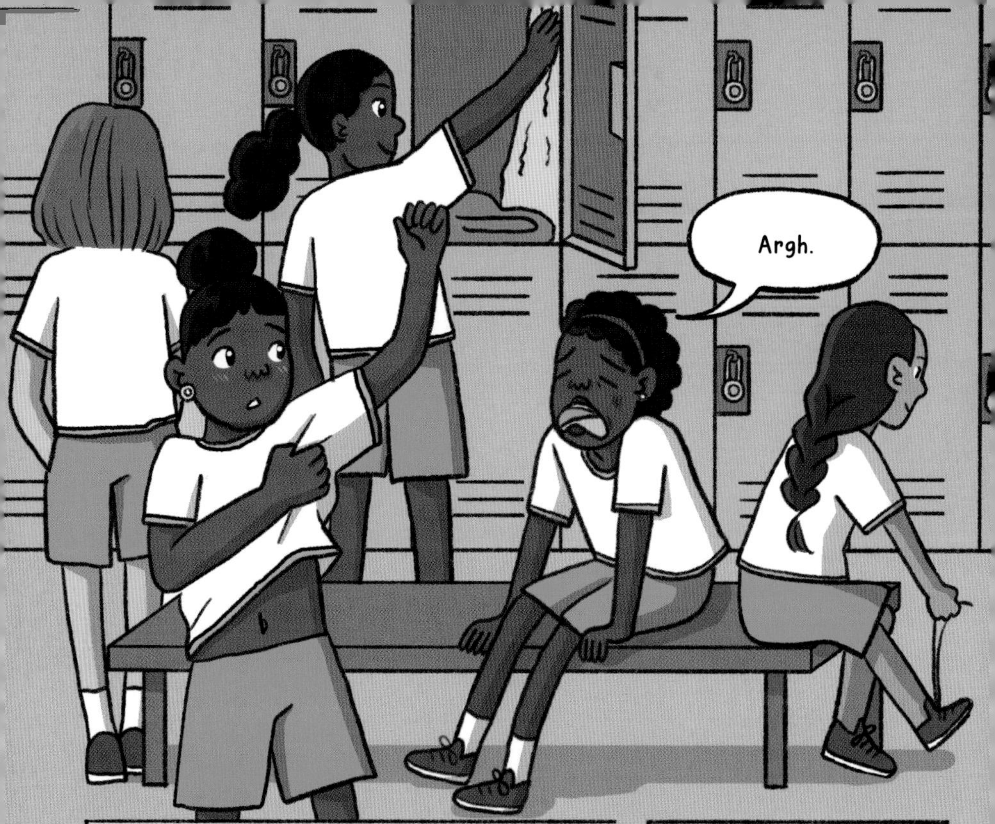
Argh.

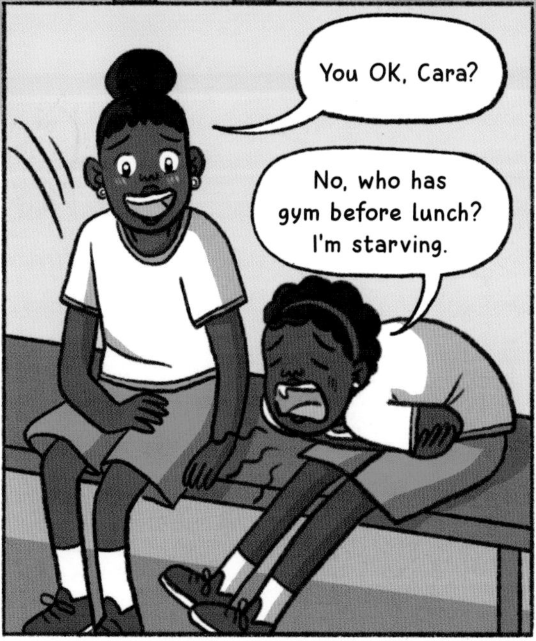
You OK, Cara?
No, who has gym before lunch? I'm starving.

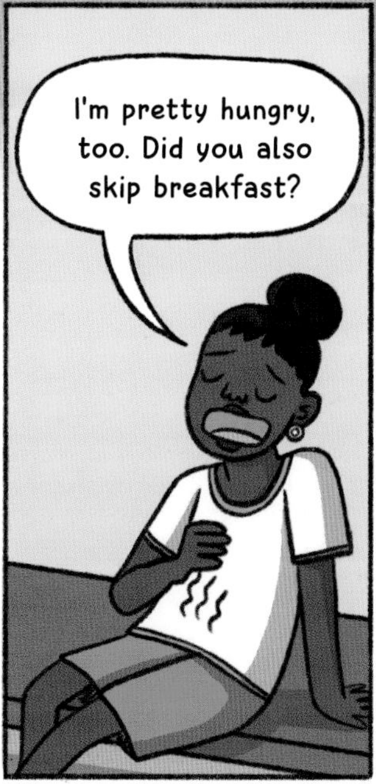
I'm pretty hungry, too. Did you also skip breakfast?

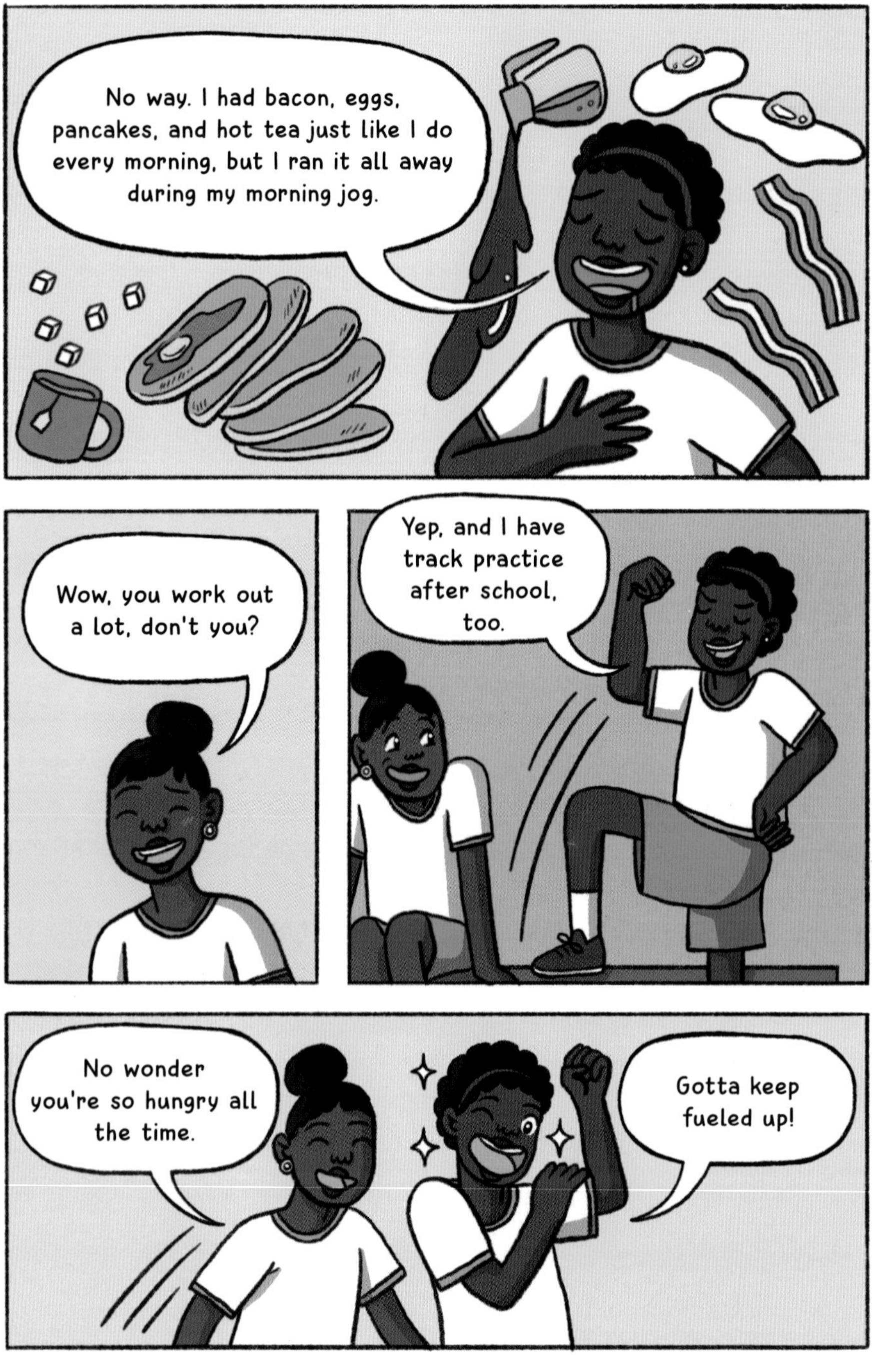
No way. I had bacon, eggs, pancakes, and hot tea just like I do every morning, but I ran it all away during my morning jog.
Wow, you work out a lot, don't you?
Yep, and I have track practice after school, too.
No wonder you're so hungry all the time.
Gotta keep fueled up!

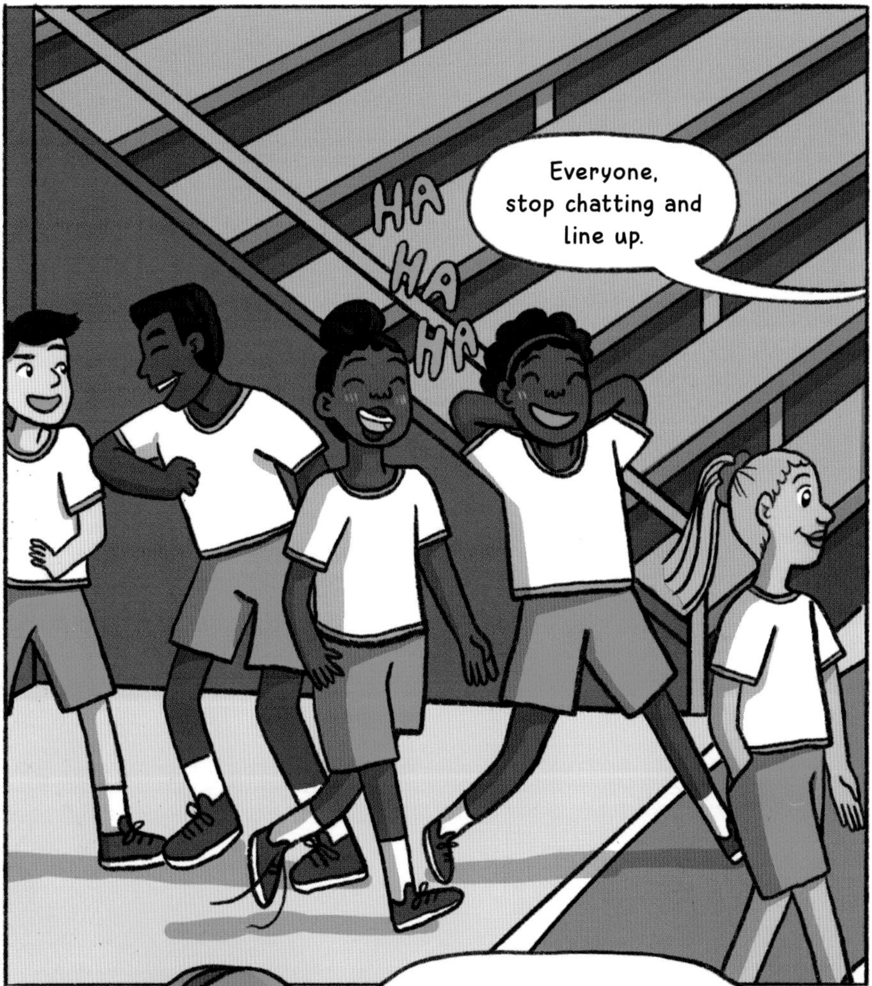
HA HA HA
Everyone, stop chatting and line up.

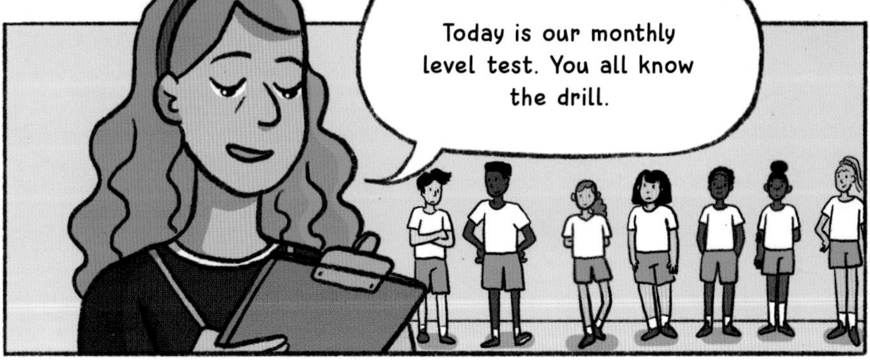
Today is our monthly level test. You all know the drill.

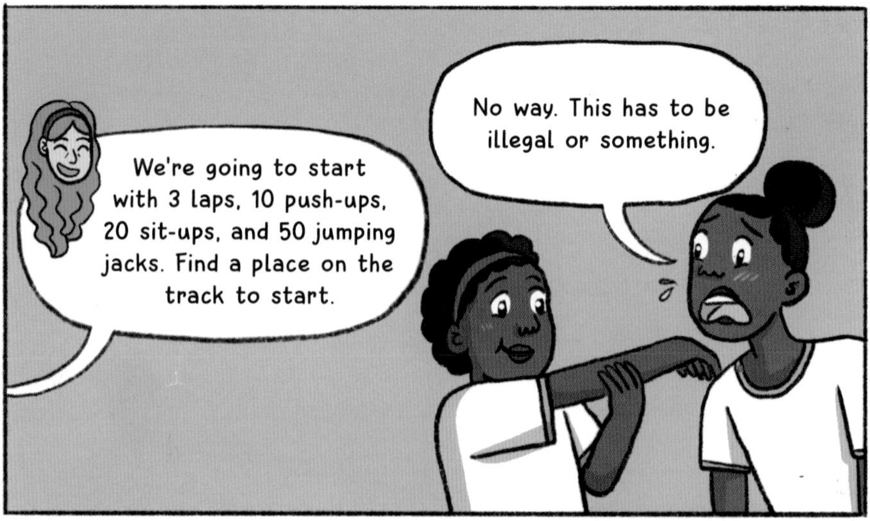
We're going to start with 3 laps, 10 push-ups, 20 sit-ups, and 50 jumping jacks. Find a place on the track to start.
No way. This has to be illegal or something.

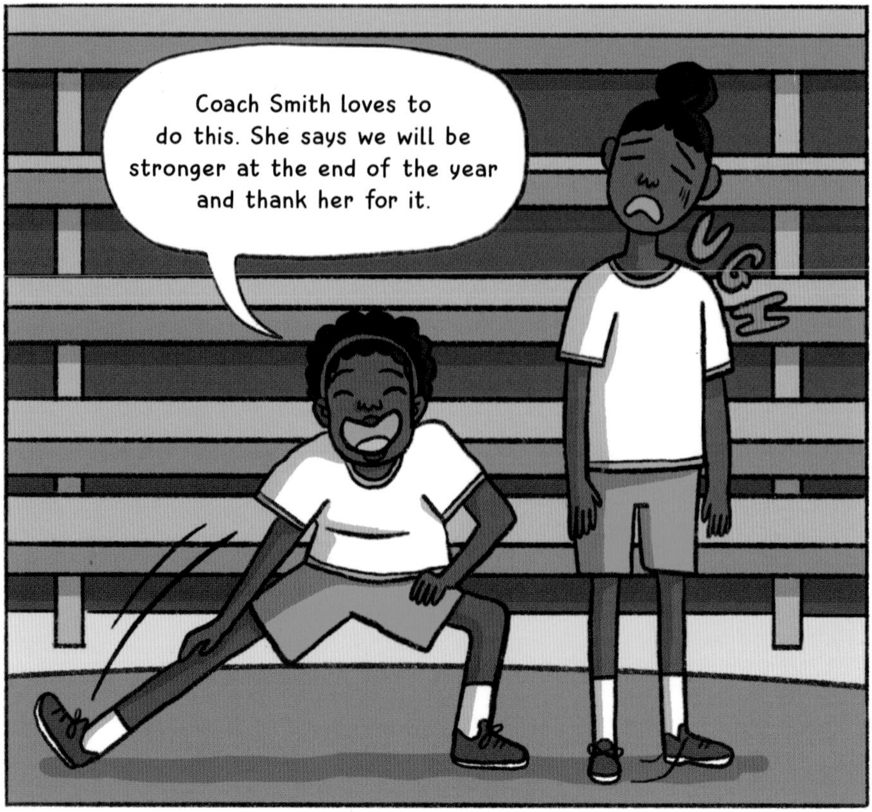
Coach Smith loves to do this. She says we will be stronger at the end of the year and thank her for it.
UGH

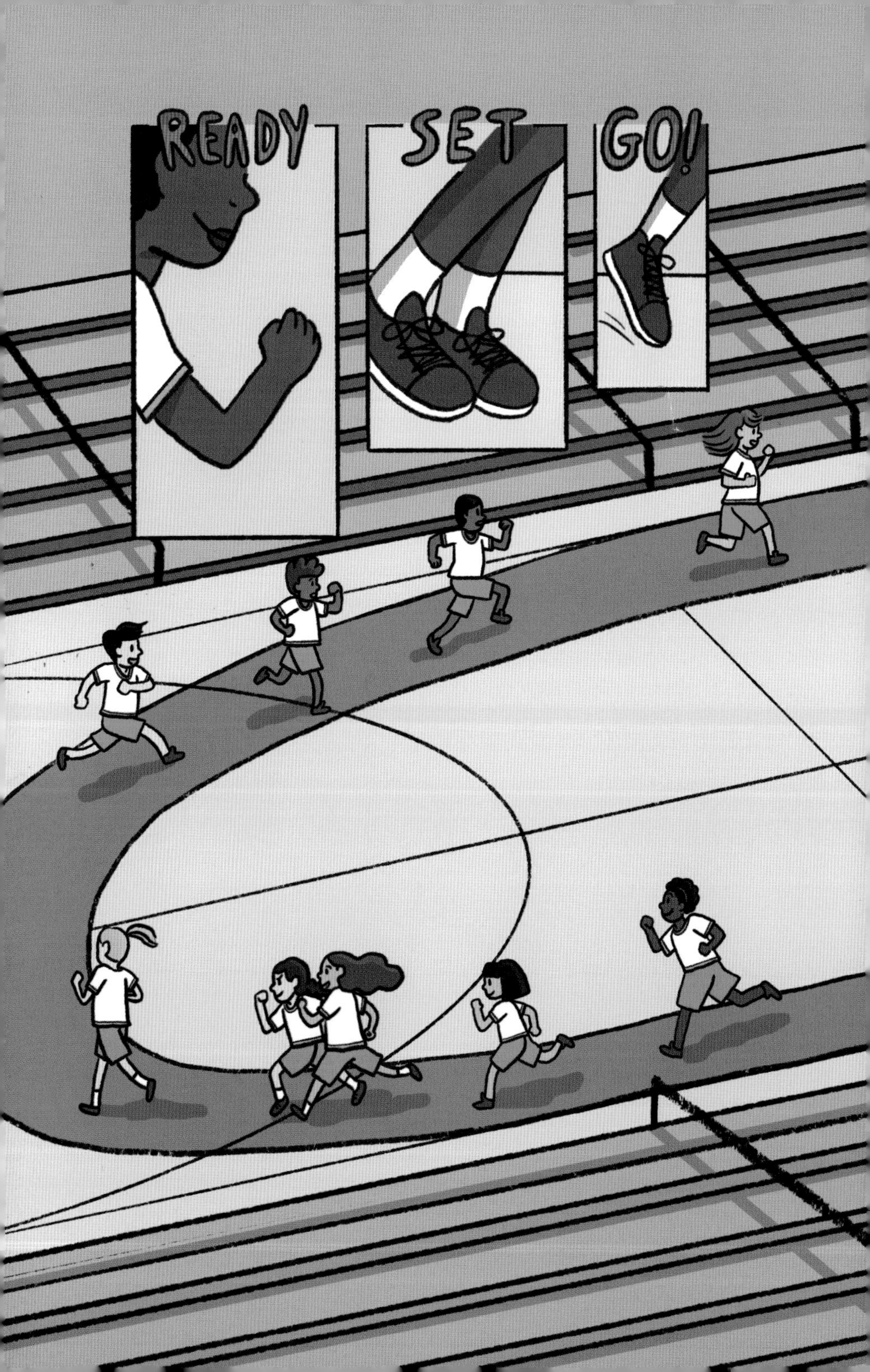
READY
SET
GO!

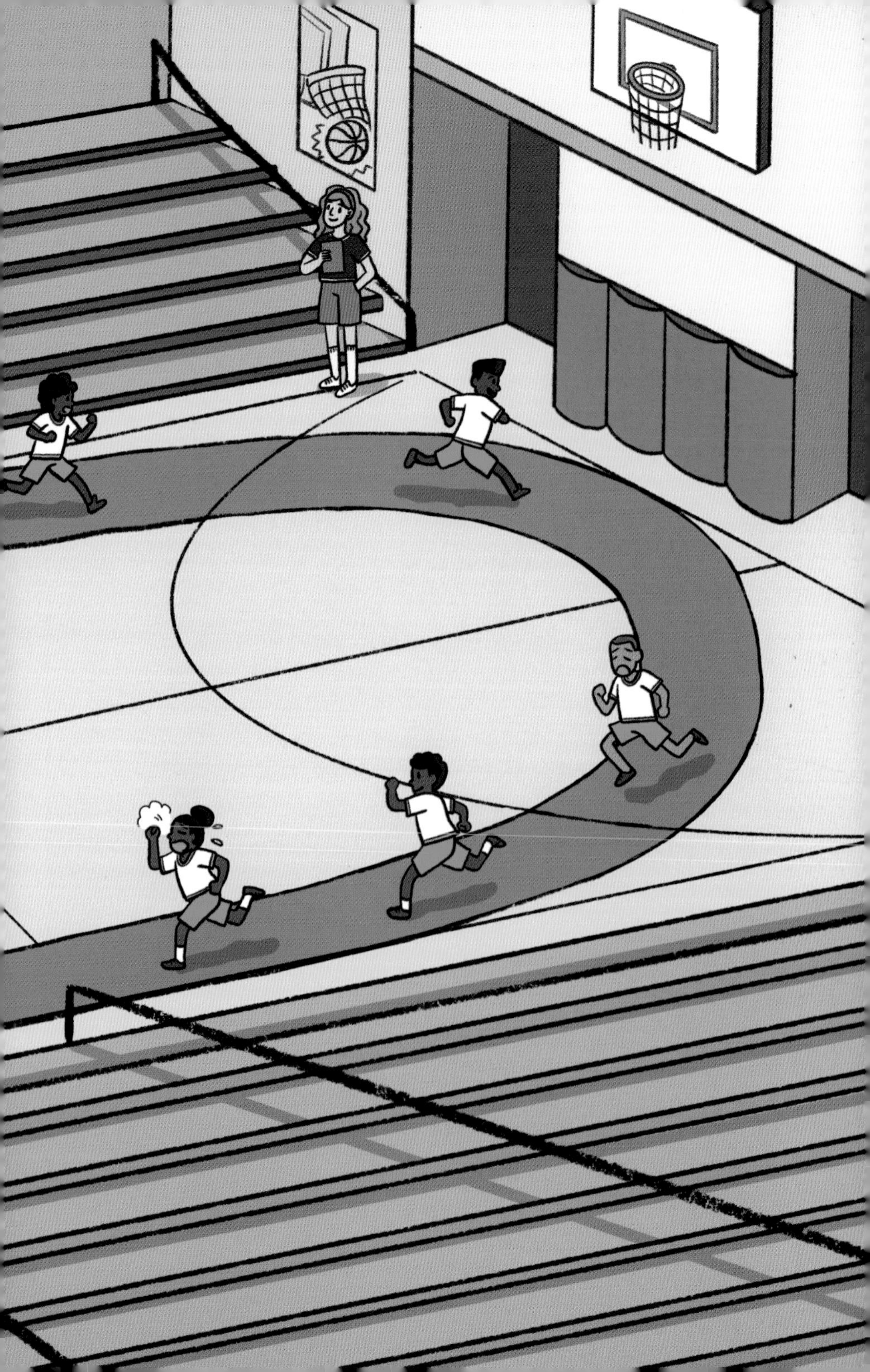

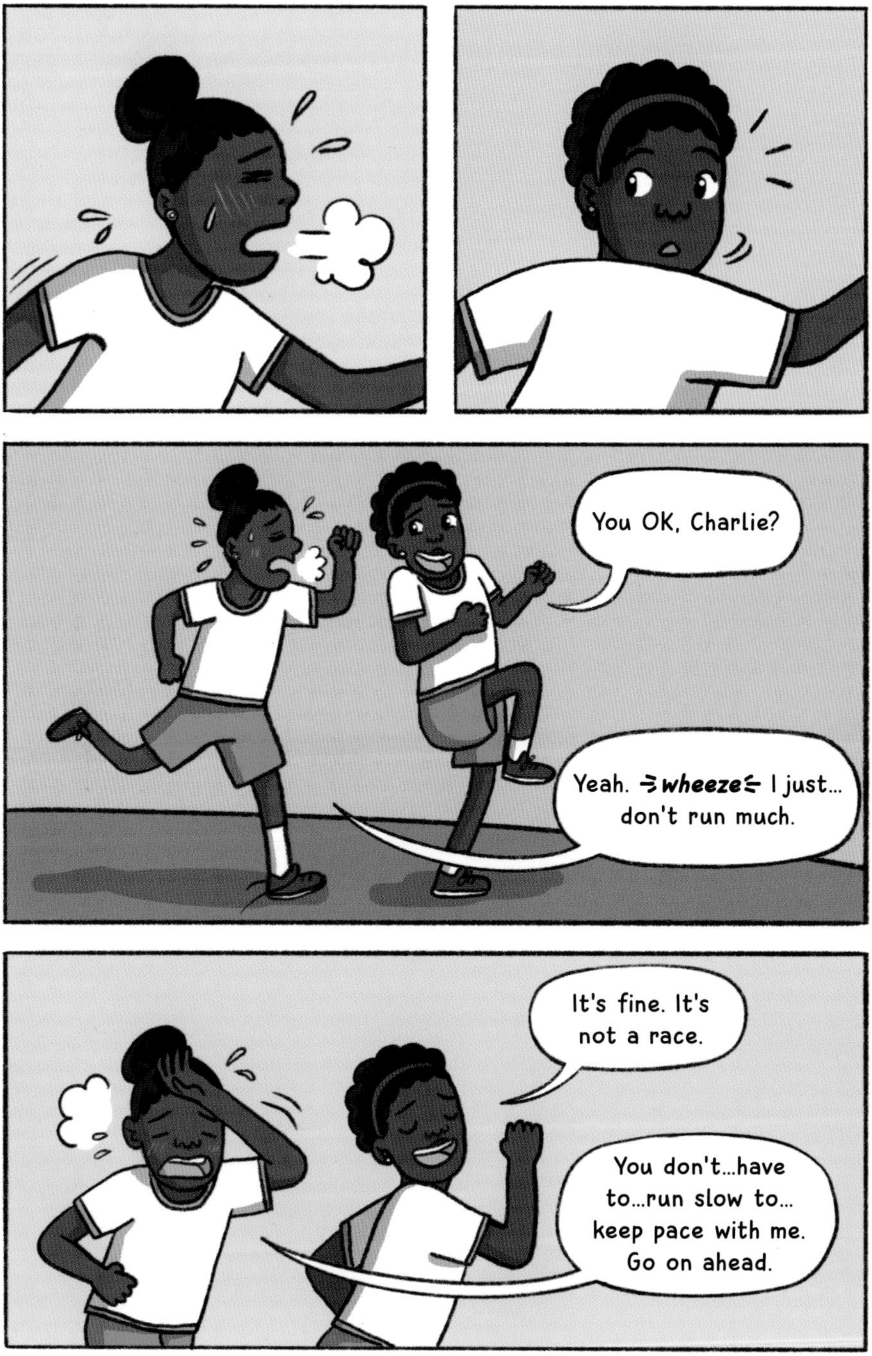
You OK, Charlie?
Yeah. *wheeze* I just... don't run much.
It's fine. It's not a race.
You don't...have to...run slow to... keep pace with me. Go on ahead.

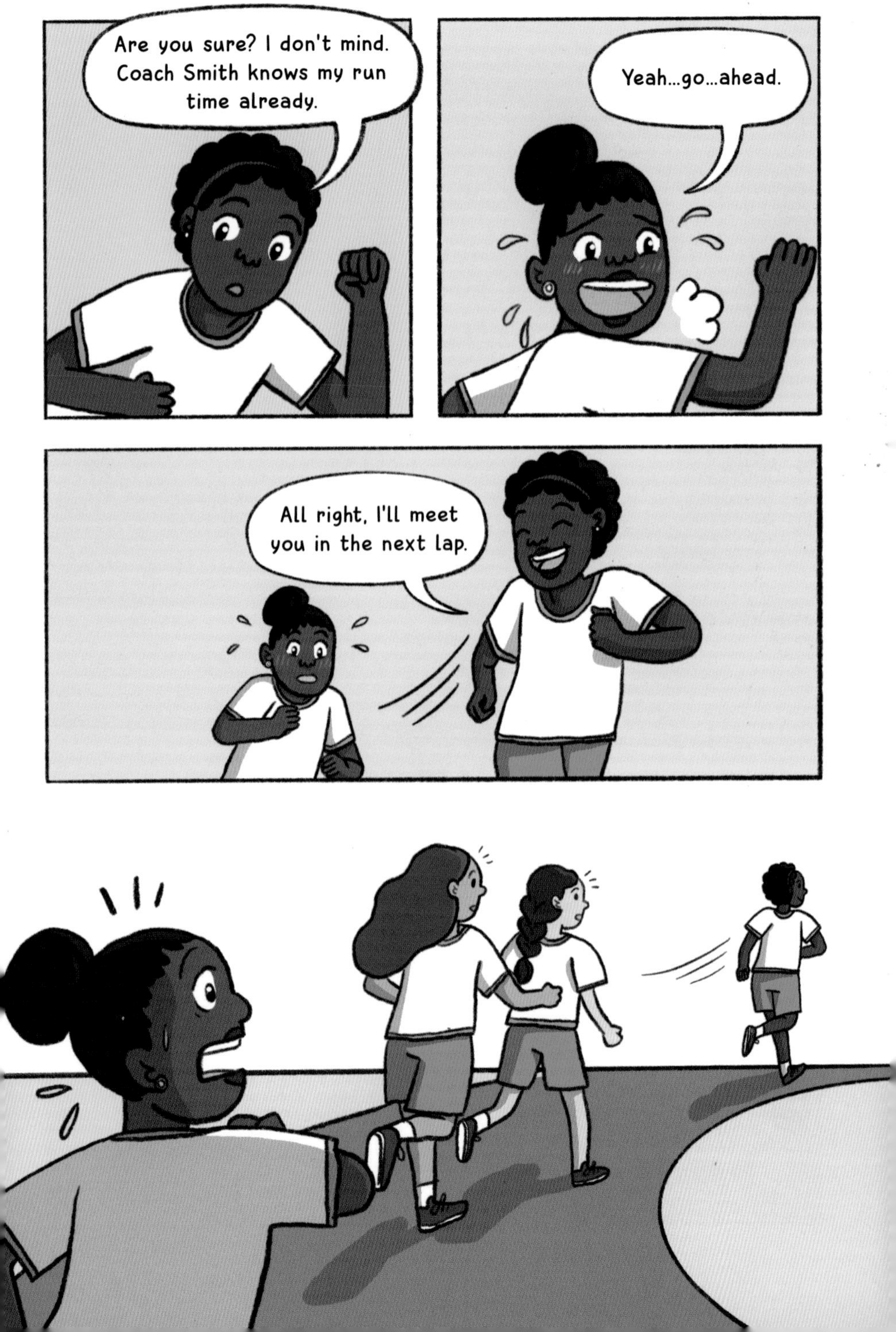
Are you sure? I don't mind. Coach Smith knows my run time already.
Yeah...go...ahead.
All right, I'll meet you in the next lap.

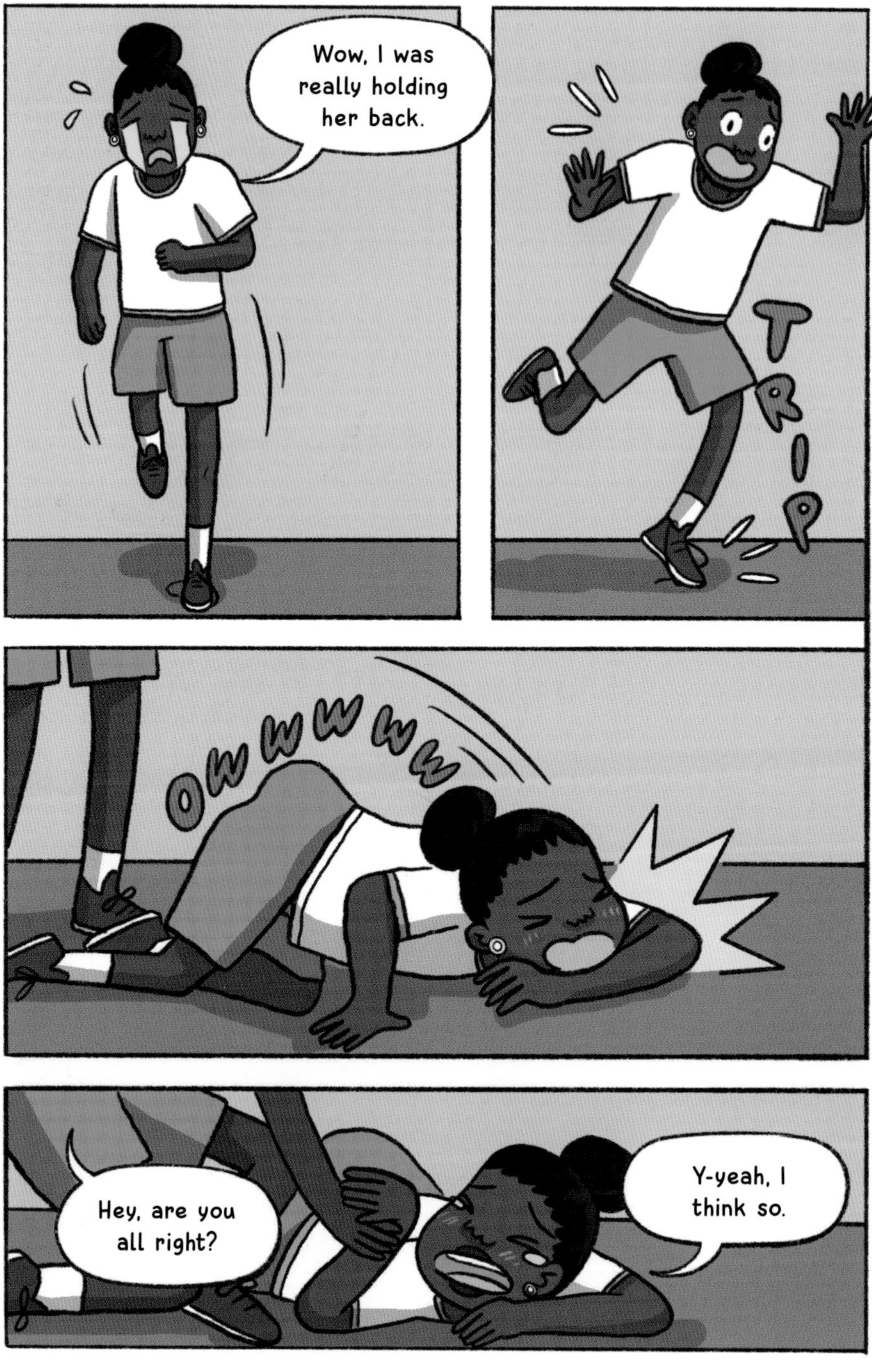
Wow, I was really holding her back.
TRIP
OWWWWW
Hey, are you all right?
Y-yeah, I think so.

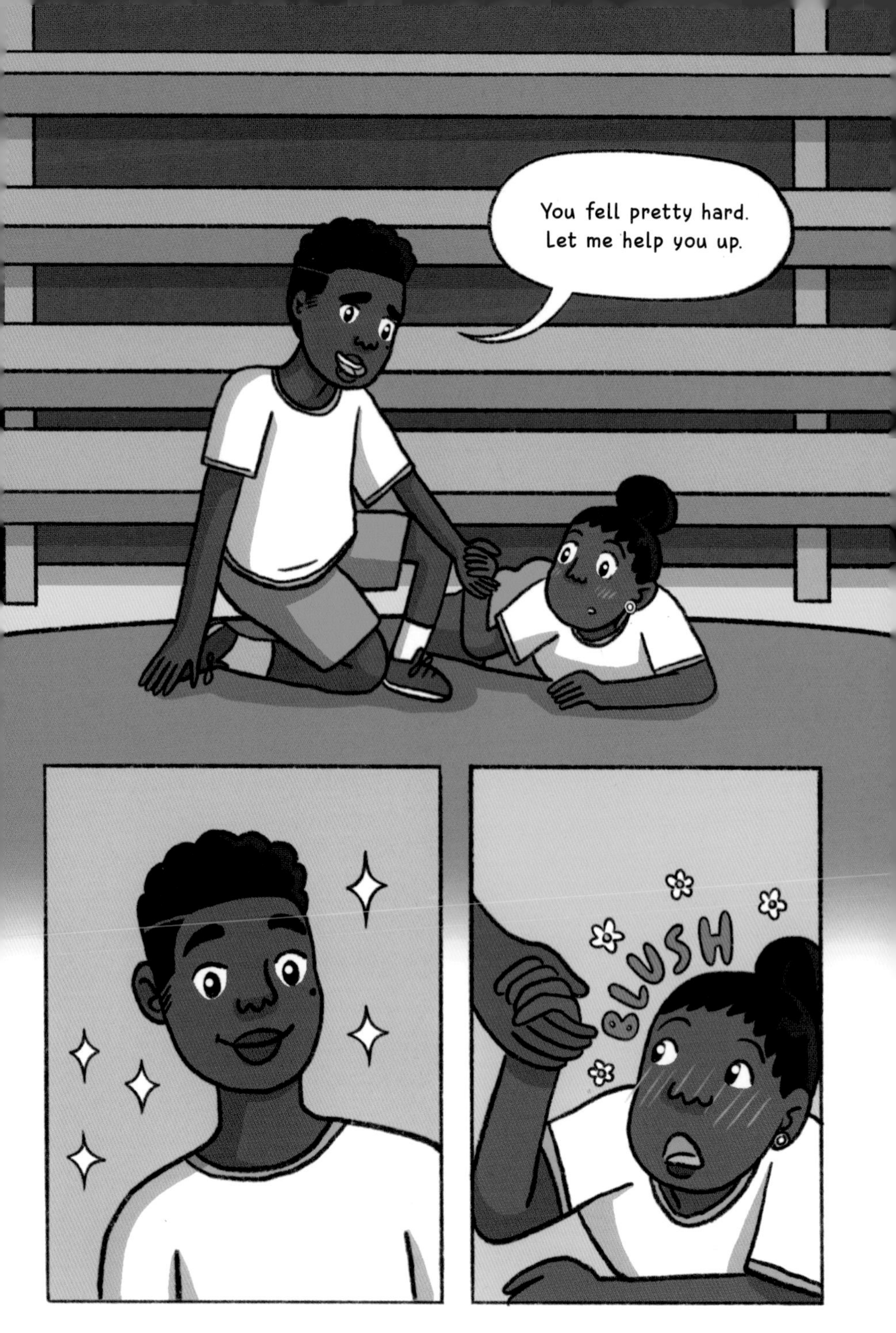
You fell pretty hard.
Let me help you up.
BLUSH

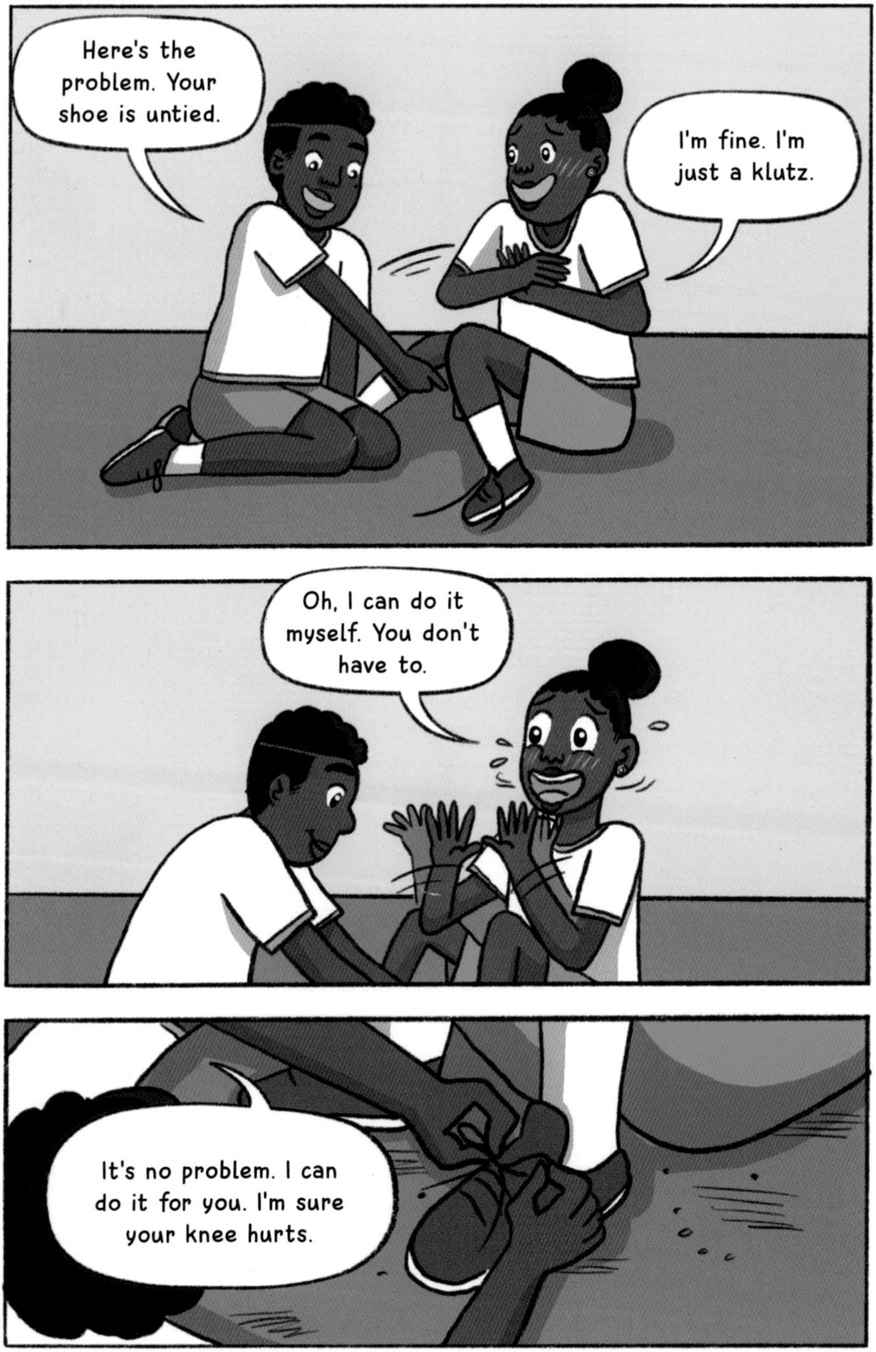
Here's the problem. Your shoe is untied.
I'm fine. I'm just a klutz.
Oh, I can do it myself. You don't have to.
It's no problem. I can do it for you. I'm sure your knee hurts.

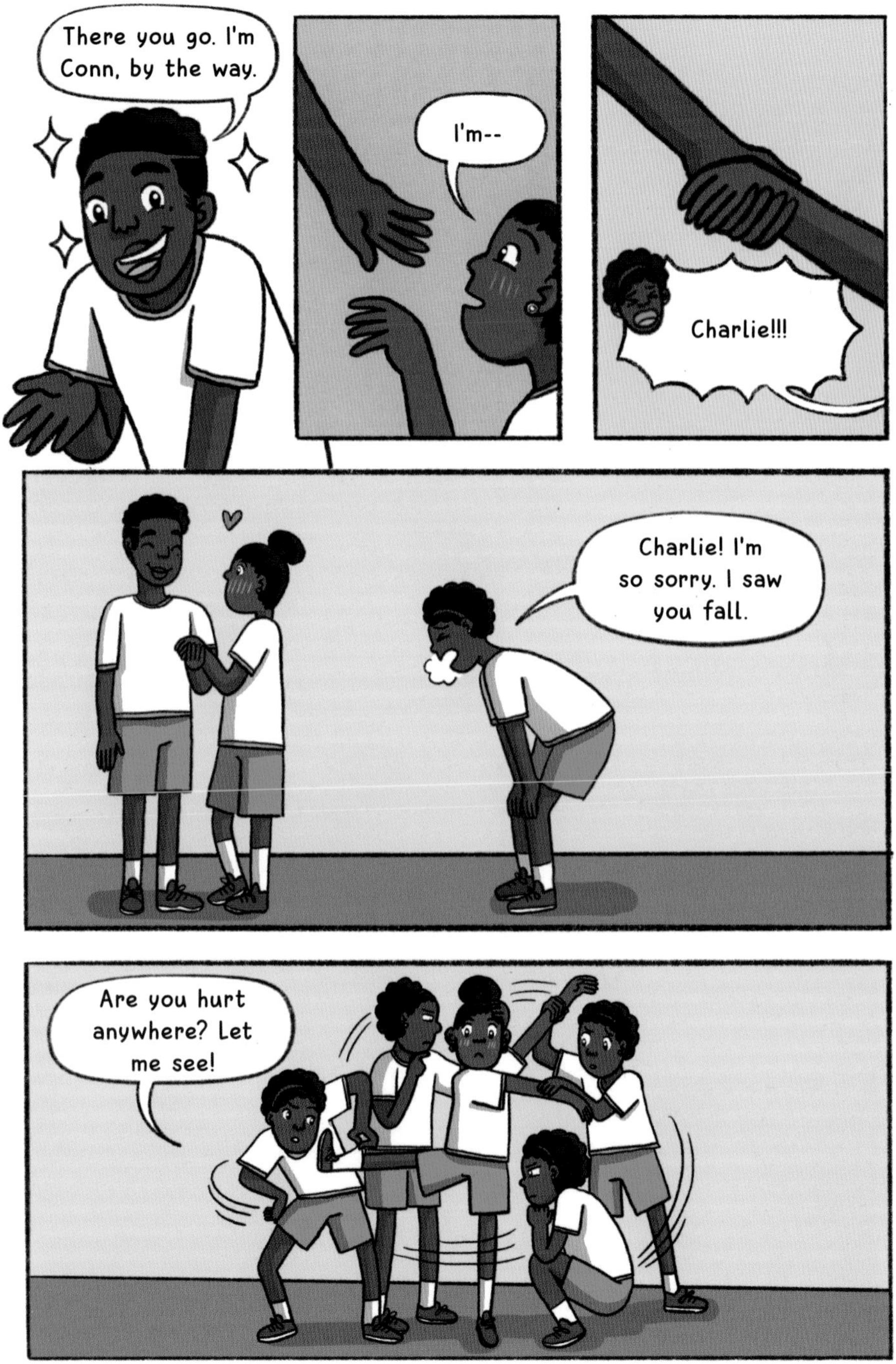

There you go. I'm Conn, by the way.
I'm--
Charlie!!!
Charlie! I'm so sorry. I saw you fall.
Are you hurt anywhere? Let me see!

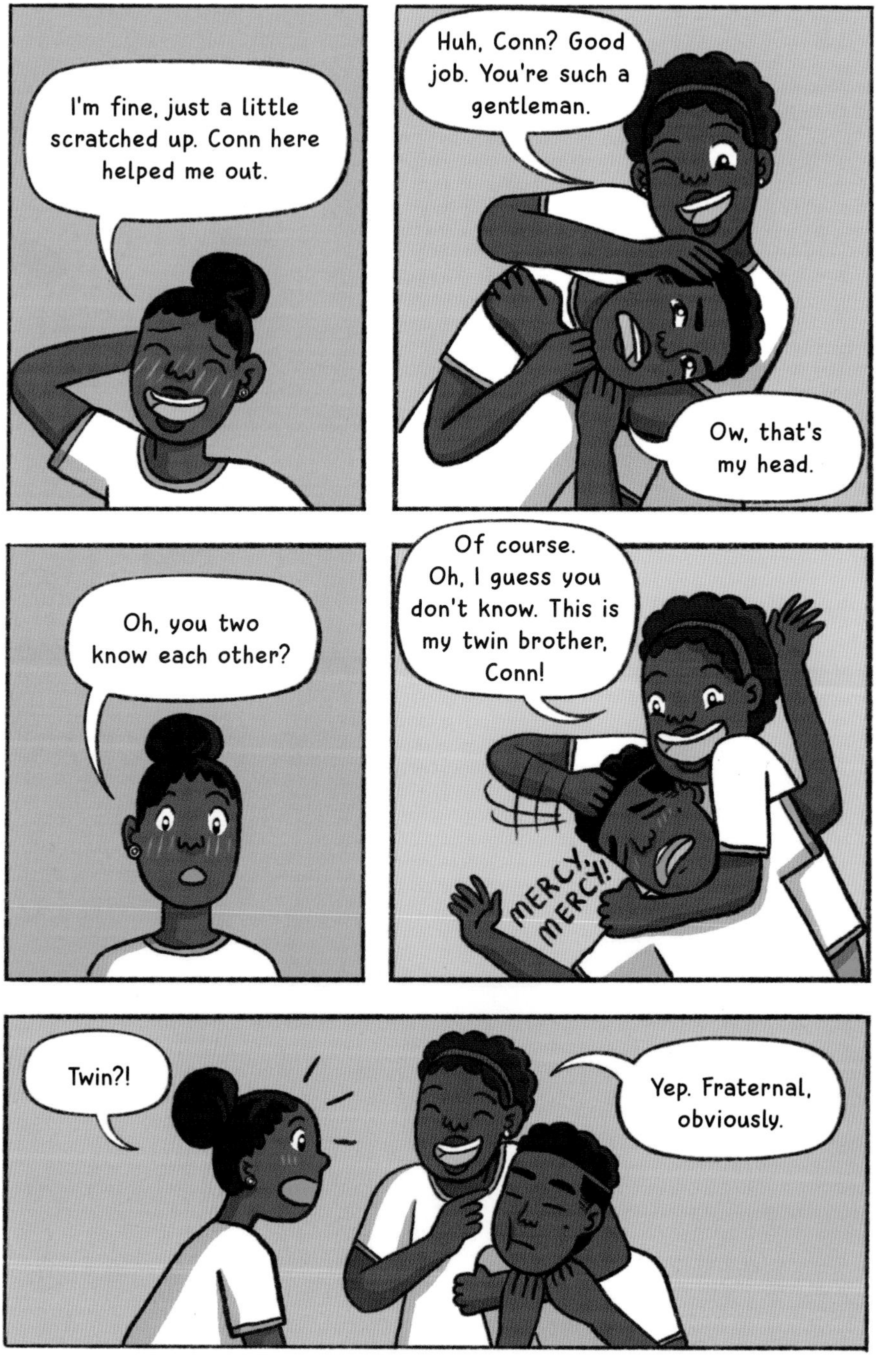

I'm fine, just a little scratched up. Conn here helped me out.
Huh, Conn? Good job. You're such a gentleman.
Ow, that's my head.
Oh, you two know each other?
Of course. Oh, I guess you don't know. This is my twin brother, Conn!
MERCY! MERCY!
Twin?!
Yep. Fraternal, obviously.

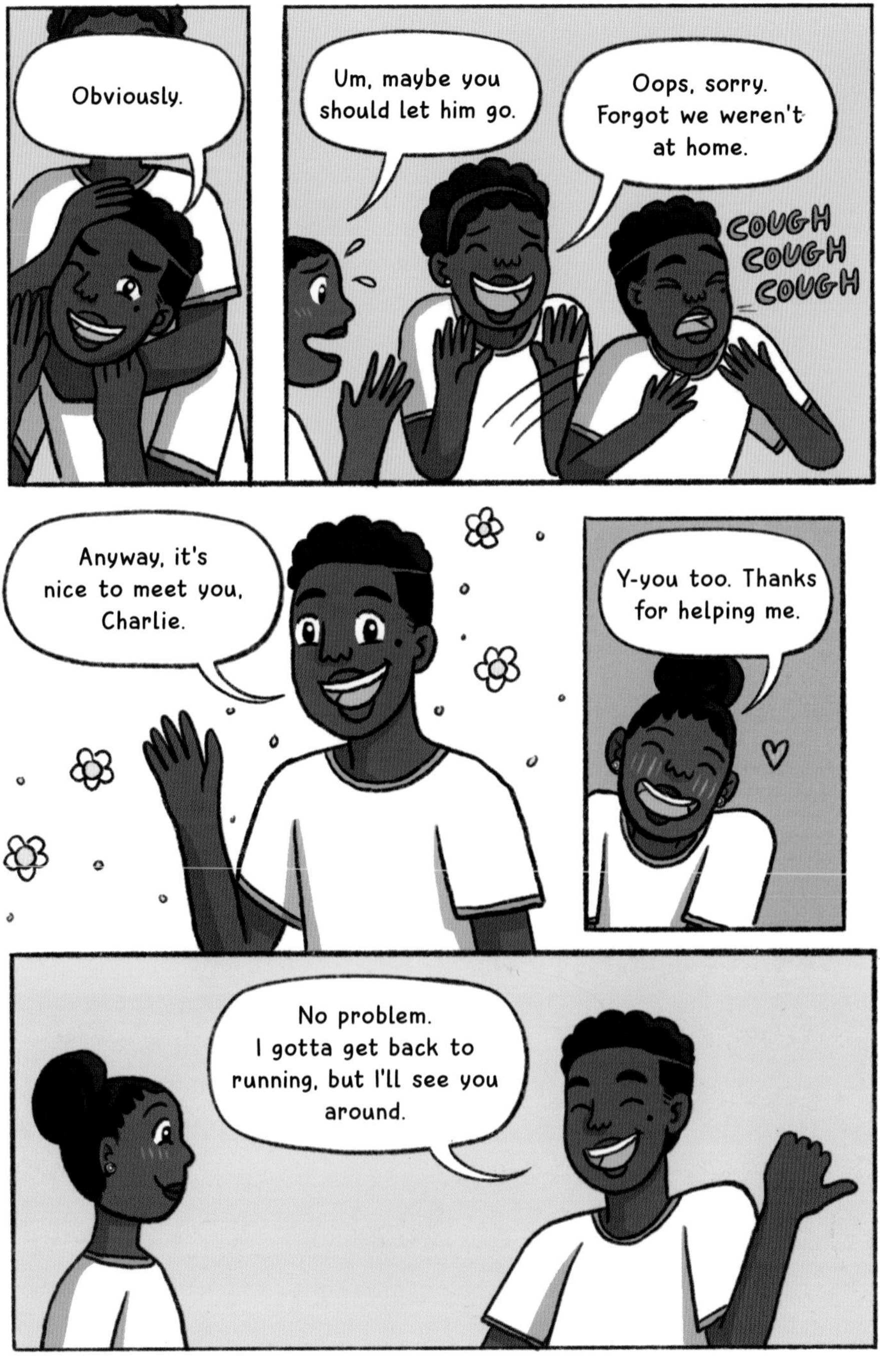
Obviously.
Um, maybe you should let him go.
Oops, sorry. Forgot we weren't at home.
COUGH COUGH COUGH
Anyway, it's nice to meet you, Charlie.
Y-you too. Thanks for helping me.
No problem. I gotta get back to running, but I'll see you around.

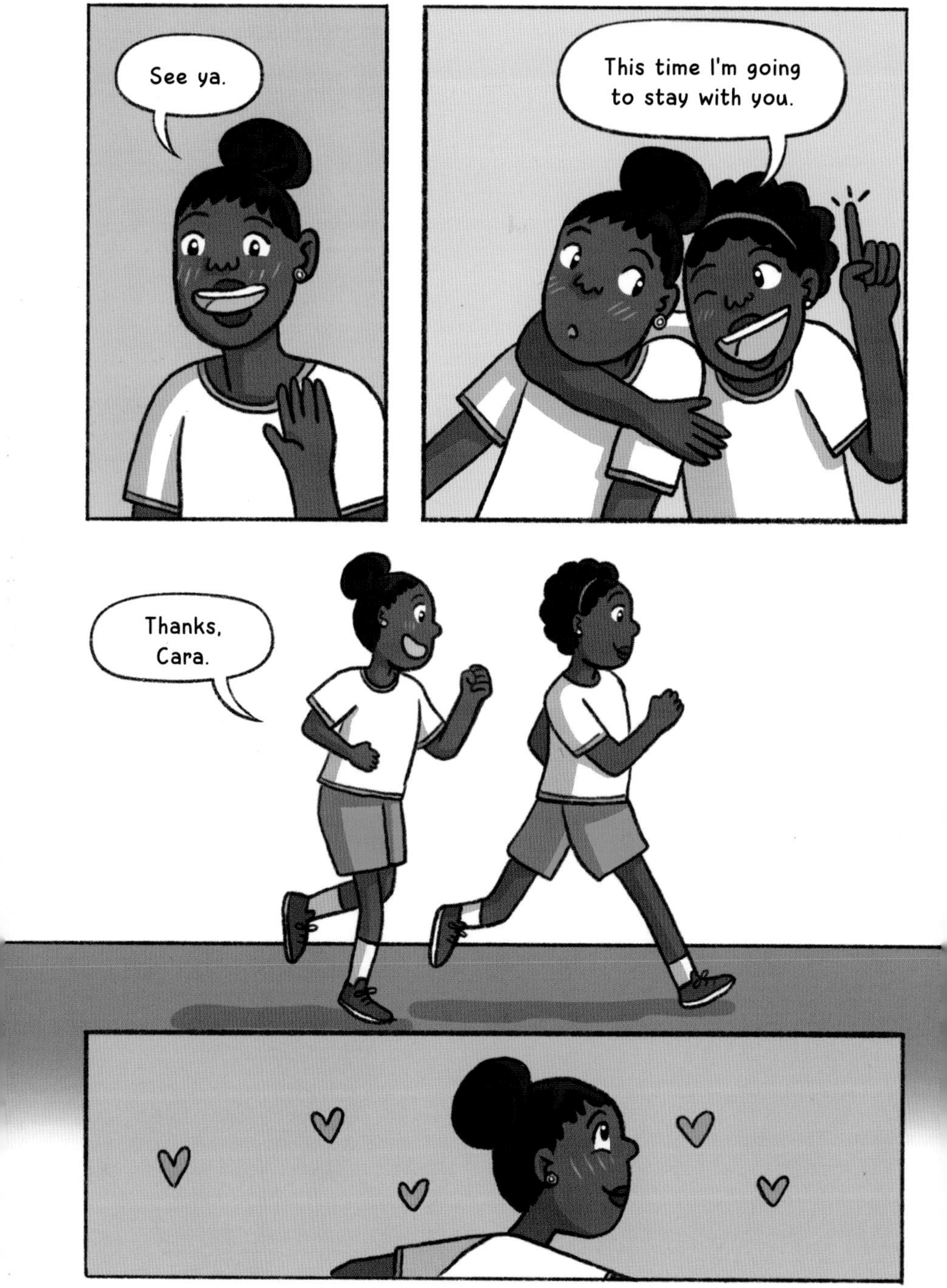
See ya.
This time I'm going to stay with you.
Thanks, Cara.

CHAPTER
7

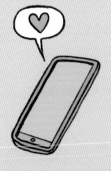

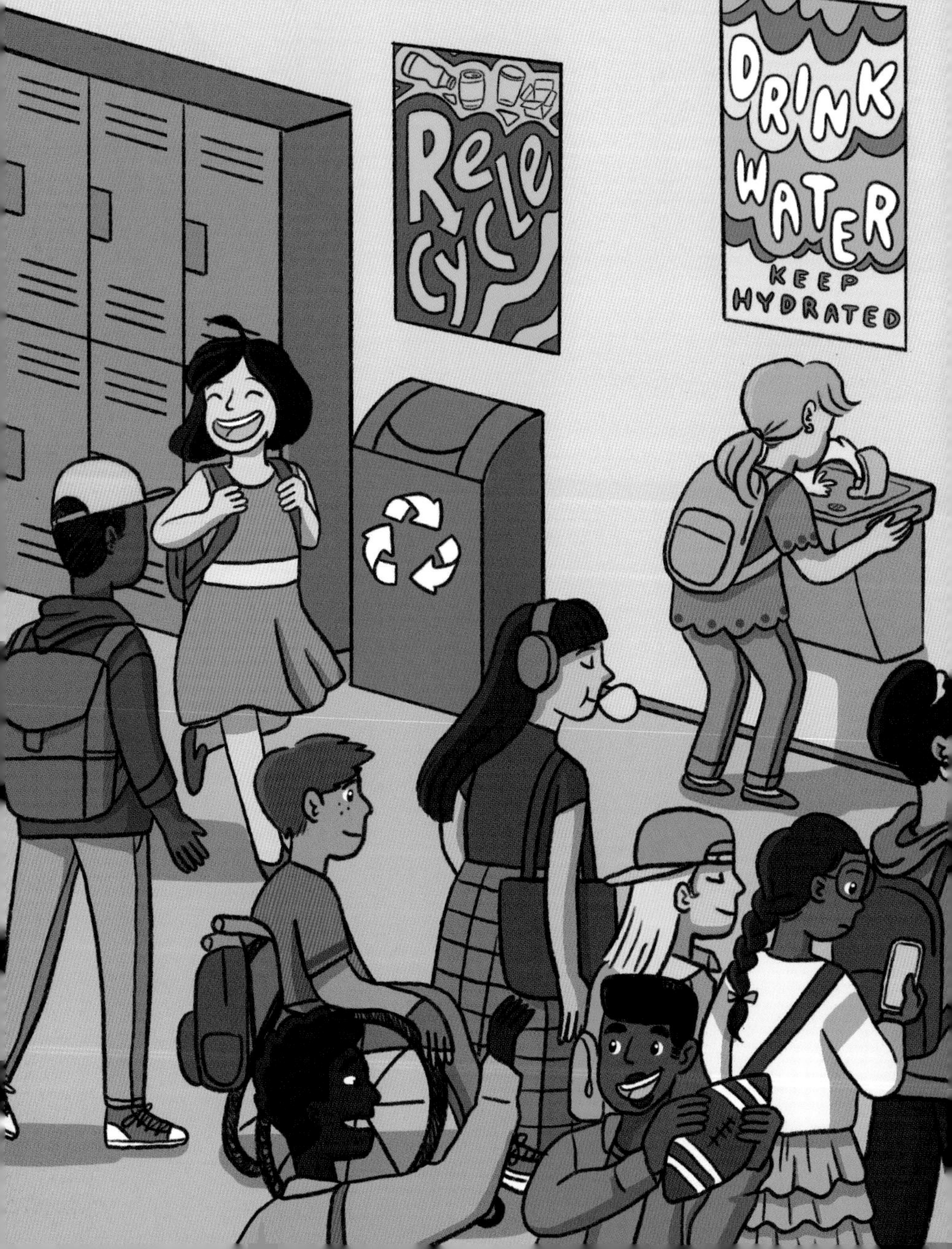
Recycle
DRINK WATER
KEEP HYDRATED

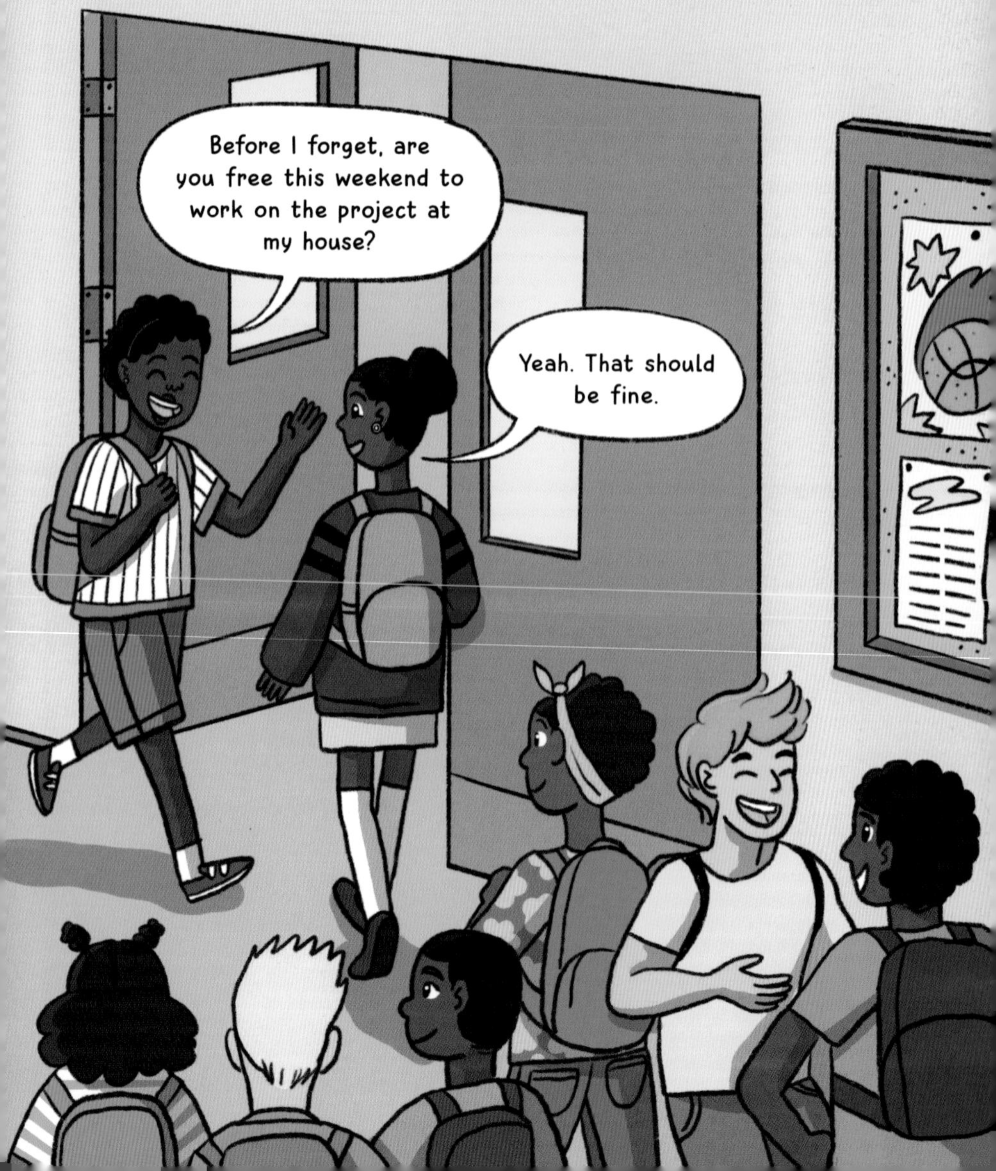
Before I forget, are you free this weekend to work on the project at my house?
Yeah. That should be fine.

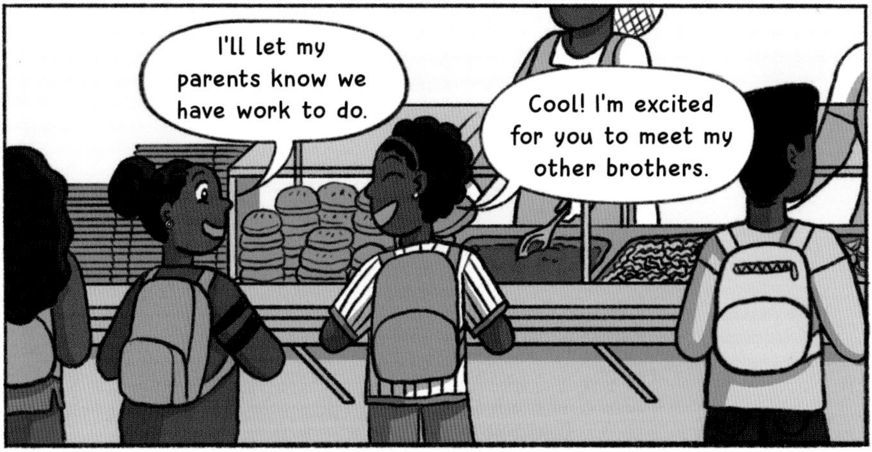
I'll let my parents know we have work to do.
Cool! I'm excited for you to meet my other brothers.

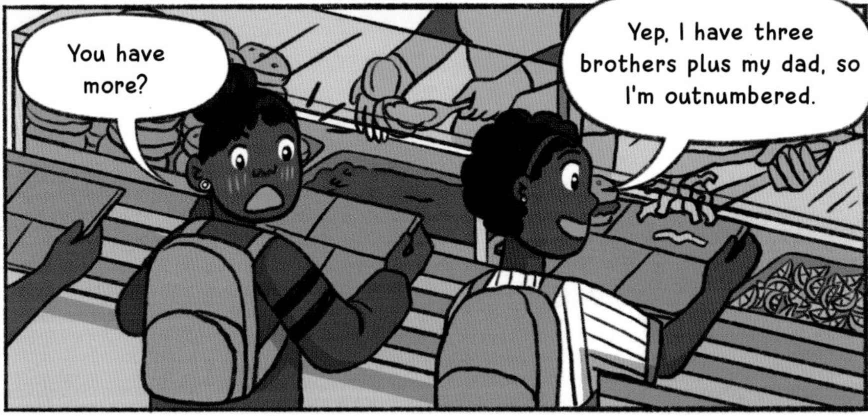
You have more?
Yep, I have three brothers plus my dad, so I'm outnumbered.

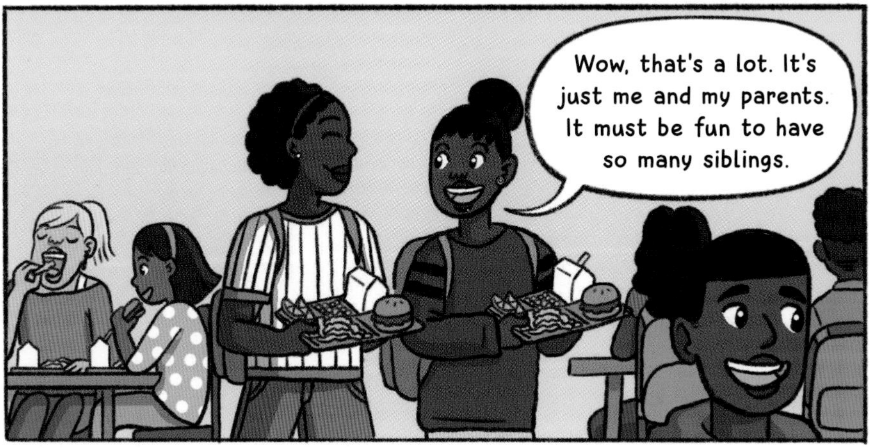
Wow, that's a lot. It's just me and my parents. It must be fun to have so many siblings.

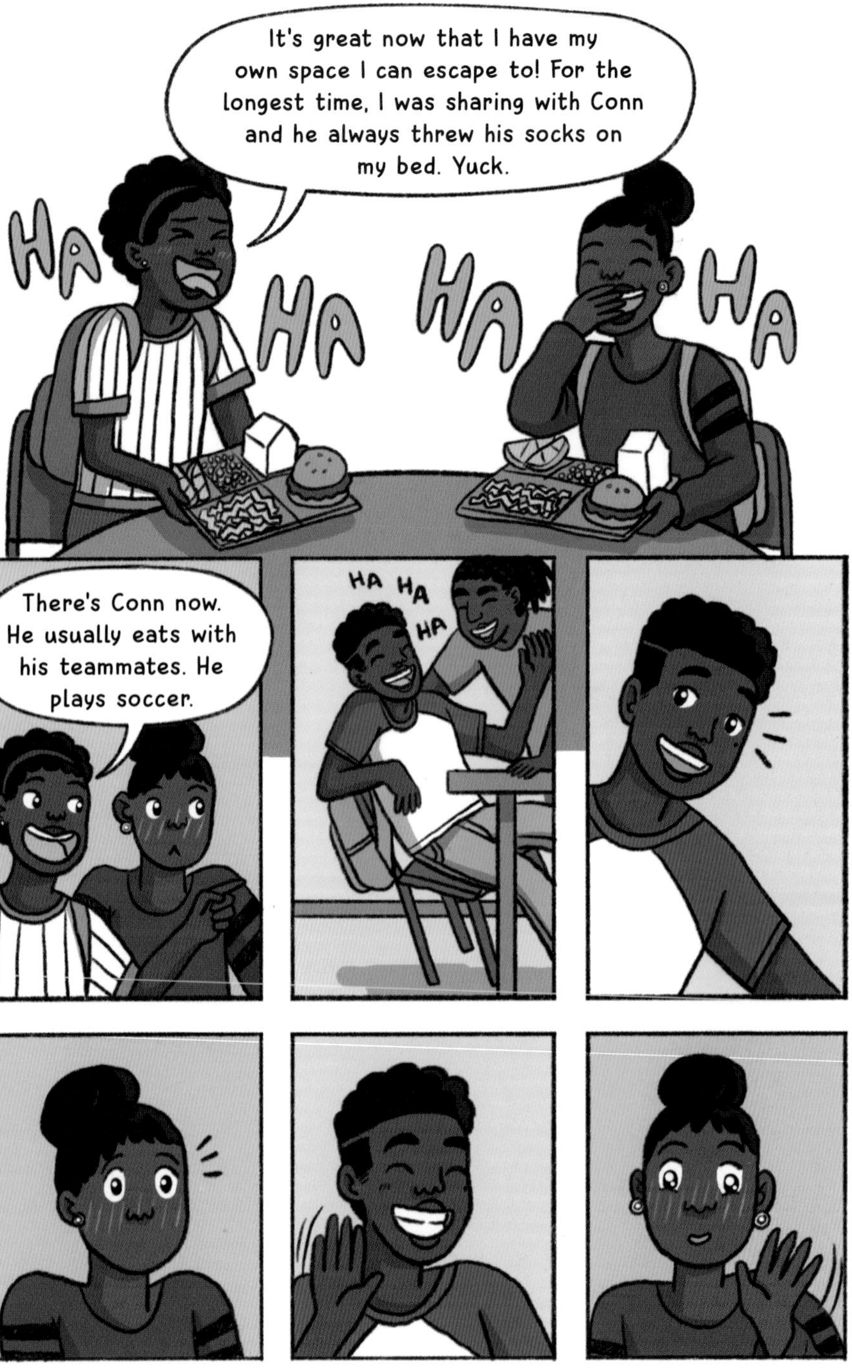
It's great now that I have my own space I can escape to! For the longest time, I was sharing with Conn and he always threw his socks on my bed. Yuck.
HA HA HA HA HA
There's Conn now. He usually eats with his teammates. He plays soccer.
HA HA HA

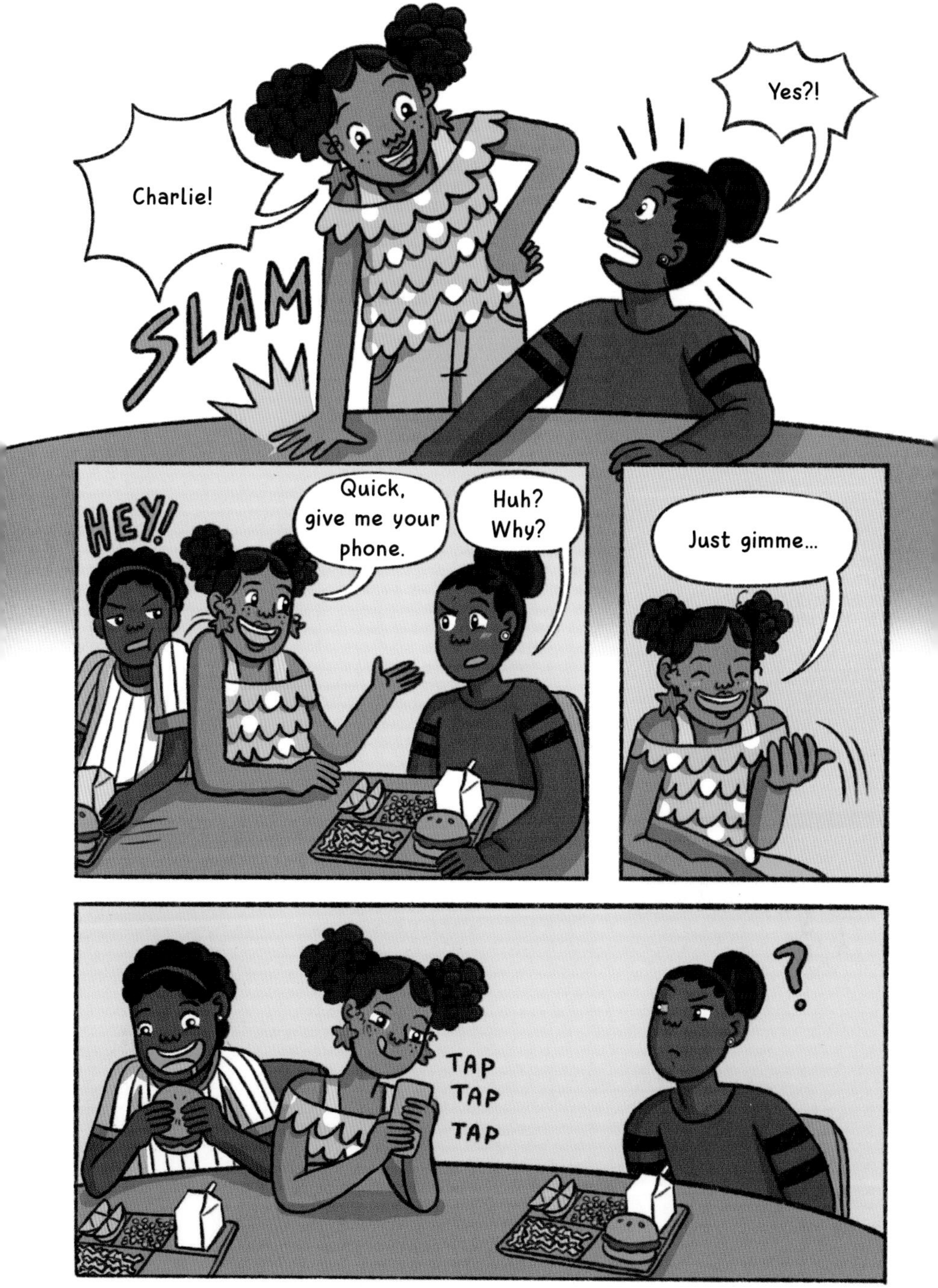
Charlie!
SLAM
Yes?!
HEY!
Quick, give me your phone.
Huh? Why?
Just gimme...
TAP
TAP
TAP
?

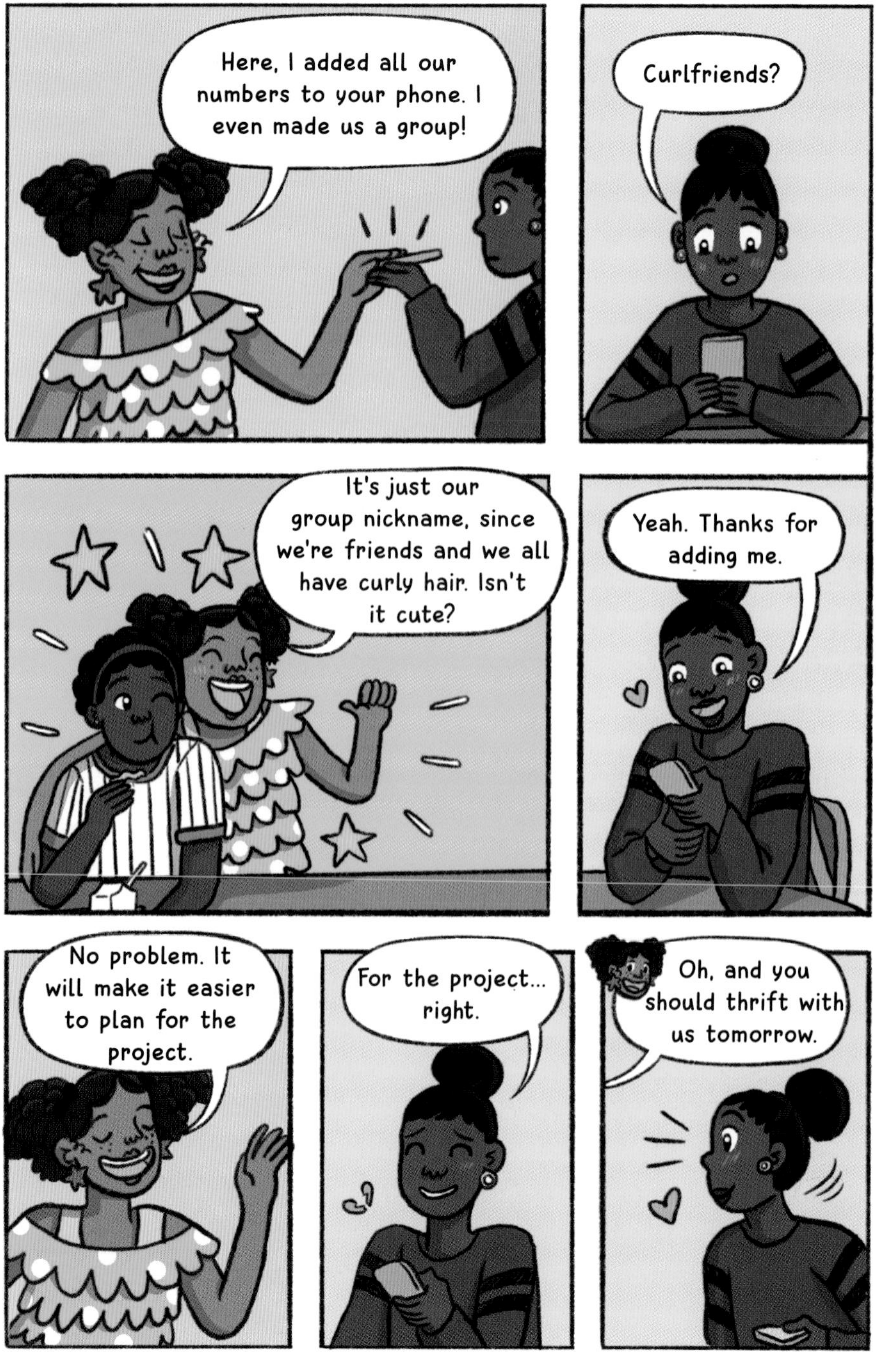
Here, I added all our numbers to your phone. I even made us a group!
Curlfriends?
It's just our group nickname, since we're friends and we all have curly hair. Isn't it cute?
Yeah. Thanks for adding me.
No problem. It will make it easier to plan for the project.
For the project... right.
Oh, and you should thrift with us tomorrow.

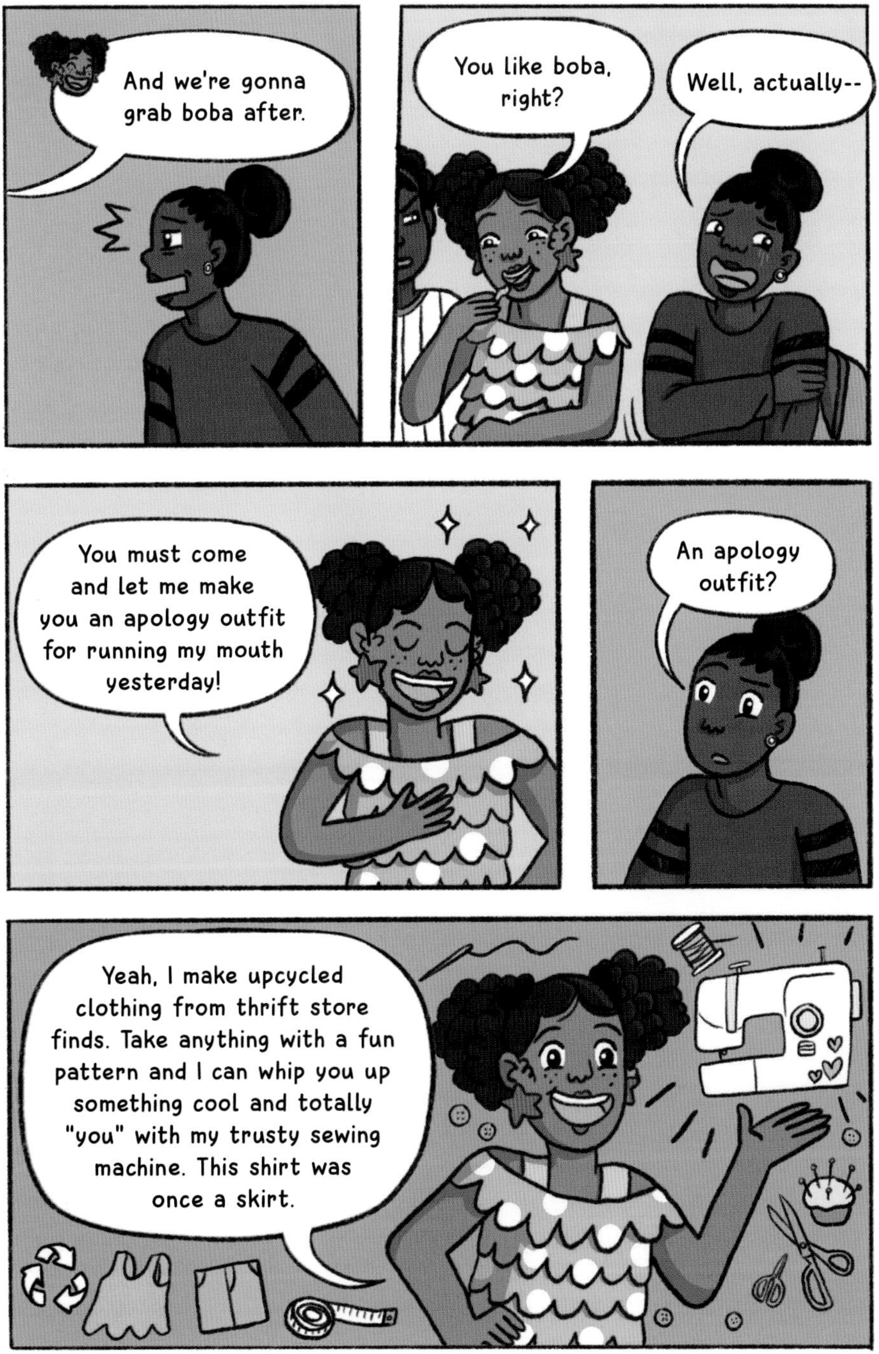
And we're gonna grab boba after.
You like boba, right?
Well, actually--
You must come and let me make you an apology outfit for running my mouth yesterday!
An apology outfit?
Yeah, I make upcycled clothing from thrift store finds. Take anything with a fun pattern and I can whip you up something cool and totally "you" with my trusty sewing machine. This shirt was once a skirt.

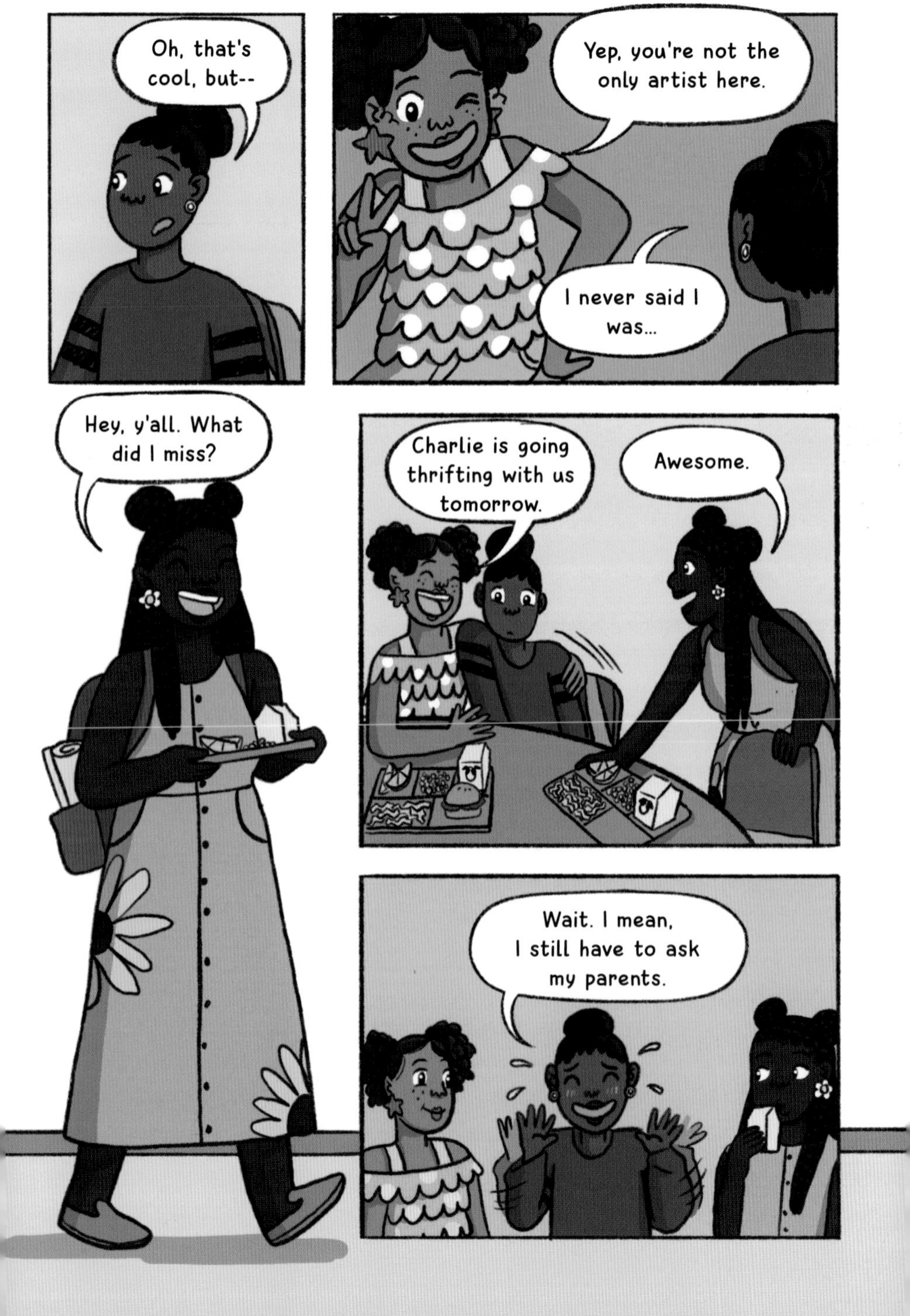

Oh, that's cool, but--
Yep, you're not the only artist here.
I never said I was...
Hey, y'all. What did I miss?
Charlie is going thrifting with us tomorrow.
Awesome.
Wait. I mean, I still have to ask my parents.

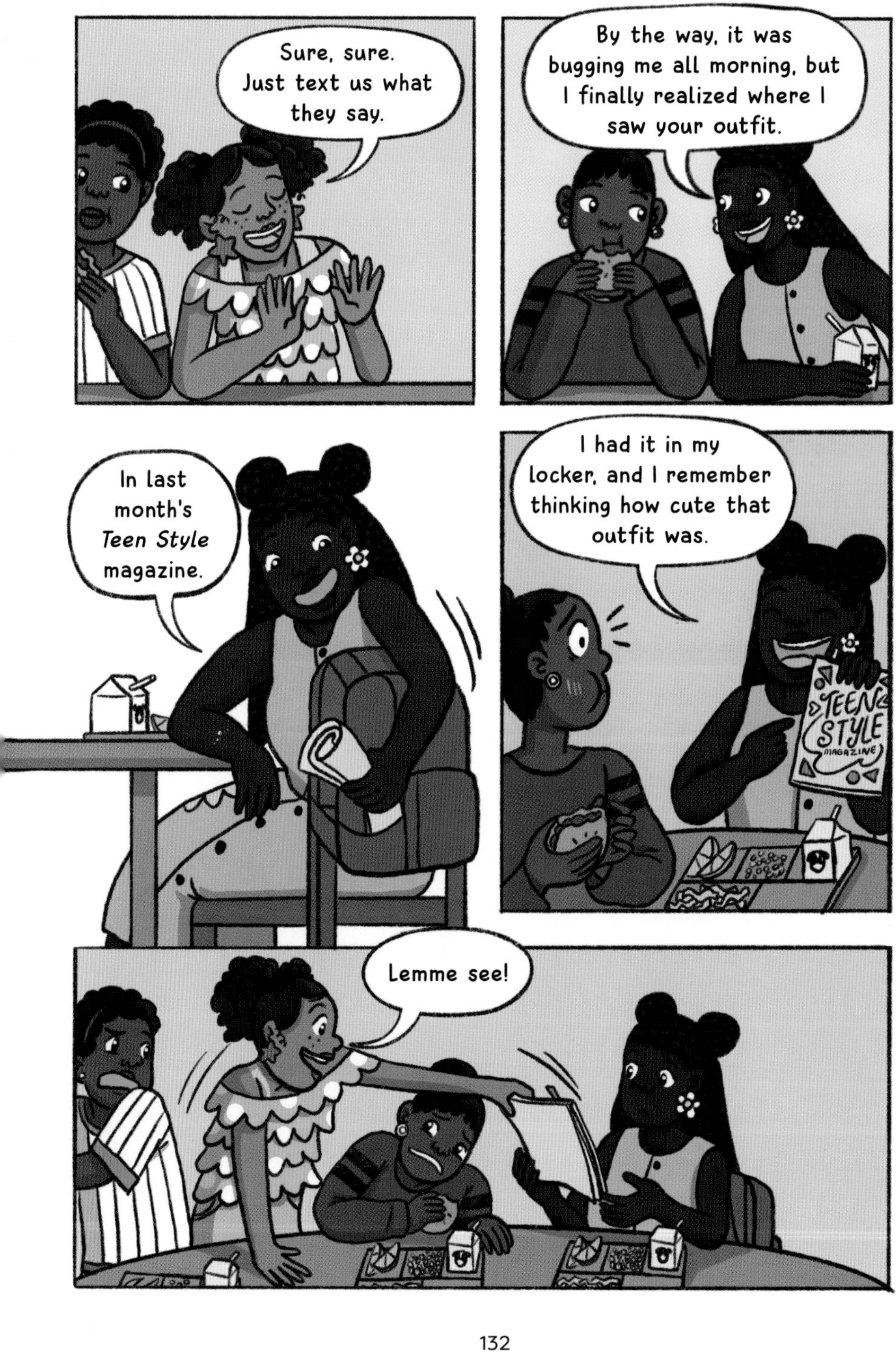

Sure, sure. Just text us what they say.
By the way, it was bugging me all morning, but I finally realized where I saw your outfit.
In last month's *Teen Style* magazine.
I had it in my locker, and I remember thinking how cute that outfit was.
TEEN STYLE MAGAZINE
Lemme see!

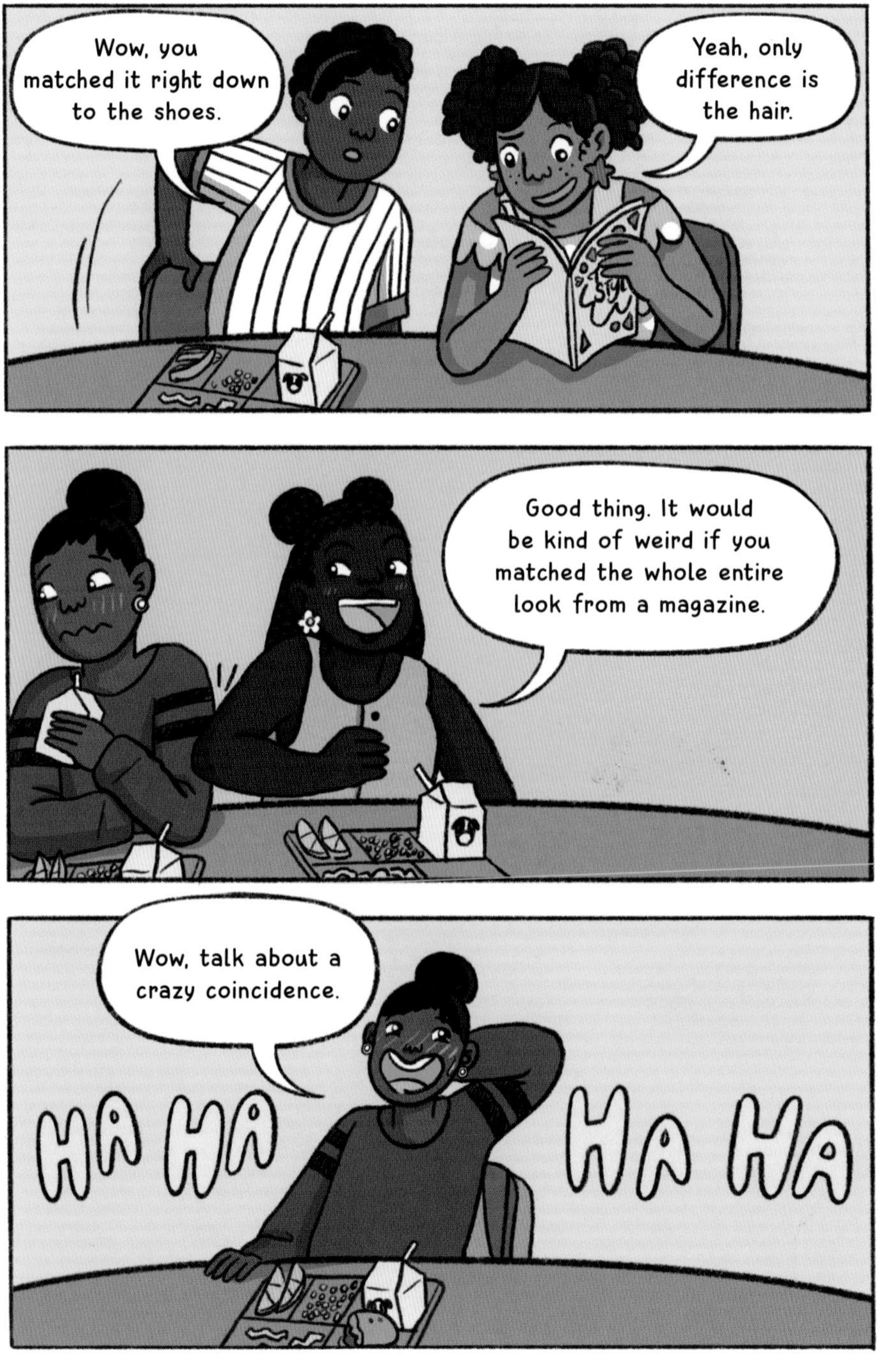
Wow, you matched it right down to the shoes.
Yeah, only difference is the hair.
Good thing. It would be kind of weird if you matched the whole entire look from a magazine.
Wow, talk about a crazy coincidence.
HA HA
HA HA

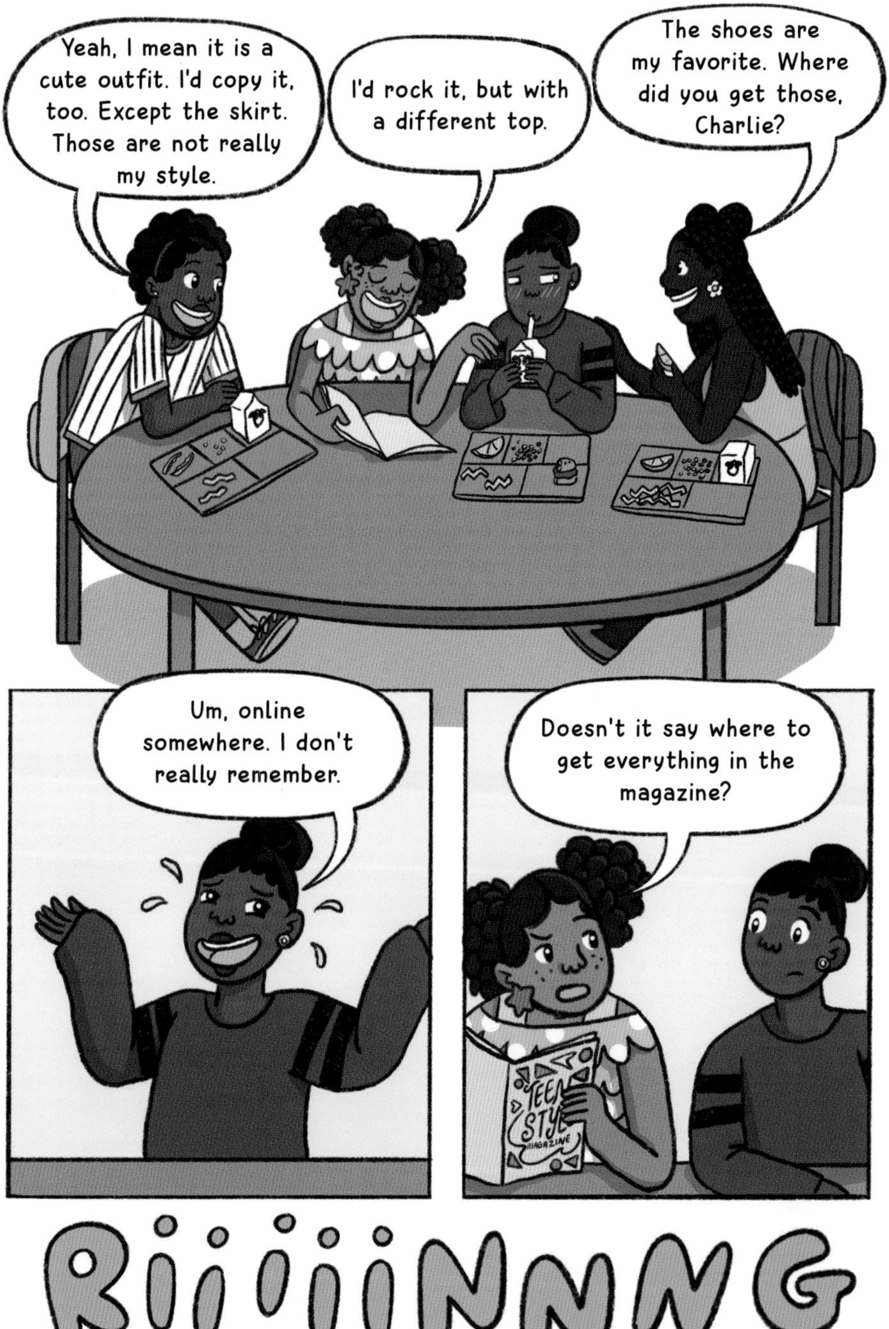
Yeah, I mean it is a cute outfit. I'd copy it, too. Except the skirt. Those are not really my style.
I'd rock it, but with a different top.
The shoes are my favorite. Where did you get those, Charlie?
Um, online somewhere. I don't really remember.
Doesn't it say where to get everything in the magazine?
RIIIIINNNG

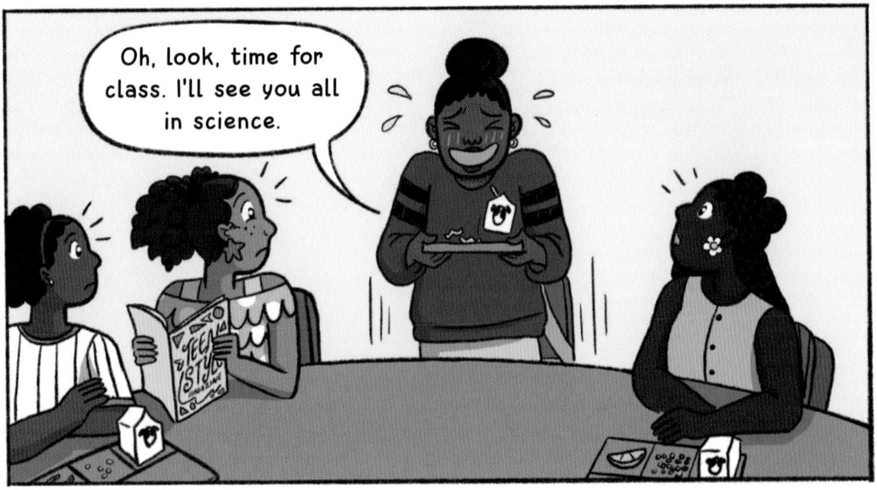
Oh, look, time for class. I'll see you all in science.

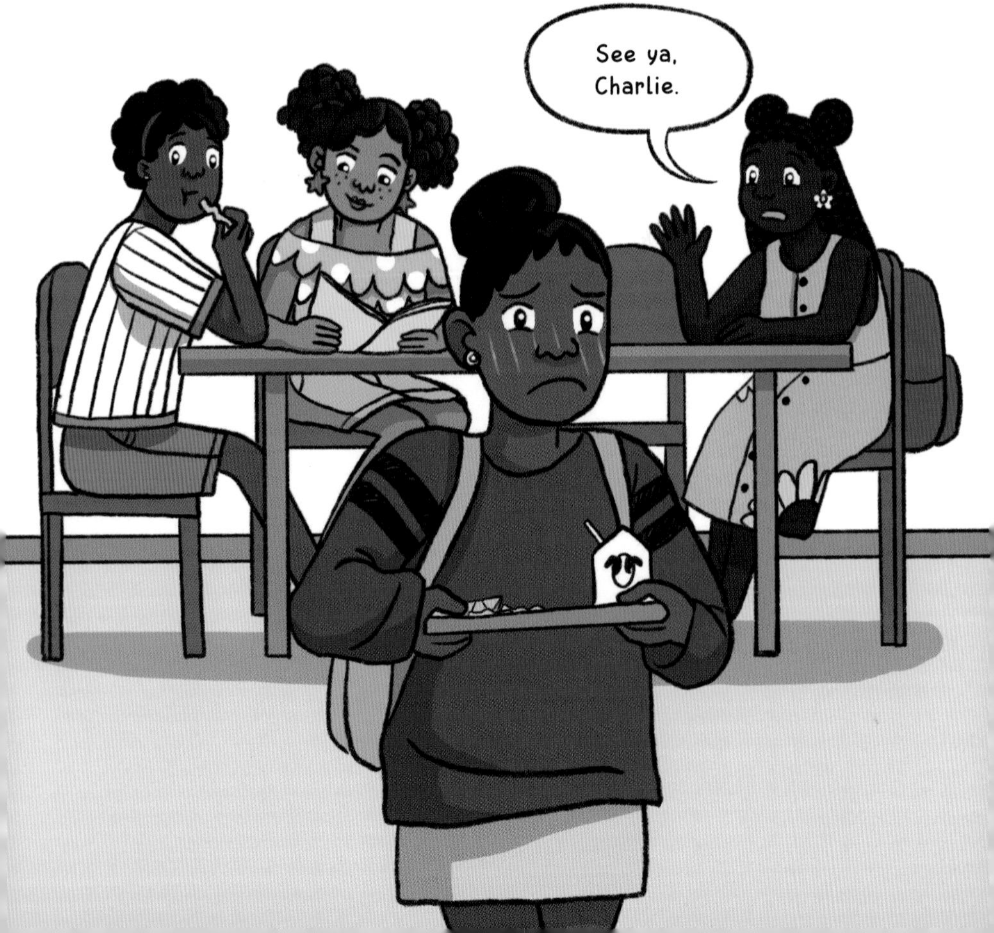
See ya, Charlie.

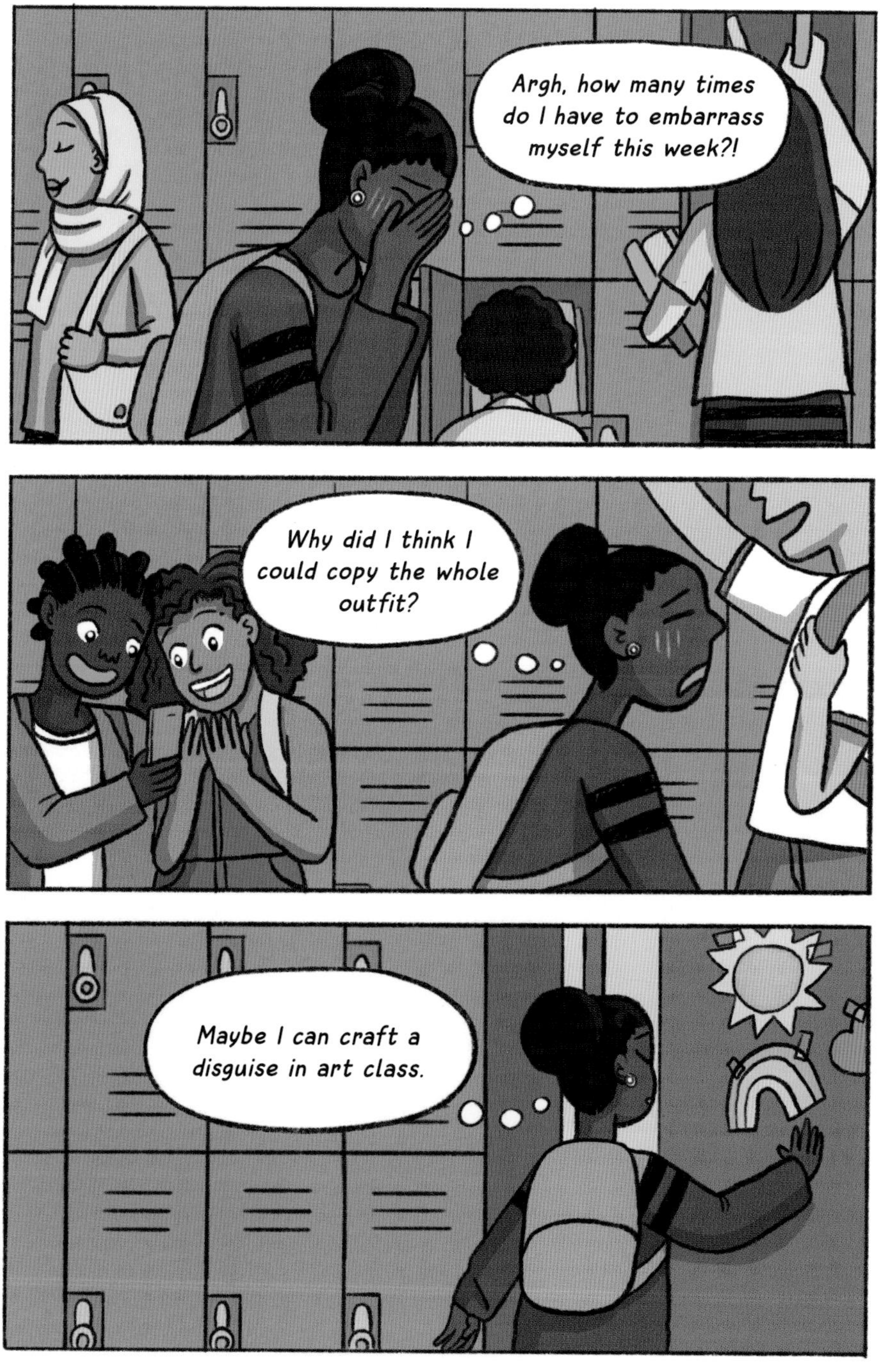
Argh, how many times do I have to embarrass myself this week?!
Why did I think I could copy the whole outfit?
Maybe I can craft a disguise in art class.

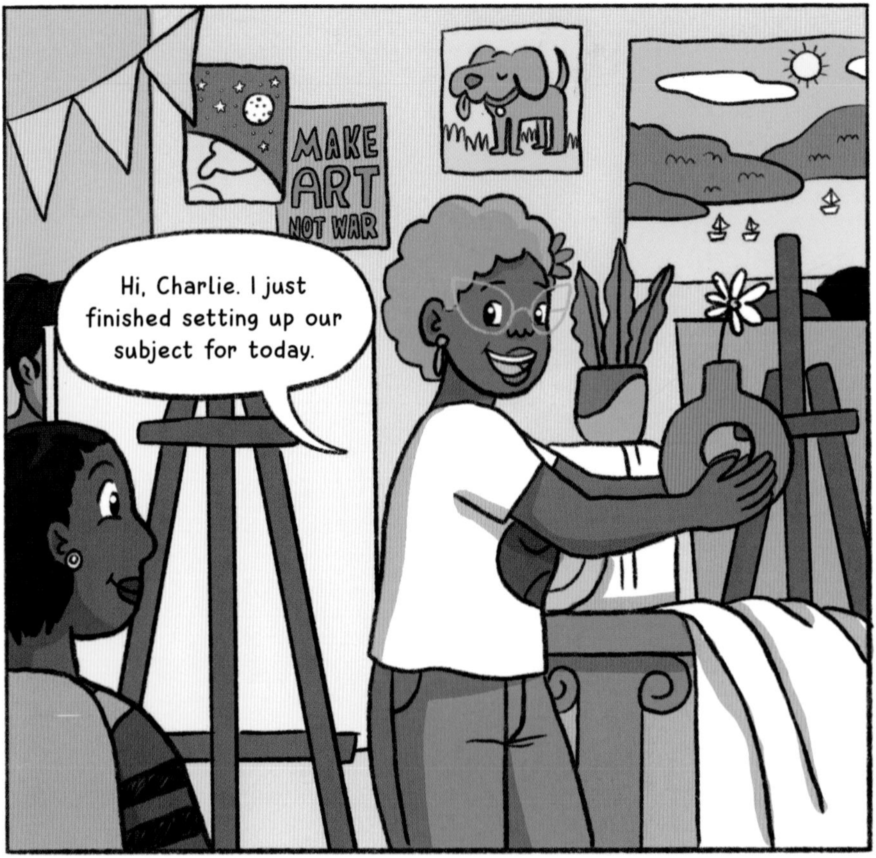
MAKE ART NOT WAR
Hi, Charlie. I just finished setting up our subject for today.

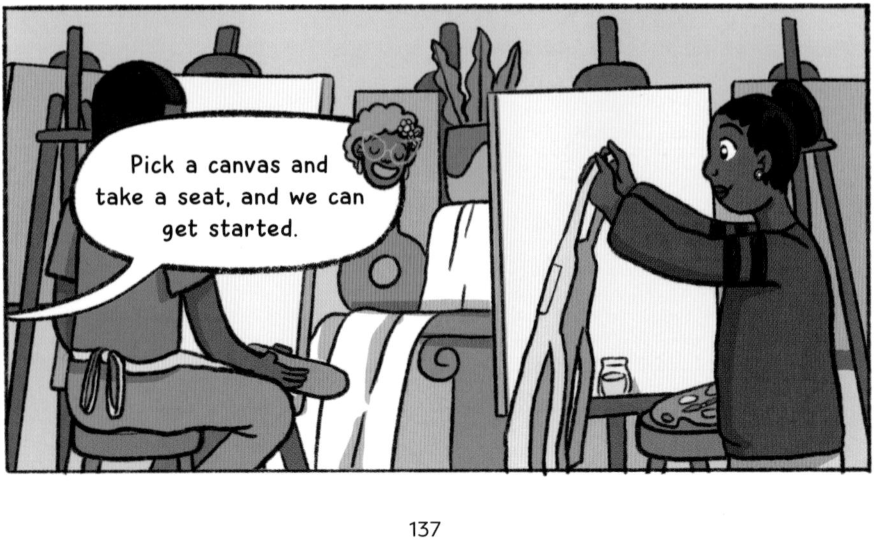
Pick a canvas and take a seat, and we can get started.

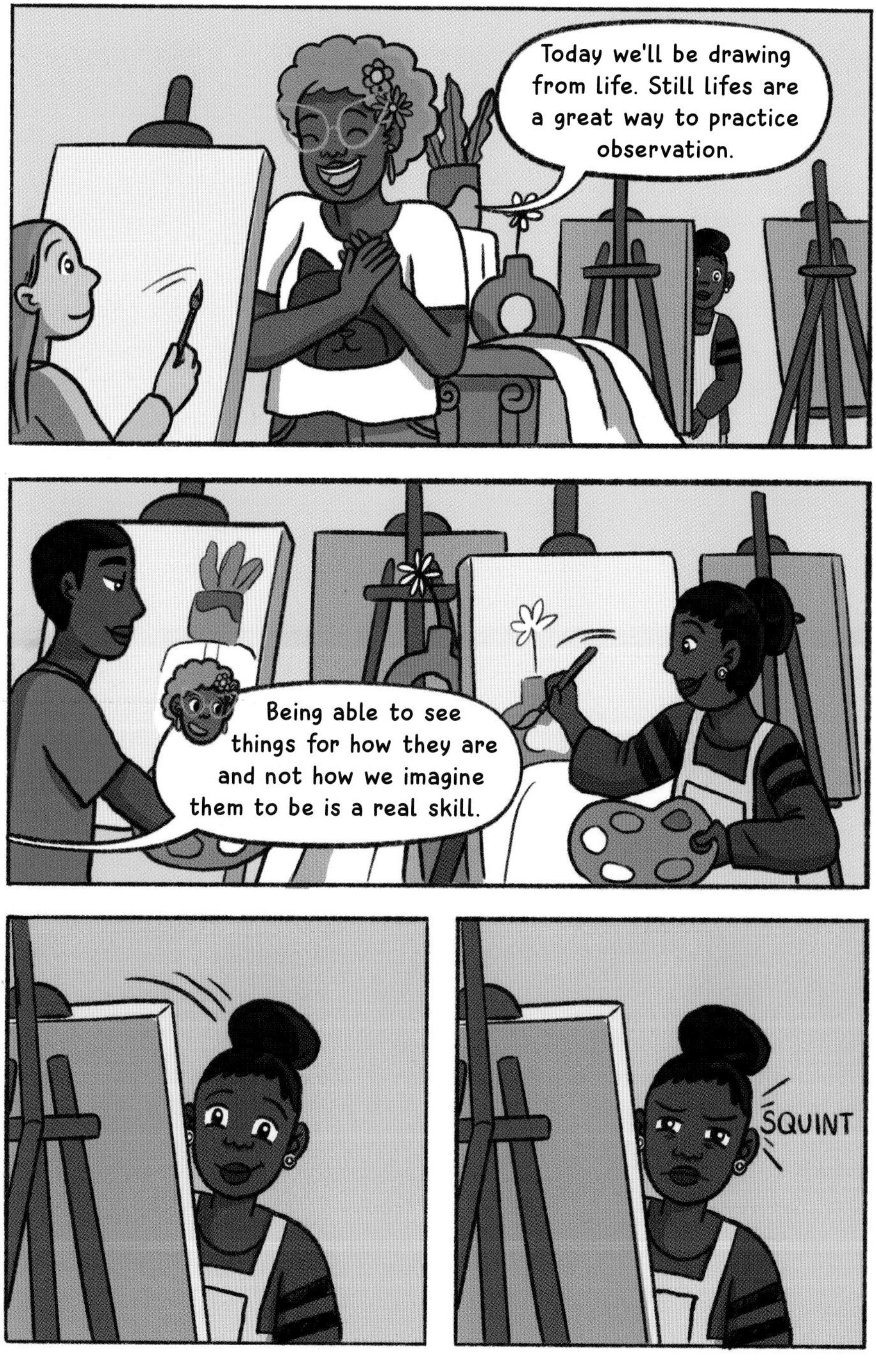
Today we'll be drawing from life. Still lifes are a great way to practice observation.
Being able to see things for how they are and not how we imagine them to be is a real skill.
SQUINT

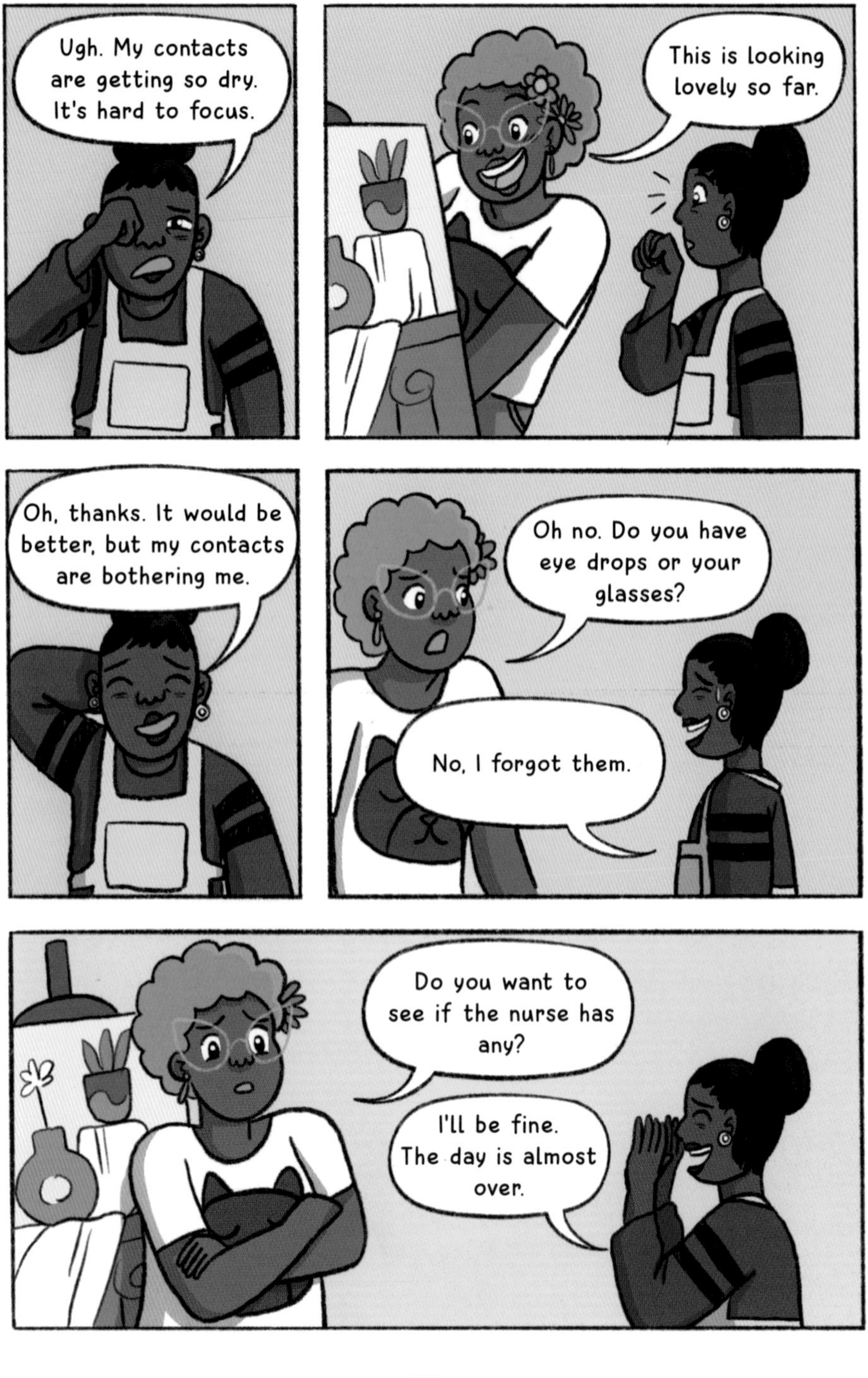
Ugh. My contacts are getting so dry. It's hard to focus.
This is looking lovely so far.
Oh, thanks. It would be better, but my contacts are bothering me.
Oh no. Do you have eye drops or your glasses?
No, I forgot them.
Do you want to see if the nurse has any?
I'll be fine. The day is almost over.

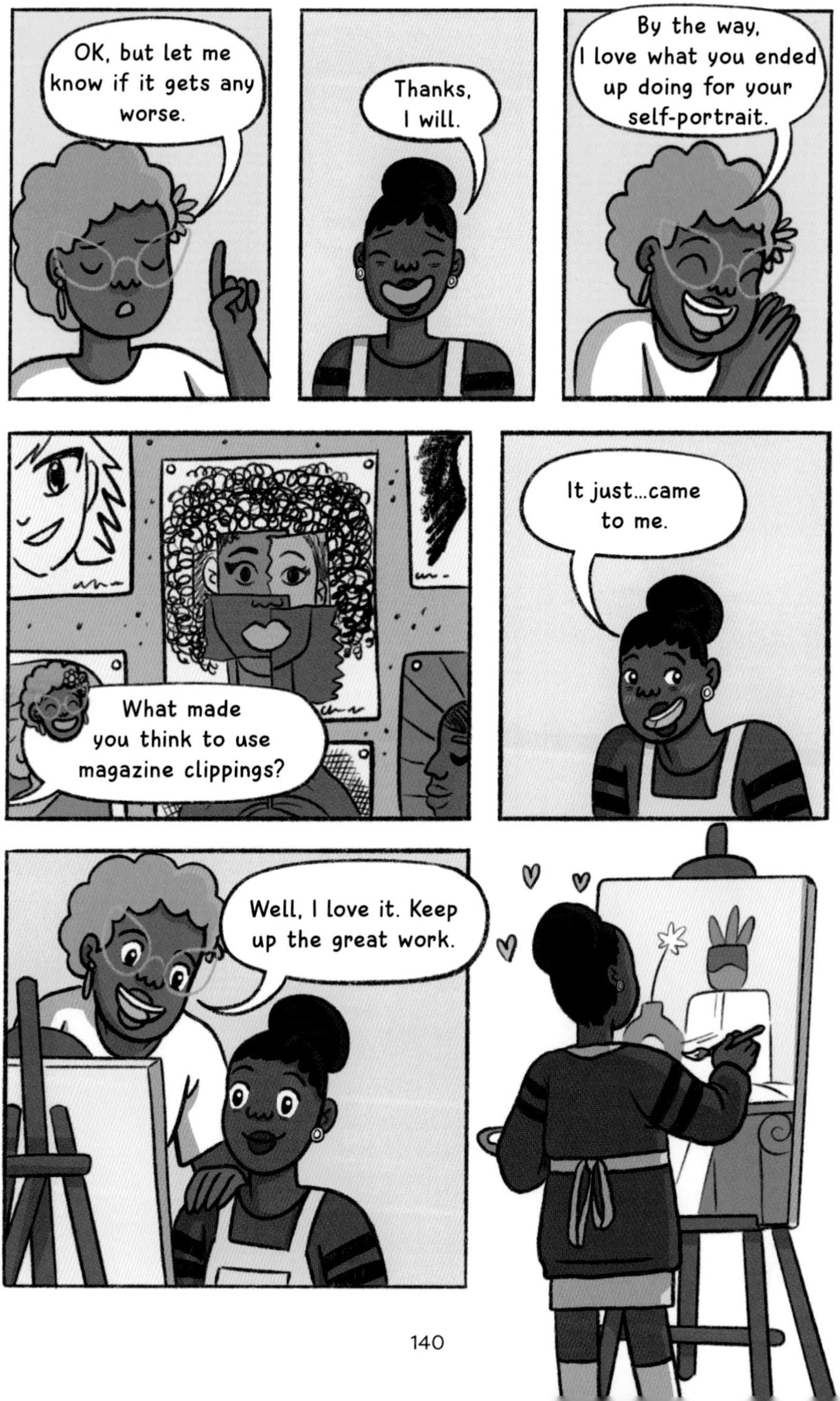
OK, but let me know if it gets any worse.
Thanks, I will.
By the way, I love what you ended up doing for your self-portrait.
What made you think to use magazine clippings?
It just...came to me.
Well, I love it. Keep up the great work.

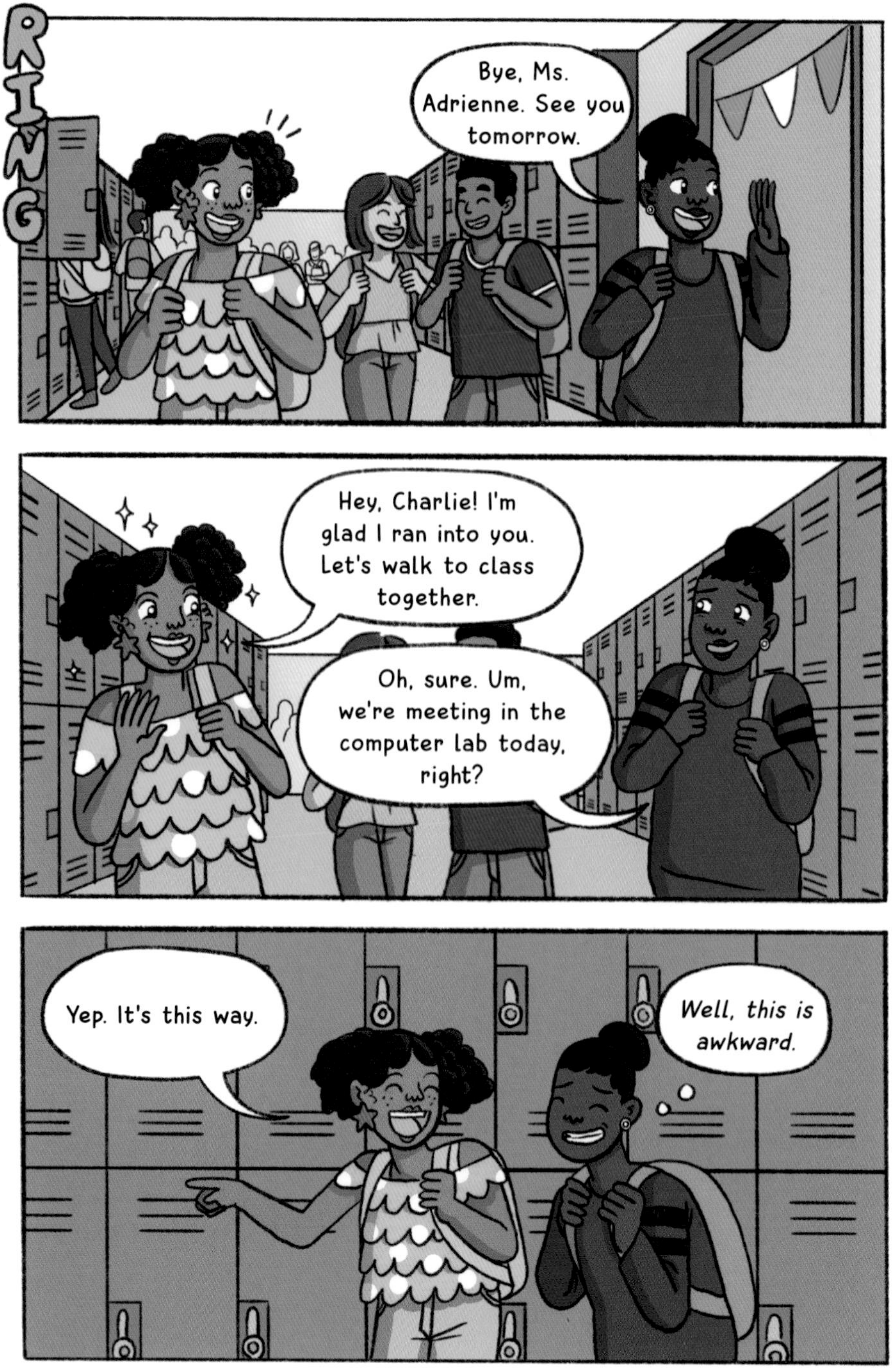
RING
Bye, Ms. Adrienne. See you tomorrow.
Hey, Charlie! I'm glad I ran into you. Let's walk to class together.
Oh, sure. Um, we're meeting in the computer lab today, right?
Yep. It's this way.
Well, this is awkward.

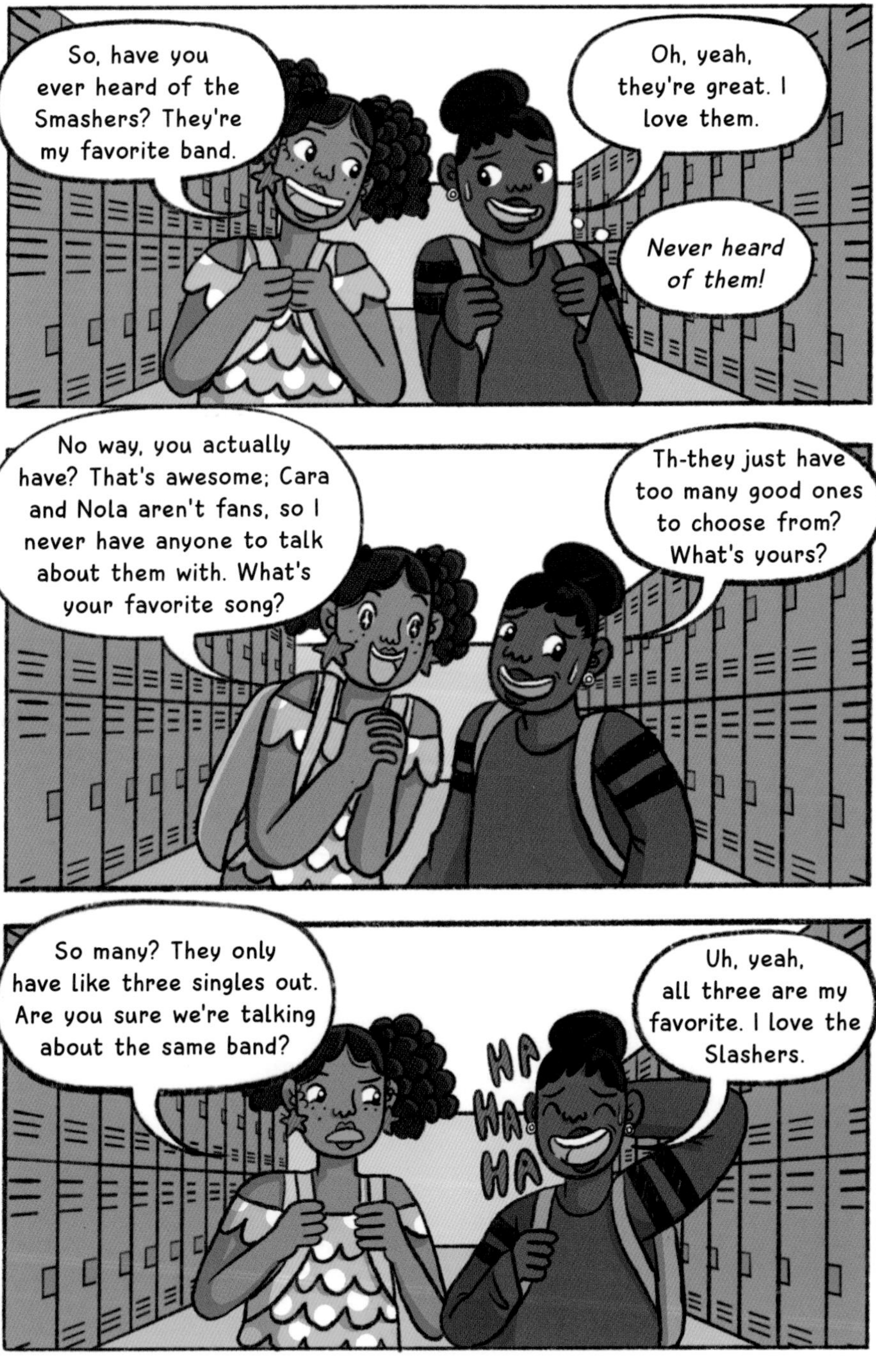
So, have you ever heard of the Smashers? They're my favorite band.
Oh, yeah, they're great. I love them.
Never heard of them!
No way, you actually have? That's awesome; Cara and Nola aren't fans, so I never have anyone to talk about them with. What's your favorite song?
Th-they just have too many good ones to choose from? What's yours?
So many? They only have like three singles out. Are you sure we're talking about the same band?
HA HA HA
Uh, yeah, all three are my favorite. I love the Slashers.

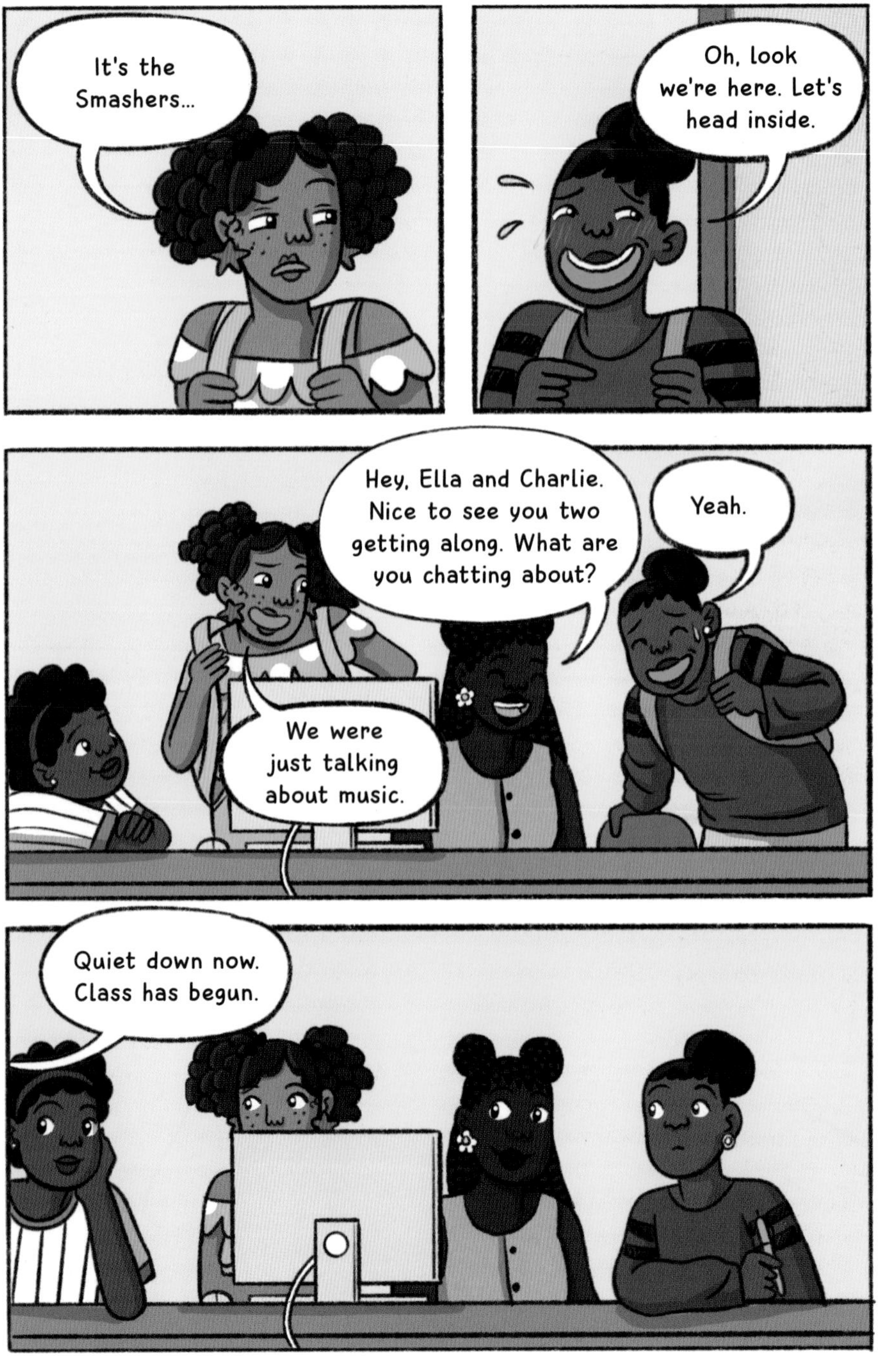
It's the Smashers...
Oh, look we're here. Let's head inside.
Hey, Ella and Charlie. Nice to see you two getting along. What are you chatting about?
We were just talking about music.
Yeah.
Quiet down now. Class has begun.

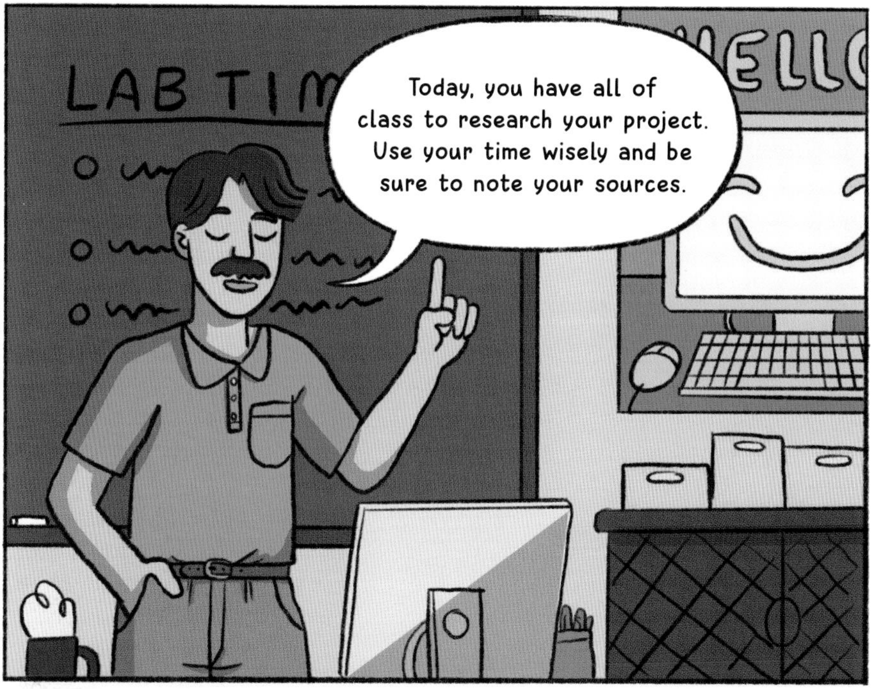
LAB TIM
HELLO
Today, you have all of class to research your project. Use your time wisely and be sure to note your sources.

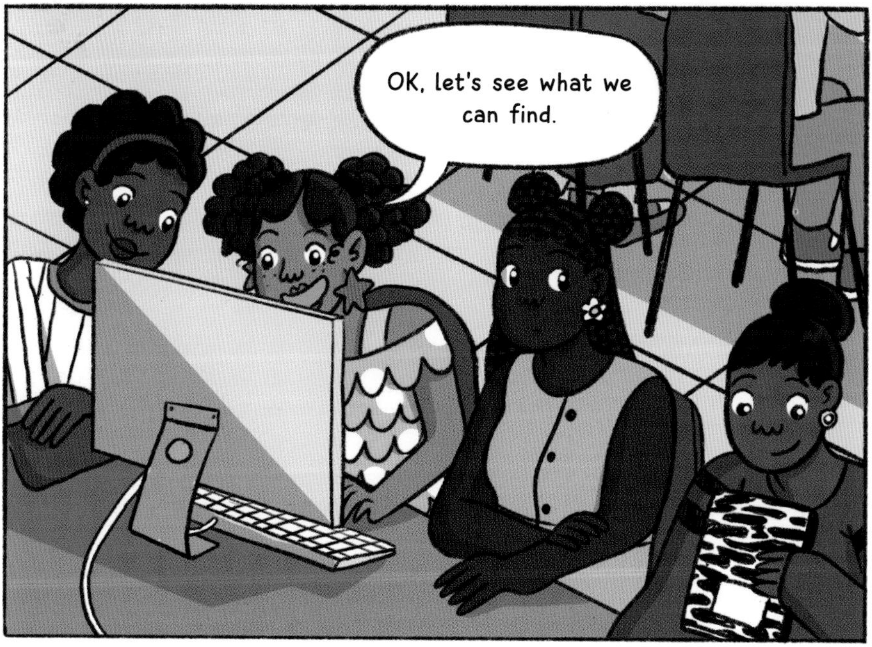
OK, let's see what we can find.

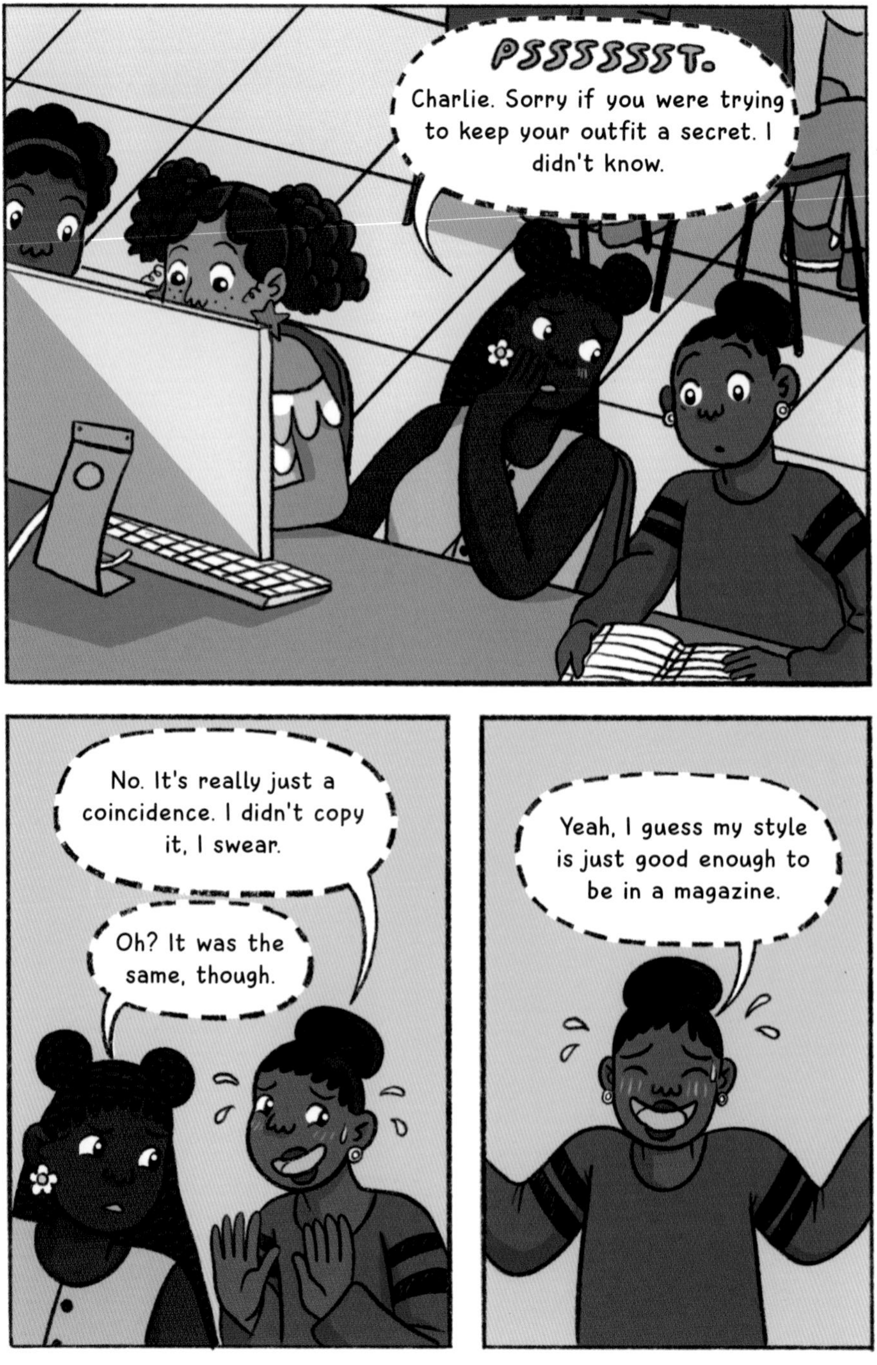
PSSSSSST.
Charlie. Sorry if you were trying to keep your outfit a secret. I didn't know.
No. It's really just a coincidence. I didn't copy it, I swear.
Oh? It was the same, though.
Yeah, I guess my style is just good enough to be in a magazine.

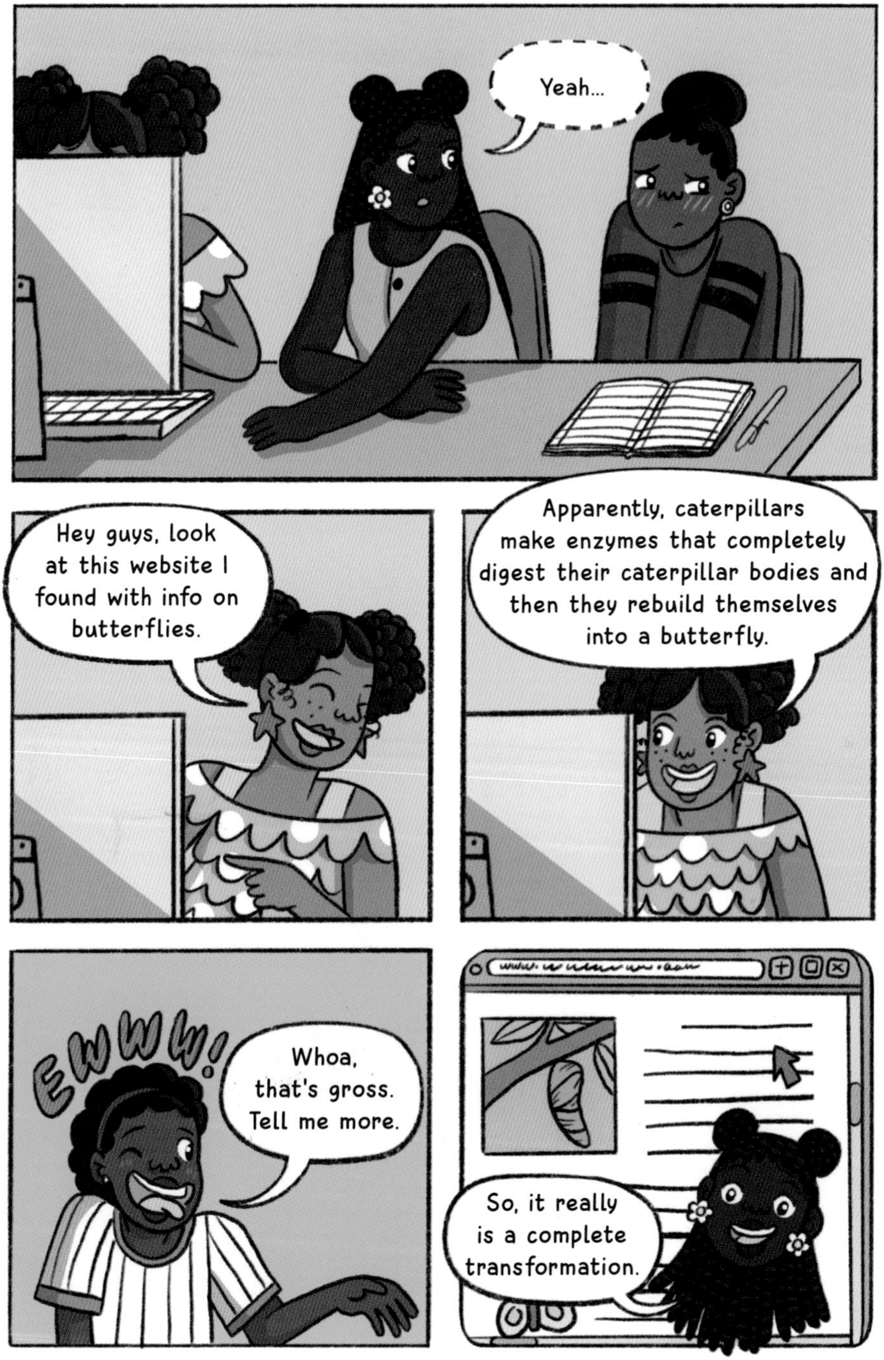
Yeah...
Hey guys, look at this website I found with info on butterflies.
Apparently, caterpillars make enzymes that completely digest their caterpillar bodies and then they rebuild themselves into a butterfly.
EWWW!
Whoa, that's gross. Tell me more.
So, it really is a complete transformation.

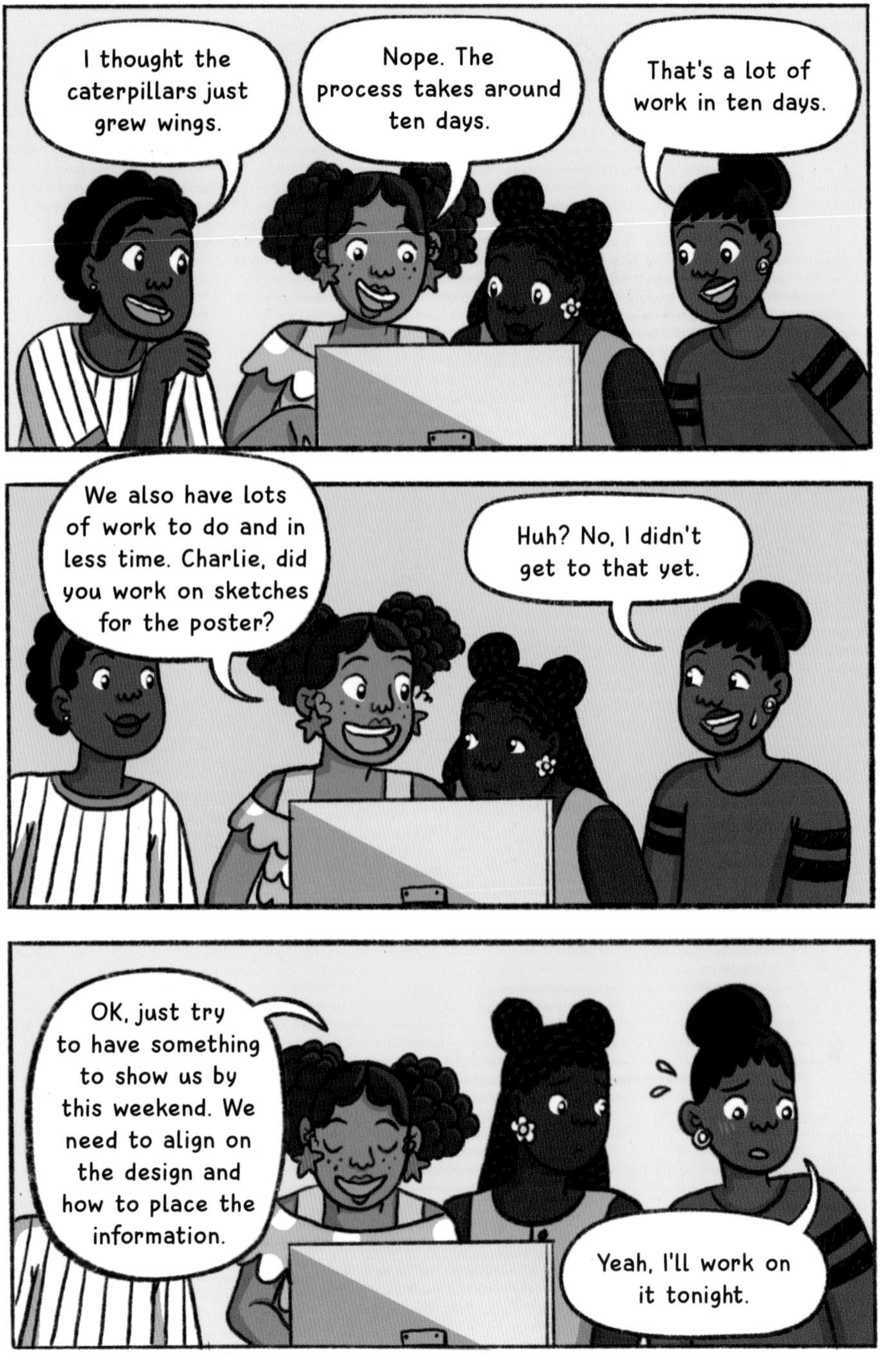
I thought the caterpillars just grew wings.
Nope. The process takes around ten days.
That's a lot of work in ten days.
We also have lots of work to do and in less time. Charlie, did you work on sketches for the poster?
Huh? No, I didn't get to that yet.
OK, just try to have something to show us by this weekend. We need to align on the design and how to place the information.
Yeah, I'll work on it tonight.

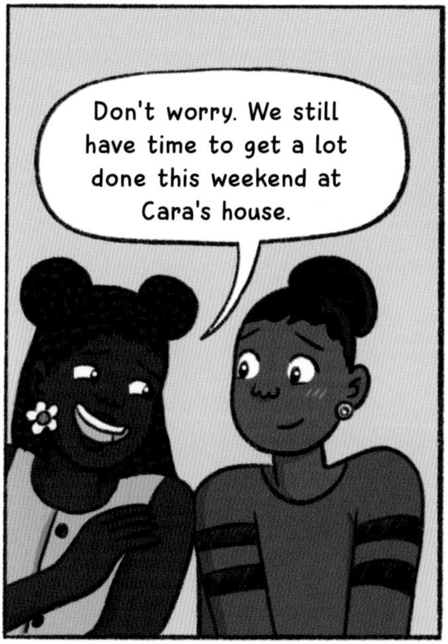
Don't worry. We still have time to get a lot done this weekend at Cara's house.

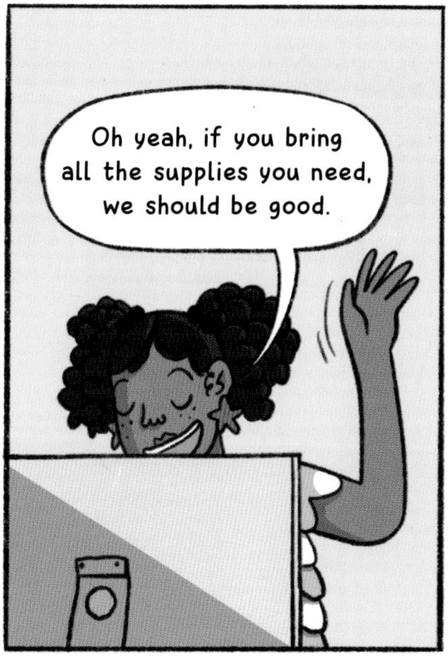
Oh yeah, if you bring all the supplies you need, we should be good.

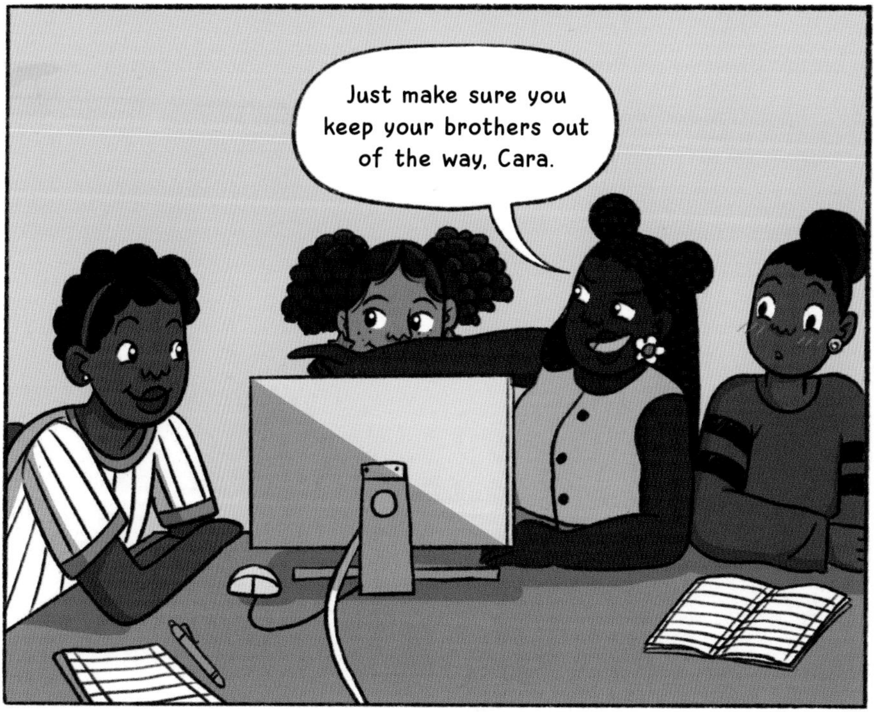
Just make sure you keep your brothers out of the way, Cara.

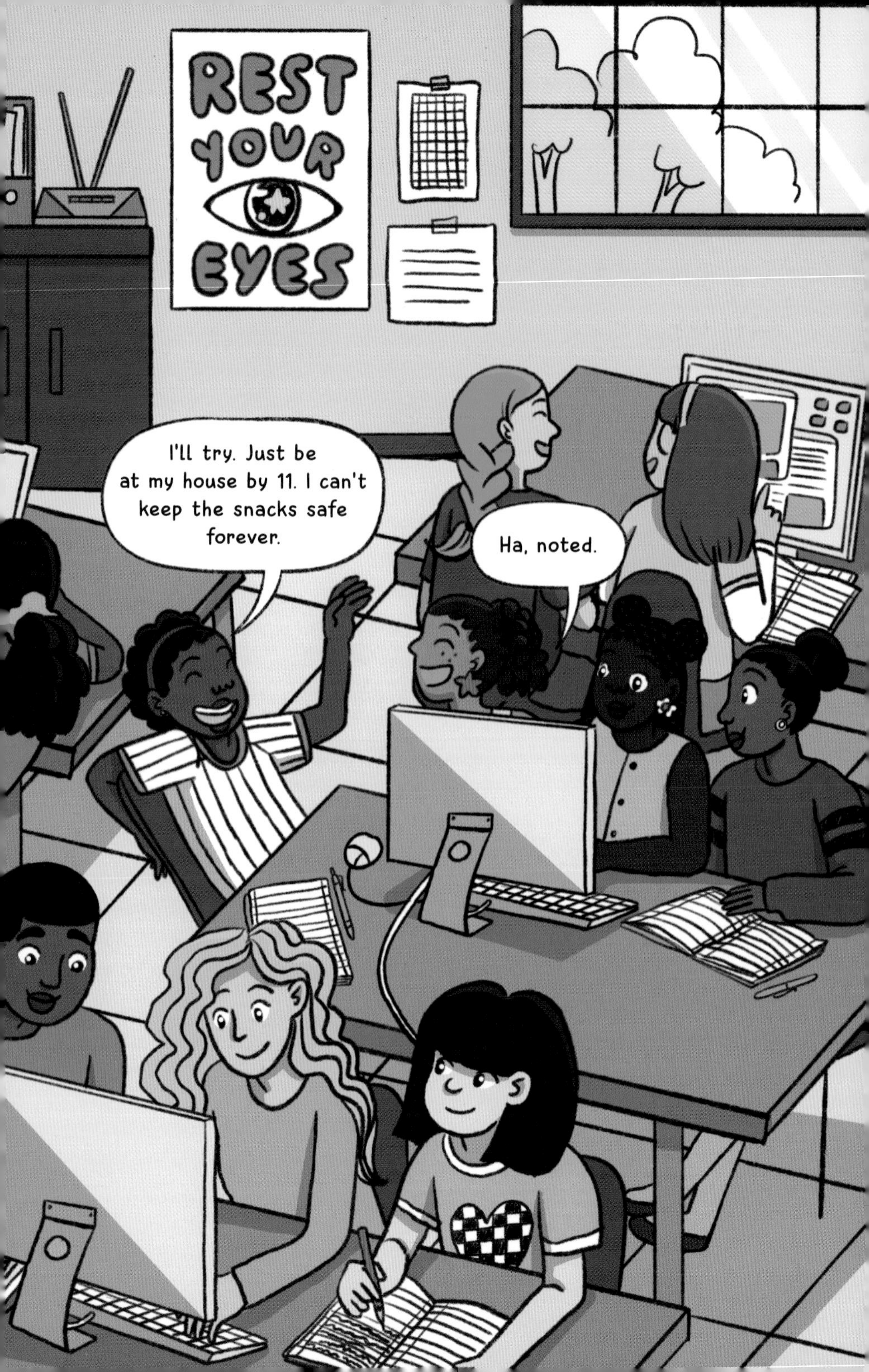
REST YOUR EYES
I'll try. Just be at my house by 11. I can't keep the snacks safe forever.
Ha, noted.

CHAPTER 8

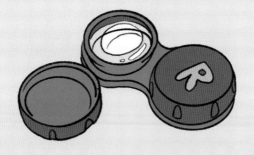

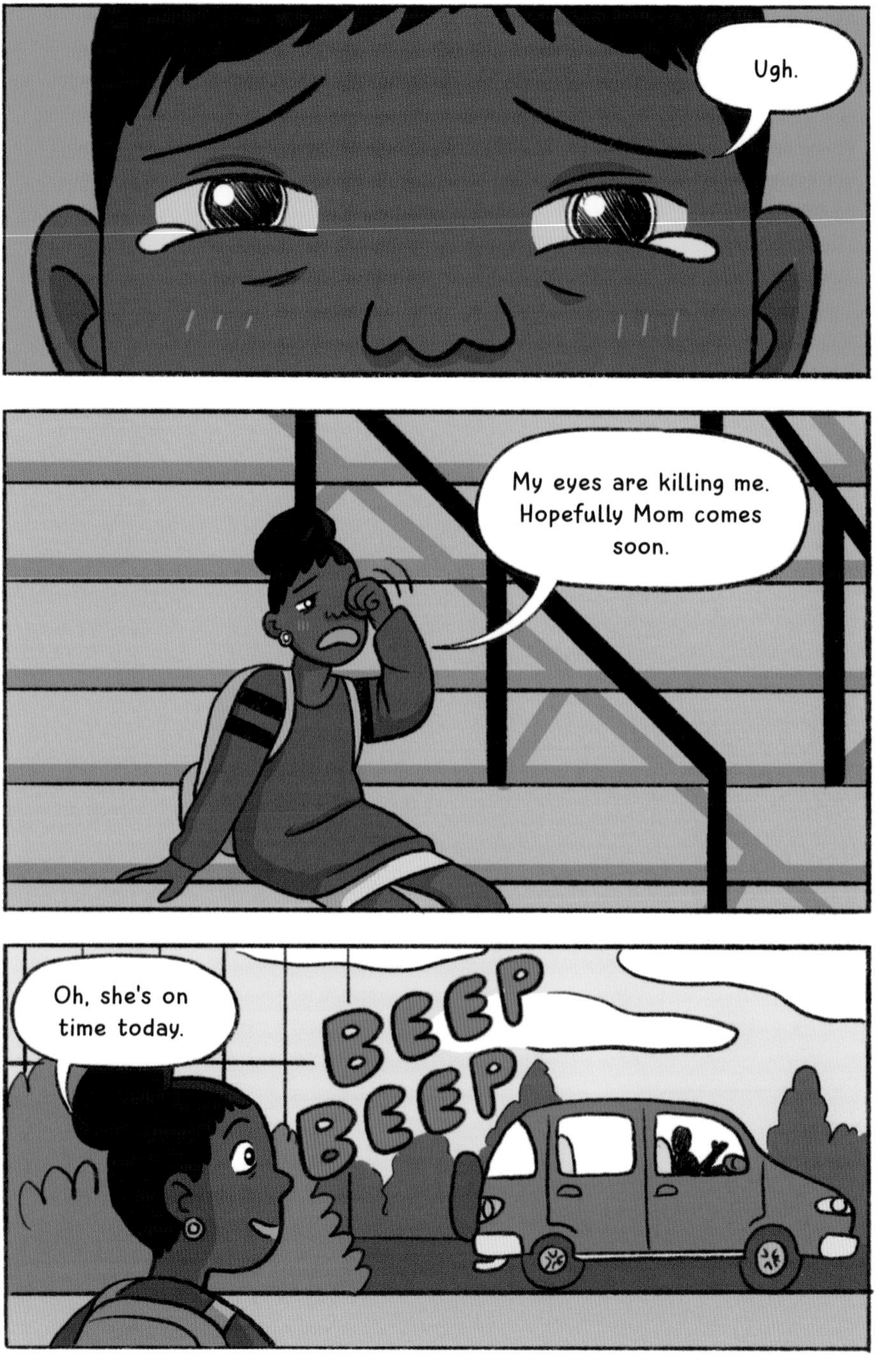
Ugh.
My eyes are killing me. Hopefully Mom comes soon.
Oh, she's on time today.
BEEP BEEP

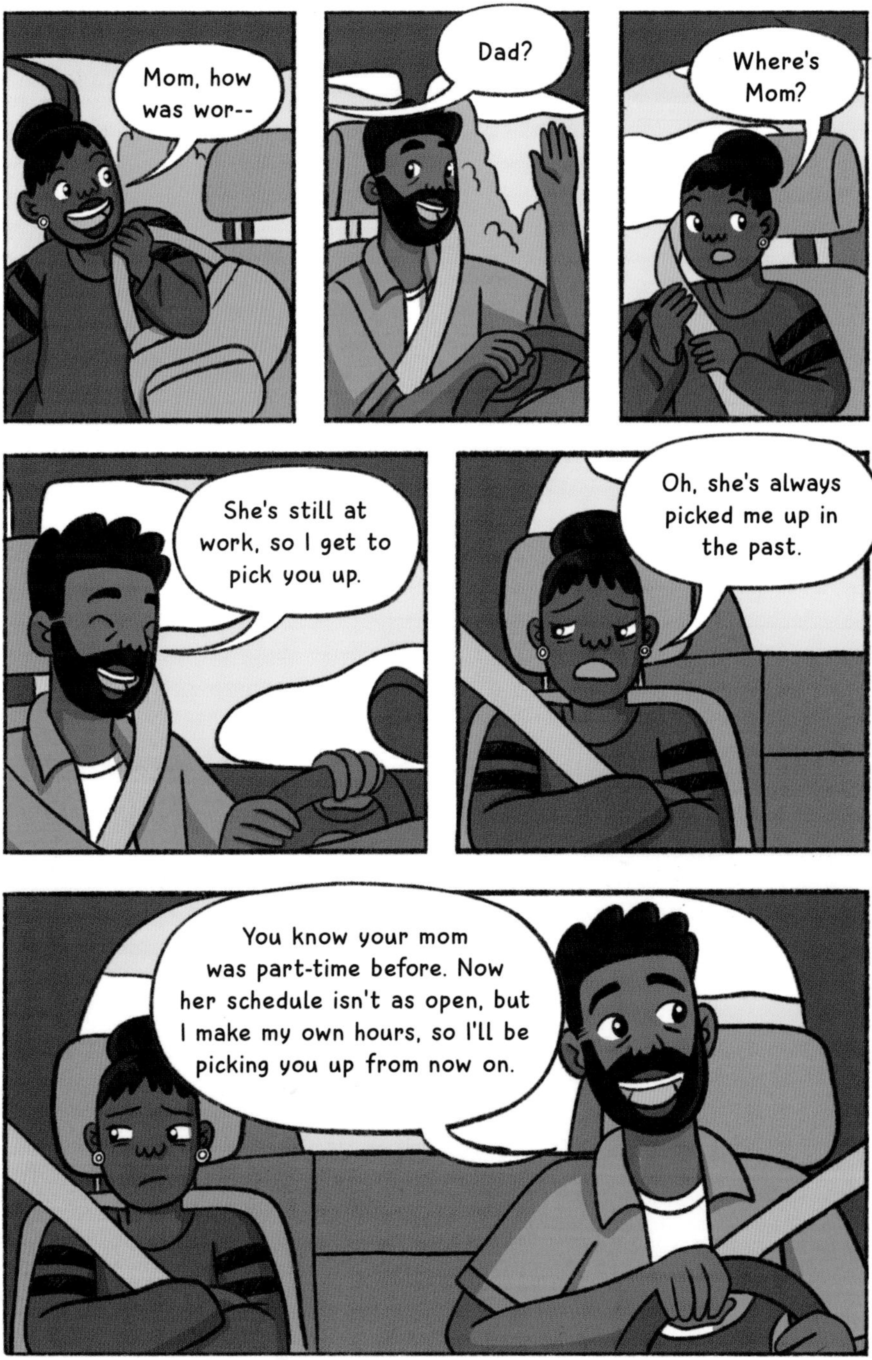
Mom, how was wor--
Dad?
Where's Mom?
She's still at work, so I get to pick you up.
Oh, she's always picked me up in the past.
You know your mom was part-time before. Now her schedule isn't as open, but I make my own hours, so I'll be picking you up from now on.

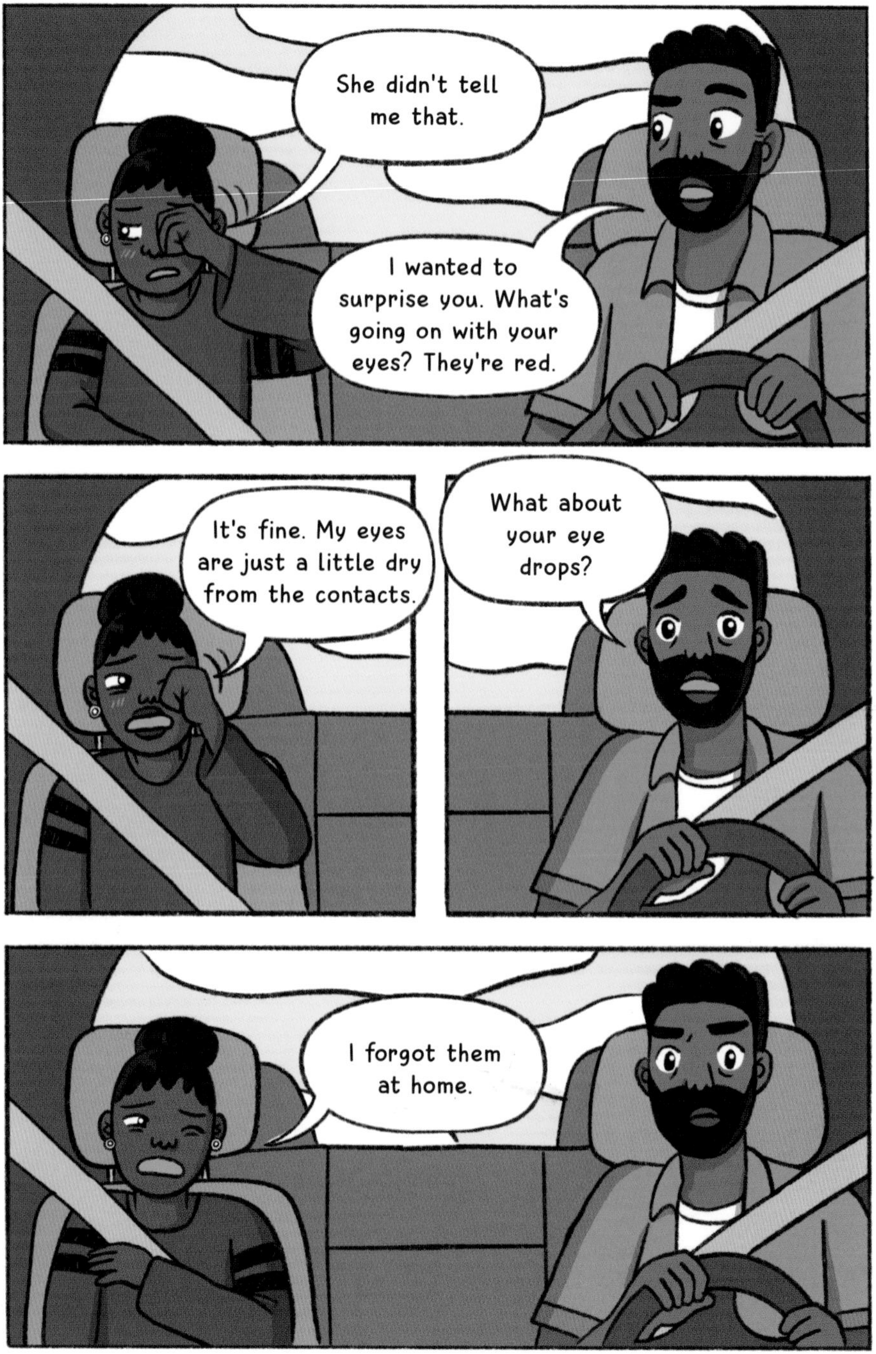
She didn't tell me that.
I wanted to surprise you. What's going on with your eyes? They're red.
It's fine. My eyes are just a little dry from the contacts.
What about your eye drops?
I forgot them at home.

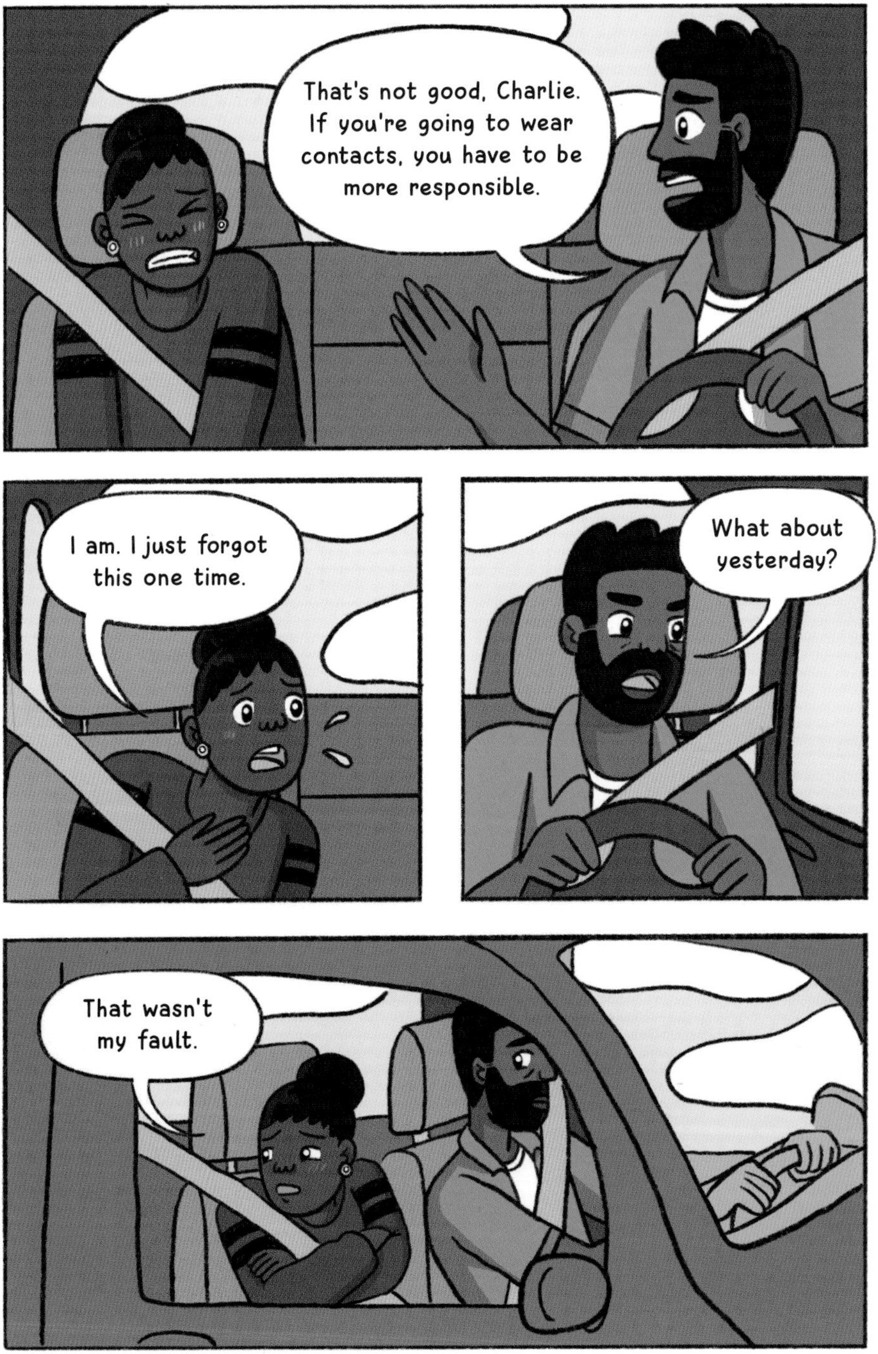
That's not good, Charlie. If you're going to wear contacts, you have to be more responsible.
I am. I just forgot this one time.
What about yesterday?
That wasn't my fault.

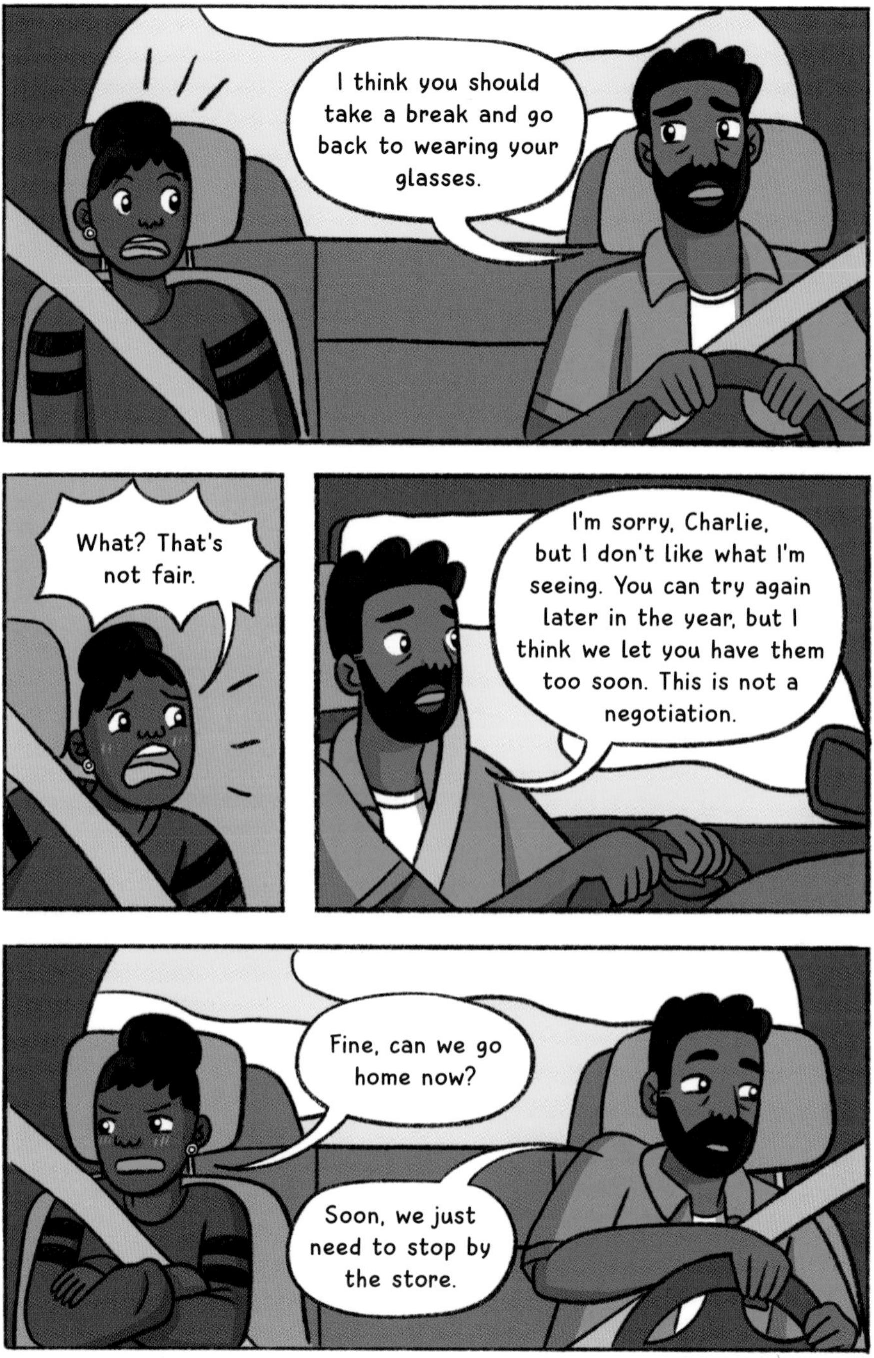
I think you should take a break and go back to wearing your glasses.
What? That's not fair.
I'm sorry, Charlie, but I don't like what I'm seeing. You can try again later in the year, but I think we let you have them too soon. This is not a negotiation.
Fine, can we go home now?
Soon, we just need to stop by the store.

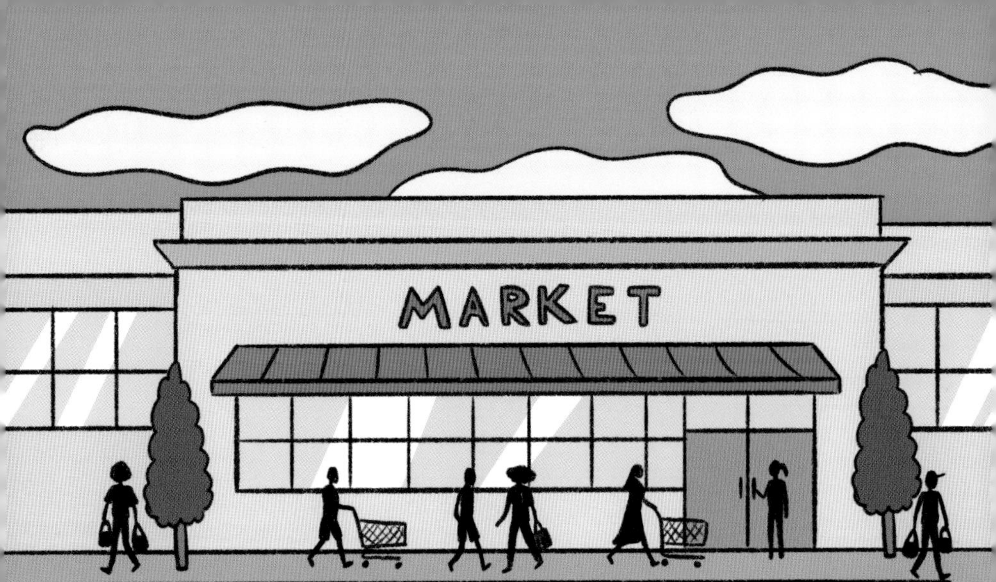
MARKET

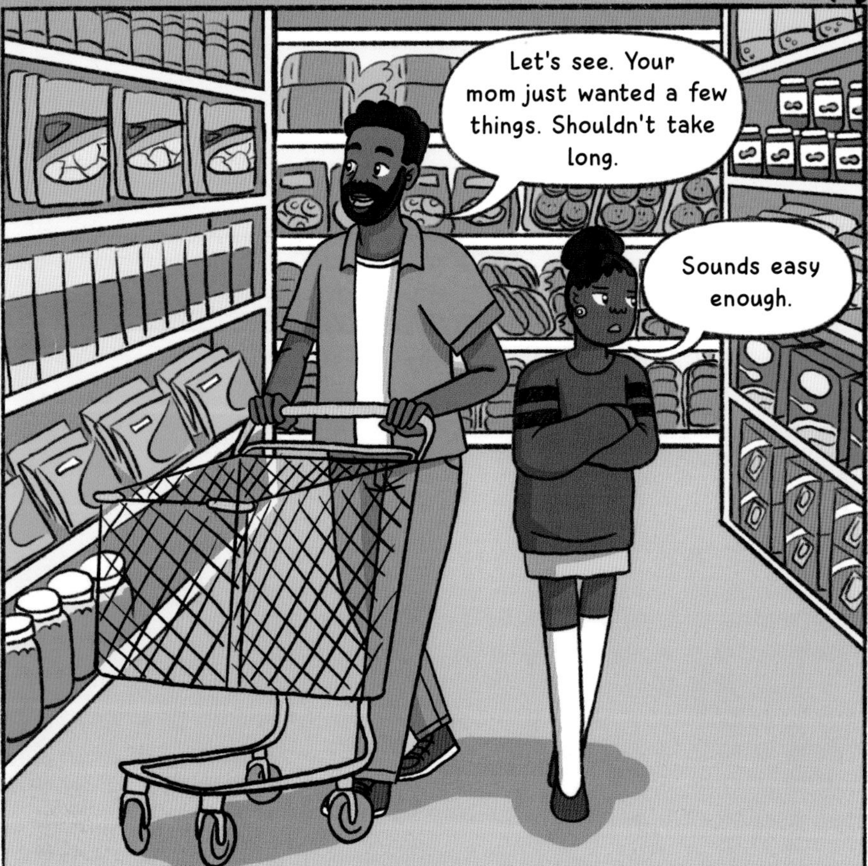
Let's see. Your mom just wanted a few things. Shouldn't take long.
Sounds easy enough.

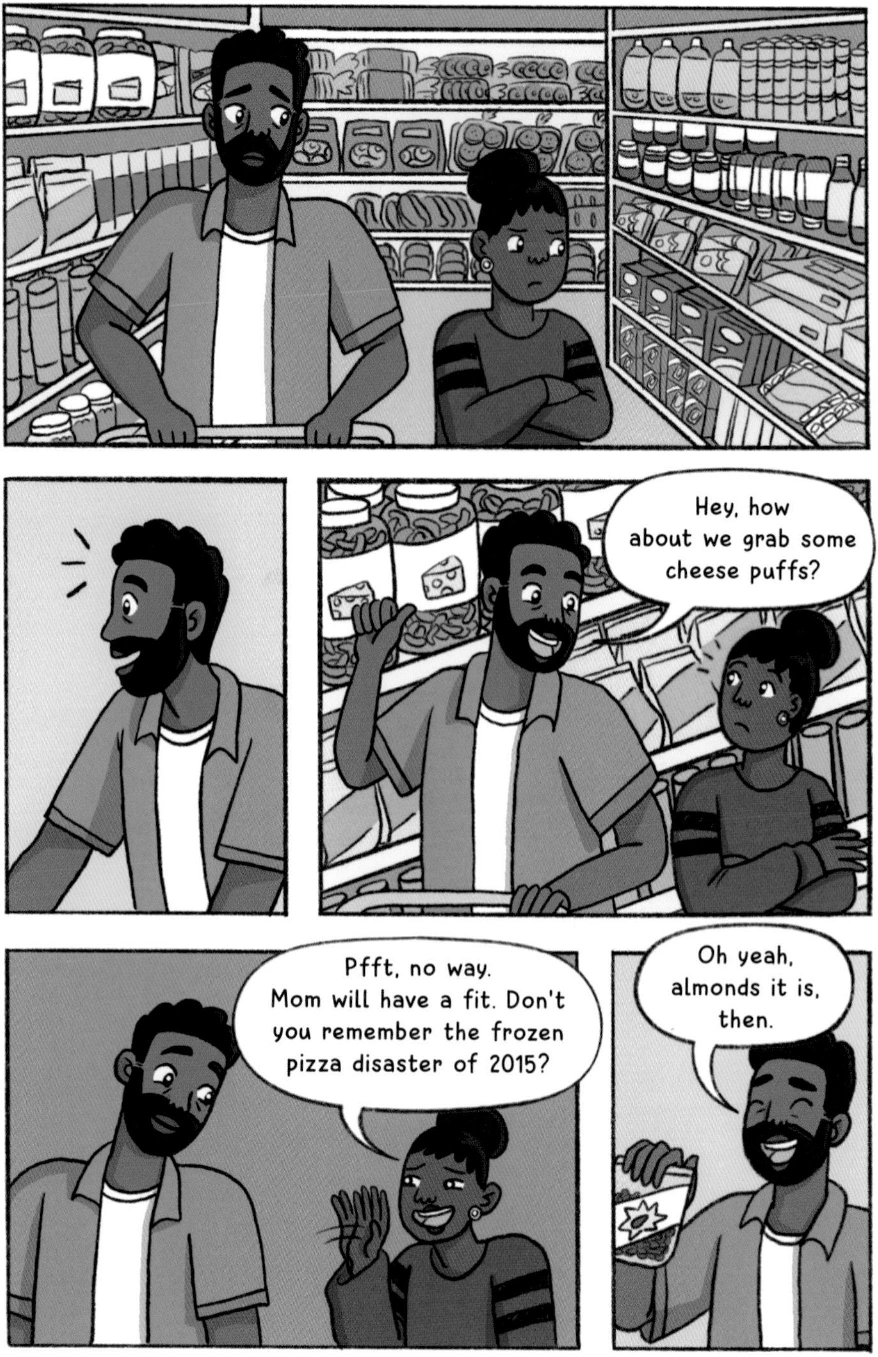
Hey, how about we grab some cheese puffs?
Pfft, no way. Mom will have a fit. Don't you remember the frozen pizza disaster of 2015?
Oh yeah, almonds it is, then.

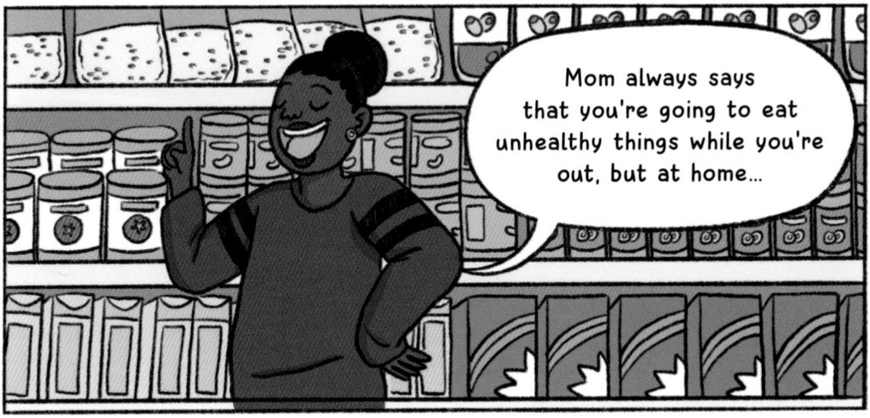
Mom always says that you're going to eat unhealthy things while you're out, but at home...

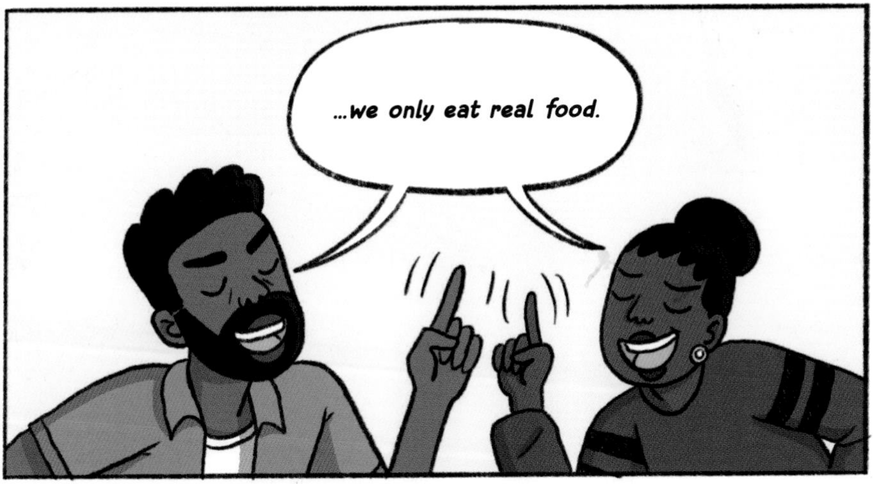
...we only eat real food.

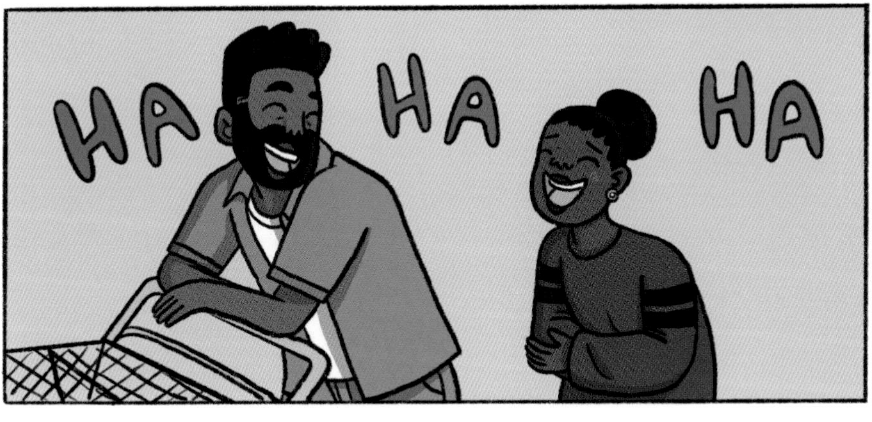
HA HA HA

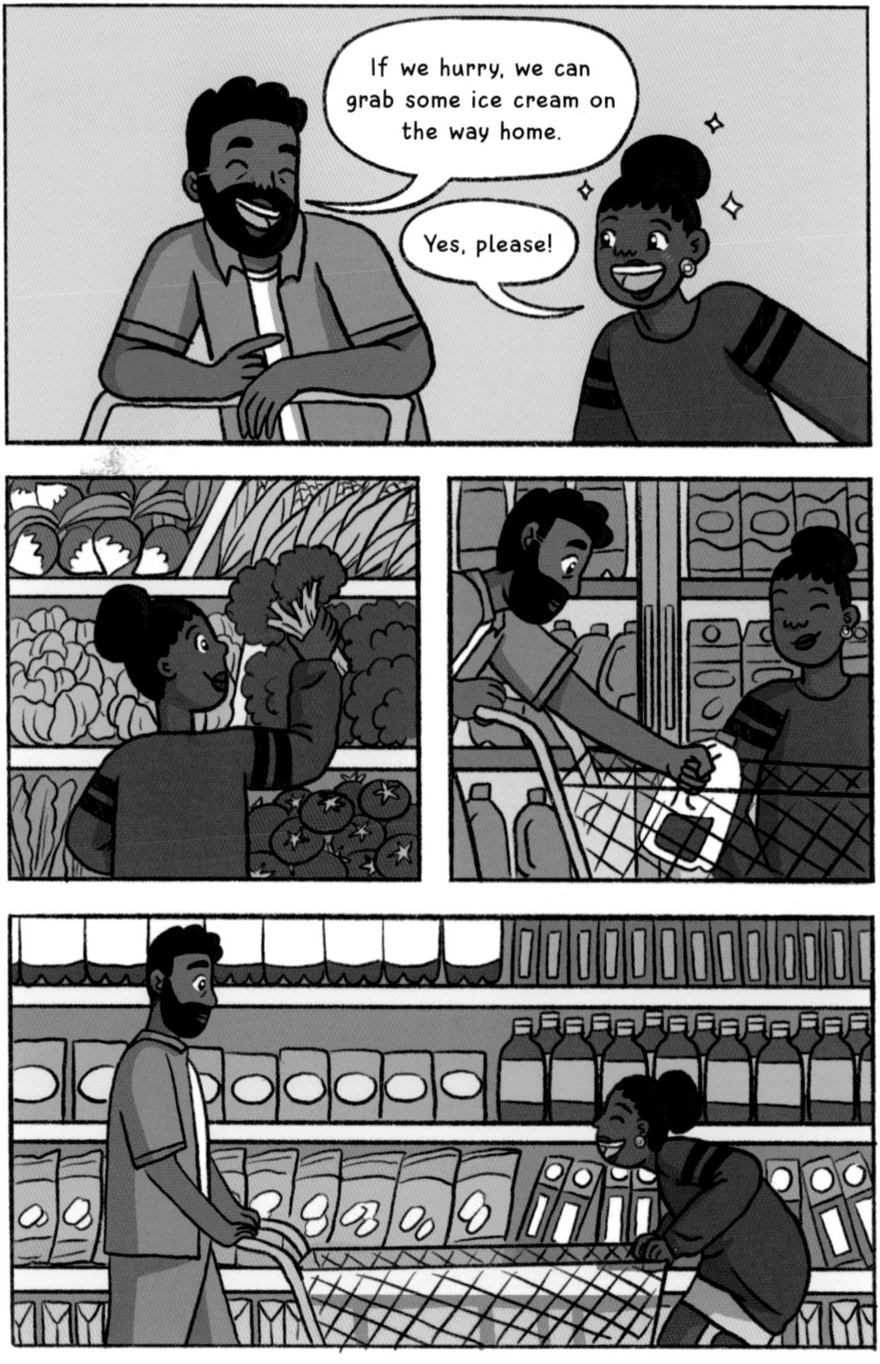
If we hurry, we can grab some ice cream on the way home.
Yes, please!

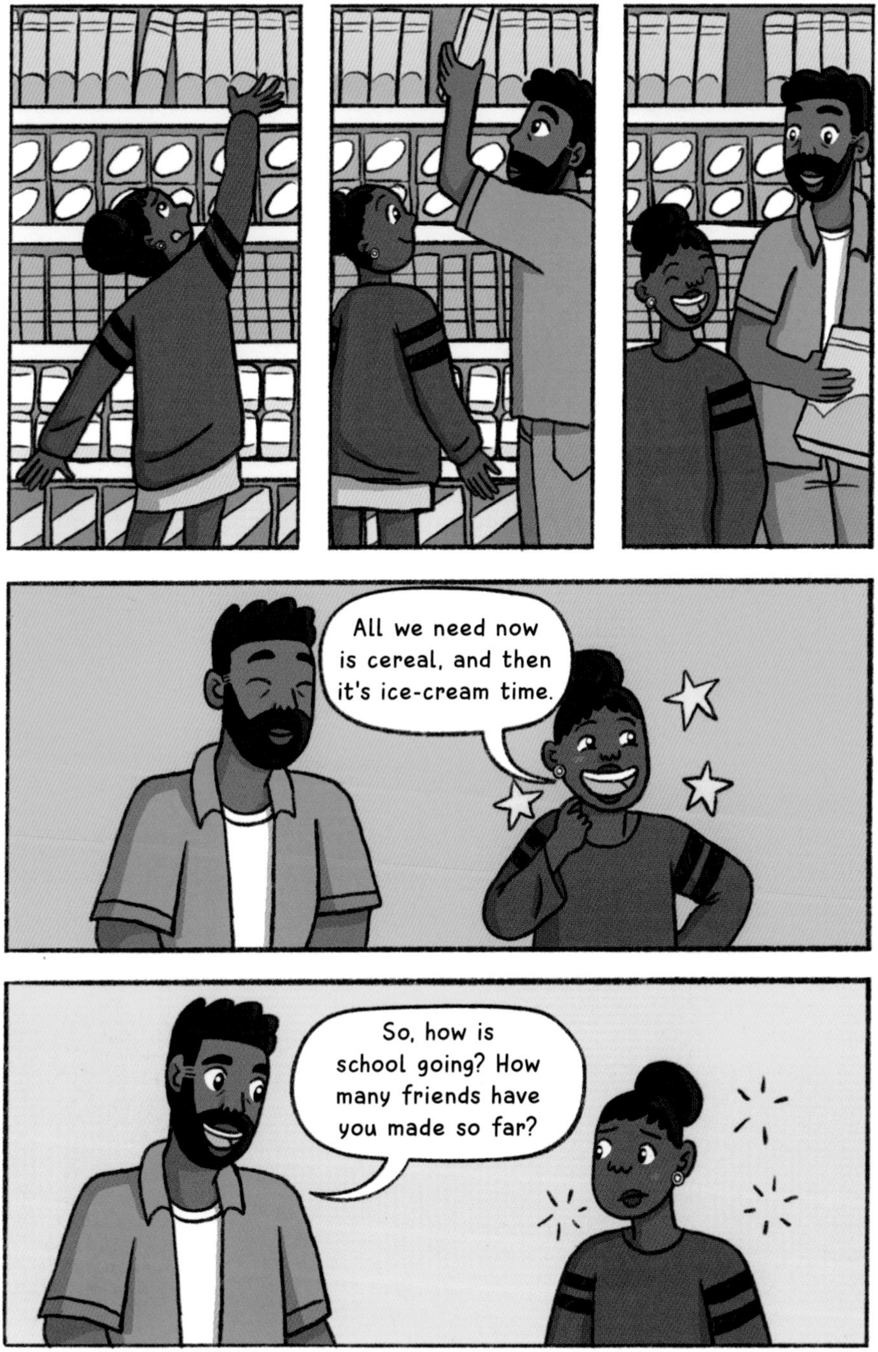
All we need now is cereal, and then it's ice-cream time.
So, how is school going? How many friends have you made so far?

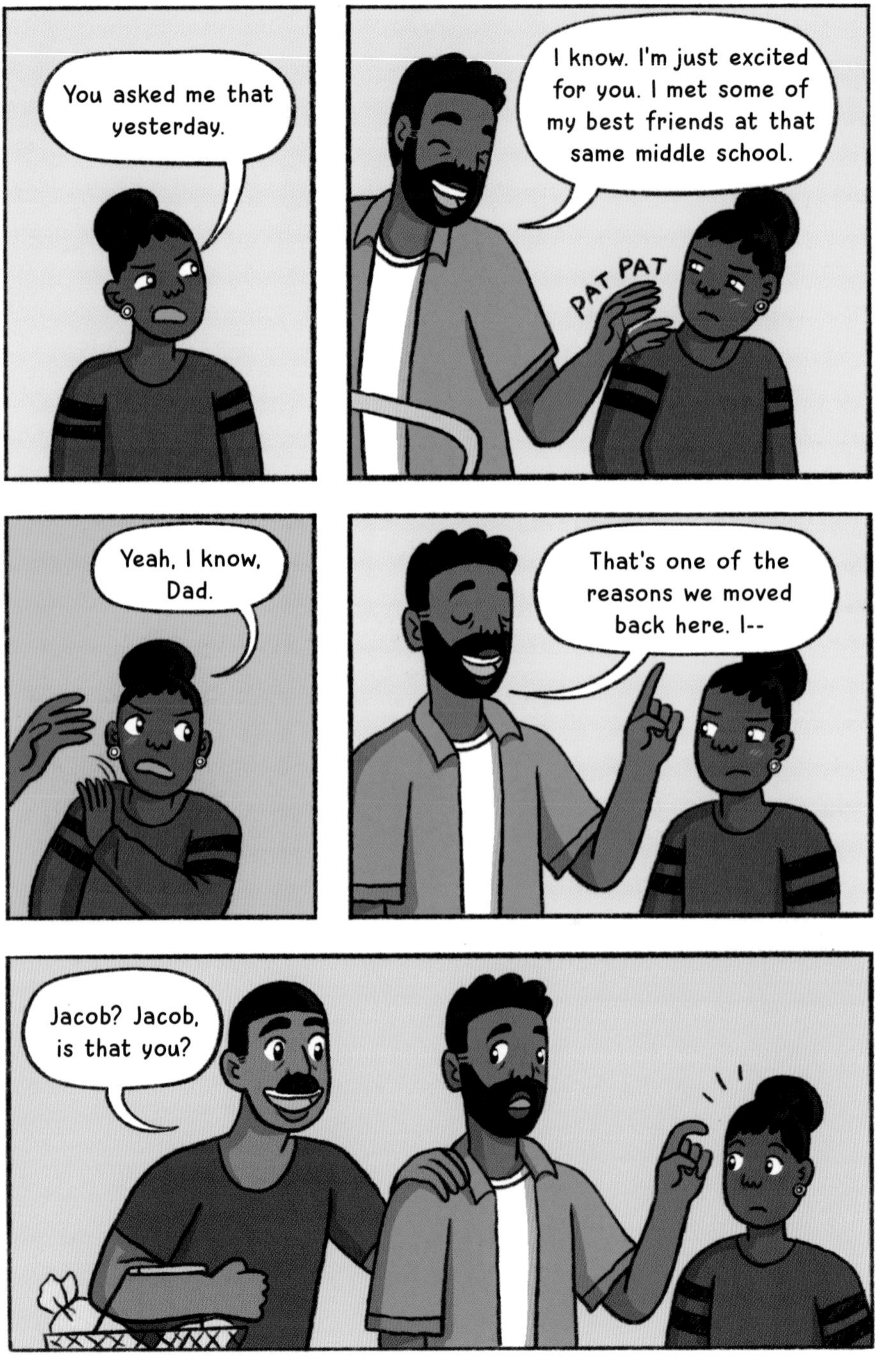
You asked me that yesterday.
I know. I'm just excited for you. I met some of my best friends at that same middle school.
PAT PAT
Yeah, I know, Dad.
That's one of the reasons we moved back here. I--
Jacob? Jacob, is that you?

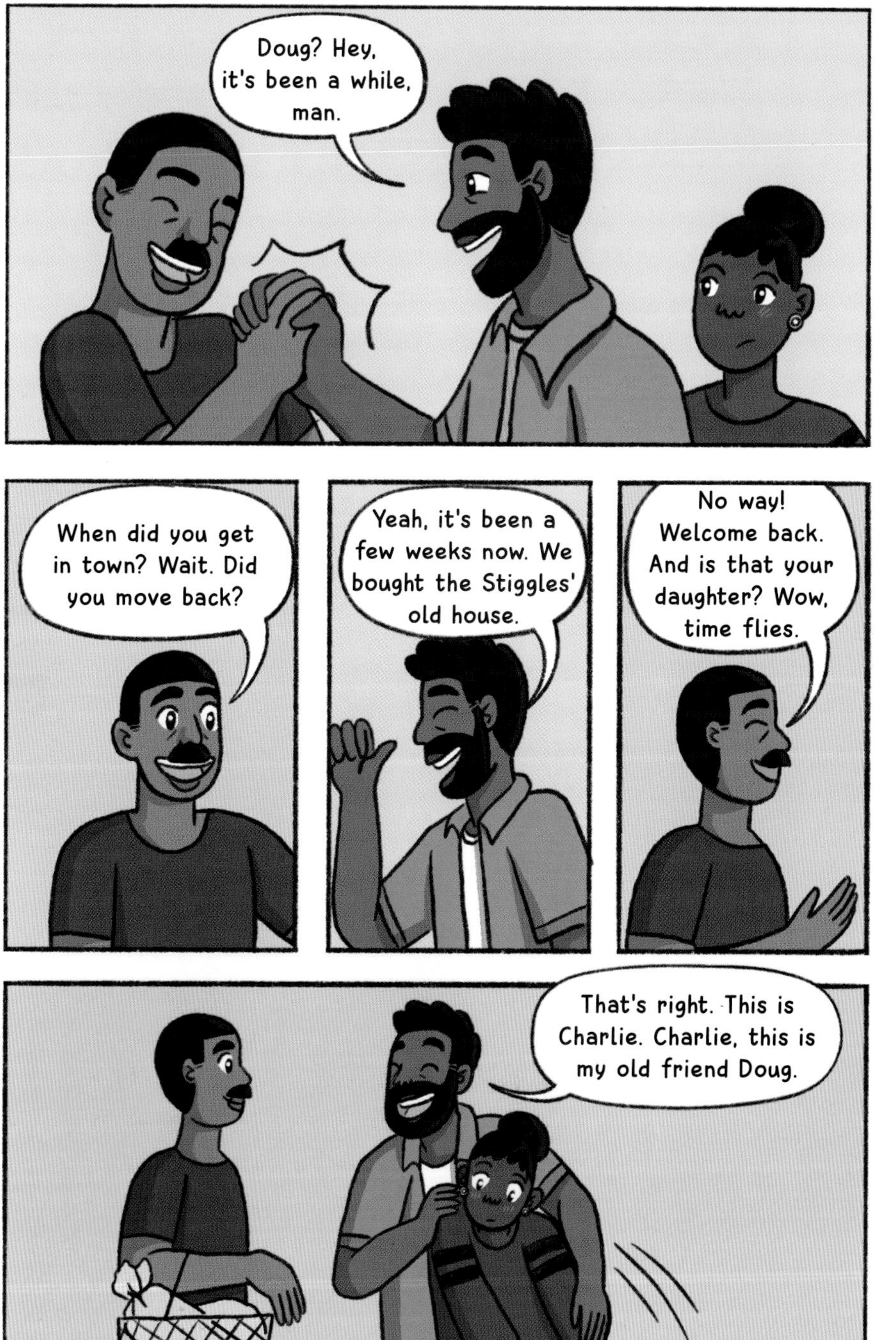
Doug? Hey, it's been a while, man.
When did you get in town? Wait. Did you move back?
Yeah, it's been a few weeks now. We bought the Stiggles' old house.
No way! Welcome back. And is that your daughter? Wow, time flies.
That's right. This is Charlie. Charlie, this is my old friend Doug.

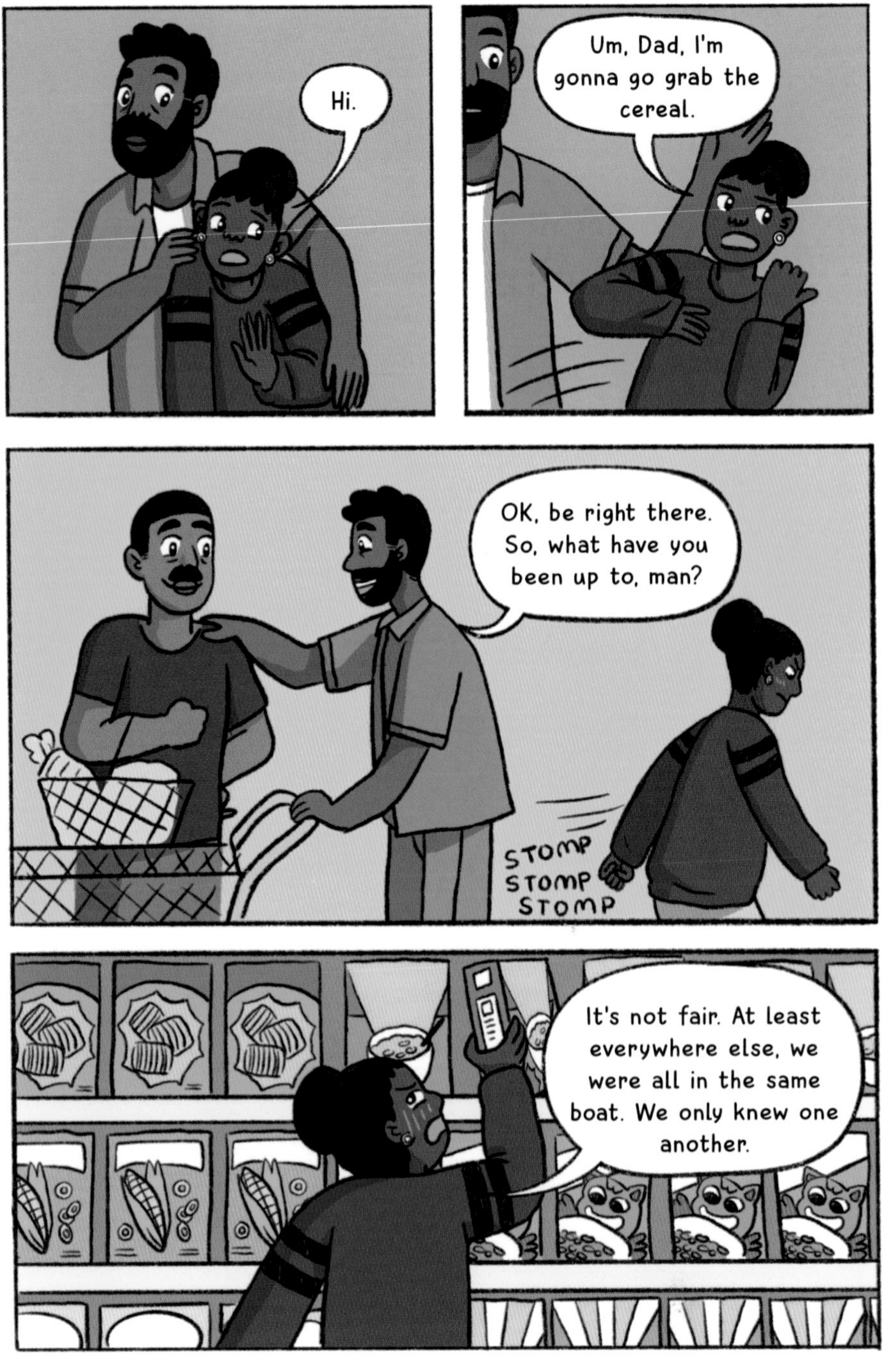

Hi.
Um, Dad, I'm gonna go grab the cereal.
OK, be right there. So, what have you been up to, man?
STOMP STOMP STOMP
It's not fair. At least everywhere else, we were all in the same boat. We only knew one another.

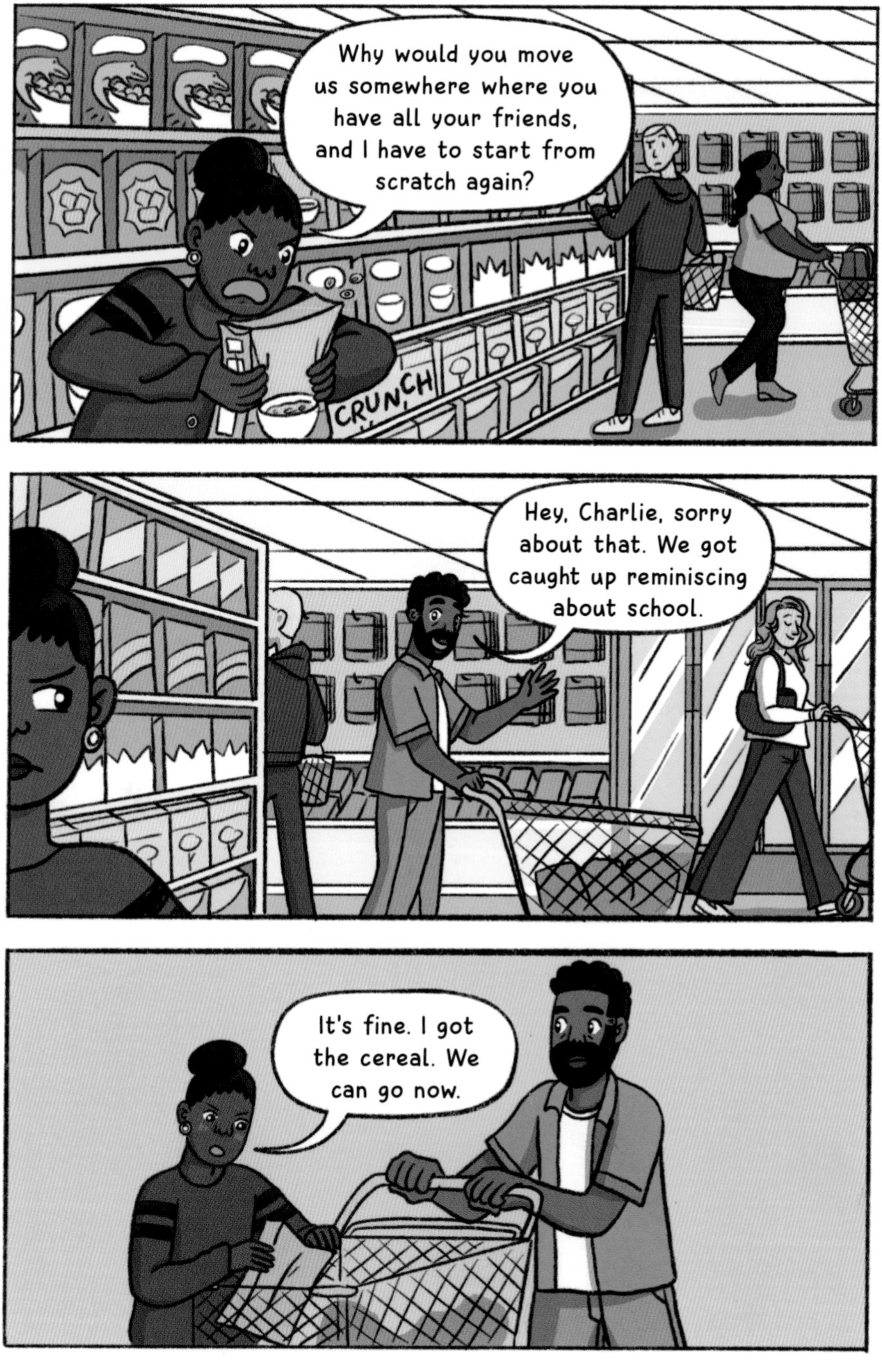
Why would you move us somewhere where you have all your friends, and I have to start from scratch again?
CRUNCH
Hey, Charlie, sorry about that. We got caught up reminiscing about school.
It's fine. I got the cereal. We can go now.

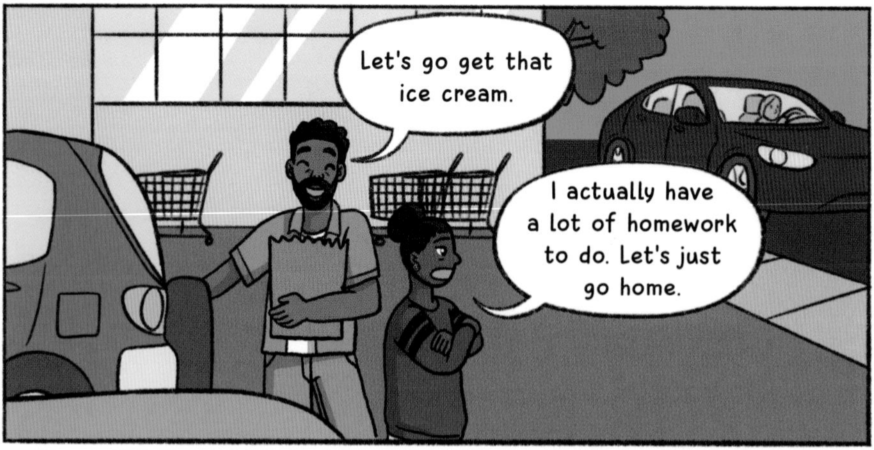
Let's go get that ice cream.
I actually have a lot of homework to do. Let's just go home.
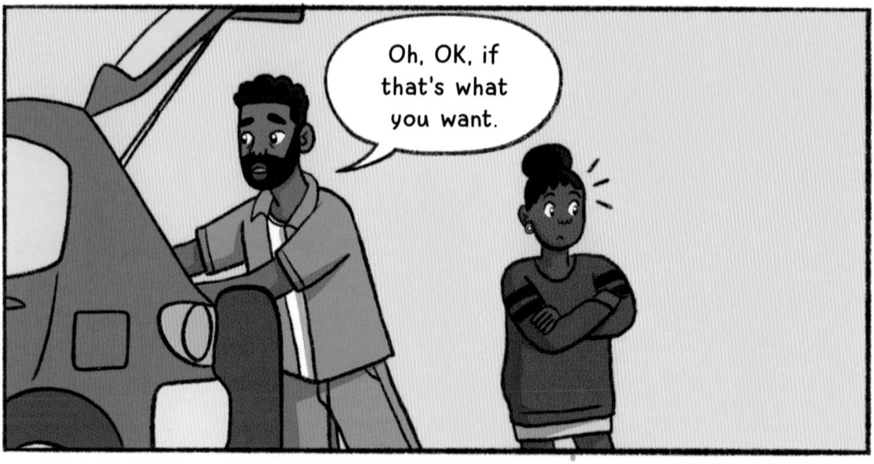
Oh, OK, if that's what you want.
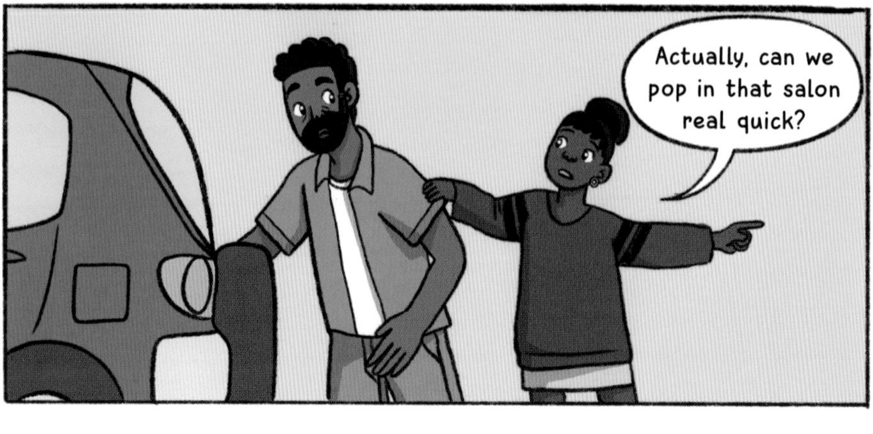
Actually, can we pop in that salon real quick?

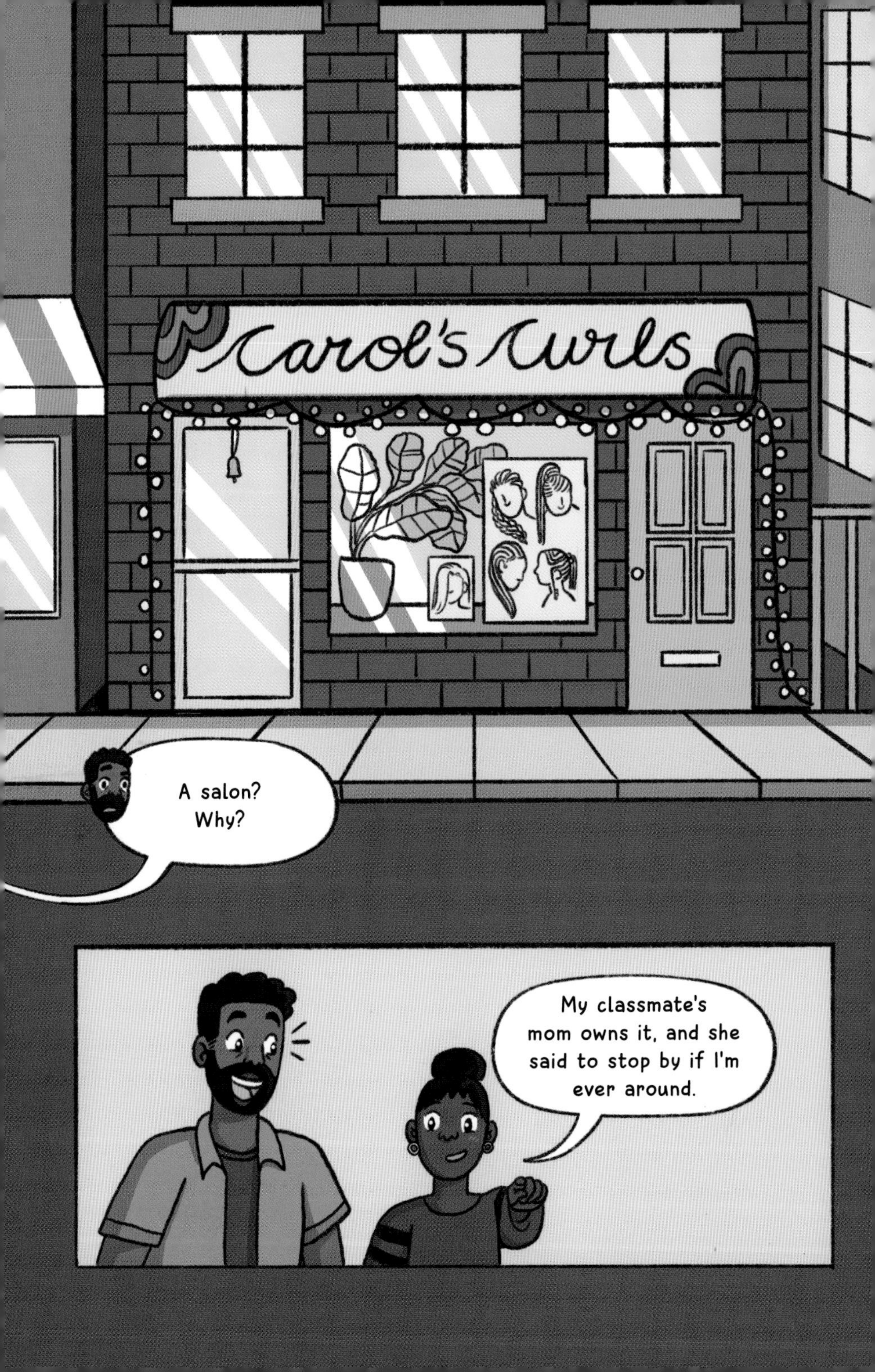
Carol's Curls
A salon? Why?
My classmate's mom owns it, and she said to stop by if I'm ever around.

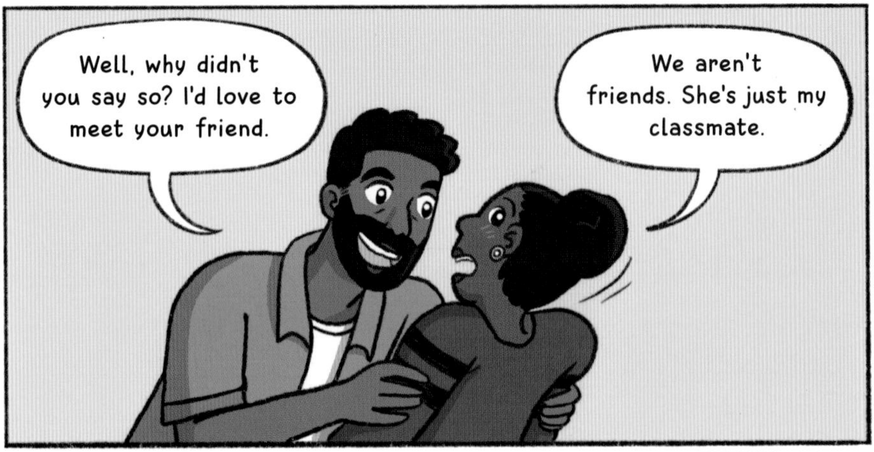
Well, why didn't you say so? I'd love to meet your friend.
We aren't friends. She's just my classmate.
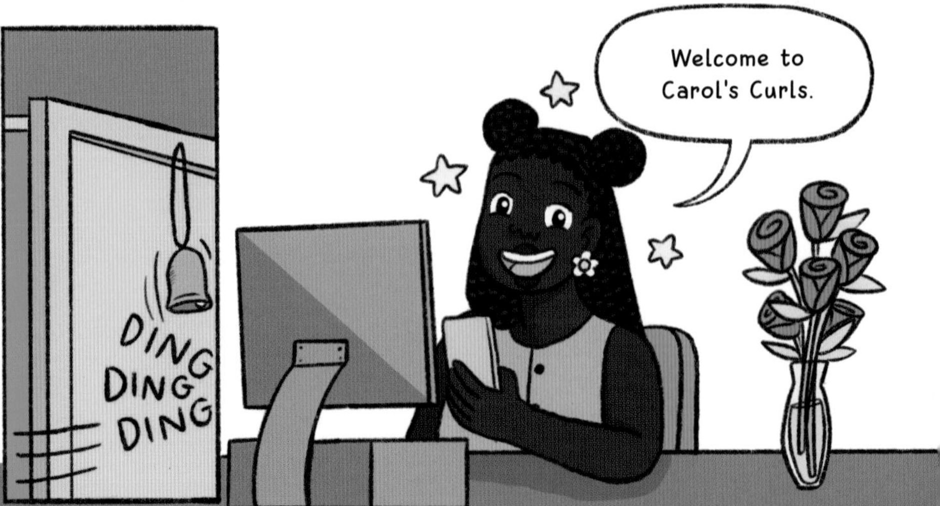
DING DING DING
Welcome to Carol's Curls.
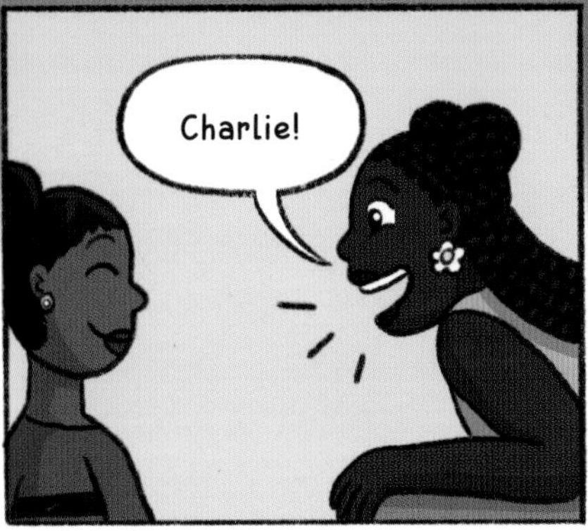
Charlie!
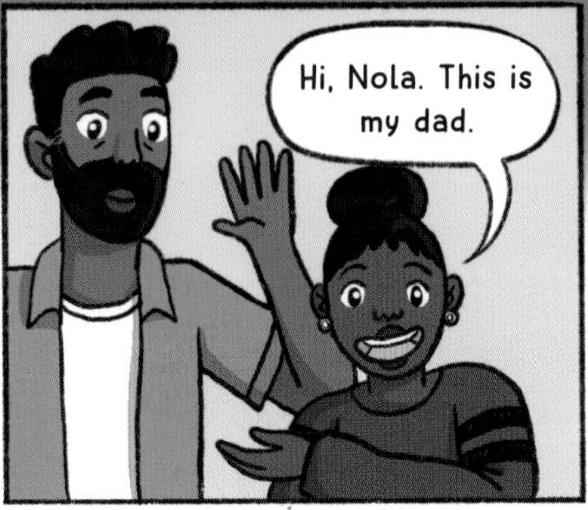
Hi, Nola. This is my dad.

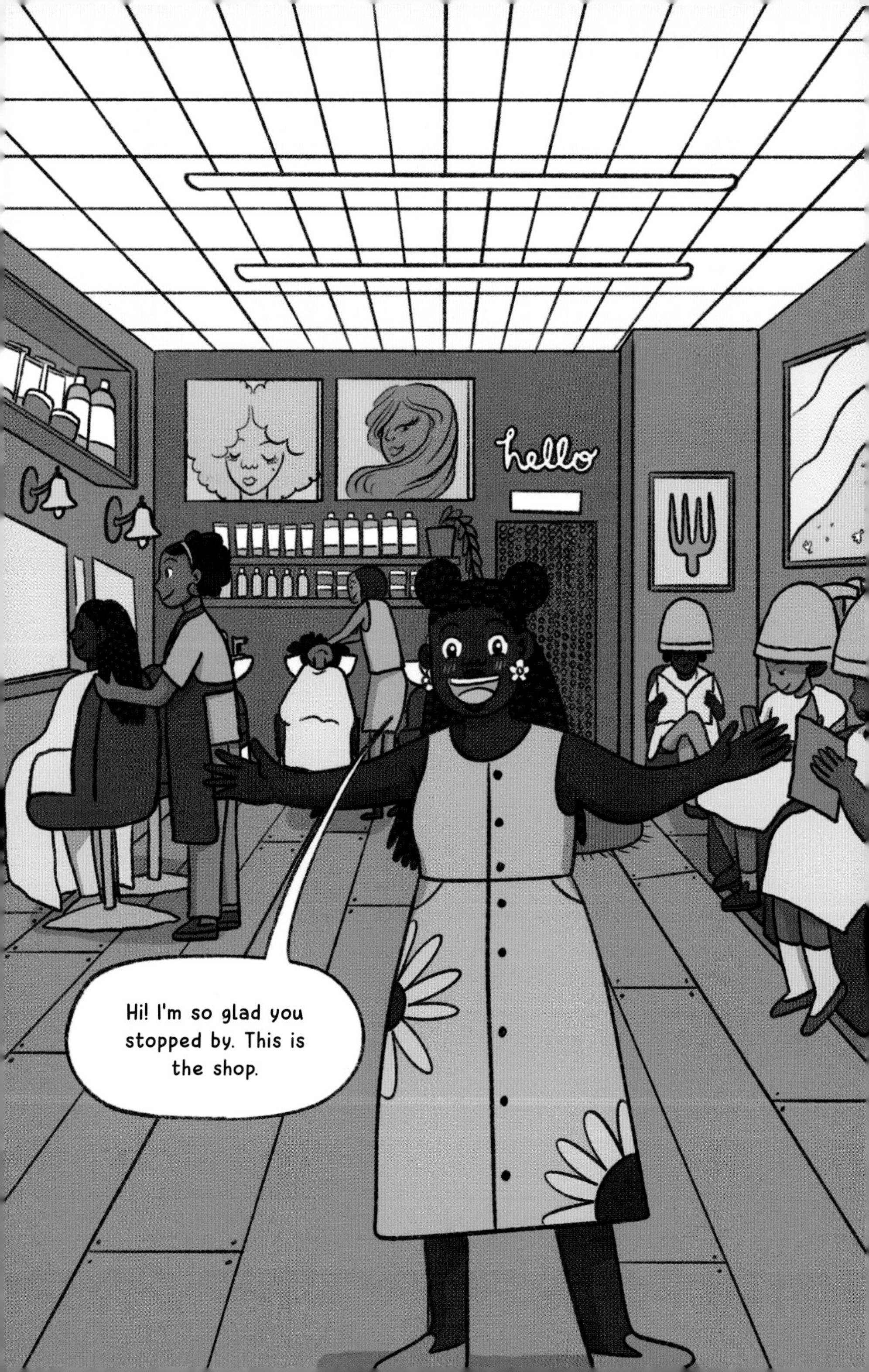
hello
Hi! I'm so glad you stopped by. This is the shop.

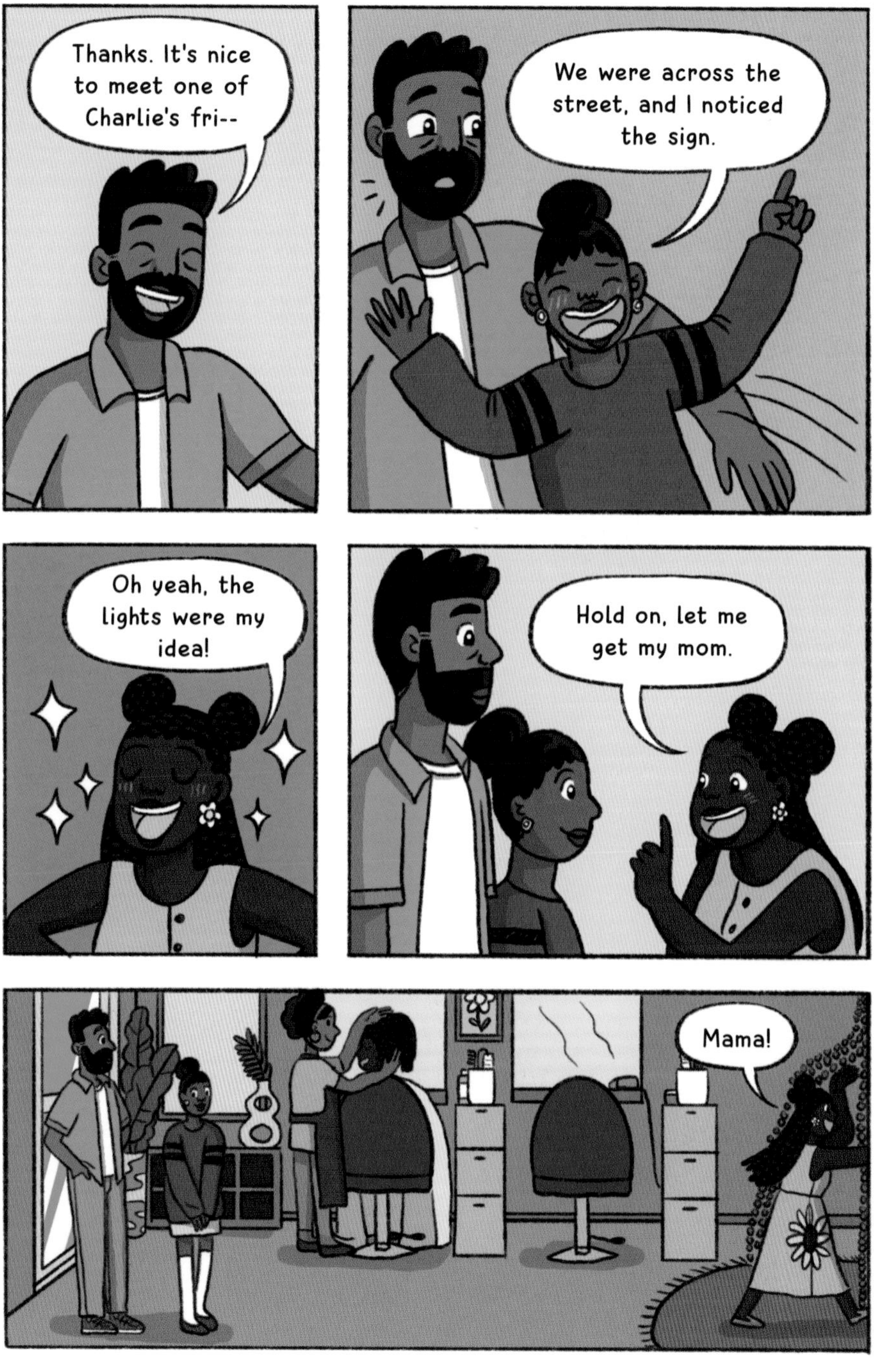

Thanks. It's nice to meet one of Charlie's fri--
We were across the street, and I noticed the sign.
Oh yeah, the lights were my idea!
Hold on, let me get my mom.
Mama!

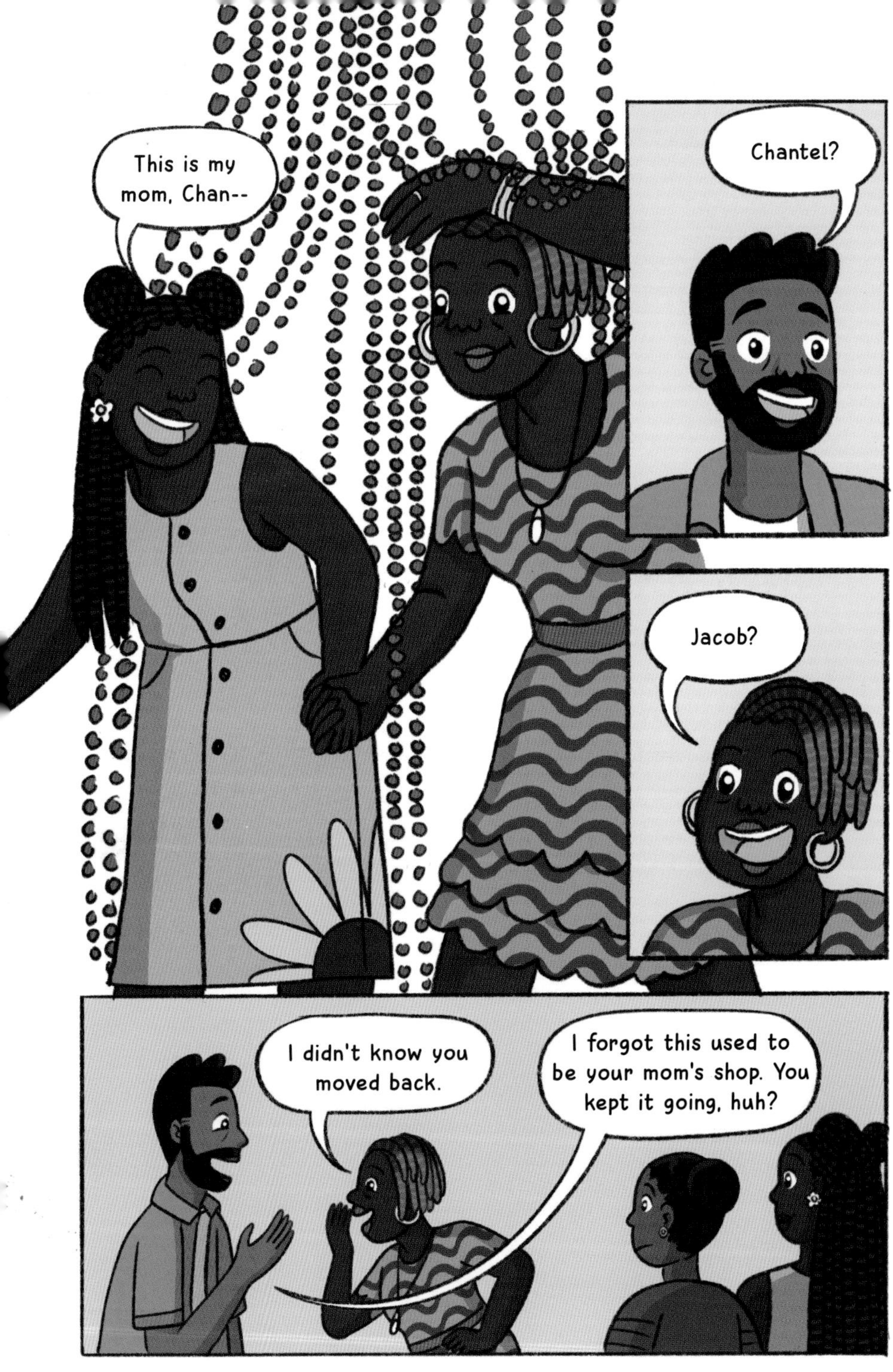
This is my mom, Chan--
Chantel?
Jacob?
I didn't know you moved back.
I forgot this used to be your mom's shop. You kept it going, huh?

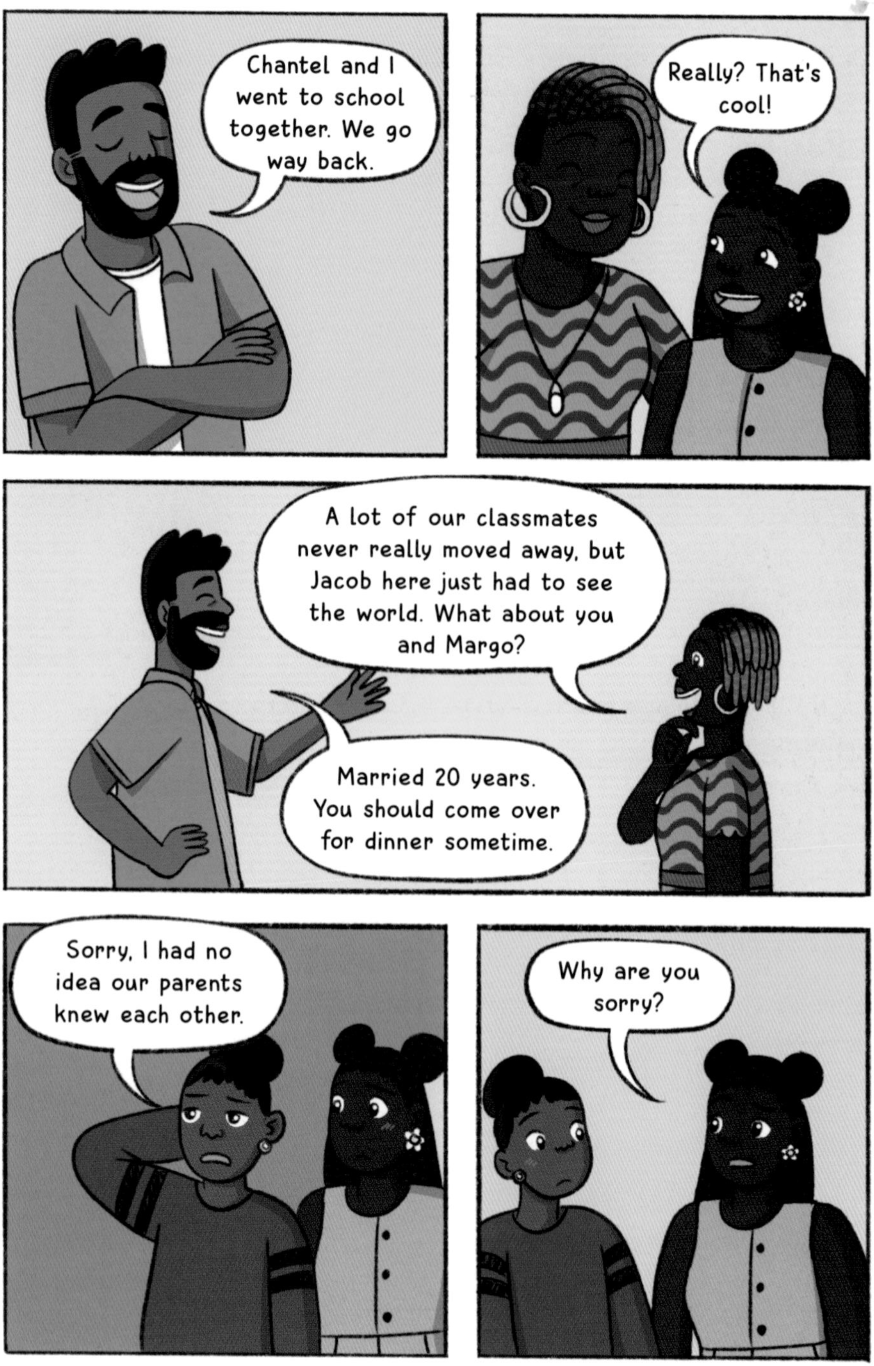
Chantel and I went to school together. We go way back.
Really? That's cool!
A lot of our classmates never really moved away, but Jacob here just had to see the world. What about you and Margo?
Married 20 years. You should come over for dinner sometime.
Sorry, I had no idea our parents knew each other.
Why are you sorry?

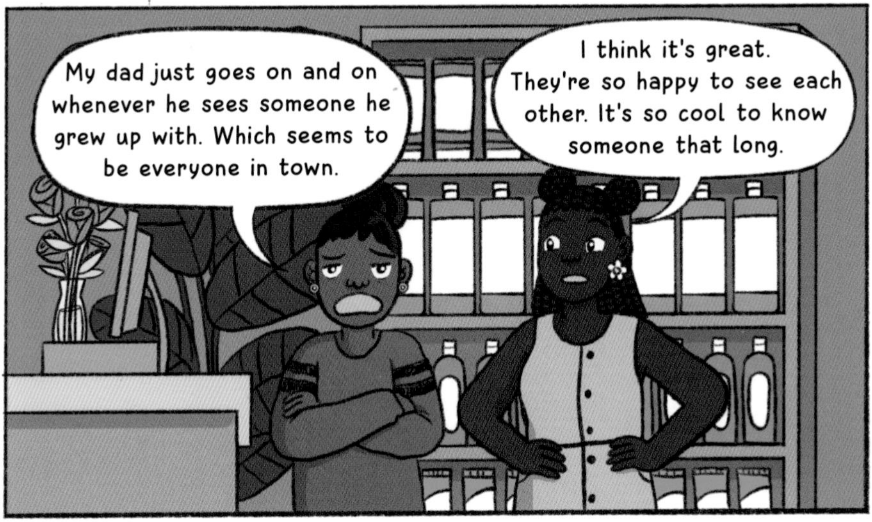
My dad just goes on and on whenever he sees someone he grew up with. Which seems to be everyone in town.
I think it's great. They're so happy to see each other. It's so cool to know someone that long.

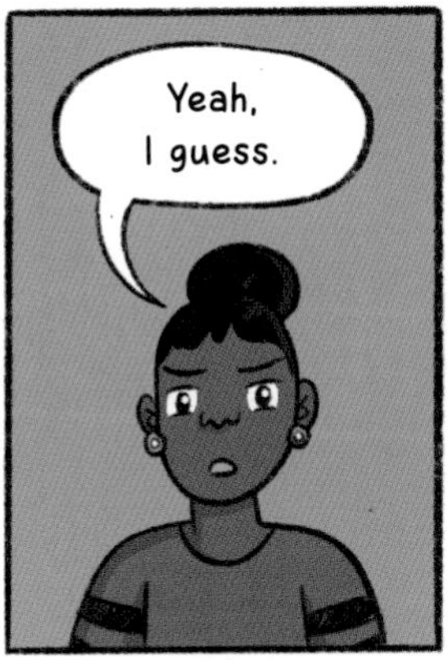
Yeah, I guess.

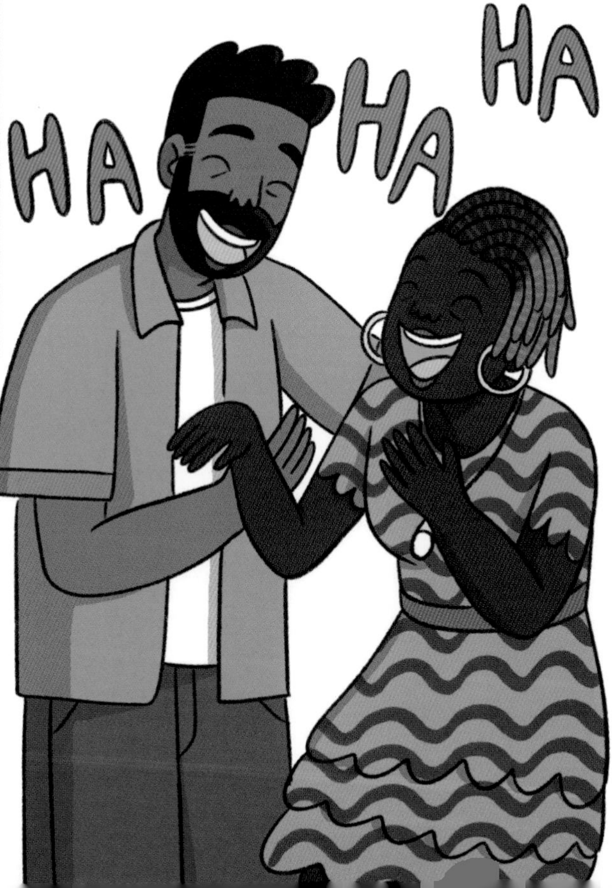
HA
HA
HA
HA

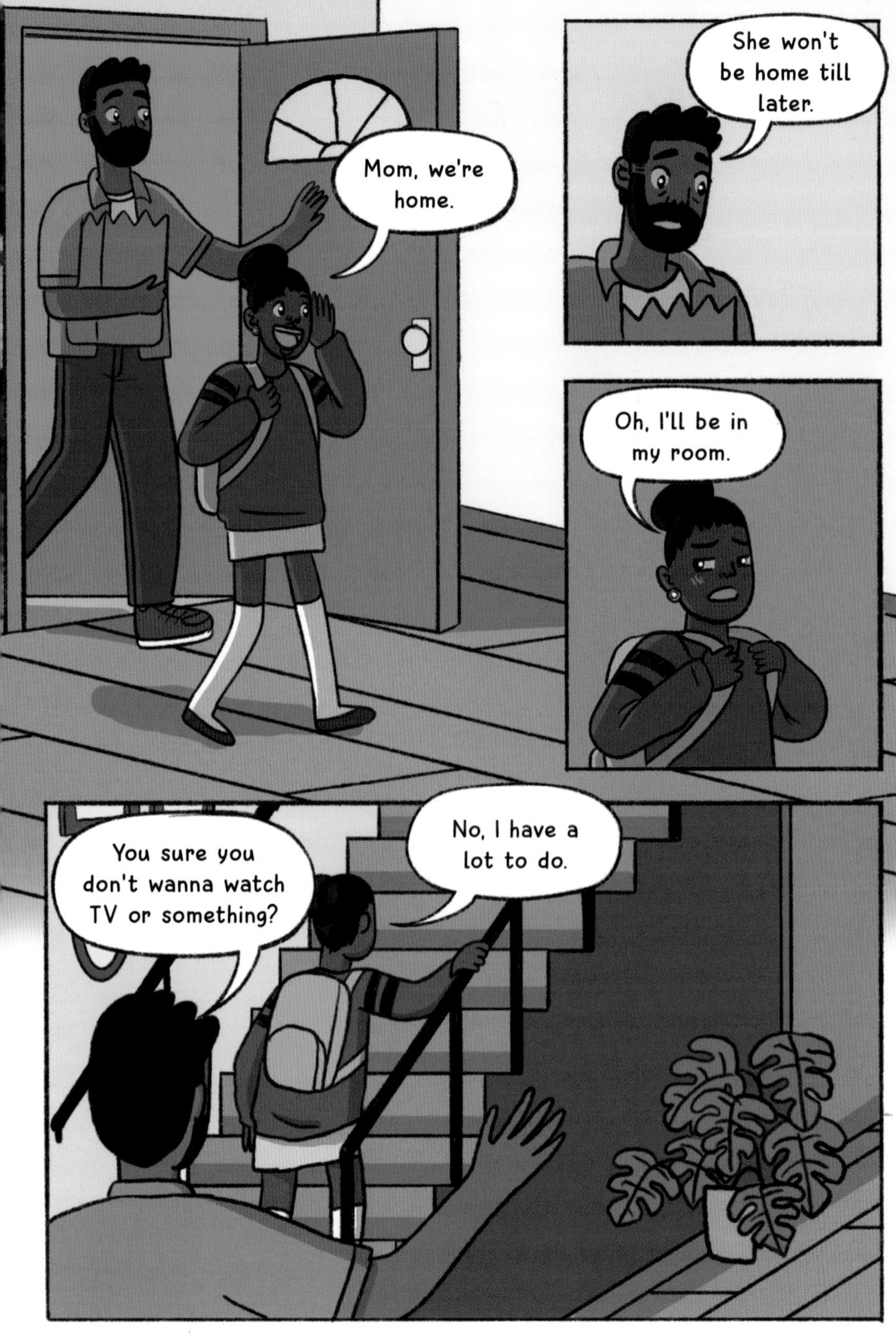
Mom, we're home.
She won't be home till later.
Oh, I'll be in my room.
You sure you don't wanna watch TV or something?
No, I have a lot to do.

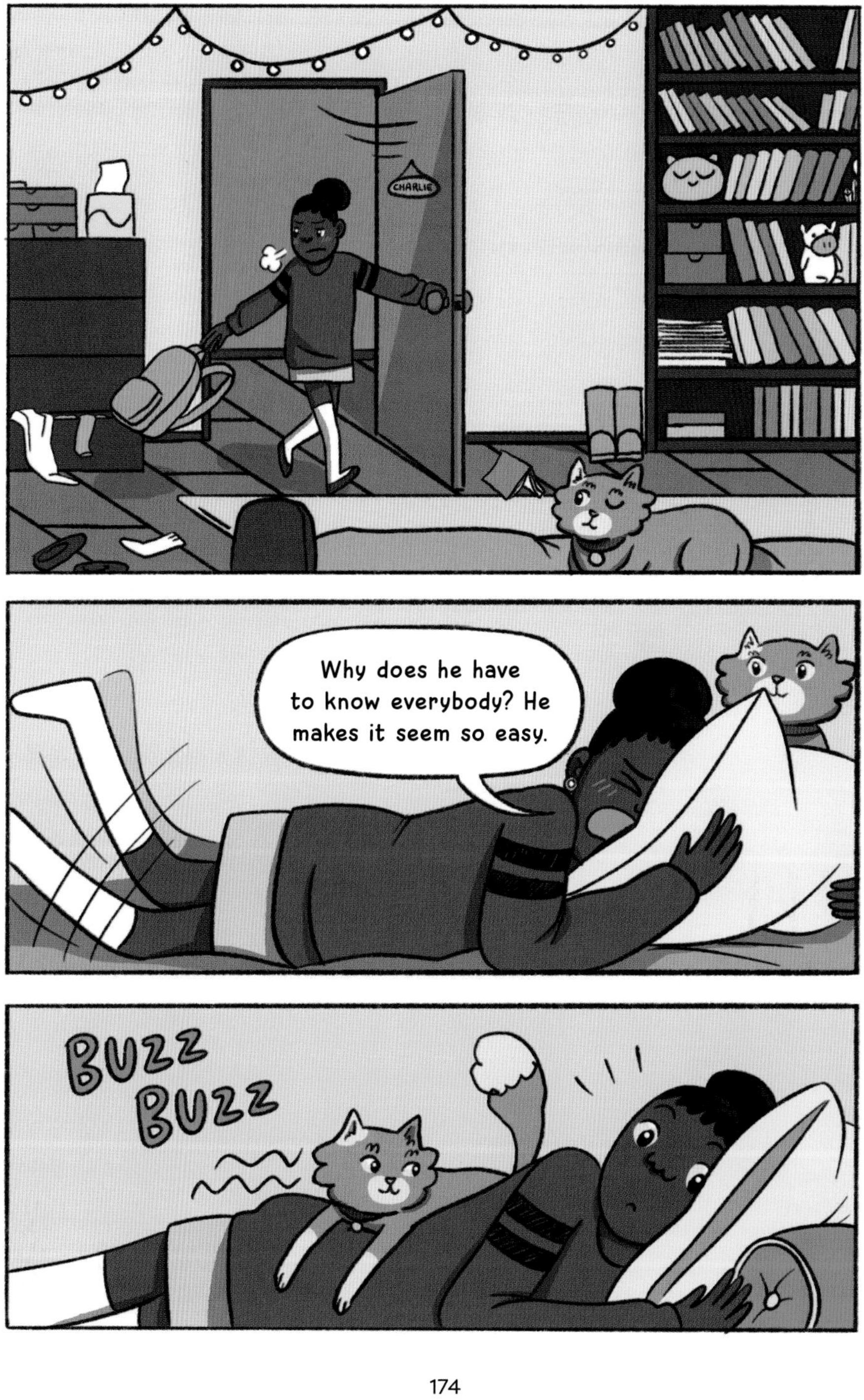
CHARLIE
Why does he have to know everybody? He makes it seem so easy.
BUZZ BUZZ

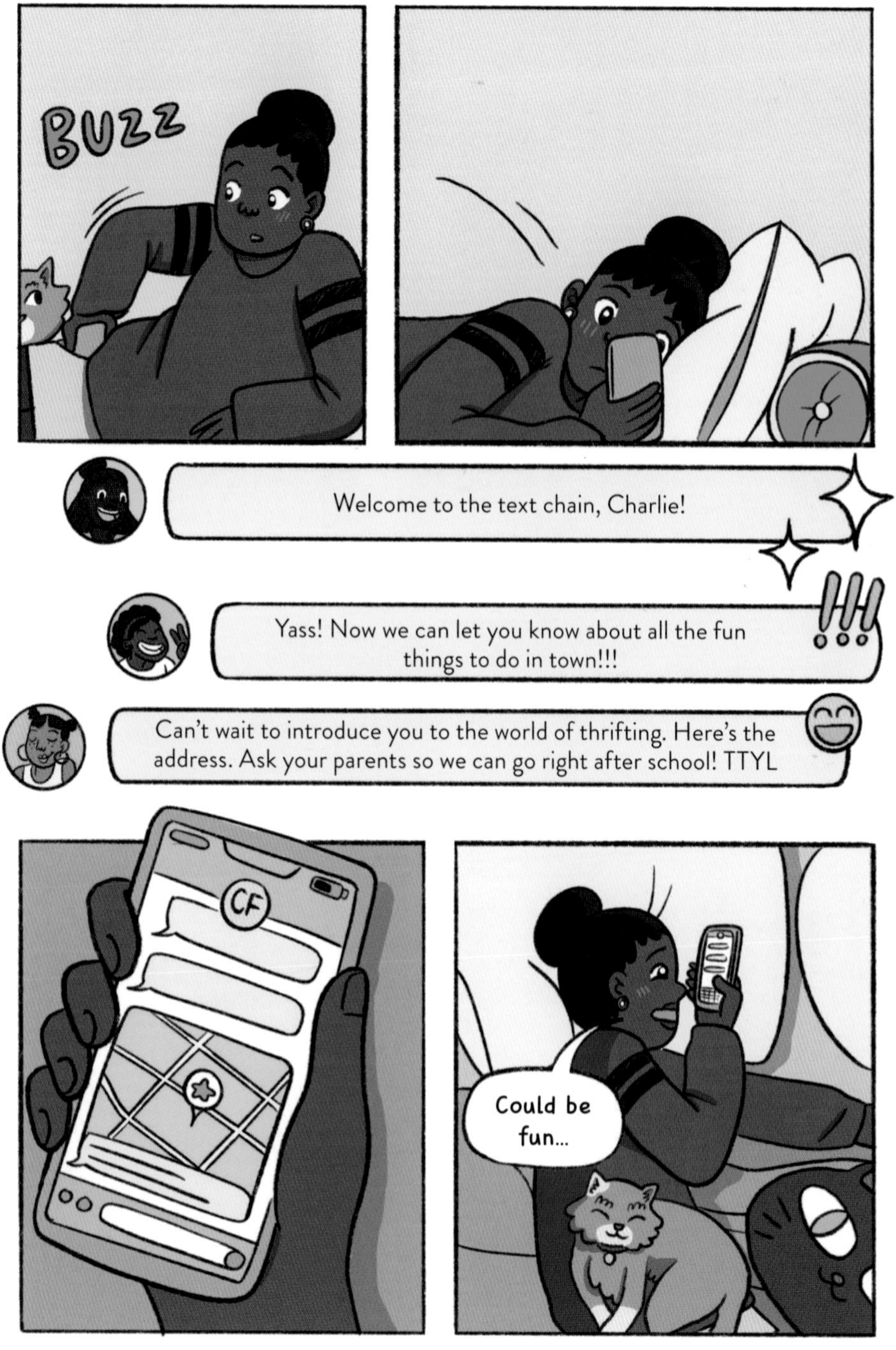
BUZZ
Welcome to the text chain, Charlie!
Yass! Now we can let you know about all the fun things to do in town!!!
Can't wait to introduce you to the world of thrifting. Here's the address. Ask your parents so we can go right after school! TTYL
CF
Could be fun...

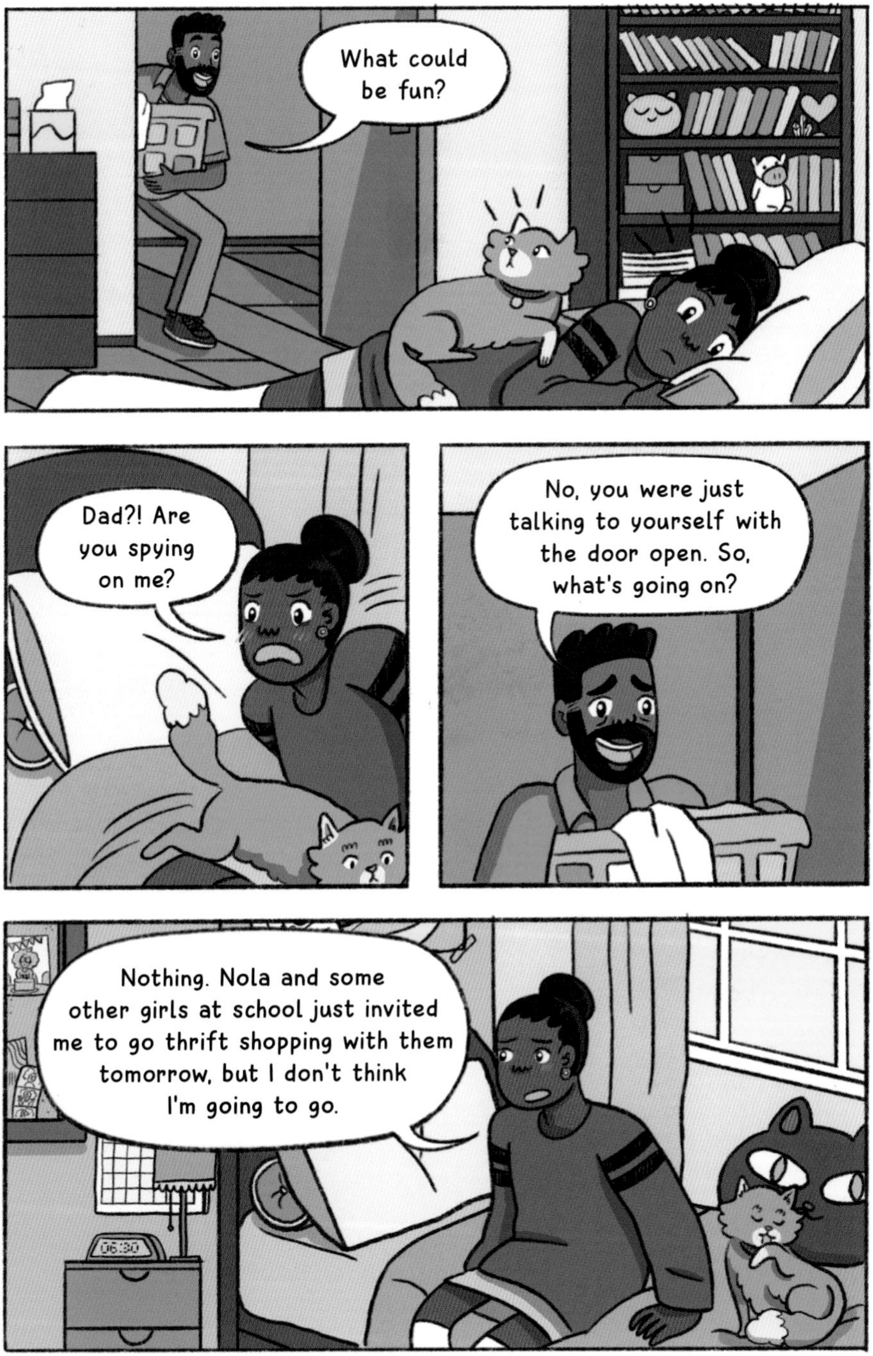
What could be fun?
Dad?! Are you spying on me?
No, you were just talking to yourself with the door open. So, what's going on?
Nothing. Nola and some other girls at school just invited me to go thrift shopping with them tomorrow, but I don't think I'm going to go.
06:30

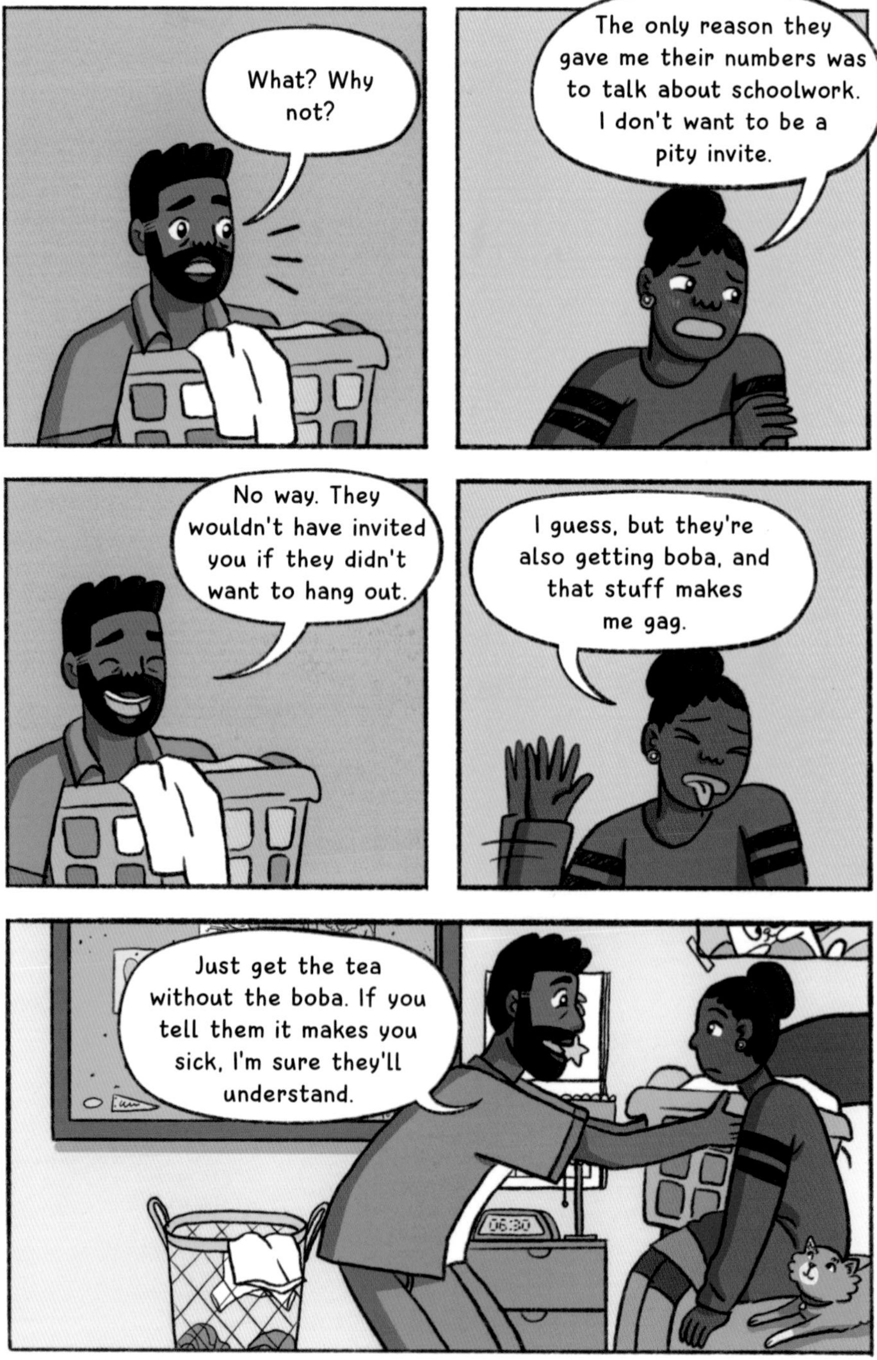
What? Why not?
The only reason they gave me their numbers was to talk about schoolwork. I don't want to be a pity invite.
No way. They wouldn't have invited you if they didn't want to hang out.
I guess, but they're also getting boba, and that stuff makes me gag.
Just get the tea without the boba. If you tell them it makes you sick, I'm sure they'll understand.
06:30

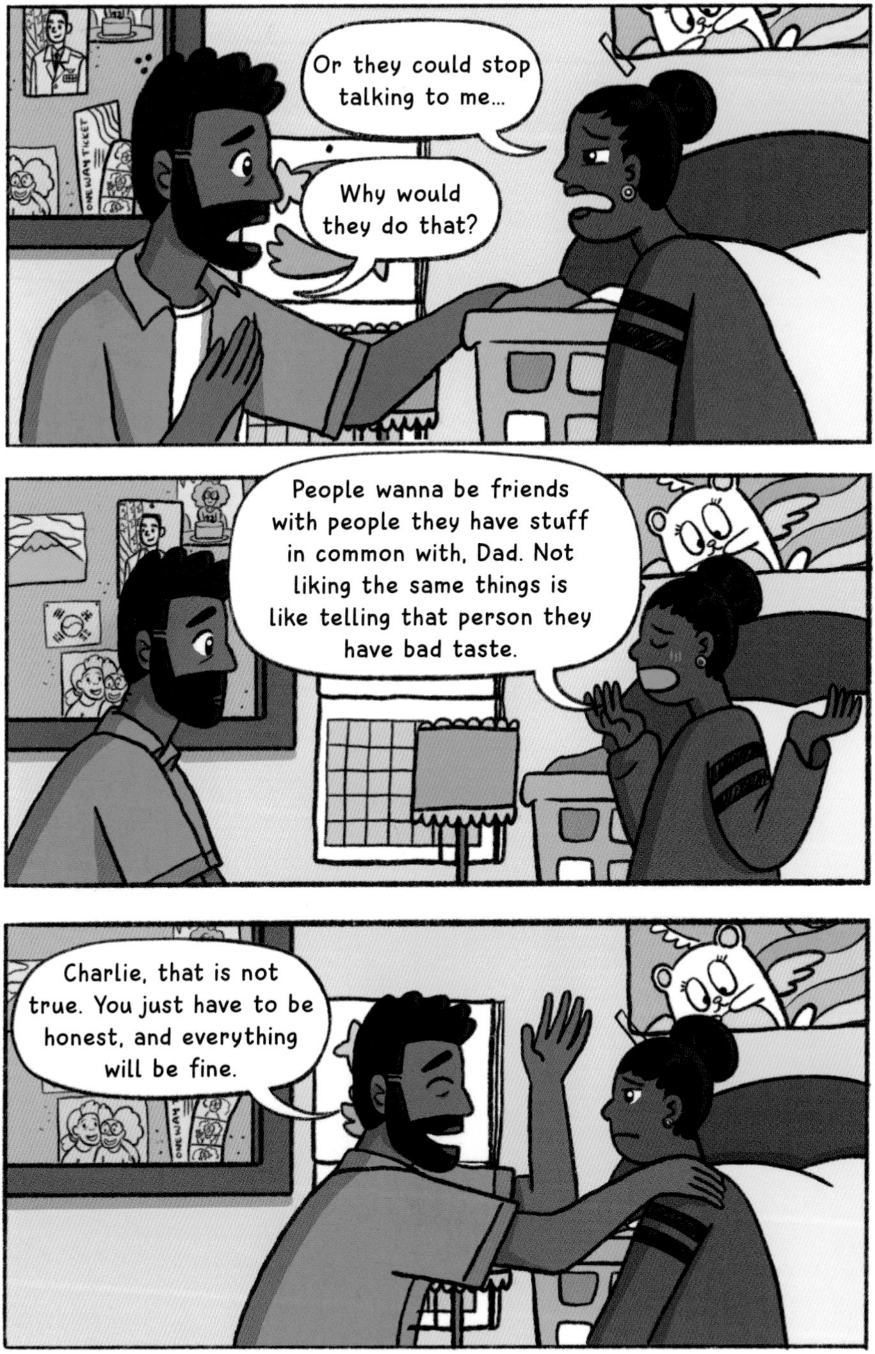
Or they could stop talking to me...
Why would they do that?
People wanna be friends with people they have stuff in common with, Dad. Not liking the same things is like telling that person they have bad taste.
Charlie, that is not true. You just have to be honest, and everything will be fine.

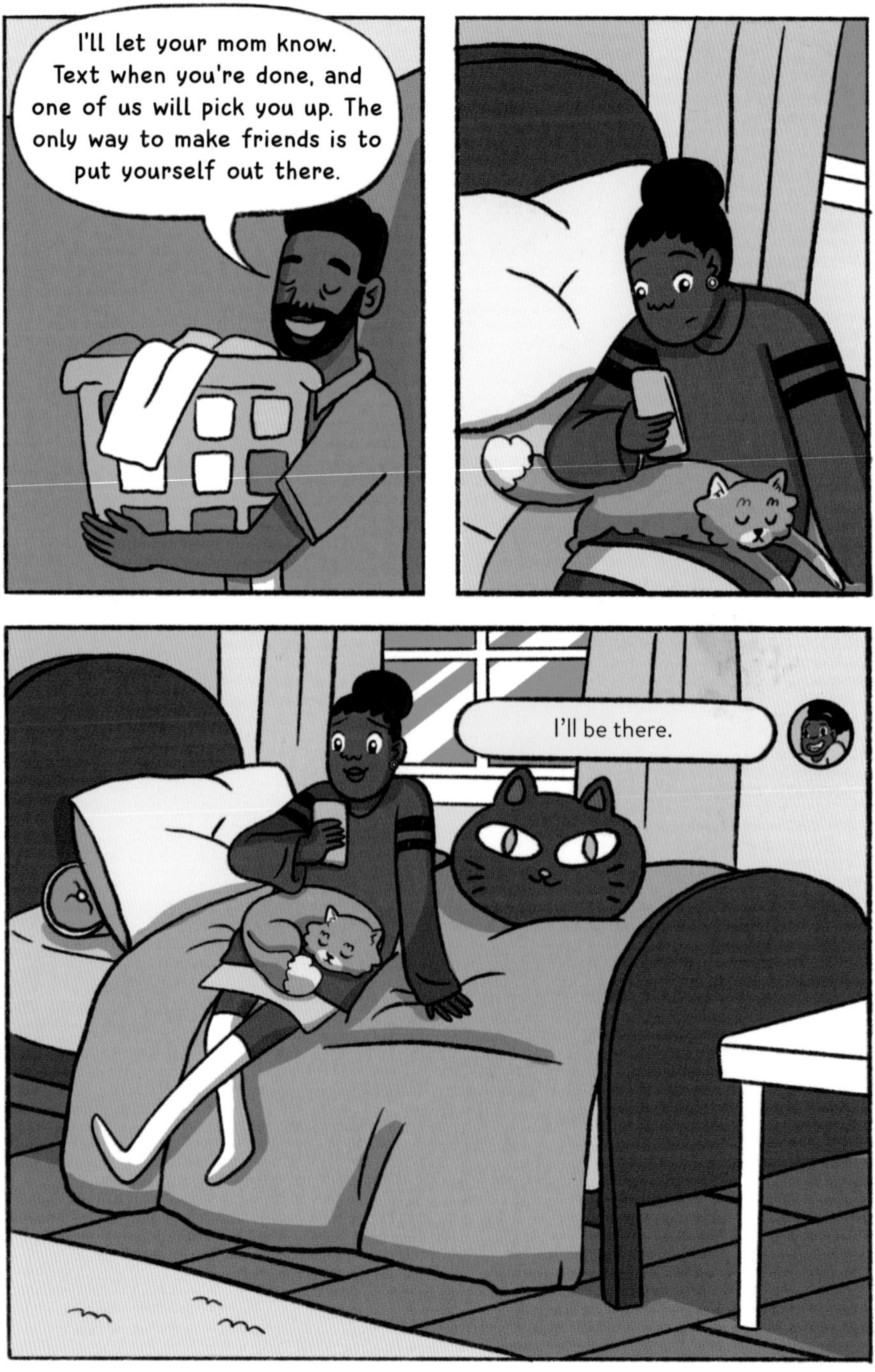
I'll let your mom know. Text when you're done, and one of us will pick you up. The only way to make friends is to put yourself out there.
I'll be there.

CHAPTER 9

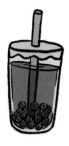

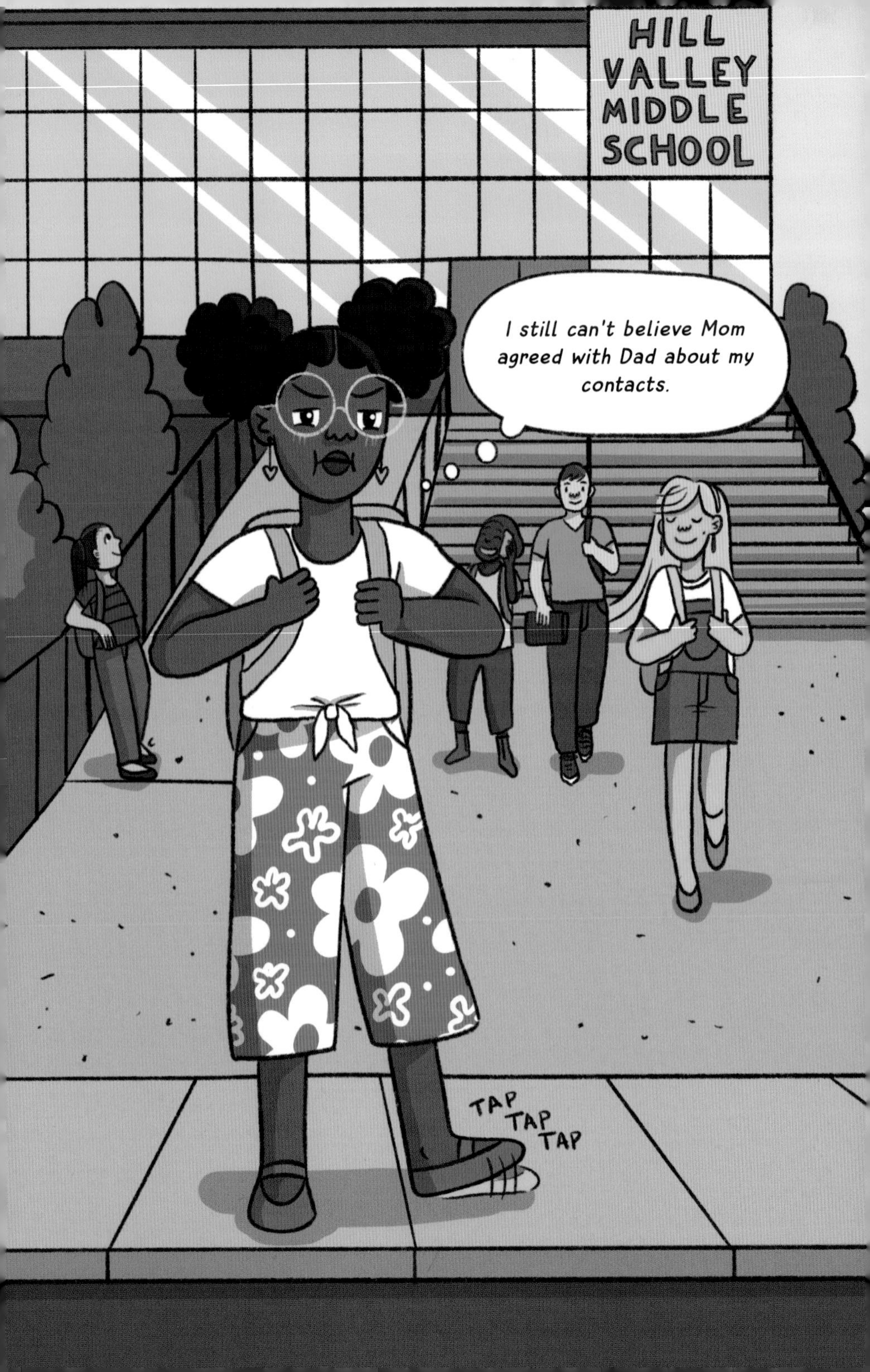
HILL VALLEY MIDDLE SCHOOL
I still can't believe Mom agreed with Dad about my contacts.
TAP TAP TAP

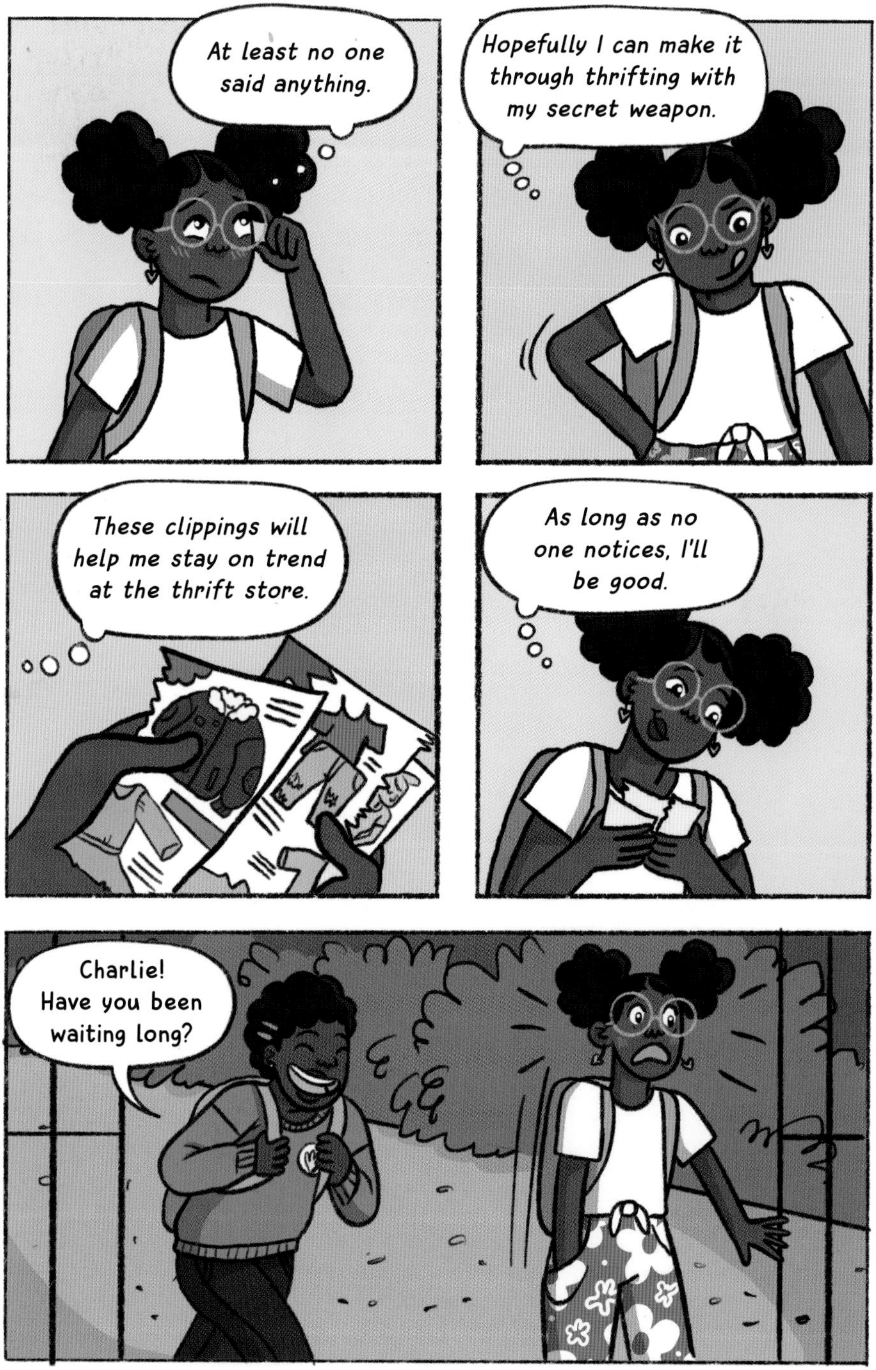
At least no one said anything.
Hopefully I can make it through thrifting with my secret weapon.
These clippings will help me stay on trend at the thrift store.
As long as no one notices, I'll be good.
Charlie! Have you been waiting long?

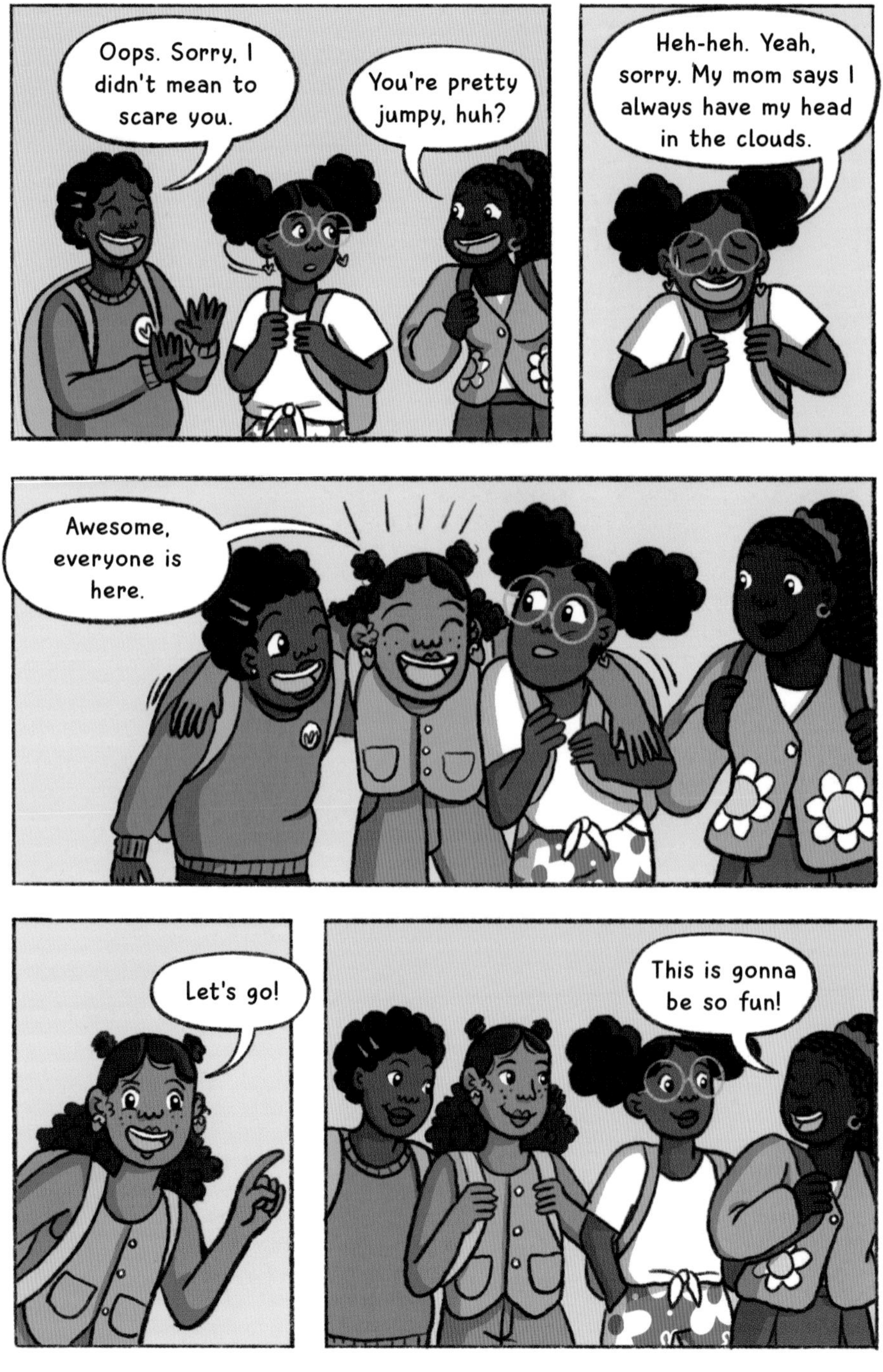
Oops. Sorry, I didn't mean to scare you.
You're pretty jumpy, huh?
Heh-heh. Yeah, sorry. My mom says I always have my head in the clouds.
Awesome, everyone is here.
Let's go!
This is gonna be so fun!

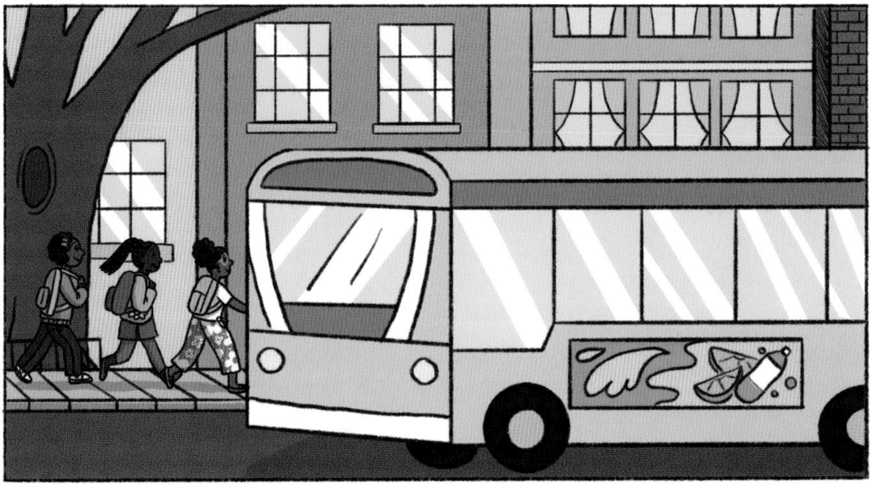

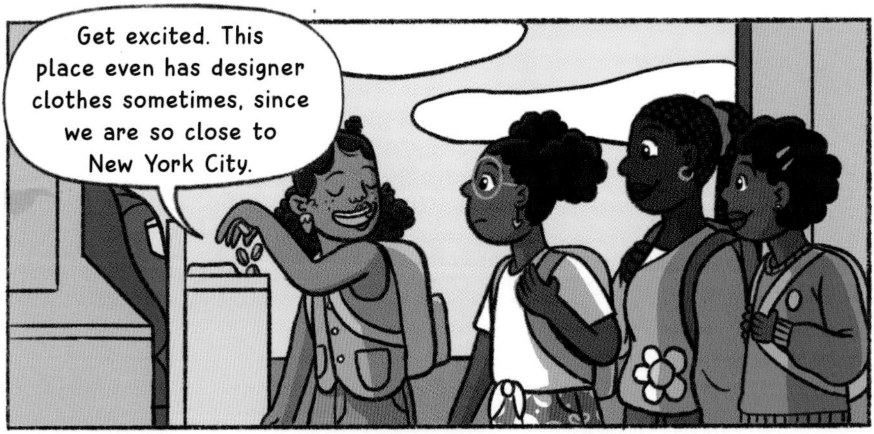
Get excited. This place even has designer clothes sometimes, since we are so close to New York City.

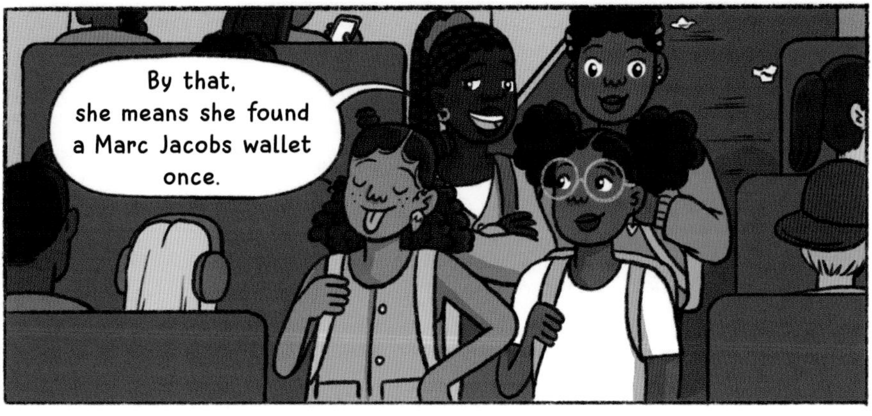
By that, she means she found a Marc Jacobs wallet once.

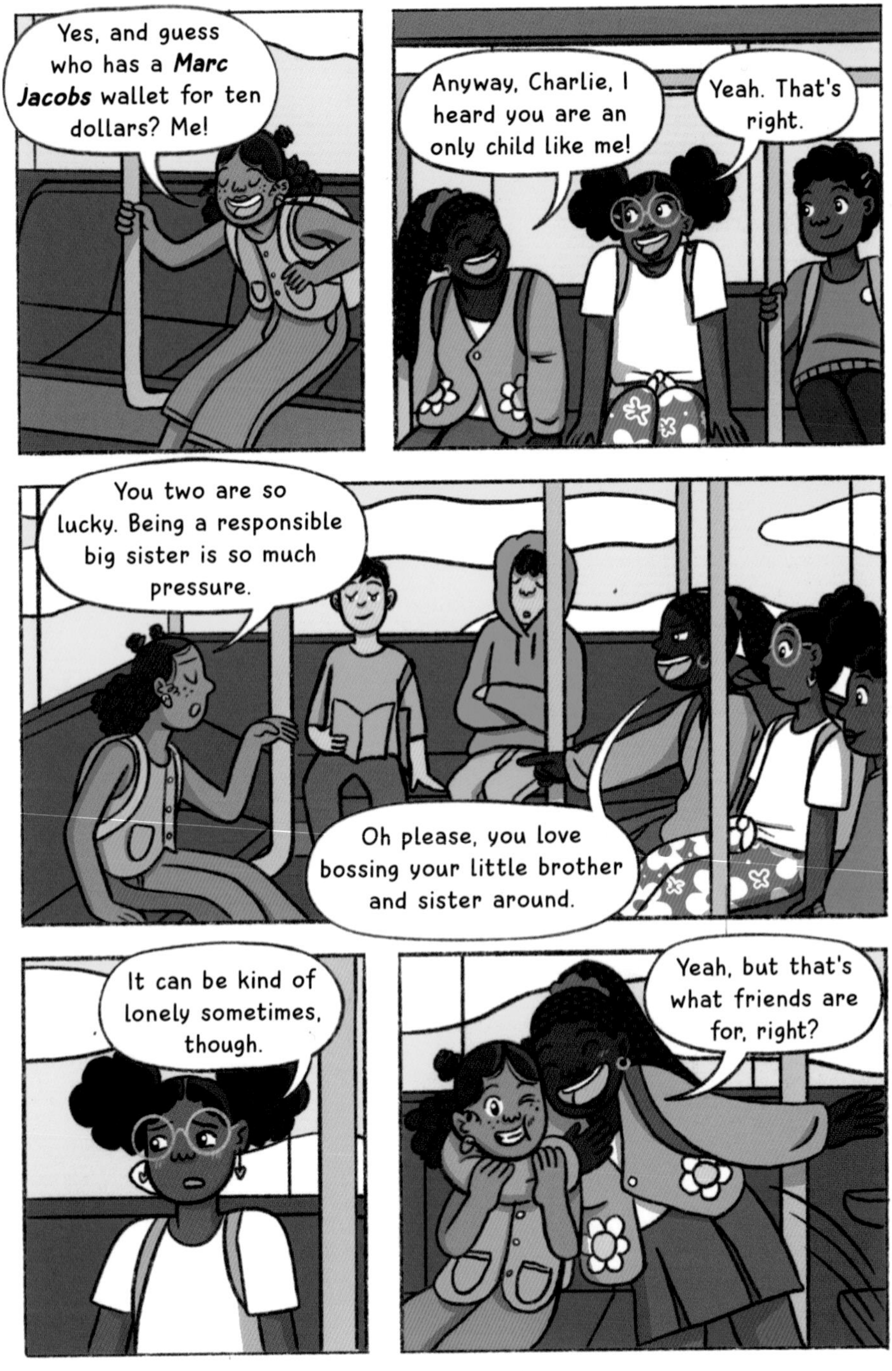
Yes, and guess who has a **Marc Jacobs** wallet for ten dollars? Me!
Anyway, Charlie, I heard you are an only child like me!
Yeah. That's right.
You two are so lucky. Being a responsible big sister is so much pressure.
Oh please, you love bossing your little brother and sister around.
It can be kind of lonely sometimes, though.
Yeah, but that's what friends are for, right?

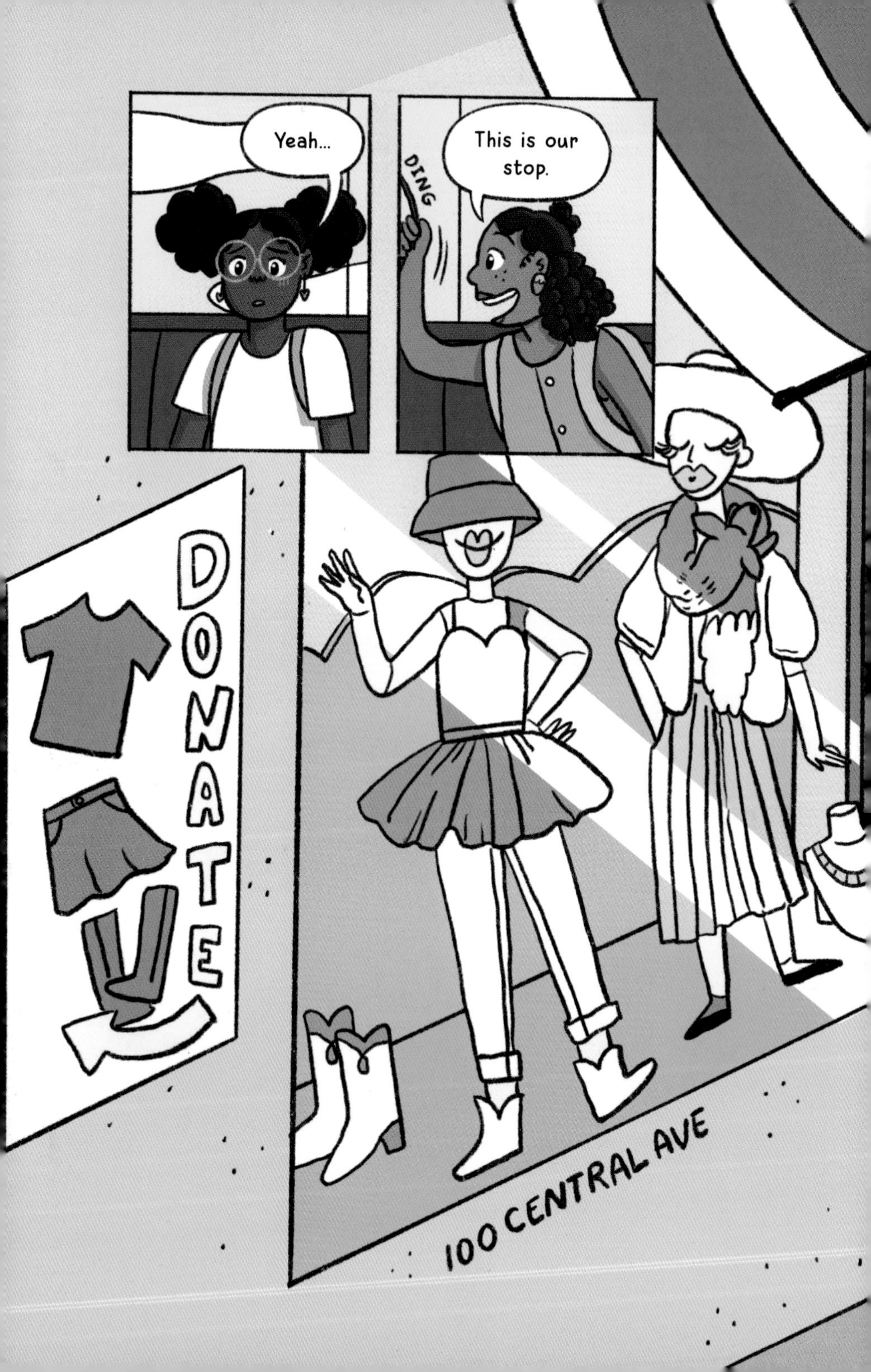
Yeah...
DING
This is our stop.
DONATE
100 CENTRAL AVE

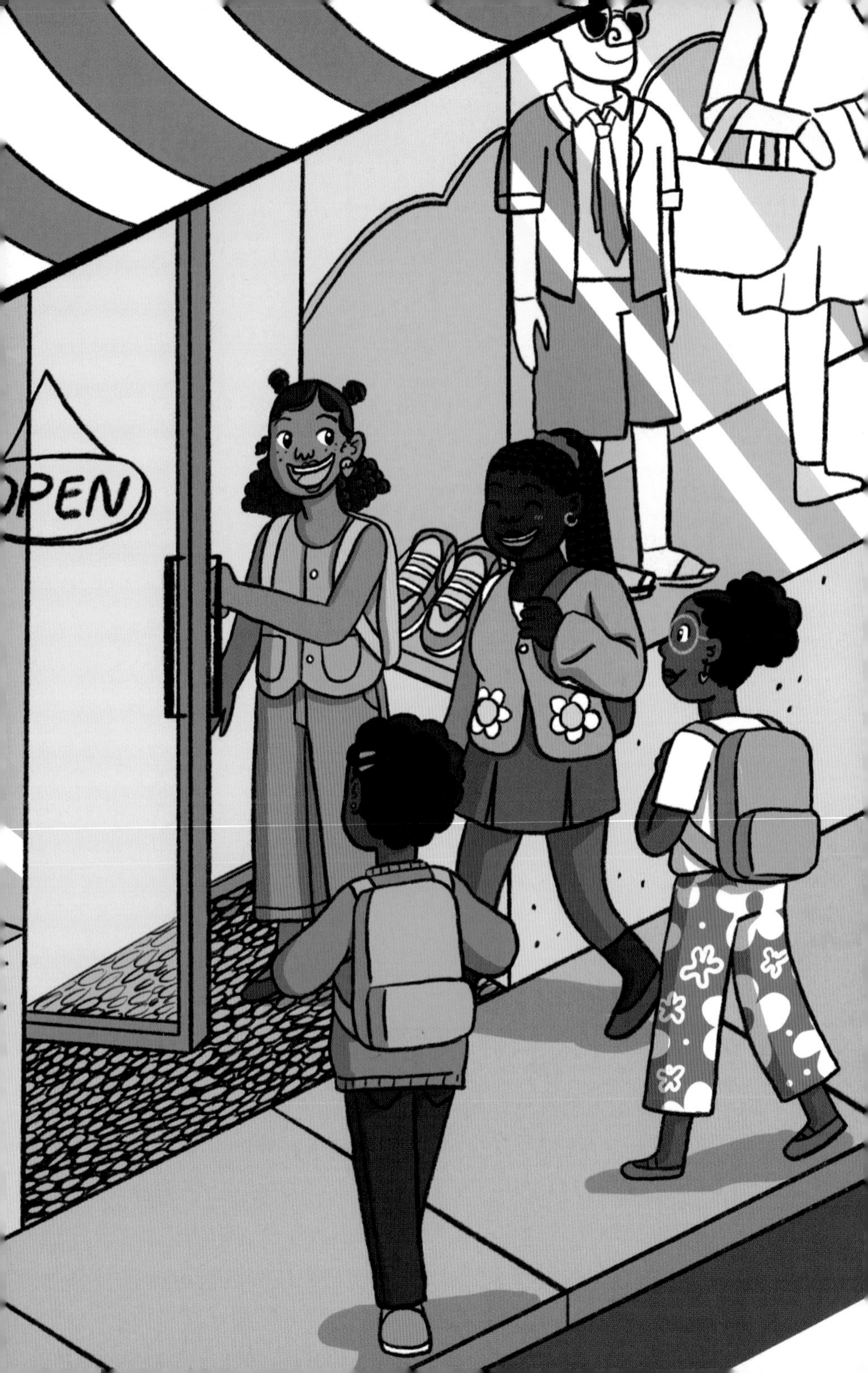
OPEN

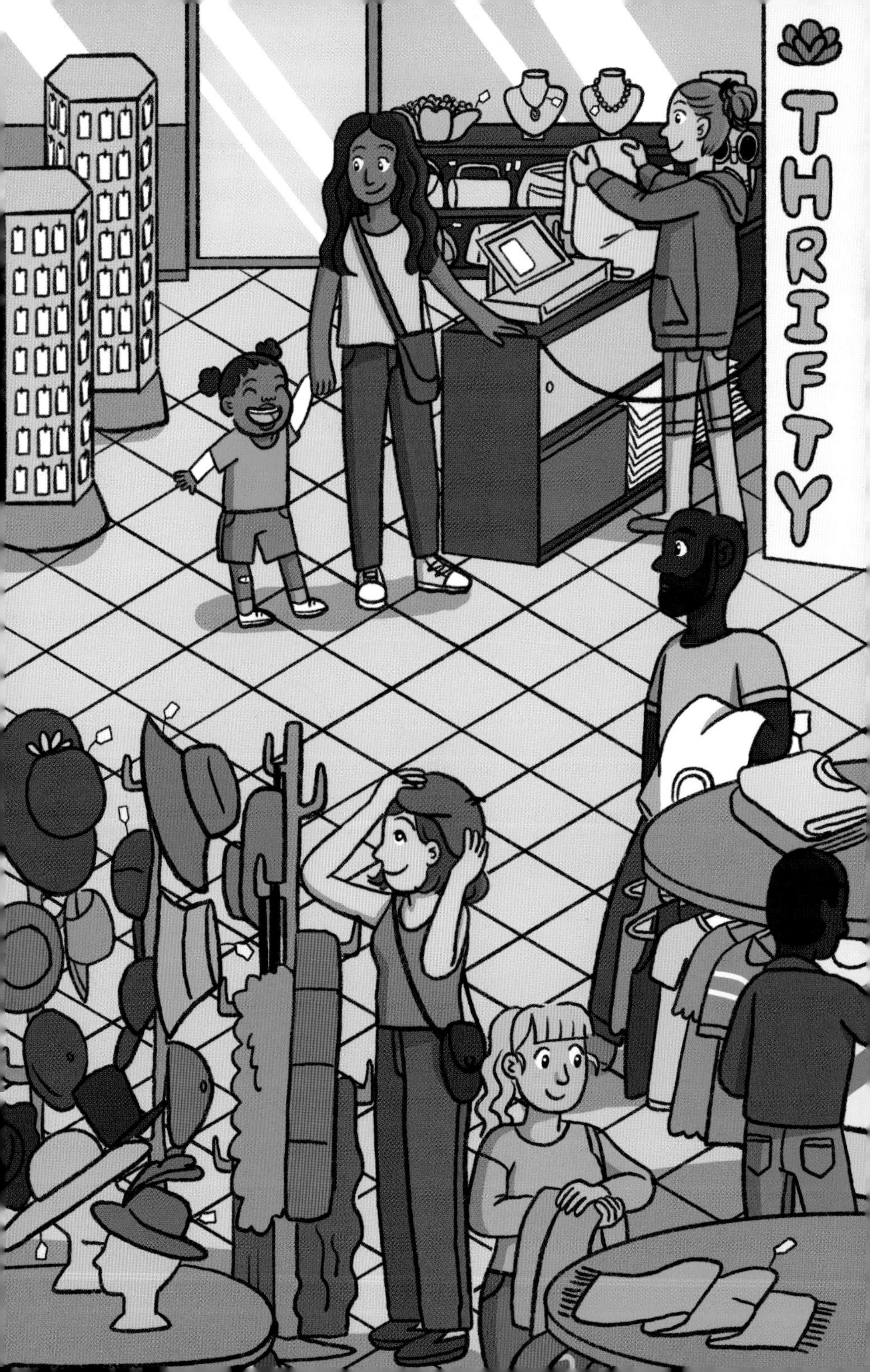
THRIFTY

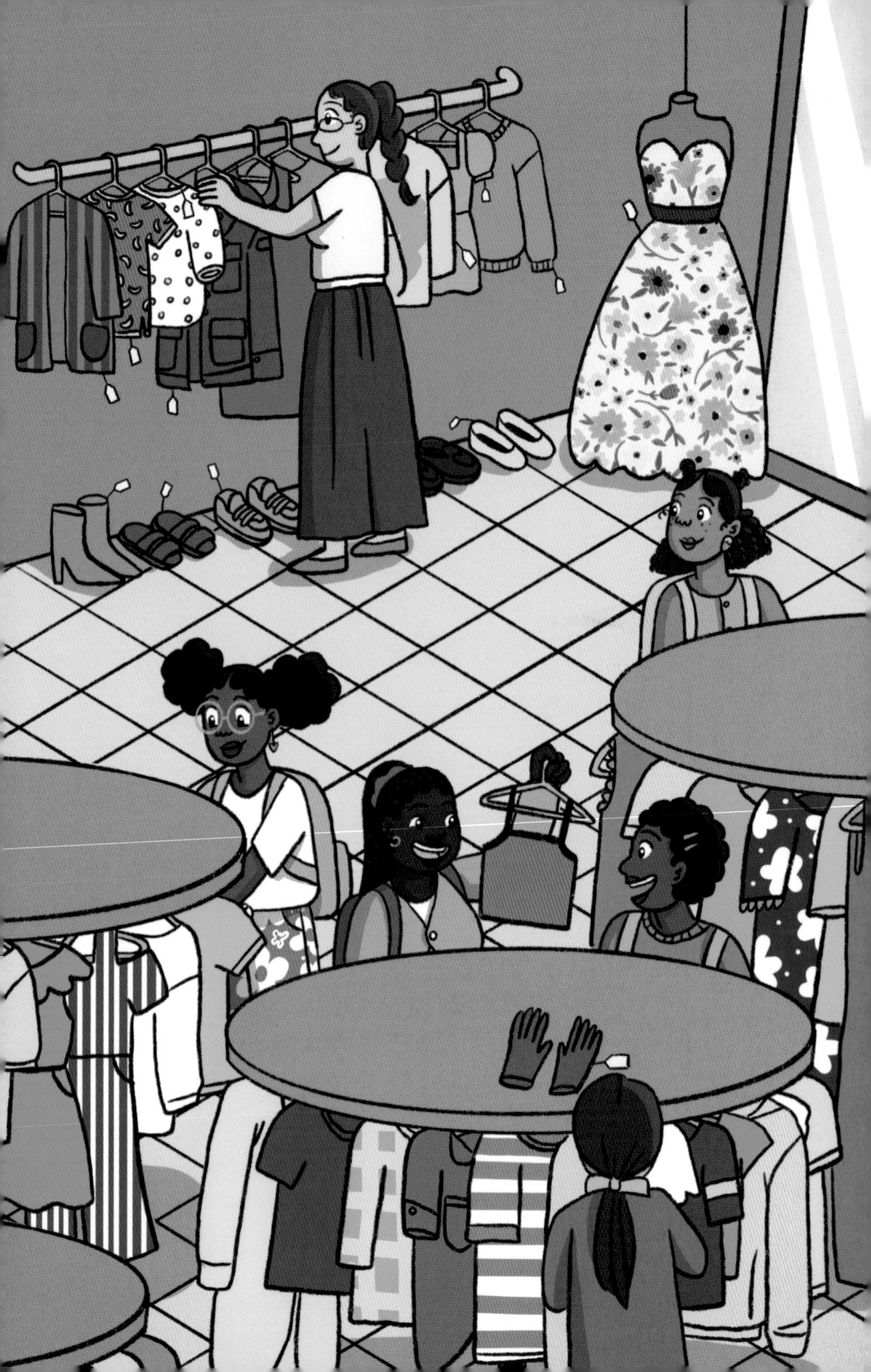

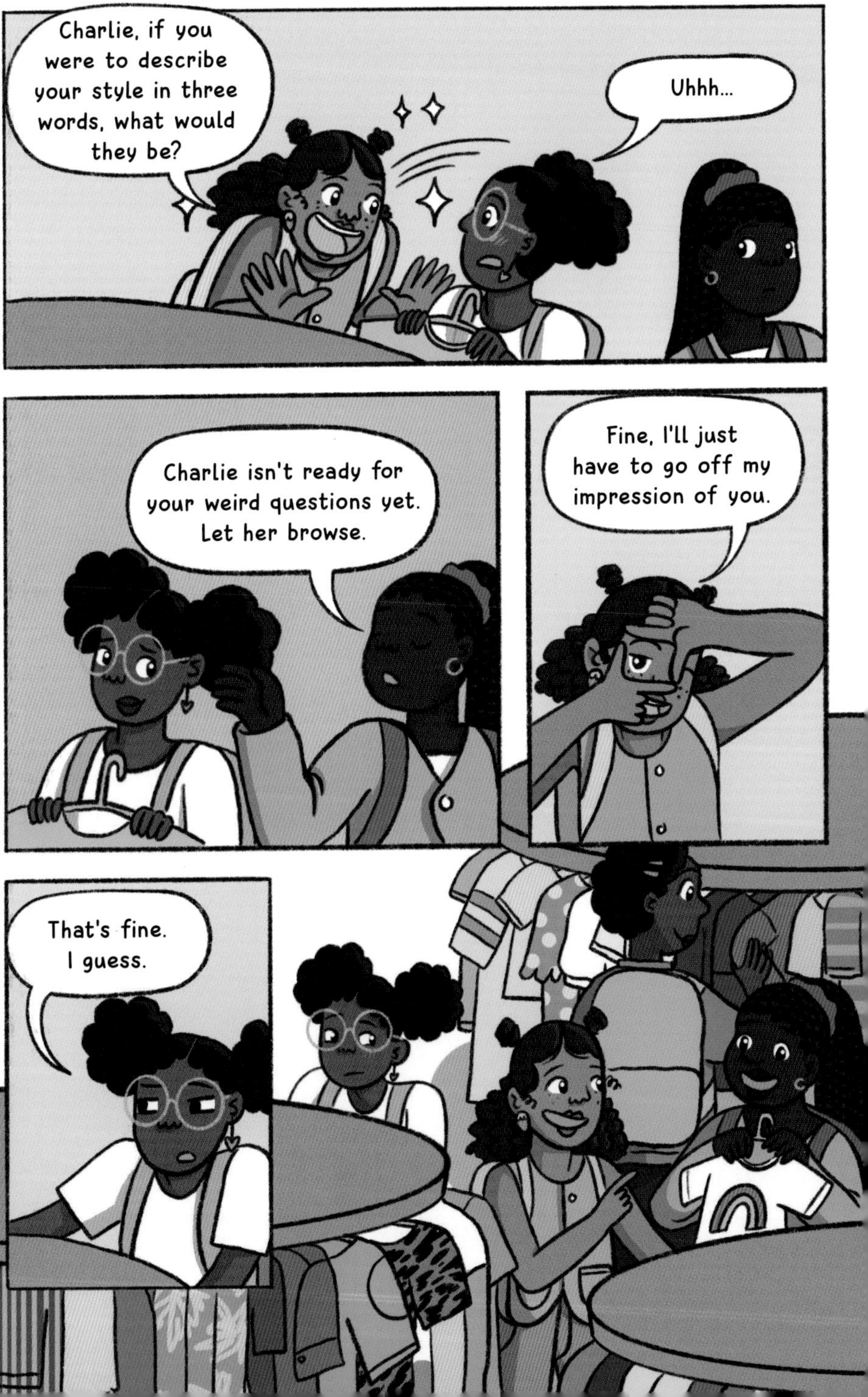
Charlie, if you were to describe your style in three words, what would they be?
Uhhh...
Charlie isn't ready for your weird questions yet. Let her browse.
Fine, I'll just have to go off my impression of you.
That's fine. I guess.

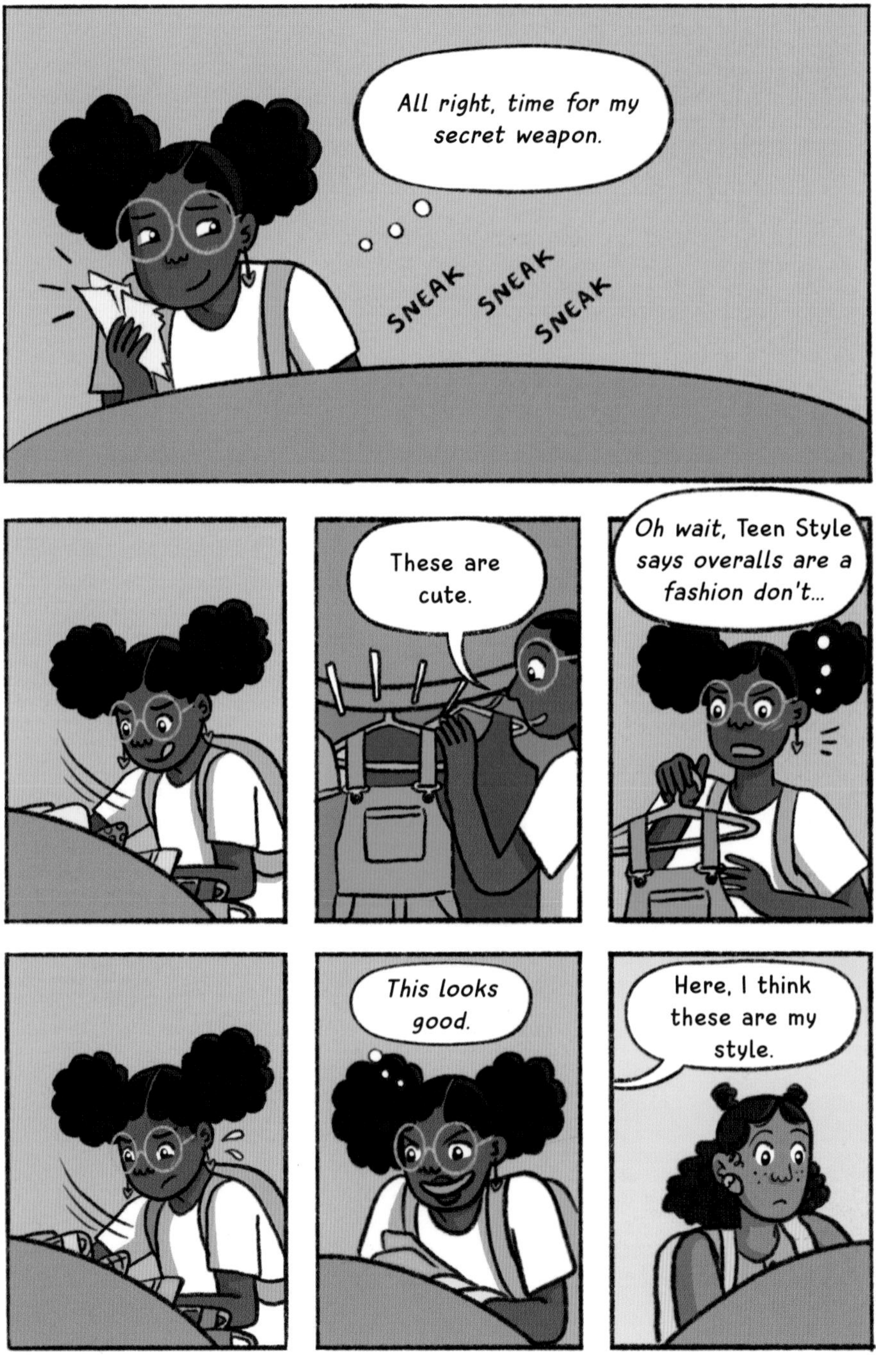
All right, time for my secret weapon.
SNEAK SNEAK SNEAK
These are cute.
Oh wait, Teen Style says overalls are a fashion don't...
This looks good.
Here, I think these are my style.

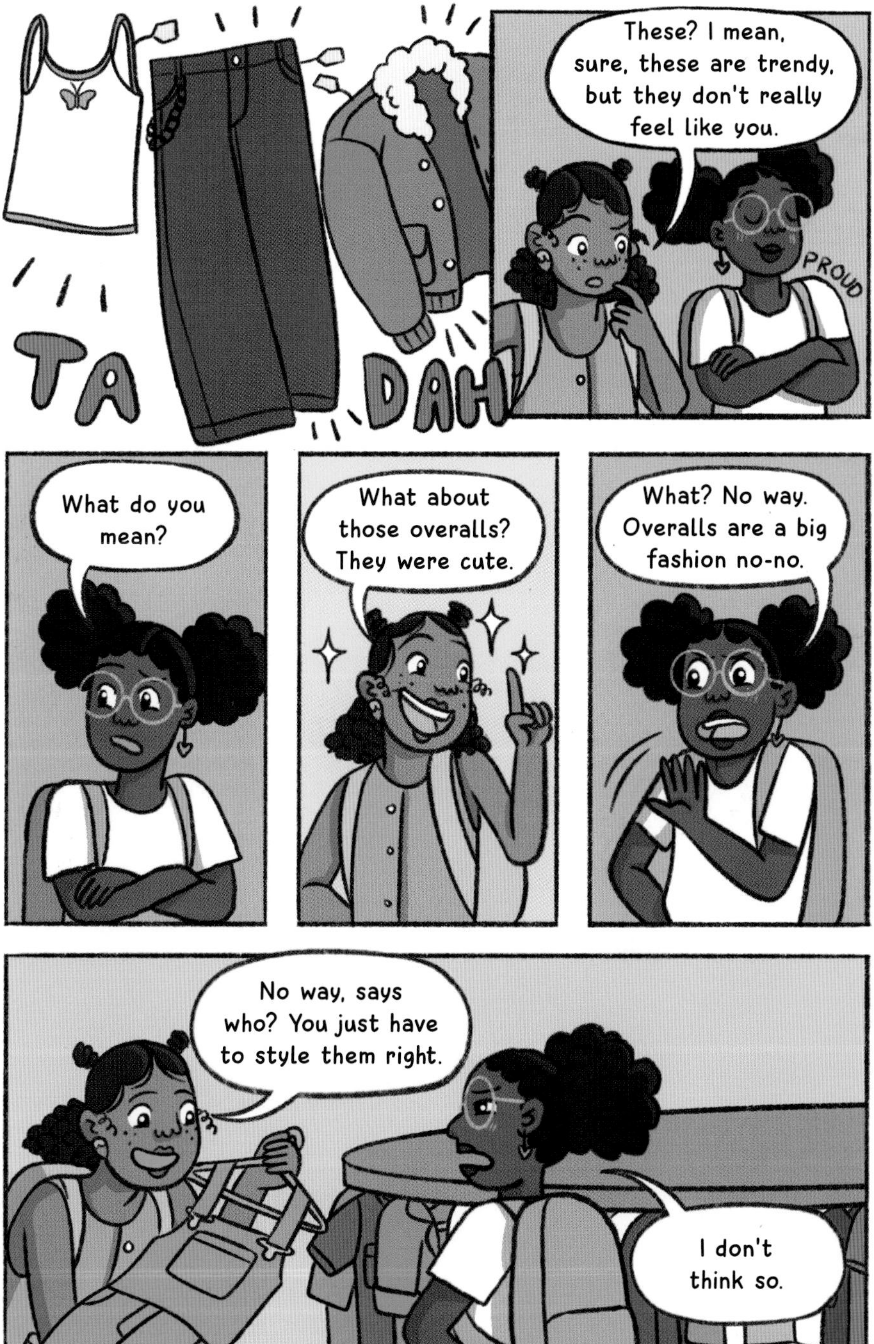
TA
DAH
These? I mean, sure, these are trendy, but they don't really feel like you.
PROUD
What do you mean?
What about those overalls? They were cute.
What? No way. Overalls are a big fashion no-no.
No way, says who? You just have to style them right.
I don't think so.

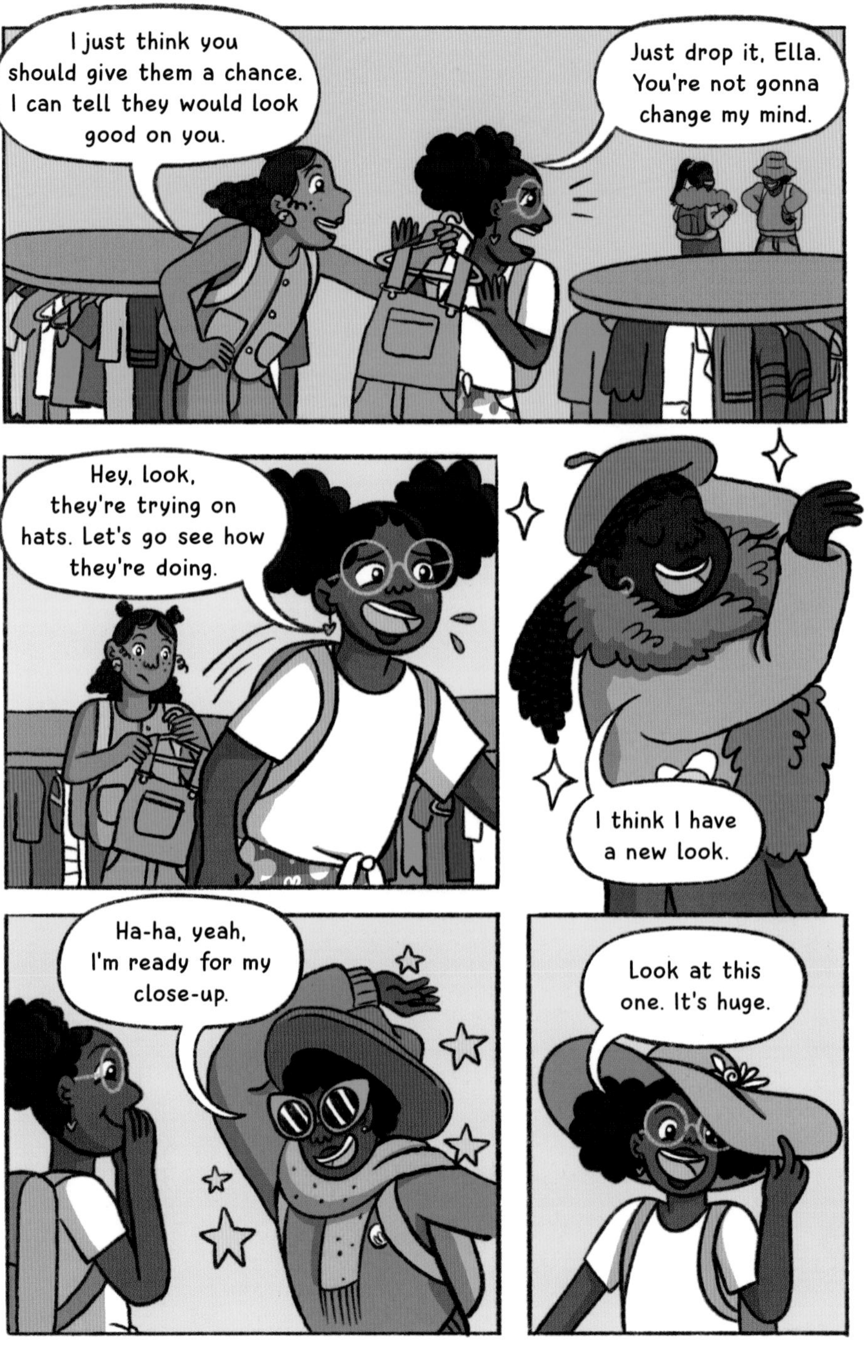
I just think you should give them a chance. I can tell they would look good on you.
Just drop it, Ella. You're not gonna change my mind.
Hey, look, they're trying on hats. Let's go see how they're doing.
I think I have a new look.
Ha-ha, yeah, I'm ready for my close-up.
Look at this one. It's huge.

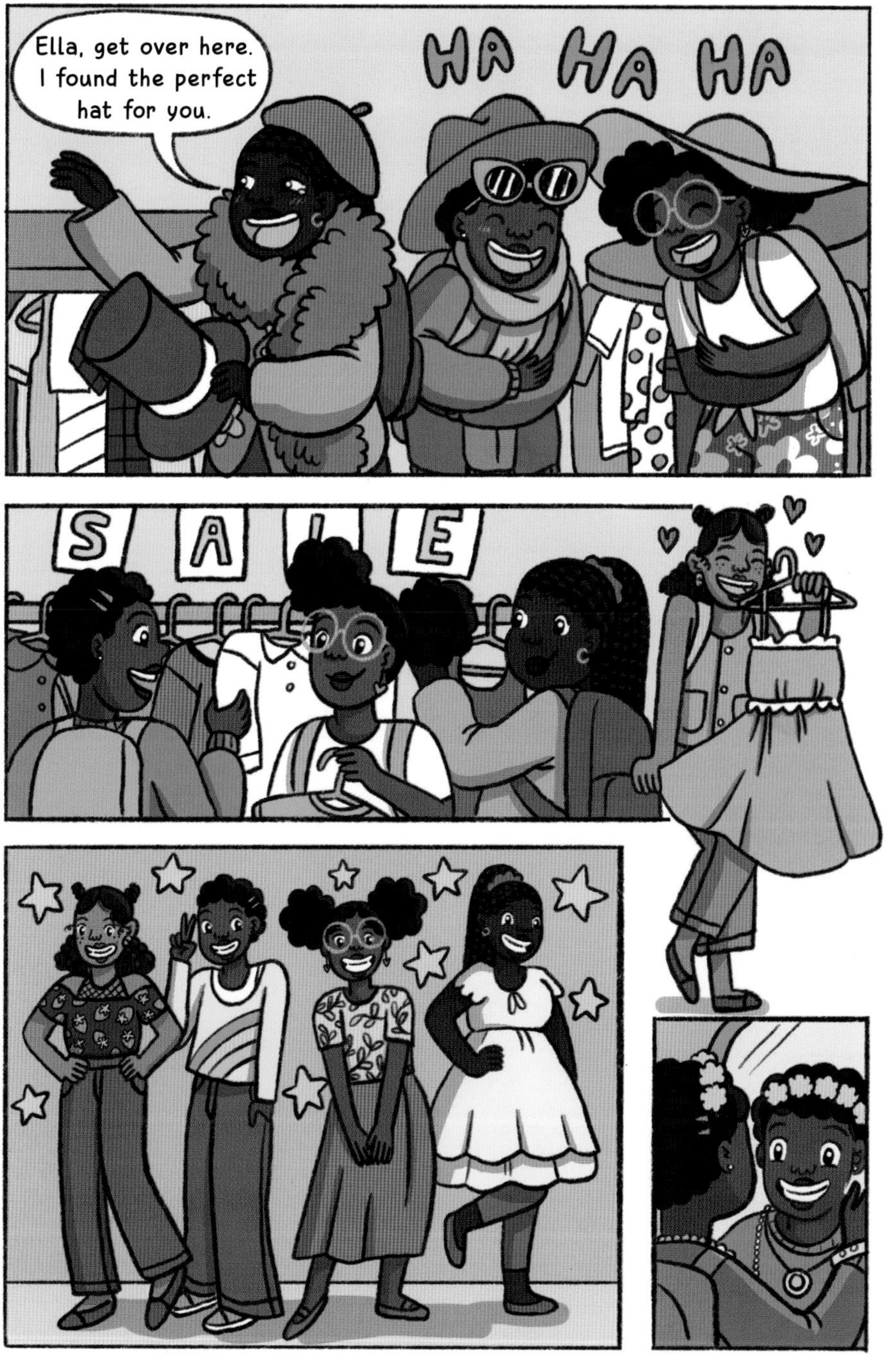
Ella, get over here. I found the perfect hat for you.
HA HA HA
SALE

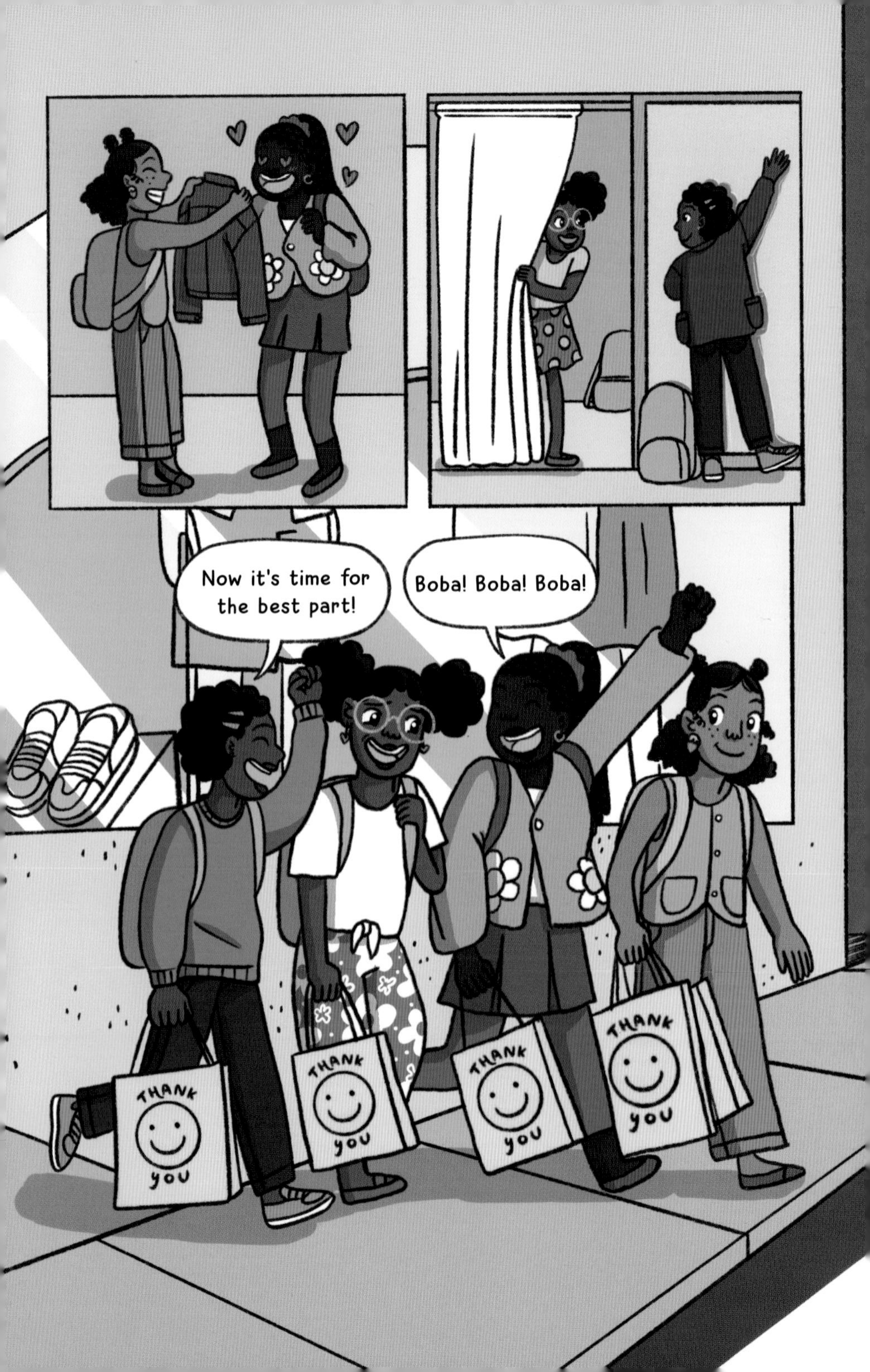

Now it's time for the best part!
Boba! Boba! Boba!
THANK YOU
THANK YOU
THANK YOU
THANK YOU

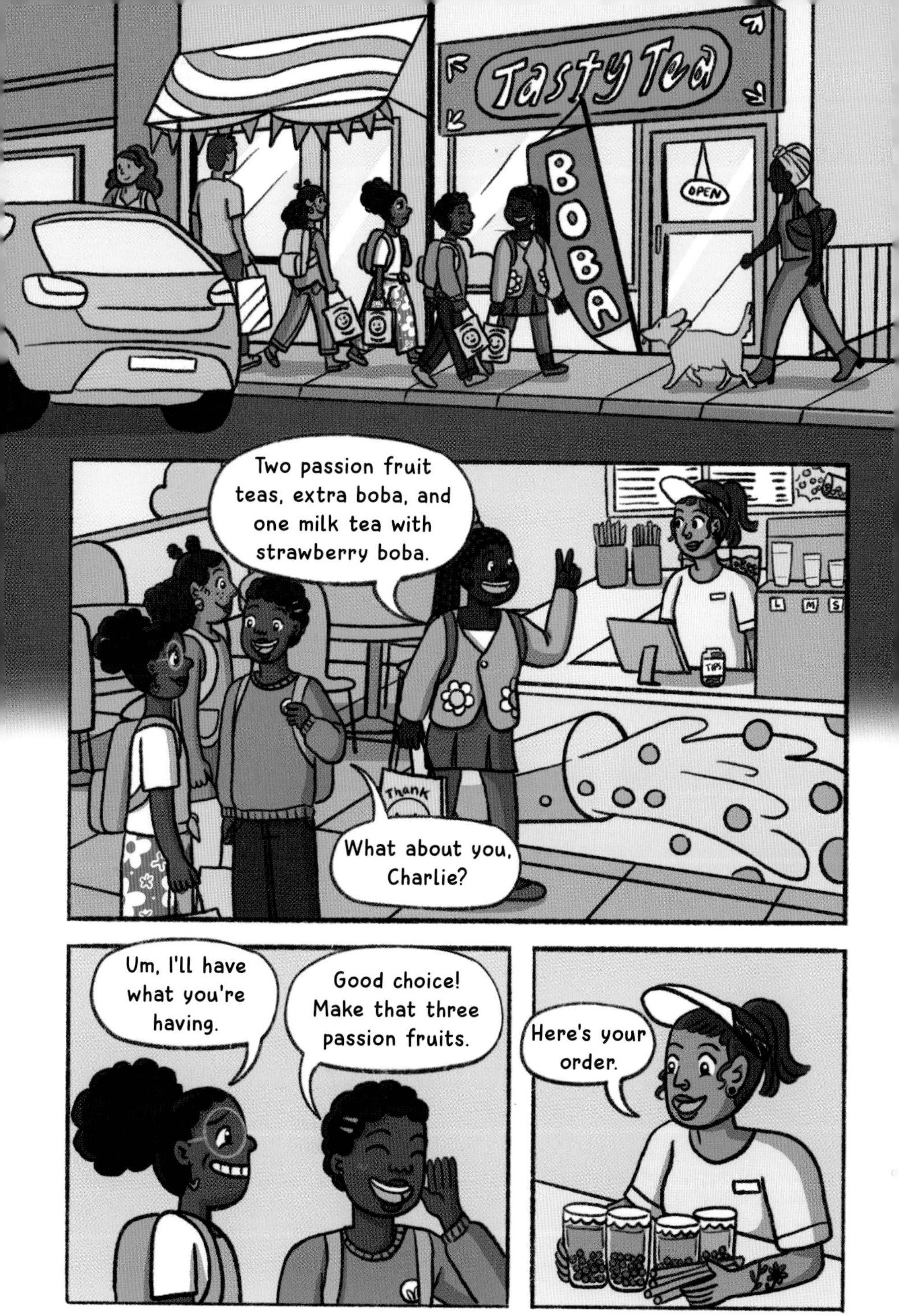
Tasty Tea
BOBA
OPEN
Two passion fruit teas, extra boba, and one milk tea with strawberry boba.
What about you, Charlie?
Um, I'll have what you're having.
Good choice! Make that three passion fruits.
Here's your order.

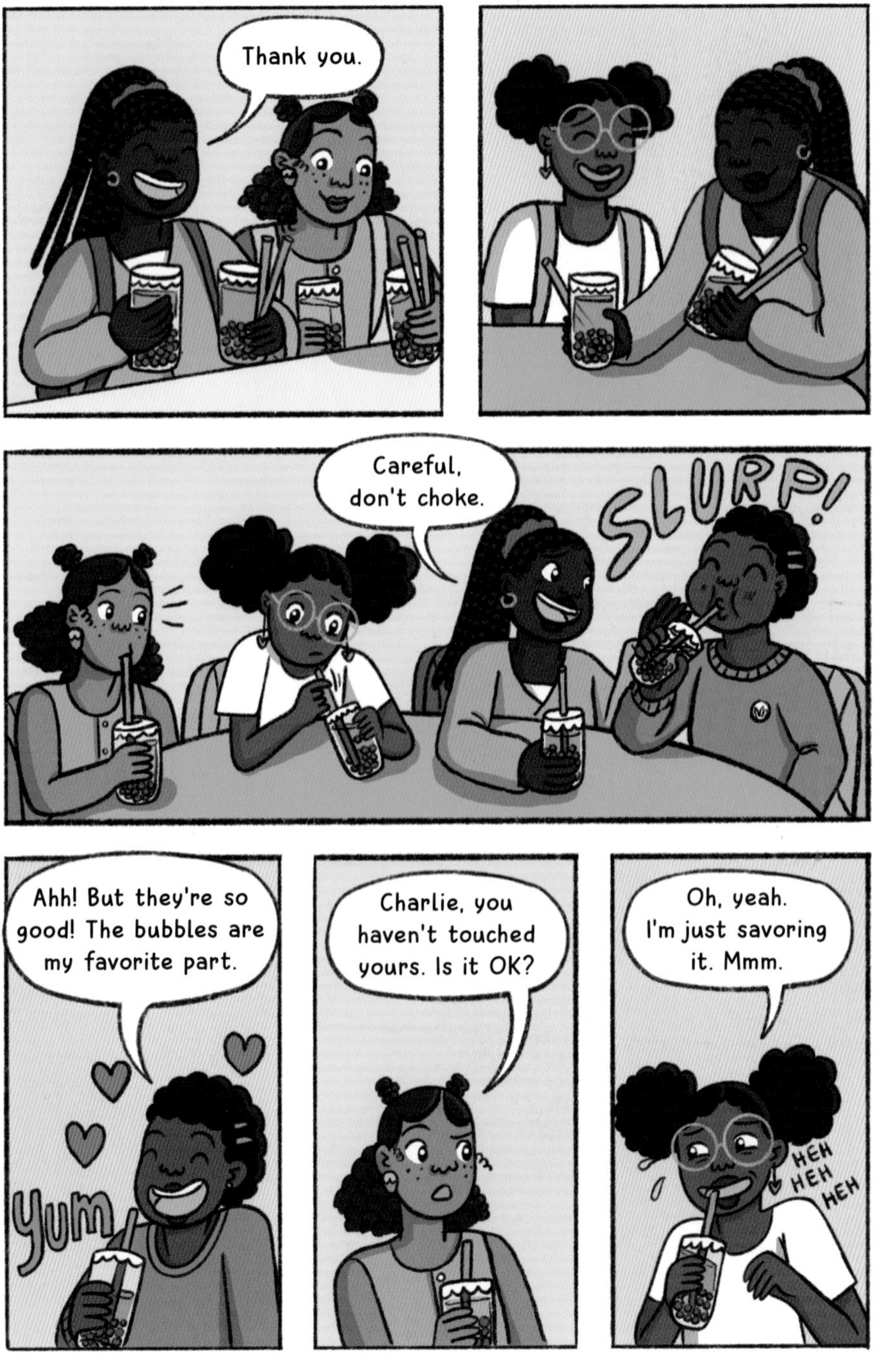
Thank you.
Careful, don't choke.
SLURP!
Ahh! But they're so good! The bubbles are my favorite part.
yum
Charlie, you haven't touched yours. Is it OK?
Oh, yeah. I'm just savoring it. Mmm.
HEH HEH HEH

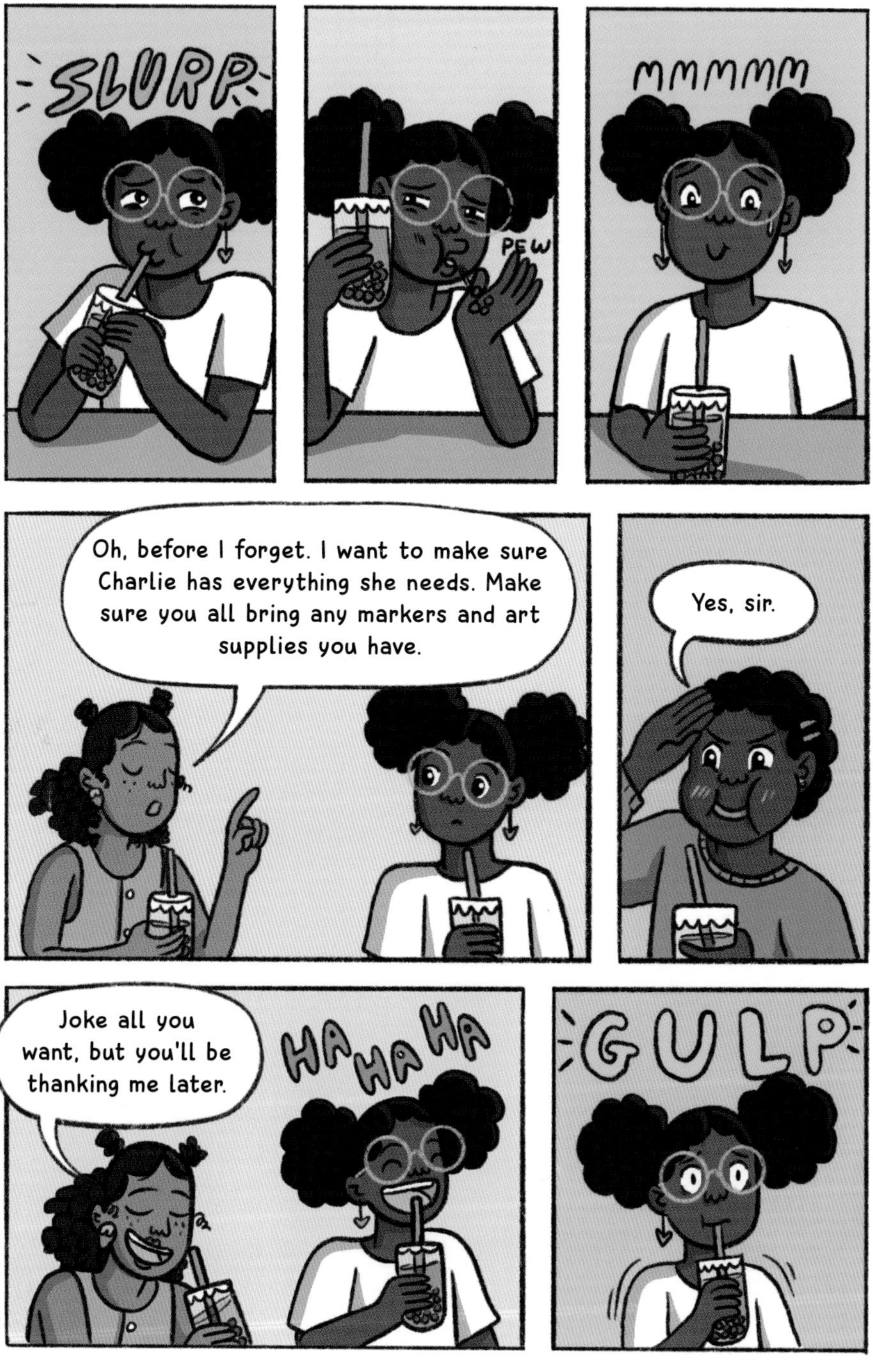
SLURP
PEW
MMMMM
Oh, before I forget. I want to make sure Charlie has everything she needs. Make sure you all bring any markers and art supplies you have.
Yes, sir.
Joke all you want, but you'll be thanking me later.
HA HA HA HA
GULP

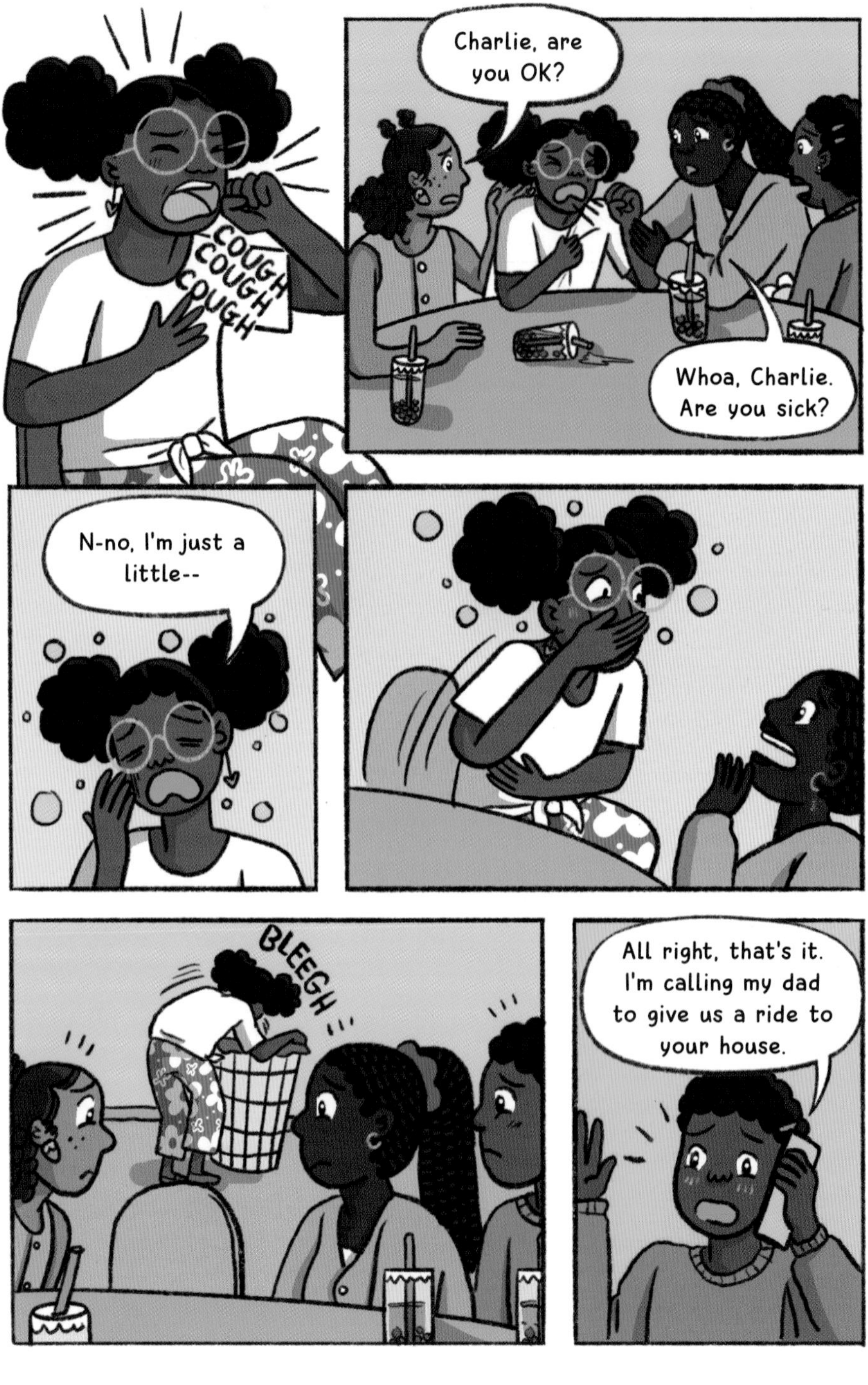
COUGH COUGH COUGH
Charlie, are you OK?
Whoa, Charlie. Are you sick?
N-no, I'm just a little--
BLEEGH
All right, that's it. I'm calling my dad to give us a ride to your house.

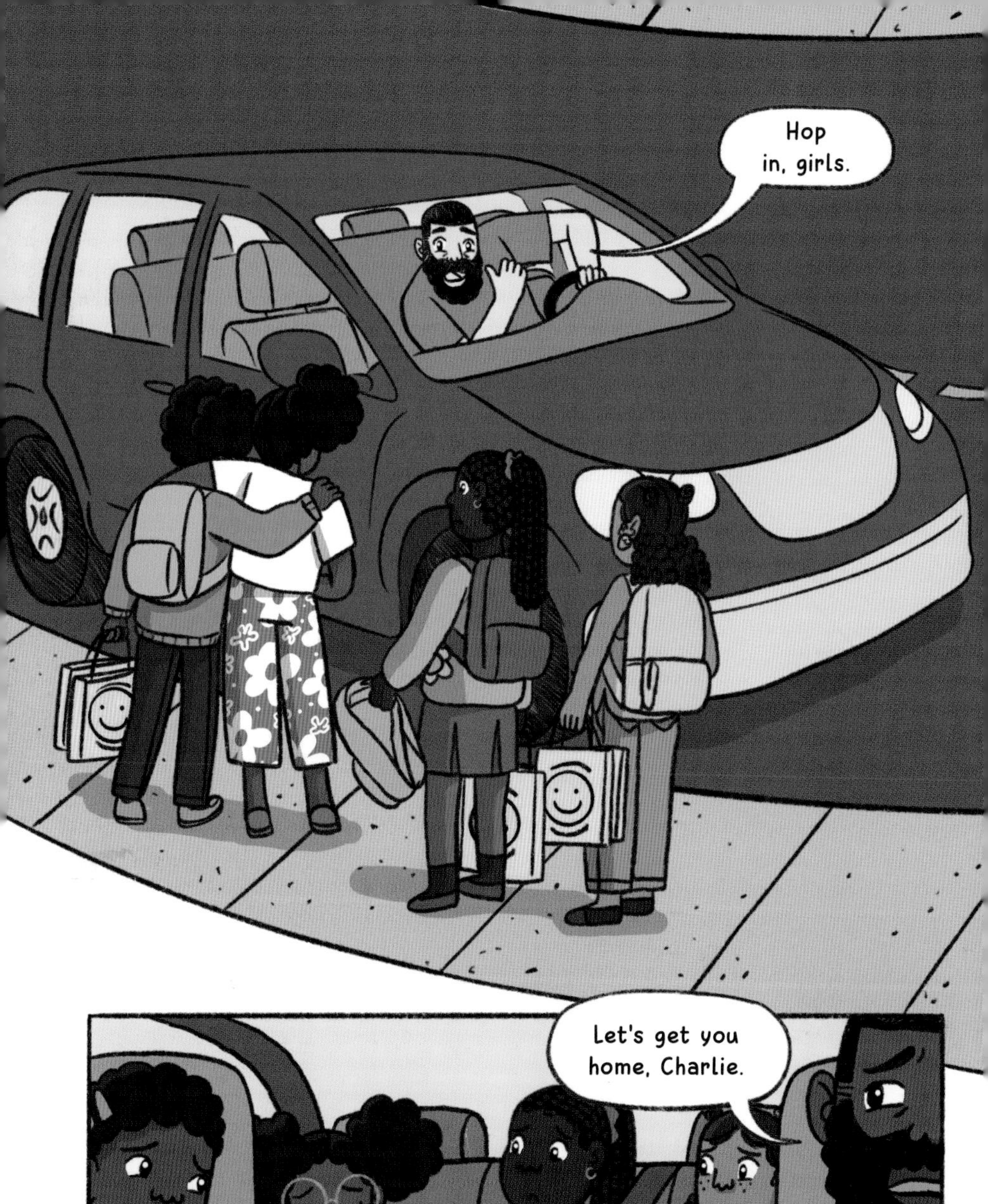
Hop in, girls.

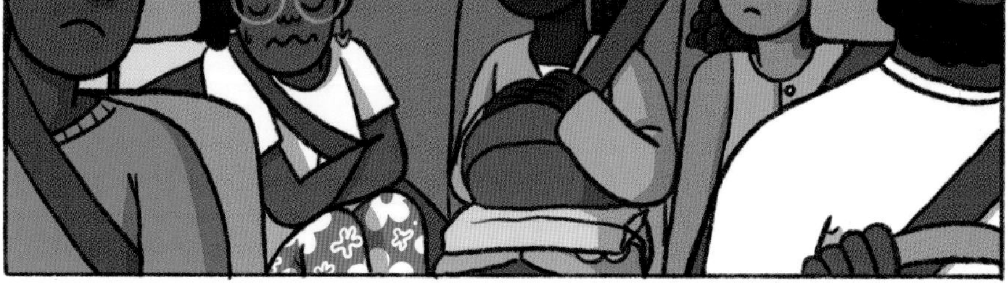
Let's get you home, Charlie.

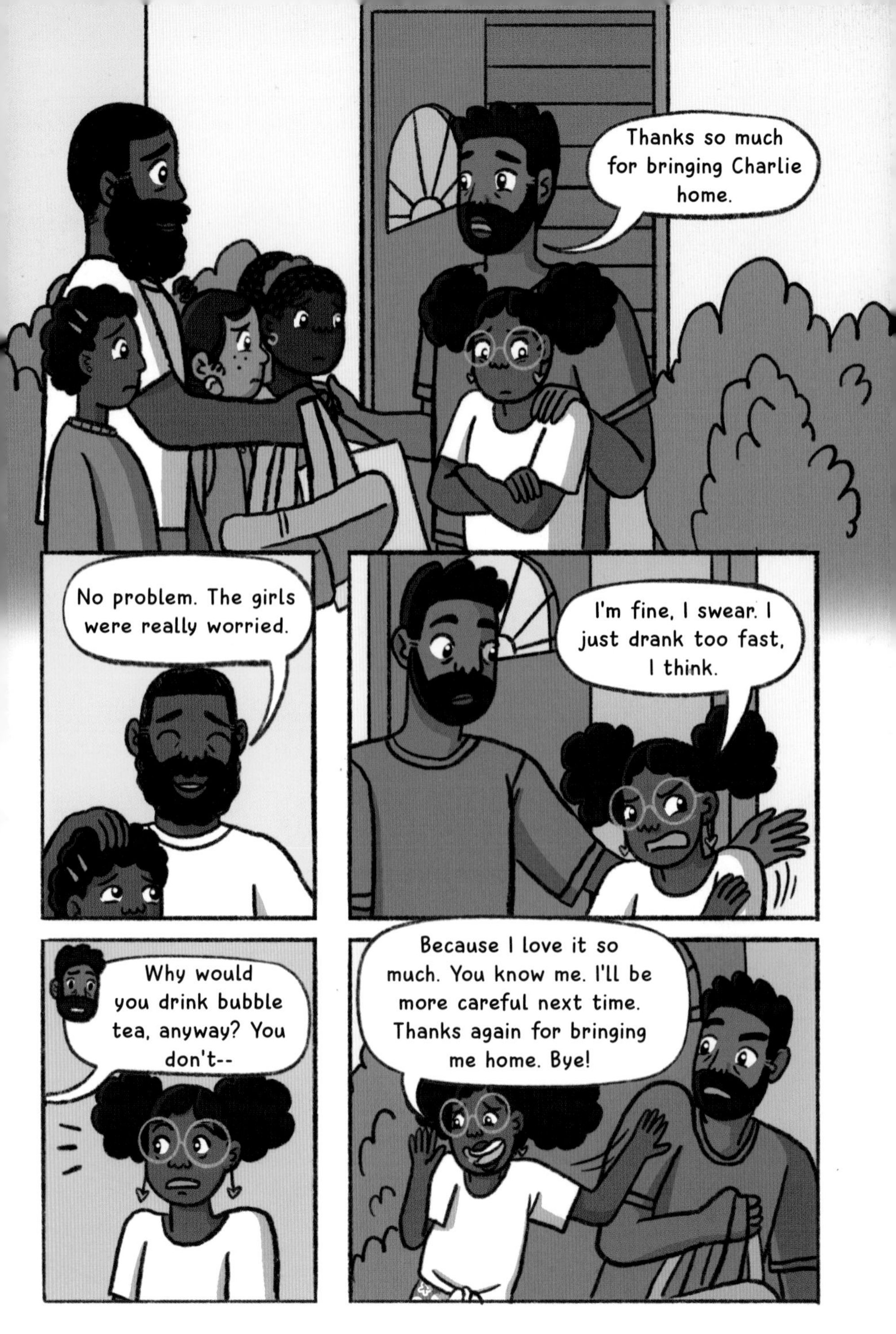
Thanks so much for bringing Charlie home.
No problem. The girls were really worried.
I'm fine, I swear. I just drank too fast, I think.
Why would you drink bubble tea, anyway? You don't--
Because I love it so much. You know me. I'll be more careful next time. Thanks again for bringing me home. Bye!

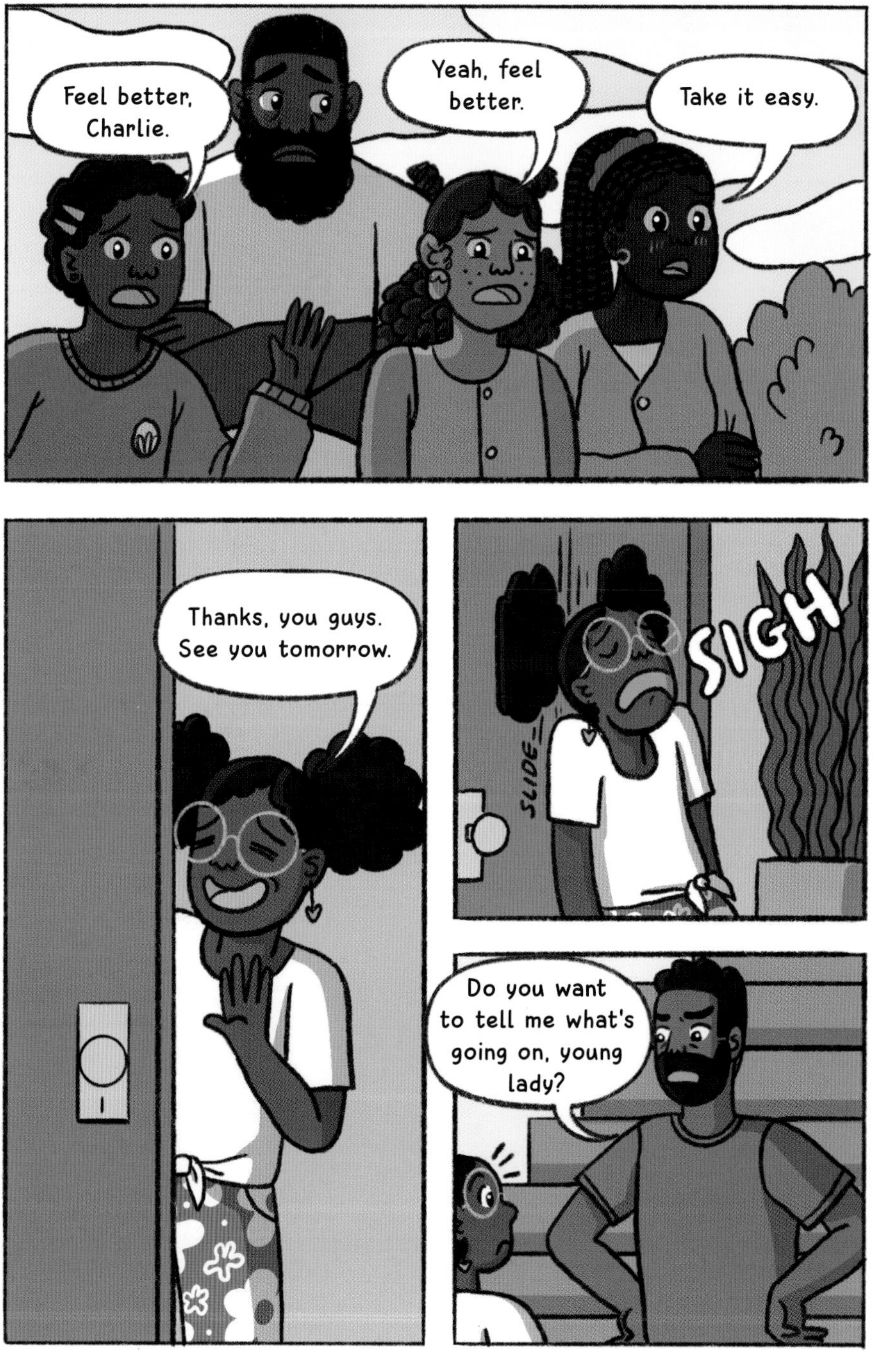
Feel better, Charlie.
Yeah, feel better.
Take it easy.
Thanks, you guys. See you tomorrow.
SLIDE
SIGH
Do you want to tell me what's going on, young lady?

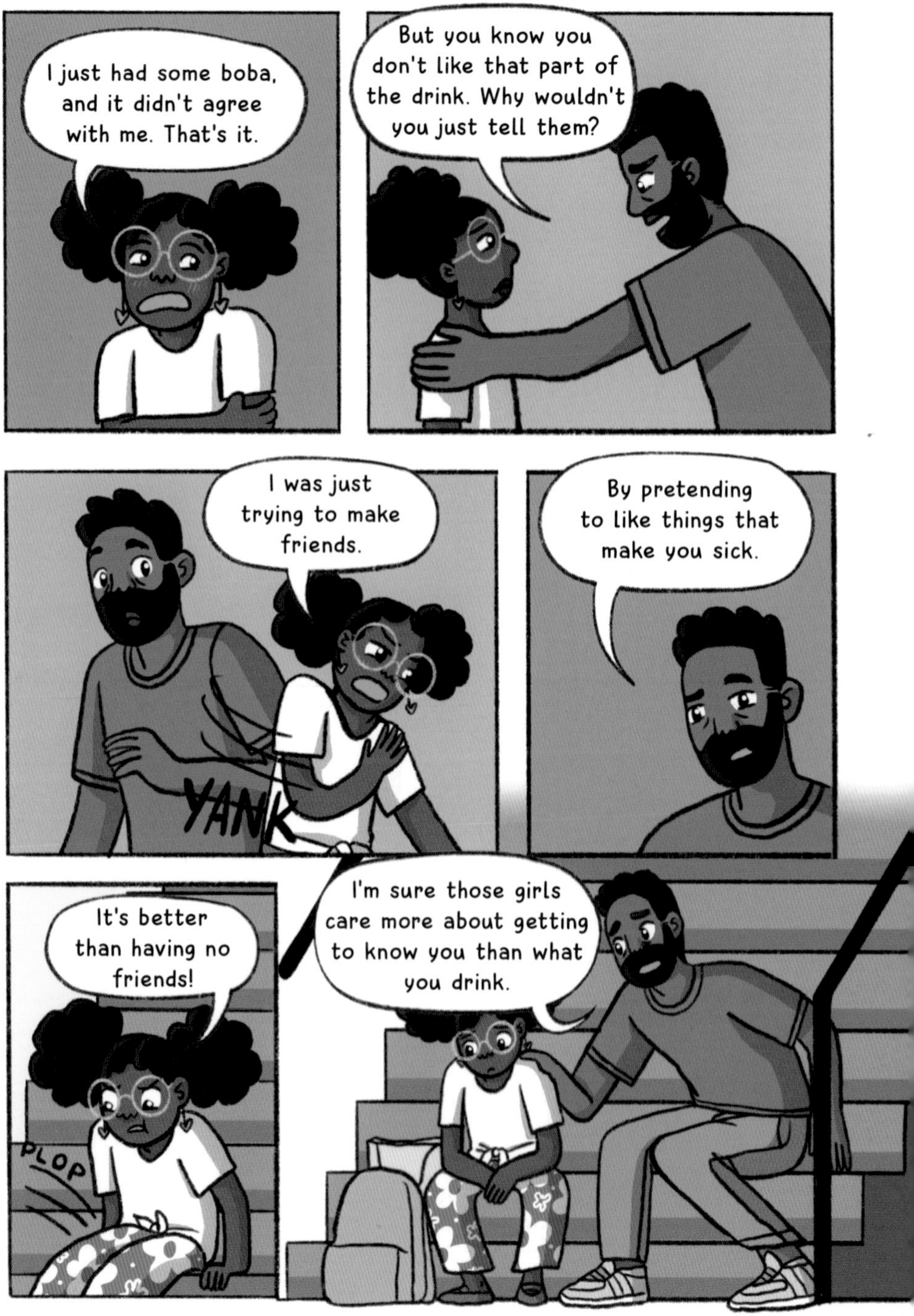
I just had some boba, and it didn't agree with me. That's it.
But you know you don't like that part of the drink. Why wouldn't you just tell them?
I was just trying to make friends.
YANK
By pretending to like things that make you sick.
It's better than having no friends!
PLOP
I'm sure those girls care more about getting to know you than what you drink.

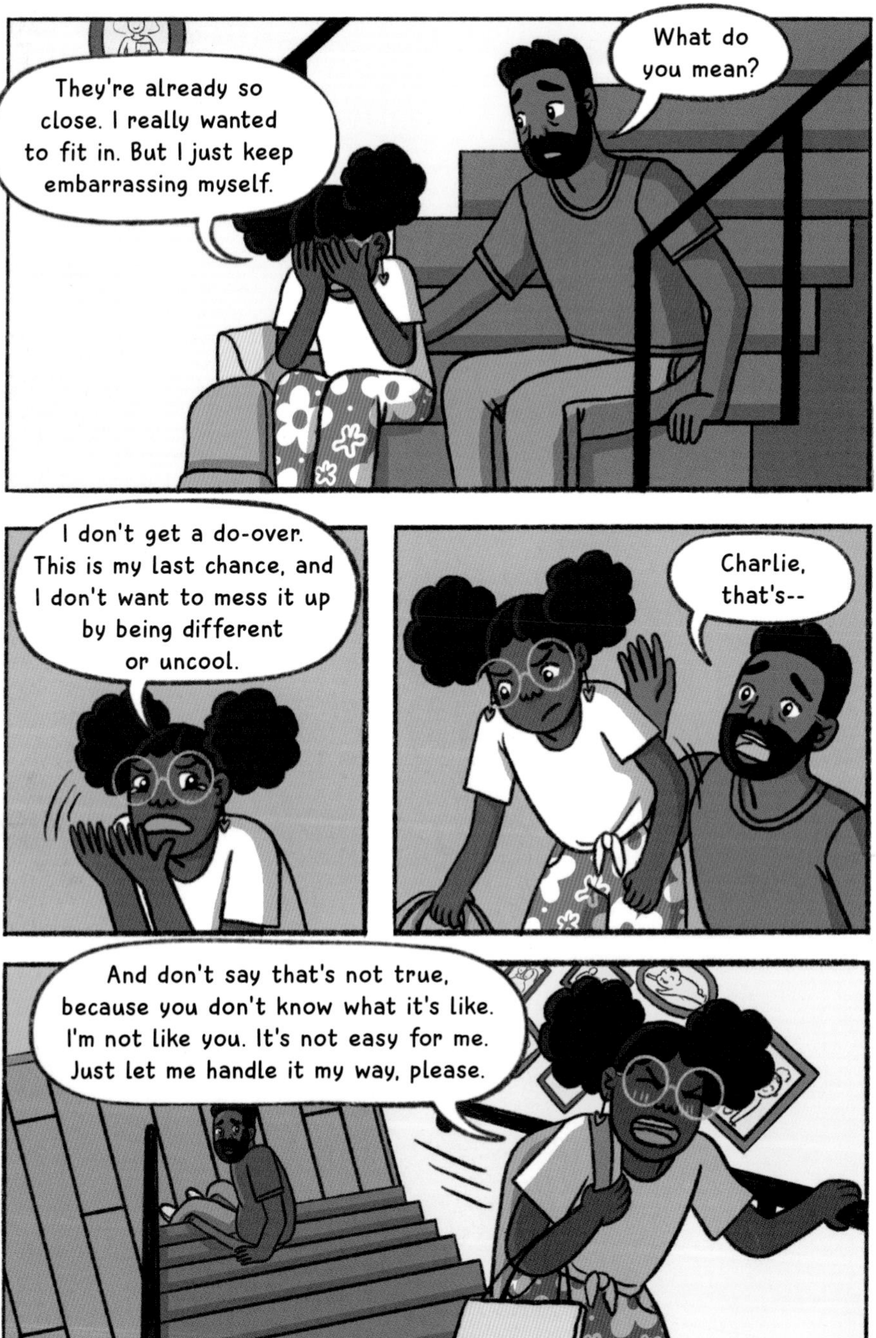
They're already so close. I really wanted to fit in. But I just keep embarrassing myself.
What do you mean?
I don't get a do-over. This is my last chance, and I don't want to mess it up by being different or uncool.
Charlie, that's--
And don't say that's not true, because you don't know what it's like. I'm not like you. It's not easy for me. Just let me handle it my way, please.

CHAPTER
10

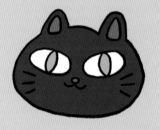

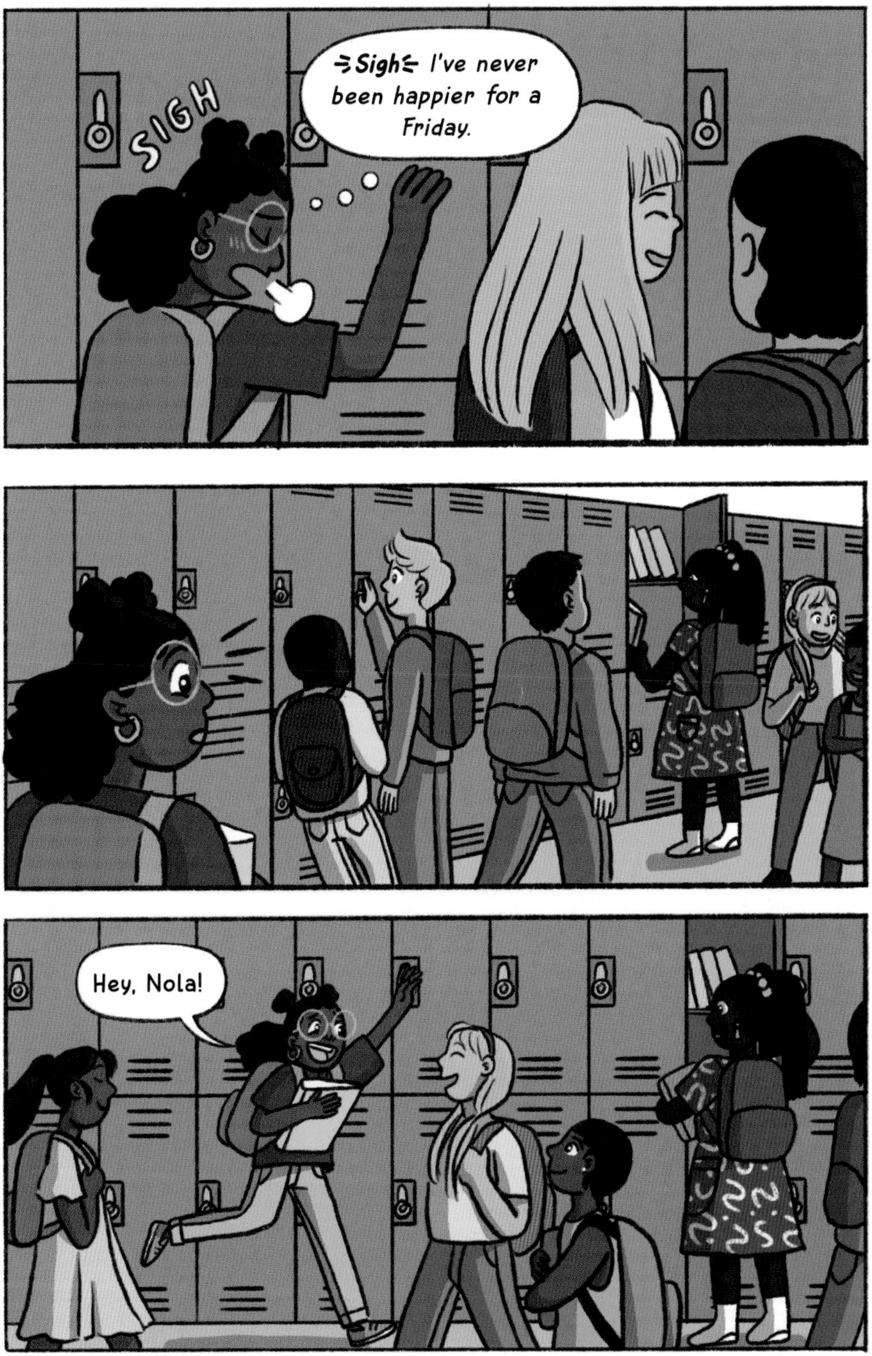

SIGH
⥱Sigh⥱ I've never been happier for a Friday.
Hey, Nola!

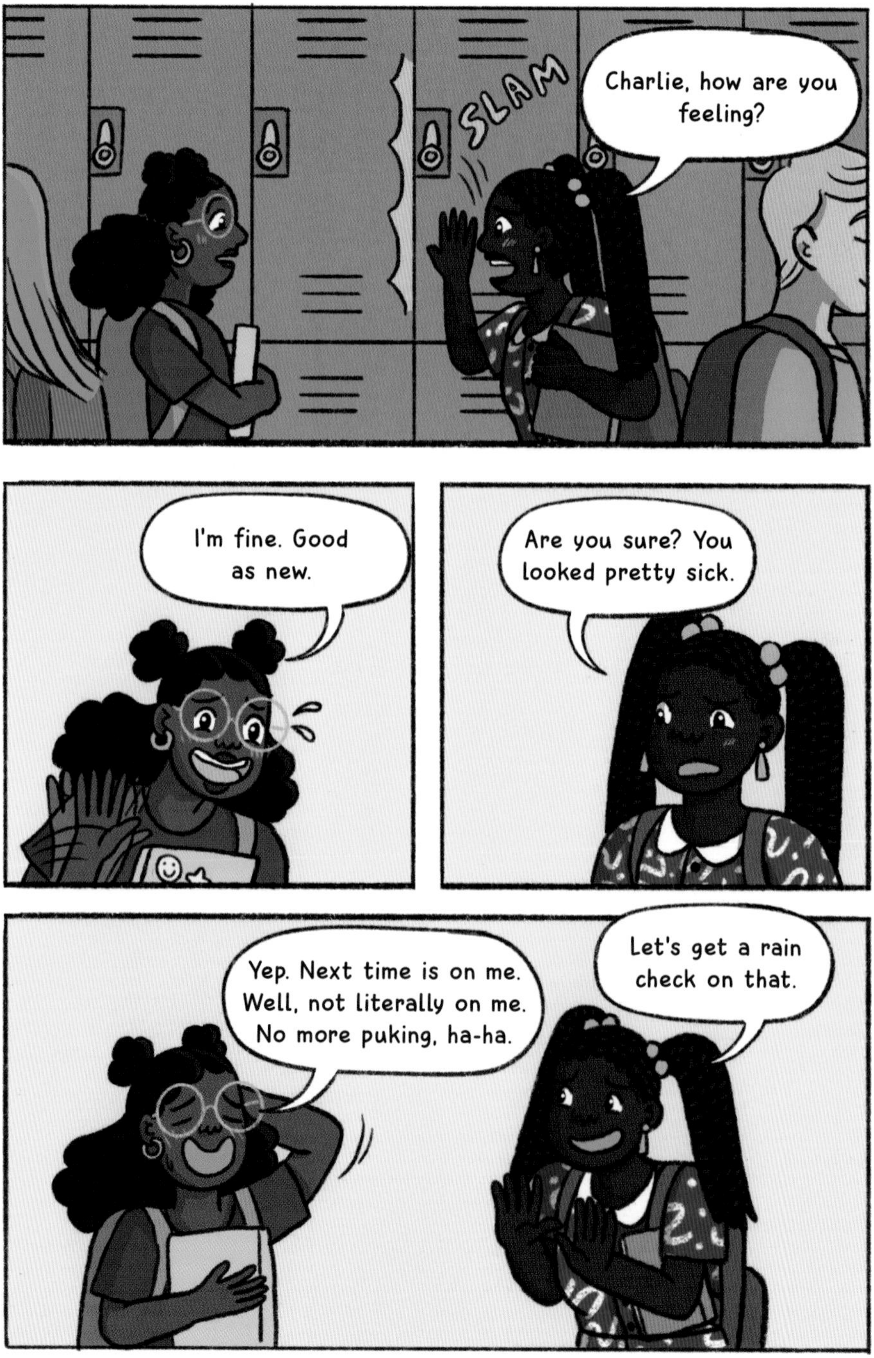
SLAM
Charlie, how are you feeling?
I'm fine. Good as new.
Are you sure? You looked pretty sick.
Yep. Next time is on me. Well, not literally on me. No more puking, ha-ha.
Let's get a rain check on that.

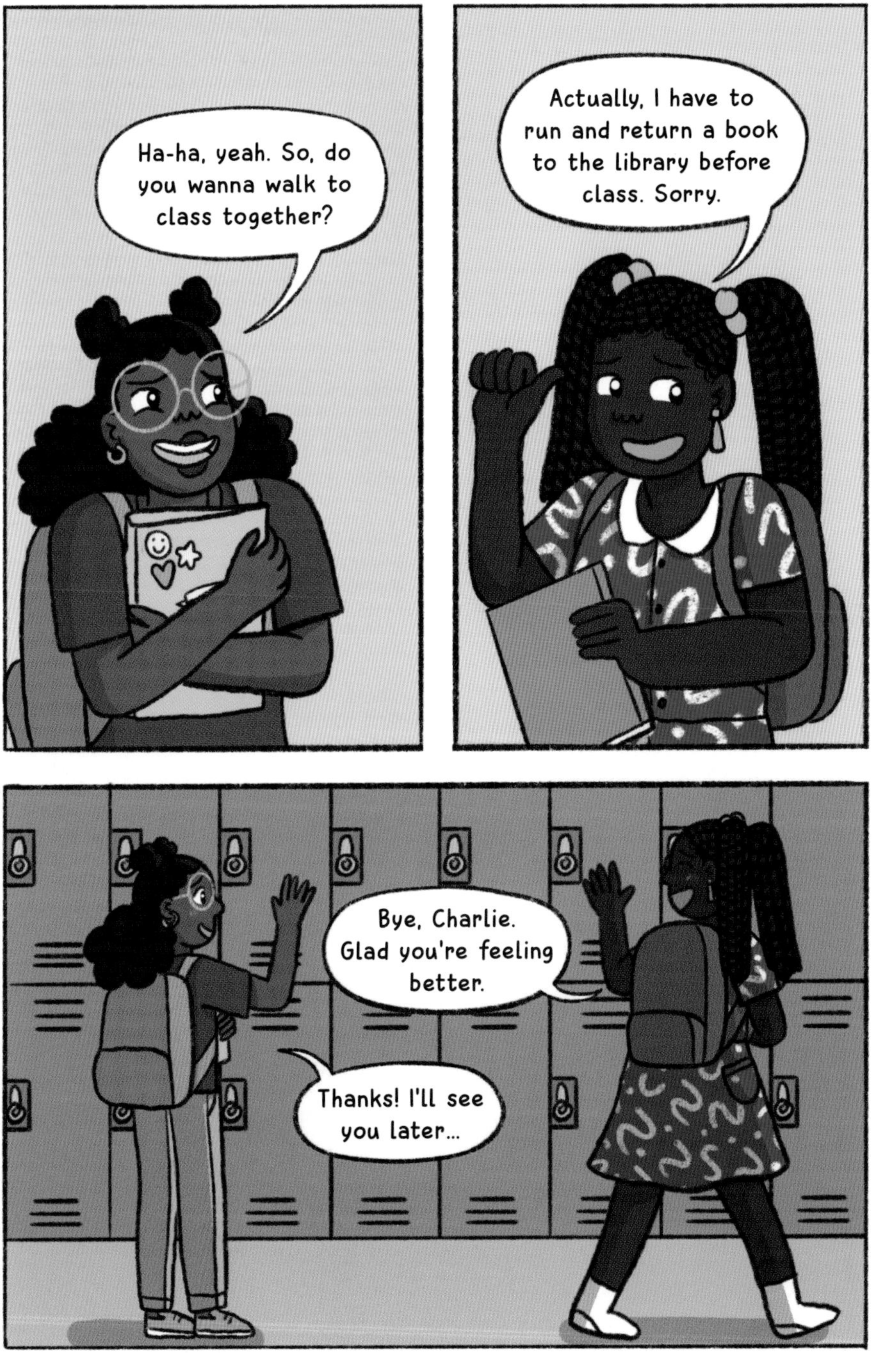
Ha-ha, yeah. So, do you wanna walk to class together?
Actually, I have to run and return a book to the library before class. Sorry.
Bye, Charlie. Glad you're feeling better.
Thanks! I'll see you later...

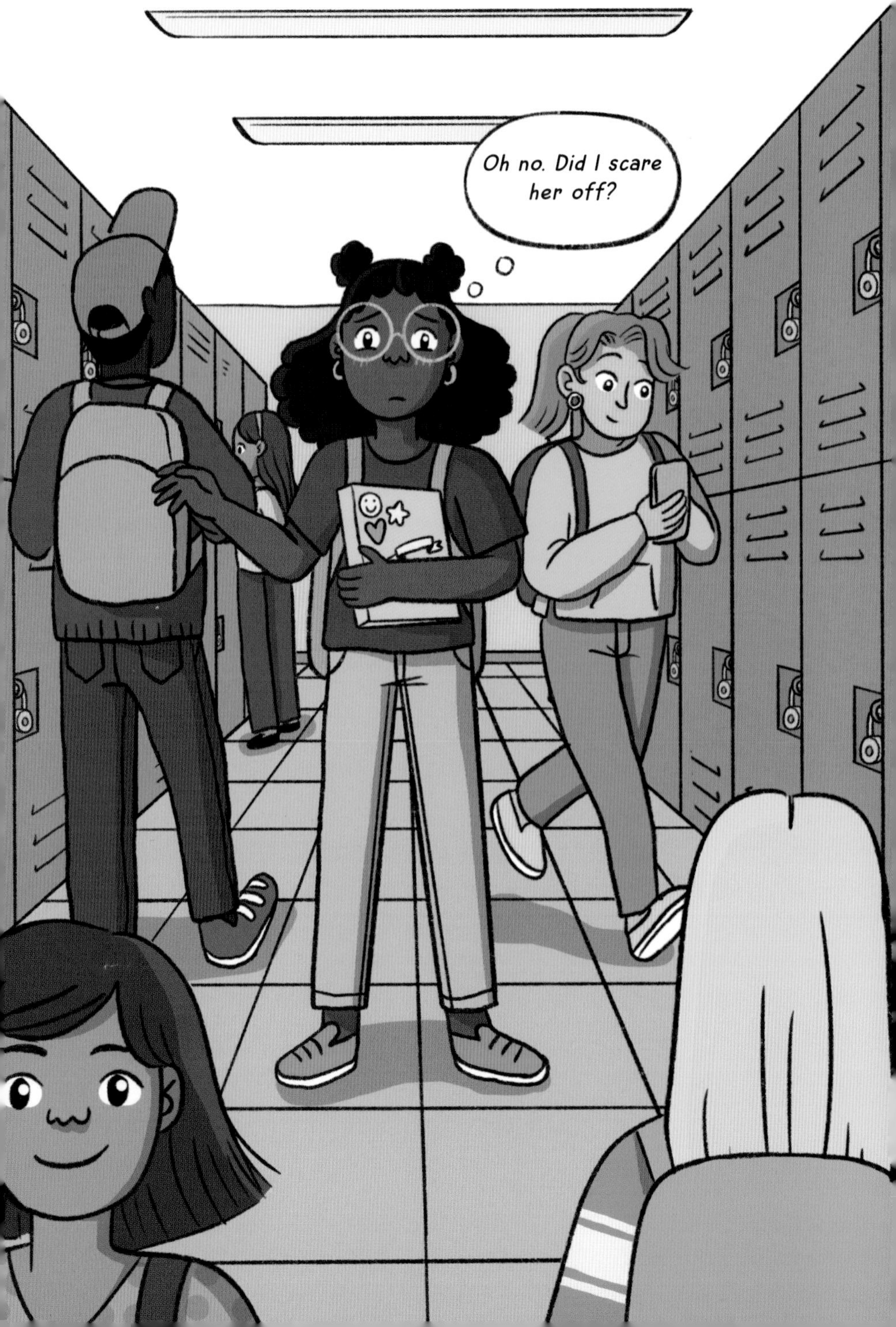
Oh no. Did I scare her off?

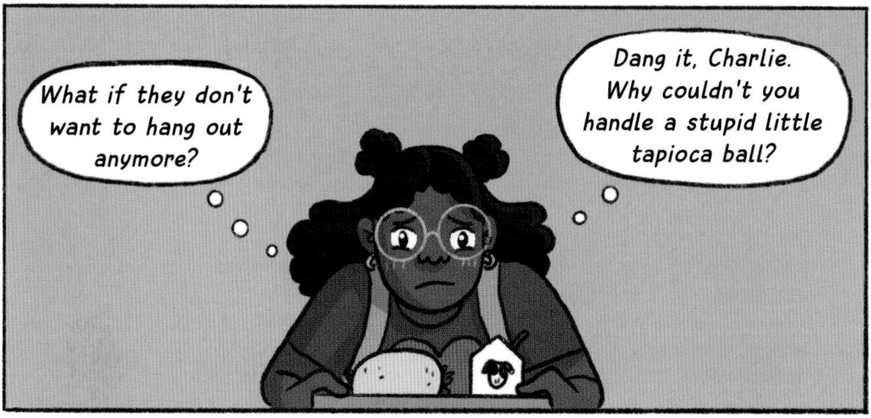
What if they don't want to hang out anymore?
Dang it, Charlie. Why couldn't you handle a stupid little tapioca ball?
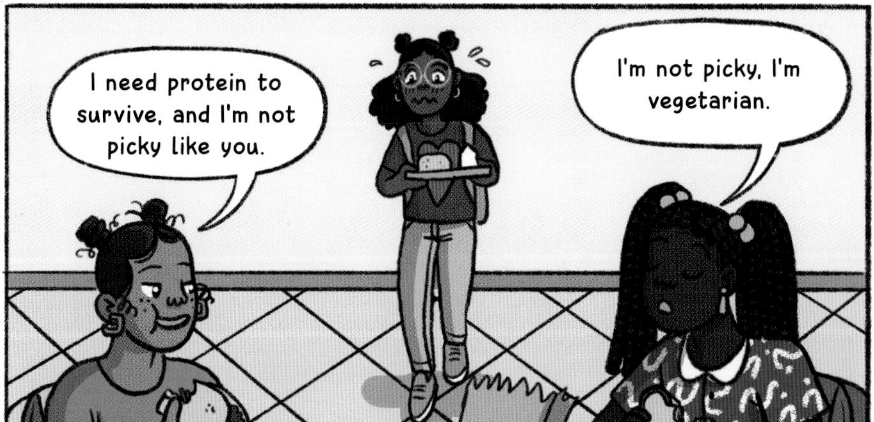
I need protein to survive, and I'm not picky like you.
I'm not picky, I'm vegetarian.
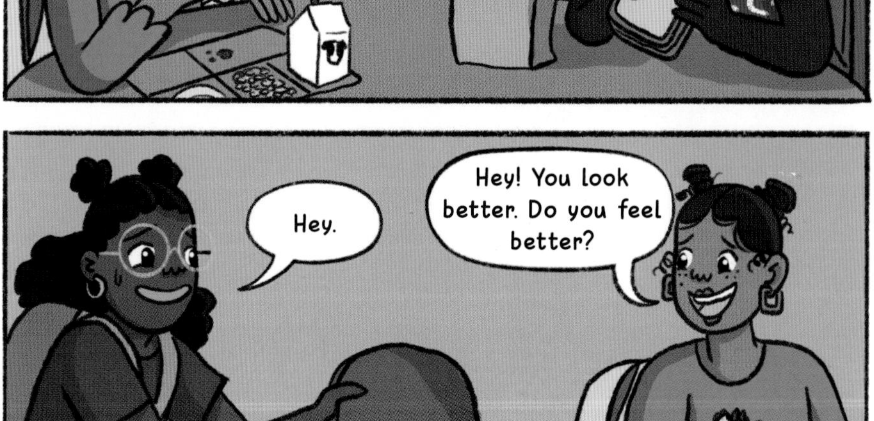
Hey.
Hey! You look better. Do you feel better?

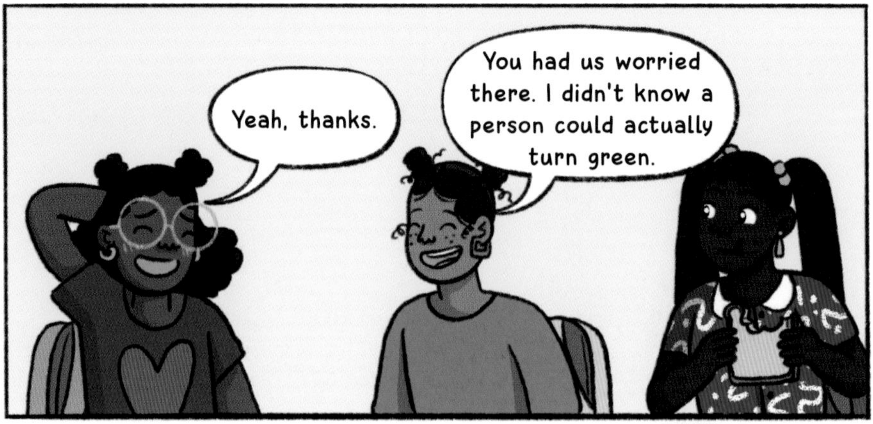
Yeah, thanks.
You had us worried there. I didn't know a person could actually turn green.

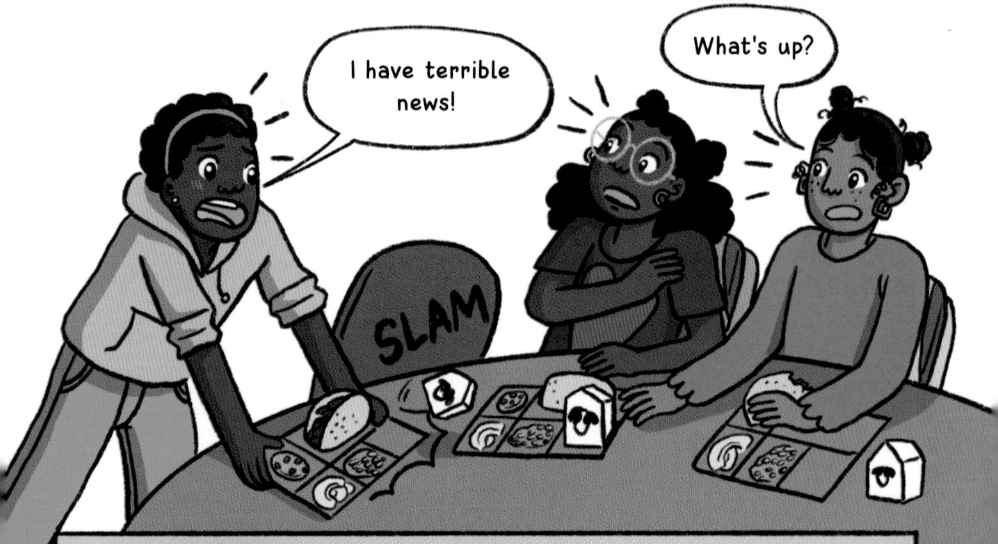
I have terrible news!
What's up?
SLAM

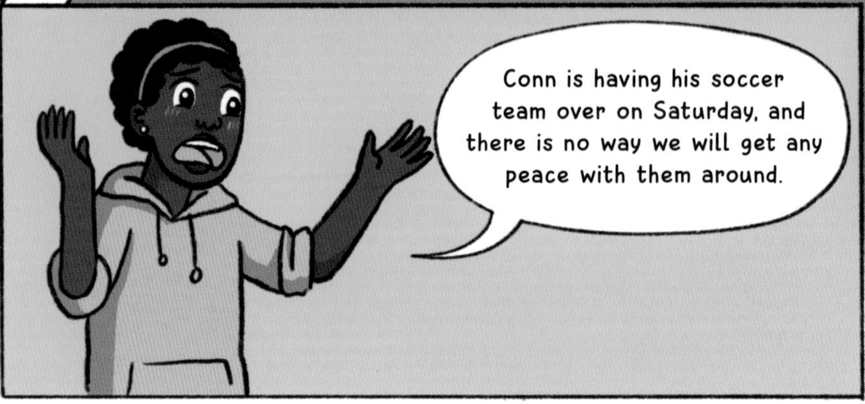
Conn is having his soccer team over on Saturday, and there is no way we will get any peace with them around.

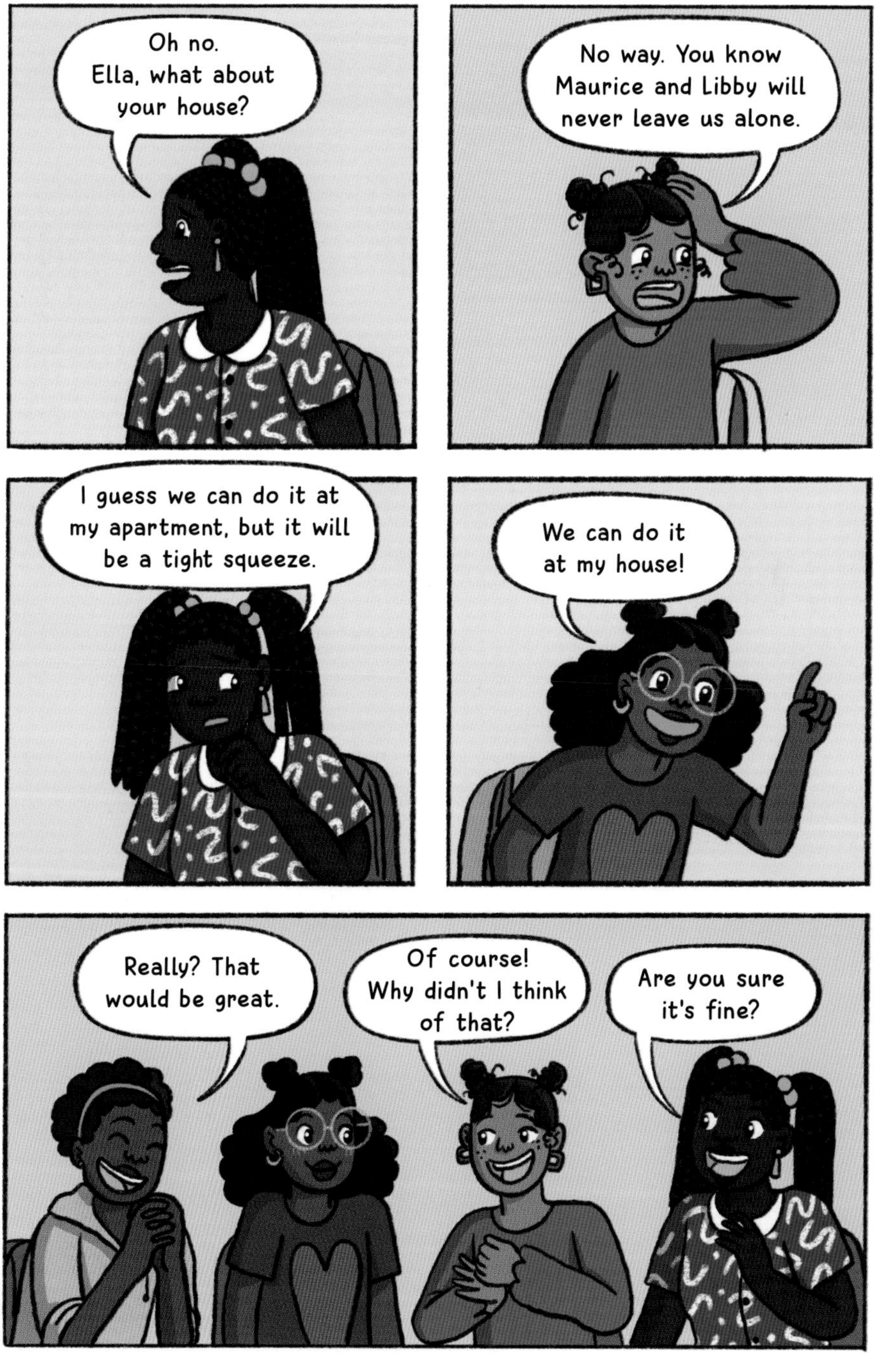
Oh no.
Ella, what about your house?
No way. You know Maurice and Libby will never leave us alone.
I guess we can do it at my apartment, but it will be a tight squeeze.
We can do it at my house!
Really? That would be great.
Of course! Why didn't I think of that?
Are you sure it's fine?

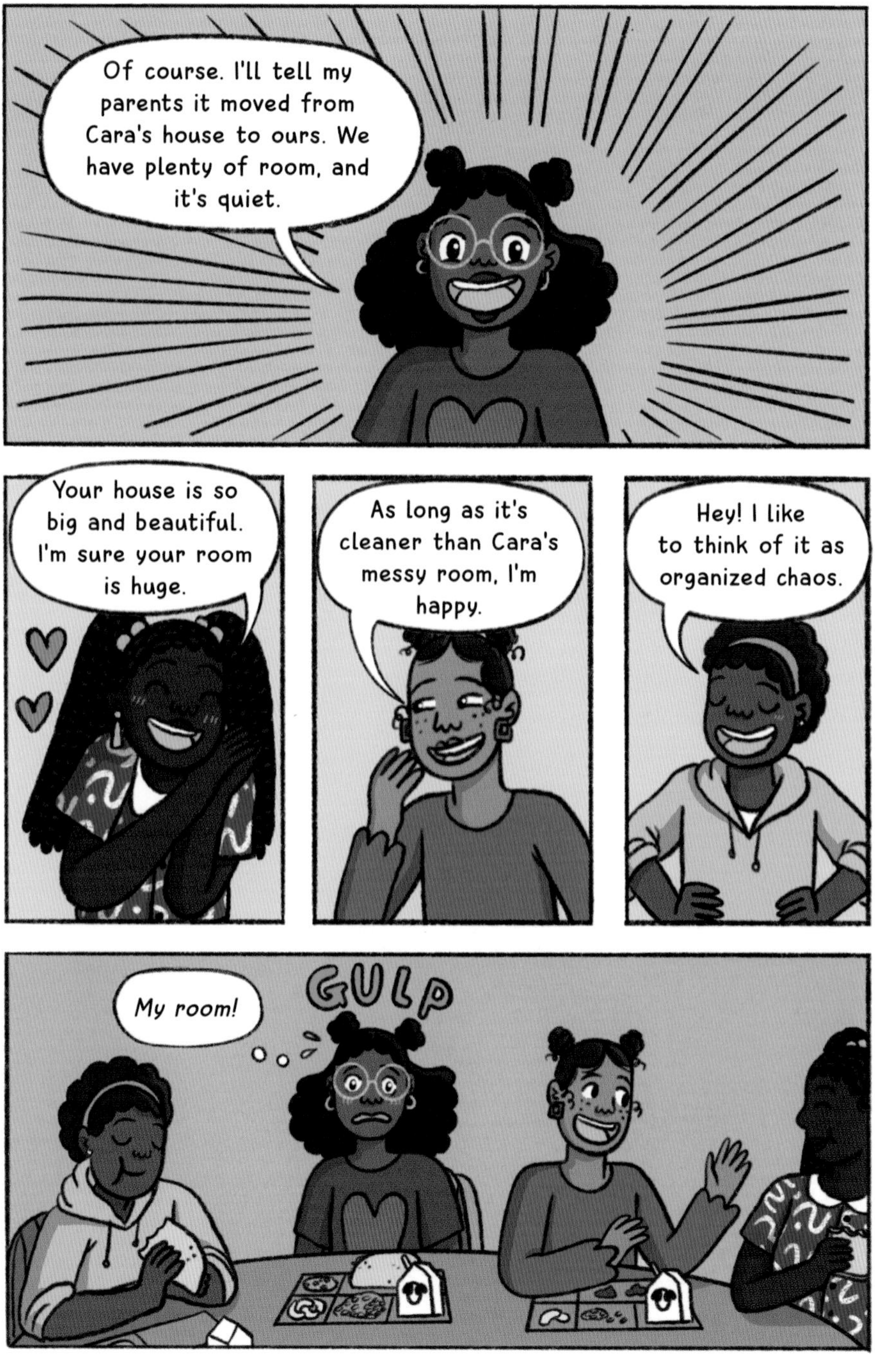
Of course. I'll tell my parents it moved from Cara's house to ours. We have plenty of room, and it's quiet.
Your house is so big and beautiful. I'm sure your room is huge.
As long as it's cleaner than Cara's messy room, I'm happy.
Hey! I like to think of it as organized chaos.
My room!
GULP

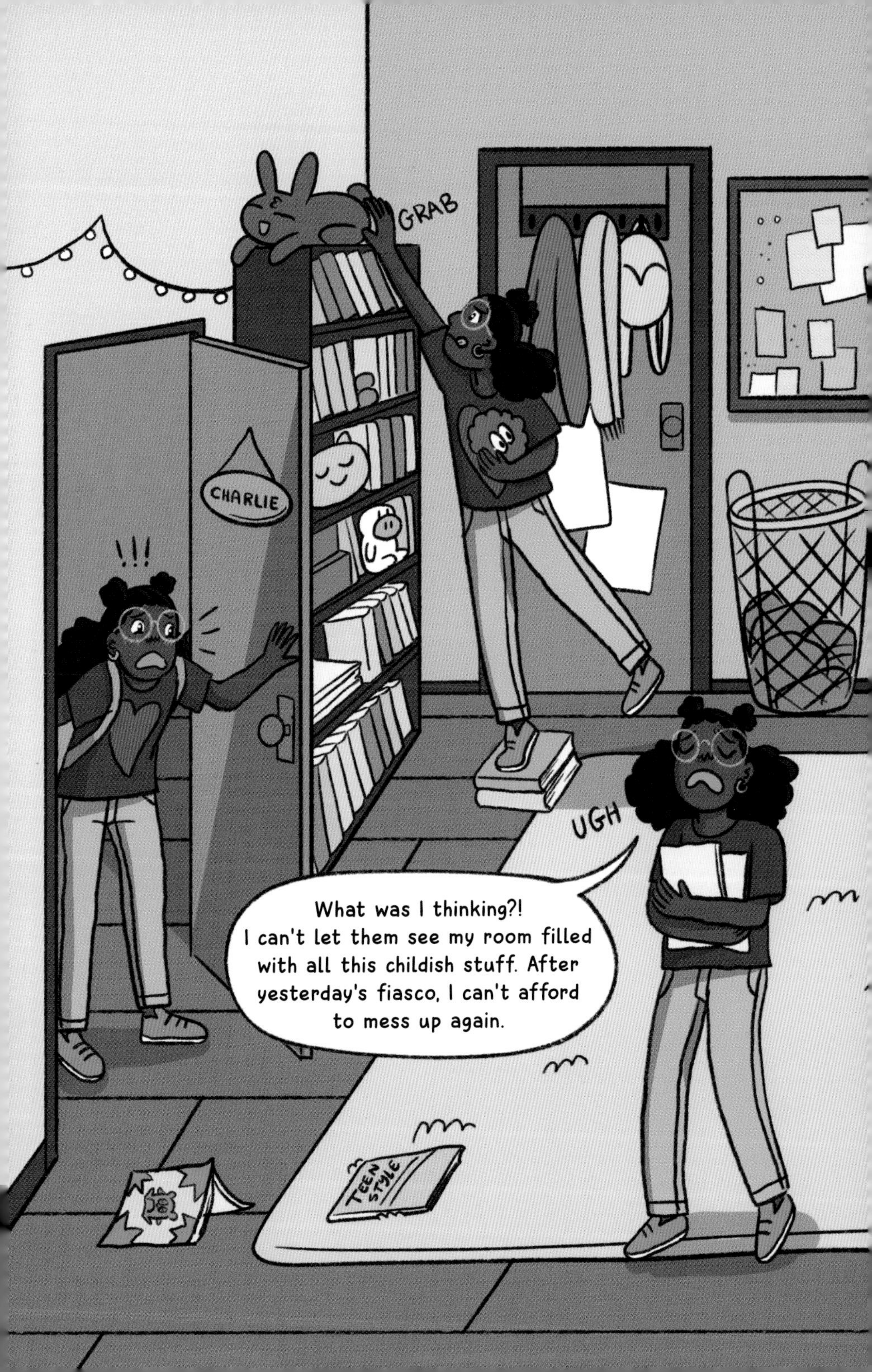
CHARLIE
GRAB
!!!
UGH
What was I thinking?! I can't let them see my room filled with all this childish stuff. After yesterday's fiasco, I can't afford to mess up again.
TEEN STYLE

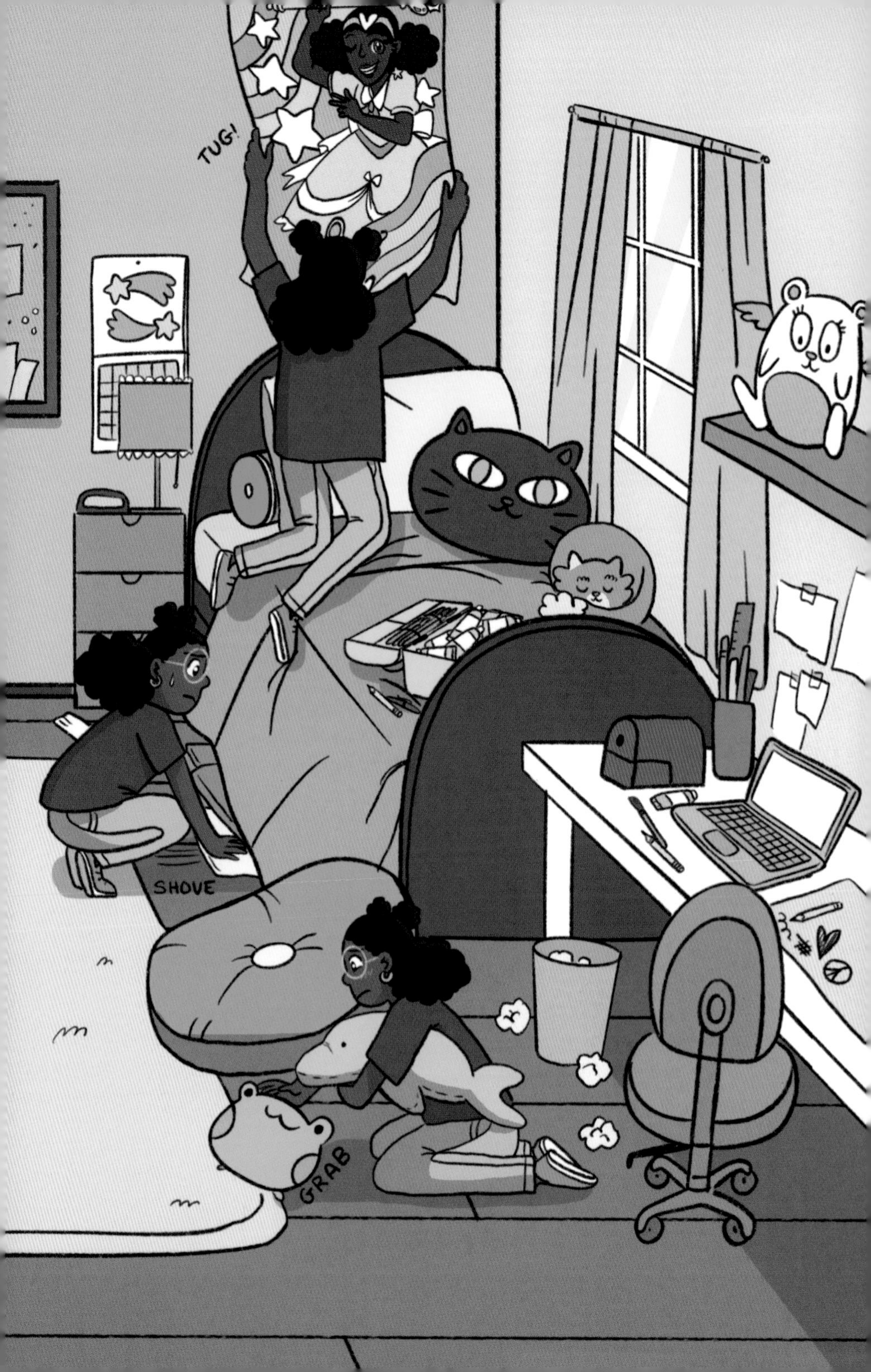
TUG!
SHOVE
GRAB

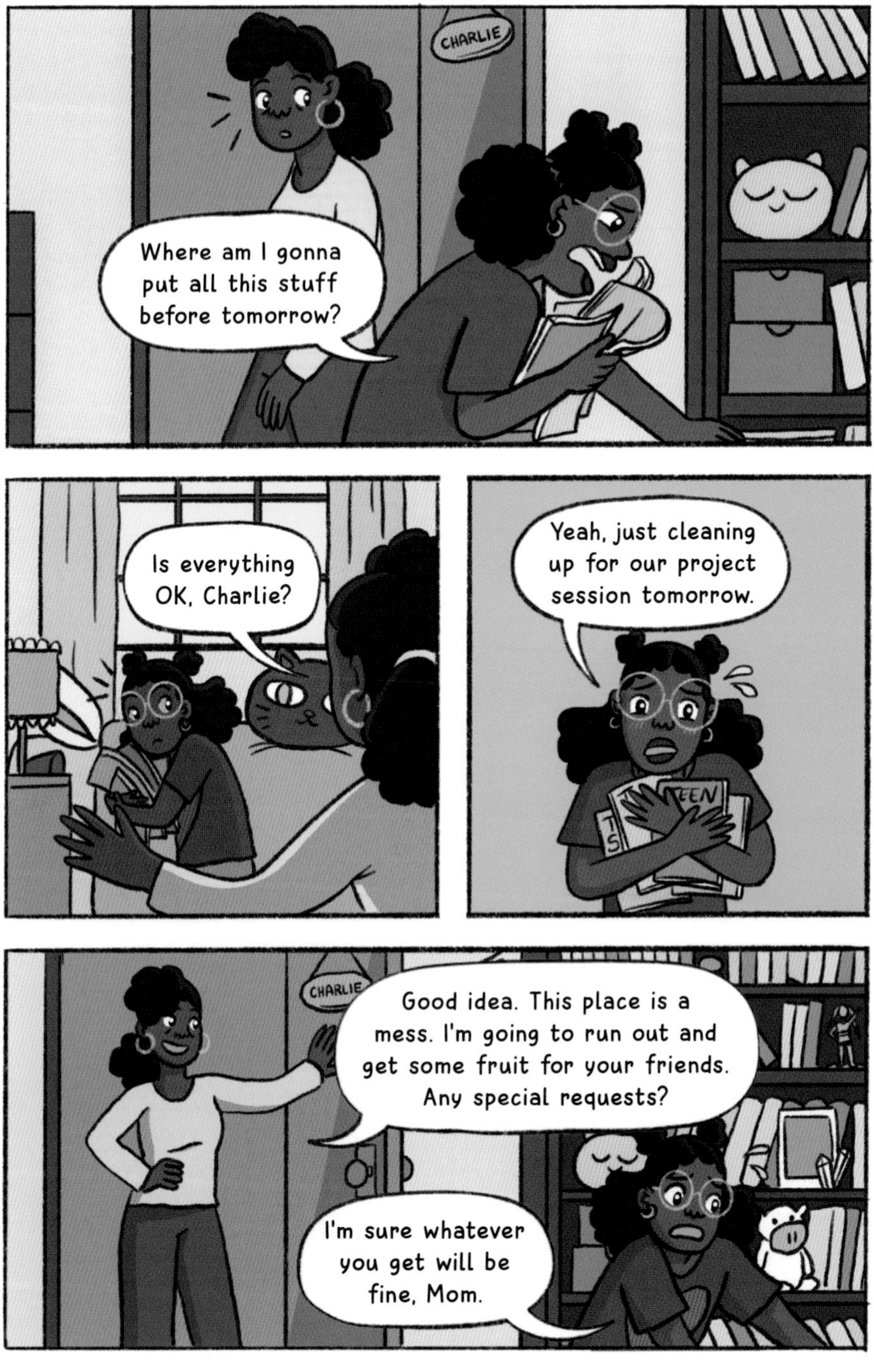
CHARLIE
Where am I gonna put all this stuff before tomorrow?
Is everything OK, Charlie?
Yeah, just cleaning up for our project session tomorrow.
CHARLIE
Good idea. This place is a mess. I'm going to run out and get some fruit for your friends. Any special requests?
I'm sure whatever you get will be fine, Mom.

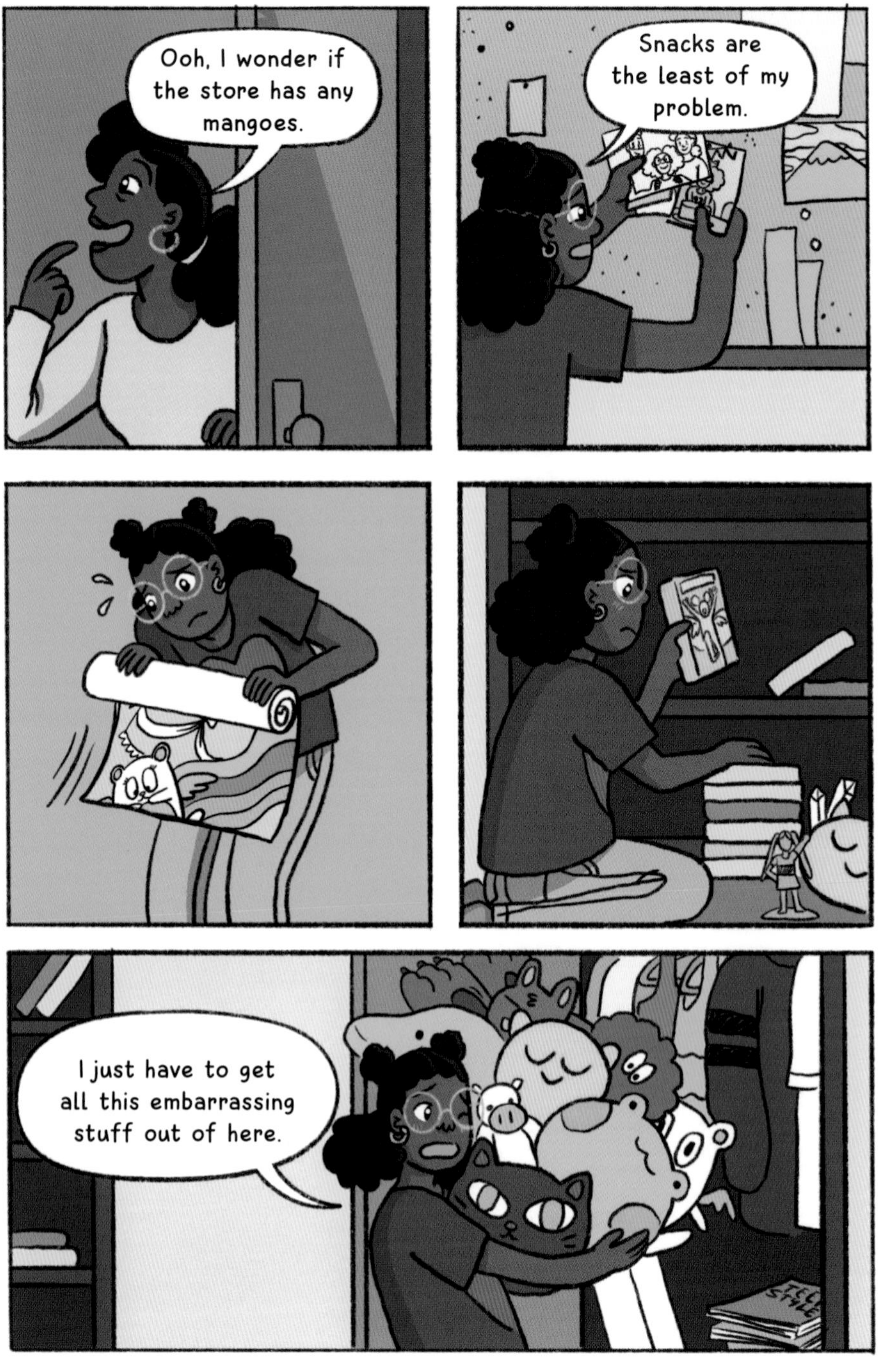
Ooh, I wonder if the store has any mangoes.
Snacks are the least of my problem.
I just have to get all this embarrassing stuff out of here.

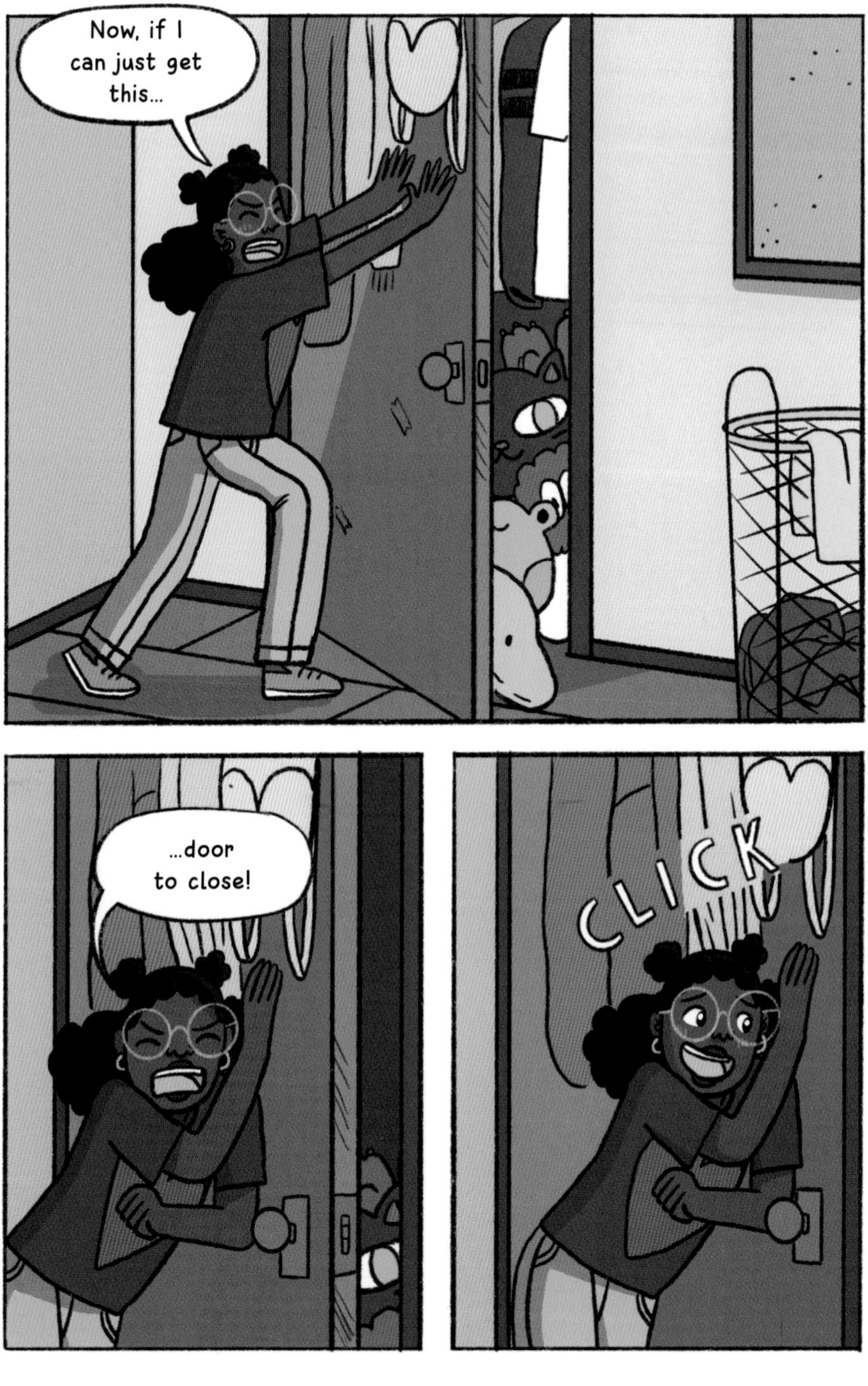
Now, if I can just get this...
...door to close!
CLICK

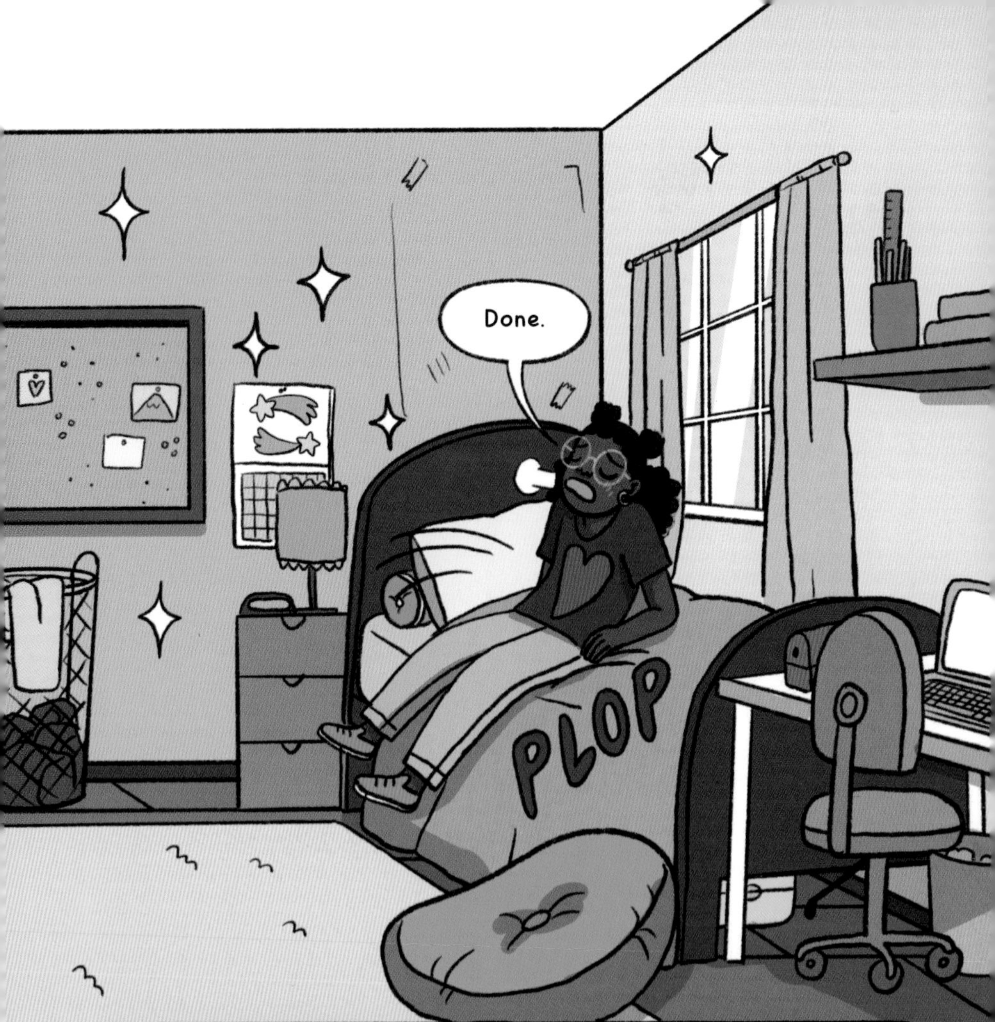
Done.
PLOP

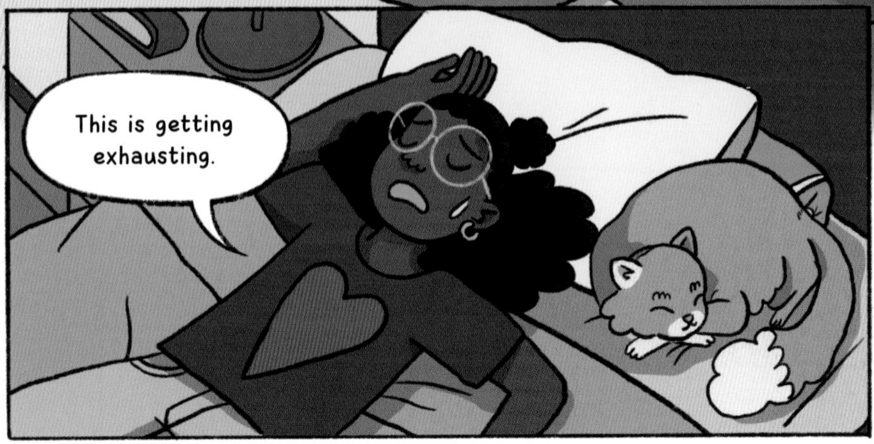
This is getting exhausting.

CHAPTER
11

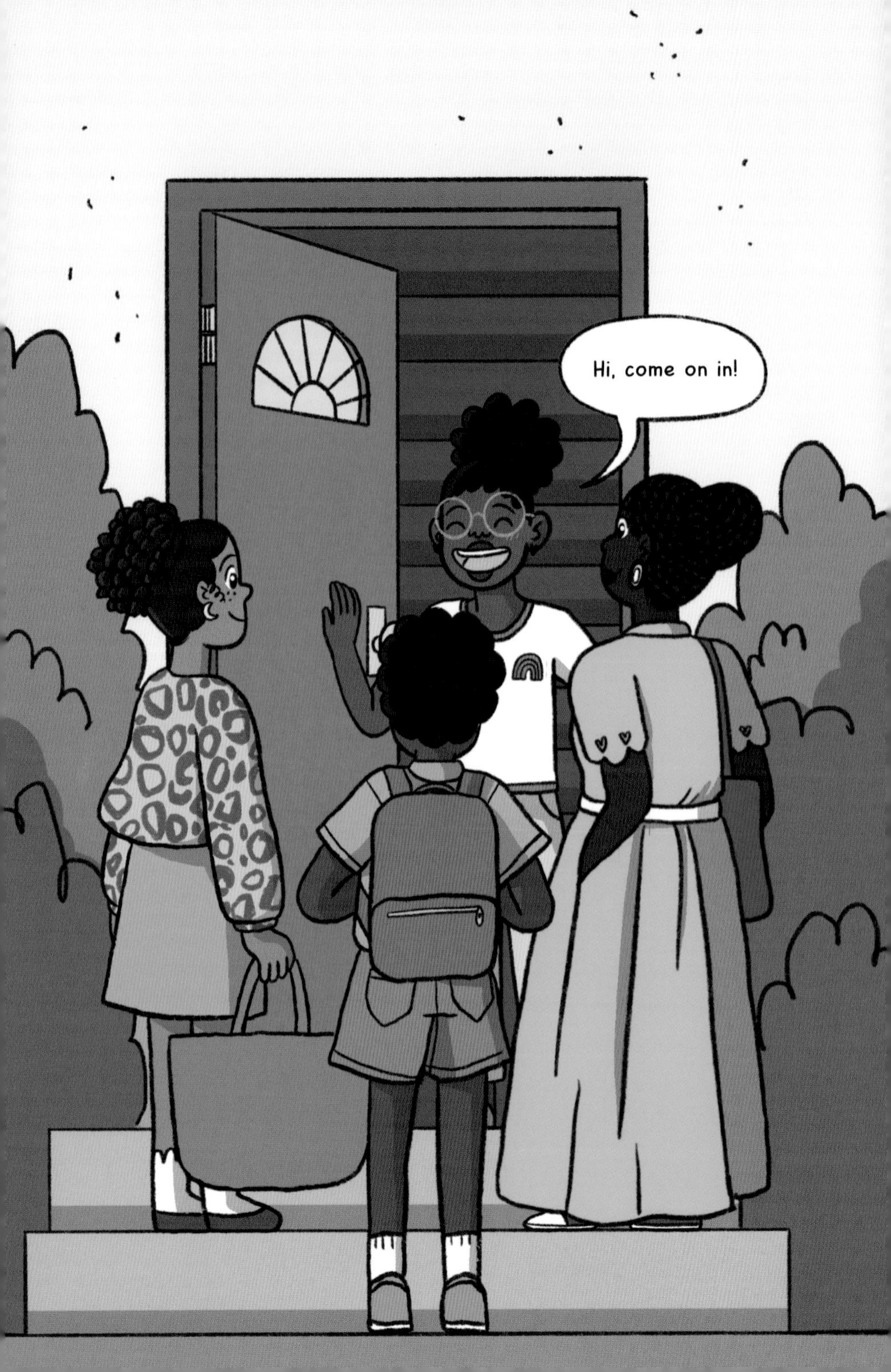
Hi, come on in!

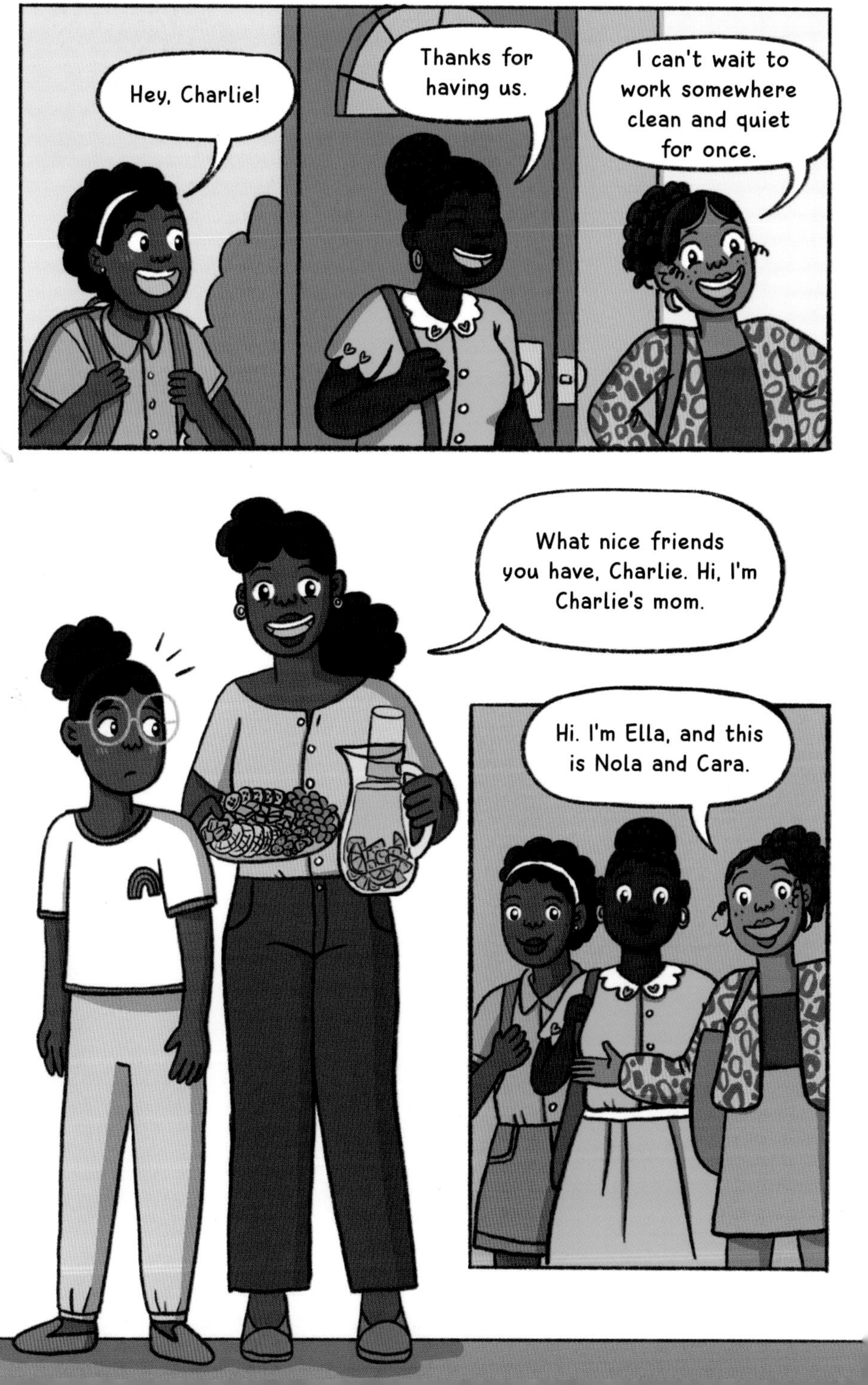
Hey, Charlie!
Thanks for having us.
I can't wait to work somewhere clean and quiet for once.
What nice friends you have, Charlie. Hi, I'm Charlie's mom.
Hi. I'm Ella, and this is Nola and Cara.

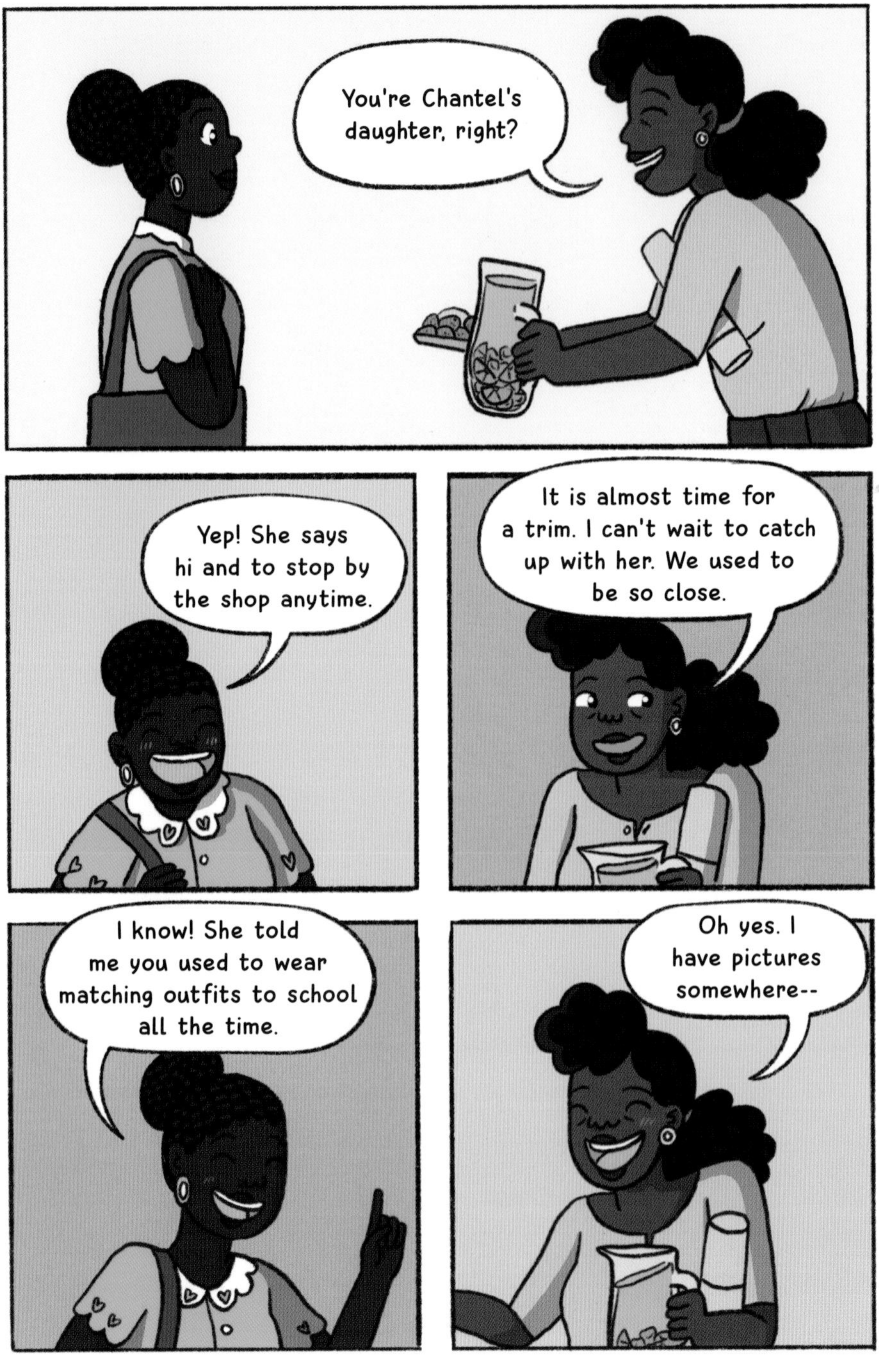
You're Chantel's daughter, right?
Yep! She says hi and to stop by the shop anytime.
It is almost time for a trim. I can't wait to catch up with her. We used to be so close.
I know! She told me you used to wear matching outfits to school all the time.
Oh yes. I have pictures somewhere--

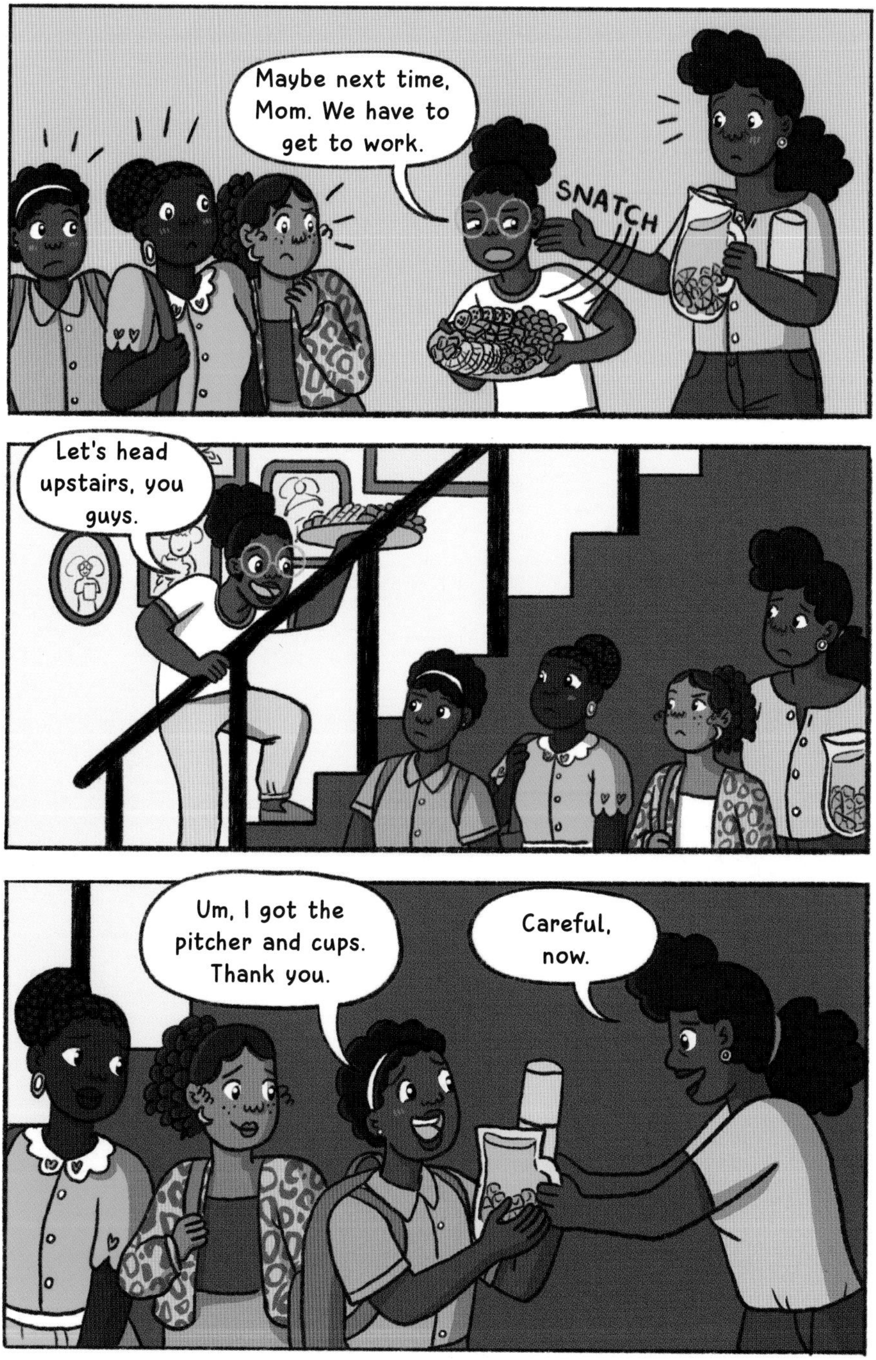
Maybe next time, Mom. We have to get to work.
SNATCH
Let's head upstairs, you guys.
Um, I got the pitcher and cups. Thank you.
Careful, now.

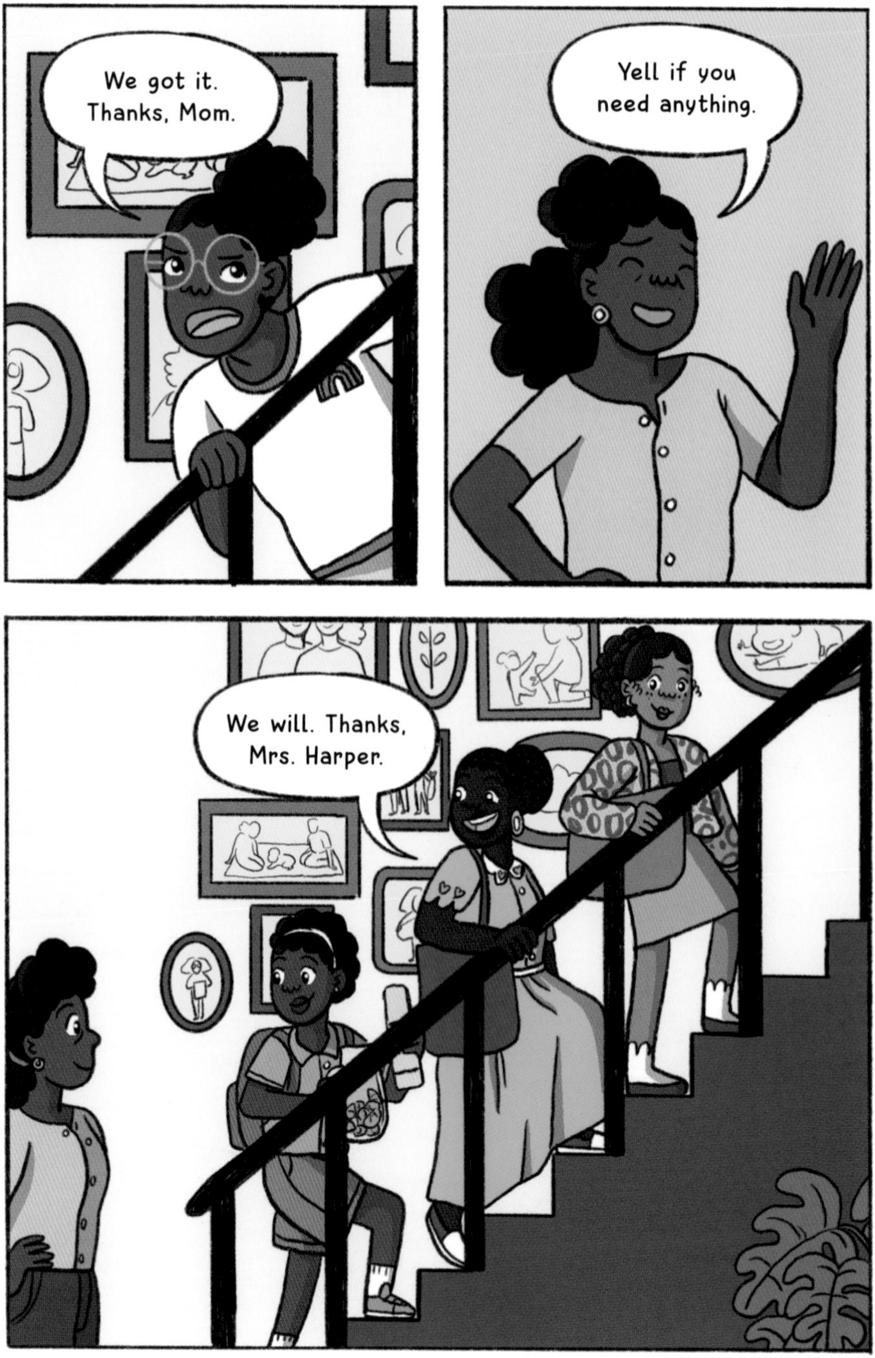

We got it. Thanks, Mom.
Yell if you need anything.
We will. Thanks, Mrs. Harper.

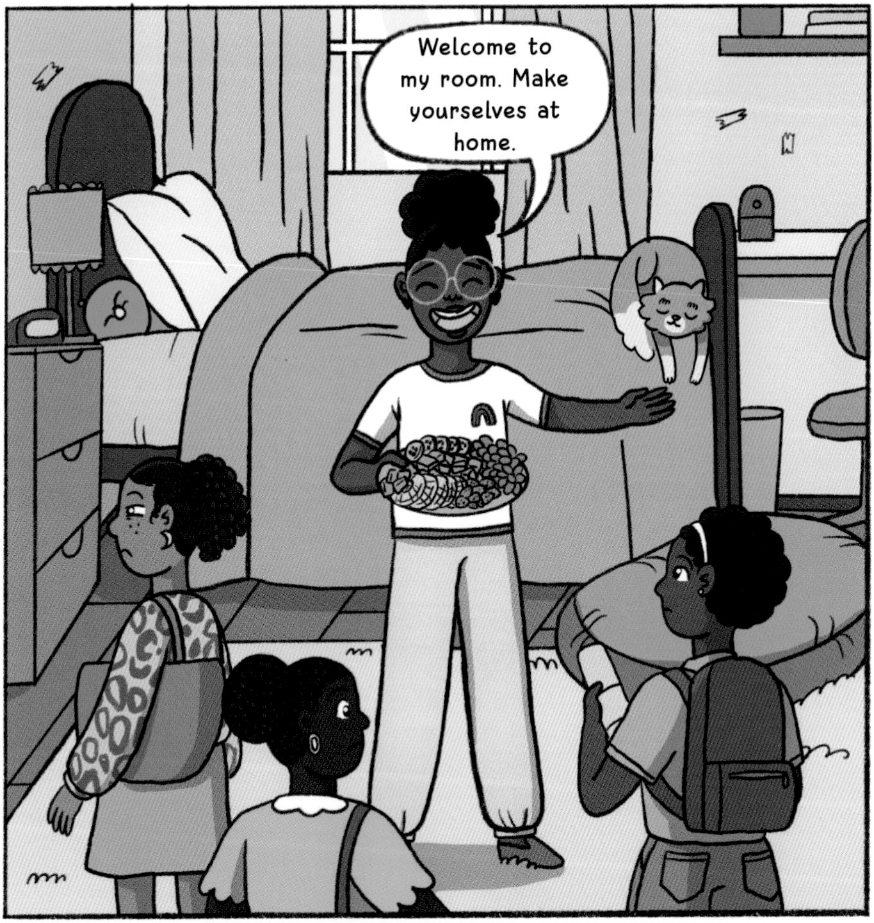
Welcome to my room. Make yourselves at home.

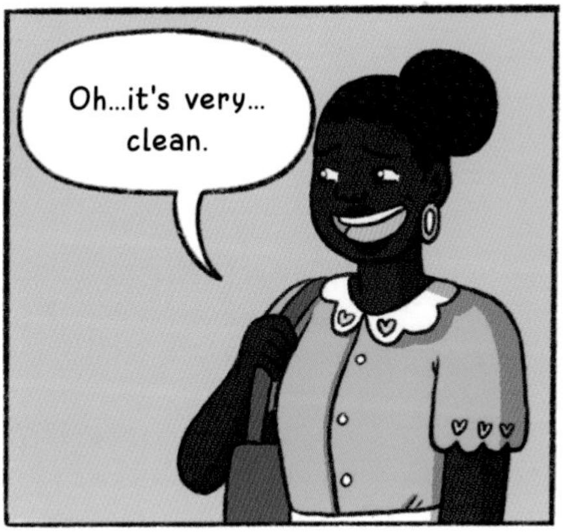
Oh...it's very... clean.

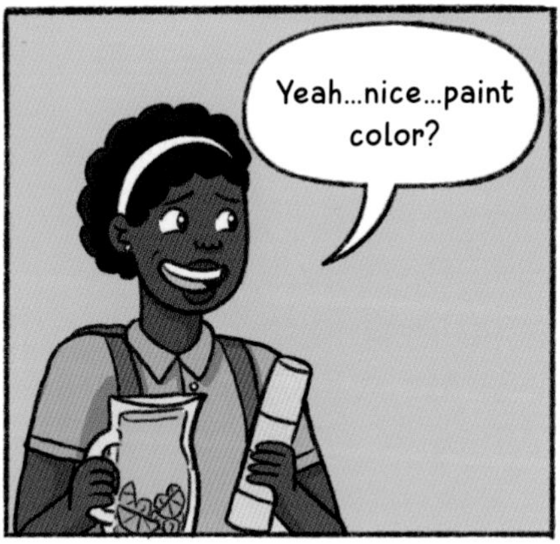
Yeah...nice...paint color?

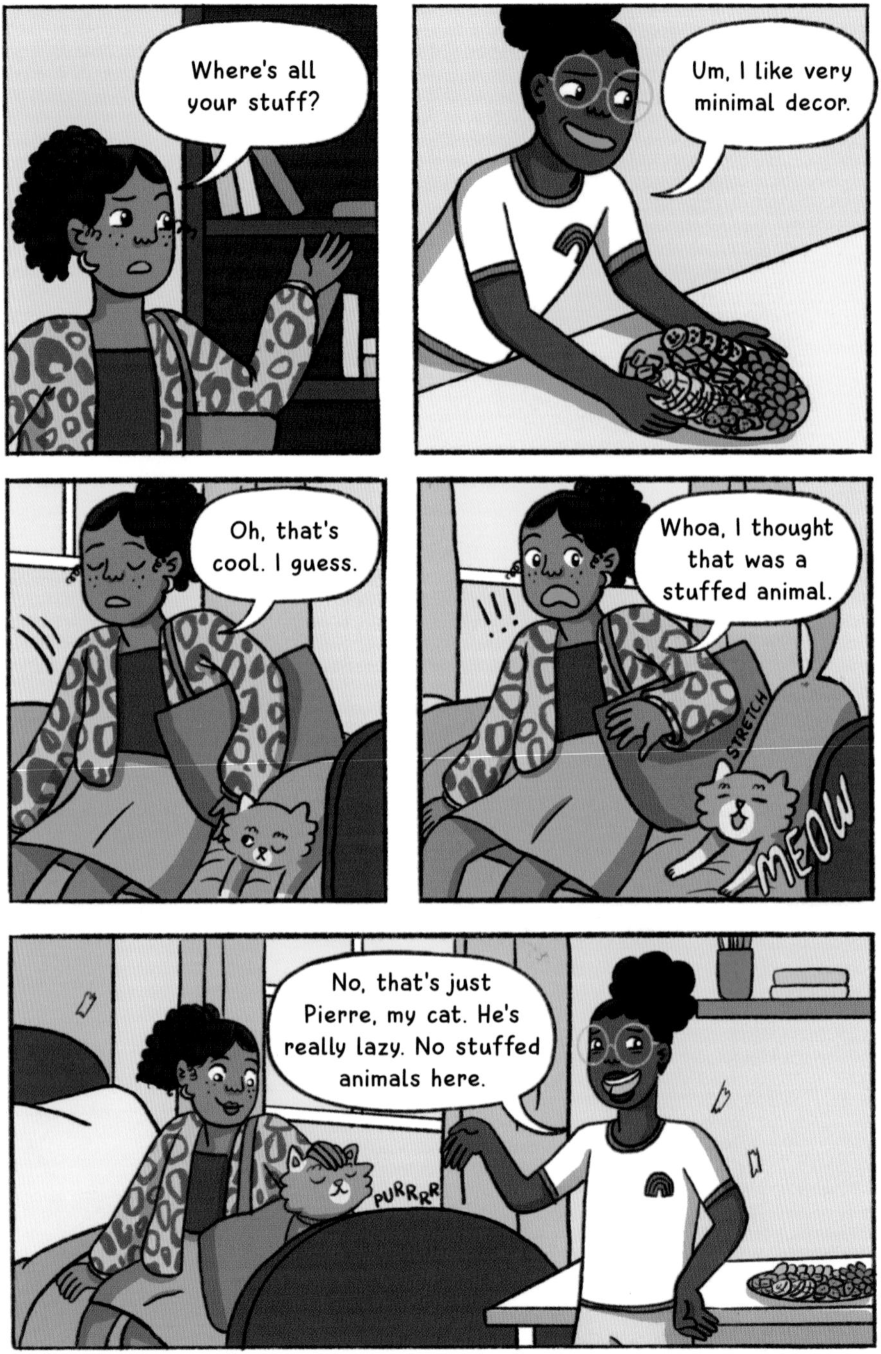
Where's all your stuff?
Um, I like very minimal decor.
Oh, that's cool. I guess.
!!!
Whoa, I thought that was a stuffed animal.
STRETCH
MEOW
No, that's just Pierre, my cat. He's really lazy. No stuffed animals here.
PURRRR

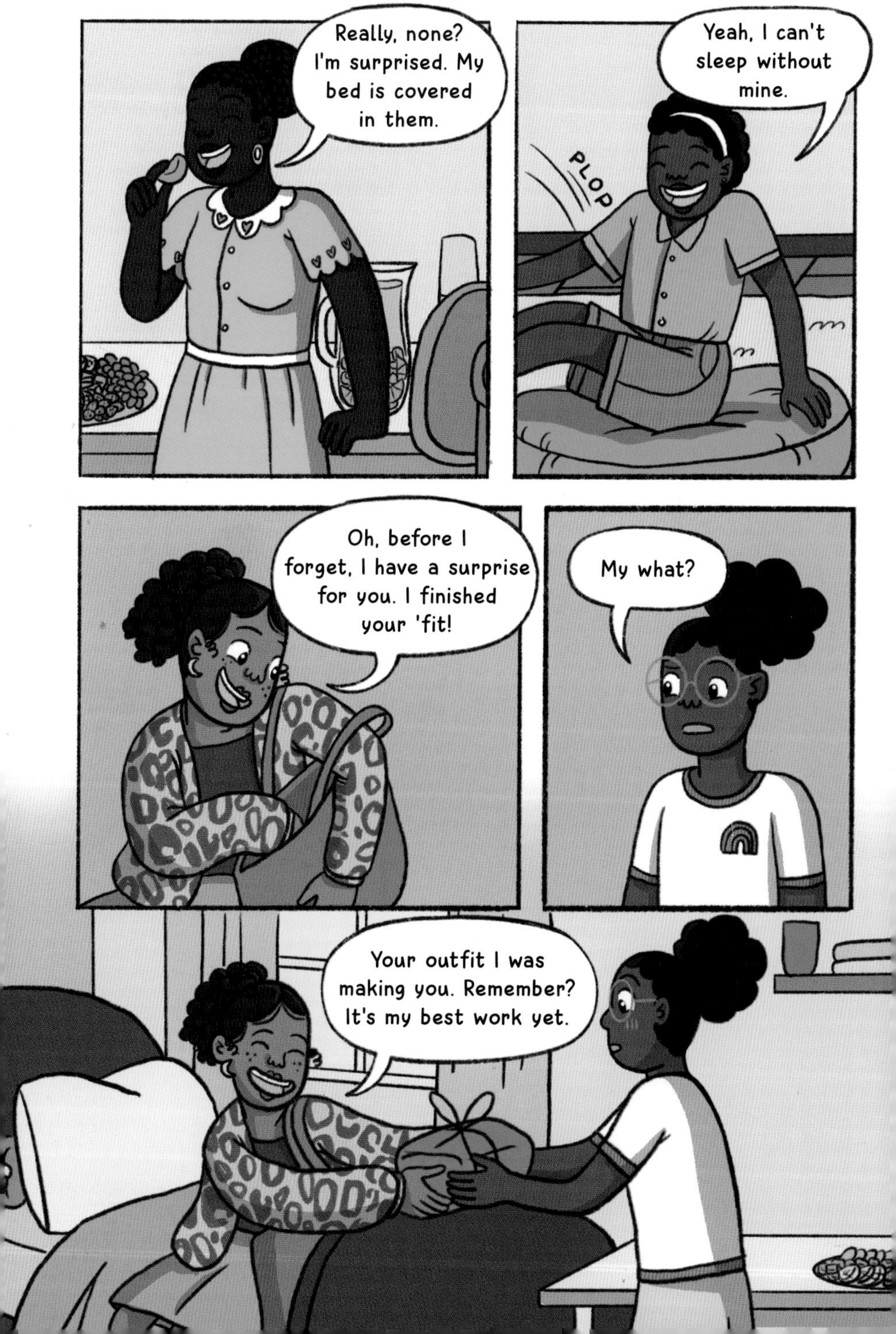
Really, none? I'm surprised. My bed is covered in them.
Yeah, I can't sleep without mine.
PLOP
Oh, before I forget, I have a surprise for you. I finished your 'fit!
My what?
Your outfit I was making you. Remember? It's my best work yet.

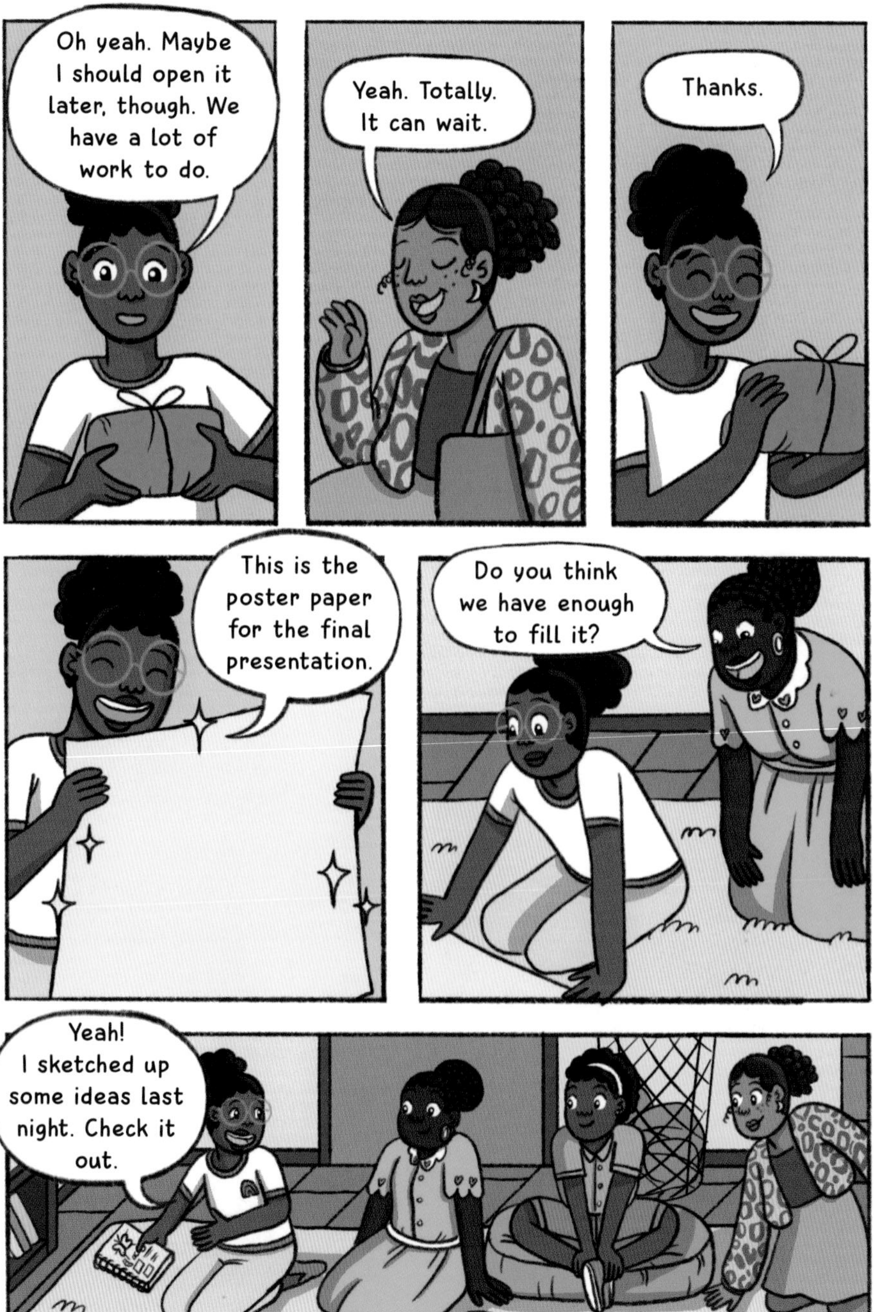
Oh yeah. Maybe I should open it later, though. We have a lot of work to do.
Yeah. Totally. It can wait.
Thanks.
This is the poster paper for the final presentation.
Do you think we have enough to fill it?
Yeah! I sketched up some ideas last night. Check it out.

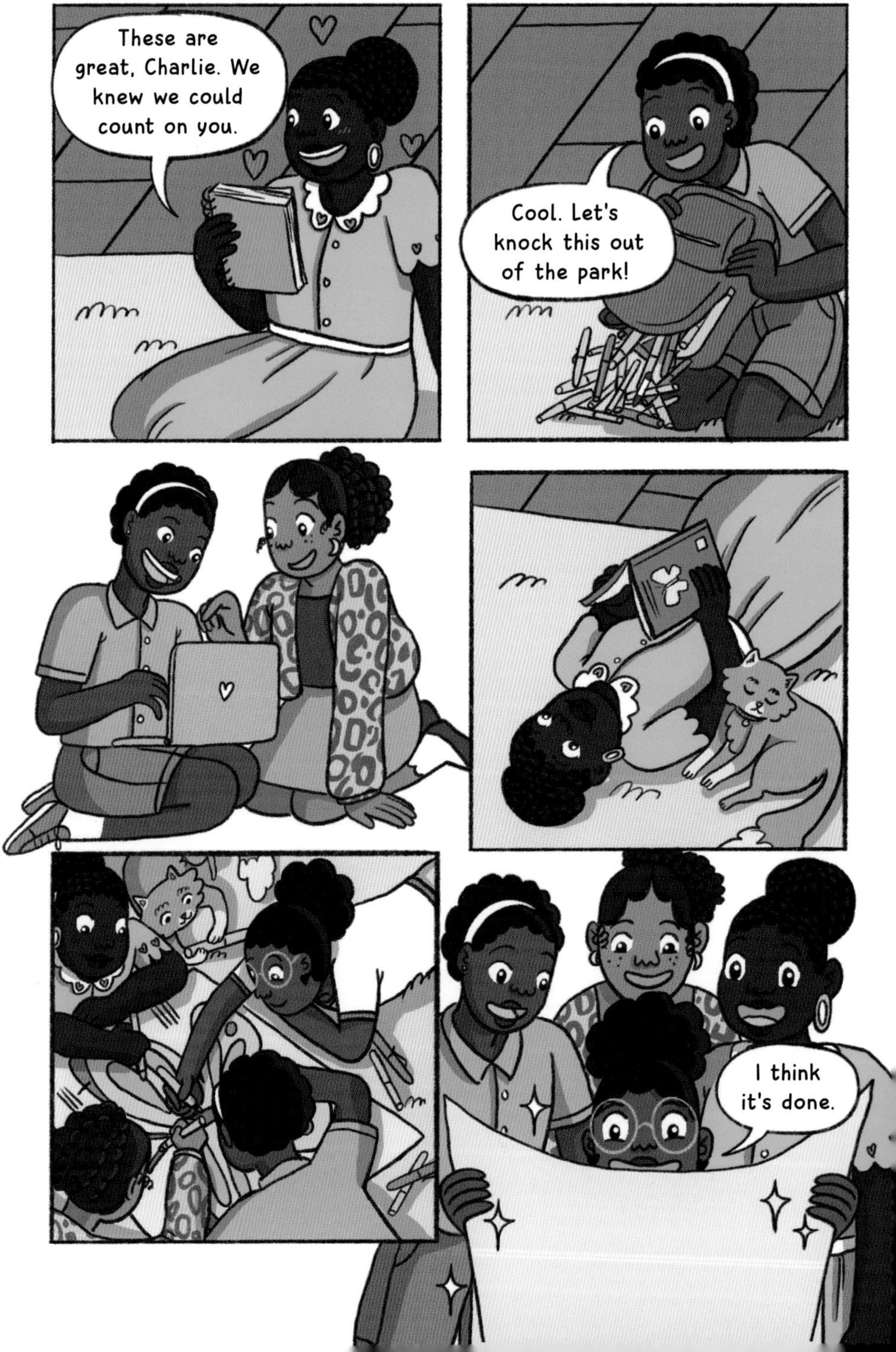
These are great, Charlie. We knew we could count on you.
Cool. Let's knock this out of the park!
I think it's done.

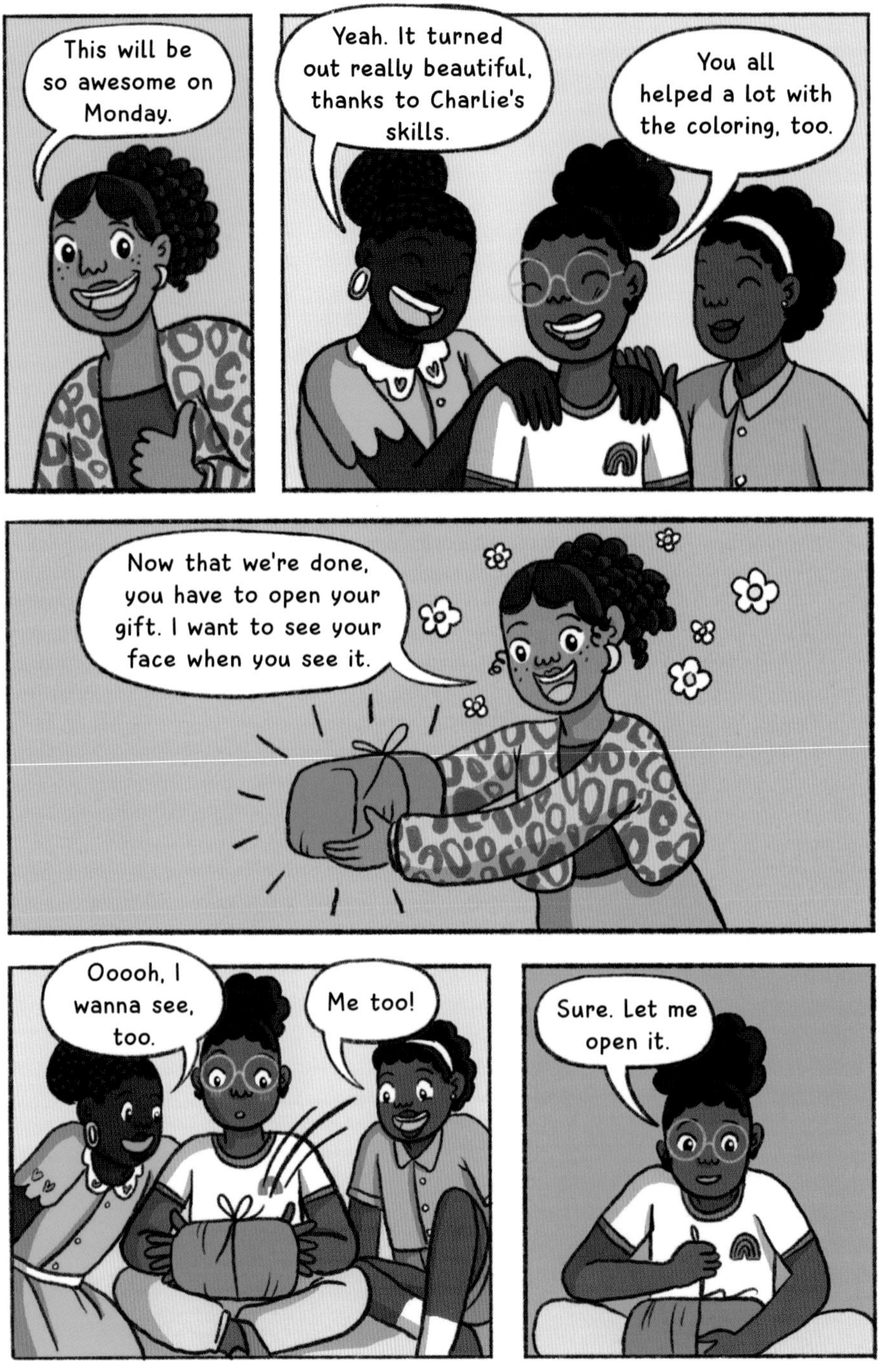
This will be so awesome on Monday.
Yeah. It turned out really beautiful, thanks to Charlie's skills.
You all helped a lot with the coloring, too.
Now that we're done, you have to open your gift. I want to see your face when you see it.
Ooooh, I wanna see, too.
Me too!
Sure. Let me open it.

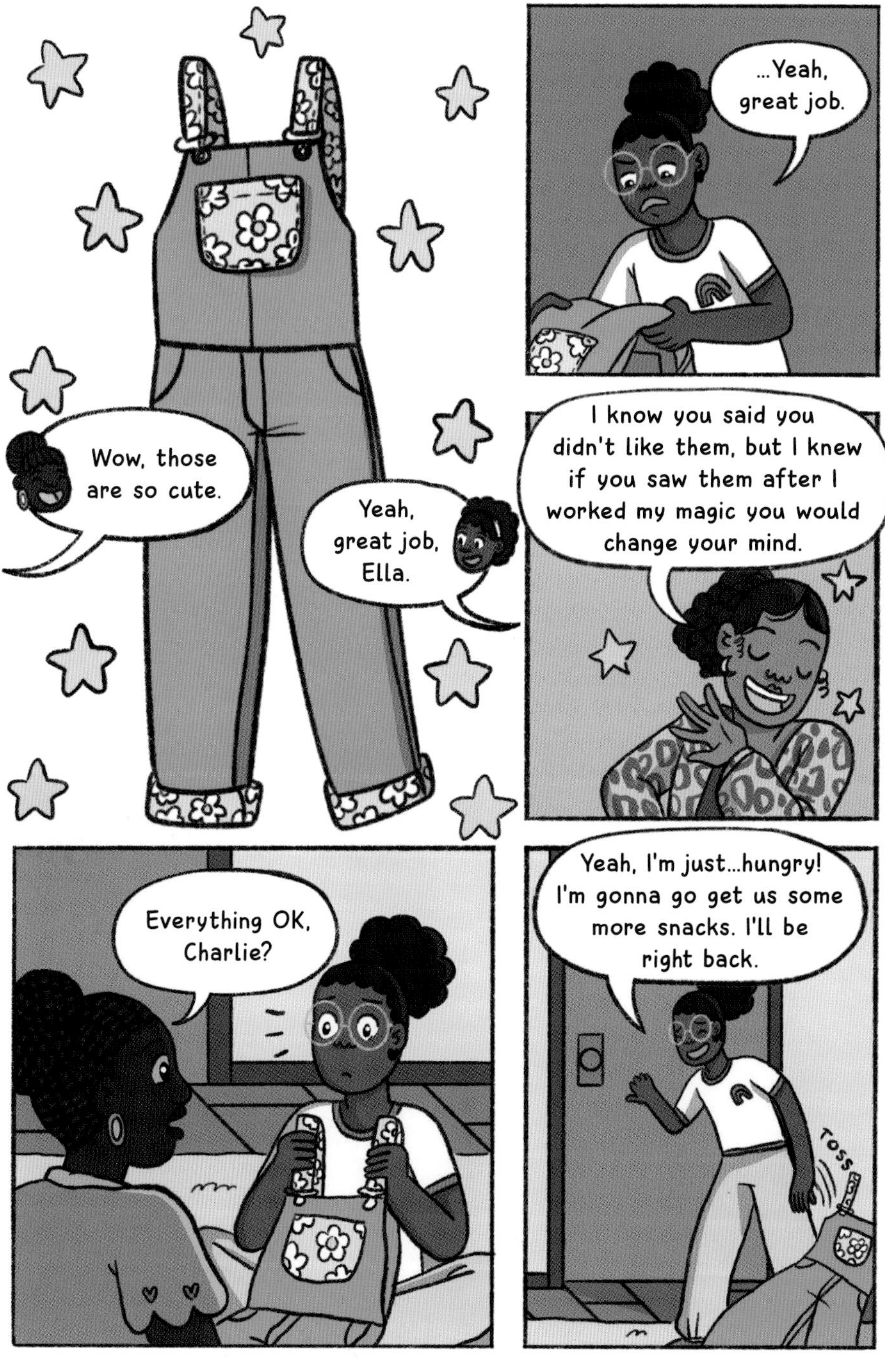
Wow, those are so cute.
Yeah, great job, Ella.
...Yeah, great job.
I know you said you didn't like them, but I knew if you saw them after I worked my magic you would change your mind.
Everything OK, Charlie?
Yeah, I'm just...hungry! I'm gonna go get us some more snacks. I'll be right back.
TOSS

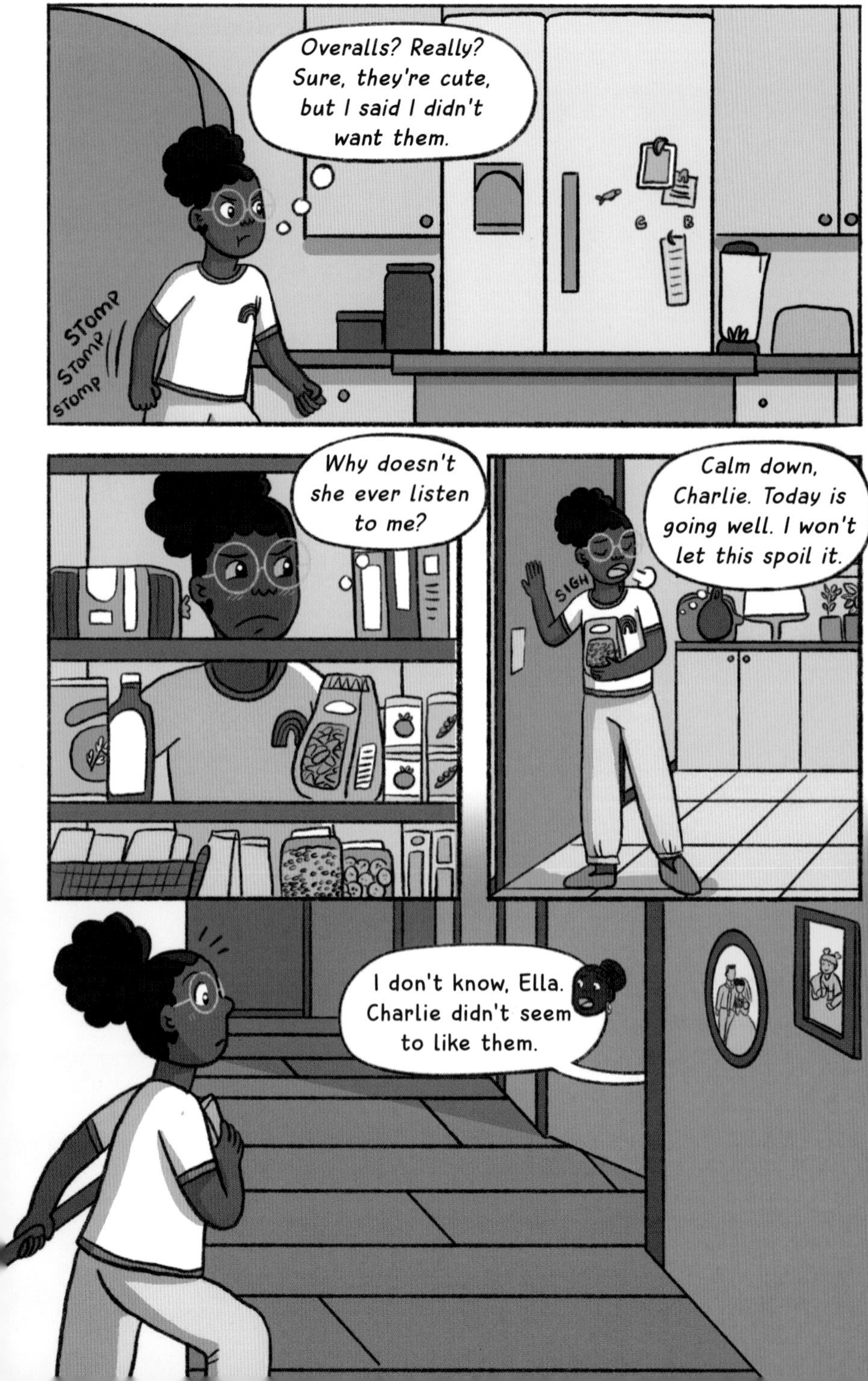
Overalls? Really? Sure, they're cute, but I said I didn't want them.
STOMP STOMP STOMP
Why doesn't she ever listen to me?
SIGH
Calm down, Charlie. Today is going well. I won't let this spoil it.
I don't know, Ella. Charlie didn't seem to like them.

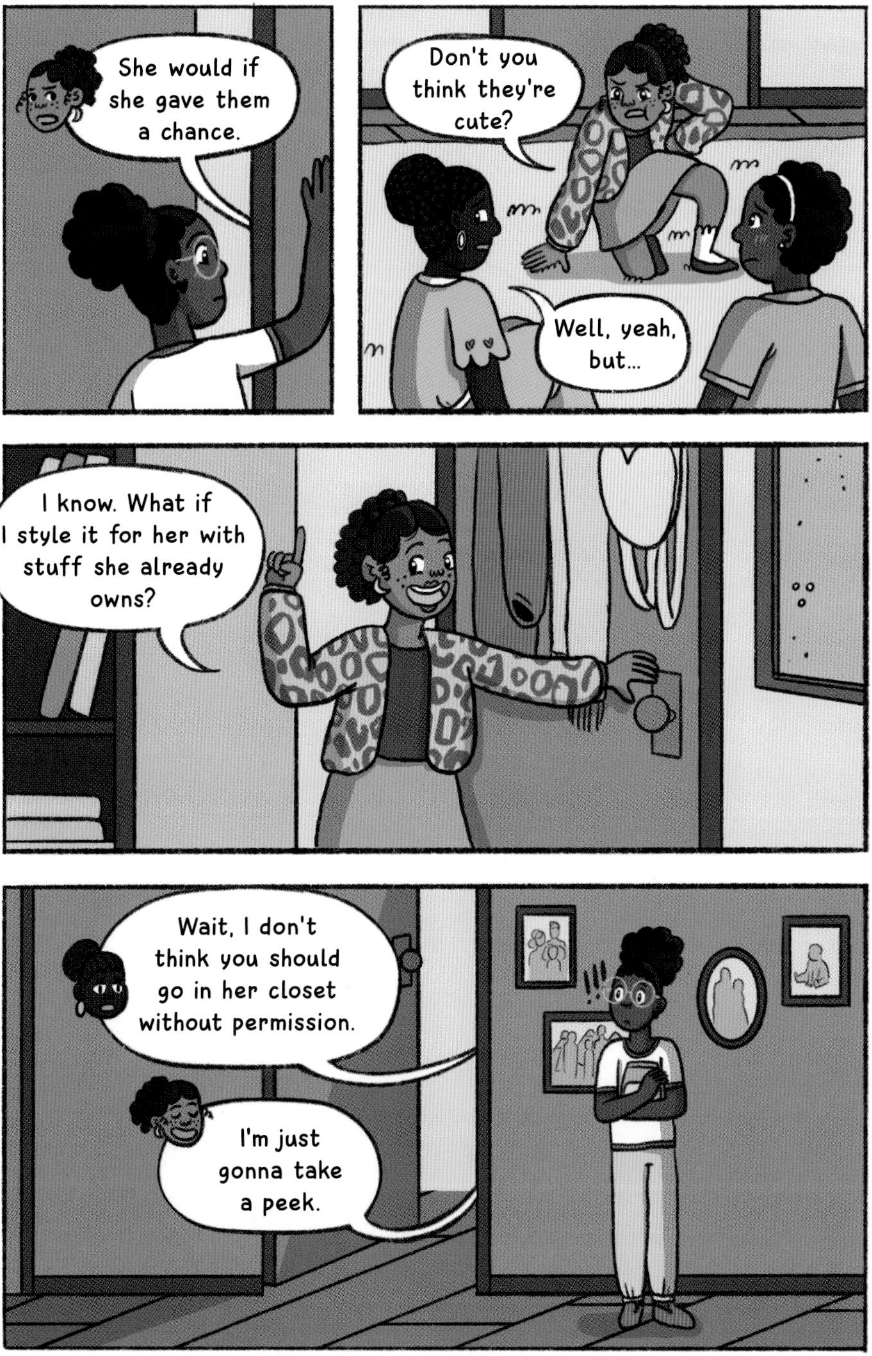
She would if she gave them a chance.
Don't you think they're cute?
Well, yeah, but...
I know. What if I style it for her with stuff she already owns?
Wait, I don't think you should go in her closet without permission.
I'm just gonna take a peek.

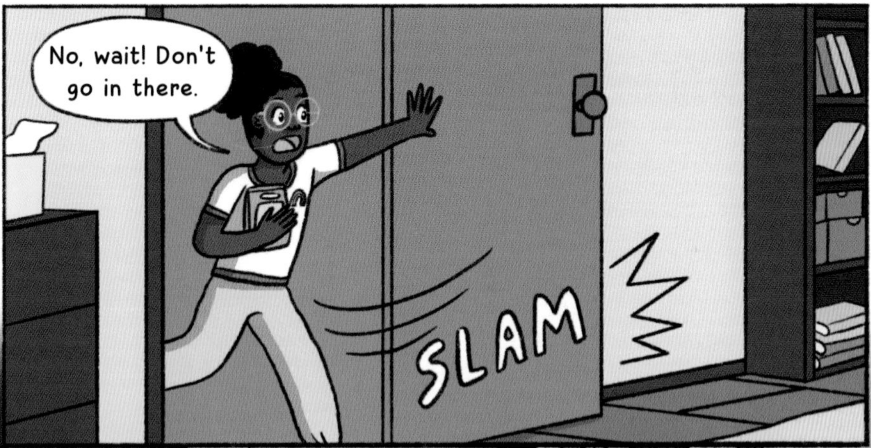
No, wait! Don't go in there.
SLAM
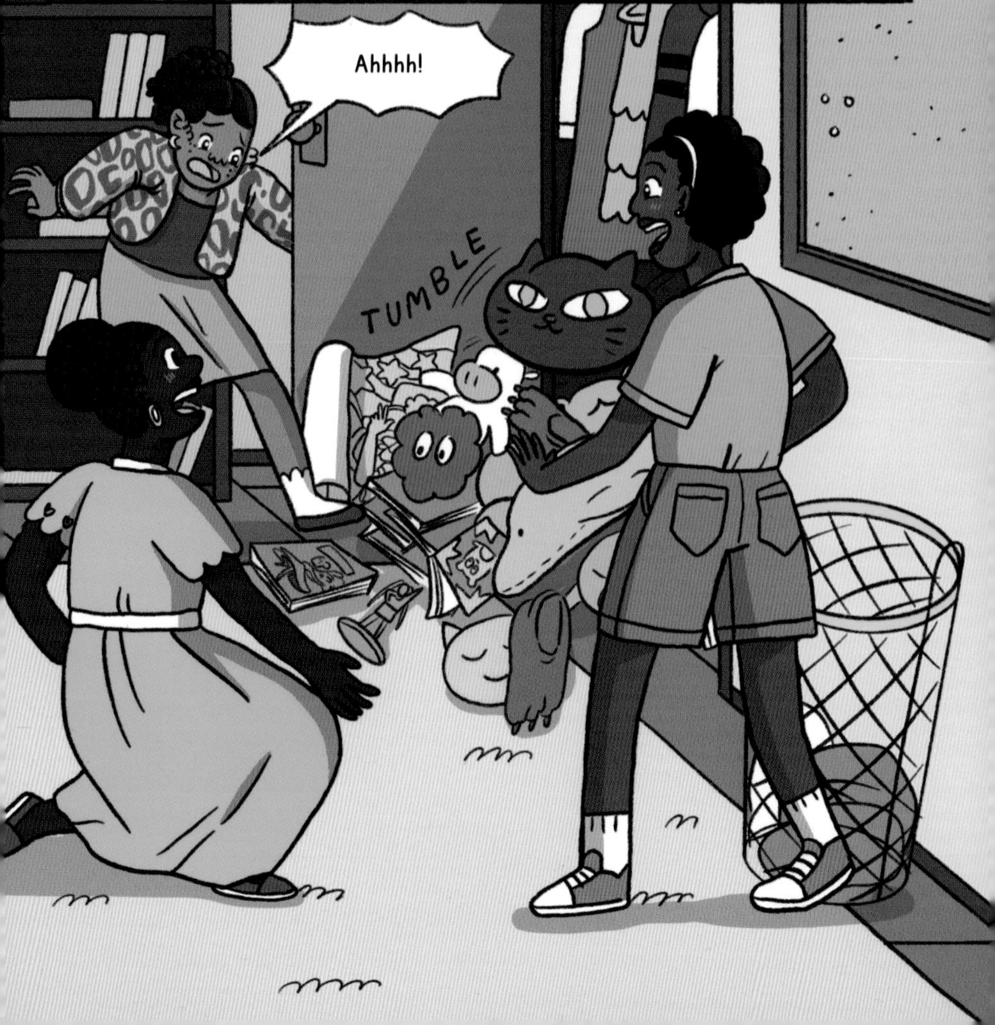
Ahhhh!
TUMBLE

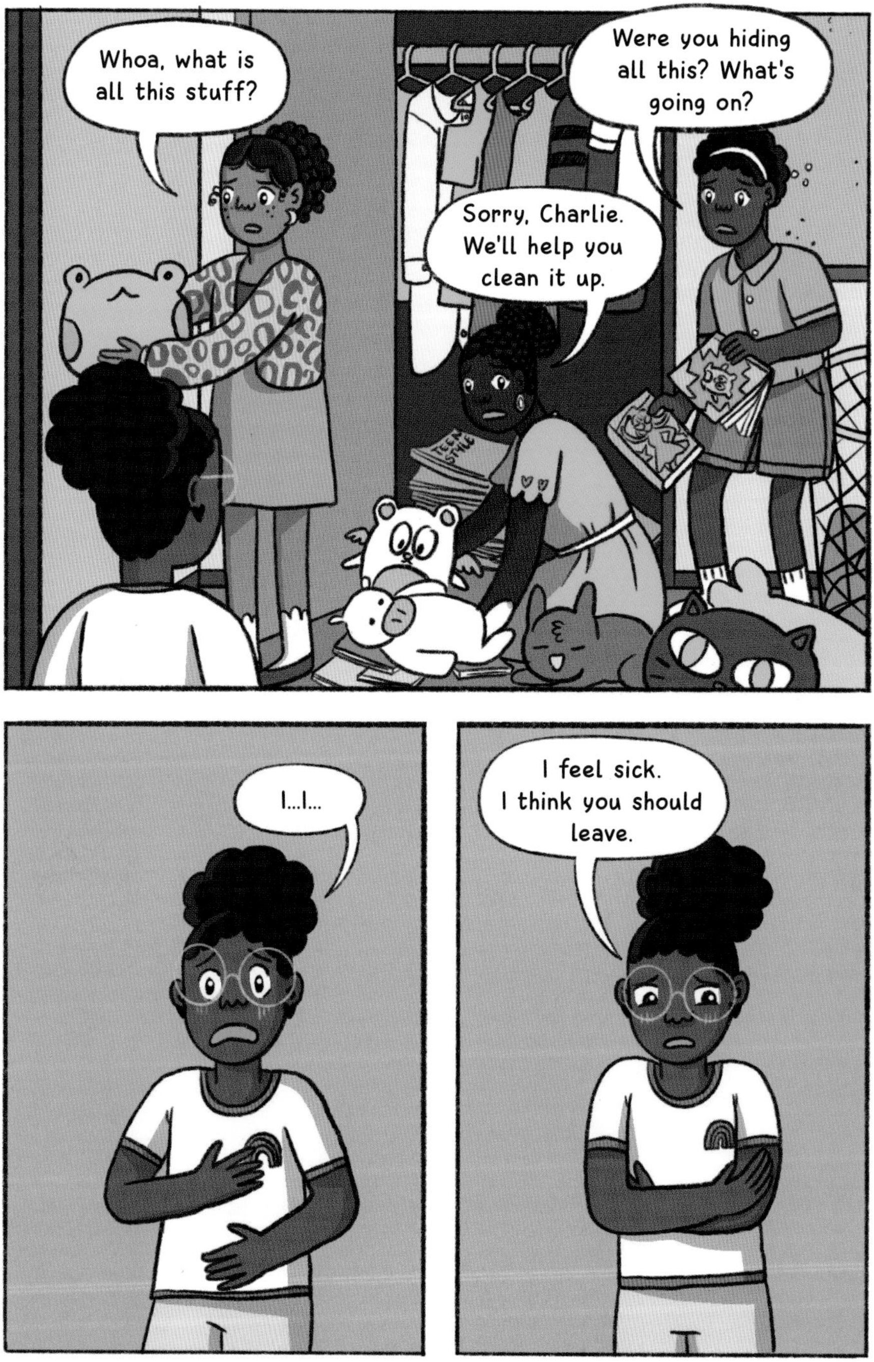
Whoa, what is all this stuff?
Were you hiding all this? What's going on?
Sorry, Charlie. We'll help you clean it up.
TEEN STYLE
I...I...
I feel sick. I think you should leave.

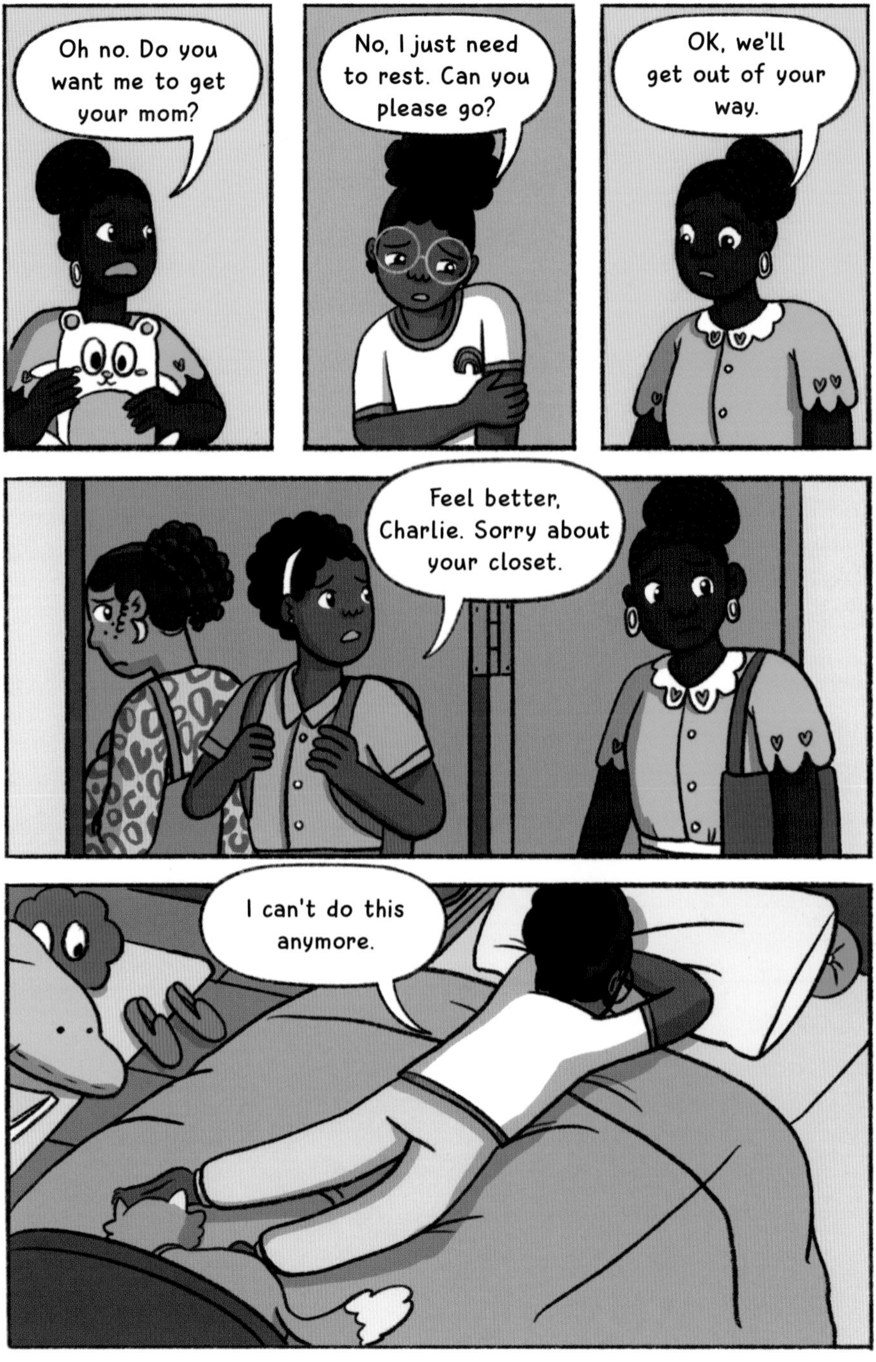
Oh no. Do you want me to get your mom?
No, I just need to rest. Can you please go?
OK, we'll get out of your way.
Feel better, Charlie. Sorry about your closet.
I can't do this anymore.

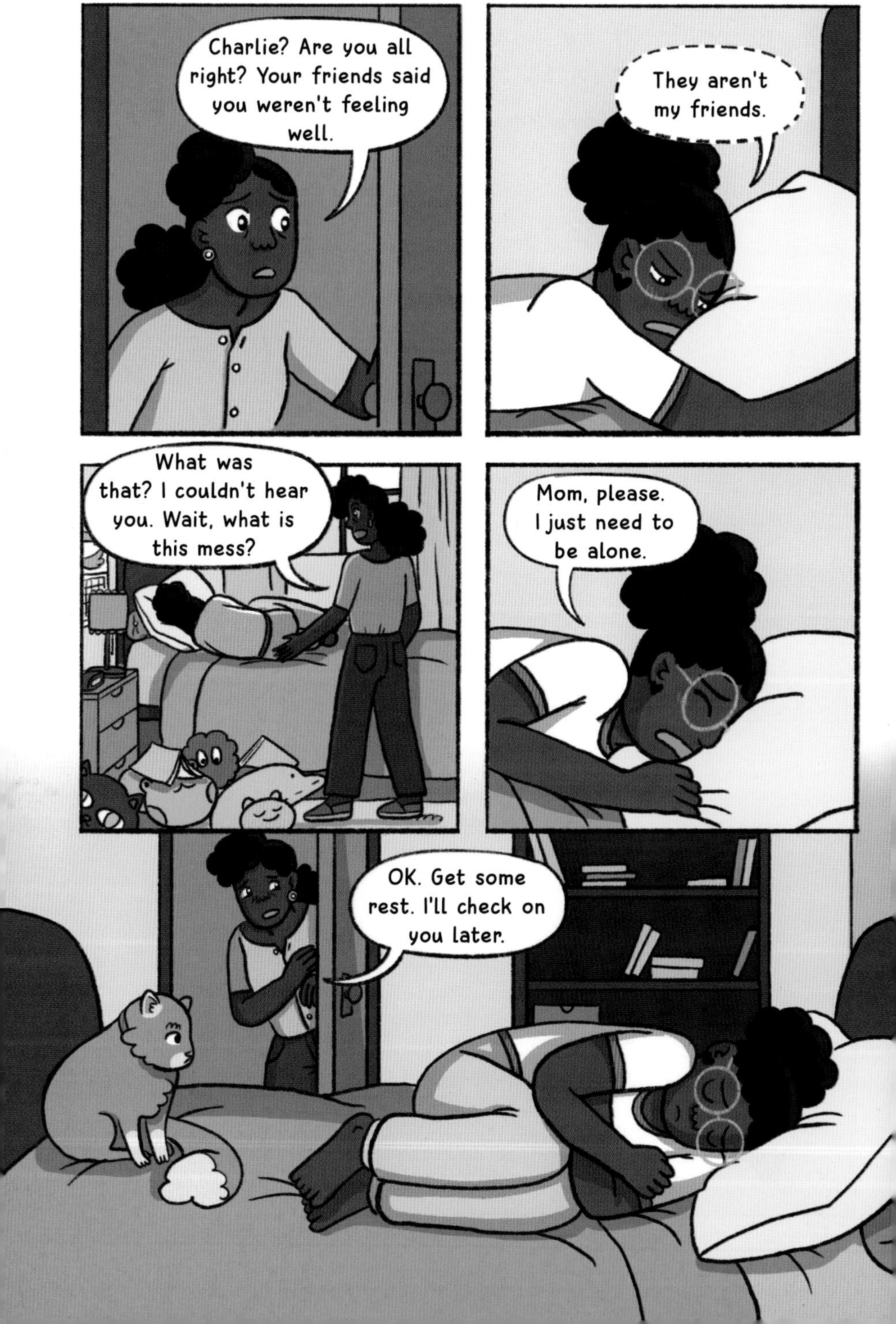
Charlie? Are you all right? Your friends said you weren't feeling well.
They aren't my friends.
What was that? I couldn't hear you. Wait, what is this mess?
Mom, please. I just need to be alone.
OK. Get some rest. I'll check on you later.

CHAPTER
12

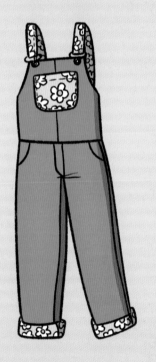

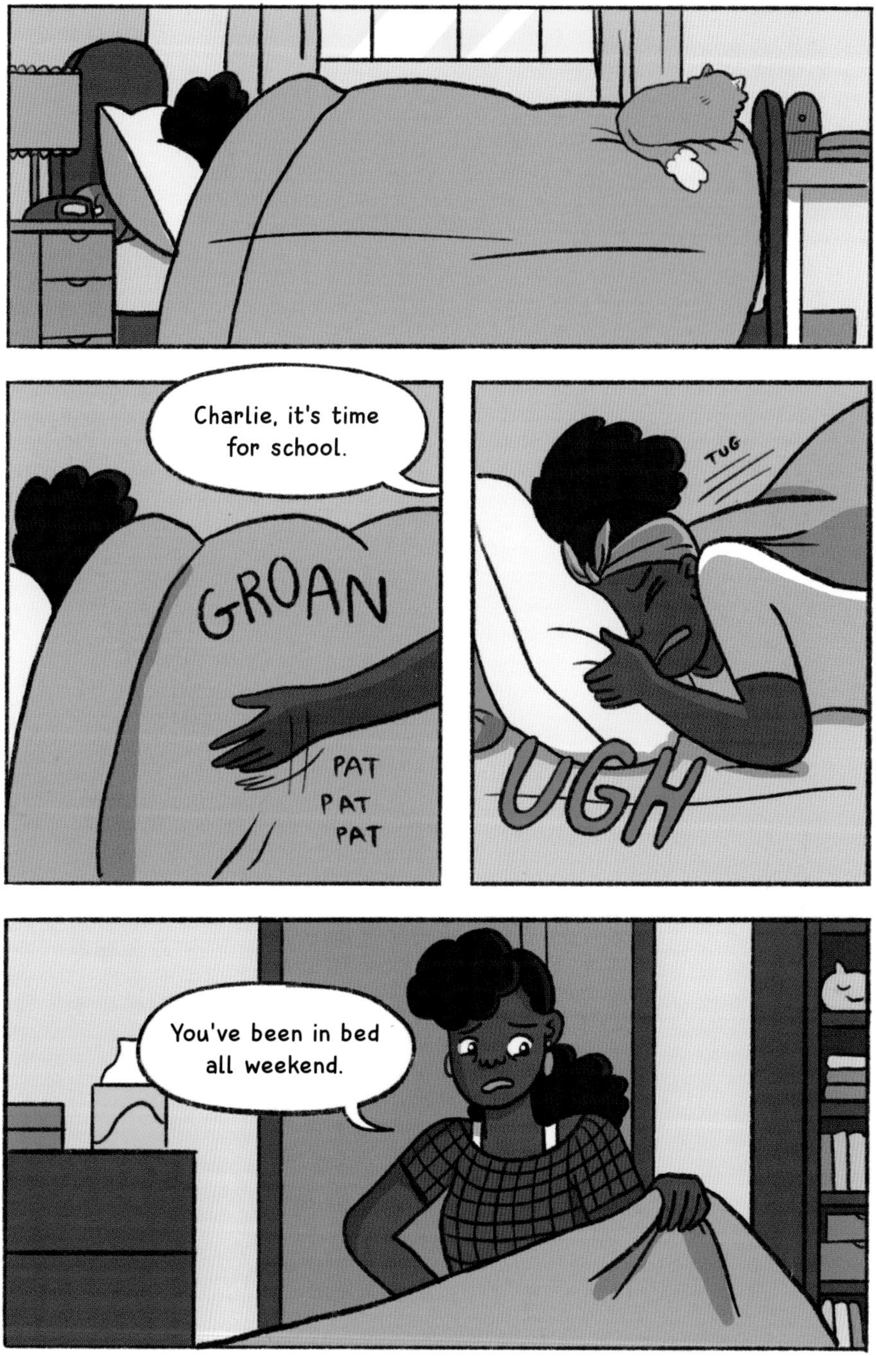
Charlie, it's time for school.
GROAN
PAT PAT PAT
TUG
UGH
You've been in bed all weekend.

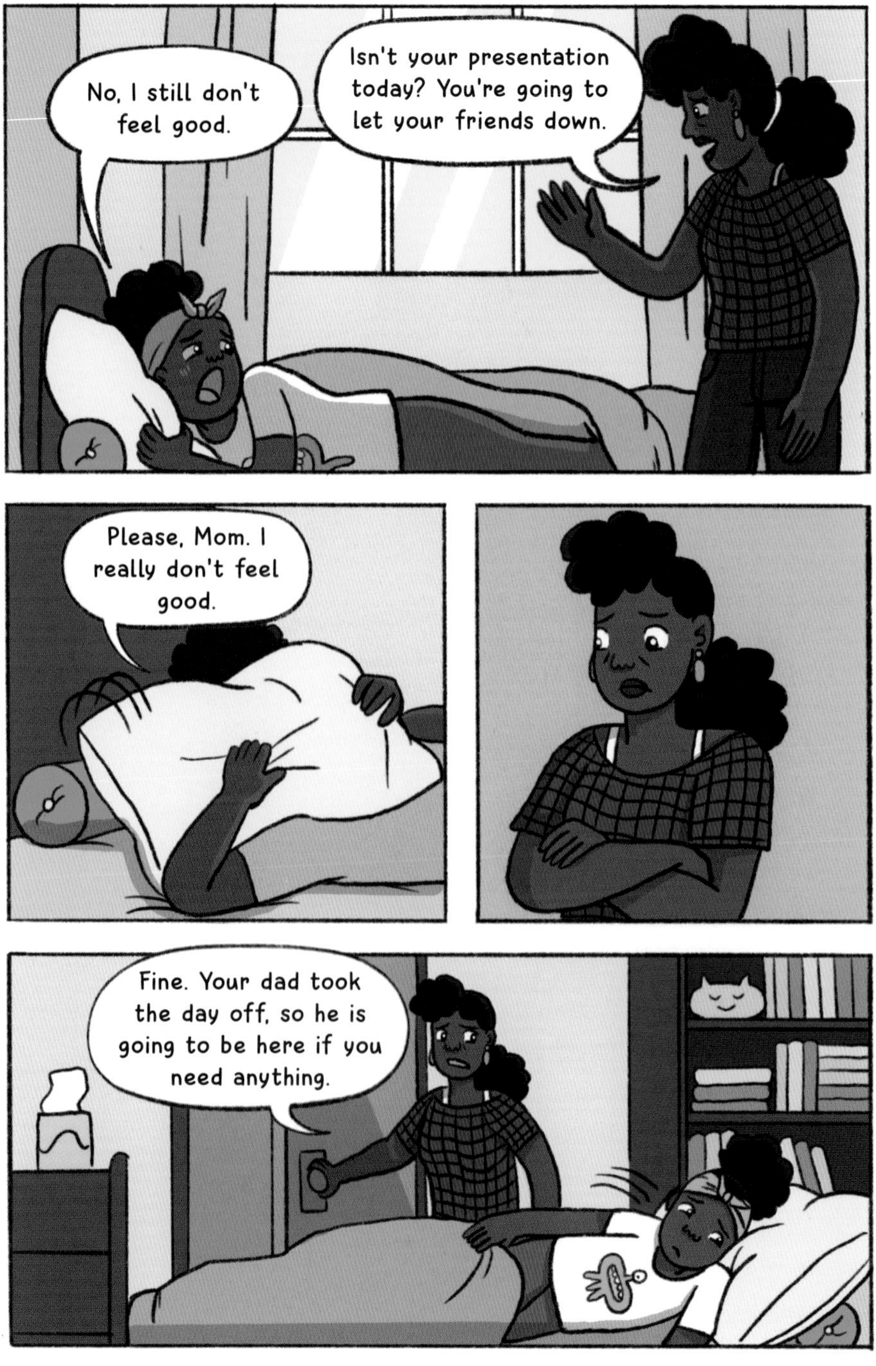
No, I still don't feel good.
Isn't your presentation today? You're going to let your friends down.
Please, Mom. I really don't feel good.
Fine. Your dad took the day off, so he is going to be here if you need anything.

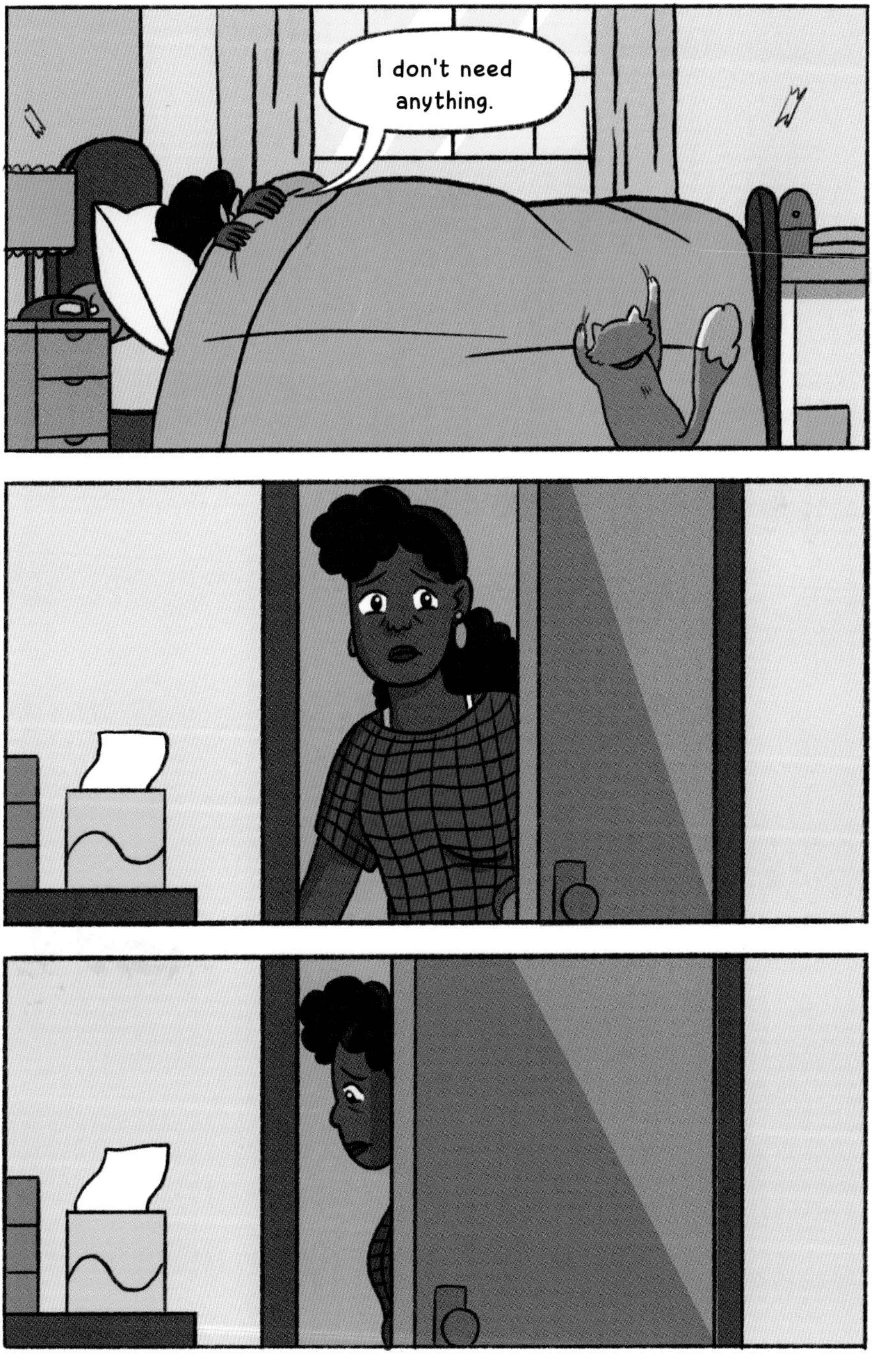
I don't need anything.

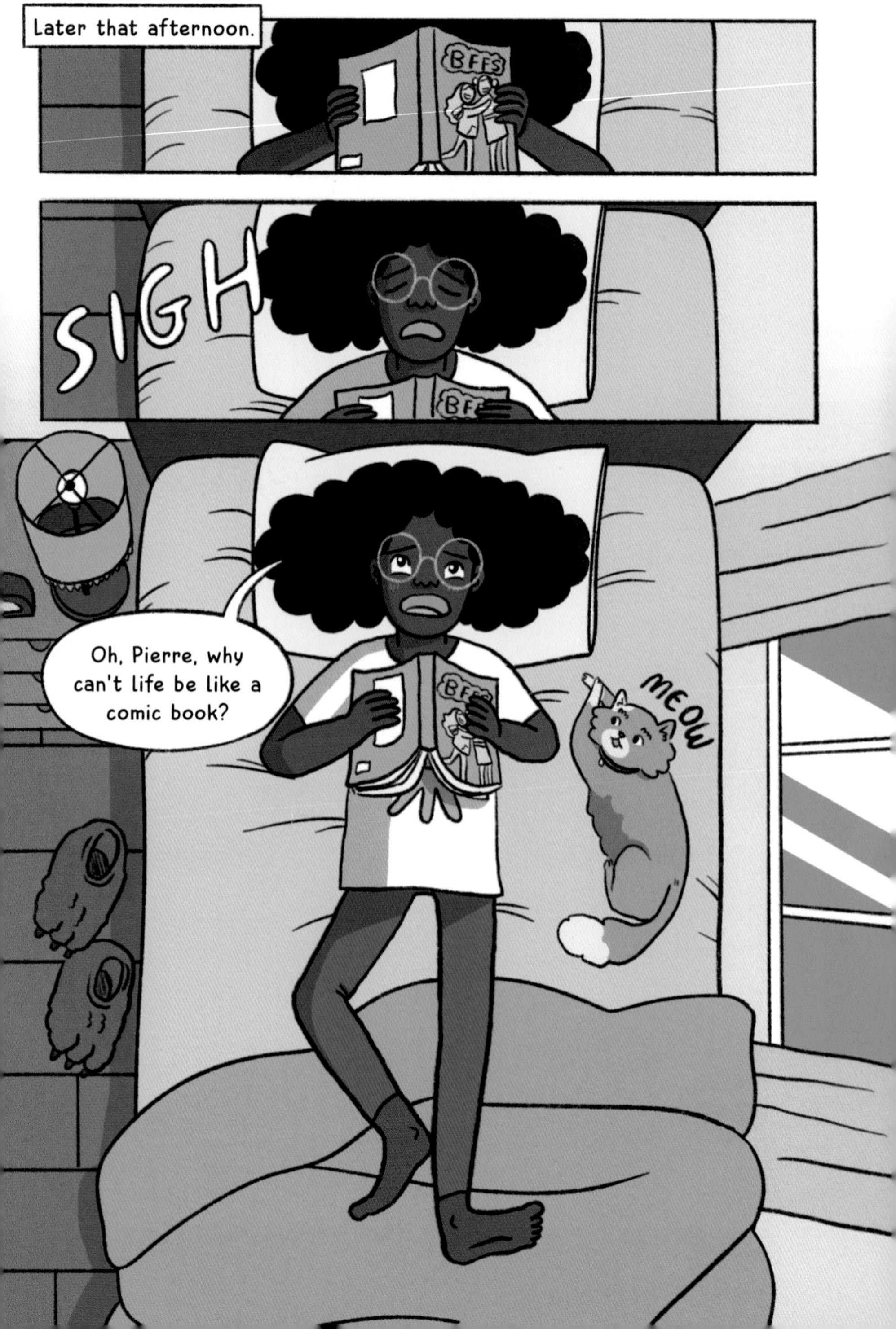
Later that afternoon.
BFFS
SIGH
BFFS
Oh, Pierre, why can't life be like a comic book?
BFFS
MEOW

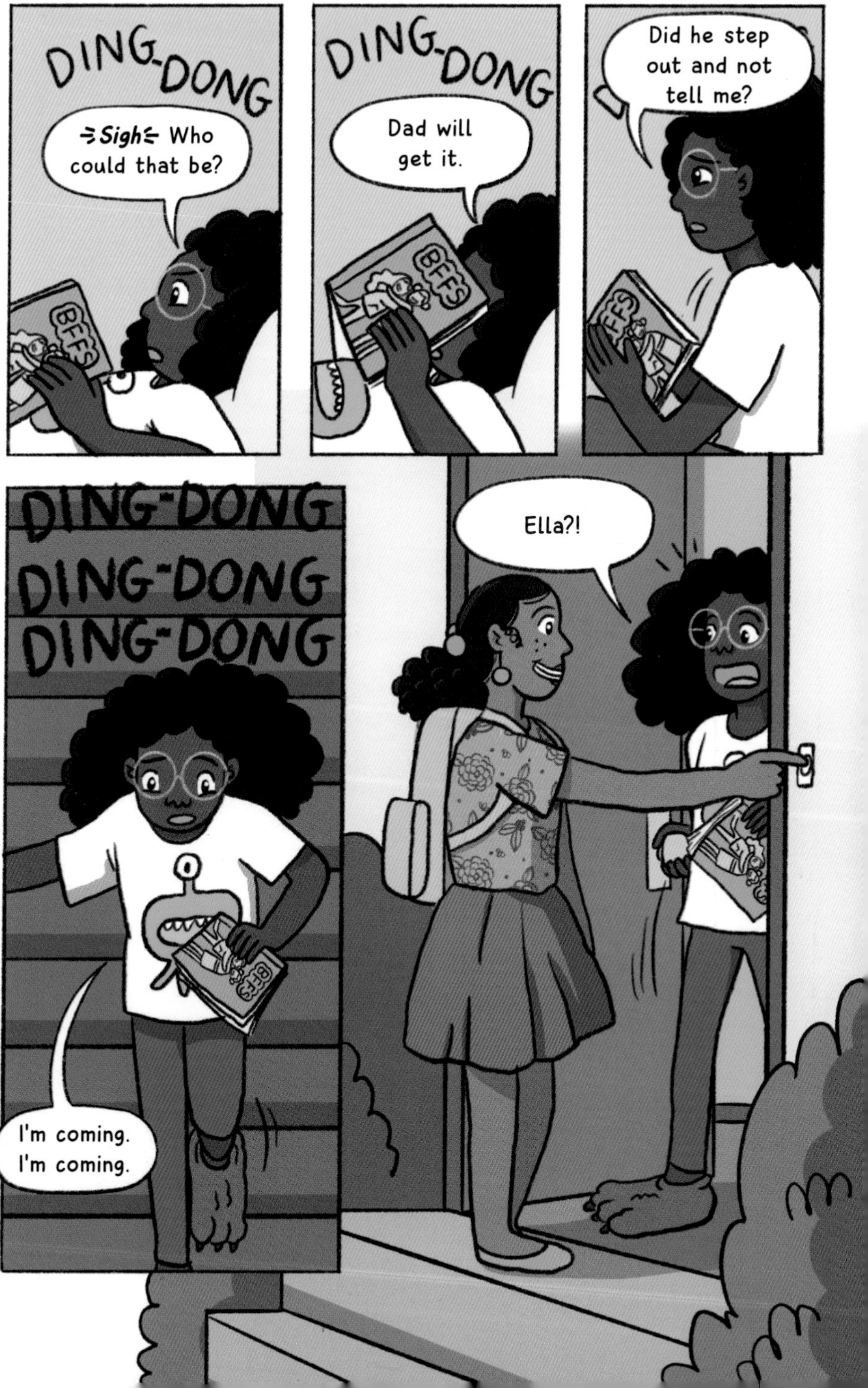
DING-DONG
Sigh Who could that be?
DING-DONG
Dad will get it.
Did he step out and not tell me?
DING-DONG
DING-DONG
DING-DONG
I'm coming. I'm coming.
Ella?!

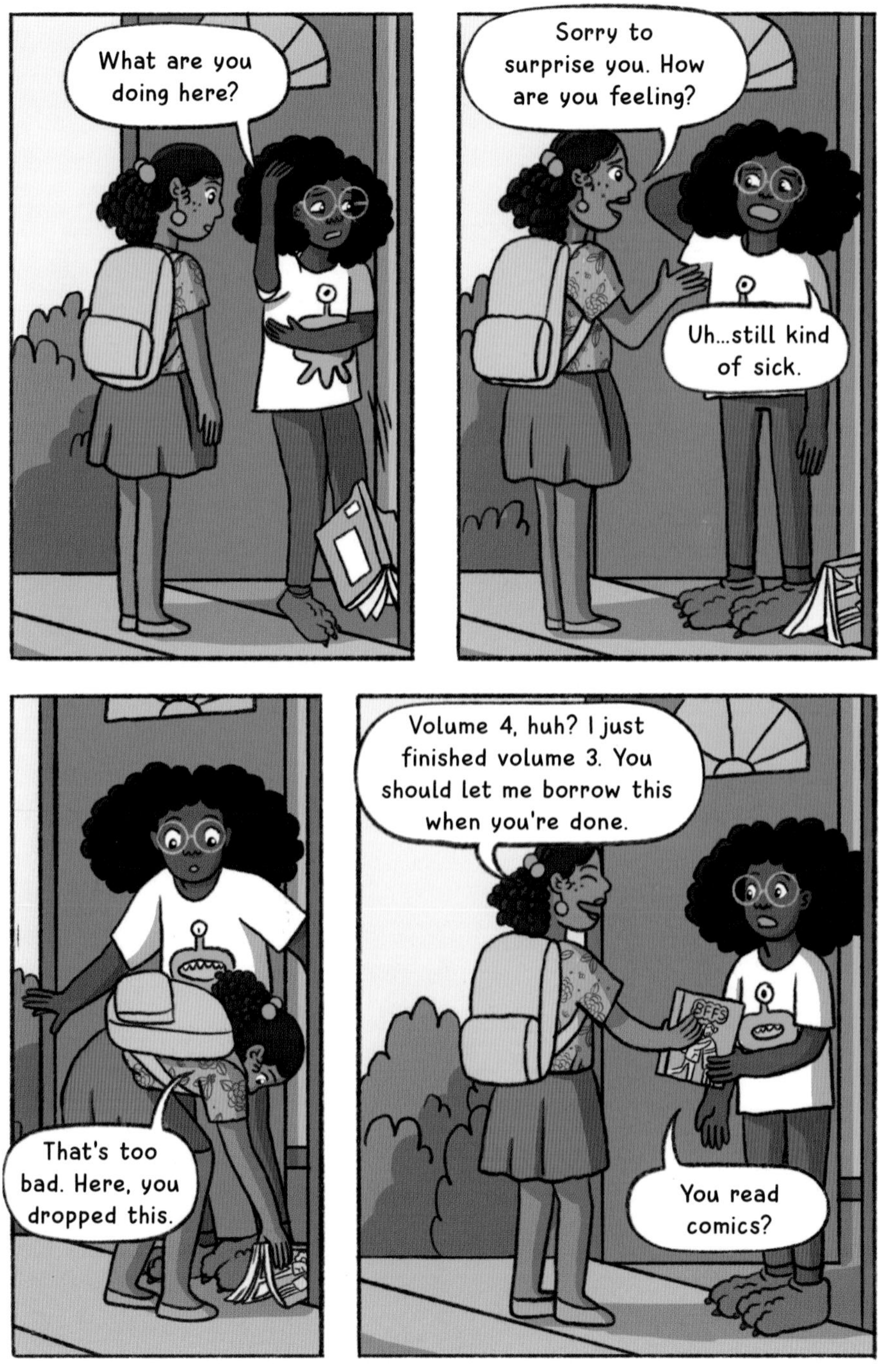
What are you doing here?
Sorry to surprise you. How are you feeling?
Uh...still kind of sick.
That's too bad. Here, you dropped this.
Volume 4, huh? I just finished volume 3. You should let me borrow this when you're done.
You read comics?

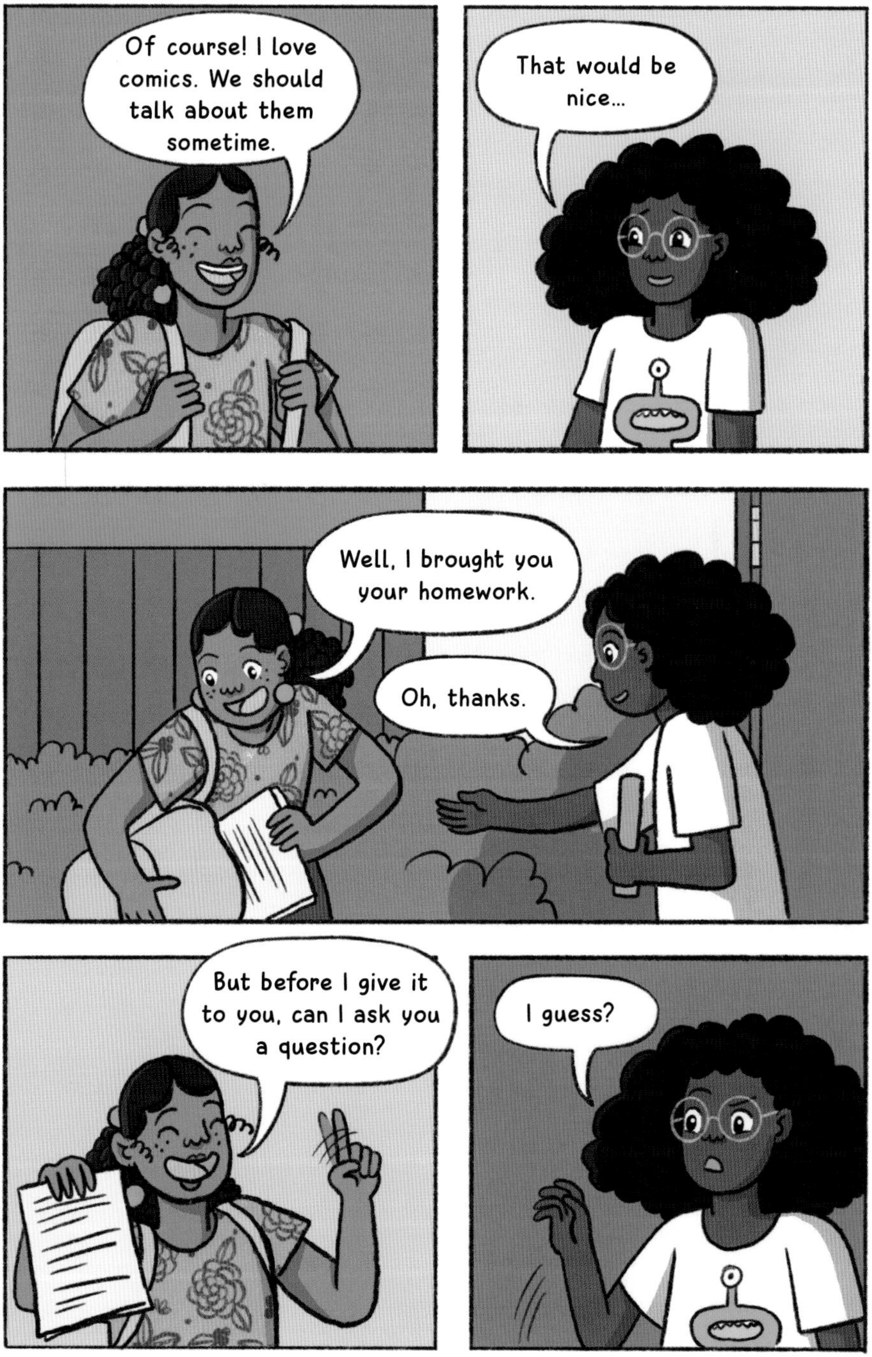
Of course! I love comics. We should talk about them sometime.
That would be nice...
Well, I brought you your homework.
Oh, thanks.
But before I give it to you, can I ask you a question?
I guess?

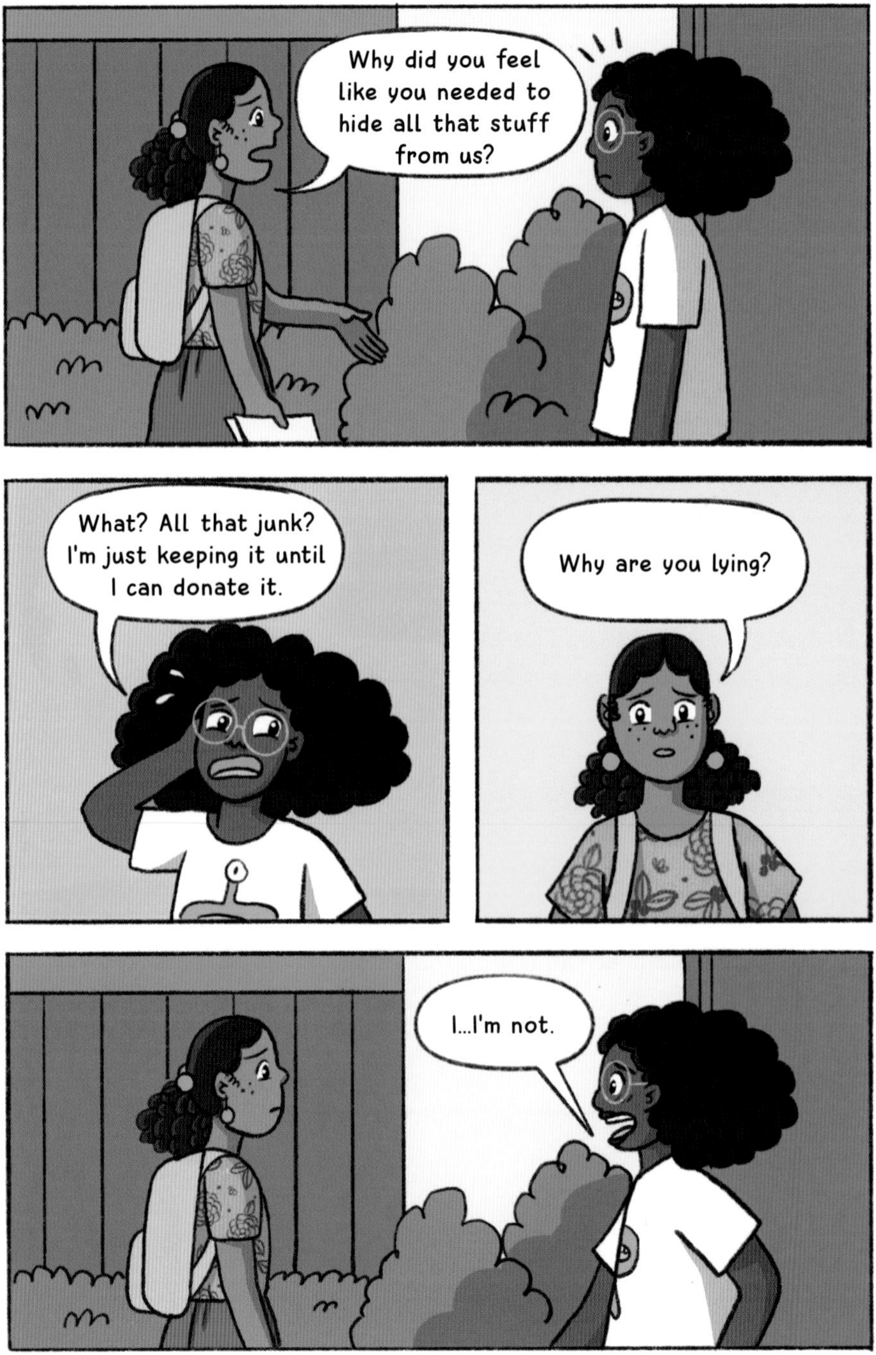
Why did you feel like you needed to hide all that stuff from us?
What? All that junk? I'm just keeping it until I can donate it.
Why are you lying?
I...I'm not.

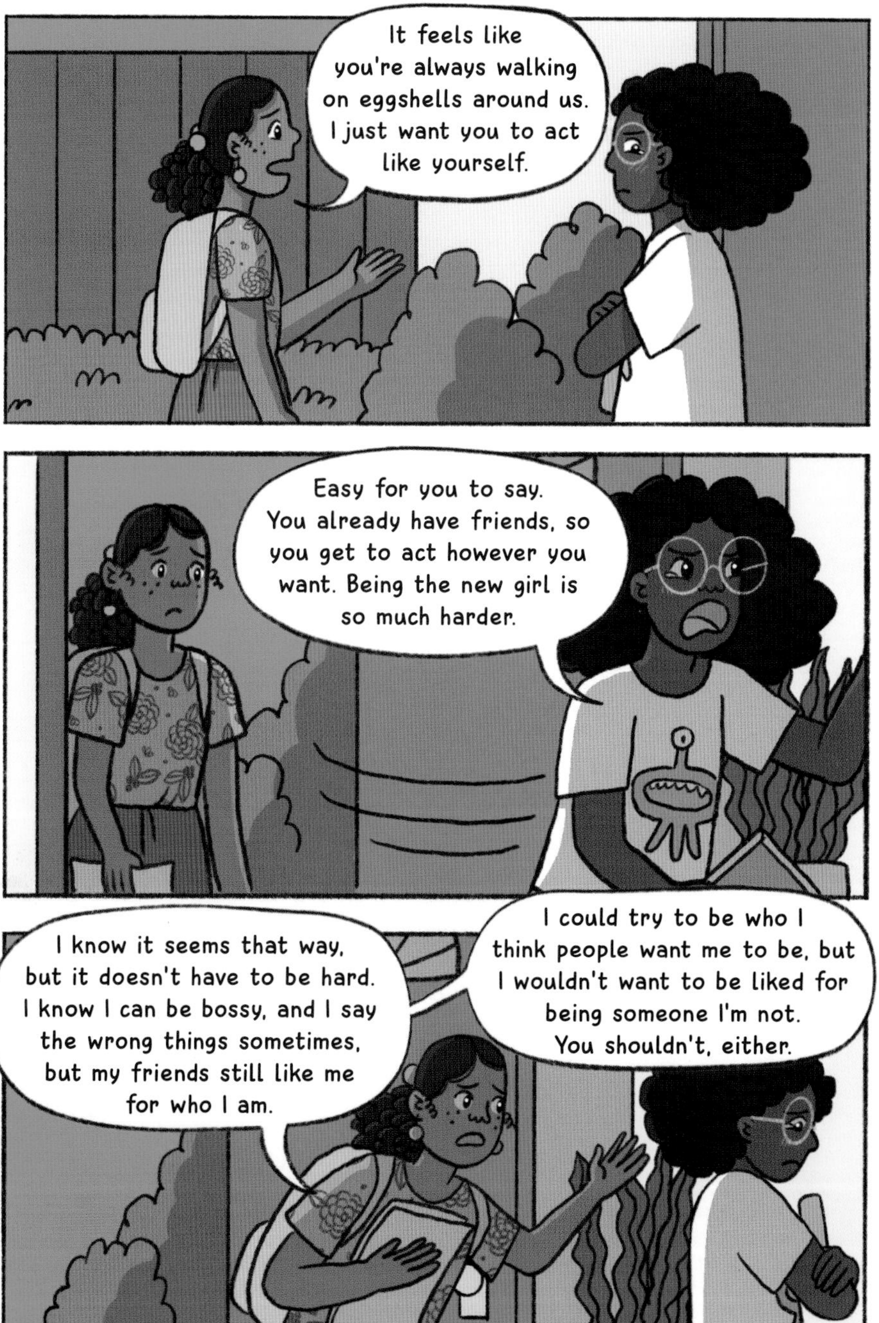
It feels like you're always walking on eggshells around us. I just want you to act like yourself.
Easy for you to say. You already have friends, so you get to act however you want. Being the new girl is so much harder.
I know it seems that way, but it doesn't have to be hard. I know I can be bossy, and I say the wrong things sometimes, but my friends still like me for who I am.
I could try to be who I think people want me to be, but I wouldn't want to be liked for being someone I'm not. You shouldn't, either.

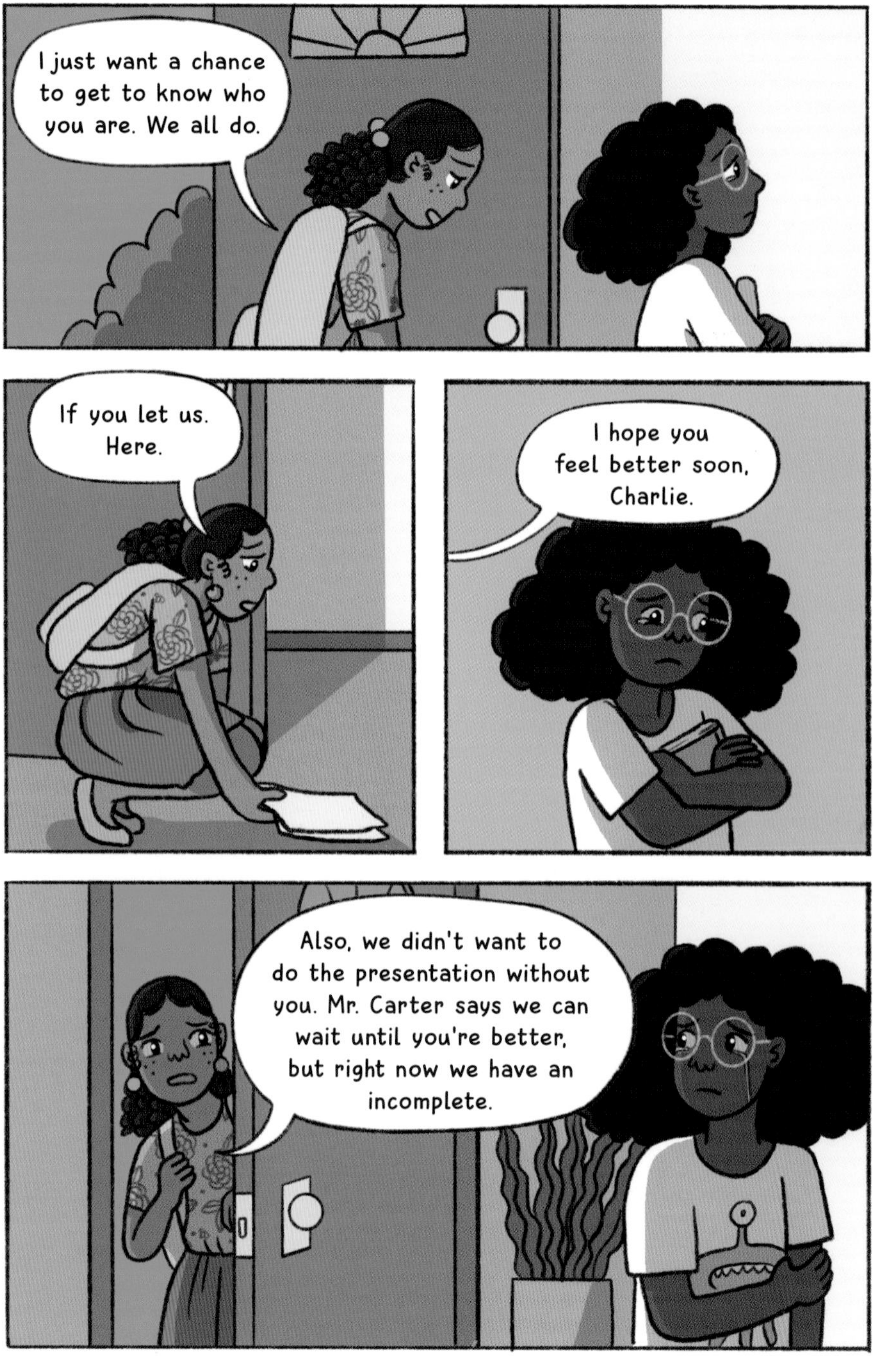
I just want a chance to get to know who you are. We all do.
If you let us. Here.
I hope you feel better soon, Charlie.
Also, we didn't want to do the presentation without you. Mr. Carter says we can wait until you're better, but right now we have an incomplete.

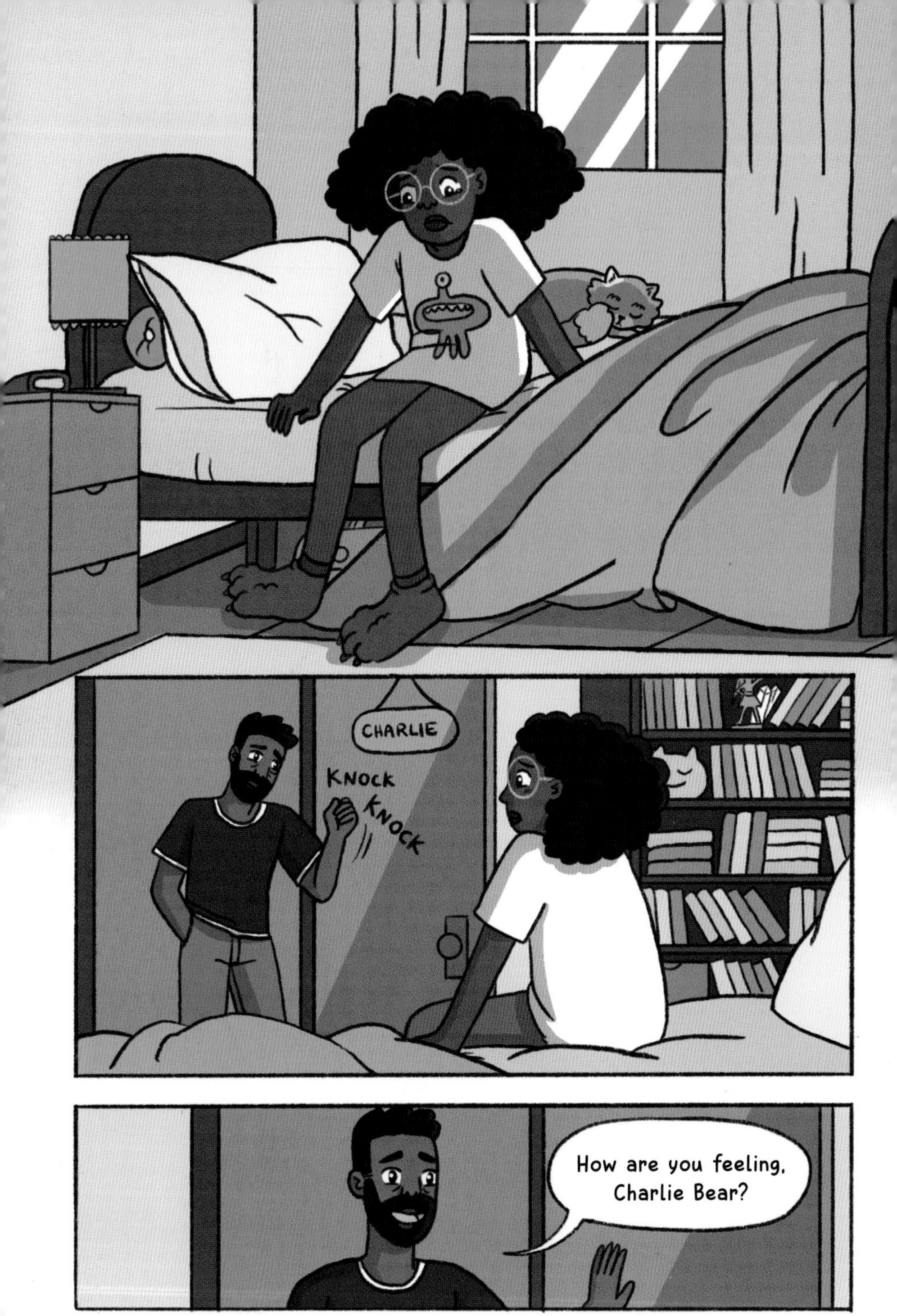

CHARLIE
KNOCK
KNOCK
How are you feeling, Charlie Bear?

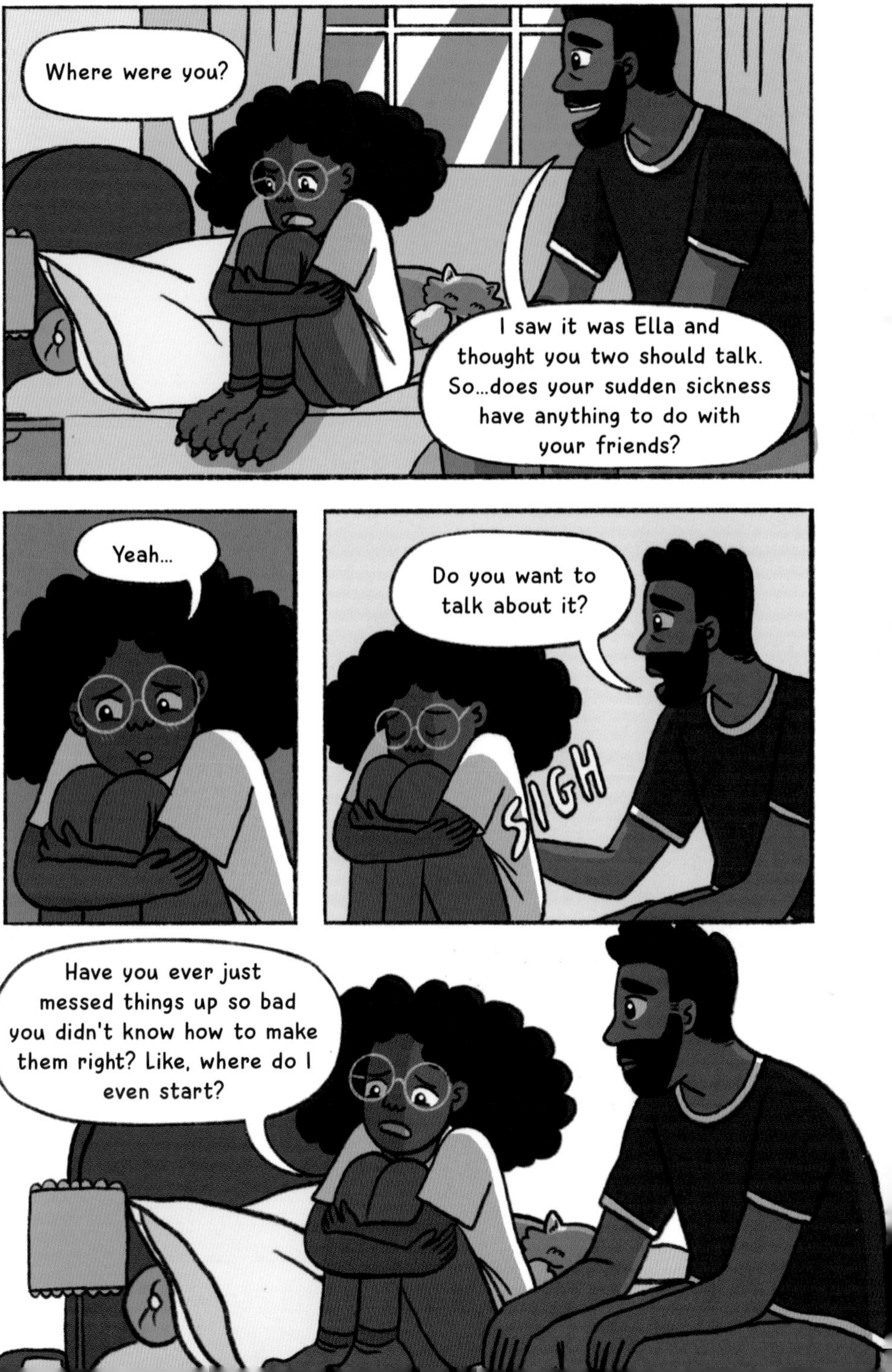

Where were you?
I saw it was Ella and thought you two should talk. So...does your sudden sickness have anything to do with your friends?
Yeah...
Do you want to talk about it?
SIGH
Have you ever just messed things up so bad you didn't know how to make them right? Like, where do I even start?

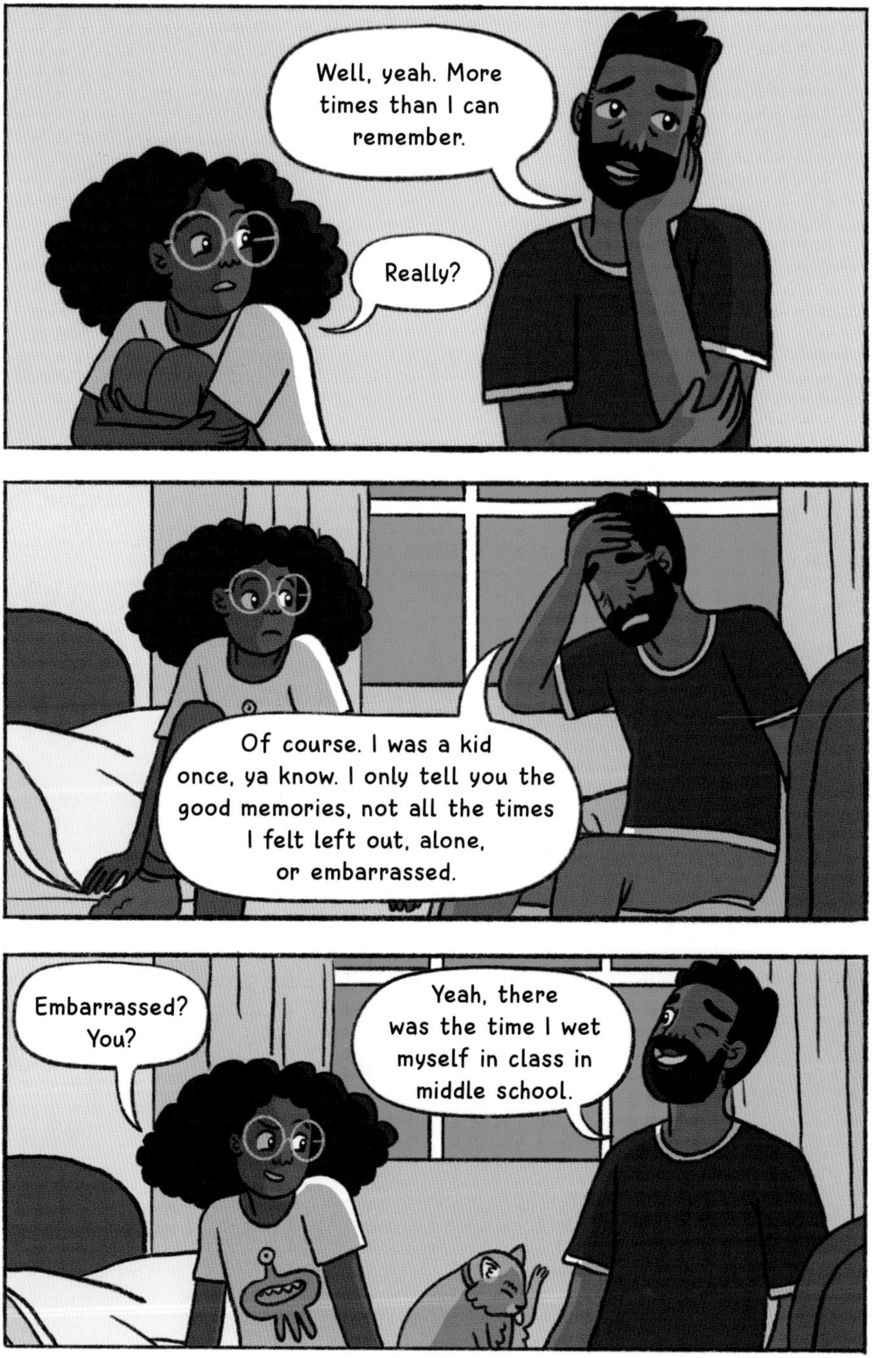
Well, yeah. More times than I can remember.
Really?
Of course. I was a kid once, ya know. I only tell you the good memories, not all the times I felt left out, alone, or embarrassed.
Embarrassed? You?
Yeah, there was the time I wet myself in class in middle school.

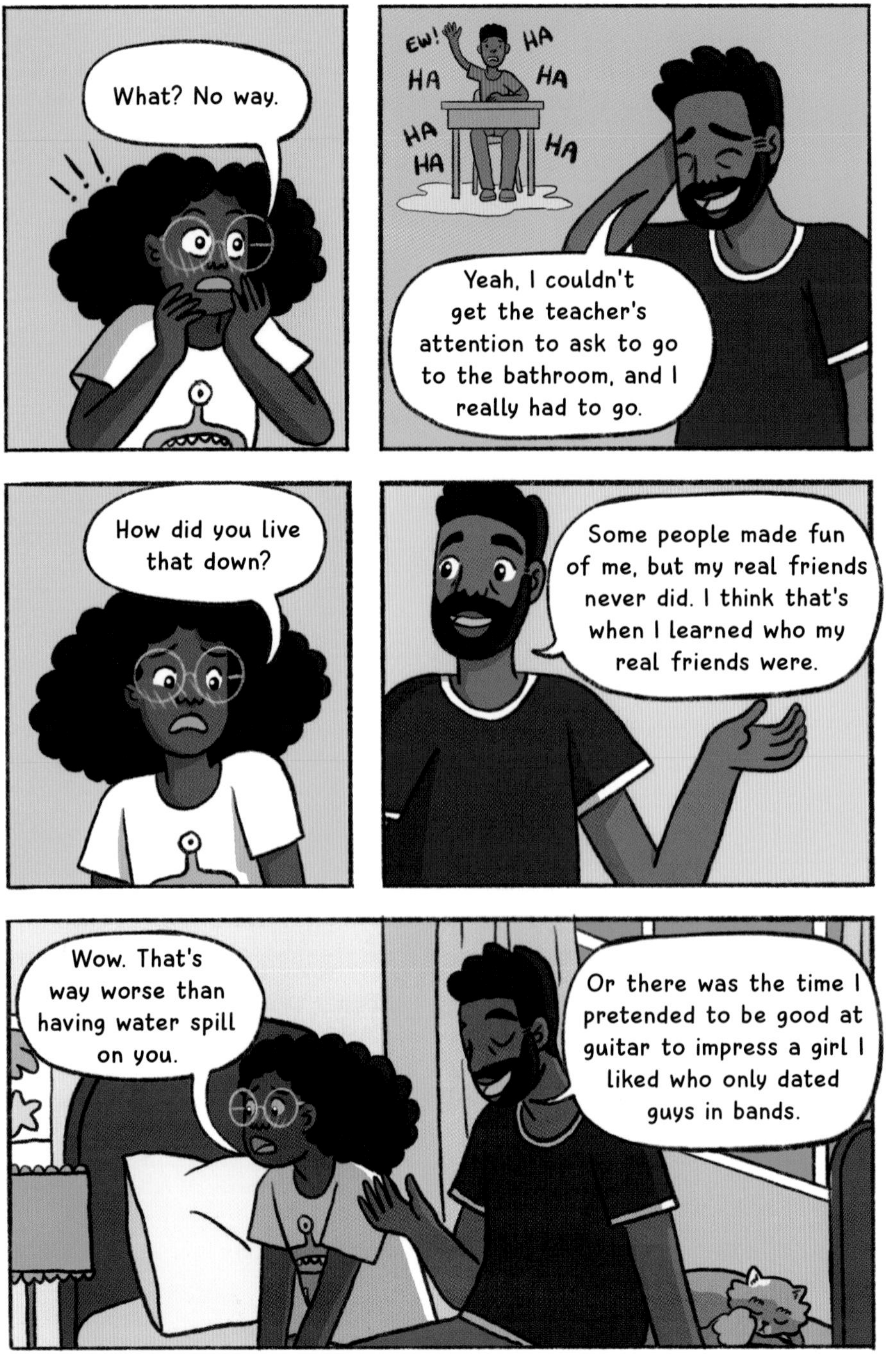
What? No way.
EW!
HA
HA
HA
HA
HA
HA
Yeah, I couldn't get the teacher's attention to ask to go to the bathroom, and I really had to go.
How did you live that down?
Some people made fun of me, but my real friends never did. I think that's when I learned who my real friends were.
Wow. That's way worse than having water spill on you.
Or there was the time I pretended to be good at guitar to impress a girl I liked who only dated guys in bands.

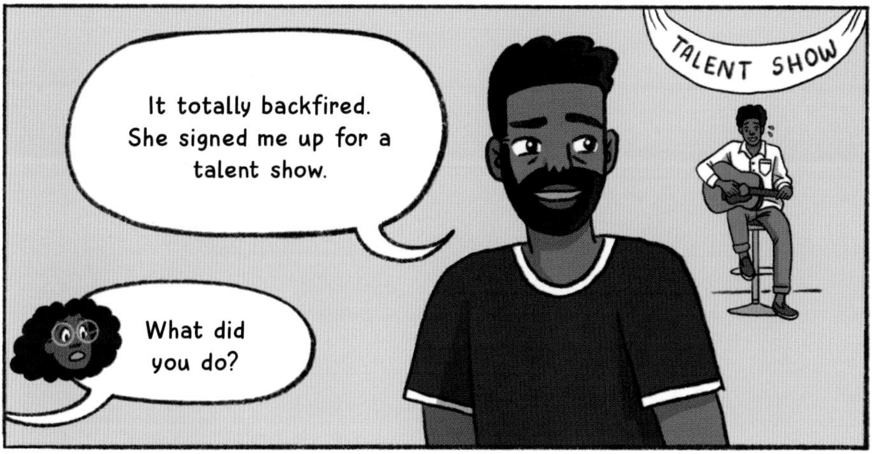
TALENT SHOW
It totally backfired. She signed me up for a talent show.
What did you do?

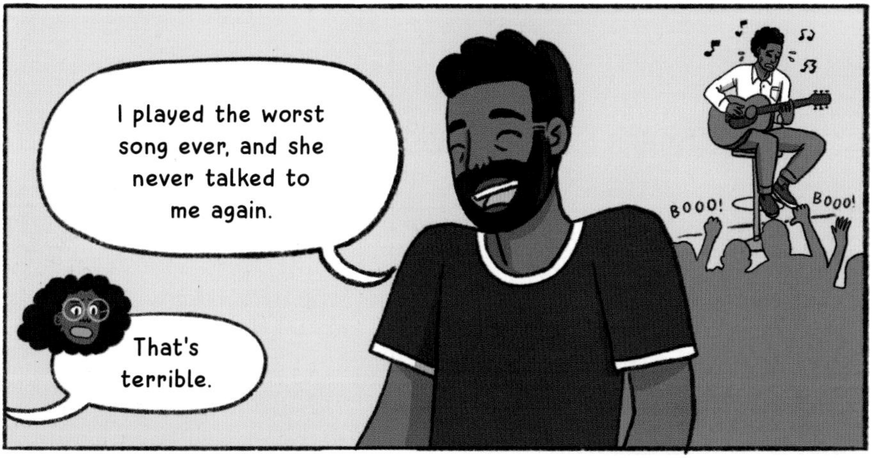
I played the worst song ever, and she never talked to me again.
BOOO!
BOOO!
That's terrible.

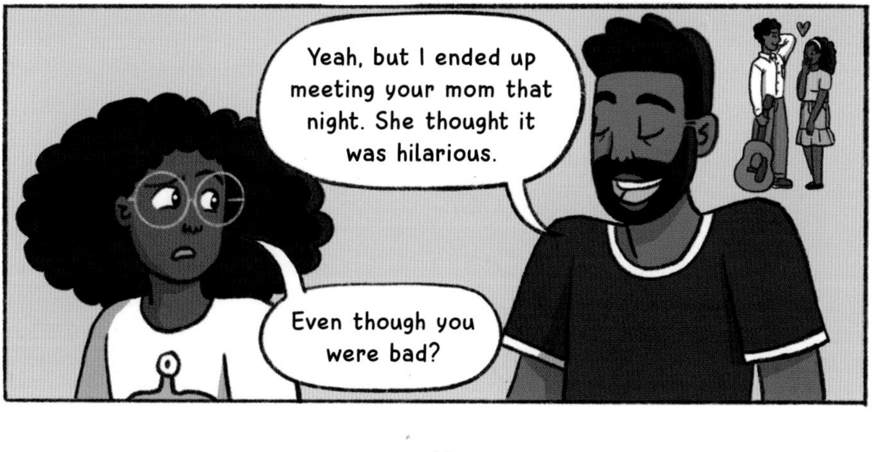
Yeah, but I ended up meeting your mom that night. She thought it was hilarious.
Even though you were bad?

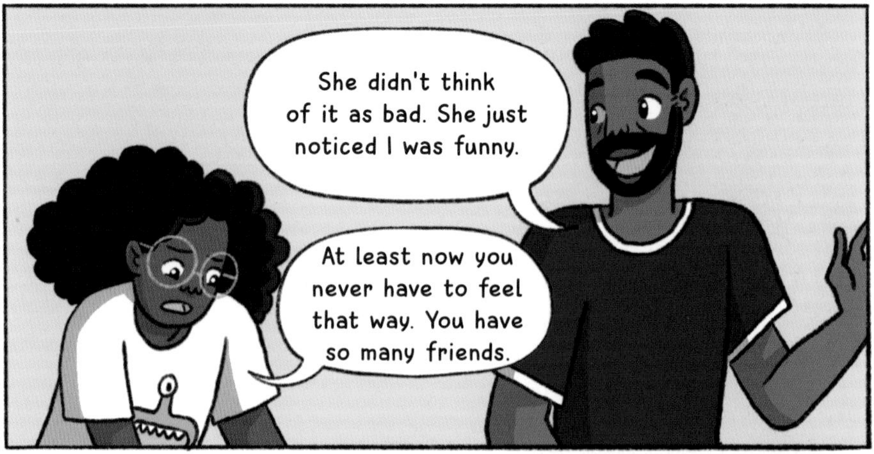
She didn't think of it as bad. She just noticed I was funny.
At least now you never have to feel that way. You have so many friends.

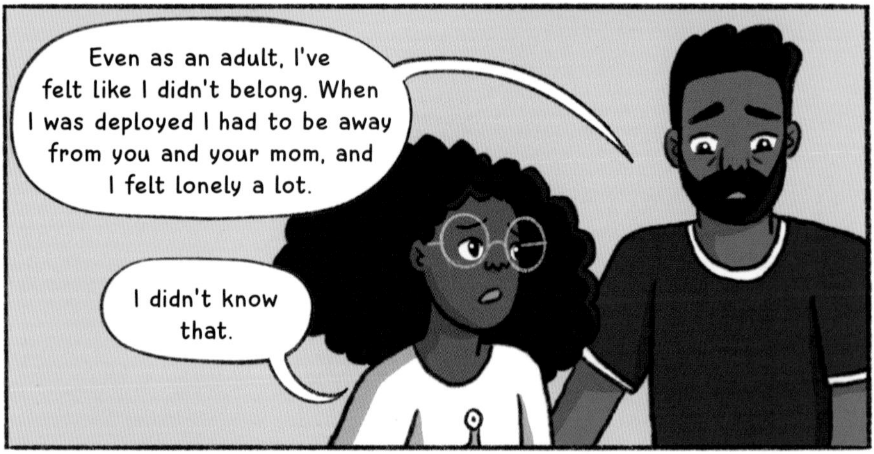
Even as an adult, I've felt like I didn't belong. When I was deployed I had to be away from you and your mom, and I felt lonely a lot.
I didn't know that.

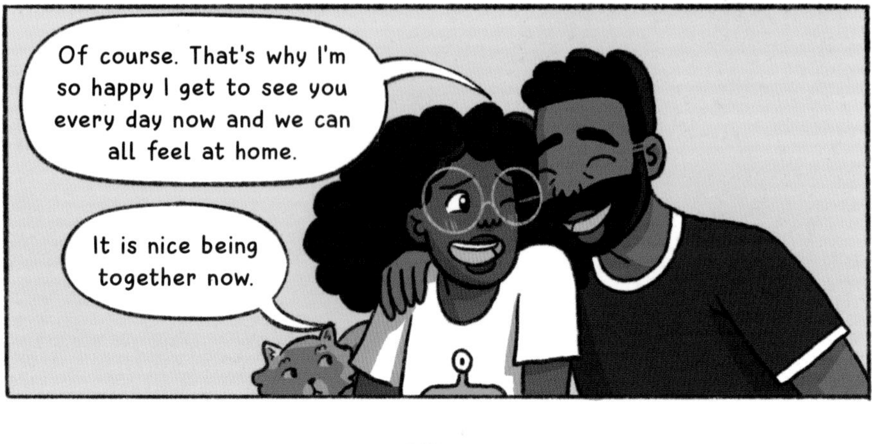
Of course. That's why I'm so happy I get to see you every day now and we can all feel at home.
It is nice being together now.

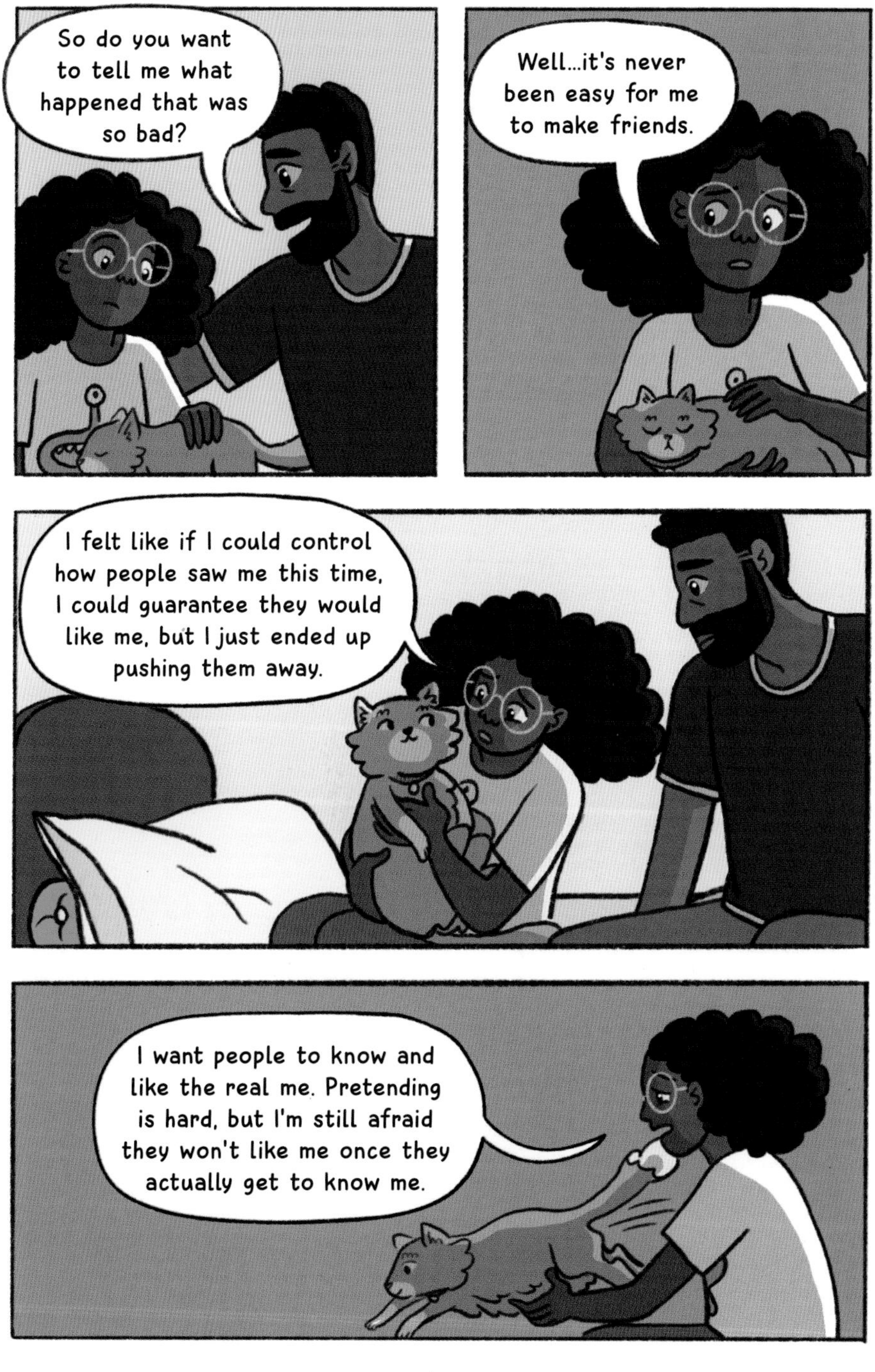
So do you want to tell me what happened that was so bad?
Well...it's never been easy for me to make friends.
I felt like if I could control how people saw me this time, I could guarantee they would like me, but I just ended up pushing them away.
I want people to know and like the real me. Pretending is hard, but I'm still afraid they won't like me once they actually get to know me.

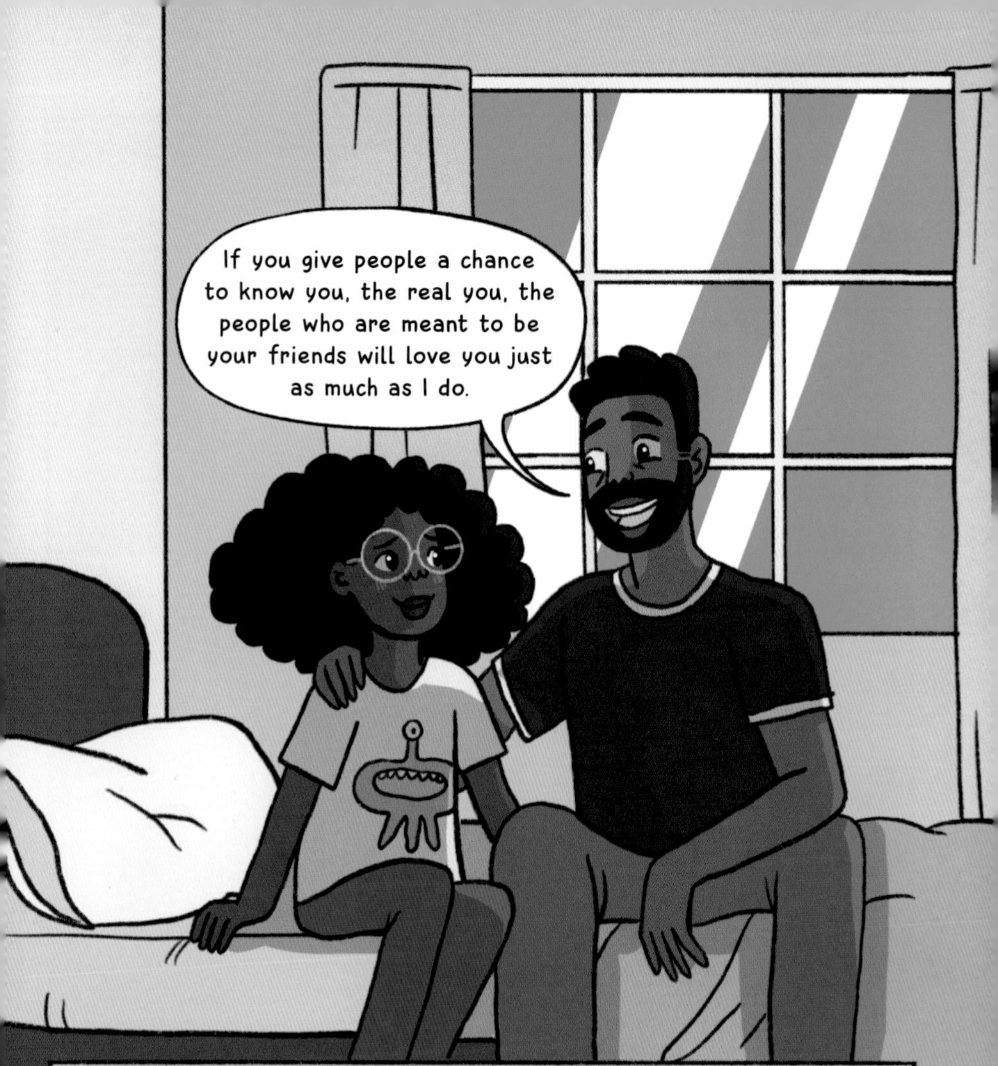
If you give people a chance to know you, the real you, the people who are meant to be your friends will love you just as much as I do.

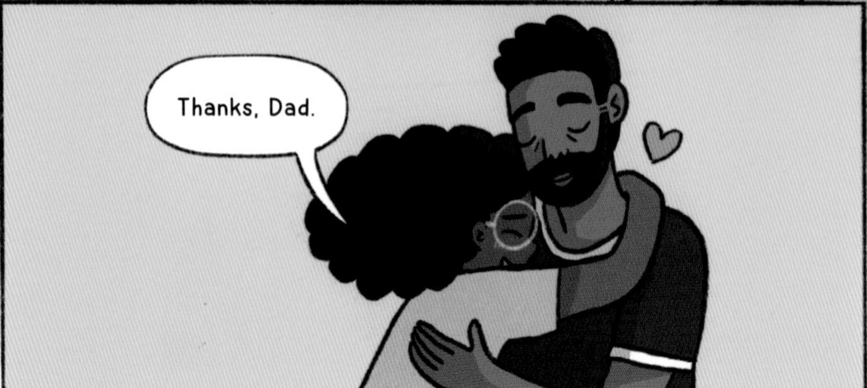
Thanks, Dad.

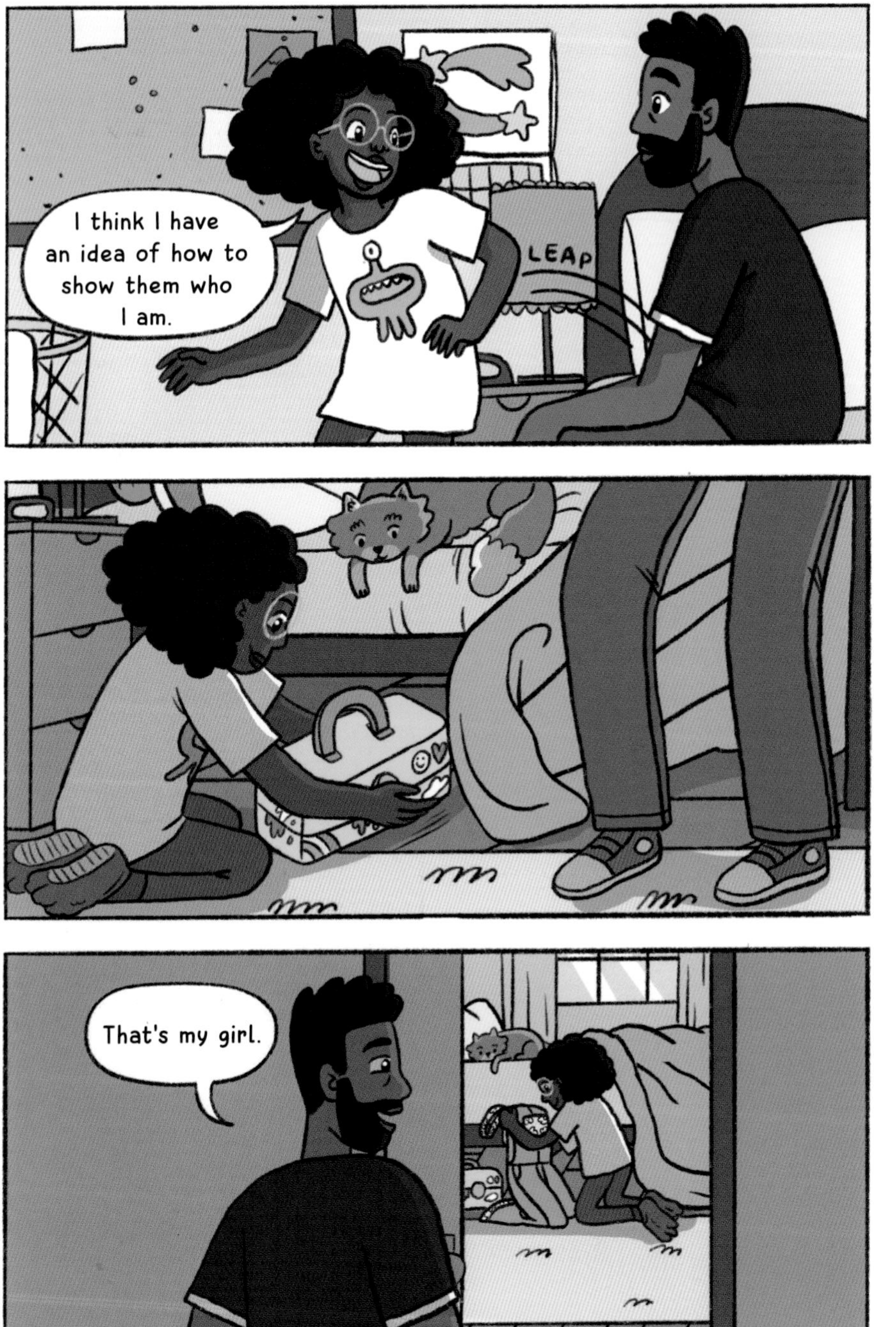
I think I have an idea of how to show them who I am.
LEAP
That's my girl.

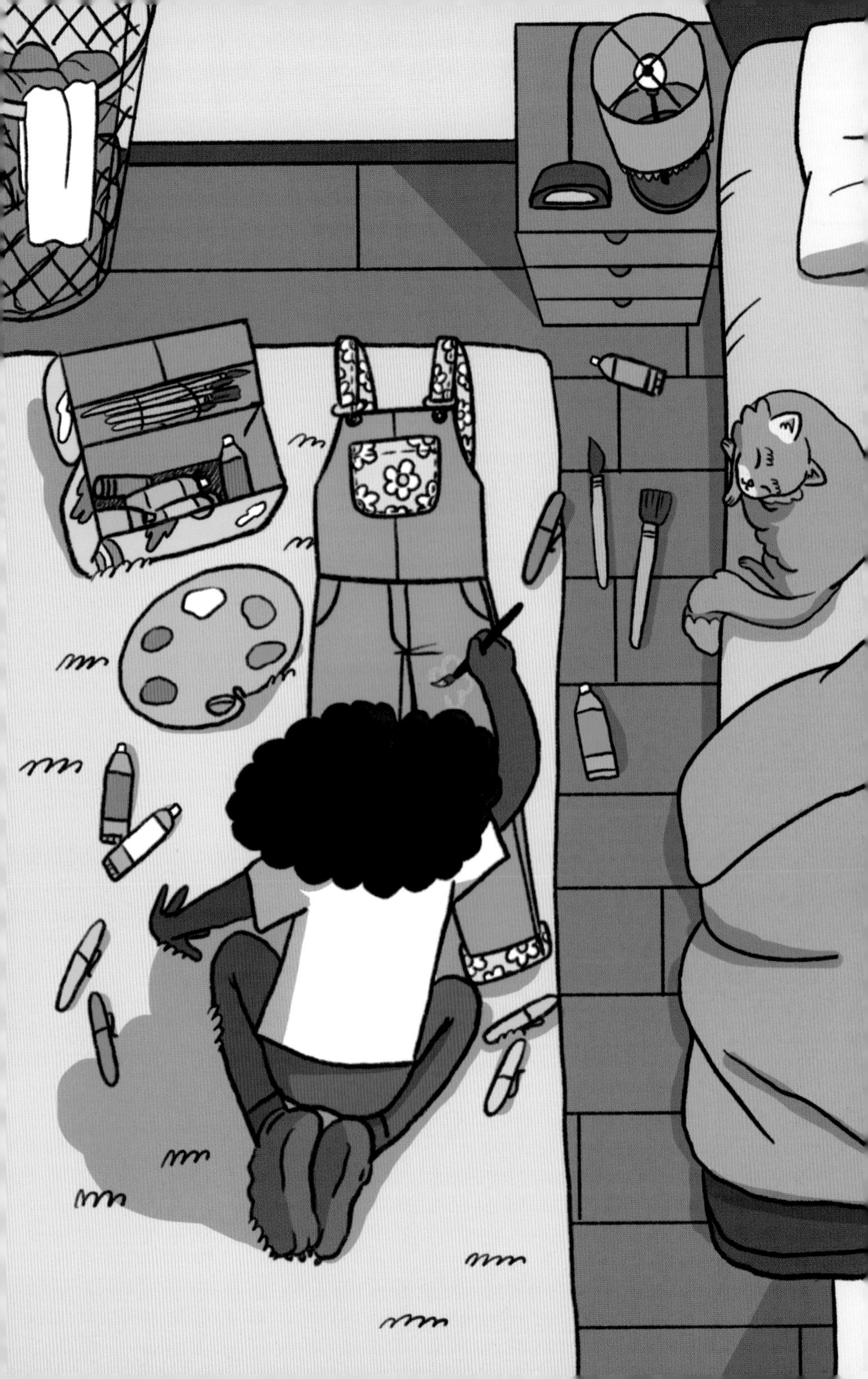

CHAPTER 13

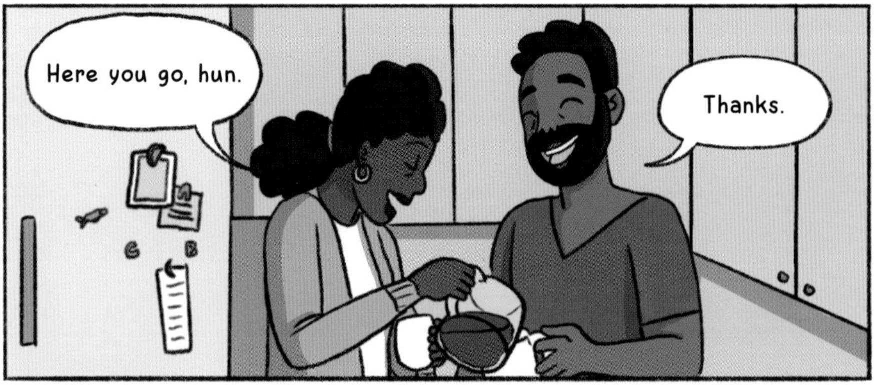
Here you go, hun.
Thanks.
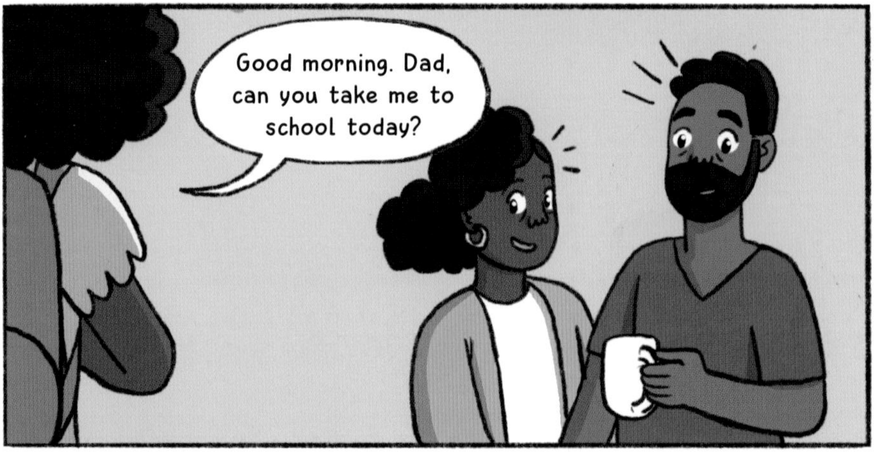
Good morning. Dad, can you take me to school today?
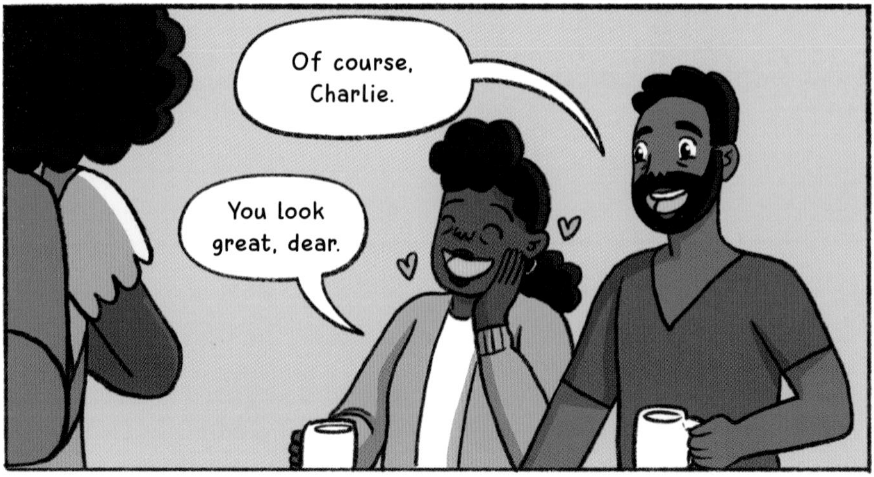
Of course, Charlie.
You look great, dear.

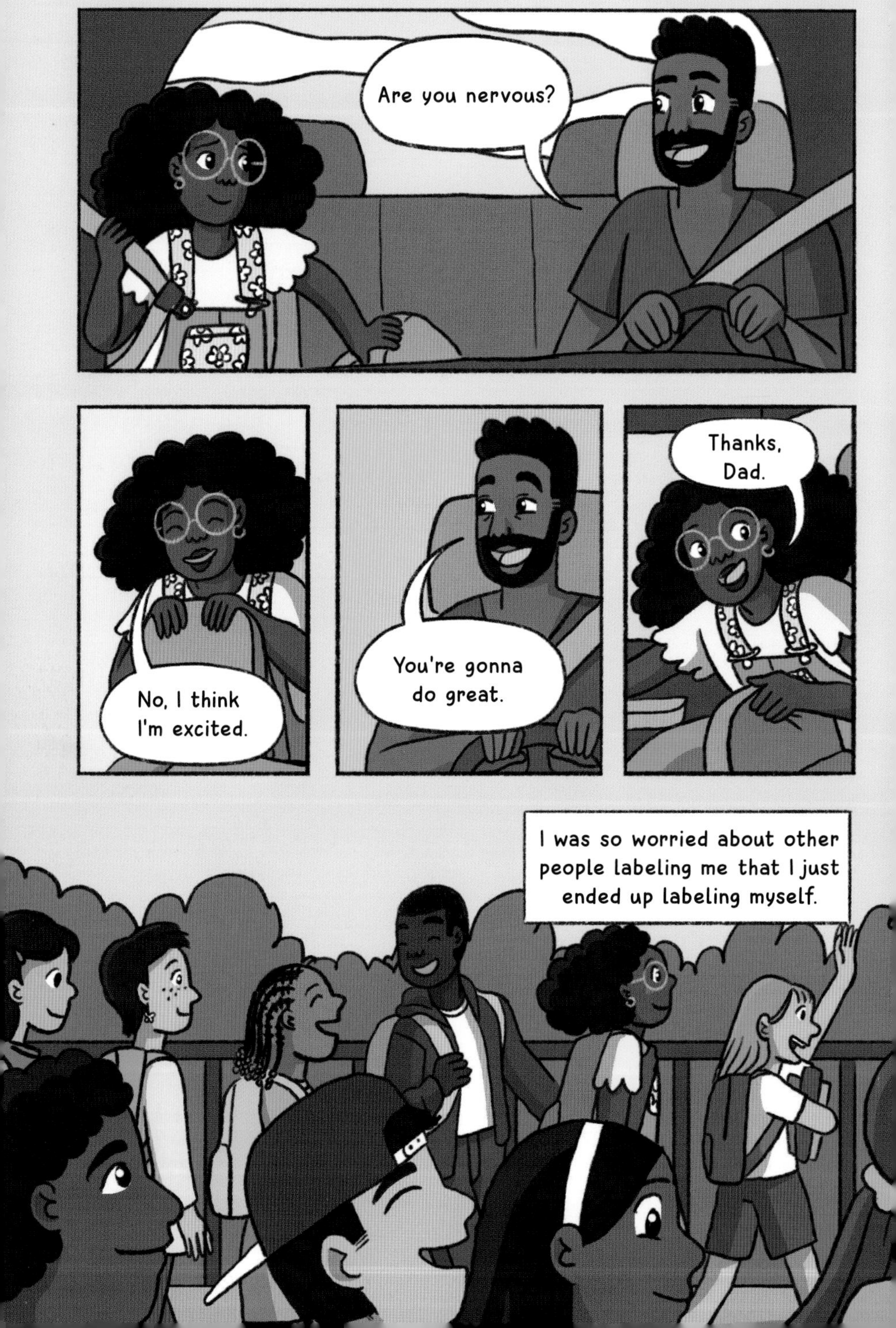
Are you nervous?
No, I think I'm excited.
You're gonna do great.
Thanks, Dad.
I was so worried about other people labeling me that I just ended up labeling myself.

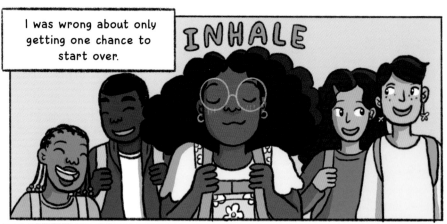

I was wrong about only getting one chance to start over.

INHALE

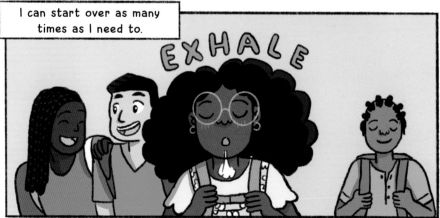

I can start over as many times as I need to.

EXHALE

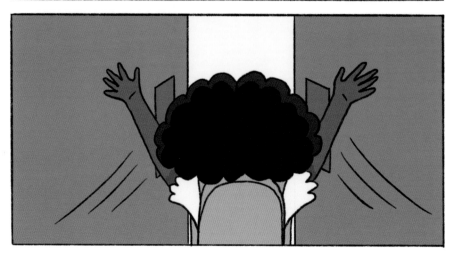

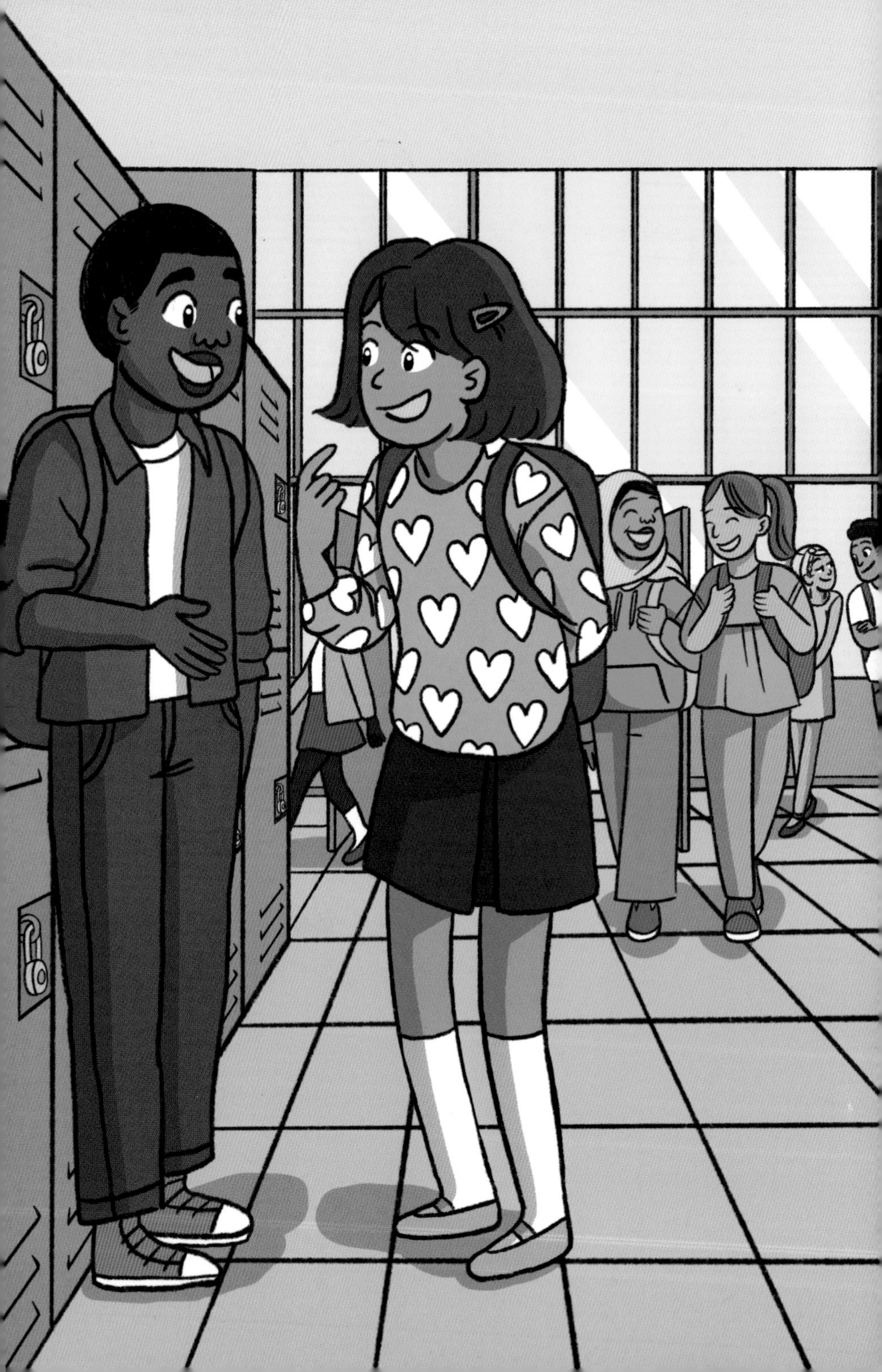

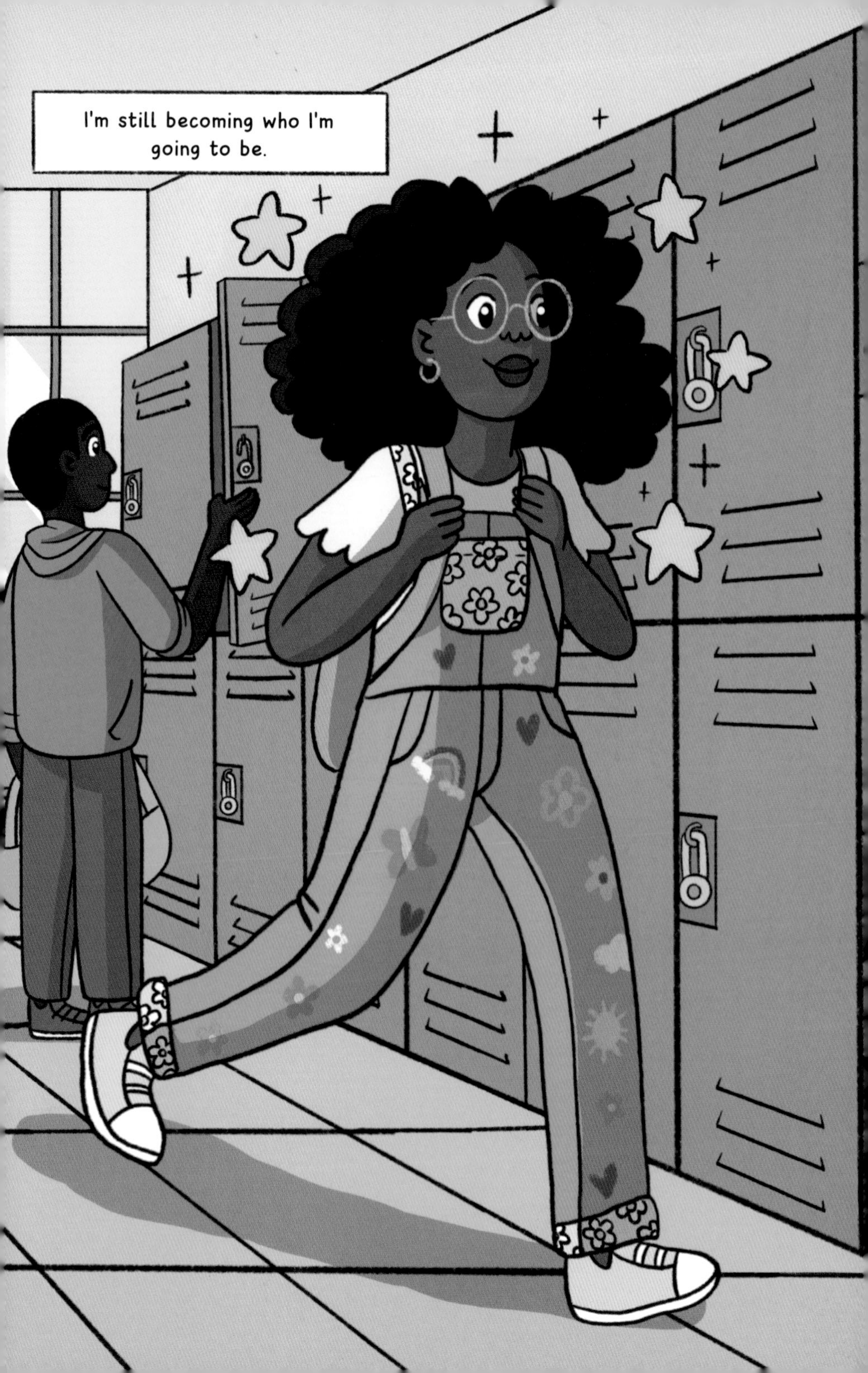
I'm still becoming who I'm going to be.

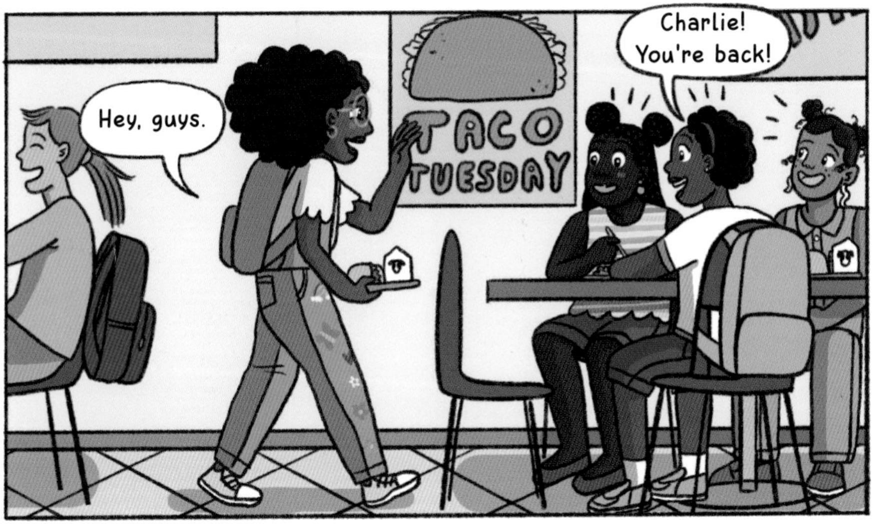
Hey, guys.
Charlie! You're back!
TACO TUESDAY

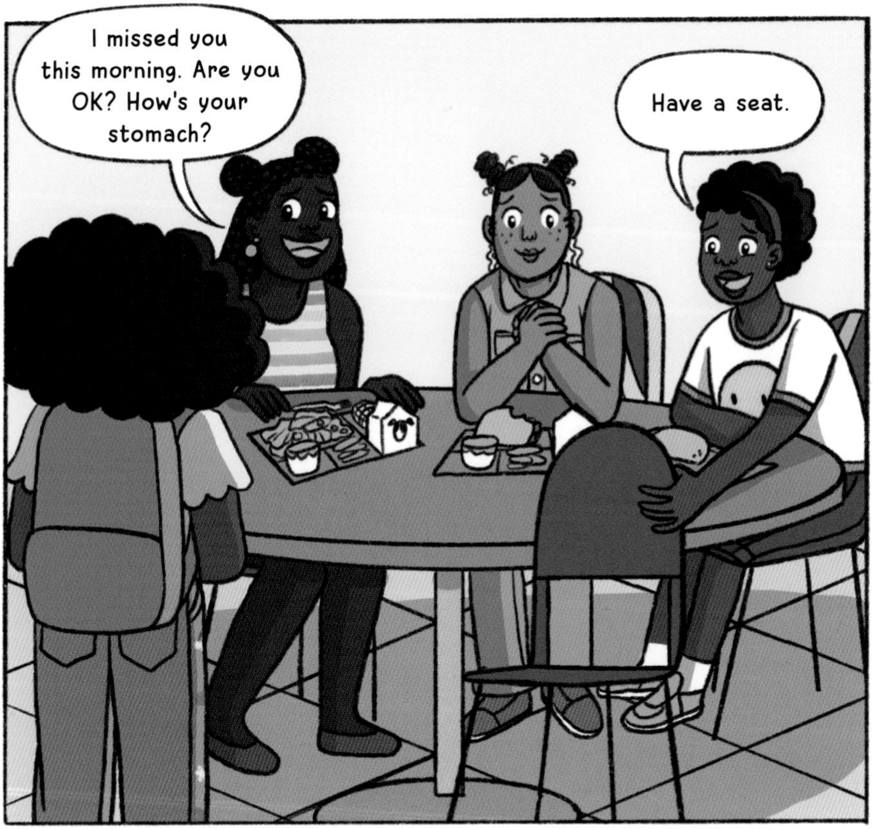
I missed you this morning. Are you OK? How's your stomach?
Have a seat.

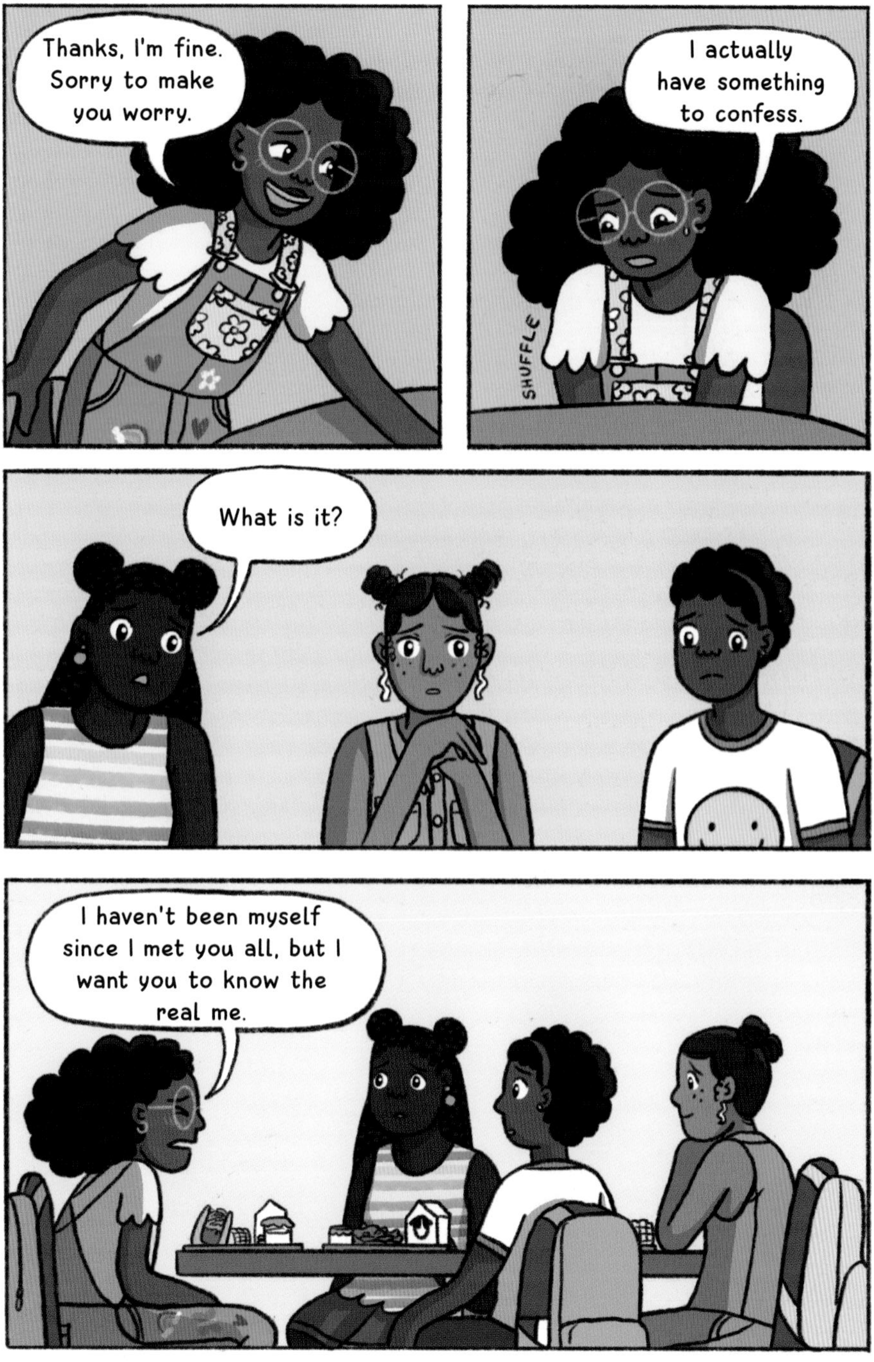
Thanks, I'm fine. Sorry to make you worry.
I actually have something to confess.
SHUFFLE
What is it?
I haven't been myself since I met you all, but I want you to know the real me.

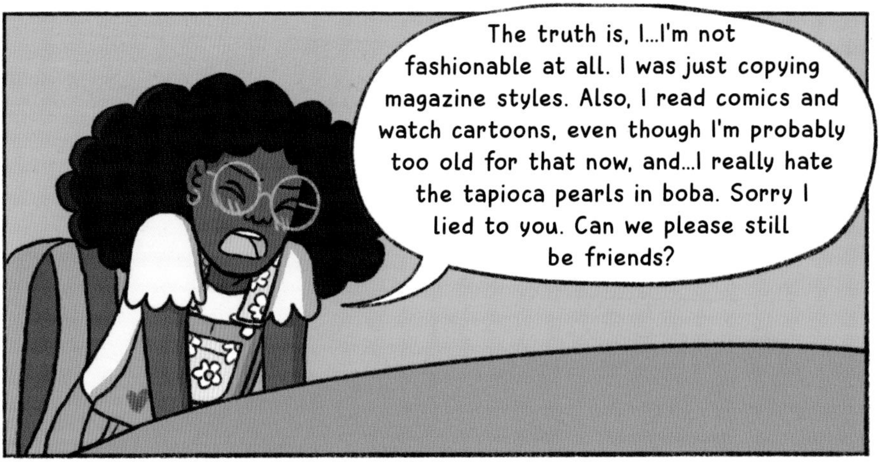
The truth is, I...I'm not fashionable at all. I was just copying magazine styles. Also, I read comics and watch cartoons, even though I'm probably too old for that now, and...I really hate the tapioca pearls in boba. Sorry I lied to you. Can we please still be friends?

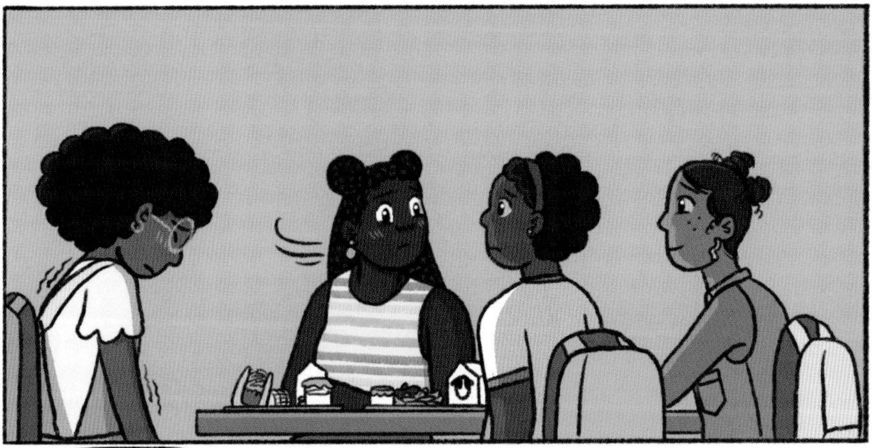

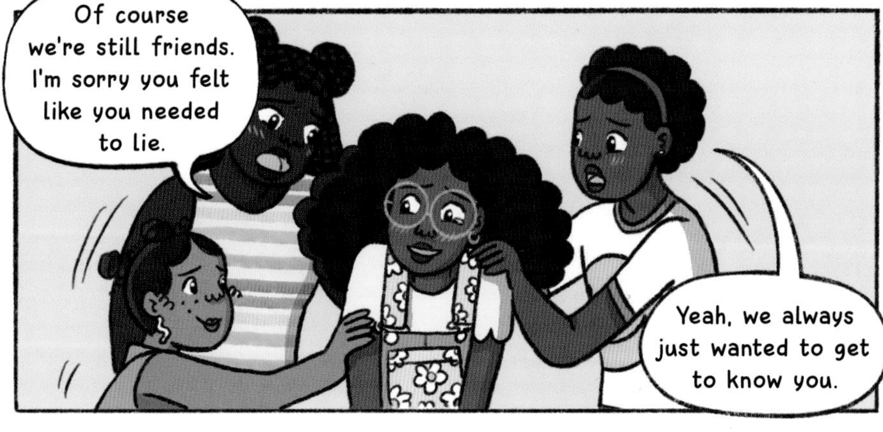
Of course we're still friends. I'm sorry you felt like you needed to lie.
Yeah, we always just wanted to get to know you.

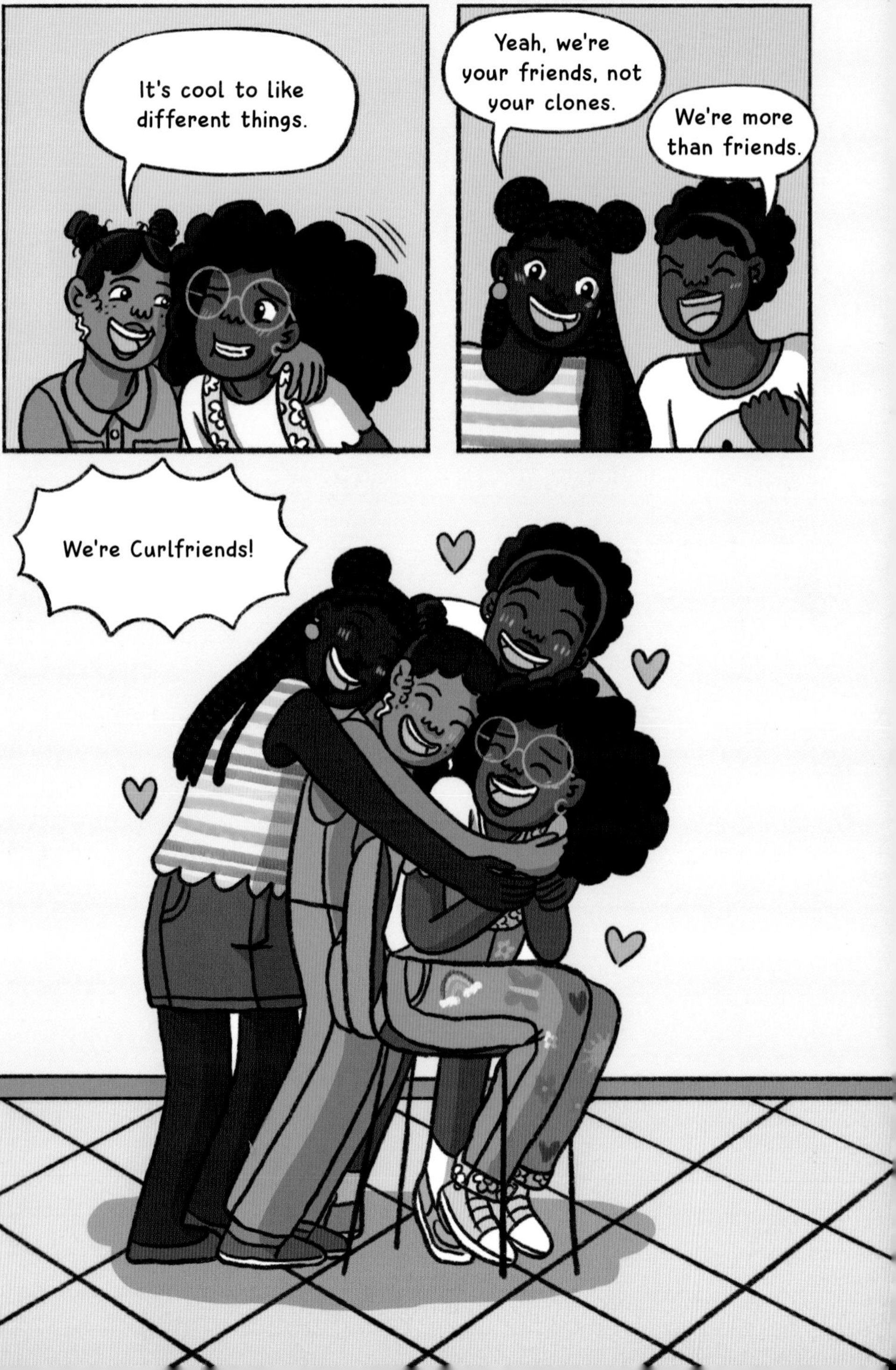
It's cool to like different things.
Yeah, we're your friends, not your clones.
We're more than friends.
We're Curlfriends!

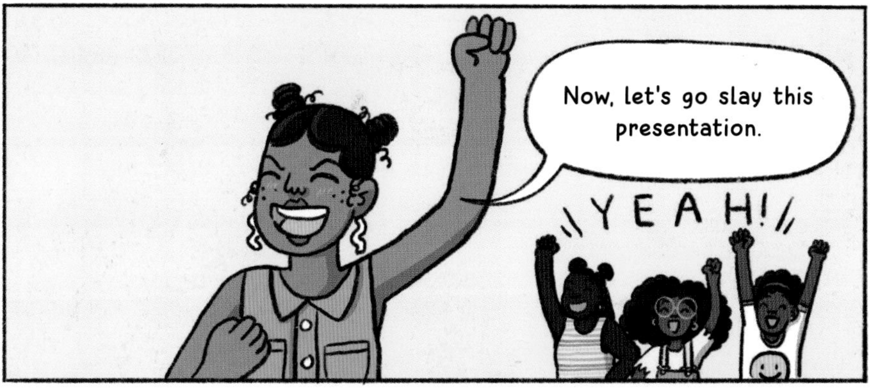
Now, let's go slay this presentation.
YEAH!

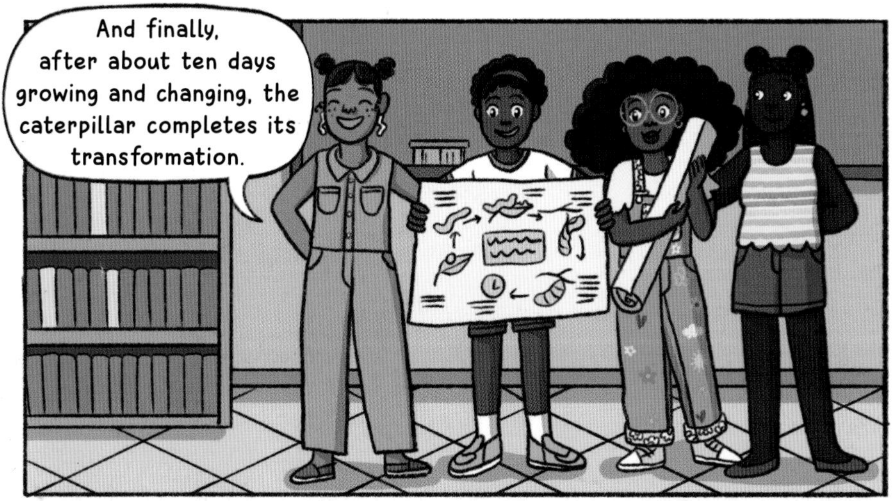
And finally, after about ten days growing and changing, the caterpillar completes its transformation.

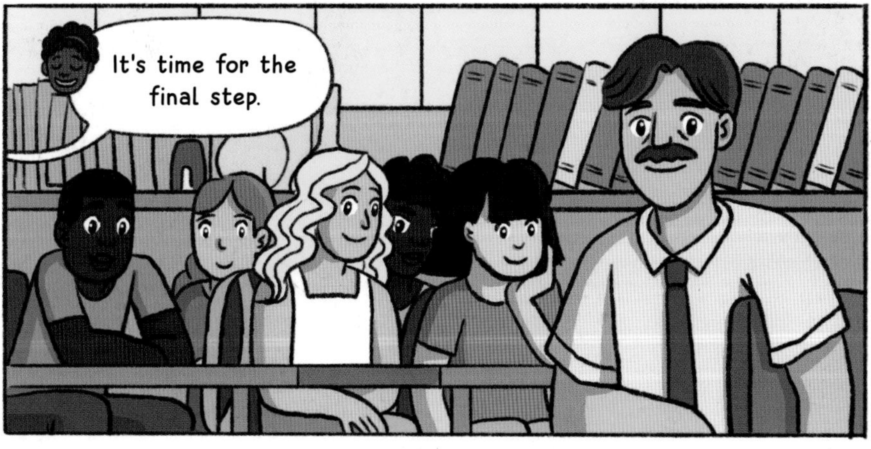
It's time for the final step.

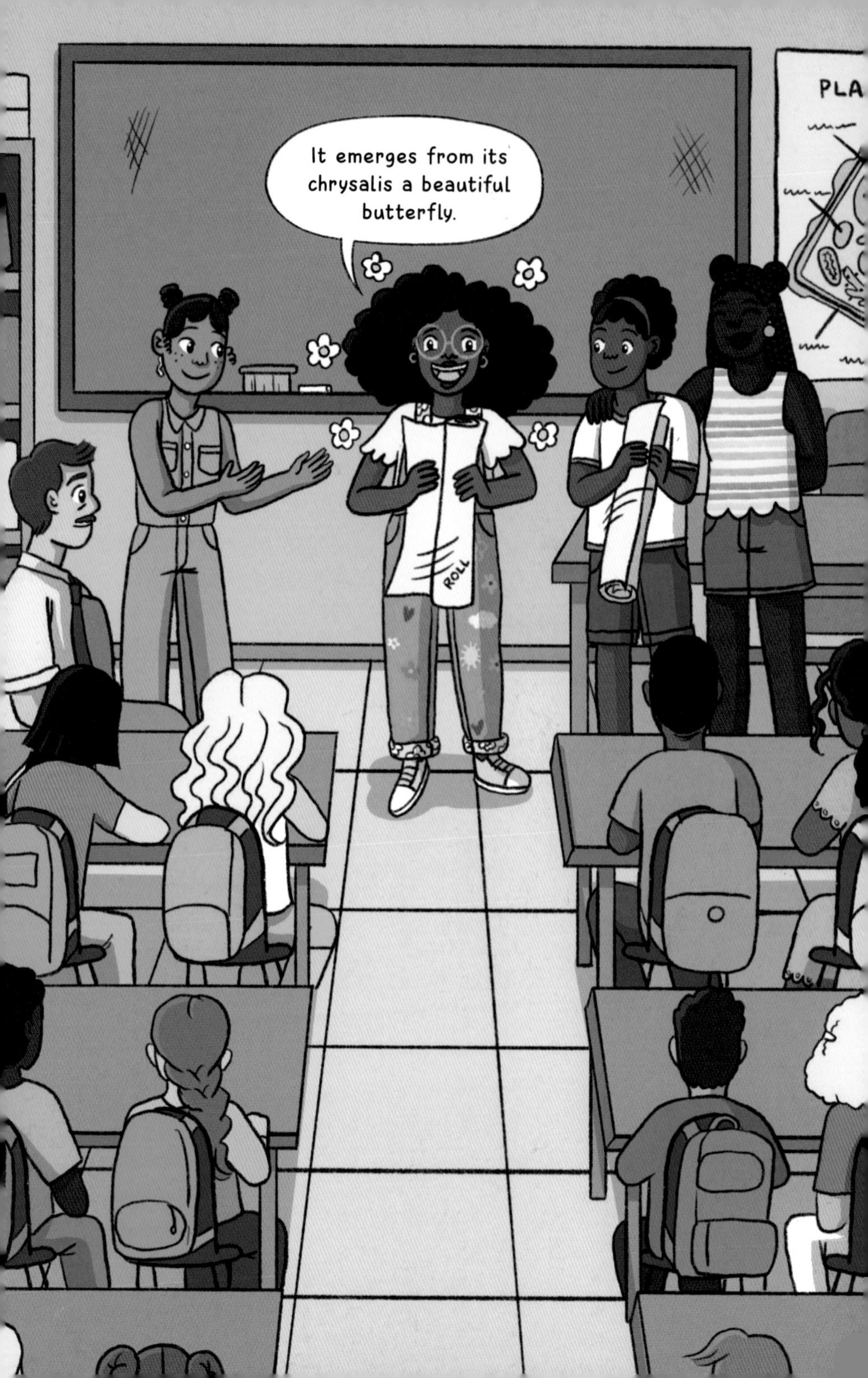
It emerges from its chrysalis a beautiful butterfly.
ROLL

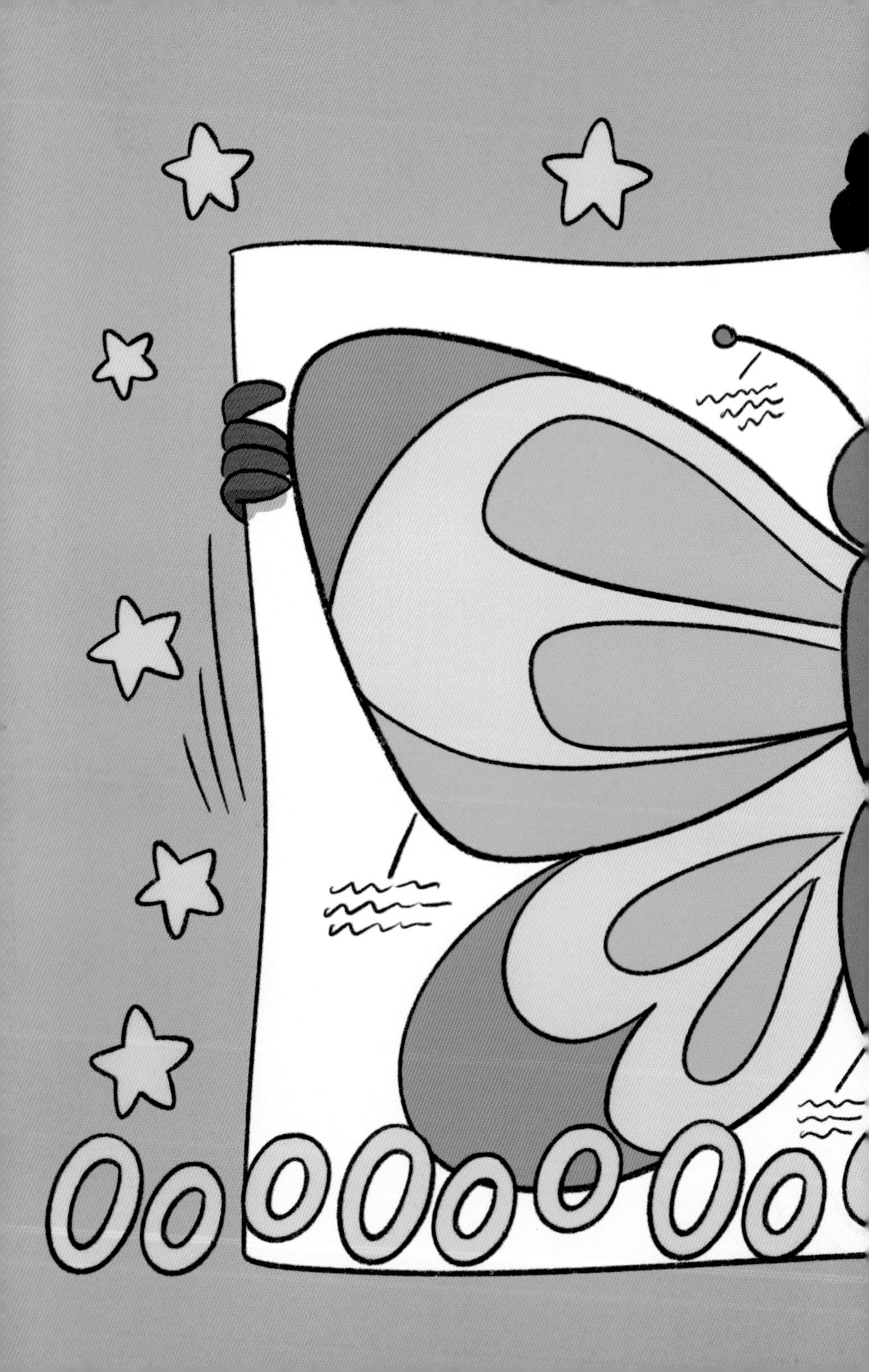
OOOOOOOO

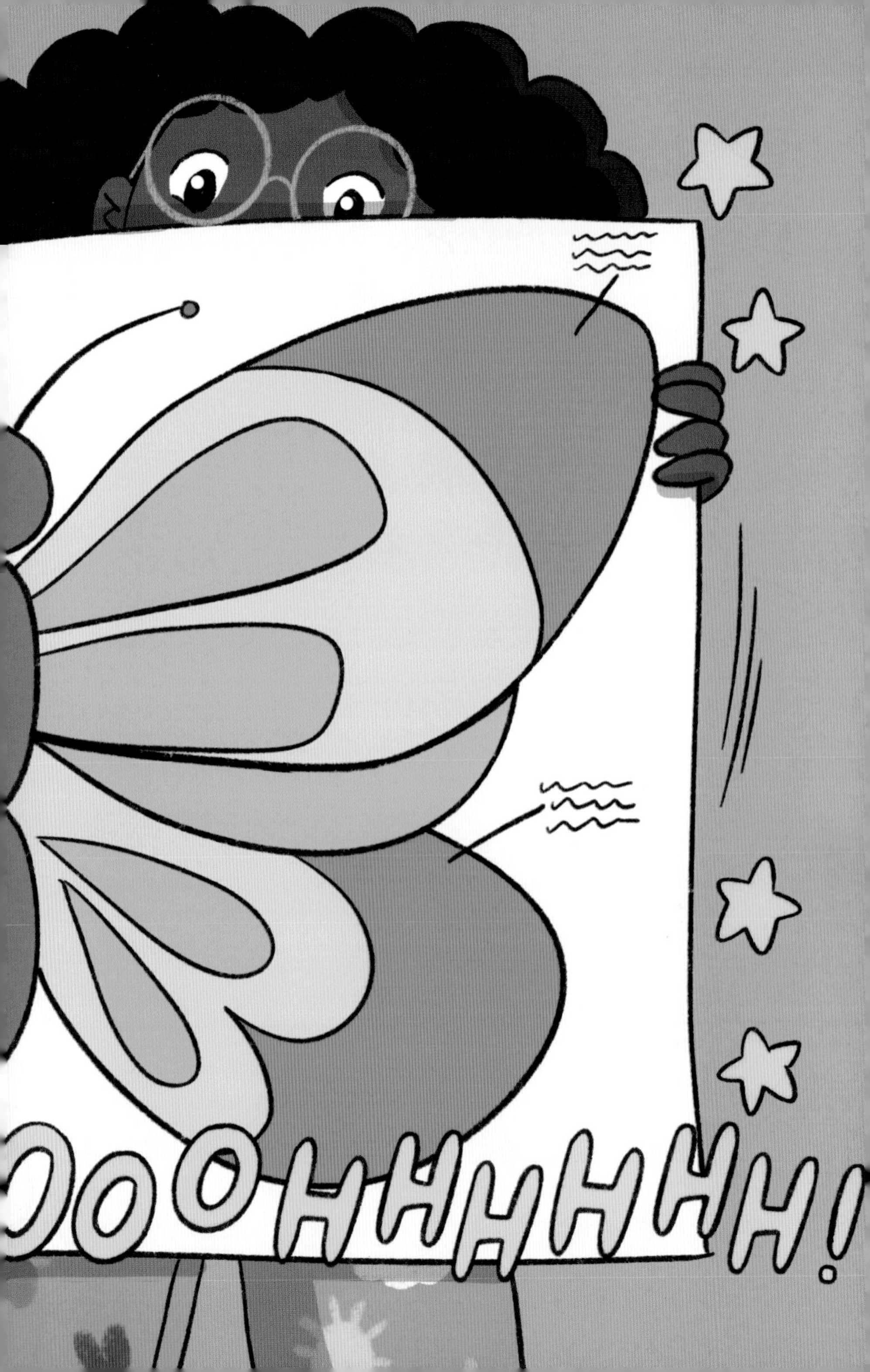
OOOOHHHHHHHH!

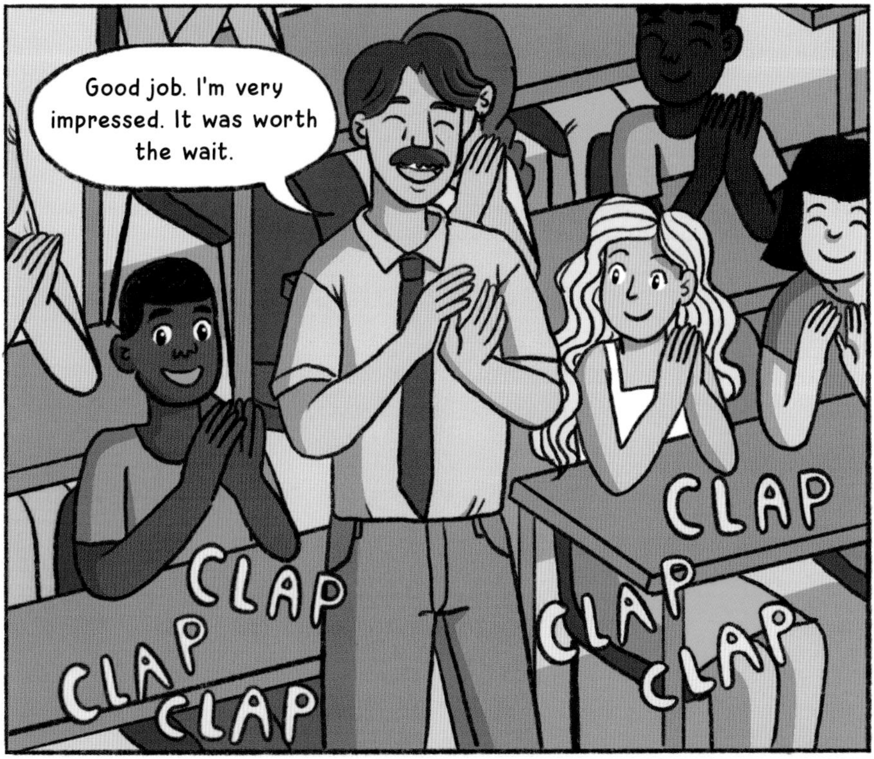
Good job. I'm very impressed. It was worth the wait.
CLAP
CLAP
CLAP
CLAP
CLAP
CLAP

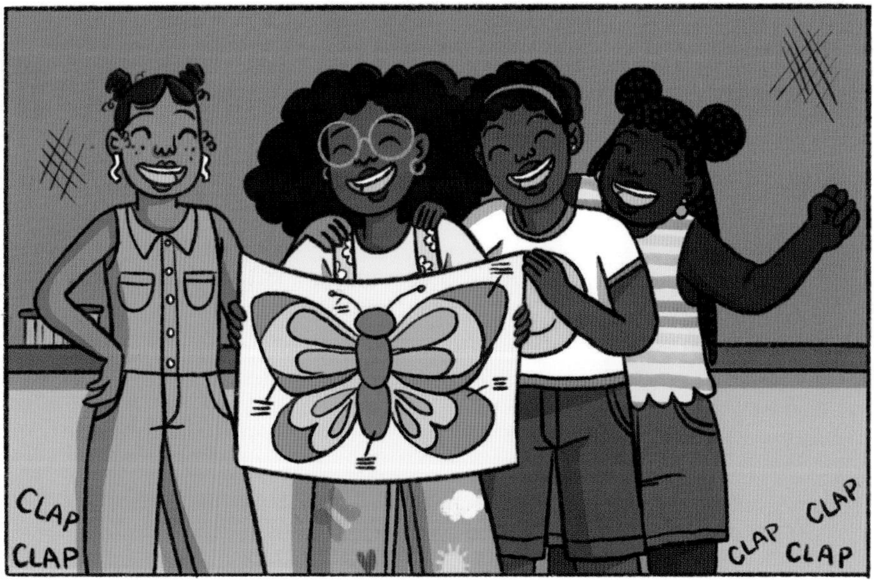
CLAP
CLAP
CLAP
CLAP
CLAP

CHAPTER
14

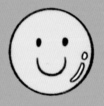

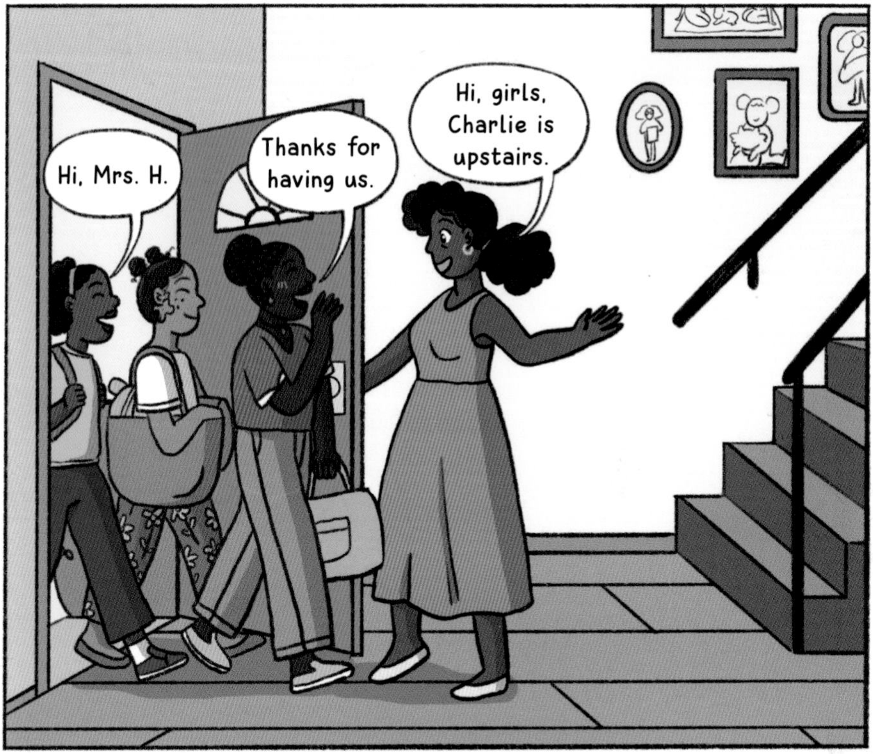
Hi, Mrs. H.
Thanks for having us.
Hi, girls, Charlie is upstairs.

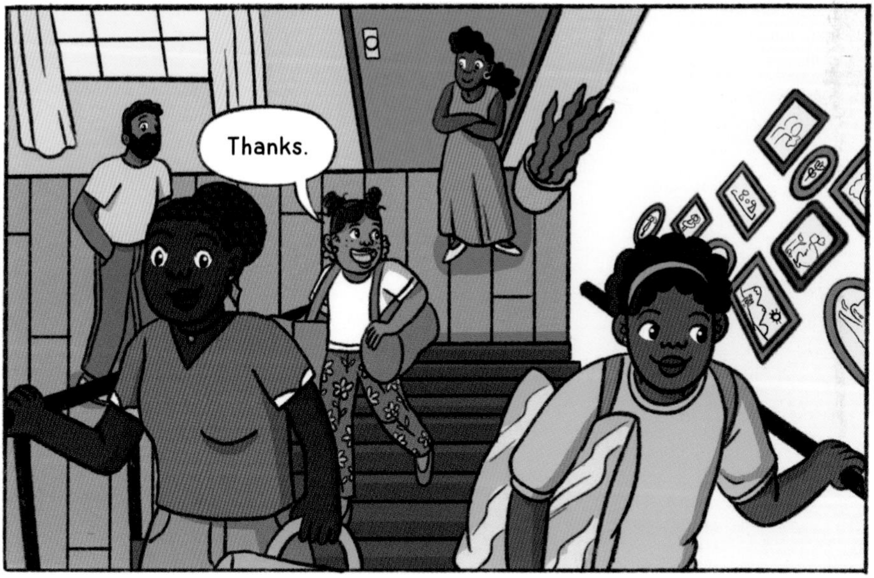
Thanks.

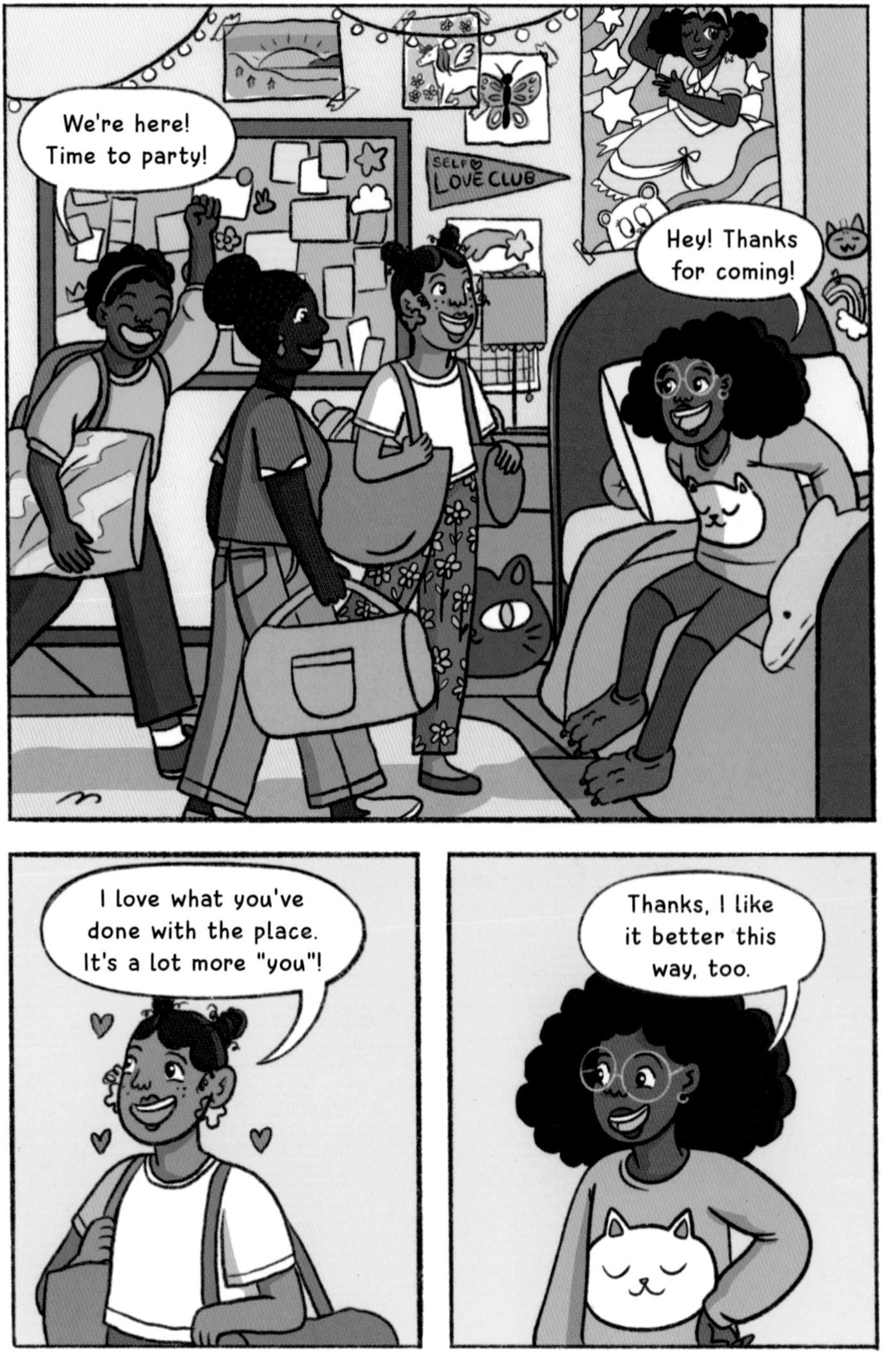
We're here! Time to party!
SELF LOVE CLUB
Hey! Thanks for coming!
I love what you've done with the place. It's a lot more "you"!
Thanks, I like it better this way, too.

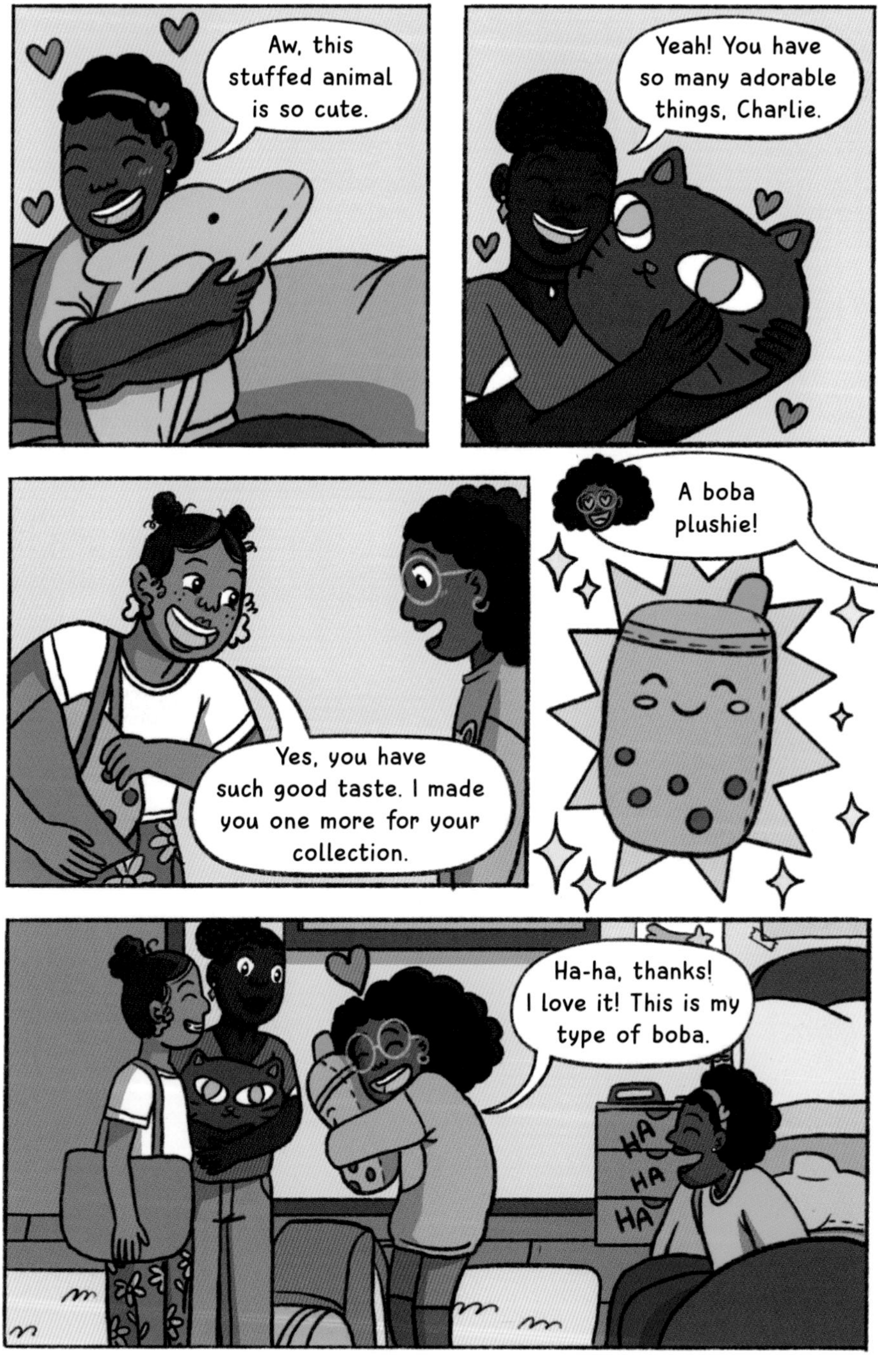
Aw, this stuffed animal is so cute.
Yeah! You have so many adorable things, Charlie.
Yes, you have such good taste. I made you one more for your collection.
A boba plushie!
Ha-ha, thanks! I love it! This is my type of boba.
HA HA HA

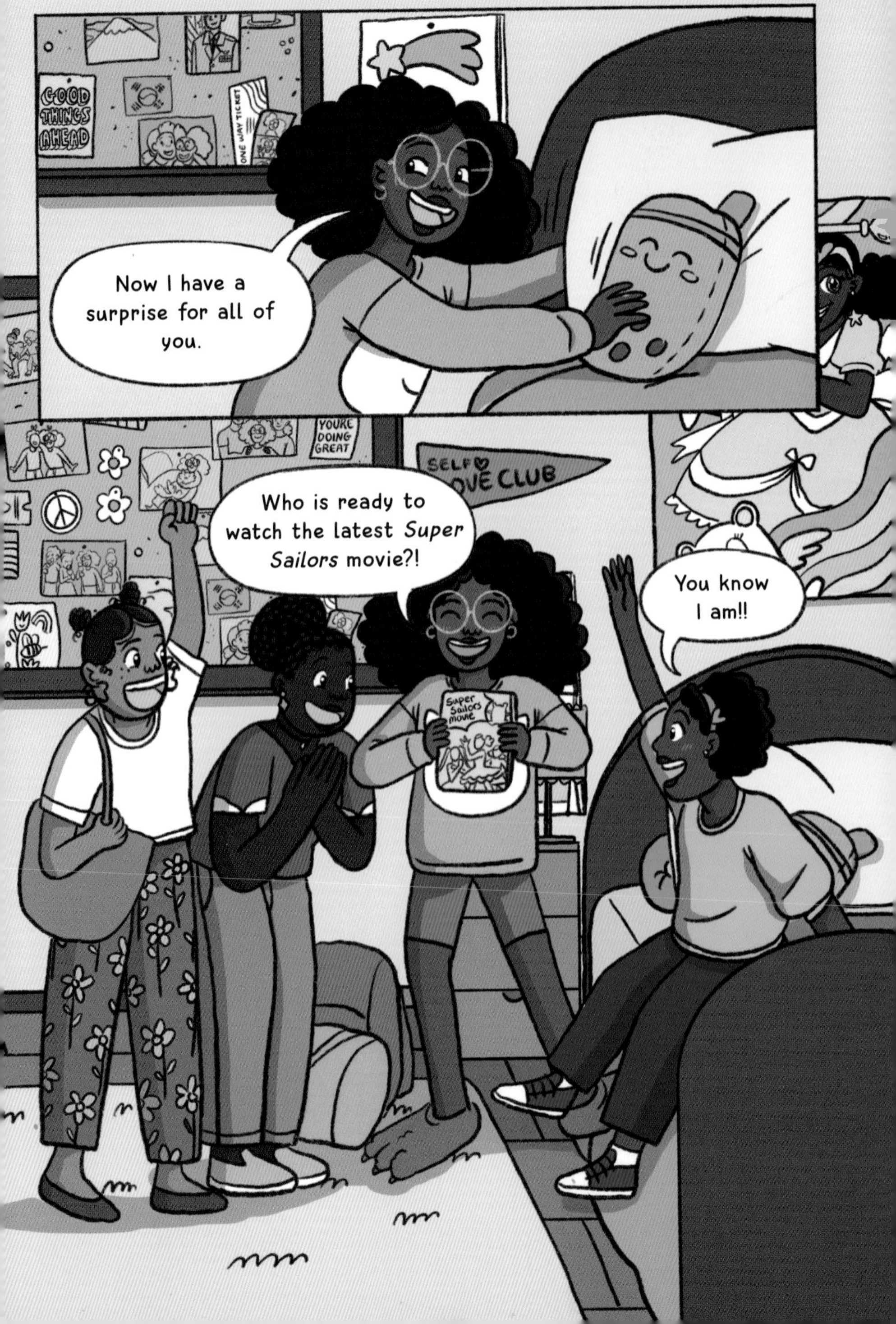
GOOD THINGS AHEAD
ONE WAY TICKET
Now I have a surprise for all of you.
YOURE DOING GREAT
Who is ready to watch the latest *Super Sailors* movie?!
Super Sailors movie
You know I am!!

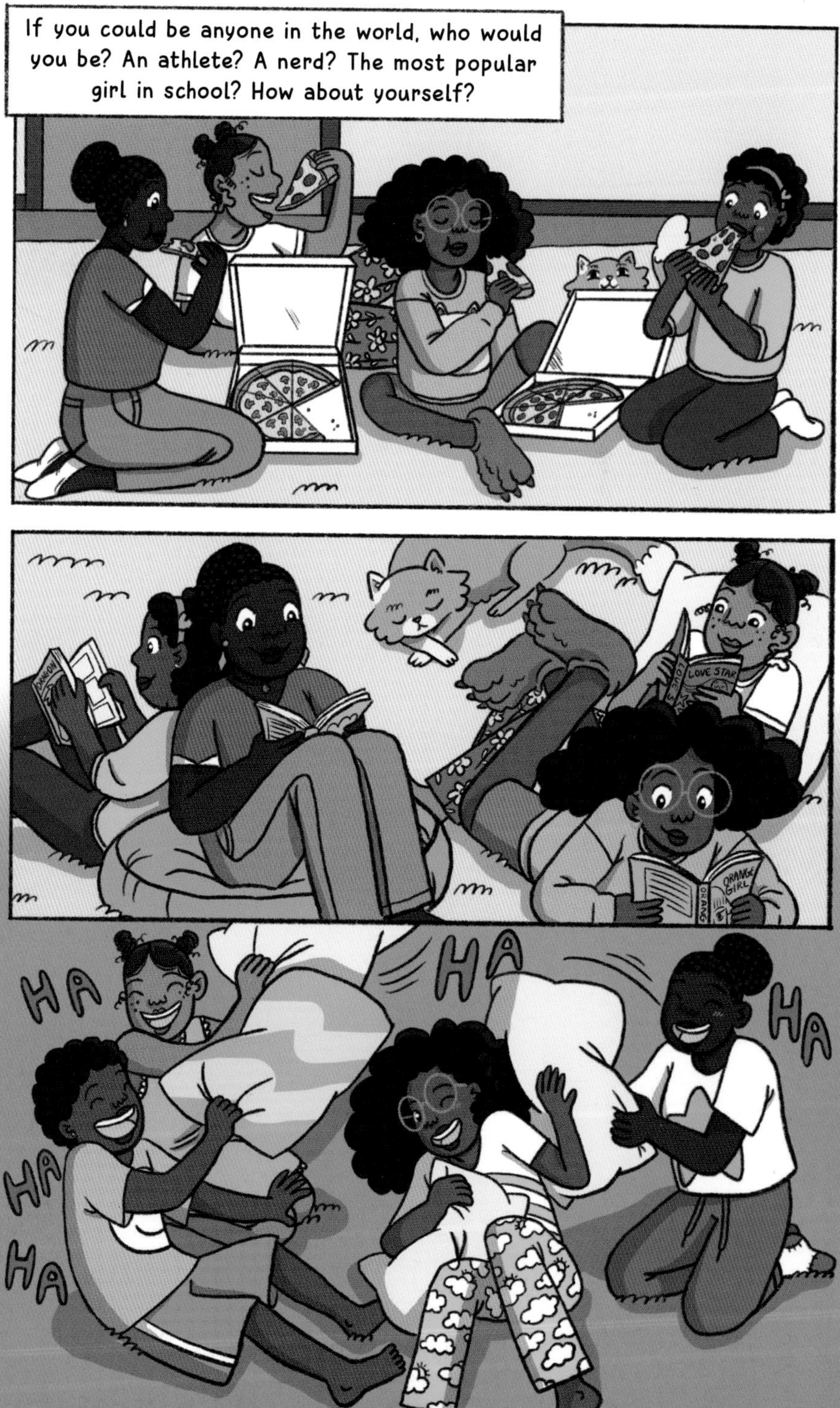
If you could be anyone in the world, who would you be? An athlete? A nerd? The most popular girl in school? How about yourself?
LOVE STAR
ORANGE GIRL
HA
HA
HA
HA
HA

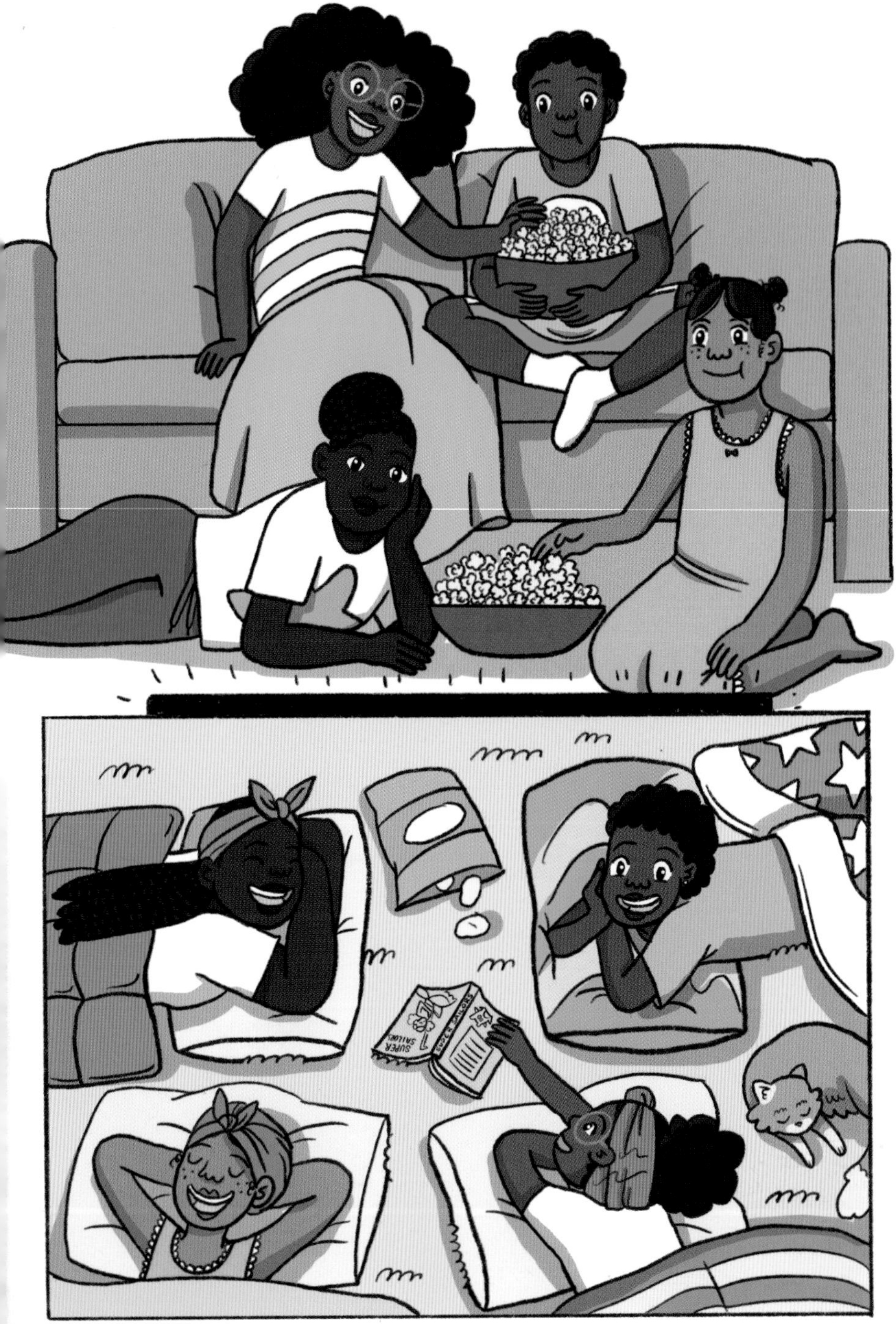
SUPER SAILORS

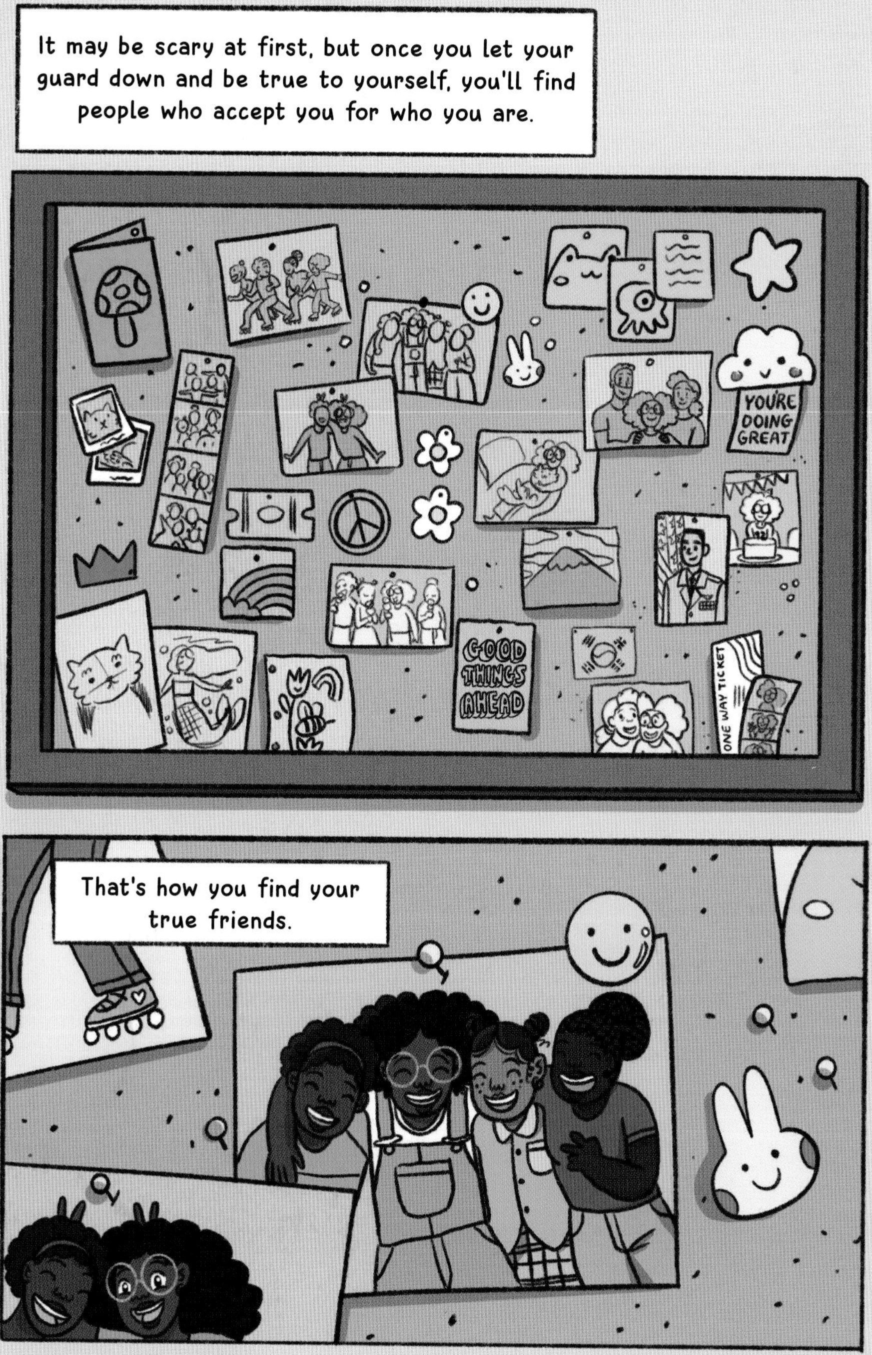
It may be scary at first, but once you let your guard down and be true to yourself, you'll find people who accept you for who you are.
YOU'RE DOING GREAT
GOOD THINGS AHEAD
ONE WAY TICKET
That's how you find your true friends.

ACKNOWLEDGMENTS

The first book in the Curlfriends series celebrates friendship, being yourself, and father-daughter relationships. I lost my father while I was working on this book, so the moments Charlie was able to have with her dad were bittersweet for me. I put so much of my father into Charlie's dad. He was in the air force, goofy, outgoing, and affectionate. I couldn't have such a sweet and open heart-to-heart with him in real life, but I am happy I could have that moment through Charlie. I also lost my sister, who was a huge influence for me becoming an artist. This was sudden and unexpected, but I also wanted to honor her. I was happy I could represent her as Ms. Adrienne, Charlie's quirky and passionate art teacher. I hope knowing the meaning behind these characters and their relationships helps you enjoy their story even more.

This book was a labor of love that I couldn't have done without all the support I received from my family and my publishing team. I want to thank my editors, Andrea and Nikki, for helping me tell this story and sticking with me through these tough times. Thank you to my agent, Monica, for always seeing the value in my work and encouraging me along the way. Thank you to my spouse and son for putting up with my long nights and weekends drawing away. Thank you to my friends who inspired my story and my mom for always believing in me.

Until next time. Happy reading!

SHAREE MILLER is the author and illustrator of *Princess Hair*, *Don't Touch My Hair!*, and *Michelle's Garden*. She is also the illustrator of the Shai & Emmie series written by Quvenzhané Wallis and Nancy Ohlin and *The Excursion* written by Lauren Telesz and published in partnership with the Make-A-Wish® program. She lives in Jersey City with her spouse, son, and two cats, Pumpkin and Spice! Sharee invites you to visit her at shareemiller.com.

741.5 C   ROB
Miller, Sharee
Curlfriends :

ROBINSON
10/23

DISCARD

W9-ASY-622